GUARD OF HONOR

JAMES GOULD COZZENS

Guard
of
Honor

> I and my fellows
> Are ministers of Fate: the elements,
> Of whom your swords are temper'd, may as well
> Wound the loud winds, or with bemock'd-at stabs
> Kill the still closing waters, as diminish
> One dowle that's in my plume: my fellow-ministers
> Are like invulnerable.
> *The Tempest*

A Harvest Book
Harcourt Brace & Company
San Diego   New York   London

Library of Congress Cataloging-in-Publication Data
Cozzens, James Gould, 1903–1978
    Guard of honor.
    (A Harvest book)
    1. World War, 1939–1945 — Fiction. I. Title.
PS3505.099G8   1983   813'.52   83-8464
ISBN 0-15-637609-1

Printed in the United States of America

B C D E F G H I J

ONE

THURSDAY

THROUGH THE late afternoon they flew southeast, going home to Ocanara at about two hundred miles an hour. Inside the spic and span fuselage—the plane was a new twin-engine advanced trainer of the type designated AT-7— this speed was not noticeable. Though the engines steadily and powerfully vibrated and time was passing, the shining plane seemed stationary, swaying gently and slightly oscillating, a little higher than the stationary, dull-crimson sphere of the low sun. It hung at perpetual dead center in an immense shallow bowl of summer haze, delicately lavender. The bottom of the bowl, six thousand feet below, was colored a soft olive brown; a blending, hardly distinguishable, of the wide, swampy river courses, the overgrown hammocks, the rolling, heat-shaken savannas, the dry, trackless, palmetto flatlands that make up so much of the rank but poor champaign of lower Alabama and northwestern Florida. Within the last few minutes, far off on the right and too gradually to break the illusion of standing still, the dim, irregular edge of an enormous, flat, metallic-gray splotch had begun to appear. It was the Gulf of Mexico.

The original AT-7's, of which this was one, were delivered to the Army Air Forces in the second summer of the war. Meant for use in navigator training, their cabins were equipped with three navigator's positions—a seat; a plotting table; a drift meter and an aperiodic compass; a radio headset and a hand microphone. On the bulkhead wall behind the pilots' compartment, placed where all three students would be able to see them, were a radio compass azimuth indicator and a simple supplementary instrument panel. In the cabin top was the miniature plexiglas dome of a navigation turret with a bracket for the pelorus. On the left wall, under, above, and around three small rectangular fuselage windows were racks for signal flares, oxygen bottles, so-called quick attachable parachutes, a long map case, and a pull-down seat on which the instructor could sit when he was not forward with the pilot. At the back, a little compartment afforded, when the door was closed, the refinement of privacy to a chemical toilet.

Though an AT-7 was designed to carry five people, this one was carrying seven. All of them were military personnel attached to the Army Air Forces Operations and Requirements Analysis Division, known as AFORAD, which the Air Forces Board had set up at Ocanara, Florida; or to the Ocanara Army Air Base. In the third fuselage window, next to the entrance door, an oblong metal plaque was temporarily attached to the glass by strips of adhesive tape. The plaque was scarlet and bore two white stars, for the plane was piloted by Major General Ira N. Beal, commanding at Ocanara.

General Beal had that morning flown up from Ocanara to Sellers Field, Mississippi, accompanied by three of his present passengers. They were Colonel Norman Ross, the Air Inspector on General Beal's Staff; Lieutenant Colonel Benny Carricker, a young fighter pilot who had served with the general overseas; and Master Sergeant Dominic Pellerino, the general's crew chief. The other three were pick-ups—Ocanara personnel who happened to be at Sellers Field for one reason or another and were now being given a ride back to their station.

Captain Nathaniel Hicks, of the AFORAD Special Projects Directorate, had been sent to Sellers Field on a project of that Directorate's Reports Section. Second Lieutenant Amanda Turck, of the Women's Army Corps, had no actual business at Sellers Field. She had come in to Sellers that morning on a plane that had given her a lift from Des Moines, Iowa. She had been at Des Moines on seven days temporary duty, taking a course in disciplinary regulations which, now that the Corps was part of the Army, must apply to the five hundred-odd officers and enlisted women of the WAC detachment at Ocanara. A young, slender, and shy Negro Technician Fifth Grade belonging to an Ocanara Base Services Unit had been on furlough at his home near Sellers Field. His name, stenciled across the side of a little kit bag he carried, was Mortimer McIntyre, Junior.

4

These passengers had disposed themselves as well as they could for the three hour trip. Lieutenant Colonel Carricker was in the co-pilot's seat, up front with the general. Colonel Ross sat in the forward student-navigator's position. He had covered the plotting table immediately with piles of papers from his brief case; and he applied himself to them except when General Beal, turning his head, addressed some remark to him. Captain Hicks sat in the middle navigator's position. He, too, had laid out work from a brief case; but he spent much of the time faced around, talking against the noise of engines to Lieutenant Turck, in the rear navigator's position. He and she knew each other, in the sense and to the extent that Nathaniel Hicks's work often required classified material from the library files which were in Lieutenant Turck's charge at Ocanara.

On the pull-down seat by the door Sergeant Pellerino's stout, short body was relaxed with remarkable completeness. His thick-featured, amiable face was vacant. Regardless of his cramped situation, he was sound asleep. In the rear compartment, visible through the open door, T/5 McIntyre sat on the cover of the chemical toilet, the only place left to sit. He did not mind. Anything satisfied him. He had been prepared to stand, or sit on the floor if that was all right; but when they were airborne, Sergeant Pellerino opened up the compartment door and told him considerately that he might as well sit on the toilet. T/5 McIntyre's uniform, which fitted him neatly and closely, was very clean; and, like his carefully creased overseas cap with the scarlet-and-white Engineer Corps piping, seemed still cleaner because of the intense satiny blackness of his face and hands. He had never flown before. Though he held a worn, paper-bound comics magazine open in his lap, he spent most of his time glancing shyly and guardedly around him, absorbing an experience that he would be able to make a good deal of, once he was back to his barracks tonight.

General Beal, his tense thin snubnosed young face—for he was at that time the youngest two-star general in the Air Force —severe and thoughtful, moved his shoulder against the padded back of the pilot's seat and turned his head to speak over it to Colonel Ross. General Beal had said nothing for almost ten minutes; but they were talking last about Colonel Woodman at Sellers Field; and it was plain that the general had gone on thinking about him. He said, his voice raised to be heard: "I wish to God I could do something about Woody, Judge. Think of anything?"

Colonel Ross, who was, in fact, a judge in civilian life, had been looking at a draft of a proposed Post Regulation 200-2. The tenth paragraph was entitled *Restricted Areas:* and proceeded: *Dogs and cats are prohibited in the following buildings: Headquarters, Operations, Officers Clubs, Barracks, Mess Halls, Kitchens, Swimming pools, or immediate vicinity.* He penciled a caret between *Officers Clubs* and *Barracks* and wrote above it firmly: *Post Exchanges.* He then initialed the sheet "NR," and put it on the right hand pile.

Plenty of men have married at eighteen and had children at nineteen, so Colonel Ross was old enough to be the general's father. He now took off his glasses, turned his large clear blue eyes on General Beal, and gave him a drily paternal look. While not stout, Colonel Ross was a big man, and he showed the heaviness of increasing age. His thick gray hair, parted in the middle, stood up enough to lengthen his lined face. Locked in his mouth was a bulldog pipe. He gave the pipe two hard puffs, removed it, and said: "You might take that bottle out of his bottom desk drawer."

General Beal said: "I know that."

General Beal wore a not-very-clean khaki shirt, open at the neck, with his stars on the wilted collar. His sleeves were rolled above his elbows. On his left wrist was a beautiful Swedish navigator's chronograph the size of a half dollar. The case was made of platinum and it had a platinum band. On his right wrist a gold crash bracelet hung loosely. The ends of the plate were joined by the heaviest possible hammered gold links. These elegant appointments contrasted with the shirt, and with his garrison cap, "raunchy" as it was then called, to a degree hardly exceeded by any new air cadet's carefully soiled and broken headgear.

General Beal removed this object and hung it on the microphone. He began to rub his brown hair, cropped in order to conceal the unmilitary curl natural to it. He said, "I doubt if they let him keep even Sellers Field. That won't be so good. He thinks he got a raw deal already. I didn't like to take the plane."

Colonel Ross puffed twice more on his pipe. "How could you help it?" he said. "It was an Air Staff directive. Woody better learn to comply with directives. He had no business shooting that TWX to Washington."

"He just doesn't get off the ground," General Beal said. "And it isn't just liquor. He always drank. He just isn't the man he used to be."

Colonel Ross grunted. "In my part of the country," he said, "they have another line to that. It goes: 'No, and he never was.'"

"I can tell you Woody was a pilot, Judge. He was my first squadron commander at Rockwell Field. He could fly and he was a right guy. Ask anyone who knew him then."

"Well, I saw a little of him at Issoudon in 1918, which is more than you did. He may be a good pilot. But he hadn't much sense. I mean, even less than most pilots. I doubt if he has any more now, in view of some remarks he made to me while you were out taking that telephone call."

"What did he say?"

The tone made Colonel Ross smile. "Not about you," he said. "It was about why he thinks they have it in for him at Fort Worth. But you're quite right; he probably would have said plenty about you if Sellers Field were in your command."

"By God," said the general, "do you know who was in command at Rockwell—I mean, the Air Depot? Major H. H. Arnold. Woody never gave a damn for anyone. He didn't like something, so he went around making cracks about the Distinguished Information Service Medal; and how we won't be over till it's over over there. I know they actually wrote up specifications for charges. Then it got fixed, somehow. Maybe he apologized. Nobody could stay sore at Woody very long. He was really a comical bastard."

7

Lieutenant Colonel Carricker said casually, "Getting way off our heading, Chief."

They both looked at the compass.

"By God, we are," said the general. He leaned and looked out. Presently he said: "That ought to be the Apalachicola River, ahead there. Let's see your sectional chart a minute, Benny." He took down his radio phones and held one against his ear. "Getting *A*," he said. "We're on Marianna still, aren't we? Well, if that's the river, we're not too far off—"

Colonel Ross returned to the pile of papers from his brief case. Among them he had information copies of the exchange of messages between Washington and Colonel Woodman, that quondam comical bastard; and it looked to Colonel Ross as though, sooner or later, people could and would manage to stay sore at Woody quite a while.

Colonel Woodman's trouble was, professedly, about letting General Beal have this AT-7, which General Beal now had, and was now flying home. However, Colonel Woodman had been twice ordered to let General Beal have it; so that was that. If Woody still went on, it was safe to guess that the real trouble was something else, of which the loss of one of his AT-7's was only a symbol.

Colonel Woodman, if he had any sense, must have recognized General Beal's conciliatory gesture in coming himself to get the plane. You would expect Colonel Woodman to meet it halfway. Maybe when he got the TWX message that General Beal was coming he meant to meet it halfway. He had, apparently, put the heat on his mess to get the general as good a lunch as they could on such short notice. He was duly down on the ramp in front of Sellers Field Operations with his Executive and his Airdrome Officer to welcome General Beal. However, while waiting for the tower to report the general's plane, Woody doubtless took a couple of quick ones from that bottle Colonel Ross later observed in his not-quite-closed lower desk drawer.

General Beal's plane was a B-25B, called *My Gal Sal*. It was beautifully kept. The general landed it hot, with plenty of dash.

8

He gunned it around, swept back to the ramp, and roared up his fine engines while Colonel Woodman had a good look at it. The only plane available for Colonel Woodman's personal use was a worn out AT-6, the advanced single-engine trainer.

The general gave Colonel Woodman a cordial wave. Then there was some delay as he got out of his parachute, and Lieutenant Michaels, his pilot, took his place, and Lieutenant Noble, another pilot, took Lieutenant Michaels' place. This made it plain that the B-25 was going right back. Finally the hatch under the radio position opened, the ladder dropped, and General Beal scrambled down and ducked out from beneath the plane.

Colonel Ross, coming out less actively, was in time to see what followed. Woody, his red face very red, his red-veined eyes glowering, his half-comic, half-ferocious cavalryman's mustache twitching, sauntered forward. The Executive and the Airdrome Officer, unprepared for this informal move, had automatically snapped up their hands to salute the general as soon as he was clear of the plane. Woody, it seemed, had sulkily decided he was not going to salute anyone, and he didn't, not even when the general answered the other officers' salute. His greeting (whose offensive force was perhaps weakened a little by the fact that the general was now face to face with him and had held out his hand, and Woody had limply taken it) was: "Well, how the hell many personal planes do you need down there, anyway?"

You could see Colonal Woodman choking on resentments and disappointments. He was sick with the long deferment—now he must know it was really more than that, it was the final demise—of hope. He was not going to get any stars. He was never going to get that overseas assignment without which there could be no kind of postwar career in the Air Force. Instead, they ordered him to Sellers Field, a poorly located tarpaper post which they were hastily transforming into an extra school to meet the increasing demand for navigators.

Probably because General Beal understood at least part of this, he answered Colonel Woodman by laughing. "Yeah," he said. "We're really putting it on." He turned and watched

Sergeant Pellerino, who was easing a wooden box out of the rear gunner's hatch in the plane. "Got some branch water?" he said. "I brought you something to go in it. Honest-to-God case of Scotch, right from London. RAF fellow gave it to me. Come on, Woody. Let's see your place. I hear it stinks."

They went up and had some of the Scotch in Colonel Woodman's office; but, probably for the first time, even whisky seemed to choke Woody. He kept mumbling parts of his argument. More than once he said, irrelevantly, to everyone else at least, "I don't get it. I don't see what they're trying to do. I don't think anyone knows what the hell is going on!" Sometimes he seemed to mean Ocanara and AFORAD; sometimes, the training program in general; sometimes, the conduct of the war. It was clear to Colonel Ross that Woody, in a practiced, unhappy way, was tight.

Someone spoke in then on the box and said that Ocanara was calling, a personal message for General Beal; so the general went to take it. Colonel Woodman immediately made an effort to sober himself. Carricker had gone to check out on the AT-7, so that they could fly it down; Colonel Woodman's Executive had been previously excused. He and Colonel Ross remained there alone.

Colonel Woodman said at once, with an air of fortitude, that he didn't want Colonel Ross to get him wrong. "Hell, Norm," he said, perhaps a little belatedly playing up their acquaintanceship of twenty-five years ago, "I'm not kicking about this assignment just because it's lousy. I can take it. I'm a soldier. I'll serve where they send me."

Colonel Ross was surprised. Though he might well kick about his assignment, Colonel Woodman had been so busy kicking about the Air Staff decision on the plane that he hadn't mentioned it before. Colonel Ross realized then that Colonel Woodman was staring, with mixed craft and tipsy ingenuousness, at the Inspector General's insignia on Colonel Ross's collar. Woody might not have understood that his old friend was at Ocanara, not from Headquarters in Washington, and so couldn't do anything for him.

Rapidly and passionately, Colonel Woodman now developed

what he was kicking about. They were the difficulties which were being deliberately put in his way at Sellers Field. "I just want to tell you a few things confidentially—just informally, in case you think some action—"

Since this confirmed Colonel Ross's guess about the stare at his insignia, and since Colonel Ross did not particularly want to hear the maudlin story of Colonel Woodman's troubles, he interrupted to say, very carefully and clearly, that he was not from the Inspector General's office in Washington, nor even AAF Headquarters' Air Inspector's office. He was just SWAAF; detached on Service with the Air Forces. He was assigned to Ocanara as General Beal's Air Inspector. Nothing outside AFORAD was in his province or power. . . .

Colonel Woodman would not listen. He went on to describe his "few things," directing whisky fumes in short explosive puffs toward Colonel Ross, clenching and unclenching his swollen hands on the sweaty leather of a riding crop which he carried around the post with him. Sometimes he rapped the desk with the crop. There was this deliberate withholding of essential equipment; unanswered requisitions; delays in meeting approved and authorized schedules. When they did let him have some of what he needed, on one pretext or another (he gave Colonel Ross a significant look) they took it away from him. They refused him qualified officers and they deliberately undermined post morale by sending in detachments of trainees for whom, as they damn well knew, he couldn't yet have provided quarters or even proper mess facilities.

Of course, Colonel Woodman did not deny that some of these things *looked* perfectly natural when a new installation was being set up in a hurry. That was part of it; they were pretty smart. By "they," he meant a certain "clique" at Fort Worth who had it in for him. The members of it were so placed in the organization of Training Command Headquarters that, dropping a word here or delaying a paper there, they could hamstring any installation and wreck any program. He knew exactly who these people were, and he could positively prove what he was saying.

Well, Colonel Ross might ask—in fact, Colonel Ross asked

nothing, simply sucking at his pipe—why didn't he go to General Yount personally with his proof? All right; Colonel Woodman would tell him why. He got up abruptly, opened the door, and closed it again. Then, with a kind of fuddled caution, he examined the box on his desk to see that it was off. The plot, it seemed, was not confined to the Headquarters of the Training Command. It would be useless to go to General Yount. The general was in no position to do anything. To Colonel Woodman's positive knowledge, General Yount had told his Chief of Staff that Sellers Field would have to sink or swim. Colonel Ross would know what that meant. In Washington, certain parties had resolved to thwart, humiliate, discredit, and ruin Colonel Woodman.

Colonel Ross, in his turn, stared. For a Regular Army man like Woody to believe that the Commanding General of the Training Command would say any such thing to his Chief of Staff, or to anyone else, was preposterous to the point of being psychopathic. If Sellers Field "sank," General Yount would be held personally responsible.

Colonel Ross did not have the facts on whatever other troubles Colonel Woodman had or thought he had; but he knew all about this episode of the AT-7—perhaps more than Woody thought. It was really all you needed to know. A routine order had gone from Washington to Fort Worth and from Fort Worth to Sellers Field; give an AT-7 to General Beal. Understandably, Colonel Woodman didn't like giving away planes; but anyone not obsessed with a persecution complex need only look at a map to figure it out. The finger was put on Sellers Field because it was the point nearest Ocanara to which AT-7's were then being delivered. Moreover, Sellers Field, as Woody so loudly protested, was not scheduled to be, and was not, ready to use all its planes. Still, standard operating procedure would be to query the order. Fort Worth grasped, at least as well as Colonel Woodman did, that basic principle of military management: always have on hand more of everything than you can ever conceivably need. If Colonel Woodman in the normal way queried Fort Worth, Fort Worth could be counted on to query Washington.

What Woody did was compose and immediately fire off a TWX message to the Chief of Air Staff. Naturally, he had known and flown with this officer back in his comical bastard days. Woody now said that every AT-7 he had or could lay his hands on was absolutely indispensable to the Sellers Field program. Giving one to General Beal was quite out of the question. He made an oblique but unmistakable reference to those fancies of his about his superiors at Fort Worth. He made another, incoherent but no doubt intelligible enough, to the duplication of effort, waste, and working at cross-purposes bound to result when exempt organizations under the Chief of Air Staff, like AFORAD, supposed to do God Knew What, were given the inside track on everything.

At the Headquarters of the Army Air Forces the second summer of the war was a nervous time. They still put up those signs about doing the difficult at once and requiring only a little longer to do the impossible. Nearly every day they were forced to make momentous decisions. On their minds they had thousands of planes and hundreds of thousands of men and billions of dollars. Their gigantic machine, which, as they kept saying, had to run while it was being built, gave them frightening moments and bad thoughts to lie awake at night with.

Now, then, toward the end of the usual exhausting day, came a long and stupid message which, if it were going anywhere, should have gone to Fort Worth. It fretted them about one training plane. It lectured them on what was indispensable to Sellers Field (the AAF had so many fields that you could not find one man who knew all the names). It informed them that the Training Command was not run properly and that the project at Ocanara was a poor idea.

Enemies of Woody's, a "hostile clique" trying to do-him-in, would have asked nothing better than a chance to make these attitudes and opinions of Colonel Woodman's known at AAF Headquarters. Woody made them known himself, in black and white, over his signature. Colonel Ross could not help thinking that the evidence showed, if anything, that there were "certain parties" at Headquarters who were still ready, for old times' sake, to cover for Woody, to try and keep him out of trouble.

An angry man (so Colonel Woodman thought a little wire-pulling could determine Air Staff decisions, did he?) might have walked across the hall, laid the message before the CG/AAF and watched the roof blow off. Even a mildly annoyed man might have supplied Fort Worth with an information copy and left Woody to explain. Instead Woody got a personal reply at Sellers Field. He was peremptorily ordered to make available at once repeat at once one of first ten subject articles delivered to him. He was curtly reminded that direct communication between Headquarters Sellers Field and Headquarters Army Air Forces was under no repeat no circumstances authorized.

Of course, Colonel Woodman had done irreparable damage to any remaining chances he might have had for advancement, or an important command. Still, there was such a thing as the good of the service; and Woody, making it certain that he had no future, might be promoting that.

General Beal, speaking again to Colonel Ross, said: "Well, the hell with it! I'm sorry he doesn't like it; but I really need this plane. I need a plane for short trips. That's what it will mostly be. There's no percentage in hopping *Sal* to, say, Orlando, or Tampa. Uses too much gas. Besides, unless I modified it, it's too uncomfortable for anyone but the pilots. I don't think I'll do anything to this. It's all right the way it is." He faced about and looked back into the fuselage. He began to laugh. "Get a load of Danny," he said, indicating Sergeant Pellerino. "When that boy sleeps, he sleeps. I wish I could do it. Just the same, I don't like rubbing it into Woody; throwing my weight around with him—hell! You hungry? I am." To Lieutenant Colonel Carricker, who had been sitting idle, staring out the side window, he said: "Let's get this on the automatic pilot, Benny. Want to see what's in that bag."

"Roger," said Carricker. He put out a powerful square hand whose whole back was a graft of glazed skin transplanted from his thigh to cover second degree burns. The fingernails, small deformed fragments of horn-like substance, were in the much slower, perhaps never-to-be-completed, process of renewing themselves. He steadied the co-pilot's wheel a moment, took away the repaired hand, and watched the instrument panel. "Nose up," he said. "They must have somebody parked in the can." He craned back until he was able to see T/5 McIntyre perched on the chemical toilet. "Make us a little elevator trim, Chief."

General Beal reached for, and moved, the control on the bulkhead behind him. "Roger," said Carricker.

To Colonel Ross, the general went on moodily, "I suppose Woody thinks I was pulling rank on him. By the time Woody needs all his planes, Materiel will have him a replacement. He's got nine others, anyway, for God's sake!" Abstractedly, he watched Carricker setting the automatic pilot. "You can't align the elevator index with the horizon bar," he said.

"I wasn't," said Carricker simply. His calm, beefy face, bent toward the panel, turned a little, allowing him to cock an eye at the general. "What's eating you, Chief?" he asked amiably. He pushed the valve handle to *ON* and held it there until he could feel the gyros take over. "Wish you were back at Colomb Bechar with the Frogs?"

The shadow on General Beal's face seemed to lift. "Nuts to you, Benny," he said. He brought up from the floor behind his seat a large paper bag. Looking into it with interest, he said: "Cream puffs! Danny must have gone and got them in town."

When the general asked for the sectional chart, Colonel Ross had put his glasses on again and gone back to his pile of papers. The largest file folder held this morning's collection of information copies of messages, office instructions, special memoranda, and daily activity reports from AFORAD's five administrative directorates and the various staff sections. Since not one in a hundred of these was of any importance or required any thought, Colonel Ross had gone on reading and initialing them while he settled in his own mind the case of Colonel Woodman.

When General Beal made his later remarks, Colonel Ross gave him looks, to show that he heard; but made no comment since comment might encourage the general to keep going over it to no one's profit—and even, perhaps, to the general's own hurt. The continued humane or fraternal concern about Woody had a nervous sound. Woody could be made into an object lesson. In Woody was that food for thought which men find in the sudden sickness and death of old acquaintances. Woody's predicament might be of his own making, and so nothing for anyone else to worry about; yet Woody went right on embodying the disquieting truth that all the breaks may go against a man. There are, or seem to be, forces affecting a man's life wholly outside a man's control (Woody certainly did not want to be where he was). Whether operating on him in spite of him, or operating on him with his co-operation, they may ruin him as surely as they may, for instance, make him a major general at forty, and bring within his reach the highest ranks and honors.

Colonel Ross had never seen in General Beal that special assurance, hard to distinguish from conceit or bumptiousness, that views ascent to a high place calmly, as no more than the just deserts of high merits, always felt at heart and now admitted (later, of course, than they should have been) by a distracted world which foolishly imagined it might do without them. Though standing in an intimate relation to him and closely observing him for many months, Colonel Ross could not say whether General Beal did or did not ascribe his fortunes to luck, to getting the breaks. Not that General Beal lacked, or would imagine he lacked, unusual abilities which he could use —had used—with confidence; but he might feel that he owed his chances to use them to something outside, rather than something inside, himself. Colonel Ross must admit that modesty of this kind was pleasing in a man who had risen to high place; yet it was not (perhaps unfortunately for the world) the basic stuff of greatness. It spoke a simplicity of nature little related to the complexities, often unpleasant, of those natures that are resolved to lead, and also, by a suggestion of mystery and power in those very complexities, apt to impose leadership—the able, queer, vain men who in large-scale emergencies are turned to, and so make history.

Beyond question General Beal had been tried by emergency

and not found wanting; but as far as Colonel Ross knew or could guess, the emergencies were the soldier's, the man of action's, immediate and personal, well within a simple nature's resources of physical courage and quick sight. Because he found himself meeting such emergencies adequately or more than adequately, General Beal might be right in holding himself, humbly, no more than a lucky fellow. Colonel Ross, too, thought (that being how it was) that General Beal was lucky. Anyone was lucky who could go a successful way without the call to exercise greatness, without developing greatness's enabling provisions—the great man's inner contradictions; his mean, inspired inconsistencies; his giddy acting on hunches; and his helpless, not mere modest acceptance of, but passionate, necessary trust in, luck.

Twenty years before, when General Beal's youthful look and his eager or active air could not have been less marked than now, fellow classmen at the Military Academy, professing a derision that few of them actually felt, nicknamed him "Buster." Every old Air Corps man still knew him as Bus, and Colonel Ross could not remember hearing any of them speak ill of him.

Yet Colonel Ross knew it would be too much to say that none of them had ever thought ill of Bus. The quality of boyish eagerness, which a man's contemporaries can just stomach if he joins it to a friendly, unassuming nature, is likely to endear him to his superiors, and if it does, it becomes a harder thing to live down.

Colonel Ross, from years of a fairly active reserve-officer's close and sometimes critical acquaintance with the Regular Army, knew what such a boy would be up against. His professional abilities as an officer and a flyer had to stand invidious scrutiny. To stand that scrutiny with complete success, he needed to excel anything yet attained by mortal flyer or mortal officer. Bus was good, all right; but with so little room at the top, and with plums so few and far between, could he possibly be *that* good? Even if the answer had to be yes; even if he stood, by really unthinkable common agreement, well above everyone who shared his date of rank, his superiors would not feel perfectly free, at least in peacetime, to reward his merits quickly. In peacetime, everyone in the Army waits. Singling out a man, merely because of his abilities, and excepting him from the general rule, may give rise to rumors of favoritism. Rather than run such a risk, why not test his character by disappointment and delay? If your man loses patience, resigns his commission, plainly he lacks something; and your wisdom in waiting is established. The Old Man's favorite often takes a hard riding for this good reason.

Of course, Bus Beal made it easier for everyone by never seeming to give a damn for his career. Colonel Ross heard about that in Washington when they told him he was going to Ocanara, and General Beal, when he got back from Europe, would be his CO. If, as time passed, Bus did perhaps get more, and did get away with more, than other young officers less happily constituted (though in their own minds not undeserving), no one could say that Bus worked it by bucking for things, or keeping out of trouble. He was in trouble often. His Efficiency Rating seldom got beyond *excellent* (which, in the Army, is pretty bad), because his Efficiency Reports kept noting undesirable traits of recklessness and impulsiveness. Since he did nothing about mending his ways, some instinct may have informed Lieutenant, and later Captain, Beal that these censures were mostly for the record, where they would be ready if evidence were needed to show that Bus got no special favors. His instinct's information was correct. When it became apparent that the Army's long winter between wars was going to end, nothing was found to prevent jumping him, by two special orders two months apart, from captain to lieutenant colonel (temporary), and sending him to the Philippines. He arrived there three days before the Japanese bombers came over and destroyed on the ground two hundred and twenty-one of the Air Forces' less than three hundred planes.

Colonel Ross had heard the general mention incidents and circumstances of the bad first months of the war. Behind the locked and guarded doors of a Council on Reports session, or a meeting of the AFORAD Projects Board, General Beal would suddenly brush aside the proposals of his Directorate Chiefs, or the contentions of the Orlando, or Eglin Field, or Wright Field liaison officers, saying: "No. That won't work." Morosely, then, looking away at the big charts on the wall, or at an unlighted cigarette which his nervous fingers turned around and around until it broke and scattered pieces of tobacco over the agenda sheet before him, he would tell them, in explanation of his view, what he saw at Ido, or what you could learn from the mistakes at Nichols Field. He meant that until those whose opinion was different had seen what he had seen, he felt entitled to overrule them for reasons quite apart from rank.

Indeed, it was not easy for a person who had never been in that situation to know how a man must feel, and they listened to him, painfully silent, sternly shamefaced, even when they thought, as some usually did, that the lessons of 1941 were out of date. Since General Beal knew this as well as anybody, indeed had helped to make them out of date, the general was misled by the distortions that pain and emotion gave to facts which were just facts to people who had been spared his experience.

"Well, the hell with all that now—" General Beal would soon say; for his accounts never went beyond a half dozen sentences, some incomplete, some highly ungrammatical in the stress of trying to express what he meant without talking about it. There would be a profound pause.

Those who were still going to object shrank from objecting at once; and even those who agreed felt the momentary inappropriateness of getting right back to business. One of them might clear his throat and say, "General, I wonder if you ran into so-and-so . . ."; or another simply murmur: "Christ!" while he tried on himself the nightmare of everything going down in ruin around you (men wept at Nichols Field when the parked B-17's blew to bits or sank to junk in the flames of oxidized aluminum and running gasoline); your friends killed; your country shamed; disaster heaped on disaster; death at every turn; nothing to fight with; nothing to hope!

Colonel Ross did not think such a picture over-painted. Lieutenant Colonel Beal, putting together again and again the remains of a P-35 (obsolete before the war began), spent January

and February flying it off a patch on Bataan to perform limping reconnaissance missions. When he somehow got back, it was
often necessary to crash-land the crate. He would then walk
away from it and report a few details of Japanese movement
which would confirm the completeness of their disaster and the
inevitability of their doom. From time to time, General Beal
probably still re-lived moments so bad that a man might expect
to die of them without assisting cause. In memory perhaps even
worse would be the hours and days and weeks of horror rather
than terror, when you had to do what you could not do; when
you were never not hungry; when you were physically too sick
to stand—General Beal had told Colonel Ross that, suffering
from dysentery, he solved one problem of those ghastly reconnaissance missions by stuffing the seat of his coveralls with old
paper.

If it were suggested to General Beal that Lieutenant Colonel
Beal had liked any of these things, which he was not able to
speak of without pain and which he winced a little even to
think of, he would have stared angrily; but Colonel Ross
thought it possible that Lieutenant Colonel Beal did like them
better than General Beal now remembered. It was fair to believe that General Beal knew no more about himself than most
men; and, out of his self-knowledge, could tell you, no matter how hard and honestly he tried, less than you could learn
from what you saw or heard of his behavior.

Considered in this light, Lieutenant Colonel Beal's situation
eighteen months ago might have been less than hell. Who but
he could have made that P-35 fly at all? Who else could have
evaded the Jap patrols? Who else could have brought the plane
down without killing himself; and then fixed it to fly again
later that week? However harrowing and hopeless looking,
everything there was capable of yielding him the gratification
of knowing that he had proved himself able to do all or more
than any other man in those circumstances could do; that he
had not flinched—or, rather, since of course he had, that no
one had seen him flinch; and that, come what might, he had
stuck it out.

Even on this last point there had been a problem to face

and a choice to make, and General Beal could know that he had not fallen down on it. About the second week in March they asked for a volunteer to take one of the last flyable P-40's and try to get to Mindanao with a packet of sealed papers. That man, if he made it, would be out of this; while everyone else was lost. It was not a good chance, God knew, but it was a chance. It was the only chance any of them would ever get. The answer, while not easy, was simple. That a P-40, in the condition of those they had, could ever make Mindanao was hardly possible. If the likelihood of its getting there was greater with one pilot than with another, then that pilot must go. He must take the one chance, he must leave his surviving friends to the Japanese; he must escape, if he could, to life and health, to food and comfort; to honors and promotions. Lieutenant Colonel Beal was fully qualified to name that pilot, and it was necessary for him to name himself.

Colonel Ross did not envy him in this situation. Picking himself meant publicly concurring in the opinion, only decent when others held it, that no one approached him in skill and resource. Moreover, he must privately go on reiterating the unbecoming boast, giving himself specific instances of his clear superiority, since it was the only final answer to the hesitant, sickening query of his own heart. His heart knew how it longed not to die, and how little it regarded any face-saving argument that this escape might be more dangerous than not escaping. Perhaps so; but what pilot there, if the chance were offered him, would refuse it? Lieutenant Colonel Beal knew, too, all that, at that moment, was being bitterly felt and heatedly said about a more illustrious officer, only last week required, by direct orders, and by a sense of the duty that his high estimate of his own abilities imposed on him, to make his getaway. Colonel Beal must accept the certainty that the story of how he gave himself orders to go would pass from contemptuous mouth to contemptuous mouth, not only then and there; but for the rest of his life—or, if tomorrow a flight of Zeros jumped him, or his rickety engine conked out above the Sibuyan Sea, as long as any survivors of Bataan lived. Still, it was simple. Colonel Ross realized that Lieutenant Colonel Beal's temperament and training fitted him to state the problem; and, in this happy case, you could guess that the conscious mind, with its concept of duty, unreservedly replied: I *can*; while the secret image, every man's fond, fantastic idea of himself, whispered low: *Thou must.*

So he left; and he got the Silver Star for reaching Mindanao safely. Very soon afterward Lieutenant Colonel Beal was promoted to full colonel and sent to Australia to organize the fighter defense, such as it was, of Port Darwin. He flew in New Guinea for a month or so, and was credited with two Japanese planes. They then shifted him to the Seventh Air Force; and in May promoted him to Brigadier General. In July they brought him to Washington; and in September or October, he was sent secretly to Colomb Bechar.

Colonel Ross supposed that the game changed and the stakes went up at Colomb Bechar. He did not know what the general went there for. The fact that he did not know, that neither the general nor anyone else had ever told him, indicated the very highest level of policy and secrecy. However, Colonel Ross did know from ordinary sources of information, and by putting various references together, that Colomb Bechar, before it subsided to its present status of a junction point on the Air Transport Command's northwest African routes, had been a French Air Force field. It was three hundred miles south of Oran on the edge of the mountains.

General Beal went there many weeks before the November invasion, so vital preparations for the air part of that invasion might have been involved, and the general must have performed his job satisfactorily, in spite of whatever difficulties Carricker had in mind when he made his reference to the Frogs. There was, of course, the annoyingly complicated political situation in French North Africa. Moreover, Colonel Ross doubted if the general would feel at home with the French; a people who, in one of their aspects probably dismayed him by being so fond of gaiety and light wines; while in others they probably irritated him by their stubborn attachment, even when they were of low degree, to elaborate formalities, or stirred his contempt by their unabashed eagerness, even when they were of high degree, for substantial *pourboires*.

Because of its nature, and the high policy level of the necessary decision, Colonel Ross did not think that Bus Beal had asked for the Colomb Bechar assignment; but it seemed likely that, pleased with him, the high command let him say what he would like to do next. He turned up with the Ninth Air Force, where General Brereton no doubt wanted him. This surely suited Brigadier General Beal down to the ground. The situation was again difficult; but the issue was clear and openly joined, and he was the man to take it on. He was young enough, and himself fighter pilot enough, to uphold, as no one else could, the hand of the air generals against a strong and well-seated opposition.

They, the foot army commanders, controlled all air elements and were benightedly destroying them piecemeal. They must be stopped. The control must be wrested from them. To do this, it was necessary to shake them, or some of them, in their ruinous concepts. To shake them, they must be shown what the right use could do, compared to the wrong use. The person who showed them must be a man able at once to plan the mission, and himself lead it; and, having by rank the unquestionable right to be present at the highest council tables, to report out of his own mouth, so they must listen. Colonel Ross knew that it was believed by the Air Staff that General Beal, more than any other single person, won that fight; and, because of that air victory, they credited air power with winning, by May, Tunis, and Bizerte, too.

This was good; this was fine. Colonel Ross could well imagine it. General Beal, behind him half a skyful of his fighters, his gun hatches open and his magazines shot empty; his hair thick with the African dirt and his eyes dark with it in a face the sun had burned scarlet, must have felt like singing, regardless of more personal knowledge than most generals', that war is hell. He would flash around, four hundred yards off the runway, coming fast, a wing dipped to the tricky crosswind, to put down like an angel on three perfect points. By the dispersal areas beyond the distant edges of the field, all the ground crews

23

jumped from their slit trenches—not long ago, approaching engines were always German. They bowled their helmets on the ground. They yelled and leaped and punched each other, all their daily gripes forgotten in the ecstasy of look the sweet Jesus at the general! Get a load of that aircraft driver! Bus is back from the wars!

II

WHEN THEY taxied out to take off from Sellers Field, Captain Nathaniel Hicks, with Colonel Ross's example before him, removed in a businesslike way some file folders from his brief case. They contained a three weeks' collection of material for a proposed revision of Army Air Forces Field Manual One-dash-Fifteen: *Tactics and Technique of Pursuit Aviation.* Though published as recently as April, 1942, this work was already obsolete—indeed, much of it was obsolete when it was written, for those who produced it had no experience in actual combat later than 1918.

There was now a general agreement about what parts of the text were wrong; but Captain Hicks had not yet found two fighter pilots in complete agreement on what would be right. He had gone to Sellers Field to talk to a Major Post, a noted AVG flyer. Major Post had lost an arm in China, and though they had fixed him up a good mechanical substitute, he did not like it; and he did not like being relegated to Operations Officer at Sellers Field. It was soon plain to Captain Hicks that Major Post, consciously or unconsciously, also disliked at sight anyone who had all his limbs, was not a fighter pilot, or came from Ocanara to bother him with a lot of talk. Seeing that Captain Hicks wore no wings and had no ribbons, Major Post stared at him in a surly way while the project was explained. He then said: "How the hell are *you* going to rewrite it?"

Captain Hicks, who was thirty-eight to Major Post's twenty-eight, and who was, in civilian life, a magazine editor whose judgment might often do much to determine what several hundred thousand people like Major Post were going to read, and so, going to think and believe, accepted this criticism in good part. Nathaniel Hicks said that he was not writing the new manual himself. He was getting the views of qualified pilots on the proper changes. He would write these up in a report and, on the basis of them, prepare a synopsis of new material. This would go to the Training Aids Division of AAF Headquarters, which handled manuals. It would be for them to write and publish the revision.

Major Post said: "What am I supposed to do?"

Captain Hicks suggested, if the major had time, that he go over the present text, of which this was a copy in case he didn't have one, and simply mark out everything he thought was wrong. Captain Hicks had already done this with Captain Wiley, at the School of Applied Tactics at Orlando; and with—

"Who the hell is he?" said Major Post, taking the manual brusquely and slapping it open on his desk.

"He was with the Eagle Squadron, flying off Malta," Captain Hicks said. "He has seven Axis planes."

"Axis!" said Major Post. "Wops, I suppose he means."

"Five of them were German," Captain Hicks said. He was a good-tempered man and ready enough to subordinate his civilian dignity or consequence to those who were in the after all important fighting end of the war. However, bumptiousness irritated him now just as much as it used to when staff writers put up loud, persistent, and foolish arguments about things that few or no writers seemed capable of understanding—what was good and interesting because it interested them personally, for instance, and what was intrinsically interesting to people at large.

Captain Hicks had a frank, round face not suited to conceal his feelings. A warm color appeared on his temples below his short, fuzzy, blond hair. His blond mustache, cropped to a stiff growth of quarter-inch hairs, stiffened more, and his eyes began to snap, for he liked a fight when he was finally forced to it.

Major Post said impatiently, "Sure, I got time. What else is there to do here?" He bent his thin dark face on the text and began to scratch his over-long dark hair. "I don't know about all this crap," he said, tapping the introductory paragraphs. "I never saw this before—Jesus, they must be nuts! What do they want all this for, anyway?"

"I don't know, sir," said Captain Hicks. "We have an AAF Board Directive. I have been ordered to prepare the material. We'd be glad to leave out some of the crap, if you'll tell me what it is."

"I think all of it's crap," Major Post said. "Well, all right. Skip all this first part. I don't know anything about that. 'Air Tactics of Pursuit Aviation.' Huh! Well, in the first place—" He paused and jerked the buttons loose on his left sleeve. "Let me take this goddamn thing off," he said. He then unbuttoned his shirt, fumbling for something with his right hand. Captain Hicks, a good deal mollified, said: "Could I help you, Major?"

"Yeah," Major Post said truculently. "Just open those two buckles there." Captain Hicks did as he was directed, and Major Post slipped the arm out and laid it on his desk. He tucked the end of his empty sleeve into the breast pocket beneath his Senior Pilot's wings. "I need the goddamn thing to fly," he said. "Rest of the time, I'd like to shove it up the Flight Surgeon's—"

Misfortunes of this type should happen to philosophers. When a philosopher loses an arm, he does not go on being sore about it; he exercises reason and patience, and trains himself with equanimity to make the best use he can of the ingenious substitute that a grateful nation has given him. Nathaniel Hicks's civilian talent for identifying and developing themes of interest to men in general was at least partly based on an instinctive grasp of their very limited resources of reason, patience, and equanimity. He grasped these limits less by special perspicacity, of which, however, he had a good deal, than by sharing them.

It required no thought at all for him to act on the impulse and offer to help Major Post—an offer which might strike a man who was in the habit of making considered judgments as tactless and likely to annoy the major more. Though Major Post had given no sign of it, Nathaniel Hicks's instinct informed him that the major was disgusted with himself and his own irritability. If Captain Hicks affected to notice no difficulty with the straps, it would be taken not as delicacy or tact but as an indication that Captain Hicks perhaps shared these

26

feelings. A casual offer to help meant that he probably hadn't noticed anything out of the way in the major's attitude or remarks.

With this crisis past, they began to get on better. Major Post remained suspicious, in his jumpy way looking for signs that Captain Hicks thought him irritable and arrogant—complaints against himself which he felt to be just; and so, which would make him ready, in a fury, to develop and release his own just complaint that Captain Hicks was not a fighter pilot, nor even a pilot.

Getting through the afternoon without incident, Major Post, at the end of it, said in a faintly friendly tone that they might as well go over to the Officers Club and have a drink. He was, however, still morose; and still, it was plain, jumpy. While Captain Hicks was giving him a hand with reattaching the arm, the door of Major Post's small office, which was at the end of the Operations Room, opened without ceremony and a young Flight Officer strode in and stopped, surprised.

"God damn it to hell!" Major Post said. "Don't barge in here when I'm busy, Mister; or you may find it in a high sling some morning!"

Later, trying to get to sleep in the stifling Mississippi night, Nathaniel Hicks was depressed by the thought of Major Post. He shared a meager Visiting Officers Quarters room with an unexplained artillery captain, who was snoring when Hicks came in, and went on snoring. The afternoon had not been very profitable as far as progress on FM 1-15 went. Major Post was in sharp disagreement, especially about combat formations, with Captain Wiley; with an RAF Group Captain stationed at Ocanara, named Cooper; and with Colonel Folsom, Chief of the Ocanara Fighter Analysis Directorate. (These three were, of course, also in disgreement with each other.) The project had begun to seem a waste of time.

Considering the conflicts in the material, Nathaniel Hicks's editorial training told him what should be done. You just shelved it; you postponed any use of it indefinitely—removed it from the magazine's schedule. Two years ago, such decisions

27

were left to him; and when he made them they were absolute. They were not left to him here. Major Whitney would listen to his objections, disliking them and worried by them. If Nathaniel Hicks fussed enough, he might even carry them to the colonel, where it would run up against the directive. Prepare it anyway! Arrange these papers alphabetically and burn them!

Though the pressure was mildly applied in AFORAD, Special Projects, it was firm. The dismaying sense of it, perhaps the one common denominator in the various feelings of several million men caught up in a war, of the steady, in the exact sense, preposterous, compulsion, oppressed the mind. It reversed accustomed order and reasoned expectation. Pulled constantly up in blank amazement, a man must ask himself what in God's name he was doing here. The answer Nathaniel Hicks needed was one beyond or behind the accessible and obvious answer, that there was a war on, and since he would probably be drafted anyway, he might as well volunteer; or any feelings about the merits of the contest (which, in a way, did not matter; once the contest began the only issue was beat or be beaten, and this easy choice could command almost anybody's best endeavor quite as well as zeal for right and justice, or the heady self-gratulations of simple patriotism).

These, the accessible and obvious explanations of how you came to be where you were, involved only motives and choices of your own. They hardly seemed good enough to settle the disquieted mind's question, or to still that primary amazement which recognized that it was preposterous. Major Post must find it preposterous to have no left arm. Major Post had always had two arms, in very much the sense that Nathaniel Hicks had always, or at least since he left college, had a rational life, a job of his own choosing which he did very well, a wife and children at a place that he had bought, though not yet finished paying for, in Connecticut; and every motive or choice would have continued him along those lines. Both he and Major Post regarded their present circumstances with dismay and incredulity—not exactly sorry for themselves; not necessarily complaining; but deeply and disturbingly aware that this they would not have chosen.

Here was nothing they had elected to do and then did. This was done to them. The dark forces gathered, not by any means at random or reasonlessly, but according to a plan in the nature of things, like the forces of a storm; which, as long as heat expanded air and cold contracted it, would have to proceed. When the tempest reached its hurricane violence, uprooting, overturning, blowing away, you must make the best of its million freaks, whose diverse results might range from riddling Major Post's arm with a burst of 7.7 mm Japanese bullets to landing Nathaniel Hicks in his sweat-soaked underwear on a cot in the dark at Sellers Field.

So he lay there, gazing amazed at the captain's bars reflecting the dim light beyond the open door, on the collar of his shirt, hung on a chair with his folded trousers—preposterous proof that it was all true, that he was here. Tomorrow he would put on those unlikely garments, move through the cooler twilight just before sunrise to an electrically lighted officers cafeteria, gulp his breakfast, sign out with the adjutant, collect his musette bag, and wait at Operations for a plane that would give him a ride back to Florida. Not back to his Connecticut house, where he might expect to awake and find that all along he had been dreaming. He would go back to an extension of the dream, which included some fairly comfortable rooms he shared with a Captain Duchemin and a Captain Andrews in an old hotel at Ocanara called the Oleander Towers.

The next day, still deep in his dream, he would be at his desk in an office—shared this time with Captain Duchemin and a Lieutenant Edsell—in the new Special Projects Directorate Building out in the sandy pine woods of the AFORAD Area beyond the Air Base. As the intolerable heat rose, the concrete block walls condensed moisture from the nearby lakes. The fans swung the dead air around under the open rafters of the low pitched roofs. Very soon, Major Whitney, Nathaniel Hicks's Section Chief, would lope in and hover, worried, to say that Washington or somebody had been asking about FM 1-15. Could they estimate an approximate date?

✦

In the morning, things stirred at Sellers Field because of the sudden word that General Beal was coming. Major Post was pestered every five minutes by Colonel Woodman for an ETA on the general's plane. At about ten, Lieutenant Turck turned up on a C-47 from the west. Entering Operations rather shyly and stiffly, she gave Captain Hicks a startled look, and then said, "Oh, hello, there! You don't know how I can get to Ocanara, do you? I think I'm lost."

Lieutenant Turck was a tall woman in her late twenties with a good figure and thin, fine-textured skin. Her hair was sandy and her profile sharp and pointed with a well-formed nose. Her eyes, a light gray, expressed a pleasant directness and her long, thin-lipped but flexible mouth gave her an agreeable, humorous air. Nathaniel Hicks understood that she had formerly worked as a librarian, and this was doubtless true, for the Ocanara Classified Files ran with a certain professional competence under her direction.

Naturally Lieutenant Turck had worn her best uniform on the temporary duty assignment at Des Moines, so she looked, though weary and wrinkled, quite smart and dressed up—instead of a shirt, a tropical worsted blouse that fitted her well. She had taken care to embellish it by pinning on the shoulder loops (already changed from the old WAAC position to run the regulation way) AFORAD distinctive insignia—a wonderfully fancy shield in variegated enamels showing, above some mountains where the sun was rising, a human hand thrust through the clouds to support on its palm a silver plane. On top, by way of a crest, was a gold gauntlet clenching a pair of silver wings; and underneath, on a gold scroll, the motto: *Nec Tenui Ferar Penna;* generally translated for those curious enough to inquire: *Stay Away from Pennsylvania.* It was known to be the invention or creation of Colonel Mowbray, General Beal's Executive Officer. He seemed to have devoted his leisure, during some idle prewar years at Maxwell Field, to designing coats and shields appropriate for Air Corps units or installations. The rumor that Colonel Mowbray got twenty-five cents commission on every set the Ocanara Post Exchange sold, though widely credited, was wholly false.

Lieutenant Turck's appeal energized Nathaniel Hicks. Before going out to the water cooler, where he met her, he had been sitting in Major Post's office, listlessly typing up his notes on the major's conversation yesterday. The major, idle and gloomy, berated the Weather Officer for some delay in the morning reports; told the Airdrome Officer, who wanted an order that no planes should land or take off while General Beal was being welcomed on the ramp, that to hell with General Beal, they had a day's work to do; found fault with a staff sergeant who reported that they were out of Form 23. Between times, he expressed his conviction that Captain Hicks might as well throw that stuff away, all anybody ever published was more of the usual crap. However, he had asked Hicks into his office and did not seem to mind his waiting there. He said he would, during the next couple of days, mark up a copy of 1-15 with his objections and suggestions and get it off to Ocanara. He then went on to add that if General Beal couldn't take Hicks back, he might fly him to Ocanara himself. If he could get a plane; which he doubted; the goddamn maintenance was so lousy.

Captain Hicks told Lieutenant Turck about General Beal, and about Major Post's offer. He would see what he could do to get her on with him. "Thank God!" Lieutenant Turck said. "I am pretty nearly AWOL. I don't think that would be too good. I am now a seven-days-expert on Army Regulations and Military Justice Procedure. I do not want to begin my new duties by advising the Staff Director on what to do with my own case."

Her vivacity was strained. She must have spent most of the night, sleeping little and probably very cold, in a bucket seat. She looked worn; and no doubt she felt miserable and dirty, and wished she could find a lavatory. Those at Operations, marked respectively *Enlisted Men* and *Officers*, were provided for males.

Captain Hicks went back to Major Post's office and explained this situation. Major Post grunted impatiently, took the telephone, and called the Sellers Field WAC Detachment Headquarters. He then said, "Tell that Joe out there by my jeep to take it and drive her up."

"Thanks very much," Nathaniel Hicks said. "It's kind of rugged for the girls."

"Rugged!" said Major Post with disgust. "I think they're nuts, having them. We bring it in, and wave it in their faces until we hot the goats up; so then we have to put the area off-limits and walk guards all night to keep them from getting any. I want that jeep back right away, tell him. I may have to go down the line."

Lieutenant Turck said: "Oh, God, what a wonderful man you are!" She walked out with him quite jauntily and got into the jeep. A chunky little Pfc saluted them, pulled out a pack of square blue cards, selected one with a big second lieutenant's bar on it and shoved it into a holder on the windshield. Then he roared away with her.

When Nathaniel Hicks got back to Major Post's office the major, who was holding the telephone, said: "Jesus Christ, Captain, is anybody left at Ocanara? They got a man of yours down at the gate who wants a ride. They think we run a railroad? He's an Engineer Corps jigaboo. He's got a furlough certificate to today, so the Provost Marshal's holding him. You want to do anything about it?"

"I don't know what I can do," Nathaniel Hicks said. "How can they hold him if his furlough certificate is still good?"

"Look," said Major Post. "He's due back at Ocanara to-night by midnight, I suppose. So, can he get there? I don't see how. He lives over in town, this dinge. So tomorrow or next day, the Provost Marshal will probably get a wire saying to look for him. He figures if he has him in the guard house, he'll know right where to look."

"That's the damnedest thing I ever heard of!" Nathaniel Hicks said. "You mean he's going to hold the man until he *is* AWOL? Why—"

"Now, don't go damning me, God damn it," Major Post said. "I'm not holding him. I don't care what they do with him. He wants a ride back to Ocanara, and we don't have any." To the telephone, he said, "Send him up! We have an Ocanara

32

officer here. He can figure out what to do with him." He slammed the receiver down. He said, "Does he think we're going to set up a flight for him? He knew when he had to be back. Why didn't he start in time to get there? The brainless black bastard! If you feel so bad about it, you fix it."

"Well, I don't see what I can do, Major," Nathaniel Hicks said stiffly. "I suppose he belongs to one of our base service units. I'm afraid I don't know very much about company administration—"

"That's your problem, chum, not mine," said Major Post. The telephone rang and he whipped it up, snapping "Operations Officer!" He listened a moment. Then he shouted through the open door: "Write up General Beal's B-Twenty-five from Ocanara for one-one-zero-zero. Find the Airdrome Officer, he's screwing around on the ramp somewhere, and tell him. Better ring Colonel Woodman's office, too."

They both busied themselves for some minutes in silence. Then, scowling, Major Post glanced out the window. "There's your jigaboo, Captain," he said. "Don't bring him in here."

Nathaniel Hicks went out to the parking space behind the building. Omitting Major Post's epithets (which made him uncomfortable, since he had no conscious prejudice against Negroes, and was even mildly irritated by the note of self-esteem necessarily present in all assertions on the subject by those who had) he could not help being much of the major's mind. It was up to the man himself to see that he got back. Nathaniel Hicks, a year or more ago, had listened, stupefied with heat and physical fatigue, to perhaps six hours of lectures at the Officers Training School at Miami, on company administration. He had the impression that there was some form or some something to authorize or excuse an overstaying of furlough; but he did not know how you got it, who issued it. He had no authority to make any arrangements for anyone, let alone Corps of Engineers personnel; and though the Provost Marshal's proposal might strike him as outrageous, what would he propose instead?

With nothing prepared, he walked across the sun-baked cinders to a truck with a couple of benches in it, from which had descended the Negro—just a kid, he saw, with T/5 stripes on his sleeves, and an MP. They both saluted. He said: "I'm Captain Hicks from Ocanara. What's your trouble, Corporal?"

The boy said: "They got me arrested, sir. I don't know what's the trouble." He bent his head aside, in eloquent sadness and worry and then jerked himself nervously back to attention.

"At ease, at ease," Nathaniel Hicks said somewhat uncertainly. He looked at the MP. "Why have you got him arrested?"

"He's not arrested, sir. You'll have to ask Captain Brooks. He said to hold him while we called Major Post."

Nathaniel Hicks said, "Have you your furlough certificate, Corporal?"

"No, sir." He brought his eyes around and fixed them anxiously on Nathaniel Hicks's chin. "I don't have that, Captain. Up to the gate, they ask for it, and they don't give me it back. I had it before they took it."

"Where is his paper?" Nathaniel Hicks said to the MP.

"It went over to Captain Brooks, sir, the Provost Marshal. He must have it."

"Well, look, Corporal," Nathaniel Hicks said, "when did it say you would report for duty?"

"Day due to return, sir, it says today."

"But how did you think you'd get back? You can't possibly make it. Do you know how far it is?"

"Yes, sir. I took two days on those trains coming."

"Well, why didn't you start back in time? Haven't you any money? Did you lose the other half of your furlough ticket?"

"No, sir. I never lost it. I give it to the man at the depot and he give me the money. First thing I did when I came here."

"Well, Corporal, why did you do that? You knew you had to go back." Nathaniel Hicks paused. "You didn't think you'd desert, did you, and then change your mind?"

"No, *sir!* But they said I can fly back, Captain. That's what they said."

"Who said?"

"Sergeant, sir. Sergeant my section. Sergeant Rogers. The lieutenant, Lieutenant Anderson, told me, too."

Nathaniel Hicks looked at him in perplexity. "Oh," he said. "You mean they told you it would be all right if you traveled by plane?"

"Yes, *sir*. They both said that, sir. I know they have this big field here, near where I live. We got a man in my platoon came back in a plane, sir."

"Yes," said Nathaniel Hicks, "that's right. If there was a plane going, and they had space, they might give you a ride. But you didn't know whether there was a plane going or not, or whether they'd have room for you. Don't you see that?"

"Well, this man came back in a plane. He said you just go out to a field, sir, and tell the officer there you want to go, and they don't make you pay, even—"

The MP said: "Colonel Woodman, Captain!" A staff car had swung in to the door and a red-faced chicken colonel with a mustache and a riding crop was clambering out of it. Nathaniel Hicks faced about with the others and saluted him. The colonel touched his cap visor with two fingers and disappeared into Operations.

Nathaniel Hicks waited a moment, trying to get space to think from the interruption. The MP shifted his feet and adjusted his fourragère of white cord. The boy waited mutely. "Well, Corporal," Nathaniel Hicks said to him, "your man didn't have it right. You should have told the lieutenant all that, and he would have explained it to you. Now, I'm afraid you're in a jam. What's your name?"

"Mortimer McIntyre, Junior, sir. Army Serial Number—"

Nathaniel Hicks took a notebook from his shirt pocket and wrote it down. "I'll have to see," he said.

The irksome thought went through his mind that Major Post's brainless black bastard here stood in infinitely greater need of a lift to Ocanara, supposing General Beal's plane had any space, than he, or probably than Lieutenant Turck, did. Irritated, for he didn't want to spend another day at Sellers Field— and why should he, just because Mortimer McIntyre, Junior (Lord, the names they had!), listened with thick-headed credulity to some moron's garbled version of his misunderstood adventures, and, never bothering to check it, never bothering to make the simplest and most obvious inquiries, turned up blithe and guileless at the Sellers Field gate ready for the AAF to fly him back! Nathaniel Hicks swallowed down his irritation as well as he could. "There may be a chance," he said severely. "Even if there is a plane, though, there are other passengers waiting, so it's a pretty poor one." He looked at the MP. "What are you supposed to do with him?"

"Well, I better bring him back to the guard house, sir, unless Major Post wants to take custody of him."

"No," said Nathaniel Hicks. "I can't ask him to do that. He'll get something to eat, won't he?"

"Oh, yes, Captain. We aren't going to lock him up, far as I know."

Corporal McIntyre looked sadly at the ground. He moved his lips a little, and then licked them. Nathaniel Hicks thought suddenly of the artillery captain snoring, a slow steady groan and sigh in the dim dark last night, and the baffled turnings of his own weary mind. Mortimer McIntyre, Junior, knew only that the white MP's still had him. The Ocanara officer had not rescued him from his inexplicable situation, but only told him that things other people told him were wrong. His sensitive, childish, black face bent lower still, as though he was trying to keep it as far as possible from being seen.

With a tremor of the nerves, a sharp painful shrinking, Nathaniel Hicks saw that he might be going to cry. He said loudly: "All right, you get him some lunch. Tell your captain—is it Brooks?—that the matter will be referred to General Beal when he comes in this morning; and he is to take no action until then. He'd better give him his paper back. The general may want to see it—" his rapid fabrication gave Nathaniel Hicks an idea "—because if we can't get him on the general's plane, I'm sure the general will indorse an overstay of furlough for him, and he can go back by train tonight. If there's anything Captain Brooks doesn't understand, ask him to call me, Hicks, at Operations here. Got that?"

"Yes, sir."

"All right, McIntyre. You go along with him and have some lunch. I'll let you know." He saw that, while he might have impressed the MP with his easy references to General Beal, Mortimer McIntyre, Junior, had not understood any of it. He lifted his mournful face and said, "They take me back to the guard house, Captain?"

"Just for a little while, so you can get lunch."

Twenty minutes later Nathaniel Hicks watched General Beal's arrival from a window in Operations. He had not known how he was going to approach the general; but when he saw Colonel Ross letting himself down the steps and coming out from under the plane, he went into the passage that led through the Operations building to the back door where the cars waited. He was not sure that Colonel Ross knew his name, but he was confident that the colonel would recognize him. Colonel Ross and his wife lived in one of the bungalows on the grounds of the Oleander Towers Hotel. Nathaniel Hicks, who brought a car with him when he came to Ocanara, had several times given Colonel Ross a lift out to the AFORAD Area.

As he expected, the party came through the passage. He stood at attention against the wall while the general and Colonel Woodman passed. Relaxing then, he was in time to say urgently: "Colonel!"

Colonel Ross, walking with the Sellers Field Executive Officer, swung his head. He stopped and said: "Hello, there, young fellow! I was going to look you up. Heard you were here." To Colonel Woodman's Executive, he said, "We weren't going in the general's car, were we? No. Well, I've something I want to see the captain about. Be along in a minute." He put a hand on Nathaniel Hicks's arm and stood against the wall with him. He said, "I went up to your quarters last night. Saw that big Duchemin fellow. He said you were at Sellers Field. When are you coming back?"

Somewhat disconcerted at the notion of being an object of a search by the Air Inspector, Nathaniel Hicks said: "That's what I was going to ask you about, sir."

"What's the trouble?"

When Nathaniel Hicks had told him, Colonel Ross said: "Three of you? Well, I don't know. I'll have to ask Carricker. We're flying back in another plane. Stay around the building here and I'll let you know. I think we can take *you*, all right."

"Well, sir, the truth is it may be more important for the others—"

"I doubt it. The Old Man wants to see you—" He laughed. "You'd better be here."

"What does he want to see me about, sir?"

"He'll tell you." Colonel Ross began to laugh again. "Well, I don't think they're going to shoot you," he said. "Not yet anyway! No, listen, Hicks. You know the general's wife?"

"No, sir. Well, I saw her at that reception. But—"

"She's Colonel Coulthard's sister, you know. He happened to be over there the other night, and your name came up. The general has an idea. All right. Have your friends here, and we'll see what we can do."

He walked on to the door, leaving Nathaniel Hicks standing in the passage disquieted, for he had, by now, a fair certainty about the ideas likely to occur when his name "came up," and they were often extravagantly unfeasible.

✦

Second Lieutenant Amanda Turck shifted in her seat. With a little difficulty, she recrossed her legs under the plotting desk. She said, her head toward Nathaniel Hicks, her low but cleanly articulated words distinct against engine noise in the well-insulated cabin: "Well, it was an incident, I tell you. I don't know whether she thought it was her duty, or whether it was just curiosity, but she came around to see us one afternoon about five-thirty, of all times! She called up and told the sergeant in the Enlisted Women's Day Room that she was coming—a very dumb child named Hogan. You know, until they finish a BOQ for us, all the WAC officers are quartered on the top floor of a barracks—the one on the end of the line there. Not the whole building, though. The Day Room and a laundry are downstairs. It is hellishly uncomfortable. Everything is always in a mess—no place to put anything."

She glanced at Colonel Ross's back, as though to assure herself that the muted yet pervasive noise kept him from hearing. "Well, Hogan, the dumb brat, didn't bother to tell us upstairs. She was in a dither, getting the Day Room policed up and scurrying around to the other barracks, and the mess, and so on, to say that Mrs. General was going to make an inspection and when the girls came in they were to wash their faces quickly and stand by. At, say, one-seven-two-nine, Hogan got back from spreading the alarm. It was a ghastly hot afternoon and Colonel Mowbray had been hanging around over at Classified Files wanting some nonsense that wasn't there anyway, so I'd just got in, gone upstairs, stripped, put on a bath robe and come downstairs to get a shower—that's a wonderful feature of the accommodations. There's no washroom upstairs, and to get at the one downstairs you have to go through the Day Room, trying as you go to give an example of dishabille becoming an officer and a lady. Well, there I was attractively garbed in Mary's old bath robe with a towel around my neck, when Hogan noticed me sneaking along the wall. She said: 'Oh, ma'am! Were you alerted? Mrs. Beal is coming—I think, there she is now!'"

Lieutenant Turck spread her hands. "Oh, really! Oh, God! She *was* coming, too. She was walking up the duck boards to the Day Room door. I suppose I could have gone right into the washroom and hidden; but nobody knew upstairs, and the place was a shambles. Coming off duty, everyone would get out of her clothes, leaving them in a soggy little pool on the floor, and half of them would then just fall on a cot under an electric fan in a state of nature and hang their tongues out for ten minutes deciding whether to die or not. So I whipped upstairs again—their pal, their buddy, bless her gallant heart!—telling Hogan for God's sake not to let Mrs. General wander around—take her to the mess, show her the kitchen; anything. But Hogan was good and flustered. There were half a dozen kids in the Day Room and just as I got out of sight, I heard her yelp: 'Te-hut!'—I'm sure that isn't right, is it? You don't call

39

people to attention for the general's wife, do you? At any rate, she did; and I burst on them upstairs with the good news."

Lieutenant Turck rolled her eyes. "Meanwhile," she said, "Mrs. General asked for the Staff Director. I suppose she expected to be greeted by somebody of more weight than poor little Hogan. Captain Burton wasn't around. As a matter of fact, she was over at the hospital trying to talk to a kid who'd been AWOL a week. They'd just found her in a tourist camp cabin where she said four enlisted men had taken her, given her dope in a glass of Seven-Up, and then all violated her for days. Which she was powerless to prevent because of the peculiar action of the drug. It affected her vocal cords so that when she screamed she didn't make any noise. Poor Burton, who is rather new to the seamy side of life, was busy swallowing this; so the command, if any, more or less devolved on Mary.

"Little Hogan knew that, and instead of doing what I told her, blurted to Mrs. General that Lieutenant Lippa was upstairs, the dope. Mrs. General came right up—honestly, the gall of the woman!—shrilling out: 'Now, girls, don't mind me.' Mary hadn't got her clothes off, so she went front and center very bravely to head her off and take her somewhere else; but that's where she was wrong. Mrs. General had probably been having a few rum-and-Cokes over at the Officers Club or somewhere. I don't mean that she was tight; she was just feeling good—big-hearted. She sat down on the end of my cot, lit a cigarette, and said to call her Sal. Oh, God, I am being very nasty; she just wanted to make friends. And she did say she would speak to 'Ira' about how they would have to fix us up the new building—.

"The thing is, and you'd expect any woman, at least, to realize it, here we are pigging it in the line of duty, and she comes down to see if she can help the poor creatures, thank you kindly. There you are all covered with sweat and your hair on end, and your GI slip wet through the back, and your wretched little rack of smart and becoming eight-point-two that all needs to go to the laundry, and a half a bottle of nail polish and a can of deodorant powder laid out luxuriously on your foot locker, and she comes in all done up and says call me Sal!

Maybe it's the heat, but a girl feels like lying down and howling. It is difficult to understand men. To my mind, the General Commanding could have any woman he wanted, and that's what he wants."

"Gracious," said Nathaniel Hicks, "is he that attractive?"

"He attracts me," Lieutenant Turck said. "But then, I think single women in barracks make themselves a musty and unwholesome atmosphere. Even the brisk ones, like Burton, have a kind of taint." She shook her head. "Who would be here if there wasn't something wrong with her?"

"Well, but what's wrong with you?"

"You say the nicest things, Captain! Remind me to tell you, sometime. The story is unbelievably long and boring." She colored faintly, and seemed to falter in her conversational stride. She said, "I don't know whether you are aware of it or not, but women are much more incomplete people than men. That's why so many of them get married."

"Is that so?" said Nathaniel Hicks. "I must tell my wife."

"Oh, I think you'll find she knows all about it. Of course, she has the advantage of being pretty, so she may only know it theoretically—"

"How do you know she has the advantage of being pretty?"

"I noticed her when she was down here last month. We are great little noticers, you know. You'd been in to the files a few times and it is always interesting to see what different men's wives are like. Lippa and I have a standing reservation at the Towers every Saturday and Sunday. You may not think much of the accommodations, but that's because you live there all the time. It is very heaven, I can tell you. Bathtubs, you know. Room to turn around in. Doors you can shut. We get down Saturdays about five and don't have to be out to the Area until Sunday night at ten. So, in the dining room, we look around. I'm quite knowledgeable, what with my files contacts. So I say: 'Don't look now, but there's Major Somebody of Bombardment. That must be his wife.' So Lippa looks now anyway and says: 'She must be years older than he is. Why do you suppose women dye their hair? They never fool other women.' So we have quite a happy time."

"It sounds divine," Nathaniel Hicks said. "But you were going to tell me why they got married."

"Yes. A girl who's pretty isn't as likely to think of it so often; but even she must occasionally pull up and reflect that a woman really has to have a man, or men. I don't mean just for purposes of romance or reproduction. You need one for all kinds of things. Your whole economy is based on it, like some primitive tribe and its domestic animal. You know, the yak, maybe. They eat it, and drink the milk, and make clothes out of its fur or hair or whatever it has, and shoes out of its hide, and use it to pull a sledge, and on and on. If you haven't got one, you are really on a spot. You can't lead a full life. You're definitely underprivileged, or on sub-marginal subsistence."

"I feel like going out and getting me one," Nathaniel Hicks said. "Only I don't know that I am pretty enough." As soon as he had said it, he saw that the idle, the labored facetiousness, spoken for something to say, touched a tender spot.

Lieutenant Turck made a bitter face—though it was plain that the bitterness was directed inward, at herself. Often she must have resolved not to be that way; and it shamed and angered her when she found that the firmly taken resolve did not protect her: "I do seem to go on about that, don't I?" She bent her lips up in a smile. The fine-textured skin, stretching away from her nose, reddened faintly; while the edges of her ears grew very red. "I get quite tired of myself, from time to time. I said that to Lippa once when we were a little out of sorts, and she said: 'Well, who wouldn't?' " She drew a breath. She said, "I think I ought to be psychoanalyzed. Except I know it all already. Things complicate themselves for me. You know, when Mrs. General said to call her Sal, I was damned if I would. Now, anyone could feel that way. There's nothing wrong with that. But I know something else. As a child I did not like my name. One very good reason why I will not call her Sal is that she would be sure to call me Mandy."

"I think Mandy is fine," Nathaniel Hicks said. "I see no objection to it whatsoever. I could tell you one about that; and just to keep you in countenance, I will. They named me for

42

a great uncle of mine; and back in the 'sixties or 'seventies when he began flourishing, it seems they called him 'Nate' for short. So my parents called me Nate. When I went away to school, I tried to get it changed to 'Nat.' It didn't work. They found out I was lying, somehow; so then, whenever they wanted to speak disparagingly of me, which was often, they called me 'Nates'—as in buttocks. I used to fight people about it, if they were smaller than I was. Didn't you have a happy childhood?"

"Yes, I did, really." Lieutenant Turck paused. She said: "Except for hating to be plain. That's hard on a girl. But I had hopes. I was a great reader, of course. They always are. I used to read in books—I can't think what books, but I read everything and maybe it was in the kind of novel they covered with dark brown muslin and passed around suburban reading circles twenty years ago—about girls who were shy, awkward, and unattractive children; and then the next time the hero noticed them they had blossomed into radiant womanhood and their beauty was breath-taking. I could see I filled the first part of the bill, all right; and it made me think hard." Perhaps feeling that her tone had become too serious for the subject, she said: "Oh, dear, it's really funny; but the thought of my wretched little self fills me with compunction."

She looked out the window of the plane a moment. She said, "Did you ever notice? Flying, you can always tell when you're getting down into Florida, if it's late in the afternoon, because of the shadows. The tops of the trees look all alike, but right beside each one you can see the little black shadow of palm fronds stretched out on the ground. Shall we talk about Florida?"

"No," said Nathaniel Hicks. "Talk about your wretched little self some more. You can tell when I'm bored, because I start yawning and looking at my watch."

"Oh, don't think I won't! I just stopped because it was bringing tears to my eyes. Well, along about then, my mother thought it was time she had a talk with me about becoming a woman, as she said. You can imagine I pricked my ears up and listened attentively. 'Aha,' I thought, 'so that's it!' I was an earnest little brat—naturally—and I had pretty well reached the conclusion that in this life you get nothing for nothing and very little for tuppence. All she said sounded quite disagreeable, and that made it plausible and convincing. Anything like radiant beauty would be bound to have some strings to it. So Mother and I exchanged a few kisses and I was very blithe and merry. I used to anticipate conversations people would soon be having about me. You know. The principal at school, quite an elegant-acting dark man, would say to my teacher: 'Gracious me, Miss Mealy, little Amanda has become radiantly lovely of late.' And she would say: 'How very true, Mr. Nibble! I find myself gazing at her constantly. Her beauty is truly breath-taking.'" Lieutenant Turck made a face. "What happened instead was that my complexion got quite bad for a while and I got much too tall. So I had to go on studying hard and being fond of reading. What my teacher actually said to the principal—I know, because I often stayed and did a little work after class, having nothing else to do, and they were talking in the hall—was: 'That poor child Mandy Smith. She's just a little book worm. I wonder if a doctor could do anything for that skin condition. It makes her so self-conscious.' I went home and looked in the mirror; and worm was right. So I bawled awhile, and then went on with my reading. Perhaps it was just as well. My father died presently and left us quite poor: So I got a part-time job in the local library, being so fond of books and all, and how the money rolled in!"

"Smith," said Nathaniel Hicks.

"Yes, Turck was my married name. I kept it because it seemed a little more distinctive, I'm afraid." She paused. "I think—"

Behind his back, Colonel Ross said: "Hicks!"

"Yes, sir," Nathaniel Hicks said, facing about.

Colonel Ross was balancing a large paper bag. He held it out. General Beal had turned in his seat. He called: "Anybody back there want a cream puff?"

"No, thank you, sir," said Nathaniel Hicks. He held the bag for Lieutenant Turck, who smiled and said, "No, thank you, General."

"How about him?" the general shouted, indicating T/5 McIntyre in the lavatory.

Nathaniel Hicks called: "Corporal! General Beal wants to know if you'd like a cream puff?"

Starting, the boy dropped his comics book. "Yes, sir!" he said.

Turning in her seat, Lieutenant Turck offered the bag to him. He looked at her, startled, making it plain that he had not heard the question, but only a voice addressing him. He looked in the bag, and then perplexedly at Lieutenant Turck. "For you. Take one," she said.

"For me?" he said, astonished. "Thank *you*, ma'am!" He plunged in his slender black hand and brought out a cream puff. On the pull-down seat, Sergeant Pellerino stirred his thick-set, slouched-out body and groaned, opening his eyes.

"Danny?" called the general.

Sergeant Pellerino pushed the back of his hand across his face. "Right there, Captain—" he grunted. He gave his head a hard shake. Everyone had laughed; and, slowly realizing what he had said, he began to grin sheepishly.

"What'd you have done if I'd yelled: 'Bail out!' " General Beal shouted, grinning back.

"Busted my thick ass, General—" He saw Lieutenant Turck holding the bag toward him and said hastily: "Excuse me, ma'am!" He took a cream puff and crammed it in his mouth.

Colonel Ross whispered to Nathaniel Hicks: "I think the Old Man's going to want to talk to you in a minute."

"What should I do, sir?"

"Well, don't go away anywhere." He gave him a mildly quizzical look. "He'll have Carricker change places with you, probably. We're going to try for a little more altitude. We're bucking a pretty hard headwind. When he gets set, he'll tell you."

III

ON THE bulkhead instrument panel in the corner behind General Beal's head, the air-speed indicator leaned right until it rested on one hundred and twenty. General Beal had opened his throttles and the whole plane shook as the engines beat harder, working to climb. The hundreds hand of the altimeter began to revolve. The short thousands hand advanced from six to seven to eight.

Below, the gray expanse of the Gulf of Mexico far to the right faded in haze and disappeared. The darker earth dissolved, losing all specific character in a vast plane of shadow. Almost sunk, the flattened lip of the red sun, which looked fifty feet wide, began definitely to rise again. The needle point went to eight thousand, five hundred and to nine thousand. Carricker murmured something and the general nodded. The minutes passed; the altimeter showed ten thousand. The racket of the laboring engines rose rhythmically groaning; ebbed and rose again, and ebbed and rose again. The altimeter came jerkily, as though its hands were sticking, to eleven thousand and passed on.

General Beal said: "That wind isn't any better. We got oxygen?" Carricker said: "Yeah, but only five cylinders." He reached under his seat and twisted the cabin heater control full on. "We're too heavy, anyway," General Beal said. "We're getting hot." He turned his head to Colonel Ross. "Feel it up here, Judge?"

"All I want to," Colonel Ross said. He looked around at Captain Hicks and Lieutenant Turck. Lieutenant Turck was having slight but obvious difficulties. Her lips were parted; she stretched her neck and moved her shoulders as the lungs tried vainly to get their fill. "That will do," he said. "You and Benny must have been born in a meteorological balloon. I'm not as young as I used to be, and I need my air."

"Check," said General Beal good-naturedly. "We'll let her rest." He straightened his arm, moving the wheel forward. The plane rocked lightly; the engines soughed and sighed louder, beat quicker, changing key. "Still hitting that headwind," General Beal said critically. "I knew we must be."

"Yeah," said Carricker. He looked at the instrument panel clock. "She did all right, though." Their casual, quiet voices answered each other, sure and contented in some airmen's world of their own. The general said: "They made a good little ship here, Benny. You get the tech orders on it?"

"In the side pocket, here."

"See what's with maximum cruise. I think we could goose it a little. I want to get home tonight. It's going to be dark, anyway. That wind; thunderstorms down the line, probably."

"Yeah." Carricker bent open a page of the pamphlet of technical orders and gave it to the general. He pulled down his radio earphones and put them on. He reached for the overhead tuning control and wound it around to the Ocanara frequency. "Yeah, static," he said. "We ought to be about an hour out. Why don't we put it in long glide?" He took off the earphones. "You'll never get over a hundred and eighty this way without blowing your top. You got your head temperatures at two-fifty now." He tapped the dial in front of him.

"Roger," said General Beal. "Look, before I trim, change with the captain back there, will you. I want to talk to him a few minutes."

"Roger," said Carricker. He leaned around the back of his seat and said to Colonel Ross: "The general wants to see your man. He can sit here, but get him up before I move. We're pretty near on our tail, anyway."

The lip of the red sun had sunk again, leaving them flying deep in a pool of sourceless light. Ahead, a little more than level with them, in the empty whiteness where it became suffused with gray, a speck shone. It was a star; and for all you could tell, they had long ago left the earth and were miles out in interstellar space, bound for it.

Colonel Ross switched on the plotting table lamp and with his arm shielded his piles of papers from Captain Hicks's passage forward, and then from Carricker's passage back. He held his pencil poised. He began to read a Letter Order draft beginning: *In accordance with Ocanara Army Air Base Regulation 85-2, all Officers, Flight Officers, and Warrant Officers reporting for Temporary Duty in connection with AFORAD Project 0-336-3 (Medium Bombardment Group X-701 Evaluation) will—*

His eyes were tired and he took off his glasses and wiped

them. Breathing the thin air, he was nearly panting. He looked at his watch and saw that they were going to be good and late—no dinner until nine o'clock, probably. Picking up his pipe, he put it in his mouth, and then took it out again and laid it down, since smoking at this altitude would, he knew, make him giddy. He sighed and replaced his glasses, compelling himself by a discipline of mind which years of reading law made second nature to go on with the Letter Order.

This was an assignment of certain buildings in the AFORAD Area for the use of officers reporting in this week, and, like the rest of the stuff in this set of file folders—the daily mass of routine memoranda; information copies of AAF Headquarters messages; office instructions; Daily Activity Reports from AFORAD's five Administrative Directorates and the regular Staff Sections—was properly no business of his. He read them, in addition to his other duties, because Colonel Mowbray, the Executive Officer, seemed incapable of performing that important part of his function which was to pick from the flood of paper those pieces which the general ought to see.

Mowbray was a wizened little man with brown leathery skin and almost white hair. He was Regular Army, and an old Air Corps officer—indeed, one of the men who got his flying instruction from Wilbur Wright himself, circling the Ohio cow pasture thirty odd years ago. Of that group, with their Fédération Aeronautique Internationale civil certificates, and the original Aviation Section Military Aviator ratings there were few still on active duty. Mowbray was one, and the Commanding General of the Air Forces was another.

It was plain, then, that Colonel Mowbray—though for very different reasons—came in Colonel Woodman's category. An insurmountable impediment stood somewhere between him and those high positions to which, in the ordinary course of things, long service gave first claim. It was certainly not of the Army's making. Except in the disordered fancy of men like Colonel Woodman, no Regular Army man passed over an old timer happily. Everyone could not be Commanding General; but in the palmy days of an AUS millions strong, even a man's personal enemies would yield their prejudices to their principles.

The Army's interests were at stake. If patient waiting through years of peace was to have no certain reward the very basis of morale was attacked.

Mowbray, who was about Colonel Ross's own age, did not seem disgruntled by his conspicuous failure to get to the top. It was even possible, Colonel Ross thought, that Mowbray was relieved that they did not oblige him to take on an important command. At Ocanara, he sat quite happily in an office with an elderly woman named Mrs. Spann, who had been his secretary at Maxwell Field for years, and Mr. Botwinick, a Chief Warrant Officer, who acted, in effect, as Colonel Mowbray's Executive. Colonel Mowbray was a hard and earnest worker. Knowing that he was, feeling himself working hard, he did not seem to be disheartened by any realization of the fact, so apparent to Colonel Ross and even to the general, that most of what he did was lost motion—a frittering of effort.

When the messengers came with the morning mail, it was Colonel Mowbray's habit to examine each separate piece closely and for a long time. He would then usually say to Mr. Botwinick: "Oh, er, would you just call Colonel Hyde, Bombardment Analysis—" (or Colonel Coulthard, Special Projects; or Major Sears, the Provost Marshal; or the Finance Officer; or the Base Signal Office; or Sub-Depot Supply; or the Judge Advocate General Section) "—and ask them for a clarifying memorandum on—." He then turned the paper over and over searching for the identifying symbols or numbers; and thus the morning passed. When Colonel Mowbray finally had everything checked and double checked and swollen to twice or more its original bulk by needless supplementary material, he would bring it all in, if the general would let him, and settle down for an interminable discussion.

In self-defense, General Beal began to ask him to see what Colonel Ross thought. Colonel Mowbray did not take offense, and he and Colonel Ross soon arranged a division of labor. Copies of all the stuff that went to the Executive Officer were directed to the Air Inspector, too. Colonel Ross would read them and decide what the general should see, and take it to him. Thus, Colonel Ross handled what came *in*. Colonel Mowbray, under Mr. Botwinick's constant supervision, took care of what went *out*, after the general and Colonel Ross made the decisions.

This relieved the tension of Colonel Mowbray's mornings and he was able to organize a group that collected in the Headquarters mess about ten o'clock to have coffee and an informal discussion of the day's problems. Colonel Mowbray enlivened the proceedings by a complicated ceremony of coin-matching to see who paid for the coffee. There was no side about it. Anyone in the Headquarters quadrangle was welcome, and often people from the offices of the Directorate Chiefs sat in to pick up items about what the general said or was planning to do. The effect of a large and happy family was achieved. Colonel Mowbray chaffed the girls—the Headquarters office secretaries were just as welcome as anybody else; they had been working since eight o'clock and would work all the better for a half hour break; helped to play little jokes on newcomers or young officers who showed that they were awed by the Brass; chortled at his successes with the coins, which were many.

The institution was generally known with impatience or contempt by those who did not attend it as "The Children's Hour," but Colonel Mowbray himself was kindly regarded in spite of the exasperating administrative difficulties he could make out of the simplest matter. He would do anything for anyone, even if he did it slowly and badly. When things went wrong he was ready to take the blame or, failing that, to find excuses for those who had to take it. Though he could not be said to serve General Beal well, he served him with an entire faithfulness and devotion not unaffecting in a man who was a distinguished pioneer of the air when the general was riding a tricycle; and who, if there was any mean or jealous part of his nature, might have found little ways of showing that he felt, in view of his record and his seniority, a just resentment at being given an assignment of relatively little account under a man his junior by almost a generation.

Colonel Ross, for whom Colonel Mowbray made more trouble than anyone else, and who might very properly, in the line of his own duty, have felt it incumbent on him to censure Colonel Mowbray's ineffective work, and to recommend his immediate removal, never thought of doing such a thing. Twenty years ago, Colonel Ross dared say, it would have been his first thought; and (not without a certain rigid pleasure in seeing duty clearly; and, every other consideration put aside, doing it quickly) he would act—hew to the line, and let the chips fall where they may!

Colonel Ross was not sure whether today's different attitude came from being twenty years wiser or just twenty years older. He had, of course, more knowledge of what happens in the long run, of complicated effects from simple causes, of one thing stubbornly leading to another. Experience had been busy that much longer rooting out the vestiges of youth's dear and heady hope that thistles can somehow be made to bear figs and that the end will at last justify any means that might have seemed dubious when the decision to resort to them was so wisely made. Unfortunately, when you got to your end, you found all the means to it inherent there. In short, the first exhilaration of hewing to the line waned when you had to clean up that mess of chips. The new prudence, the sagacious long-term views would save a man from many mistakes. It was a pity that the counsels of wisdom always and so obviously recommend the course to which an old man's lower spirits and failing forces inclined him anyway.

Colonel Ross, asking himself what the end in view was, and what means would, in light of all this experience, best promote it, could anticipate the answers. They would depreciate the value of change. They would suggest alternatives. They would argue reasonably that firing Colonel Mowbray must, in the circumstances, promote not administrative efficiency, but confusion, ill-feeling, and crippling uncertainties to plague the whole organization while a new man was being found, while he acquainted himself with the job, while he was allowed some weeks' fair chance to show whether the people who said he would be good were right or wrong. The alternative was already to hand. As long as Colonel Mowbray did not insist on doing his own work, they could make out. It was only necessary for Colonel Ross to do it for him.

When he was fifteen years old Norman Ross, a big strong farm boy had felt it incumbent on him to say that he was eighteen (he did not have and knew he could not get his parents' consent) and so to join a volunteer regiment which took him to the Philippines—too late for the Spanish-American War itself, but in time for the Samar reprisal operations under that formidable commander then known as Hell-Roaring Jake Smith. Private Ross came back a veteran in 1901 and soberly went about reading law.

While he regarded the whole adventure as a piece of youthful folly, and even cited it to his own sons as an example of the kind of damned foolishness boys who act without consulting their elders get into, he had been willing to accept the assumption of the people back home that he was an old soldier, and so an expert on military matters. There was no difficulty in persuading him to join a militia regiment, and he soon became an officer with more and more widely recognized abilities in organization and administration. Though he really had no time for these duties, added to a growing law practice, he found himself unable or unwilling to lay them down. The only man available to replace him as regimental adjutant would certainly make a complete mess of all that he had painstakingly put in shape.

In 1916 he went to the Mexican border, and in 1917 to France, where he ended as an Air Service supply officer at the Third Aviation Instruction Center at Issoudun. This was not originally due to any special interest in flying, but to the fact that the Signal Corps, which fostered what Army flying there was before the war, was desperately understaffed in the face of the new demands on it. Things worked out well enough. The consciously devil-may-care young pilots of the 103rd Aero Squadron called Captain Ross Grandpa (he was thirty-four), and respected, even loved, him for his feats in diverting to them scarce and desirable supplies. The equivocal Army mess term, "beverage," was locally celebrated. By appropriating an automobile and disappearing for a day, the Supply Officer could make beverage mean, depending on the meal or the mood, all the champagne, or all the fresh milk, or all the real coffee anyone wanted. As a token of appreciation, they took him flying, and before the war ended he had, most irregularly, soloed several times.

Flying in those days was a business set apart by its unexampled dangers; and those who flew were joined in the bond of their undefined, informal co-operative effort to shut their minds to the plain fact that if the war continued they were all going to die—perhaps by enemy action, perhaps by accident; perhaps this week, certainly next month. They supported each other in fending off the normal animal despair; now by braving it with cumbersome and elaborate humor—*take the piston rods out of my kidneys and assemble the engine again;* now by a solemn, deprecatory indirection which did not blush to use such euphemisms as "grounded for good."

For those who survived it was a bond. Major Ross, returning to the law, was elected a county judge. He really could not spare time to go on with the National Guard, and he resigned his commission. Getting rid of his Regular Army connections was not so easy. Issoudun flyers remaining in the service assumed and asserted that he was one of them. As a matter of course they expected whatever support they thought he could give to projects that advanced the interests of military aviation. Thus, though he rarely saw any of these people, he was always in touch with them and with Army flying. They had the use of any influence he could bring to bear. They had little trouble inducing him to work personally for the establishment of National Guard aviation.

When the new war broke out he was not surprised to be offered a colonel's commission and told that his services were urgently required. This needed thinking over, of course. Ostensibly, he was to reflect on his various duties, consider all the factors involved, and so determine his proper course. Actually, there was never any doubt about what he was going to do. The only thing he had to think over was how to tell his wife. Cora was worried enough already, since they had two sons in their twenties, one of them married and the father of a child. She

53

was aware that both would probably have to go. A third son, not quite eighteen, who had just entered college with the plan of studying medicine, might, she thought, be deferred; but it was hard to be sure of anything in a world which she regarded as mismanaged by and for men. Judge Ross realized that his wife, like most women, in the privacy of her mind, or better, heart, set against this male world the concept of a reasonable and tidy female one, run as she ran her well-run household. Firm domestic discipline ordered the daily living. She determined the location and furniture of her man's home, his diet, his apparel, his amusements, his expenses, his savings, and the upbringing of his children. Men were certainly much better off under this tutelage; presumably the world would be.

It was, of course, only a dream. Cora was not by any means perfectly satisfied with the Judge, in spite of many changes and improvements she had made in him; but she was pretty well resigned. It was, after all, necessary to her happiness as a woman that he should retain that male ascendancy of strength, courage, and intelligence, in the notion of which she could take refuge when she was tired of exercising her superior wits. She had found no practicable way to separate from the male ascendancy the male willfulness, with its readiness to wreck everything just to prove its independence, or to show off.

Though not many women ever bother to formulate this dilemma, only a very young and very silly one would hope to change the ascendant male's decision by arguing. When, showing familiar signs that he was not at ease (since he was a little ashamed of himself for planning to do what she did not want him to do; and since he wondered if he looked foolish in agreeing with such alacrity that the Army's need for him was urgent) the judge introduced the word "duty," and enlarged on his duty to go, Cora Ross knew that it was all up. There were sons to send, and he already had the definite duties of his judgeship, and perhaps even a duty to his wife to cherish her and to take care of himself. He meant, then, that he had duly considered and duly rejected these claims. They had stopped being duties. He was going to go; so he solemnly rechristened his wish and intention, and looked at her with an absurd air of sorrowful reluctance, asking her to agree.

This she would never do. It was one of those moments, fairly numerous in life, when a normal woman must wholly and heartily hate men for their folly and hypocrisy, their callousness and their conceit. There he sat, talking away—all that nonsense!—and who would want him, who would mind losing him? The heavy answer was: she would. As soon as tomorrow she might be faced with the time-tried, humiliating need. She could not, or did not want to, live without this stupid old man.

Cora Ross controlled herself. She was a handsome woman— one of those women who, not unattractive when young, still improve with age. Her mature face lost the slight plump softness which never went well with her classically regular features. Her thick, carefully tended hair, now more white than blonde, became her. She had been resourceful and competent all her life and the resulting expression of good-tempered firmness suited fifty better than twenty. She made her mind up instantly.

She said: "Well, I suppose you are going, then. Where are they sending you, Norman? Do you know?"

He said he did not know. She observed that he was still avoiding her eye, and this mollified her somewhat. She had been nerving herself to support some complacent show of relief or even glee at getting away with it so easily. She went on crisply: "If it is in this country anywhere, I'm not going to stay here. I will close the house and get an apartment or something near the camp or whatever it is. I won't have you at your age living in a tent. Someone has to see that you get proper food and take sensible care of yourself."

He said, "For all I know, Cora, they will send me overseas."

He was still not meeting her eye; so she wondered an instant if he did know where he was going. She decided not; for he was by nature a very truthful man. When he lied, you always knew. She said: "Well, it would seem more sensible to me to send younger men overseas." She paused again, reminded of her briefly forgotten worries about her sons. Not averse to reminding him, too, in case he was by some chance capable of grasping this enormity he aggravated and abetted, she said:

"I suppose Tom and Hubert will have to go. Thank Heaven Jimmy is still too young. Doctor Potter says they will probably defer him if he is taking a pre-medical course."

Judge Ross did seem to grasp something. He shifted in his chair without replying.

"Won't they?" she said sharply.

"Well, Cora," the judge said, "I don't know whether they would or not. Boys farther along, actually in medical school—"

"Doctor Potter said—"

"Well, as a matter of fact, Cora, I had a telegram this morning. He says he is enlisting in the Air Force. I was going to talk to you about it. He feels—"

"How can he do that without his parents' consent? I know he can't. Mabel was telling me about Godfrey—" She broke off abruptly, and looked at him again. There was a dreadful second's silence. To his distress and great consternation, she stood up then and burst into tears.

"Now, Cora—" he said, getting up himself hastily.

"No, no, no!" she said. "Just don't talk to me about it. I don't want to hear about it!"

She walked out of the room. Following her into the hall, he found her knotting a scarf over her hair. She picked up a fur coat and put it on. "Now, Cora—" he repeated.

Without turning, she shook her head several times. She looked in the dark mirror, adjusted the scarf a little, and walked to the front door and opened it.

"Cora!" he said. "Where are you going?"

"I am going to the library to get a book they have for me," she said.

She closed the door and left him listening to her sharp heel taps on the verandah, and then on the steps. He went back down the hall, through the shadowed dining room to the pantry and took a glass from the shelf. In his study he unlocked a small oak stand and got out a bottle of whisky that some legal friend had sent him for Christmas. He peeled off the wrappings and extracted the cork. He poured the glass a quarter full. He put the bottle away and sat down heavily.

"Well," he said aloud, "that's that." At least, he no longer had to worry about how to tell her.

Colonel Ross's orders, which came early in February, directed him to proceed to Washington. A week before, the old friend who had put-in for him to the Adjutant General went to Savannah where they were preparing to activate the Headquarters and Headquarters Squadron of what was to be the Eighth Air Force. While the old friend was making plans that called for Judge Ross, others made plans that called for *him*. As sometimes happened in those days, he heard about his new job for the first time late one afternoon and took a plane south two hours later. Behind him he left nobody who knew about the plan to use Judge Ross—probably it was no more than a Table of Organization sketched out on a scratch pad, anyway.

In the office of the Chief of Air Staff there were people with whom Judge Ross was slightly acquainted, and they welcomed him warmly. They asked him what he was doing in Washington. Shown his orders, they scratched their heads; to no avail, called up a few people; and then said that they could only suggest that he stand by.

Colonel Ross resolved to go higher. Next day, the Assistant Secretary of War for Air had a ten minute talk with Colonel Ross and told him a little about the imminent reorganization of the War Department. Things were not quite settled yet; but it seemed likely that the Air Force would come out of it very well—in a strong position, with broader scope and new openings. He suggested that Colonel Ross stand by. Where could he be reached?

With difficulty, Colonel Ross had found a room at the old Lafayette Hotel. The Assistant Secretary made a note of the telephone number on his desk pad. The civil implication seemed to be that he might need to reach Colonel Ross at any moment. He would not be able to wait while Colonel Ross was notified through ordinary channels. With the slight dry embarrassment and the shy courtesy that distinguished

57

him, the Assistant Secretary then eased his visitor out. Colonel Ross heard no more.

By the time the reorganization finally took place in March, Colonel Ross had been doing nothing for more than a month. Every morning he got into his uniform with his colonel's eagles and last-war ribbons. He ate breakfast slowly and read the poorly disguised bad news from the Pacific. Then, unless it was snowing or raining hard, he walked down to the Munitions Building, taking care to arrive after ten o'clock. Before ten the various people he knew would be busy with office conferences, or the mail. Plodding the dark and shabby corridors he showed himself to a few secretaries and executive officers.

Sometimes, to keep him quiet, he was given long unimportant memoranda or obsolete reports and asked to read them and jot down any ideas or opinions he might have. At noon, Colonel Ross would walk, the day being fine (if not, he would take a taxi), to the Army and Navy Club and eat a light lunch of soup and salad. At first he went right back to the Munitions Building. After a week or so, he usually walked around the corner to the hotel and took a short nap. He would then telephone various offices. Sometimes they suggested that he come down and meet somebody. If they did not, he often left word that he could be reached at the Cosmos Club. Here he would read in the library until dinnertime. It was impossible to avoid the reflection that he might much better have stayed home.

The trouble, of course, was his colonel's commission. In early 1942, full colonels were not yet a dime a dozen. Anyone could fit in another captain, and perhaps even a major. Higher rank was hard to dispose suitably. A colonel not on flying status was by regulation ineligible for most Air Force commands, even if they had nothing to do with flying. Colonel Ross understood the problem. He would have to give them time.

When it was plain that the reorganization was fully accomplished, and still nobody had anything for him, he began to pull strings to get an appointment with the Commanding

General. This was not as hard as he expected and he was told to come around at ten o'clock tomorrow. Unfortunately, at ten o'clock tomorrow, the Commanding General, very angry about something, had reached his boiling point. While Colonel Ross waited, blows on the desk and shouts were audible through the doors. The general's secretary rolled her eyes and shook her head. The shouting died at last. Then two red-eared brigadier generals trooped out in a flustered way, dropping papers and bumping into each other. Colonel Ross was admitted.

The general had mislaid, or could not be bothered looking for, the note he presumably had been given telling him who Colonel Ross was and why he had come. When Colonel Ross (you couldn't be sure how having three stars might affect a man) ceremoniously advanced, halted, and saluted, the general, still warm and red, barked: "Skip all that, skip all that! Just show me what you've got!" Something buzzed by his desk, and he shouted at the box: "I'll be there in a few minutes! They'll have to wait! Don't ring in again! Now, Colonel, tell me quickly what you want."

Though taken aback, Colonel Ross was not affronted. He had, instead, a feeling of guilty compunction to be troubling a man so sorely tried already. He said that he had reported for duty a month ago; but he was afraid that whoever sent the orders had been transferred, and—

The general said: "Colonel, I can't handle the individual assignments of all Air Force personnel. You must see that. Tell the major out there that I want your case looked into. The Chief of Appointment and Procurement Division must know something. I don't. Now, why have I got to be the one to explain all this? I wish you could tell me—" He changed his face into the grin for which he had been noted in less trying times. "Please don't go away sore, Colonel," he said. "I tell people things. That's my job. And they have to try to like them. That's their job—" He struck a switch on the box. "Major, I want you to fix up the colonel here. He's coming out. He'll talk to you. I'm going now. Don't arrange anything this afternoon. I may have to fly over there."

59

Colonel Ross said: "Thank you very much, sir."
"Yes, yes. Tell him. He'll take care of you."

Colonel Ross supposed that, in one sense, the major out there, an Executive Assistant, or something, did take care of him. The following day he was summoned by a Deputy Chief of Staff. It seemed that the Inspector General was in a jam. Over there, they were raising heaven and earth to get their hands on competent men. How would Colonel Ross, a judge and all that, just what they were looking for, like to help them out, pending a proper assignment on the Air Staff, or elsewhere?

What must be the file on Colonel Ross lay in front of this little fellow with a mustache, a brigadier general. He was not stupid. He had probably been wondering, in view of those first urgent telegrams, how Colonel Ross would take this virtual about-face. It led him to go on, longer than necessary, emphasizing the Inspector General's predicament, and the temporary nature of the transfer to the Army Service Forces.

Colonel Ross took it well enough. The principal point, he told himself, was that he should be usefully employed. He understood the good and sufficient reasons why the Army Air Forces found him at the moment unemployable. They were not reasons that reflected on his capacity or ability. Unfortunately this understanding could not quite remove a melancholy of mind, a sad, umbrageous discontent. To save their lives, they couldn't think of anything to do with him! The Commanding General's major must have reported that nobody wanted the old gaffer; and he mustn't be allowed to bother the CG again. So let's get him off on the Service Forces.

Colonel Ross said that he would be glad to serve wherever he could be of use. This was the proper spirit; but to adopt it as well as to express it took a little time. The new orders were cut and ready for him—they hadn't been running any risks!— and he could report in the morning. In the morning, in his hotel room, holding his blouse while he removed the Air Force insignia from the lapels and prepared to substitute a set bearing the wreathed sword and fasces of the Inspector General, he caught sight of himself in the mirror. His large and sufficiently dignified old face below the gray hair was set in a hurt and sulky pout; and suddenly he had to laugh. He had seen that expression before. A generic resemblance in some of the features reminded him sharply of the face of his son Jimmy, adolescent spirits dashed, plans spoiled, standing disgruntled before his father while he digested the unwelcome news that he could not have the car tonight.

In a frame of mind improved by this amusement, Colonel Ross centered the new insignia neatly on the US's, put on his blouse and went to breakfast.

This, this tincture of amusement, was perhaps the real right spirit. If Colonel Ross needed it then to restore a dignity and self-command both ridiculously shaken by the kind of pique a school boy might feel, he was to need it just as much two months later. Two months later, he had to keep in hand a similarly unsuitable glee or triumph. By that time the Air Staff was doing everything possible to get him back, while the Inspector General was doing everything possible to keep him. The Army Air Forces and the Army Service Forces locked themselves in a battle of giants, with Colonel Ross for the prize. Colonel Ross maintained a disinterested attitude. He hoped he was not being too demure about it; for, after the first exchange, he was only the occasion, not the issue. The contest was carried up the line by both sides with the warmest resolution. Considerations of prestige, of precedent, of who-could-push-whom around were more and more deeply involved. No compromise could be reached below the highest level. When the dust settled, Colonel Ross was found reporting back to the Air Staff, thus maintaining the important principle that nothing can stop the Army Air Corps. However, he went back not by transfer, but by assignment to duty with the AAF. The AAF might have his valuable services for the duration; but the Inspector General had said flatly that he would not transfer Colonel Ross, and he didn't. The important principle maintained here was that the Army Service Forces truckle to no one. Everybody, including Colonel Ross, if that mattered, was satisfied.

Now, a year and a half later, Colonel Ross could fairly say that he was still satisfied. Things might have been easier with the Inspector General—he would probably not be doing two or even three jobs all at once. His anxieties might have been fewer—he was not altogether easy about the state of the Operations and Requirements Analysis Division which in the six months of its existence had naturally created an opposition—men of more consequence and resource than Colonel Woodman felt that AFORAD overbore them and aggrandized itself at their expense. In ways still more indefinite, he felt concern about General Beal who, though jumpy enough, seemed less than clearly aware of the possible threats to his position.

Colonel Ross was even concerned about the progress of the war, a matter clearly unconnected with his duties and responsibilities. At Ocanara the material pouring in often suggested, in the course of its analysis by men of opposite opinions, disastrous possibilities. Colonel Ross knew, for instance, what must happen to the Eighth Air Force if someone in Germany recovered his wits and ordered simple and obvious changes in the fighter defense tactics. Though far himself from the scene, and no doubt unqualified to appraise rightly the odds for or against this gigantic bet on German obtuseness, Colonel Ross pondering the analysis of the Regensburg-Schweinfurt mission a couple of weeks ago—sixty Forts down, sixteen per cent of all the bombers airborne, nineteen per cent of the force actually attacking—was uneasy in his mind. His son Jimmy was in England as a B-17 bombardier, and Colonel Ross, since he could do nothing, would have been willing to know as little about the matter as people outside AFORAD and the Air Staff would normally know.

In the gloom of the cabin Colonel Ross replaced his glasses. He looked down at the paper under the plotting table light and read again: *In accordance with Ocanara Army Air Base Regulation 85-2, all officers . . .*

His head was tired. He held his pencil, however, feeling a mental remonstrance that meant (and it was never wrong)

62

that despite his disinclination he ought to read again, he was missing something. He looked at the diminished yet still considerable pile of unread papers, as though he hoped they could excuse him from the effort. His disciplined mind, rejecting excuses, came heavily to heel. Here was an assignment of buildings to be used as quarters—right! It concerned Project O-336-3, due in this week—right!

The buildings were listed in a short column. They were identified by numbers which in their digits indicated the type of building and where it was, in the area, and in relation to other buildings. Colonel Ross went from number to number. He looked to see whether they were scattered over the map in some absurd or inconvenient way; or whether the unit officer in charge of billeting had mistakenly designated a mess hall or a school building as a BOQ barracks. He came then to the listing: *T-305 Club Building*.

With instant relief he put two red lines beside the item. He wrote on the margin: *Policy?* He initialed it and transferred it into the creditably thin folder of papers General Beal should see. From the unread pile, he took a fresh sheet and read: *To: CO's All AFORAD & Ocanara AAB Tactical Units. Subject: Many Happy Returns.*

Colonel Ross winced. This was Colonel Mowbray's "surprise" scheme to greet (and not impossibly annoy) General Beal Saturday, which would be the occasion of the general's forty-first birthday, with an elaborate parade at Retreat, usually no more than a token ceremony. Since Colonel Ross had not the heart to override Colonel Mowbray's plot when, chuckling and rubbing his hands, he first proposed it; and since he grudgingly refrained from warning the general (who had probably forgotten that Saturday was his birthday), it was too late now to do anything.

This must be the fourth or fifth memorandum. The plan naturally got fancier as Colonel Mowbray indulged the same imagination that produced the AFORAD insignia. He was now arranging to bring in a few flights of C-46's from Tangerine City, one of Ocanara's satellite fields, and jump paratroopers as a sort of backdrop to the big military formation on the

63

ramp. He had persuaded AFSAT, the School of Applied Tactics at Orlando, to pass over two squadrons of new P-51's at 1630 precisely, at three thousand feet. Hendryx Field had been importuned to produce simultaneously at six thousand feet as many flights of B-17's as the school's ordinary duties might leave free. Colonel Mowbray was counting hopefully on forty or fifty heavy bombers. Hearing of this improvement, Major Sears, the Provost Marshal, grunted in an aside to Colonel Ross, that, one more thing; they ought to get the bombers to drop sticks of demolition two-fifties and blow the whole place to hell. That would end everybody's troubles.

IV

HAVING MORE glass, the pilots' compartment was brighter than the cabin behind, but General Beal had switched on the panel lights. Absorbed in resetting the automatic pilot, he tipped his head toward Carricker's empty seat indicating to Nathaniel Hicks that he should sit down. The faint glow from twenty illuminated dials gilded the general's intent face.

Looking with him, Nathaniel Hicks saw the air speed indicator at 200. On the turn and bank indicator the air bubble quivered dead center. The rate of climb indicator was six points under level flight; the altimeter's hundreds hand crept deliberately backward. Nathaniel Hicks watched with interest. Over on his side, a fuel pressure warning lit up suddenly. General Beal put a hand on the selector valve and said, "Hit the pump a couple, Captain."

Appalled, Nathaniel Hicks looked hastily around. "Wobble pump! Right there, under you," General Beal said. "That handle. Work it back and forth."

"Yes, sir," Nathaniel Hicks said.

"You'll see it come up on the pressure gauge. We've been burning a lot of gas. We had a headwind. Still have. That's fine." He clicked the fuel selector gauge to 3, left it while the engines took hold; then turned it to 4. The needle twitched over to ten tenths. "Would have been just too bad if somebody forgot to fill those. A hundred miles is a long walk. Cigarette?" He drew a package from his shirt pocket and held it out.

"Thank you, sir," Nathaniel Hicks said. He was mortified to have shown the general so clearly that he was not at home in a plane; or, at least, it would have been pleasant if, when the general spoke, he had known what to do and done it as a matter of course. He fumbled for a match, but General Beal had produced a gold lighter, and to his increased confusion, held the light for him.

Though not exactly awed by rank, Nathaniel Hicks had learned to have a regard for it. He had seen the same thing in a good many other amateur officers—a diffidence or wariness, whose object was less a show of respect (whether felt, or not) than the cautious wish to give no colonel or general occasion to exercise his right or duty to dress them down—a situation which most of them would not have faced since their school days and so would hardly know how to handle after some years of being treated with a strictly civilian consideration for whatever dignity and consequence those years might have brought them. He felt shy.

So, he realized presently, did General Beal. Of course the general's state of slight uncertainty didn't involve the awkward possibility that Captain Hicks might see fit to admonish or reprimand him; but it was plain that these civilians made General Beal uneasy. He said: "Colonel Ross tell you what I wanted to talk to you about?"

Nathaniel Hicks said, "No, sir." He felt his face drawing into a not-quite-genuine expression of obsequious interest.

"Well," said the general, "it's a thing we've been thinking about. I'm not sure I'm in favor of it—for us. Understand that. It isn't settled, and we'll have to see how it shapes up before we can settle it. Only we have to have something to go on, so we can see what it looks like. Understand what I mean?"

The honest answer would obviously have to be no; but the general had better be encouraged to get into his subject, whatever it was. Nathaniel Hicks said, with an intelligent air, "Yes, sir."

"Good. Now, I talked to Colonel Coulthard about this. He says you have your hands pretty full. I forget what he said you were doing; but I don't want to interrupt any regular work. Not for a thing like this. It has to be handled pretty carefully. What we've got to decide is whether it's in the best interests of the AAF. I don't want you to drop your regular work, at least not at this stage. If we decide to go through with it, I'll put you on temporary duty with my office. I think we can make a place in with Colonel Mowbray. However, that will have to wait until we see what's what."

"Yes, sir," said Nathaniel Hicks.

"O.K., here it is. You have a fair idea about AFORAD, haven't you—objectives, and so on? Get the AAF Letter on it, if you haven't. That states it. Now, we think it's pretty important, and some of our men, and some members of the Air Staff in Washington, think people ought to know a little more about it. Of course we have a lot of stuff that's just as top secret as it comes. We can't go talking about that, naturally. What they think we can talk about, is the overall set-up—the idea back of it. Of course we'd have to get it approved in Washington. But what they think is, that we could put a fairly concrete proposition up to Washington—show them what we have in mind, and how we would go about it. We don't want to ask them to do it; because we think we can do it better. Coulthard says you're a magazine man. Now, what they think is, you would have the experience, background, to get up something showing how we could get, inside security limits of course, some good stuff up about AFORAD and Ocanara that could go in different magazines, maybe. A lot of pictures, maybe. The Photographic Section could do them."

"You mean, sir," Nathaniel Hicks said, speaking with forced brightness, "that you'd like to find out what possibilities there were of getting stories about Ocanara into the big circulation magazines?"

"Now, hold on," the general said. "We don't want to promise them anything we can't deliver. And anyway, I don't know whether I can go along with this. There's been stuff about Orlando, for instance. I hear from Washington that right now

66

the Training Command is getting itself written up for a magazine. I don't know that we want to go blowing our own horn so much. Still, they think we ought to. The Air Force is a damn big organization—" he broke off. "I know the Old Man himself is behind this. You know, we haven't got our own Public Relations set-up any more. I mean, the AAF hasn't. There's an Air Forces Group under the War Department Bureau. I think the Old Man isn't satisfied that the AAF story is being put over as well as it could be. He personally wants every AAF activity to do what it can to fill in the big overall story—"

The general's face was frowning and intent, strained around the mouth and eyes, and Nathaniel Hicks could see that he was repeating a lesson that he had made himself learn in a field entirely foreign to him. General Beal probably did not see any real need to fill in big overall stories, or did not see it until the Commanding General ordered him to. The need then became, of course, actual and absolute. It occurred to Nathaniel Hicks that General Beal, though accepting the order, felt the indignity of any obligation to "put over the AAF story," to assure the public that the AAF was good, on its toes, doing its duty. General Beal's own instinct might be to shut up and get on with the war. They were going to win it; so do that first, and tell the story, if you had to, afterward. Nathaniel Hicks was obliged to admire a simple, unlimited integrity that accepted as the law of nature such elevated concepts as the Military Academy's Duty-Honor-Country, convinced that those were the only solid goods; that everyone knew what the words meant.

They needed no gloss—indeed it probably never crossed General Beal's mind that they could be glossed, that books had been written to show that Country was a delusive projection of the individual's ego; and that there were men who considered it the part of intelligence to admit that Honor was a hypocritical social sanction protecting the position of a ruling class; or that Duty was self-interest as it appeared when sanctions like Honor had fantastically distorted it. In his simplicity, General Beal, apprised of such intellectual views, would probably retort by begging the question; what the hell kind of person thought things like that?

Formal logic was outraged; but common sense must admit he had something there. Few ideas could be abstract enough to be unqualified by the company they kept.

Nathaniel Hicks said: "I see, sir."

"Yes," said General Beal. The strain on General Beal's face increased a little. Nathaniel Hicks, his eyes politely on the good though slightly snub-nosed profile, noted that the effect was not the ordinary one of making the young face look older; it made it look younger. The general had the expression of a troubled boy. This was engaging, showing more of the simple-minded integrity; but the virtue graded into the accompanying fault. A more adult way to handle states of personal uncertainty was to cover them at once with an extra positiveness, to crush arguments that might aggravate uncertainty before they were heard. While this made other people angry, it also relieved them of a responsibility which it was not their business to bear. General Beal said: "I don't know what they want to put in magazines. That's where you're supposed to come in. Coulthard says you're well known. He says you're a top-flight man. That's what we want."

To deprecate this high estimate would, under the circumstances, be silly. It was certainly tempered by the general's indication that Nathaniel Hicks in his top-flight capacity was not well known to him; and probably not even to Colonel Coulthard, who showed the human tendency to make as much as he could of what was his. Colonel Coulthard had in his Directorate a lot of officers that both he and General Beal must consider queer characters. Colonel Coulthard, with no soldiers or flyers to offer, could excuse himself best by claiming command of eighty or ninety commissioned geniuses, at least one "top-flight" man in any non-military field in which the vagaries of modern war might impel the general to take an interest. All accomplishments of theirs became, in effect, Colonel Coulthard's accomplishments. Nathaniel Hicks said: "I have done a good deal of editing, sir."

Perhaps wondering if the temperate statement showed lack

of confidence, General Beal frowned faintly. He said: "Well, you know what the magazines want, don't you? I guess you probably know men running big magazines, don't you? You'd know what would appeal to them. So, as I see it, what we have to do is see whether we've got it here, see how we could fix it up. What sort of stuff do they want, anyway?"

"That depends on the magazine, of course, General," Nathaniel Hicks said. "You can judge pretty well by what they publish. On a big magazine you have to bear in mind that several million people are going to read it—you hope. It has got to be interesting—" He broke off, not sure that he could or should give the general a lecture on what constitutes reader interest.

"You think they'd be interested in Ocanara?"

"People are interested in anything they didn't know before, when you can show them how it affects them personally, sir." Nathaniel Hicks saw the Tech. Orders of the AT-7 in the side-pocket where Carricker had pushed it. "A magazine wouldn't publish those tech orders because they're full of stuff the average person wouldn't understand. Why would they want to know about it? The answer is, they wouldn't—unless you could show them that here was a plane that after the war was going to make safe, cheap flying possible for everyone."

"Don't get that idea," General Beal said. "I guess they'll have that kind of plane sometime; but this isn't it."

"No, sir," said Nathaniel Hicks, "so that wouldn't be an article."

"O.K.," said General Beal. "Is there any article? You're the doctor."

With a sense of inadequacy Nathaniel Hicks said: "I don't know, sir, now. I'd have to find out what we have. I know a few things; but we've been pretty busy and I don't know too much about what goes on outside the Special Projects Directorate—" Or inside it, either, for that matter. Colonel Coulthard, speaking to his officers when he took command, read laboriously what somebody had written for him. Their vital function was to analyze and evaluate the practicability, adequacy, and economy of such projects as might from time to time be authorized by the CG, AFORAD; and to prepare full plans, specifications, and other necessary material to assist and expedite their implementation by appropriate AAF commands or agencies in the event of their approval and adoption by the AAF Board.

As far as Nathaniel Hicks could see, this meant in practice that anyone could fire off to AFORAD any idea that came to him. If it had nothing to do with anything practical, like bombardment, or gunnery, or air-ground co-ordination, the Special Projects Directorate, with its staff of assorted geniuses, could have a crack at it. At the desk next to Nathaniel Hicks, Captain Duchemin, for instance, was busy preparing a report to cover the practicality, adequacy, and economy of Pigeon Units.

"Check," said General Beal. "Now, what I think you'd better do is give yourself an overall orientation on AFORAD— the whole works. Go anywhere, see anything you want. Well, no. Keep away from any radar stuff. There might be one or two other things. I'll have the Security Officer brief you. Go up to Tangerine City—we have airborne stuff there. Go out to Boca Negra—Air Ground Cooperation has some amphibious projects. Get to Chechoter and look at the gunnery ranges and the Demonstration Area—well, I doubt if we could use much of that; Eglin sends us stuff they've tested. Better not touch that; but anyway, go and see it. You might get an angle. That what you mean?"

"Yes, sir," Nathaniel Hicks said. "Any unusual angles—"

As though distracted by his effort to recall them, General Beal said: "Well, we've got a lot of things, Hicks. Now, here's another job we've just been directed to do. Shows the different kinds of things they use us for. We have a project in this week —started getting here yesterday. It's about Negro flyers. We've been training some at Tuskeegee, you probably know; we've even activated some fighter squadrons that did all right in Africa. Still, there's a morale problem. The Air Staff has been asked to consider activating an all-Negro medium bomber group. Now, they're sending us a picked bunch, some Tuskeegee washouts, but all with GCT scores of one-thirty or better. Personnel Analysis is going to set them up in a kind of skeleton group organization and see whether it clicks. We might not be able to clear anything about it very soon; but go around and find out about them from Colonel Jobson. It's all part of AFORAD. See what I mean?"

"Yes, sir. Is there any hurry about this?"

"Is there—" General Beal turned his head. The questioning manner that sought Nathaniel Hicks's assent or agreement was transformed, though with no transition, with utter naturalness, as easy to General Beal as breathing, into an anger of amazement. "Wasn't I just telling you to get onto it!"

"I beg your pardon, sir," Nathaniel Hicks said. "I thought you told me, first, that I was not to stop my Special Projects job. It won't give me much time for the next week or two. I have a lot of material I got yesterday from an officer at Sellers Field. I have a Captain Wiley I was working with over at Orlando probably coming in Saturday or Sunday on some formation diagrams the Charts and Plans Section was going to rough out. Colonel Coulthard has arranged for an informal co-ordination with a Navy man at Jacksonville. I was supposed to go up there next week."

Alertly, sharply speaking on Nathaniel Hicks's last word, General Beal said: "Why doesn't he come down here?"

"I believe he's a commander, sir; and the Navy was doing it more or less as a favor to us; so—"

"Well, Coulthard's a colonel. And we don't want favors from the Navy. We'll fly on our own gas. What is this project, anyway?"

"Recommendations for the revision of Field Manual One-dash-Fifteen, sir."

"What's that?"

"*Tactics and Technique of Pursuit Aviation,* sir."

"There's no such thing any more! That term is out! Don't use it for anything; let alone in a manual."

"Yes, sir. We're recommending retitling it 'Air Fighting.'"

"I want to see it. Tell Colonel Coulthard anything you do on that is to come to me personally before he submits it to the Board, or it's sent to Washington, or anywhere. And wash out that Navy business. That type of co-ordination is on AAF

Headquarters level. If Ocanara can't do its job without running to the Navy we'd better bust up. I don't want any more of that. Bring all your stuff to me tomorrow morning. I want to see what's going on."

"Yes, sir. And what do you want me to do about the magazine matter, sir?"

"Oh—" General Beal said. His sudden unbending might, under other circumstances, have struck Nathaniel Hicks as amusing. General Beal's tone changed. He visibly relaxed. "I want you to go ahead with that as fast as you can. See Colonel Mowbray. He'll arrange any transportation. See Colonel Howden on Security. I think we'll have you sit in on the Staff Conference Monday morning. That's when all Directorates report on progress, and future projects are assigned. It would be a quick way for you to find out what's going on. And I'd like you to come to me directly if you get any ideas, or if you have any trouble getting what you need. O.K.?"

"Yes, sir." Nathaniel Hicks made to get up.

"Wait a minute," the general said. "We'll get Benny here first. It throws the trim off if you're both back there." He glanced at his instrument panels and raising his chin peered ahead into what had become deep night.

Down to the right Nathaniel Hicks saw three scattered lights, which went under the wing. "About ten minutes out," General Beal said.

Nathaniel Hicks became aware of a change in the plane's motion. A slight strong lifting sensation was followed by a soft, somewhat shaky jolt. Through the slanting rectangles of the windshield a broad illumination broke in the west. Nathaniel Hicks could see the right engine nacelle bulk from darkness behind its glinting disk of propeller arc. To the east, a similar glow immediately flared. Before the eastern glow died, a far brighter one awoke due south among mountainous masses of cloud, some black in silhouette, some fuscous and livid in pale radiance. The light vanished; and instantly winked on, fainter, to the west—once, twice, three times. In this half minute of wavering twilight the riveted metal surface of the plane's right wing appeared stark and rigid, wagging sedately in the void above a steely or leaden landscape below. They took a new, harder jolt.

General Beal called: "Benny!"

He put his radio earphones on, reached up and rocked the tuning crank back and forth. Carricker, stepping carefully to the motion of the plane, came forward. He stood peering ahead at the lightning in the southern sky. Then, brusquely, he tapped Nathaniel Hicks's shoulder and jerked his thumb toward the cabin behind.

Nathaniel Hicks obediently got up and pressed past Lieutenant Colonel Carricker. In one sense, Carricker probably meant no offense by his manner; but, in another, he certainly meant all that the manner implied. Like Major Post at Sellers Field, he had undergone dangers and suffered injuries. He thought little of all these jerks over here who didn't know anything, outside their rank and serial number. Unlike Major Post, who was riding low, a discard from the fighting air force, his luck out, stuck in a dull job at one of hundreds of training fields, Benny was, of course, riding high with General Beal. Where Major Post was touchy and resentful, Benny was spirited and imperious.

✦

These qualities of Lieutenant Colonel Carricker's were not new to Nathaniel Hicks. He had happened to see Carricker in action soon after Carricker's arrival at Ocanara. Carricker came back from Europe with General Beal, but he had been sent to some special hospital for treatment of his burns, and he reported a few weeks late.

At that time Special Projects, like several of the AFORAD Directorates, was using office space downtown in Ocanara while the new Area was under construction. Special Projects had a former five-and-ten-cent store, a circumstance that gave pleasure to lighter hearted members of the staff, like Captain Duchemin. It was not very convenient, for a good deal of the business was out at the Base or the new Area and that meant a lot of running back and forth. Those who had cars used them; and since the Motor Pool was unpleasant about supplying transportation, those who hadn't cars used, if they could, those who had.

One morning, Nathaniel Hicks, about to take some papers out, was hailed loudly by Captain Solomon, Colonel Coulthard's Adjutant. Captain Solomon came dashing through the five-and-ten-cent store doors crying: "Wait for baby! Wait for baby!" It developed that he had to see the Base Flight Control Officer, name of Carricker, about the Unsatisfactory Reports on one of the three planes assigned to Special Projects, and he wanted a ride.

Captain Solomon was a swart, perky little man with Service Pilot's wings. His job before the war had been persuading civic organizations in small cities to establish airports, and thus avoid being left behind by the Air Age. If his persuasion proved successful, he was ready with plans, and could put them in touch with contracting and equipment firms. Captain Solomon's nature was free and friendly; when he met anyone he began the conversation by asking that person to call him Manny. As Adjutant he was in a position to do people small favors and he did them willingly. He had the successful—though perhaps small-time—promoter's facility with smiles, compliments, and slaps on the back, which after all cost nothing. In the end, they usually paid off, even with people who recoiled at first from the pushing good fellowship and friendly inquisitiveness. Captain Solomon knew that what every man is most interested in is himself; and if you want to please him, you must show the same interest. In the end, the merry smiles and warm indications of liking would win.

Captain Solomon, whose head must have been a remarkable file of thousands of useful little facts about hundreds of people was, though he had never seen or met Carricker, able to tell Nathaniel Hicks a few interesting things about him. Carricker had the Distinguished Service—not Flying—Cross, and furthermore, he had an oak leaf cluster on it. According to Captain Solomon, Carricker was the only man in the Army who did have that. A Distinguished Service Cross *with* a cluster made the Congressional Medal look like a Good Conduct Ribbon. Captain Solomon then told Nathaniel Hicks a little about the policy regarding the Medal of Honor. They had to see that a few people in each theater got them—for morale, so when it was time for your theater to have one, you might get it for something you might get the Air Medal for if it wasn't time. That was not the case with the Distinguished Service Cross—no, sirree!

It was clear that Captain Solomon looked forward to meeting and perhaps being called Manny by this almost unique hero. He hummed under his breath; he beamed on Nathaniel Hicks, and sucked with relish on a cigar left over from the several boxes he had passed around a couple of weeks before when he had been promoted to captain.

After Nathaniel Hicks dropped off his papers, they drove down to the ramp where it was suggested that they might find Lieutenant Colonel Carricker. They found him standing on the wing of a P-38 bawling out a civilian mechanic who had just succeeded in getting a smear of grease on Lieutenant Colonel Carricker's tropical worsted shirt. "God damn," he said, "do I have to put on coveralls every time I look at a plane?" Hearing that he was wanted, he got down by way of the little cockpit ladder, which swung with him, as it had a dangerous habit of doing, and almost dumped him on his back. He swore some more, and came over to Captain Solomon and Nathaniel Hicks.

It was true that he had the Distinguished Service Cross *with* a cluster. He was wearing it. Captain Solomon ingratiatingly explained his business and Carricker said at once: "How the hell should I know?"

In fact, as everyone learned later, Carricker had been written into the T/O as Base Flight Control Officer merely as a matter of form. His job was to be the general's flying companion and general utility man.

Although Captain Solomon knew now that he had, in his own phrase, come to the wrong address, Captain Solomon smilingly stood upon his going. Nathaniel Hicks had noticed before a certain wistful eagerness in Captain Solomon to approve himself to military pilots, to get on flyer-to-flyer terms with them. Apparently he felt at a disadvantage with his Service Pilot rating. He made a number of adulatory remarks and then in a bold but friendly way, implying that it was something that might happen to any of us airplane drivers, asked with sympathetic interest about Carricker's very noticeable burns.

Carricker looked at Captain Solomon with calm amazement. He let his eye drift over the Service Pilot's wings. He snapped a cigarette end into the flower bed before the Operations Building. For a minute he said nothing at all.

Though not himself involved, Nathaniel Hicks winced; and even Captain Solomon wilted. Carricker said languidly then: "Why, thanks for asking, Mac. Why, one day here was all this gasoline they put in planes, see? And here I am, at fifteen thousand feet, flying upside down. Then here was this match I just found. So I was thinking how's if I set the match to it? Rougher than a cob, pal!" He waited another instant. He said then: "Throw that cigar away, Captain! What do you mean by smoking on the ramp? Can't you read the sign? Now, get out of here!"

V

NATHANIEL HICKS made his way back to the vacant navigator's position. Colonel Ross's plotting table light was on but the colonel, he saw, was asleep. Lieutenant Turck's light was on, too, and she was looking restlessly at her *Manual for Courts Martial*. Nathaniel Hicks fitted himself into the seat and she said to him: "Oh, dear, I don't like it too much when it bounces. Thank Heaven I didn't eat that cream puff! Is this going to get worse?"

"We're nearly in," Nathaniel Hicks said heartily. From the pocket of a flying jacket which he had hung on the drift meter eyepiece beside him he took some sticks of gum. "Try that," he said. He took the radio earphones down from the hook on the wall. "Let's hear what they say."

Sergeant Pellerino said to T/5 McIntyre: "You better come out of there now. Might be a little rocky. Close the door and park yourself on the floor here."

Nathaniel Hicks put on the earphones and snapped around

the jack box switch. General Beal's voice, flat, mechanically syllabified, broke on his ear: "Ocanara Tower, this is Army—what is it, Benny? Where's the card?—this is Army three seven six three. Over—"

A long empty blaring and cracking on the frequency followed. "They don't say nothing," Nathaniel Hicks said to Lieutenant Turck.

Beneath them the plane took two hard bounces, yawed left jerkily, rolled level, and bounced again. The fuselage windows went from darkness to a pale electric glare and back to darkness. Nathaniel Hicks groped for the ends of his dangling safety belt and clamped them together across his stomach, which had contracted somewhat. The slight nausea was, however, mental not physical. Unless you start to fly when you are very young, you are unlikely to feel complete confidence in the strength or stability of any airplane. When the flimsy contraption begins to take a knocking around it disquiets you.

He turned and made a casual gesture to Lieutenant Turck, indicating that she might as well fasten her own belt. Her face, he saw, was very pale. She found the straps and fumbled with them. Her lips moved and Nathaniel Hicks bent toward her, pushing up one earphone. In the other, General Beal was trying again: "Ocanara Tower, this is Army—" Making a comic face, Lieutenant Turck shook her head. She said, "I just said to myself: I will not be sick. I simply will not be sick. I would rather die—oh, don't let it do that! For another thing, it really scares me to death."

"Chew your gum," Nathaniel Hicks said. "I will tell the general to stop it. Don't you see that card with the stars on it in the window? That means you're perfectly safe. Major generals take care of themselves."

On the whole, Nathaniel Hicks concluded, his pleasantries had a feeble sound and he might reassure her better by being calm and silent—or at any rate, silent. With exaggerated unconcern, but with a persisting inner qualm of distaste and apprehension, he looked around the constricted, unsteady cabin, saw the lightning-lit sky through the small ports, felt the careless slam of fragile wings on the hard air, and reflected that the only part of flying he had ever liked was that fine moment when he could slide back the cockpit canopy, or when someone opened the door, and he could jump down with a reassuring jar on solidly paved ground, telling himself as he strolled away: *all right this time!*

He became aware, in his earphone, of a small, childish, female voice floating through the crash of static. It came clear then, speaking with a marked Southern accent: "This is Ocanara Tower. I hardly read you. Over—"

There was no response for a moment, and Nathaniel Hicks looked forward, wishing General Beal would attend to business now that he had the Tower. The general's head and Carricker's were mounting against a brightly flash-lit sky. The plane's tail swung with the motion of a thermometer being shaken down. General Beal's bare brown arm, the oblong wrist held rigid under the twitching gold crash bracelet put the wheel firmly forward, eased it, put it forward again. They bumped with great violence, but he appeared unconcerned. He brought the microphone in his left hand to the side of his mouth and Nathaniel Hicks could hear him saying casually "—I am about three zero north at two thousand, contact. Estimating field in five minutes. What is your weather?"

A clicking and roaring prolonged itself while Nathaniel Hicks waited apprehensively. If the weather wasn't good— and how could it be?—they might have to go around and this could continue for an hour, or hours. The little girl's voice— some Wac in the Tower—proved to be saying: "—thermal thunderstorms centered south southwest approaching. Nil precipitation. Winds light variable east and southeast—." There came a pause, presumably while she consulted someone. "Are you the B-Twenty-six with radio malfunction attempting previous contact? Advise immediate nine zero turn east, easy, and hold heading five I say again five minutes and contact us for conditions. Wait." She resumed: "Unless you are in distress, this will be considered an order."

"Ocanara Tower," the general said, "you have the wrong plane. This is General Beal speaking. I am low on gas. If the field is still open I am coming right in. Oh! Have somebody see my car is at Operations."

A male voice replaced the female: "Yes, General! This is the Airdrome Officer, sir. The storm is some distance off. By present indications, your runway will be seven."

General Beal bent his face to the side window. His wing dropped off a little, the sky lit up, and he said: "I am over Lake Armstrong, contact. Let me hear if the wind changes and give me runway lights in three minutes. Is it raining yet?"

"Not yet, sir. The lights will be on, sir. We will advise you of any changes. Please let us know when you are ready to turn on base leg—"

"Roger," said General Beal. He laid the microphone in his lap. Turning his head, he called: "Put out all lights back there, please. We get a reflection—" he noticed Colonel Ross's nodding head then, pointed at Nathaniel Hicks, and made a shaking motion with his hand. Nathaniel Hicks pushed Colonel Ross's shoulder gently. The colonel lifted his head and said: "What goes on here?"

"Three minutes out, sir," Nathaniel Hicks said. "The general wants your light turned off. A little rough," he added. His laugh sounded aimless to him and he breathed and swallowed.

"Rough is right," said Colonel Ross. "What are they trying to do, break us up? I was sound asleep. Better strap down." Looking around, he said to Sergeant Pellerino who had placed himself on the floor, "Who's going to hold you?" The sergeant smiled placidly. "I got me a good brace, sir." To T/5 McIntyre he said, reaching over and pushing him: "Get your back on the bulkhead. We're going for a ride." He put up a hand carefully and felt the oxygen bottles in the rack above him. "Hope they stowed them good. One of those crown you—"

He broke off, reached into the corner and brought out the paper bag that had held the cream puffs. He looked at Lieutenant Turck kindly and said: "Maybe you better have that, ma'am."

General Beal turned and said again, "Put your light out, Judge. We get it on the windshield." Nathaniel Hicks saw

79

Lieutenant Turck grasp the bag. She gave him a tense and anguished look and said between her teeth: "I will not be sick. I will not. I will not—"

Colonel Ross's light went out. In the darkness, the plane, as though punched in the nose, staggered. Off balance, it took two more punches, fell forward, groggily rolled level. Nathaniel Hicks could see the general and Carricker, dark against the dim instrument panel, paying no attention, making nothing of it. Colonel Ross, looking at the dial of his watch, said: "Nine o'clock. I knew it! We won't get anything to eat in the dining room. You get it fixed with the general?"

"He said he wanted me to look around, sir."

"What do you think?"

"I think it depends on what we can clear with security, a good deal."

"You might be able to clear the general," Colonel Ross said. "Youngest major general in the Air Force. If the war keeps on, he may go a long way. What would you think about that?"

"I hadn't thought about it, sir." Nathaniel Hicks found it difficult to give the conversation proper attention in the mute miserable wish that the next few minutes would just hurry up and be over. "You mean, an article about him personally?"

"Why not? I've seen articles about different generals." The plane canted left giddily and came back.

"It might be done," Nathaniel Hicks said, "but I think we'd have to get somebody with a name to write it. Would he like it?"

"I haven't asked him. I'll talk to you about it tomorrow. It might be a useful thing."

From the pilot's compartment Carricker's voice sounded. "Tail wheel locked."

"Well, here we go," said Colonel Ross.

"Gear down," General Beal said. Carricker must have thrown the switch, for Nathaniel Hicks could immediately feel the energetic grinding of the mechanism. After a moment the little green panel light came on past Carricker's shoulder.

With the throttles cut, there had been a moment's smoother motion; now, with the wheels down, the plane seemed to trip on itself, falling from one little lurch to another. Nathaniel Hicks, who had started to breathe easier, with exasperation steeled himself again. Lightning lit up the dark cabin and Nathaniel Hicks turned to give Lieutenant Turck a smile. He was in time to see her duck her head convulsively, cram the paper bag to her mouth and nose. The cabin went dark, and he could hear her, with a choking, sobbing sound, being very sick. In his earphone, General Beal said: "Tower! This is Army three seven six three turning on base leg—"

The wing went up, tilting them hard. Lightning flashed; and Nathaniel Hicks had a prolonged toppling glimpse down through the opposite fuselage windows of Ocanara slanted in a clear but ghastly radiance. The little huddle of tall buildings downtown seemed to project, almost perpendicular to an incredibly steep dark hillside laid out in rectangles of house roofs and tree tops. High above he saw the sprawling shape of the old Oleander Towers Hotel with its absurd domes and minarets clear against the lake water standing on edge behind it.

The sky went dark, and the tableau of Ocanara on its side vanished. Still tipped at an angle that wracked his nerves, Nathaniel Hicks looked over an interminable double row of runway lights swinging like the spoke of a moving wheel. The sky lit up again and showed him the great camouflaged hangar roofs ranked down the side of the field, and the Base's radiating acres of low buildings.

General Beal said: "Landing light, Benny!" The wing, tilted so far under them, came up strong and steady. "O.K. Flaps!"

"Right on the nose," Carricker said with satisfaction. Beyond their bent heads and busy hands in movement between the glowing instrument panel and the control pedestal, glare from the landing lights in the wings filled the windows.

At this instant a driving flaw of rain tapped the metal skin, and water poured down the glass. Straining his eyes past the general's head and Carricker's, Nathaniel Hicks, with a grateful fading of those tremors of mind (the ignoble affections of a fear unfortunately distinguished from the fear brave men often felt by being a folly too; an alarm when not in danger; a fleeing when nobody pursued), was looking hard for that good broad mile-long runway, right on whose nose the general had expertly put them. He could see only the strong landing light beam reflected on sheets of silver rain. Though this was nothing, it gave his confidence a cool little pause. To get himself over the critical seconds, he began to count, knowing that by the time he reached thirty or forty they would jar down soft and fast, running free and easy, safe home.

He had counted ten when the shining curtain of rain dissolved—a little shower sweeping on across the field—and, with a swelling new ease of mind, he saw the level runway well aligned, right where it ought to be, coming up at them. He counted eleven; he counted twelve; and he saw, flooded by their lights, sharp and dark against the concrete expanse ahead, a mottled green-brown object pushing itself slowly out, below and to the right of their nose.

For a full second, this peculiar moving mass was nothing recognizable—an object on the ground, perhaps, brought in view by a change in perspective; a solid construction of flat surfaces, smooth curves, and sharp angles covered with camouflage paint. In front, they must have seen it the same way, unable to make anything of it.

Carricker, in a perplexed voice, started to say: "What the hell—"

Nathaniel Hicks saw a glint of light then, a propeller spinning, and the peculiar shape became at once a twin-engined medium bomber, a B-26, in fact, pushing determinedly ahead of them.

Carricker cried out: "Chief! He's landing. The wheels are down—"

In fact, he had landed. He touched; he left the runway with a low, slow bounce; he touched again, and quick smoke puffs burst up behind his racing tires. At once, a fearful nightmare-like phenomenon of reversed relative motion began. The bomber, slowly floating ahead while it was in the air, appeared to go faster now that it was down. The level, stubby wings swept like the wind along the flat pavement; yet, at the same time, the slow pushing-ahead ended. Then suddenly, as though the B-26 were standing still, they started to overhaul it.

Nathaniel Hicks sat paralyzed. He was disembodied, a conscious but stunned presence, a pair of seeing eyes fixed thoughtless in the close little fuselage filled with dim reflected light. He saw Colonel Ross's gray head and the broad back of his khaki shirt which, below the arm pits, showed a dry, faintly-white, crusted staining of old sweat. He saw General Beal's tanned boyish face, lips parted on his straight white teeth, the gold bracelet hanging loose from the thrust-out wrist. His other hand, higher, was clenched on the upper cross bar of the segmented wheel. The Military Academy class ring with its colored stone shone over the knuckles.

Then they ran into something—not the ground; they were as high as the great hangar roofs; overtaking the bomber, but still above and behind. They hit very hard with a bucking, buckling violence. One wing went down. The cabin roof became the side; the opposite wall became the ceiling; and from it, with a crashing slam, came Sergeant Pellerino, striking Nathaniel Hicks's plotting table. In Nathaniel Hicks's earphone a panicky voice was shrilling: "B-Twenty-six on runway; B-Twenty-six on runway! There is an airplane directly behind you. There is an airplane—"

The wing came back with equal violence and threw the sergeant away. He sat down against the other wall, looking dumbly at Nathaniel Hicks while, distinct in the wavering gloom, a dark wet trickle of blood ran down his cheek. Nathaniel Hicks looked back at him, dumb too, in a numbed release, in the amazing, almost grateful, torpor of helplessness. There was no need to do more; you could stop straining away, and let yourself softly and peacefully smash.

Carricker's sharpened, roaring voice said: "—his prop wash! His prop wash! Can't do it—let go . . ."

The wing began to dip again, shuddering in the terrible air. Reaching sideways, really reaching down, Carricker's hand with the glazed skin and little knotted nail buttons covered both throttle knobs and shoved them forward to the stops. The hand went accurately on and hit the landing gear switch. Clean-fingered and quick, it snatched and jerked the cowl flap controls. It came nimbly over, and, with calm care, began to milk the wing flaps up.

A convulsive roar of engines hammered Nathaniel Hicks. His teeth cracked together; he was pinned to his seat. Sergeant Pellerino tumbled and came against T/5 McIntyre and the lavatory door. With a skidding, skating motion they bounced past the bomber moving under them. Heeling away, they missed the high fronts of the hangars which swung traversely not far below. Then they were hauling hard, hand over hand into darkness. The lights of the field swerved off; the hangar roofs shrank down; they mounted the night in long slugging bounds. Out of the din, General Beal's voice carried urgently: "Forty inches! Watch it! You got more than forty inches—"

Carricker's roaring voice answered: "—God damn right I have—"

But he must have pulled his throttles back, for a sense of quiet came over Nathaniel Hicks. He started to swallow and stopped in pain. His mouth and throat were completely dry. Gingerly, he tried again, his dry tongue touching and catching at his dry teeth. His earphone, still clamped in place, began to squawk: "Army three seven six three! Army three seven six three—"

General Beal was bent, looking for his microphone which had fallen off his lap. The click of the contact button came and he said: "Tower! General Beal speaking. We are going around again. Hold that B-Twenty-six crew at Operations. I want to see the pilot. Out."

Aware now of the earphone pinching his right ear, Nathaniel Hicks slipped the headband off. After two inaccurate tries he hung it on its hook. Colonel Ross said: "All present or accounted for?" He leaned forward and said to General Beal: "We'd better have a light. Somebody got knocked around. All right?"

General Beal said: "Ask Benny. He's running it."

"Ah," said Carricker, "nuts, Chief!"

Colonel Ross snapped on his table lamp, and Nathaniel Hicks put his on, too. Sergeant Pellerino, back now against the wall, had his hand to his head. He lowered it, looked at the smear of blood on his fingers and grinned. "Forget it, sir," he said. "Got me a couple of bumps is all." To T/5 McIntyre he said: "How about you, you hurt?"

T/5 McIntyre must have had his overseas cap knocked off. He had found it again and held it tugged tight between his hands. His thick lips were parted and he said doubtfully: "We have an accident, sir?"

Sergeant Pellerino said: "You don't call me 'sir,' son. No, that wasn't no accident. Just keep your chin up. We're still flying—"

Nathaniel Hicks looked at Lieutenant Turck, and she turned her face away. "Don't!" she said.

"All right, young lady?" Colonel Ross said, turning around, too. Lieutenant Turck in the shadow brought one cheek against the wall and laid both hands over the other. "I'm all right," she said.

Facing front, Nathaniel Hicks could see General Beal saying something to Lieutenant Colonel Carricker. Beyond their heads the southern sky was filled with bright quiet lightning flares. Lieutenant Colonel Carricker moved his shoulders in a shrug, turned his face to look at the compass, and they began to bank gently.

General Beal's face had turned in profile, set stern, and angry, the lips in brief limited movement. Lieutenant Colonel Carricker, his face front, said audibly, "Ah, cut it, Chief! Go on, take over."

General Beal said something else; sat back and folded his arms.

Looking straight ahead, Lieutenant Colonel Carricker said, brusque and angry, "Flaps coming down! You damn well better take it, Chief; because I'm not going to. She won't land herself."

For the first time audible, General Beal said, "That was an order. You're in arrest."

"All right; so I am. Go ahead. Take it."

Colonel Ross said, "Come on, you two! That's enough of that."

General Beal put a hand on the wheel before him and edged it forward precisely. With his other hand on the throttle knobs, his eyes intent on his instrument panel, he called out calmly enough: "Nothing for you to worry about, Judge. When I'm in command, I'm going to be obeyed."

No one said anything; and suddenly under them came a quick short brush of wheels, a soft little speeding jolt, and the runway lights flicked fast right and left. General Beal gunned around in the darkness and they moved rapidly past the long line of hangars. In front of the Operations Building floodlights were turned on the ramp. The B-26 stood dark and motionless, poised on its tricycle gear. General Beal swung in nearby and ran up his engines. A handful of military police and an officer with the AO band on his arm were out in front.

General Beal cut his engines and Sergeant Pellerino knocked up the catch and opened the door. A warm moist wind, carrying long rolls of thunder, blew in. Nathaniel Hicks breathed it deeply. He undid his belt and dropped the ends. Sergeant Pellerino, his voice loud in the stillness, said: "Don't bother, ma'am. Just leave that. They'll clean it all out."

Lieutenant Turck said faintly: "Thank you."

"All right, you people, get out," General Beal called. "You, too, Benny. I'll be along in a minute. I can give anyone who's going to the Oleander Towers a lift."

Colonel Ross said to Nathaniel Hicks: "You're going down, aren't you? Wait around in front."

"How about you?" Nathaniel Hicks said to Lieutenant Turck. Swinging his musette bag over his shoulder and tucking his flying jacket under his arm, he had followed her out. She stood uncertainly on the wet concrete. "How are you going to get home?"

She said, still faintly: "At the gate here I can get a taxi over to the Area, I think. They put my bag in front. I'll have to wait until they get it out." She looked at him sadly.

"I think I'd better see you to it," Nathaniel Hicks said. "You don't feel very well, do you?"

"Tolerable," Lieutenant Turck said. "I am so ashamed of myself. I am all right. Would you do this? Would you help me get that bag to the gate? I feel a little weak in the knees—"

"They're getting the stuff out now," Nathaniel Hicks said.

Two men had come up with a wheeled stage and were opening the luggage compartment in the plane's nose. There was a vivid flash of lightning, a crack of thunder, and somewhere far across the field, the sound of rushing wind. "We'd better get into Operations," he said. "It's going to rain like hell in a minute."

Moving heavily but quickly, Lieutenant Colonel Carricker brushed past Nathaniel Hicks, walking away from the plane. He headed with purpose across the ramp, and Nathaniel Hicks saw that he was going toward the B-26. A group of men, the crew, were standing together with a couple of military police under the wing tip. "I think somebody is going to get burned," Nathaniel Hicks murmured. There was a breath of moist wind, more lightning to the south, and a reiterated bang of heavy thunder. Nathaniel Hicks stared at the men under the wing a moment and said: "Well, I'm damned!"

"What?" said Lieutenant Turck.

"They're black. I couldn't be sure because of the light, there, at first. They're Negroes. Do you know what that is? It's part of a project the general was telling me about—a Negro medium bomb group they're thinking of activating. Poor bastards, they got off to a fine start—"

Carricker's heavy swinging strides had brought him up to the group, perhaps thirty yards away. He stopped and he must have spoken to them, for there was a stir, and then a tall thin figure stepped forward. In the glare of the floodlights Nathaniel Hicks could see that he had a small black mustache. His skin seemed fairly light. There was a second lieutenant's bar on his shirt collar, and wings over his pocket. He brought his hand up and saluted. Behind him, the other four figures hastily saluted. Carricker stood planted, his feet apart, his head forward, saying something.

Nathaniel Hicks heard a movement behind him. General Beal, who had just got out of the plane, said: "All right, Judge. I—" He stopped short.

Over by the B-26 Carricker moved abruptly. He dropped one hand, his shoulder swung, and he hit the lieutenant in the face with a clear, solid smack. The tall figure went down backwards. The other four recoiled. The two MP's stood gaping.

"Benny!" shouted General Beal. Then he shouted: "What are you MP's doing? Get in there! Break it up!" To Colonel Ross, he said, "Now, by God, he *is* under arrest!"

At that instant the wind freshened. Lightning filled half the sky; the thunder crashed, and louder than the last echoes of the thunder, drove the racing beat of tropical rain.

Colonel Ross said: "Better run for it, Bus!"

The two men with the stage on which they had placed the luggage were already running, pushing it in front of them. Nathaniel Hicks caught Lieutenant Turck's arm and ran with her. Colonel Ross began to run himself. As he ran, he called to the group by the B-26: "Inside, all you!"

Looking that way, Nathaniel Hicks saw them getting the man who had been knocked down to his feet. They began to run; and Carricker ran too. Looking back, Nathaniel Hicks saw General Beal running; and, behind, a tempest of rain, a thick curtain of falling water on which the lights shone, coming rapidly after him.

TWO
FRIDAY

THE CLEAR gold morning was of extraordinary, though for Ocanara at that time of year, not unusual, beauty. Last night's rain washed every leaf and every roof. All dust was laid. The sandy gray or white soil lay damp, clean and firm. Light breezes, delicate and fresh, moved the tranquil air. The senses, enchanted, hardly believed that newness, coolness, softness would be all gone in another hour.

Through scraggly pine woods, across rippling ponds, the sun poured level in splendor on the ample, close-fenced AFORAD Area. Over the yellow-painted wood walls and mottled composition roofs of the close-set long ranks of barracks and temporary buildings; over the permanent construction of concrete block sprayed with dull shades of green which housed the Directorate Centers, the administrative offices, the work shops and drafting rooms, the libraries and laboratories, the auditoriums and demonstration halls, a profound bright hush hung.

The hush was deepened, rather than broken, by scattered occasional noises. Metal bumped metal and water splashed in kitchens and mess halls. Somewhere someone whistled emphatically the tune of a song called "Paper Doll." Now and then cars or trucks left the motor-pool sheds and racketed away down the open, empty streets.

In the Headquarters quadrangle a lined-up platoon of the Headquarters Guard, white sun helmets, white pistol belts, white leggings, all spotless, dressed right, dressed!

Neat and motionless, they waited on the voice. It cracked proud and snappy across the radiant sunshafts on the clipped grass: "Ready—front!"

"Left—face!"

"Forward—"

The platoon moved. Steel heels hit in unison through the

gap between the buildings. They clicked smartly over the paved road.

At the flag staff, two privates of the Flag Detail fell out and joined the sergeant. They unlashed the halyards and shook them clear. They attached the top hoist buckle of the post flag, held, exactly folded, in the sergeant's arms. Then they stood and waited.

From the polished saluting cannon the Gun Detail stripped the tarpaulin. With formal movements of a drill as old as the Civil War, they charged the piece. The corporal stepped back, grasping the lanyard ring in his hand.

Down the front steps of Headquarters walked the Commander of the Guard, and the Senior and Junior Officers of the Day. They stopped talking and stood at attention.

In the empty Guard Room the Sergeant of the Guard kept his eyes on the electric wall clock. Prolonged, the bright hush held on, suspended. Silently, rhythmically jerking down, the clock's big minute hand came to, then covered, the mark of 6:25. Now the Sergeant of the Guard let the reproducing needle drop in the spinning groove.

All over the Area clustered horns of the amplifying system emitted a gritting, vibrating hum. Abruptly, with the volume of a hundred bugles, notes of reveille crashed rousing out of them.

The post flag lifted, shaking its folds on the lee side of the staff. The flag's long, bright fly swelled away. It climbed, wavering in the breeze. The saluting cannon uttered a puff of smoke and boomed, shaking the ground.

✦

The mechanical bugle notes, blared in the open windows, started Amanda Turck from her thick, uncomfortable sleep. She stirred in the distress of one of those dreams in which the poor dreamer's every struggle to escape from a disagreeable or dangerous situation is prevented by a torpid helplessness. In

92

this case, the situation involved a water moccasin, an ugly, thick-bodied snake. About a month before, a water moccasin had indeed appeared between two of the enlisted women's barracks. No doubt it was confused by all this building, which was not here last year; and perhaps it was inconvenienced by the drainage of a swampy hollow below. One of the WAC Area guards came and killed it quickly with his rifle butt; but before he arrived there had been enough squealing and shrieking to attract Amanda Turck's attention. Though not herself a company officer, she had been passing and she recognized her duty to get the matter in hand. The excited spectators, advancing and recoiling at a considerable distance from the sluggish and bewildered snake, included one girl who had collapsed in what appeared to be a perfectly genuine faint.

Lieutenant Turck strode up and gave a few crisp and matter-of-fact directions about the care of the girl who had fainted. She then stated loudly and authoritatively that the snake, while venomous, would never think of chasing or pursuing anyone. Unless stepped on or handled, it would not bite—snakes did not "sting"; they bit, using fangs rooted in their upper jaw. To bite, they had to strike; and no snake could strike beyond a half and probably not beyond a third of its own length. Reassuringly bored by the schoolteacher's tone and the dry learning, the audience readily fell in with a suggestion that they ought to get back to what they were doing before, and let the guard, who now trotted up, deal with the snake.

In the dream version, however, it was she, and not the calm, lumbering guard who had the snake to deal with. Though she hit at it repeatedly with a file drawer full of index cards which she was for some reason carrying, she struck with no force, and the snake's gross folds kept edging closer—not with any apparent hostile intent, yet with a loathsome dumb determination. A Girl Scout leader she had known twenty years ago told her, tapping her shoulder, that rattlesnakes seeking warmth sometimes crawled into the blankets of campers sleeping on the ground.

The convulsive start of waking left Amanda Turck sitting on her cot, bugle notes ringing in her ears. The light dew of sweat in which she slept here every summer night crept on her face and soaked the pajama top she wore. She shook her head, ridding her mind of the bad dream. She put down her feet and worked them into straw slippers.

On a cot five feet to her left, Lieutenant Mary Lippa lay face down. Lieutenant Lippa had on nothing at all; but across her brown back and over her neat buttocks the brassiere and shorts she wore swimming had shielded two bands of white skin from the sun. Since the rest of her was burnt brown, the effect was of a kind of costume. Lieutenant Lippa's face, small, snub-nosed, was pushed well into her damp pillow; but she was more or less awake. She lifted a hand and pressed it over her ear. She screwed her eyes tighter closed and groaned: "No! No! No!"

"Yes, yes, yes," Lieutenant Turck said briskly. "Wake up. Hurry. You won't get a wash basin."

"I don't care."

"Yes, you do. We went into it all last night, remember? Get up!"

"No."

"Yes. Up, now! That's three times."

"No!"

"O.K.," Lieutenant Turck said. "This is it!" She slapped Lieutenant Lippa as hard as she could on the untanned buttocks.

"Damn you, Amanda!" Lieutenant Lippa said. "That really hurt!"

"You ungrateful wretch," Lieutenant Turck said. "Did you ever get up at all while I was away? It hurt my hand, too, if you want to know. I will use a hair brush next time, if I am ever kind enough to bother again. Now, are you going to be late to your formation?"

"Oh, God, no!" said Lieutenant Lippa. "Thanks, darling! Here, where's my wrapper; where are my slippers?"

Two miles to the west, in the hospital area of the Air Base, Lieutenant Werthauer, the Night Duty Officer, was yawning

94

and listening for the gun. He did not hear it, because, at that moment of its firing, another of a flight of B-24's, folding its gear up and thundering down a racket of not yet quite synchronized engines, took off and passed a few hundred feet above the hospital roofs.

Lieutenant Werthauer, a short pale youth with a bush of black hair, thought that intelligent planning would not have put the hospital area directly up the prevailing winds from the air field. Yet the fact that there they had it afforded him a regular bitter pleasure. A hundred times a day his poor opinion of the military mind was recalled and increased by the moment's necessary pause while you could not hear yourself think. Lieutenant Werthauer was a neurologist. Though still in general practice, he had done post-graduate work in the field, and last year he had been invited to read a paper to the Neurological Society detailing a new theory about causative factors in somatic choreas, a signal honor for a man of his age. He did not see any sense in an assignment that kept him sitting around treating blisters and prescribing laxatives.

As the racket of the B-24's take-off died away, a nurse came in, obligingly bringing, along with the night report sheets, a cup of cocoa for him and a cup of coffee for Captain Raimondi. Captain Raimondi, a fat little fellow and a first rate surgeon, appeared on her heels, whistling cheerfully. He said: "Thanks, honey-bunch!" to the nurse. He took a long swallow of the coffee and held up the report sheets. "Got anything I don't want to know about, Doctor?" he said to Lieutenant Werthauer.

"No," Lieutenant Werthauer said. "There's a T/4 who dropped a cylinder block on his foot; and a belly-ache observation."

"What's this Willis, Second Lieutenant Stanley M.? What's he got a room for?"

"Oh, that! Ask McCreery. Subject officer is a smoke. McCreery didn't want to put him in Fourteen for fear some sensitive Southerner would wake up next to him and be sore. He's a pilot who brought a plane in last night. He had a knock in the face. Maybe he bumped a gunsight, or something; but somebody said somebody slugged him." Lieutenant Werthauer yawned and finished his cocoa. "If so, it was a solid slugging. McCreery took a stitch in his lip; and he has a well-fractured nose. McCreery asked me to help him with the splints on that. The fact is, McCreery hadn't the haziest idea of how to put them in. When I finished, he took a lot of plaster, he already had a dressing on the lip, and was going to slap it on the nose. I asked him what that was supposed to do; so he mumbled something, and finally decided not. The damn fool!"

"Tut, tut," said Captain Raimondi. "Rank hath its privilege, Doctor."

"You know a cheer they give over in Communications? Just heard it. It goes: 'Three dits, four dits, two dits, dah; Ocanara, rah, rah, rah!'"

"I do not catch."

"Study up your Morse code, Captain." Lieutenant Werthauer put his cocoa cup down and got to his feet. "Here, you can have the place. I'm going to bed."

The thudding jar of the Morning Gun went up the highway that passed southbound between the AFORAD Area and the Air Base. The highway soon became Tropical Avenue, entering Ocanara in a brick-paved, shaded tunnel of big live oaks and camphor trees. Reaching the intersection with Sunshine Avenue, the boom went west over the business blocks, and east to the park-like, though much overgrown, grounds of the Oleander Towers Hotel.

These twenty-odd acres bordering Lake Armstrong were, through shortage of labor and neglect, largely a jungle of Jacaranda and Turk's cap, bamboo, banana trees, silk oaks and oleanders, crotons and poinsettias. Tumbledown arches and walls and cement gazebos were covered with magenta-colored bougainvillaea and yellow bignonia. Years before, an attempt had been made to establish a royal-palm avenue. It was found in due time that, north of the Everglades, these trees survived with difficulty. Only three or four, sheltered by the bulk of the hotel, were left. As they died, Washington palms had been planted. In their accumulated stacks of dead fronds they formed a shabby double line from the gate on East Sunshine Avenue to the main entrance.

The hotel itself was large, though smaller than when it was built. The not-very-practical scheme of the owner and builder had been to exceed, if only a little, in size and elegance the then-new Flagler constructions on the east coast. The not-very-practical ambition of the architects seemed to have been to exceed, if only a little, the ornate absurdities of the Tampa Bay Hotel. By adding to the Moorish some features of other Oriental styles, this ambition had been largely realized. The original shape was that of a letter E whose center arm was joined to those east and west by a great curved verandah with horseshoe arches and spindle supports inspired by the Alhambra's Court of Lions pavilion. This verandah faced south on East Sunshine Avenue. The back of the E was encrusted with balconies looking on Lake Armstrong. The roofs were a jumble of domes, towers and minarets.

In the '90's a fire, only prevented from destroying the whole structure by the ample supply of water right at hand in Lake Armstrong, burned down the west wing and part of the north front on the lake. These were never replaced. The building was left truncated—reduced to the center wing, with the lobby and dining room, half the north front, the east wing, and half the curved verandah. The insurance money was used to put up a dozen bungalows in the park. They were supposed to offer what was then called the utmost in luxury, privacy, and convenience.

As time passed, people preferred newer and more modest hotels; some in Ocanara, but many of them, unfortunately for Ocanara's dream of becoming the biggest and best-known winter resort of central Florida, at Orlando and Winter Park. Had there been no war, and so, no Ocanara Army Air Base and no AFORAD, the winter of 1942–43 would probably have seen the Oleander Towers closed and perhaps torn down. Instead, by the summer of 1943, it was doing a business not known there since 1900. Its guests were almost entirely officers stationed at Ocanara, or those down on conferences, inspections, and junkets.

For accommodations they could have done worse; and, indeed, at most AAF installations they did do worse. The vast corridors, the old-fashioned lofty rooms with ceiling fans and slatted doors were fairly cool. The high, screened balconies got some breeze off Lake Armstrong most nights. A large staff would have been required to keep the hotel clean, and since large staffs could not be hired, it was not kept clean; yet the food and service were better than you would expect in trying times. There was a fairly new tiled swimming pool with plaster arches around it; a dozen tennis courts, on six of which some sort of game could be played; and a bar with two fountains, one working, which had been taken over as a downtown Officers Club. The luxury, privacy, and convenience of the bungalows was enjoyed by the top brass—General Beal in the best, and nobody less than a full colonel in any of the others. Though there was occasional talk of requiring all unmarried officers, or those whose families were not with them, to live in the AFORAD Area BOQ's—an idea whose disagreeableness anyone who ever lived in a BOQ could understand—nothing had so far come of it.

✦

The boom of the Morning Gun was audible at the Oleander Towers, but faintly. When it sounded, two Negro bell boys accomplished reveille by rapidly plugging in and ringing room after room from the hotel switchboard. At the same time the dining room doors, under an arch resembling the portal of the Taj Mahal, were parted enough to let out the aged colored headwaiter whose tufts of white wool and striped waistcoat had long delighted those of the all-too-few peacetime Northern visitors who knew a real, old-time darky when they saw one. His name was Nicodemus. Limping, bobbing his head, he got the dining room doors pushed back and hooked. This was hardly done when the screened doors of the front entrance to the lobby swung and admitted Colonel Ross, who lived in one of the bungalows with his wife, but found it more convenient to get breakfast, since he ate it so early, at the hotel. He went to the newsstand, helped himself to a copy of yesterday's New York *Times* and of today's Ocanara *Morning Sun,* and marched to the dining room.

Nicodemus greeted him with extravagant pleasure. Beaming and ducking, he said: "A very good morning to you, Colonel. I am in hopes I see you well, so bright and early this fine morning, sir." He hobbled quickly ahead, down toward a table by one of the west windows, calling as he advanced: "You, there, girl! Fetch the colonel's juice! You, there; pour out the colonel's coffee! You, there; get the colonel's eggs on the fire!"

With a flourish, he drew back Colonel Ross's chair, seated him, snapped open a napkin and laid it across his lap. Turning in time, he intercepted a mulatto girl carrying a silver bowl of crushed ice in which was embedded a tall glass of dark fluid. He took it away from her, his tremulous old hands slopping some of it, and put it down ceremoniously before Colonel Ross.

Colonel Ross looked at the dark fluid with disgust.

"Nick," he said, "I'd like to ask you a question. Why the devil is there no orange juice in Florida?"

Nicodemus broke into a rich noise of laughter, a spasm of hearty yeh-yehs. "Colonel, they tell me out there in California, that's where they buy it all. Yeh, yeh, yeh—"

"Then you better go out there and get me some tomorrow." Colonel Ross took a swallow of the juice, a puce-colored slop, tasting as you would expect anything that color to taste, and turned his attention to the Ocanara *Morning Sun.* He opened it at once to the editorial page and a column headed: *This & That by Art Bullen.*

Mr. Bullen was the owner of the *Sun.* He was not a native of Florida; but he had come to Ocanara as a young man, and few people born there were so aggressively, in Mr. Bullen's own term, Ocanarans. Perhaps he felt that all was definitely right about a place where a young fellow with nothing but energy and ambition could do so well by himself in less than twenty-five years. Just out of the Army after the last war, he was supposed to have bought the paper, a weekly with a circulation of about one thousand, for fifty dollars. Ocanara's hopes of becoming a great winter resort were already gone, perhaps fortunately, for the subsequent real estate boom had no special effect and those who bought land around Ocanara mostly wanted it for citrus fruit and truck gardening. Of course, a real estate operator could and did make money. Mr. Bullen made some to go with the other money that came from his success in putting the *Sun* on its feet and his marriage to a local girl, the daughter of the president of the most prosperous bank, and the majority stockholder in the Ocanara Gas and Electric Company.

Success had never led Mr. Bullen to put on airs. He now employed a managing editor and a fair-sized staff, but he still worked hard on the paper. A rich man, he continued to wear old shirts and wash pants; and his recreations were still pitching horseshoes and playing poker. He was quiet spoken, with a spare dry frame, an angular impassive face, and a mild, civil manner. Though not himself an active politician, his friends were the ruling faction and it was a safe bet that Mr. Bullen's energy and acumen had much to do with keeping them in power. Colonel Ross, as an elected judge, had been himself at least partly in politics for many years. He understood politicians perfectly. He could not feel that the military authorities had always shown wisdom in their handling of Mr. Bullen's friends.

Colonel Mowbray, along with his unquestioned integrity and upright innocence, had a child's, really, you might think, an infant's, ignorance of any businesses or human activities which were not an ordinary part of life on a peacetime Army post. Colonel Mowbray was uneasily aware of this defect in knowledge and experience. Just as deaf people sometimes allow themselves to become obsessed with the suspicion that most of the talk they cannot hear consists in plottings and schemings to overreach or get around them, Colonel Mowbray was warily inclined to believe that any proposal, particularly any long and carefully detailed proposal, was on the face of it made to fool you, deliberately complicated so you would not see its dishonest purpose.

One day, a few weeks before General Beal arrived to assume his command, Colonel Mowbray had found in his hands just such an elaborate proposal. A Mr. McCormack was offering to provide bus service between downtown Ocanara and the Air Base and the new AFORAD Area. Colonel Mowbray gave one of his worried mornings to a futile meticulous scrutiny of the proposed contracts. Then he asked Mr. McCormack to come out and see him.

The interview did not go well.

Colonel Ross knew only what Colonel Mowbray afterward confusedly recounted to him; and there was now no way of distinguishing what was fact from what might be Mowbray's misapprehension. Colonel Mowbray, who had neither the time nor the inclination to find out anything about his visitor's standing or local position, seemed to have jumped to an *a priori* conclusion that here was a crook. He said that this McCormack admitted to being a big stockholder in the Ocanara Transit Company; and though the contracts were with a man named Waters, Waters was nothing but a dummy. The Army was to furnish Waters with vehicles for the extra bus service. Waters then would lease these vehicles to the Transit Company (that is, Mr. McCormack) for operation. The lease was at an extremely high figure; thus giving this Waters a handsome profit for doing nothing but passing along government property to someone else. Obviously, Mr. McCormack must have a deal with Waters on the side, Colonel Mowbray knew enough about business tricks to see that. "The whole thing smelled," Colonel Mowbray said with virtuous indignation. "I gave him back his contracts, and I told him that if he was still on this post five minutes from now, the Provost Marshal would put him off."

With a knowledge of Colonel Mowbray's limitations and ordinary habits of thought, it was possible to reconstruct the incident as it might have been; and to reconcile the wild implausibility of Colonel Mowbray's report with the fact that Colonel Mowbray would probably see himself shot before he told a deliberate falsehood. In the first place it was obvious that Colonel Mowbray, fantastically unbusinesslike, had never thought of finding out whether the people offering to make this contract were responsible—with the financial and other means to carry it through and provide an adequate service. Asked if he knew who these men were, he would doubtless reply that he did not know and he did not care. The circumstance that

Mr. McCormack was a leading citizen of Ocanara, respected, well-to-do, consequential; and that what Colonel Mowbray slightingly called "this Waters" was a former longtime member of the state legislature, former chairman of the State Democratic Committee, or in other words, one of the most powerful men in Florida politically, cut no ice with Colonel Mowbray. Anyone who thought he could be swayed by venal considerations of that kind had another think coming.

Mr. McCormack, for his part, must have assumed that Colonel Mowbray knew already, or at least had taken care to find out, something about his standing and responsibility. Colonel Mowbray's own standing and responsibility appeared in his uniform and rank. Both uniform and rank probably caused Mr. McCormack to feel constraint. Perhaps he was apologetic, since he probably regarded himself as too old to take part in this war; yet here was a man, clearly of his own age, who was taking part in it. Mr. McCormack might have, too, a sense of being out of his business element—during peacetime he knew, of course, that there was an Army somewhere; but he never saw it or had anything to do with it.

At any rate, whatever the cause, the effect had plainly been to provoke in Mr. McCormack a surely unusual ingenuousness. The elderly officer Mr. McCormack saw facing him looked composed, impassive, with alert eyes and an air of severe efficiency—a front which Colonel Mowbray had long used to cover bewilderment. Mr. McCormack must have explained freely; when, in fact, he needed to do nothing but let the contract speak for itself—Greek, to Colonel Mowbray. Colonel Mowbray would never have admitted he didn't understand, not from vanity or a wish to deceive; but because he represented the Army and he owed it to the Army to see that no kind of discredit ever came to it through him. Naturally, he could not sign when he did not understand; but he could have promised Mr. McCormack a decision before the day was over. After Mr. McCormack left the Judge Advocate's Section would tell him whether it was "legal."

Colonel Ross didn't doubt that it was "legal." Mr. McCormack, a man of fairly large affairs, would have lawyers who knew how to get him what he wanted in ways scrupulously regardful of all pertinent Federal or Florida statutes made and provided. If Colonel Mowbray had it anything like straight, what Mr. McCormack wanted was obvious. There was no faintest intention of defrauding the War Department. He wouldn't stoop to such a thing. Mr. McCormack merely intended to defraud the Collector of Internal Revenue by causing the Transit Company to "lose" a good deal of money and thus eliminate taxable profits. Who but Colonel Mowbray, a simpleton, would confuse this kind of common sense with common cheating? Mr. McCormack must have been astounded at Colonel Mowbray's explosion of virtue. In a frank and agreeable way, he had probably come right out, or nearly right out, and said something like: "You see, Colonel, we feel we can undertake this because, even though it is unprofitable to the Transit Company, the stockholders aren't out anything. That would just have gone in taxes—"

He then had five minutes to get off the post before the Provost Marshal threw him off.

Colonel Ross thought it was significant that Mr. McCormack swallowed the affront so quietly. He would not have lacked for the means to take it to Washington, so he must have decided that it wouldn't pay. This pretty clearly showed that Colonel Mowbray, doltish and ignorant as he was, had, only knowing that right was right, outsmarted a smart man. So far: so good. But, of course, like Mr. Waters, Mr. McCormack, the outsmarted smart man, was a close friend and poker-playing companion of Mr. Bullen's. As it happened, he was also Mr. Bullen's father-in-law. The next day, the Ocanara *Morning Sun*, speaking in sorrow more than anger, started needling the Military.

Opportunities came often. Two large diverse and independently directed communities, not merely side by side but actively overlapping and elbowing each other, cannot live without friction. Colonel Ross's first article of business each morning was to see what aspects of this friction had come to Mr. Bullen's attention during the last twenty-four hours.

Colonel Ross did not entirely blame Mr. Bullen. The inci-

dent of the bus contracts, even as it was described by Colonel
Mowbray, let alone as it must have been described by Mr. Mc-
Cormack, might justify an honest conviction that military stupidity and Army arrogance should no longer go unprotested.
Yet Colonel Ross would have been glad to put a stop to it;
both because Mr. Bullen's style was irritating, and because Mr.
Bullen often seemed too well informed about matters, which
while they might not involve actual military security, were no
concern of Mr. Bullen's, and must involve a leak somewhere
among AFORAD Headquarters personnel.

Folding the paper to today's column, Colonel Ross saw with
a comprehensive glance that they were in for it again, and at
length. This could give him no pleasure; but he noted next,
by an automatic, hardly conscious lawyer's habit of cross reference and classification of material performed even while he took
in the sense, that this time he might have what he had long been
looking for.

The leak was there, all right. Somebody who saw those
memoranda of Colonel Mowbray's talked to Mr. Bullen; and
those memoranda happened to have been classified *Confidential*.
Happened, Colonel Ross must admit, was the right word. By
that stamp, Colonel Mowbray meant that everyone was to hush
it up; not that here was information affecting the national defense of the United States within the meaning of the Espionage
Act, 50 U.S.C. 31 and 32 as amended.

Colonel Ross smiled faintly.

He immediately knew the answer to that—troop movements!
Future activity of military units! Well and truly classified! "Its
transmission or the revelation of its contents in any manner to
an unauthorized person is prohibited by law." Colonel Ross
began to read with attention.

Tomorrow, Mr. Bullen wrote, *our military friends out
Tropical Avenue are planning to celebrate the birthday of a
certain distinguished General Officer whose headquarters are
not a thousand miles from this Scribe's office. In case you could
be wondering who it is, I will come right out and elect myself*

a delegation of one to tender to Major General Ira N. ("Bus")
Beal the mass felicitations of the good citizens of Ocanara, city
and county, on the occasion of his forty-first birthday. We be-
lieve he is still the youngest Major General (not to be con-
fused with Brigadier or Buck General) in the Army of the
United States. We know from his brilliant record, both in the
Pacific and in the European Theatres, that he is a top-notch
fighting flyer. Those of us who have been privileged to meet
him and his young, attractive, and gracious wife can testify that,
in addition to being an airman and a soldier he is every inch a
gentleman, modest, courteous, and affable. We are honored to
have him at Ocanara, and we wish him many more years of
honors, health, and happiness.

No one, Colonel Ross must admit, could say fairer than that.
He gave a grunt, recognizing that Mr. Bullen (whether he
knew about the relentless scrutiny, the menacing patient attention that was given every word of every aspersive comment in
the *Sun,* or whether he depended only on his instinct for adroit
moves to stop his opponents) here neatly posed Colonel Ross,
his chief and most dangerous opponent, by this conciliatory
paragraph. What Mr. Bullen said left unchanged the fact that
he must get information from someone who got it from pieces
of paper stamped *Confidential;* but Colonel Ross recognized his
own dilemma. The point was to abate this nuisance. Colonel
Ross had to confess that long irritation made him relish the idea
of the abatement that might be managed if he just once caught
Mr. Bullen with his foot fairly in it. Mr. Bullen would not be
easy to scare; but Colonel Ross was ready, and even a little
eager, to try scaring him. Colonel Ross nodded to himself and
read on:

We only hope General Beal is enjoying his tour of duty here.
The reason this Scribe can only hope, instead of being, as you
would expect, dead certain that all sojourners here enjoy them-
selves, is that a man who has flown against the enemy and led
combat units doesn't usually take kindly to assignments with
the chairborne troops. Now, I'd better say right away; please
don't get me wrong! Most of these chairborne officers are fine
patriotic men, many of whom answered the call to arms at

great personal sacrifice, and they are doing a devoted job. The Nation is fortunate to have them in the Service, and Ocanara is glad to have them here. Everybody happy?

Well, not quite, now I think of it; and since it might have a bearing on the general's own happiness, I may as well admit that in this vale of tears, even in Ocanara, where every prospect pleases, the bitter comes with the sweet. Let us face it! Along with so many fine officers and men, the AAF has assigned us a good few who might be described as a horse, or part of a horse, of a different color. You know them. Old Army unemployables who never did anything but live this long. Thickheaded stuffed shirts recommended into commissions so their home towns wouldn't see them for a while. Pinheaded playboy types who got certified as officers and gents one jump ahead of the draft and may be found upsetting their drinks every evening in our best bars. As I say, I pause to mention these sad exceptions to the rule above because if you think (and you're right) it's tough on Ocanara having them, still and all it is probably even tougher on General Beal. You can't tell me he likes them any better than you do. . . .

Down the shadowed dining room, quick, firm steps echoed closer and Colonel Ross looked up over his glasses. He saw, as he expected, Major Sears, the Provost Marshal. Gesturing with the paper toward the other chair, he said: "Come here, Johnny."

Major Sears, though not an Army man, but appropriately enough a former State Police lieutenant, stood and moved in that perfect position of the soldier which is seldom seen outside pictures in *New Infantry Drill Regulations*. With no visible effort or strain, Major Sears carried his head erect on the correct vertical axis; his neck and head squarely to the front, chin in, eyes level. His straight shoulders, lifted chest, and narrow, evenly-held hips set off the fresh creases of his khaki shirt and trousers. His shoes gleamed. His brass belt buckle shone colorless as a clean mirror. The insignia on his collar tabs were centered to at least one thirty-second of an inch.

Colonel Ross, though he didn't, and didn't purpose to, practice himself any such excesses of bearing and grooming, looked at Major Sears with an approving eye. If you are going to do a thing—especially if you are a young man in your thirties and have a chance of doing it successfully—you should do it right. In performing his duties, one of which was to see that Ocanara personnel looked, as well as behaved, like soldiers, Major Sears properly began with himself.

Major Sears, who held a copy of the *Sun*, sat down and said: "I see you're reading it."

"I just began it," Colonel Ross said. "It looks pretty long."

"Come to the crack about my MP's?"

"No."

"I want to tell you about that, when you do. It's a thing I think we ought to crack back about, Judge. I came over to tell you yesterday; but they said you'd gone flying with the general. Another thing. Do you realize all those memos on the birthday business were classified *Confidential?* Lot of nonsense, of course, like the rest of it; but that was the classification. See what I see?"

"I see what you see," Colonel Ross said. "I was thinking about it. It might do. The Hendryx Field B-Seventeens and our airborne people are, in fact, troop movements. If the classification had to be defended. We might make him trouble. But I want to consider it very carefully. Trouble isn't what we're here to make."

Major Sears said, "I admit it couldn't matter a damn who knew about the plans; but anyone who gets to see those memos probably gets to see a lot of other stuff that does matter. Judge, I think we ought to nail that guy."

"It's a girl, of course," Colonel Ross said absently.

In his mind, he began now to plan his morning. He would have to get to Bus right away to see about Benny's business last night—a tiresome little difficulty. Last night, out of patience, Bus could put Benny in arrest in quarters and direct charges to be drawn; but this morning he would be more likely to want to drop the whole thing. The colored officer was in the hospital; not, they thought last night, very seriously hurt. He'd better check that. He said: "I'm probably going to be tied up with the general for a while; but if you see Howden, ask him to come to my office with you about ten. I think we might investigate all civilian women in Headquarters who are natives of Ocanara. I want to find out if any of them ever worked in any capacity for the Ocanara *Morning Sun;* and if the parents of any of them are especially close friends of Mr. Bullen's. You might tell Howden to get his people after that. But I don't want him to put the heat on. I'll decide which ones better be questioned directly, and I'll question them. I don't want a lot of tears and hysterics." He looked sharply at Major Sears. "If you see what I mean," he said.

"Howden is a little rugged," Major Sears said, "but you can't expect Counter-Intelligence to fool around."

"You still catch more flies with honey than with vinegar," Colonel Ross said. "Let me finish this, will you?" Looking down again, he read:

Now, it is clear that if the general lets any characters of the types sadly mentioned give orders for which the Army is going to hold him responsible, the next thing he knows, he may be on a spot. There have been instances of people speaking for the general without showing much judgment. I have had something to say before about the bus service mess. Men with passes sometimes wait hours, and this isn't helping morale any. You know why it's that way. A local citizen, putting himself to a great deal of trouble and being actually ready to see himself out of pocket if it would help the Army, presented a plan, sensible and efficient, based on years of successful experience with transit problems. He found himself kindly kicked in the teeth and practically called a crook for his pains. Then, we have repeated cases in which our local police, trying to do their duty, are prevented by high-handed, arbitrary action on the part of the Provost Marshal's office. While in some instances it might have been just MP's acting injudiciously, there was one the other night in which the Provost Marshal himself took a hand in threatening and attempting to humiliate an officer whose years of faithful service to this community would entitle him to a fairer hearing of his side of the case.

"I see it," Colonel Ross said to Major Sears. "What did you do, Johnny?"

"I really didn't do anything until afterwards. Lieutenant Day did exactly right. He's a good kid. I want to try again to get him a promotion. This city police officer, Tyler, was drunk. I have five people who can testify to it, including the barkeep at Jimmy's, where they wouldn't serve him any more. I don't know what he told them at the station, but they certainly must know that he's been an old sot for years. See?"

"I see," Colonel Ross said.

"All right, he, Tyler, was on patrol Wednesday night. He picked up an officer, a lieutenant, who had a couple of drinks, it's true, but who wasn't drunk, for going into the shrubbery in Floral Park—it was half past nine at night and dark; he was waiting for a bus to go out to the Area so he didn't want to go far away from the stop, there—and taking a leak. This Tyler, you can judge the condition he was in, put handcuffs on him, and was staggering along with him, when two of my MP's were passing in a jeep. They stopped to see what the trouble was. The policeman, weaving back and forth—my men say he was absolutely blotto—told them—they could hardly understand him—that he was going to charge indecent exposure!"

Major Sears sat back and snorted. "They thought he must be kidding, at first. I wouldn't have blamed them too much if they'd just taken the officer away from Tyler and told him to go jump in the lake. But they didn't. They tried to reason him into handing the officer over. He wouldn't. So one of them got Lieutenant Day on the walkie-talkie in the jeep and asked him to come down. Day may have scared the guy a little—said if he didn't remove those handcuffs instantly and hand over his prisoner as provided by our agreement with the Chief of Police, he, Day, would personally go to the station and charge Tyler with being drunk on duty. At any rate, Tyler did take the handcuffs off, and Day gave him a lift to his home, the cop's. We weren't going to make any trouble, once we had our man out of this crazy drunk's hands. But if they want to, just let them start!"

Colonel Ross nodded. He recognized that common, much litigated type of human disagreement in which each party to it insists on reducing his opponent's position or contention to its bare essentials—yes or no; did he, or did he not, still beat his wife?—while asserting the right to state his own position or contention with every circumstantial distinction preserved. High indignation and conflicting strong senses of righteousness resulted. Colonel Ross looked at the paper again. "Well, what did Bullen mean about the Provost Marshal stepping in?"

"It's just a plain lie," Major Sears said. "Except, of course, I suppose Day said he was acting on my orders. He would have been, too, if he'd called me—which, of course, he didn't do; because he's an officer you can depend on to show initiative and accept responsibility. I approve of everything he did."

"Did Bullen just guess that?"

"I don't give a hoot in hell about Bullen! Why is he in this, anyway? I suppose he got on to the Chief of Police, Lovewell. A lot of those old coots pitch horseshoes almost every night behind the Police Station there. I hear that's when most of the city business is done. I suppose Lovewell gave him an earful."

"I suppose," Colonel Ross said. "And where did Lovewell get the earful to give him. From this Tyler?"

"Of course. Tyler probably sobered up some the next morning—he never is entirely sober, I hear—and must have given him a song and dance about us taking a prisoner away from him. So Lovewell called me up."

"That was a long time coming," Colonel Ross said. "So, what did he want?"

"He had the gall," Major Sears said, "to say he wanted, for their records, a memorandum on the disciplinary action which the Army took in the case of what he called the culprit turned over to us by Patrolman Tyler."

"That was part of the agreement," Colonel Ross said. "You haven't stopped giving them that information, have you?"

"We give it to them if there is any action," Major Sears said impatiently. "But what action did he think we were going to take in this case? Does he think we're going to assemble a General Court Martial every time a man goes out in the dark and takes a leak behind a bush? We didn't hold the officer. There weren't any charges against him."

"That's what you told him, then?"

"That's what I told him, in substance. I didn't use those words. I simply said we had no grounds for charges and we weren't making any; that we considered the case closed. I didn't even point out to him that his patrolman was cockeyed drunk. I just said Tyler had been under a misapprehension."

"Sometimes," Colonel Ross said, "I feel this world would get on as well without liquor. That is, until I feel like having a snort myself. Did I understand you to say that this misapprehended lieutenant had been having a couple of drinks?"

"And I meant two. I talked to him, and I checked on that. He was at the Officers Club in the hotel here with another man. The barkeep remembered him and says he was served—"

"Two short beers," Colonel Ross said.

"That's right," Major Sears said, looking at him, surprised.

Colonel Ross laughed. "Johnny," he said, "this is like old times to me. When I used to sit in Quarter Sessions and a defendant was pleading not guilty to charges involving being drunk—drunken driving, for instance—and we had, say, a State Trooper's evidence that he smelled liquor, the District Attorney used to give me a wink before he asked the defendant on the stand what he had to drink prior to his arrest. Nobody ever had anything but two short beers. You could see every last one of them thinking that would be just right—it explained the arresting officer's smelling something on them; but it showed they couldn't be drunk."

Major Sears gave a reluctant answering laugh: "Yeah," he said. "We used to have that, too. But it was the barkeep who told me this."

"Indeed?" Colonel Ross said. "Maybe your barkeeps used to be different; but with us it was a very unusual one who testified that, thanks to the drinks he had served him, his customer was intoxicated."

Major Sears gave him a mild reproachful look. "I know," he said. "And it's true I didn't even see our officer until the next morning. After Lovewell called, I went around and had a talk with him. If Lovewell was going to make something out of it, I wanted to be sure I had my facts straight. But I believed Day and the MP's. I wasn't going just on what the lieutenant said himself, or what the barkeep said."

"I don't doubt you're right, Johnny," Colonel Ross said. "Who was this lieutenant, by the way? What's his organization?"

Major Sears unbuttoned the pressed flap of one breast pocket and took out a notebook. "Edsell," he said, "First Lieutenant James A. Edsell. It's the Reports Section of the Special Projects Directorate, Colonel Coulthard. The Section Chief, Lieutenant Edsell's immediate superior, is Major William W. Whitney. I had a talk with him, too. He says Edsell is a valuable officer. He's a writer or something. Major Whitney said he never saw anything to make him think Edsell was a heavy drinker. In fact, quite the contrary; he said he had several times heard Edsell refuse an invitation, when they were leaving at night, to join other officers in a drink. Edsell lives out in an Area BOQ. He's married, though separated from his wife. Thirty-four years old. Major Whitney says he believes he spends most of his time off duty writing a book, or something. Incidentally, he's Officer Candidate School, not Officer Training School."

"And you deduce?"

"Well, for one thing, he earned his commission; it wasn't just given to him."

"That's Captain Hicks's section," Colonel Ross said. "In fact, I think I know the man. Funny looking fellow. Lot of dark hair."

"That's it," Major Sears said. "Well, at any rate, I'm satisfied he wasn't drunk."

"Still, I guess he must have been pretty well tanked up with something if he couldn't wait to get to a latrine. Don't mistake me, Johnny. I think it was handled all right; and it certainly isn't likely Mr. Lovewell will want to make an issue out of it. But every now and then, remind your people it's essential to keep on good terms with the Police Department here. If that patrolman was in the state your MP's and Lieutenant Day said he was, it might have been a smart thing for them to have gone along with him—that is, taken him and Edsell in the jeep and driven right to the station and let the desk sergeant, or whoever was on duty, see for himself."

"Those bastards stick together," Major Sears said.

"And you bastards don't, I suppose?" Colonel Ross said amiably. "Johnny, it's very annoying; but whenever possible I want to meet them more than half way. If the police officer, Tyler, was drunk to the point described, reeling around and hardly able to talk, the desk sergeant, whatever he might want to do, couldn't pretend to your men that he didn't see anything."

"Some of those old sots, give them a ride in the fresh air for a few minutes, could get to be what passes for sober in a hurry," Major Sears said rebelliously. "I wouldn't mind if somebody could tell them that, while maybe it isn't essential, it would be nice if they just occasionally tried to keep on good terms with us. Anyway, Judge, this jerk Bullen doesn't go down so good with me. I don't know whether that next thing is true or not, but all that sarcastic language about military security—God damn it, does he know there's a war on, or doesn't he?"

"I'll see," said Colonel Ross. He read:

Then, not two days ago, this Scribe was visited by a bright young shavetail from the Public Relations Office and had to take quite a dressing-down for printing in this paper an item which it seems my young visitor thought I ought to have got cleared out there first.

This, I admit, hurt. At my testy age, I don't like having a lad fresh out of, as near as I could see, kindergarten pulling me around by my long white whiskers. Moreover, if I have to take a licking, it would gratify my amour propre (French) if they would give the barrel stave to anyway a captain. To make me feel worse, when I composed said wicked item, I actually imagined I was using the Power of the Press to do the AAF a good turn.

Well, in order to indicate the nature of my offense I'm afraid I'll have to repeat it just a little by printing the gist of this item again. I observed that there had been several (my word) operational accidents around here recently. Could there be any secret about that? When, two weeks ago, an AFORAD plane unfortunately hits a residence in one of our suburbs and both of them burn for half an hour, throwing up a big black column of smoke visible all over the city, a lot of people notice it. Being aware of public interest, and perhaps some alarm, over such incidents, I took a hand-out the shavetail's office sent me showing that the AAF accident rate is improving all the time, that taking into account the hours of flying done, accidents are very rare. I then observed that some accidents must be expected, because tests and projects had to be run; and it should be remembered that very often one accident here would have the direct result, from the lesson learned, of obviating many losses in combat theatres . . .

"What he doesn't see," said Major Sears, watching Colonel Ross read, "or maybe he does, the sarcastic bastard, is when he puts that in the paper, he's just raking it all up again, for no good reason."

Among the duties of the Provost Marshal were the formulation and direction of the standard operating procedures for handling crashes. Major Sears was constantly having bucked over to him those sad, bitterly suspicious, and altogether futile demands for additional, non-existent information from which the parents of dead flyers (or their ministers, or their Congressmen) hoped, as nearly as you could judge, to show that the Army and not their boy was wholly to blame for what happened to him. Like most people in the Air Force, Major Sears felt that publicizing an accident served no good purpose. Colonel Ross grunted, not unsympathetically, and read on:

Now this shavetail visitor of mine told me that by this item I was giving valuable information to the enemy, who were exceedingly anxious to know what our losses of this kind really amounted to. Since I don't know that myself, I don't hardly see how they would get it from anything I wrote. But, there he was, all twenty-two or -three years of him, speaking for General Beal, and doing his little best to make this Scribe think twice before he went to bat for the AAF again. I might be wrong, but I don't believe the general gets any good out of these various misuses of his authority. So you see he has his troubles. Every day, maybe a dozen people are making him

*say what I'm pretty sure he wouldn't think of saying, and do
what I'll bet he wouldn't want to do.*

*So, remember then, when the party breaks out tomorrow,
that being a general isn't all parades and big doings and punch
at the Officers Club. I'm sorry you won't see much of the show,
because you aren't invited. I think they might have invited you,
because by all accounts it is going to be a real honey, an
inspiring martial and patriotic spectacle involving quite a layout of the taxpayers' money. Still, you may see some of the
planes, for they have fleets of them coming from all over the
great state of Florida to wish Bus Beal many happy returns of
the day. This Scribe will now cease his carping, and warmly
join them in that wish.*

Colonel Ross grunted again. He looked at his watch. "Well,"
he said, "there go the beans! I think the general better call
Bullen personally and tell him we'll be delighted to have any
visitors who want to come and see the parade. He can get it
in the paper tomorrow morning."

"My God, Judge," Major Sears said, sincerely appalled,
"I don't think we can! Where are we going to put them?
We can't pass maybe three or four thousand people onto the
Base. I haven't the men to handle them."

"We don't pass them onto the Base. We'll knock out some
of the fence on the west side of the field on the bend of the
highway there, throw up a low barrier on the old hard stand
and maybe move in seat sections from one of the Demonstration Areas. Half a platoon would be enough to see they
didn't wander around. You won't have to have anybody downtown while this is going on."

Major Sears' regular firm face reddened. "You know what
I'd do, before I went brown-nosing this bastard—O.K., Judge!
Who'll see about the fence, and all that?"

"That's for the Post Engineer. Ask Colonel Hildebrand to
call me. You just work out your MP assignments." He arose.
"The general's probably down swimming. I'd better catch him."

"There he is now," Major Sears said, nodding out the
window.

Up a curved concrete path through the shrubbery beyond

the arches of the swimming pool, General Beal, clad only in a tight pair of blue shorts, his bare back and lean strong legs shining with water, was walking carefully in loose sandals toward the brick drive and the open stretches of lawn before the row of bungalows. On his left shoulder he carried lightly and easily his tubby, much tanned, blond-headed son, who was about three.

"You know, that kid is wonderful in the water," Major Sears said. "He really can't swim yet; but he just goes right in head over heels and slaps around until somebody pulls him out. You'd think he'd be scared. Not him. I guess he takes after his old man."

General Beal now reached the drive and was crossing in a blaze of flat sunlight to the path that led up to his bungalow. The guard, walking post there, saw him coming. The guard came to a careful, formal halt by the gate, snapped his heels together and, with admirable precision, presented arms.

General Beal responded with an easy, humorous gesture of salute. On his shoulder, the child, letting go his father's wet hair, saluted, too.

"Cute little devil!" said Major Sears.

He was smiling with pleasure at the sight, but he kept his eyes thoughtfully on the guard. The guard, though the general's back was now toward him, went through the motions of returning his rifle to shoulder arms with the same commendable precision.

Major Sears gave a little nod. "Be around at ten, then, Colonel," he said.

✦

The distant but distinct boom of the Morning Gun awakened Nathaniel Hicks in his bedroom on the third floor of the Oleander Towers Hotel. He lay a moment, feeling a stir of lukewarm air on his sweaty forehead. He waited for, and almost immediately heard, the telephones begin to ring. They moved moment by moment nearer and louder along this hall, and along the hall below. With perfect timing, he stretched out a hand. He caught his own telephone off the bedside table at the first burst of the bell. "Captain Hicks," he said.

"Morning, sir. Past six-thirty."

Nathaniel Hicks got up immediately.

His bedroom, narrow but lofty, was one of three, constituting, with a bathroom, a small kitchen, a big living room, and a screened balcony looking on Lake Armstrong, what the hotel called a de luxe light-housekeeping apartment. Though old fashioned—there was only one bathroom—these apartments were great prizes. Shared by three officers, the cost was no more than a mere bedroom, and you had the comforts of the living room, the balcony full of wicker furniture, and the kitchen. The fact that you shared your comforts with two other people —and, indeed, the living room and balcony with half a dozen others, since officers down the hall wandered in at will, and the more or less obligatory camaraderie of the military service made you make them welcome—was desirable or undesirable according to your general temperament, or your mood of the moment.

Sometimes it was cheerful when you came back at the end of the hard day to find that you had company—laughter and loud conversation; the rattle of ice in the kitchen; and Captain Duchemin's powerful radio-phonograph combination charging the fan-stirred air with music. Sometimes it was tiresome to have to face up to this gratuitous good fellowship, this forced intimacy whose only basis was War Department orders assigning duty at Ocanara, and whose one common circumstance was these men's enforced separation from their homes, their families, and their ordinary business.

From what they all said, you might get the impression that this common circumstance did wonderfully unite them in attitude and feeling. Everyone emphatically deplored the situation. What else could he do? Who cared to confess that he was happy? The loss of face would be irremediable. What? Were your abilities so small, your earning capacity so low, your intelligence so limited, and your former consequence so little that you relished this dog's life? Never! Duties, responsibilities, and any poor perquisites of an Army position, whether it was private first class or full colonel, might be grimly and patiently supported for the duration of the emergency; but let no one make the absurd mistake of imagining that the present status of this subdued creature, meanly paid, regimented in uniform, always at someone's beck and call, was normally or naturally his in civilian life.

But some of the officers who expressed these conventional sentiments were making more, not less, money than they made in whatever jobs they left, and were enjoying a freedom and an authority both greater than they had ever known before. Their exuberating zest was ill-contained and their attempted complaints unconvincing. These happy people could be irksome to men who were straining to meet expenses and obligations out of an income half, or less than half of what they used to have; or to those who, with profound sadness, were parted from wives and families on whom they were accustomed to depend psychologically for comfort and support, and whose absence made them feel that they worked to no purpose and lived to no end; or to those who bore the lesser, yet not inconsiderable, strain of finding themselves put to work which gave them few or no occasions to use special abilities they might have developed. Their developed abilities actually handicapped them, since they would, as a rule, have developed them at the expense of other abilities, very ordinary ones, yet now the only ones called for.

Nathaniel Hicks was in this last category. He doubted if either Colonel Coulthard, the Directorate Chief and his commanding officer, or Major Whitney, Chief of the Reports Section, and so his immediate superior, grasped the fact that writing, editing, and publishing were not somehow all the same thing. Nathaniel Hicks, thoroughly investigated by personnel procurement experts before being given his commission, duly certified to the Army as a competent and even important editor, nevertheless had limited abilities as a writer.

Nathaniel Hicks was ready to do what Major Whitney set him to do, but he was not easy or assured about doing it. It often involved research, which he was used to having done for him by experienced experts; so he could see the poor quality of what he did himself; and writing, for which he never had any particular gift, and which he had done little of for fifteen years.

Of course Colonel Coulthard and Major Whitney, incompetent writers themselves, and not even competent readers, might think it did well enough. So, perhaps, it did; for its purpose. This was no more than a proposed draft. If the draft was approved, somebody else would do the final writing; and he might very well be a professional writer, since the Army Air Forces had provided themselves with any number of them. That the final writing would then be good, unfortunately didn't follow.

Nathaniel Hicks was acquainted with professional writers and their difficulties. A few could and would write acceptably on anything; but for good work from most of them, what they wrote had to be, or had to be made to appear to be, exactly what the man wanted to do at the moment. The chance that a professional writer (uniformed and probably commissioned for the purpose) would, at the moment of receiving Nathaniel Hicks's material, find it exactly the thing he wanted, that moment, to do, seemed remote. It was necessary to fall back on the not-very-encouraging reflection that a new FM 1-15 was unlikely to be of any importance or use anyway, under any circumstances.

All fighter pilots had received, and perhaps some had read, the present version of FM 1-15. It told them a number of things which, remembered and heeded in air combat today, could have disastrous results. Here, at first glance, was a serious situation; but, of course, it wasn't. No pilot ever paid any attention to tactical data in a book once he had flown in combat. Unless he was shot to hell right away by somebody smarter and more experienced than he was, he started, little by little, to get smart and experienced himself. If he managed to stay alive long enough, the day came when it just so happened that he always saw the other fellow first. By thoughtless automatic compensations and adjustments in the handling of his plane, he kept his opponent in the gunsight ring. Nicely timed short bursts that he hardly noticed firing then scissored the target to bits. What good was reading going to do?

Nathaniel Hicks's work, too poorly done to please him in its present state, and certain to be of no practical use whatever, even if someone fitted for the job later took it and fixed it up, might make a sensitive man, in this daily round of lost motion, more and more lumpish and sulky. Nathaniel Hicks was not so constituted. He understood well enough that he belonged to that undistinguished majority of men for whom it should no doubt be a mortification that work was an end in itself, not a necessary detested means to make a living, certainly not a shrewd enterprise whose motive and hope was some blissful future state of living without work. His bliss was here and now; there was no pastime like the press of business.

Free to choose, Nathaniel Hicks would never, never be here, doing this; but, hardly off his bed, he was busy in his mind with what he had to do, actively planning out a bustling day, sure to be much too short. He must try to get out to the Special Projects Building a little early, to catch Major Whitney before eight, and tell him that the general wanted to see 1-15 at once; and incidentally, that the general was putting him on another project, so Whitney must count him out for an indefinite period.

Whitney would be grievously disconcerted—not angry, but sunk in baffled anxiety as he digested the news and tried to think what to tell Captain Pound, his plump, amiable, empty-headed Assistant Chief. Captain Pound, forgetting things and getting those he remembered wrong, maintained an unclear and disorganized schedule of tentative assignments to future projects.

Then it might be necessary to see Colonel Coulthard, or at least Whitney might think it necessary. Then Nathaniel Hicks would have to bring the 1-15 material to the general's office and impress somebody with the fact that the general was waiting for it; and here it was; and did the general want to see Captain Hicks, too? Then he might as well go around to the Directorate Centers and again, by the general's authority, get in to see the several Chiefs and acquaint them with what the general had in mind, and so, that co-operation with Captain Hicks was incumbent on them—or, no, on second thought, he'd better draw up a letter and have Colonel Mowbray's office authenticate it. It would order, over the general's signature, all Directorate Chiefs to do anything Captain Hicks wanted them to. Never mind why! The general might not want everyone in AFORAD to know of the project, in case it didn't pan out. Then, perhaps, he'd better have a plane put at his disposal —or, no: why get himself killed?—a staff car, and go to one of the satellite fields this afternoon—

To abhor this fantastic existence, to miss his wife and home, to regret the work, so much more important and interesting, that the war had interrupted, Nathaniel Hicks would have to wait for the proper moment, the unforeseen lull in the bustle, the speaking trifle's abrupt impression on the mind, to tell him the truth that there was a war on, and that he, amazingly, was in it.

The bright morning sky, suddenly racked with supernal thunder as a big formation of heavy bombers went over the Area, could make you think of a man crouched under the spouting fountains of debris, the avalanches of toppling walls, the winds of fire, following on concussions that flattened the lungs and jarred the rooted teeth in your jaws.

Being fancy free, you could then just as well sit yourself down, nerves dumbly shaking, in a flexible gunner's position and gaze from the sub-zero skies dotted all around you with soft puffing flak bursts to small ground conflagrations started by planes over earlier. The hits made then already welled narrow but long streamers of thick smoke, showing the way the wind was blowing across the target splotch, whose clearly defined polygonal margins, granulated grayish texture, and serried little street-lines identified a densely populated urban area. While you waited for your plane to end its run with a bound, freed of bombs, you could wait, too, for a near, perhaps audible, explosion to jolt you nearly senseless. Through a rimed port you might see an engine nacelle drop off the great wing, or the great wing itself break away bodily to usher in the crazy first spins of the miles-long fall, with or without a winding sheet of flaming gasoline to warm a moment the air in which you gyrated before it played on through the aluminum shell, damped any shrieks, and set the electrically-wired, sheepskin-lined, flying suits on fire.

Toward noon, an armed guard, moving bored and silent down a long heat-baked Base street, listlessly driving thirty men who speared up bits of paper, each man with the letter P in white paint on the back of his coarse blue jacket, might with appropriate intimations of mortality, occupy another flat, stale, unprofitable moment.

Toward evening, with the low spirits of weariness to remind you that you were no longer young, that the course was half or more run, and the run-half surely the better half, you could come back to your recent acquaintances, lounging about in their underclothes, joking such truths away, or dissolving them, and with them all other bodings of the downhearted—the browner horror, the brooding tempest, the crack of doom, the article of death—in a little whisky.

Though this was surely wise of them, they might look less wise than foolish to the tired eye. Here shone the undaunted spirit of man, brightest in dungeons, never saying die—indeed, going further, saying with the resolute cheer of good fellows got together: This is the life! Only, how could it be? This might have been the life, years ago, back at college; so it gave you quite a turn to look at your boon companions' grossened faces, thinned hair and thickened waists. You had your choice of joining them, or of sitting in your bedroom.

Nathaniel Hicks and the officers who shared his apartment with him had not known each other a year ago. In the ordinary course of events they would surely never have known each other. Captain Donald Andrews was a statistical expert for a firm of consulting engineers. Captain Clarence Duchemin, several years younger than the other two, had handled public relations and directed publicity for a chain of hotels. All three had been at Miami together, though without knowing it; for the AAF Officer Training School classes each numbered fifteen hundred at that time. You were unlikely to know anyone who was not assigned to the same hotel or the same academic section or tactical squadron.

Reporting for duty in Washington to that headquarters division that was to become AFORAD, they found themselves, together with dozens of other officers, in an unpartitioned room which occupied a whole wing of the immense and flimsy AAF Annex No. 1 at Gravelly Point. In the room were two hundred filing cases, fifty desks, and fifteen chairs. They sat on the edges of the desks for a week and wondered what was going on. Later, more familiar with the mysteries of administration, they could understand that they had come in on one faction's final struggle with another faction to get control of them, and of the great projected organization for which they were earmarked. They were told nothing because, until the struggle ended, there was nothing they needed to know.

At the end of the week the colonel, a harassed, fattish man with thin, slicked hair, named Van Pelt, brought them together —there were nearly three hundred of them—and told them that he was glad to announce that an AAF letter had finally been signed establishing the Operations and Requirements Analysis Division at Ocanara, Florida; and that orders were even now being cut for them to proceed there.

He did not look glad; he looked sick and weary and he must have lost weight, for his shabby summer blouse, with both Command Pilot and Senior Balloon Pilot wings sewed on it, and the old Air Corps triskelion patch on the shoulder, hung in folds on him. In fact, it became clear that he had lost the struggle, that someone else would command whatever AFORAD was going to be at Ocanara; for he began awkwardly to take formal leave of them, thanking them for their loyalty and co-operation, and expressing his conviction that they would do a great job and an important job.

Startled—many, perhaps most, of those assembled had never seen the colonel before, and would never see him again—they listened in silence. Then somebody began to clap, so they all clapped loudly.

Colonel Van Pelt paused—general applause at the announcement that he was leaving might strike him first as equivocal; but he must immediately realize that they meant to reciprocate the compliments just paid them. They expressed, in the only way they could think of, civil regret at his going, and good will.

His tired, flabby cheeks showed pink blotches. He bit his gross lip. His face worked for a moment. Lifting his hand at last, he said unsteadily: "Thank you, gentlemen; thank you from the bottom of my heart." He turned then and went into the corridor. His deputy, a gray-headed lieutenant colonel, stood up and said that full information was now being posted on the bulletin board.

On the bulletin board, among a hundred other paragraphs of advice, direction, and warning, travel by private automobile was authorized. Nathaniel Hicks had a car he could take. He had come to know another first lieutenant, who was Andrews, by the accident of idling in the same corner of the room, often sitting on the edge of the same desk. Andrews knew a second lieutenant named Duchemin, who had kindly got Andrews a room at the Washington hotel where Duchemin was staying—not, at that time, an easy thing to do.

Because of the luggage, Nathaniel Hicks could not take more than those two. Thus, after a three day drive, they arrived at Ocanara together. Lieutenant Duchemin's useful connections in the hotel business, shown when he got Andrews a room in Washington, were shown again. Reaching Jacksonville late at night, the hotel desk clerk told them there were no accommodations, and no chance of any; but Duchemin dug a business card from the back of his wallet and wrote a few words on it. The manager came down immediately and escorted them to a suite. They were soon followed by a waiter with a tray of sandwiches and a bottle of bourbon.

In Ocanara, things were in great confusion, with the Billeting Officers at their wits' end. Seeing them getting nowhere fast, Duchemin finally cleared his throat. He said he thought he could fix up something for himself and Hicks and Andrews, if that would be all right with the major. It was a little irregular; but they were glad to let him do it. Lieutenant Duchemin settled them within an hour in the best suite the Oleander Towers Hotel had vacant.

This worked well. Duchemin and Nathaniel Hicks were both in Major Whitney's Reports Section; Andrews was Acting Chief of the Statistical Section; and now there was little remaining danger of being ranked out of the apartment. During the first weeks, while Ocanara filled up, it had been a daily threat. Probably it would have happened, if the hotel manager had not kept forgetting to enter that apartment as occupied by, or available for, military personnel on the lists furnished the Billeting Section. Presumably the manager felt that after the war Duchemin might be willing and able to do something for him sometime.

Nevertheless, it had been a near thing. A week after their arrival, a full colonel—Nathaniel Hicks identified him later as Colonel Jobson, Director of Personnel Analysis—happened to observe their desirable apartment. The colonel, who had just got down, was in the act of locking his not-very-desirable bedroom door. The door of the apartment at the end of the corridor was open. A number of officers, all first or second lieutenants, were cheerfully, and perhaps from Colonel Jobson's standpoint, over-luxuriously, having a drink before dinner in the big living room. Nathaniel Hicks came out while Colonel Jobson, his morose face drawn down, stared. When Nathaniel Hicks was near enough, Colonel Jobson said to him: "What's that up there; a common room, or something?"

Though, in fact, that was just what it seemed to be much of the time, Nathaniel Hicks, in the Army only four months, did not venture a pleasantry. He said: "No, sir. It's part of an apartment."

"Who lives there?"

"I do, sir. With two other officers."

"You in AFORAD?"

"Yes, sir. Colonel Coulthard's Directorate."

"Hm!" Colonel Jobson said. "Flying pretty high for a first

lieutenant, aren't you?" Without waiting for an answer, he turned and clumped off down the hall.

As it happened, Colonel Jobson's irritation was disinterested. The next day, he was moving into a house where his family would join him. But if no house had been waiting, if he had needed to live at the hotel, the little dodge of being left off the list would hardly have availed them. The irritation was understandable enough. Colonel Jobson could not be unaware of the fact that lots of these amateur officers had for years, and as a matter of course, flown much higher than men like himself, who devoted their lives to serving their country, could ever hope to fly.

Nathaniel Hicks opened his bedroom door of thin louvered slats. He went down the little passage to the kitchen where he put a kettle on the electric burner and snapped a switch. The kettle had a device that whistled when it boiled. Nathaniel Hicks came back up the passage and pushed ajar the door of the big bedroom, which Captain Andrews had drawn when they divided the accommodations. Captain Andrews would hear the whistle and get up and make coffee.

These were some of the practical arrangements of living together—the switchboard rang Nathaniel Hicks; he would put on the water, and shave first. Captain Andrews would make the coffee when the water boiled. Captain Duchemin would clean up. He had what was, to him, the advantage of being able to sleep perhaps twenty minutes longer. Nathaniel Hicks went past Captain Duchemin's closed door to the bathroom. Glancing into the living room, he saw then that Captain Duchemin was not in his room.

Prone on the couch, his vast and solid rump covered by a pair of GI khaki shorts, Captain Duchemin lay profoundly and peacefully asleep. His face in repose, large and full, showed a stern sadness not in accord with his ordinary waking spirits. His dark, soft hair was cropped all over his head until it was no longer than short fur. His nose, thick and bold, was almost

Roman. His large, firm lips were relaxed, open a little. He breathed quietly through them, with a sighing sound.

Looking at him, Nathaniel Hicks was obliged to laugh, and Captain Duchemin instantly opened one eye. He said composedly: "Hi."

"Well, well!" Nathaniel Hicks said. "Enjoying a debauch, Captain?"

Captain Duchemin reared his great naked torso from the couch and put his feet on the floor. He rubbed his cropped hair, gave his head a shake, and broke into a serene smile. "You mean you didn't wake up?" he said. "I thought you were just being indignant, in there. What you see here is old-fashioned Southern hospitality, or the law of the tribe. I gave him my own bed, pulled my cloak about me, and lay on my Spartan couch."

"Come, come, Clarence," Nathaniel Hicks said. "What are you talking about?"

"Don't know," Captain Duchemin said. "What am I talking about? Oh, we have a house guest. Wilmer P. Pettie, First Lieutenant, Signal Corps. He is my pigeon officer. Say, he has to get up! We're fixing a flight this morning. We're parachuting some pigeons to the astonished troops at Boca Negra. Manny's going to give us one of the Special Projects planes. Time's a-wasting! Out of my way!"

"No, you don't!" Nathaniel Hicks said. "I shave first."

"Ah!" said Captain Duchemin, arrested. "Something I was saving for you! Just thought of it last night. There she was, all lathered up, so I had to shave her! Some trope, eh, kid? She was, too; but much good it did me. For reasons I will see you hear later. Before you dig yourself in, have I the captain's permission to answer a couple of calls of nature?" He got to his feet. "Oh, say; Colonel Ross, the Air Inspector, came here looking for you. He said charges were going to be filed about that voucher you put in for twelve days per diem at Orlando, when you were only there three days."

"Thanks, pal," Nathaniel Hicks said, "but I flew back from Sellers Field with him and General Beal last night. Hurry up. The general wants to see me this morning."

"Mercy!" Captain Duchemin said. "Whatever for?" He went trotting into the bathroom.

Down the passage, Captain Andrews's door opened wider, and Captain Andrews, in a pair of striped pajamas loosely hung on his lean frame, came out. He put on his glasses, and his face, flat-cheeked, faintly freckled about his sharp nose, brightened cordially. "Hi, Nat!" he said. "Saw you were in last night. Hope we didn't wake you up."

"You didn't. What goes on anyway?"

"It's a fellow the Signal Corps sent here on TD for Clarence's project. The pigeons, and some enlisted men who take care of them, got in several days ago, and yesterday this young lieutenant who commands the outfit came down. Clarence took him out last night and got him pretty tight. He's supposed to be staying at the Area; but Clarence thought he'd better keep him clear of the MP's, so he brought him here. It was a little before twelve. I'd just come in myself. Personnel bucked us a job at the last minute and we weren't through until after eleven. I don't think this lieutenant has quite Clarence's capacity. He kept falling down; and then he got sick; and finally we put him in Clarence's bed. I don't believe he has to report anywhere at eight, so we might as well let him sleep. I'll make some extra coffee and take it in to him when we go. Have a good trip?"

"It was all right until we got here. Then we nearly cracked up, landing. Gave me that miserable alarmed feeling."

"No! Some of these airplane drivers! I wouldn't go flying with them. Who was the pilot?"

"Well, as a matter of fact, General Beal was."

"No! Gosh, that must have been something! What happened?"

"A B-Twenty-six cut in and landed ahead of us, just as we were going to land. We hit the prop wash and practically turned over. The general—" About to comment on that, Nathaniel Hicks cut it off. The unplanned, instinctive checking both surprised and amused him since it could only mean that, all unknown to him, he had decided (presumably while asleep) to use the general's scheme for the chance it was to buck for something

128

at Headquarters. If that story got around, there would be very little difficulty in determining who had to blab everything he knew. He said, "The general was put out."

"I'll bet he was! Lord, I don't think I'd want to be that other pilot!"

"I don't think you would either. The general's little tough nut, Carricker, was along." (While this might also constitute blabbing everything you knew, Nathaniel Hicks went on, glad to gratify the hostile feelings Lieutenant Colonel Carricker aroused in him.) "As soon as we got down, he walked over to the other plane and hung one on the pilot, who, believe it or not, was a colored boy. I guess it was quite a one. They took him away in an ambulance."

"No!" said Captain Andrews. "Say, that's interesting about his being colored. That was what Personnel had us on last night—a control analysis on Negro flyers. They wanted a lot of stuff processed right off Statistical Unit reports on Negro fighter pilots in Africa last spring—every damn thing; percentage airborne effective; aircraft aborting by type of cause; operating rates figured on required maintenance and return from maintenance. I don't know what they wanted it for. Jim Edsell thinks it's a plot to ease Negro flyers out of the Air Force. The truth is, they didn't stand too well compared to some white squadrons. Edsell says it's because they were given old P-Forties."

"Edsell is a great friend of the downtrodden," Nathaniel Hicks said. "How did he get in on it? I wouldn't mind too much if you're going to say they transferred him to your section."

"No, it came to you. Whitney finally figured out that it must be because the R and R was for report, and when Woolsey or someone saw the word 'report' he checked off Reports Section on the buck slip. Incidentally, the time stamp showed nine in the morning. Whitney said he didn't get it until four. There's really no excuse for that. At any rate, Whitney put Jim on it; and since it was all figure work, he brought it in to us."

"He would."

"I don't mean I minded that. That's what we're for. I don't

even mind helping out Personnel Analysis, though they have a much bigger statistical section of their own, if they'd give us a little warning. But this made me sore; there was so much of it, and no work done on it at all; and I particularly wanted to leave at five. Did I get Katherine's telegram before you left? She had to change her plans and come this weekend. I've got to find some place to put her and I was going to scout around last night."

"You mean tomorrow?" Nathaniel Hicks said. "That's a tough one!"

"I know it," Captain Andrews said. "Of course I had the other reservation, two weeks from tomorrow, at the hotel here; and maybe Clarence could work something late Saturday night if someone checked out. Of course, as far as they know now they're full up over Saturday and Sunday. Twenty-three names on the waiting list." He hesitated and said then: "Nat, would you mind terribly if I put her in my room here? I know it will be a damn nuisance, having a woman around, especially if the fellows want to play poker."

"I don't know about you," Nathaniel Hicks said, "but I'm getting fed up with those Saturday night games. Let them go somewhere else, and keep going there. It's certainly all right with me, if your wife can stand this mess we always seem to have. Anyway, I think I can fix it not to be here. General Beal is going to use me on a new project. I'll have to get around to all the AFORAD installations. I could just as well start to-morrow. And God knows Clarence has places to spend the night. We'll both get out."

"No, you can't do that, Nat. Didn't you say you had that Orlando pilot coming in tomorrow on your manual?"

"Forgot about him," Nathaniel Hicks said. "However, we may not have any manual by tomorrow. I have to show the whole thing to the general this morning and he may throw it out. Anyway, Captain Wiley, if he comes, would be at the Area. I could probably get to stay with him in Visiting Officers Quarters."

"I don't think they'd let you."

"I think they would. The general's going to sign a letter

telling all these jerks to do what I say and give me what I want. It will be a honey. I'm going to write it myself this morning. If I want to stay in VOQ to expedite my personal survey of the Area, let's see any Charge of Quarters stop me."

"No," said Captain Andrews. "Nat, I won't do it at all if it's going to mean you move out. I have the big bedroom—and speaking of that, I think we ought to draw again for it now. I've had it long enough. It's a lot cooler than your rooms, you know. So, I mean, there's lots of room. We'd have a place to sit. We won't have to be in the living room at all—"

"That's silly," Nathaniel Hicks said, "you can have the whole apartment. Your wife won't want us around. She's coming down to see you."

Captain Andrews shook his head stubbornly. It was clear that he now lost sight of his earlier point about the damn nuisance of having a woman around—traipsing back and forth to the bathroom; making it necessary to wear a little more than a pair of shorts; and, in general, just as much there, and just as inescapable, if she ostentatiously hid in the big bedroom, or if she came and sat in the living room. The lesser inconvenience was moving out. Captain Andrews could easily enough be made to see that. However, made to see it, Captain Andrews would, without a doubt, inflexibly resolve not to bring her here under any circumstances. He would be quite capable of making arrangements (the only ones he now had much chance of making) for them to sit up two nights in some hotel lobby—a procedure by no means unusual.

"All right," Nathaniel Hicks said. "Have it your way. We'll straighten the place up as well as we can."

"We ought to ask Clarence if he minds. After all, in a way, it's really his apartment. We never would have got it without him."

"That's as it may be," Nathaniel Hicks said, "but here we happen to have the Army. I am senior in grade. I say he doesn't mind. If he gives me any lip, I'll doubletime him around Lake Armstrong."

Captain Andrews responded with a partly relieved smile. "That, I'd like to see!" he said. "Well, I hope you really don't mind. I didn't know what to do. I won't get any time to look anywhere this morning. I'm going to have to stand by with Edsell, because Personnel may not think the analysis I made is clear. When they don't tell you what they want it for, you can't be sure. I don't think Jim understands statistical work very well. Katherine's due in at Orlando at three tomorrow morning. It's the only plane she could get on."

"How's she going to get over here?"

"There's a bus she can take later."

"Look," said Nathaniel Hicks, "use my car. It's only fifty miles. You could start about one o'clock and meet the plane when it lands, and be back here long before you had to report in the morning. Manny can get you a curfew pass and write you out a basket leave. He can do anything. He got a new full C-book out of the Board for me; and the truth is, I've still got half the one I had before. So there's no trouble about gas."

Captain Andrews colored a little, plainly shaken by this generous sweeping away of difficulties. "Gosh, thanks, Nat," he said doubtfully. "I appreciate your suggesting it; but I don't see how I could take your car, use your gas. You might need it yourself. How'd you get out to the Area?"

Nathaniel Hicks said benevolently: "I explained that. You'll be back here by five or six o'clock. Anyone who thinks I'm going out to the Area before quarter to eight is crazy."

"Yes, but suppose the plane was late, or we had a flat, or something—"

"People get out there on the bus every day, I hear. Now, why don't you just tell me what a prince of a fellow and a true pal and a swell guy I am, and let it go at that? And why not start some coffee? And what happened to Clarence? Did he fall in?" He turned and banged on the bathroom door.

It immediately opened, and Captain Duchemin peered cautiously around the edge. His face was decorated with remnants of lather. He had almost finished shaving. "Caught again!" he said. "I could have sworn that chatter would last three more minutes. Make a deal with you. You let me finish; and then I'll let you shave. Hi, Captain! Say, I'm sorry about last night. I was sort of on a spot with my friend."

"That's all right," Captain Andrews said. "You couldn't send him out there, that way. The guards at the gate would have grabbed him. But what did you get him so tight for?"

"I get him tight?" Captain Duchemin said. "I like that! He did it his own little self. How do I know what he can hold? I never saw him before yesterday morning—"

"Come on, shake it up!" Nathaniel Hicks said.

"Yes, sir!" said Captain Duchemin. He leaped back to the basin, brought up his razor, and peering in the mirror began to scrape his full chin energetically. He said, "It was this way. We'd been out in the fresh air and sunshine, playing with the pigeons. They have to be remobiled. I could tell you what that means, but why bother? Just remember that a pigeon's desire to do some homing is based, it says here, on natural urges of hunger and reproduction. Well, at any rate, this went on and on. We had a grueling day. Finally we piled in a jeep I commandeered and, feeling the natural urges of hunger and reproduction, we started homing ourselves. So, soon, we were taking a few mouthfuls of beer and maybe a drop of bourbon."

"Hurry up," Nathaniel Hicks said.

"I'm hurrying. You don't want me to skip any, do you? Well, the scene was the Scheherazade Bar and the loot seemed to be in fine fettle. He was goggling at some chicks there; but you know how I shrink from the gross taint of commercialism. Bless his little heart, I thought, the old AAF can do better than this for a brother officer of a sister arm—"

"Keep shaving, pal."

"I am. So then I just happened to remember June." Beaming broadly, he broke into song, laying his hand on his fleshy chest and waving his razor: "Oh, June, like the mountains, I'm blue—" he broke off and hastily began to run the razor down his cheek. "In fine voice this morning!" he said. "Wait till I soar and sing in Manny's flying machine! Then, there was some unfinished business with my lovely little Emerald, and something about their aunt going to Tampa. So I rang up, and aunty had sure enough gone. The occasion offers and the youth complies!"

Captain Andrews's face showed signs of uneasy strain.

Captain Andrews led a chaste and sober life, and though it was not in his nature to take a censorious attitude about what other people chose to do, he did not approve. He did not want to listen. On the other hand, he did not want to appear priggish. Nathaniel Hicks was sure that Captain Duchemin recognized and relished this little dilemma. Like Captain Andrews, Captain Duchemin did not take a censorious attitude about what other people chose to do; but, after all, a belly full of beer and a girl in bed were solid goods, suited to the nature of man. People who really did not want them had something wrong with them; people, a good deal more numerous, who really did want them, but refrained for various artificial reasons from getting them, struck Captain Duchemin as ludicrous.

"So," Captain Duchemin said, "quick as a flash, we whipped out there. The loot looked all right to me. He joined heartily in the introductory inquiries about each other's healths and the exchange of compliments. I prepared some refreshments; and we extinguished a few lights to avoid eye strain—" he wiped his razor and began to splash his face with water. When he could, he said, "My lovely little Emerald and I drifted out to a fine broad hammock on the verandah to study the stars, unfortunately at the time obscured by a few thunderstorms. I left the loot going good." He buried his face in a towel, wiped the basin out with it, and threw it on the floor. "Look!" he said, pointing beyond Nathaniel Hicks, who involuntarily turned his head. Captain Duchemin darted his hand up to the shelf and, taking Nathaniel Hicks's bottle of shaving lotion, poured a quantity into his other palm. "Never touched it!" he said, putting it back and applying the palmful to his cheeks.

"Well," he said, beaming again, "now, comes catastrophe! The shame of it! I just hope it never gets back to the Chief Signal Officer! Clear case of conduct unbecoming! There was June, her warm little heart pitter-patting, ripe for romance, and halfway through some sweet nothing he was whispering to her, the loot goes to sleep! Mind you, I don't say I cared about him; but I cared about me. My lovely little Emerald, studying the stars (in absentia) with pleasing enthusiasm and eager soft abandon, had about completed the course. Her able mentor was on the verge of tendering her the diploma, when out pops June, sore as any lady would be. The cup is dashed from my lips. I have to start resuscitating the loot and getting a taxi. What an end to a beautiful evening!"

"Come on," Nathaniel Hicks said, "get out of here."

"We'd better make a lot of coffee," Captain Andrews said. "I believe your lieutenant is going to need it."

◆

From upstairs General Beal's voice called: "Sal! Where are those pants you were going to fix? They aren't in my room."

"Yes, they are, too!" Mrs. Beal, downstairs at the breakfast table, shouted back. "They're hanging in your closet! The car's here. So's Norm and Botty. Oh, *Ira*, I have to go out to Red Cross this morning. Please send the car back for me."

"I will not!" General Beal called. "It's contrary to regulations, and you know it. If I started doing it, everybody would. You want to get me court-martialed? If the garage doesn't get through with the Buick, you take a taxi, hear?"

"I never heard anything so silly!" Mrs. Beal shouted. "They have twenty cars in that old pool just sitting there—" She rolled her eyes, looked at Colonel Ross, and giggled. "He's scared of you, Norm," she said. "He wasn't always that way, I can tell you." She tossed her mop of flaxen hair which fell smoothly to a profusion of curls at the level of her shoulders and widened her blue eyes engagingly.

Colonel Ross did not think it would be fair to call this kittenish manner an affectation. The hair, the eyes, the smooth, doll-like little face, were actually a child's. Sal was not putting it on. There was no art in it. When she posed, and she often did, it was in the role of a grown-up person, an efficient housekeeper, a woman of the world, or a great lady; but she posed on the whim of the moment, sustaining it poorly, and soon, forgetting what she was supposed to be, dropping it. She seemed to do nothing by design.

At the moment her slight, childish figure was amply displayed by the careless way in which she wore a negligee of sky-blue chiffon. The exertions of eating her breakfast, pouring coffee, taking things from the maid, petting her son, turning to shout upstairs to her husband, had pulled it in here and shrugged it off there until Chief Warrant Officer Botwinick did not know where to look. Sitting on the other side of the table, Mr. Botwinick had only to lift his eyes to see most of Mrs. Beal's small, pretty left breast. In an anguish of constraint, he was avoiding the sight by studying a cup of coffee she had poured for him. Mrs. Beal now noticed Mr. Botwinick's constraint.

"Botty," she said, "what's wrong with that coffee? Why do you keep looking at it? Are you sure you don't want some cream?"

Lifting his eyes shyly and coloring, he said, "No, ma'am. Thanks very much."

Mrs. Beal grinned suddenly. She said, "What's in there, anyway? Here, let me see it!" She shot out her hand and seized a brown manila War Department envelope sealed with red wax, which Mr. Botwinick had laid on the table. She caught up a knife and made to open the flap.

Mr. Botwinick jumped.

In hasty dismay, he cried: "Ma'am, I can't give you that. That's top secret, in there. I have to give that to the general, ma'am—"

"Bang, bang! I'm dead!" Mrs. Beal said. She giggled warmly and sailed the envelope back at him. "Don't be so scared, Botty. I wasn't going to look at it—" she screamed: "Junior! No, no!"

Her son, wandering around the room, had come up to Mr. Botwinick from behind. "Bang, bang!" he echoed. With both hands he seized the holster flap covering the butt of the .45 automatic hanging at Mr. Botwinick's side and attempted to open it. Upsetting a sugar bowl, Mrs. Beal snatched him away. "My God," she said, "he'd just as soon shot us all! That's loaded, isn't it?"

Mr. Botwinick said confusedly: "Yes, ma'am, I'm sorry. I have to have it because of the papers." He hitched the belt around, brought the holster onto his lap, and folded his arms over it for safer keeping.

Mrs. Beal said, bending her head down to the level of her son's: "Mustn't ever touch Botty's gun, precious." She rubbed his nose with her own.

He said, running his fingers through her hanging curls: "Marmadale!"

"You mean marmalade," Mrs. Beal said. "All right, you little pig! Here." She put marmalade on a fragment of toast and gave it to him. "Oh, damn!" she said. "There's the telephone!" She bounded from the table, the negligee lifting about her, and ran into the hall. Her high clear voice came back, saying solemnly, with assumed hauteur: "This is Mrs. Beal speaking—"

Colonel Ross and Mr. Botwinick sat silent. Colonel Ross, who held his copy of the Ocanara *Morning Sun*, looked with distaste at Art Bullen's column again. Mr. Botwinick, his arms folded over the gun in his lap, was watching Ira, Junior, warily. Soon bored, the child went into the hall.

Mr. Botwinick immediately cleared his throat. In a careful low voice he said: "May I ask, Colonel, if you are acquainted with this matter involving Lieutenant Colonel Carricker?"

"I was there," Colonel Ross said, looking up from the paper.

"That, I deduced," Mr. Botwinick said. "I was at my desk last night when the general called the Duty Officer in Colonel Mowbray's office and directed the preparation of charges and specifications." He looked at Colonel Ross inquiringly. "I wondered, sir, if you had—ah—any suggestion?"

Colonel Ross said, "I think you'd better turn it over to the Staff Judge Advocate. I'm going to speak to him about it after I've seen the general. Colonel Mowbray's office wouldn't be expected to draw the charges."

"No, sir," Mr. Botwinick said. "Perhaps I should explain about that, sir. Colonel Mowbray feels strongly that it is not good staff work, when the general directs something to be done one day, to tell him the next morning that somebody else is responsible for that, and will do it soon. There is no one on duty in the Judge Advocate's office in the evenings. I considered calling the Judge Advocate at his quarters, but concluded against it. Therefore, I roughed out a charge and specification myself. Colonel Mowbray would want that done, so the general would not find, if he asked in the morning, that no action had been taken."

"All right," said Colonel Ross. "In the present case, I think that's enough. Don't call the Judge Advocate unless the general tells you to."

"In that connection, sir," Mr. Botwinick said, "I wonder if the general remembers that if he is preferring charges himself, if he is the accuser, the court would have to be appointed not by him, but by superior competent authority, in this case, the Commanding General, AAF, I presume."

"I will remind him, if necessary," Colonel Ross said. "I think you can dismiss the matter from your mind."

"Yes, sir," Mr. Botwinick said. He lowered his voice still more. "There are, however, certain circumstances bearing on the case which were brought to my attention this morning, and which I would like to lay before you, sir."

Colonel Ross, who had looked back to his paper, looked up again. "Lay away," he said.

Mr. Botwinick glanced around him. "It concerns the other personnel who came in with the officer Colonel Carricker assaulted, and who witnessed the assault. When they arrived at the quarters assigned to Project zero-dash-three-three-six-dash-three, they communicated the incident in a very excited manner to project personnel who had arrived earlier in the day and the day before. Much resentment was expressed. At an informal gathering in one of the rooms, at least fourteen or fifteen officers concurred in some plan, whose details unfortunately didn't reach me, for a demonstration of protest."

"I don't know how they ever got fourteen or fifteen officers in one of those rooms," Colonel Ross said. "I daresay they'll think better of it this morning. They must know Carricker was arrested." He looked thoughtfully at Mr. Botwinick.

"I should perhaps add, sir, that one or two of the men had

already expressed resentment or indignation at the assignment of separate officers-club facilities for project personnel."

Colonel Ross said: "Who told you all this, Botty?"

"Charge of Quarters in one of the BOQ's, sir." Mr. Botwinick cleared his throat. "I wonder, sir, if it is advisable to have white non-commissioned officers as Charges of Quarters while the colored officers are occupying the buildings? A few of the colored officers appear to have gone out of their way to order them around unnecessarily. They don't like it."

Colonel Ross said: "Charges of Quarters are assigned specific duties. If they are asked to do anything that isn't part of their assignment, they are quite free to tell the officer, politely, of course, that they can't accommodate him. That should take care of that."

"It should, sir," Mr. Botwinick said, "but in the interests of avoiding friction, I was wondering about the possibility of getting some colored non-coms from the Base Service Units temporarily assigned to Headquarters and Headquarters Squadron—"

"There isn't any such possibility," Colonel Ross said. "Base Service personnel wouldn't know the duties and couldn't do them efficiently. I might say that if I find any of the present detail aren't performing all their assigned duties promptly and cheerfully, I'll see that their CO busts them to privates and finds them jobs that won't involve sitting around on their tails all day. You might pass that word along." He paused. "One other thing, Botty. Colonel Mowbray's office should keep itself informed of conditions around the Air Base and the AFORAD Area. I have a very high regard for your intelligence and zeal in doing this in addition to your other duties. We get more work out of you than any three men in Headquarters, and I don't suppose there's a day when you're not asked to show someone, anyone from the general down, how the Army wants things done. Most traditional methods have something to be said for them; but there are a few I never thought good, even in the Regular Army. With AUS troops, not professional soldiers, they can't be countenanced. At many posts there used to be a sort of spy set-up. You know; certain enlisted men and non-coms who got soft jobs and other little favors for tattling. I guess you remember that it was never a secret very long who they were."

"Colonel," Mr. Botwinick said, "I hope you don't feel that I am doing wrong when I listen to a man who comes to me and tells me, because he thinks it his duty, that he has observed certain things which might lead to trouble or disturbance?"

"Not at all," Colonel Ross said, "and the man who does his duty has the reward of knowing he has done his duty. I hope that satisfies him, because I don't think any changes in Charges of Quarters are practicable at the moment—except, of course, for incompetence or neglect of duty. They will then be changed so fast they won't know what hit them."

"Colonel," said Mr. Botwinick, "I hope you will believe that I have never used my position; that is, taking advantage of the trust Colonel Mowbray reposes in me, to play favorites with Headquarters personnel. It is true that it sometimes falls to me, in practice, to name men for certain jobs. To the best of my knowledge and ability, I have tried to see that every job went to the most competent and reliable man available. I would never do anything so improper as to expect more from them than their best efforts in the job."

"Good," said Colonel Ross, "I believe you, Botty. There's a line there, and I just want you to watch it."

"Yes, sir," said Mr. Botwinick. "Here comes the general, sir."

General Beal, in the hall, called: "Let's go. Sorry I'm late." His face was sober and preoccupied. "Hello, Judge," he said as they came out. "What have you got there, Botty? More trouble?"

"The Washington TWX's, sir."

"Anything in them?"

"There is a top secret alert on an expected capitulation by Italy at any moment. It is not considered advisable to encourage celebrations when the announcement comes."

"Huh!" said General Beal. "Celebrations! I only hope it

isn't true. Keeping the Eyeties going took plenty of German divisions. If there hadn't been Wops in Africa to punch through, the foot army'd probably still be outside Tunis. Anything else?"

"Brigadier General Nichols, Deputy Chief of Air Staff, will arrive today on a special mission."

"For God's sake, what do they want now?"

"That is all the message says, sir."

"I guess he'd better stay here. Sal!"

Mrs. Beal came from the back of the hall, her mules clacking loosely under her small bare feet. He said to her: "Jo-Jo Nichols is coming down today. We'll have to put him up here. You better get that other room fixed."

"He's the funny one," Mrs. Beal said. "Oh, I like him! Well, I'll be at Red Cross at the Officers Club. Bye-bye," she said. "Kiss." She turned her face up, and when the general bent hurriedly to kiss her, entwined her arms suddenly about his neck, hanging on him. "Love me?" she said.

By a common impulse, Colonel Ross and Mr. Botwinick moved on toward the wide screened door. They waited, looking at the general's car, which waited, too, in the shade of the live oaks on the brick-paved drive at the end of the path. The driver was busy polishing the shining metal staff on which the general's small, white-starred, scarlet flag hung limp.

Colonel Ross said: "Know anything about this Nichols business?"

Very guardedly, Mr. Botwinick murmured: "Yes, sir. They are sending him down, representing the Chief of Staff, with the Distinguished Service Medal for the general. Colonel Mowbray wishes to keep it part of the secret. General Nichols is going to say he just came to look around. Then he will formally present it at the Retreat ceremonies."

Annoyed by this latest refinement of what he had to consider as the regrettable childishness, so often the obverse of the military mind's tough cold thinking in terms of personnel, not people, casualties, not dead men, Colonel Ross said with impatience: "There isn't any secret. The part about the parade is in the paper this morning. I've got to show it to the general.

141

Tell Colonel Mowbray he'd better come clean with the whole business."

II

BEFORE THE north gate of the Area at five minutes of eight the line of halted automobiles grew longer. In a last rush, they were coming up the road from Ocanara faster than the MP's could check their passengers and pass the double line through. Under the wide, white-painted wood arch, lettered AFORAD, and surmounted by the Air Forces' winged star, the MP's worked in pairs on both sides. They saluted. They stepped forward to glance at the held-up AGO cards. They stepped back. They saluted. They saluted again. They stepped forward again to the next car.

Inside the gate a train of military trucks and weapons-carriers mounting machine guns, and slender nosed anti-tank guns, blocked half the wide asphalt avenue that ran straight to the flag pole in front of the AFORAD Headquarters quadrangle. The trucks were jammed with colored troops in full field equipment. Steel helmets hung on their haversacks. Gas masks hung on their chests. Though the sun fell full and hot, and they were apparently not allowed to leave the crowded trucks, they seemed in very good spirits, laughing and chattering, grinning and gesticulating. Around the occasional jeep bearing a red, swallow-tailed, Corps-of-Engineers company guidon, little knots of white officers, sleeves rolled up their bare brown arms, olive drab painted helmets pushed back on their heads, looked at maps. Motorcycle riders, going slow enough for their machines to wobble and backfire, moved noisily up and down the long column.

The other half of the road was partly blocked by an overflow of a stream of people, civilians and military personnel, who filled the walk on that side. They were on the way to their offices from the bus stop. Nathaniel Hicks, at last through the gate, was obliged to drive his car at a crawl. Captain Andrews, sitting beside him in front, said: "What a dumb place to park a convoy at this time of the morning!"

From the back seat, Captain Duchemin said: "Speak to the general about it; have Captain Hicks speak to General Beal about it! Besides, what's your hurry? You aren't going any-where. Look at the happy jigaboos! They do not give a damn. Why don't you be like that—wait! Just remembered. Nat, you might let us out down there. We have to get some bicar-bonate of soda. They'd probably have it in the main Post Ex-change." To Lieutenant Pettie sitting beside him he said: "You told your sergeant you'd bring him some this morning for that bird."

"That's right," Lieutenant Pettie said. He passed his hand over his moist forehead. He breathed in deeply and heavily. Probably he was regretting his decision to get up and come right out. Under the sun-reddened skin his face was very pale; his wide apart blue eyes were set in a half-stupefied misery.

"It's a mighty sick pigeon," Captain Duchemin said zest-fully. "Sour crop, it has. How about you, Lieutenant? Could it be contagious?"

Lieutenant Pettie managed a miserable smile. He said, "That's the last time I ever mix beer and whisky—"

"And rum," said Captain Duchemin. "Topped off with some mellow old rum! About ten years ago, I used to take that su-pine it's-the-last-time-I-ever attitude. All you really need is more practice."

Lieutenant Pettie said: "Was that rum we had out there? I never knew that. I never would have drunk it if—" His voice died out. Nausea born of the shame that covered him no doubt aggravated his outraged stomach's physical nausea; the pain in his mind joined hands with the pain in his head; and he was really overwhelmed, speechless.

Captain Duchemin glanced sidelong at him, marking the glazy eye, the cold sweat, calm and amused. Here was one of those follies of man that Captain Duchemin enjoyed only a little less than beer and girls. He did not tire of the traditional comedy—indeed, it was always sure-fire—of the devil when sick. He was tickled by the falseness and fatuity of these ring-ing vows, so regularly, and through all time, taken by man after ludicrously glum and comically abject man; and then so regularly broken as soon as this self-dedicated individual felt better.

Lieutenant Pettie did not know half as much about what he was going to do as Captain Duchemin, laughing to himself, had learned by watching the lieutenant's antics last night. Lieutenant Pettie said it was the last time; but to Captain Duchemin it looked a good deal more like the first. By tomorrow, or possibly even by this evening, Lieutenant Pettie's young and robust constitution would clean up his hangover. Lieutenant Pettie's simple mind would then review the supposedly closed case. Of course, he would not do *that* again. That was out! Still, the matter ought to be considered dispassionately. What he wanted to avoid was not, after all, drinking; but drinking too much, and mixing his drinks. Then, there was the matter of those girls. That was pretty risky; anyone would tell you you stood a much greater chance of catching something from girls of that type, who weren't professionals. Probably he had been lucky to pass out when he did. He wouldn't have gone along if he hadn't been drunk. Since he wouldn't get drunk this time, he wouldn't have any trouble in refusing suggestions of that kind.

So now he was all set. He need not deny himself that delightful, man-of-the-world feeling which Captain Duchemin must have seen him radiating innocently as he stood to the bar (like every honest fellow, he takes his whisky clear) and exchanged a couple of dollars for a skinful of bliss and courage. This was right! This was for him! If he had known the other night what he knew now, all would have been well. He should have stopped at this point. Thinking back, calmly and carefully, he could see that it was really only when he went out to that bungalow and drank that rum—even the first glass of that hadn't bothered him, he thought. He hadn't been sure what this was all about—the house was furnished in a way that put him on his good behavior. Even after Duchemin had gone on the porch with the one with brown curls all over her head, he did not know exactly what to do. That somehow solved itself when the other one, the blonde one, got him a new drink—

144

Duchemin had mentioned his pigeons; and he came to be telling her some things about raising them, which he began to do on a roof when he was a kid. She brought back the drink, and sat down on the couch beside him. Hugging this warm, soft, pleasant-smelling girl then proved as easy as pie; and though she giggled and protested, yet she resisted less and less, and finally she was consenting to all the liberties his hands could invent; and then (it was like one of those things he had only dreamed of) she was more than consenting, she was helping and coaxing, and teaching and compelling—and this time, this time, instead of passing out like a fool, he would—

Captain Duchemin was chuckling. "Don't let it get you down," he said. "We'll have a return engagement, by popular demand. That's still unfinished business—"

"Not me!" Lieutenant Pettie said. "Never again! Say, I certainly want to apologize to you all about last night. I certainly appreciate—"

Captain Andrews, turning his head, said kindly: "Forget it, fellow! You aren't the first one who couldn't stay with Duchemin. Look at him. He weighs two hundred pounds on the hoof."

"And all whipcord and steely muscle," Captain Duchemin said. The car in front of them stopped, so Nathaniel Hicks stopped too. Captain Duchemin opened the door and stepped out onto the road.

"Brains, I know it isn't," Captain Andrews said, suddenly and irritably.

While Lieutenant Pettie got out, Captain Duchemin stood regarding Captain Andrews with a surprised but happy smile. "Brains?" he said. "Who dat?" He began to shake with new chuckles. "No brains at all," he chanted, "no brains at all! She married a man who had no—"

The car ahead moved and Nathaniel Hicks let his clutch in. "Hey!" Captain Duchemin shouted after them. "Tell Whitney I'm off on a mission, will you?"

Turning down the road to the Special Projects Building, Nathaniel Hicks could see that Captain Andrews had reddened. Captain Andrews said: "Clarence doesn't really make me sore, whatever he thinks. He just makes me tired, sometimes. He's always trying to show everybody that they're no better than he is."

"And are they?" Nathaniel Hicks said. He swung into the parking space behind the building.

"I notice you don't have to go out helling around all the time."

"The point there," Nathaniel Hicks said, "is if I wanted to, would I have to?"

"Yes," Captain Andrews said, "it's what you want. You do what you want. I see that. But people can want different things. He thinks everybody wants what he wants, only they haven't the nerve to say so. What he's working for, I don't want; and you can be sure of getting pretty much what you work for."

"Since when?" Nathaniel Hicks said.

"Since always." Captain Andrews looked at him seriously. "You reap what you sow. Nothing would make any sense if that weren't true."

Nathaniel Hicks ran up to the guard rail. "If you don't mind my saying so," he said, "what you have there is the formal or logical fallacy known as begging the question. You say that the reason it's true is that you'd feel bad if it wasn't. So anything is true that makes you feel good."

"Well, truth does make you feel good," Captain Andrews said earnestly. "I'll say that. I suppose mathematics is what I know most about. Truth there makes the difference between your being all balled up with a lot of equations that won't come out, and having everything come out right, which is a pretty good feeling. I don't say in life it is always as simple as it is there. I mean, they used to say: figures can't lie; but liars can figure—"

He looked brightly, though a little diffidently, at Nathaniel Hicks, as though he felt that this bon mot was a venture in Nathaniel Hicks's field of literary expression, and he hoped it was all right. He went on in haste: "Well, I mean I know you can't get a mathematical proof of anything in religion, or things like that. I never studied logic, but I guess any mathematical proof has to be a logical proof. And I'm no expert mathematician. I don't have time to keep up with a lot of interesting things. I know there is a lot of work being done on the tensor calculus. There are things in physics that they can't develop any further until somebody works out new mathematical expressions—well, I mean, there's a lot I don't know. But I've had enough training to understand what they're up to; and I can say that I've never seen a mathematical proposition that I couldn't get through my head, if I took time to study it—"

Nathaniel Hicks removed the ignition key and put his hand on the door latch, but he did not open the door. Captain Andrews would not take it badly if he were cut off. He was always disarmingly ready to believe that he was being boring, that he was wrongly and inconsiderately taking up someone else's valuable time. Though this was already boring, and would plainly get more so; and though, today, he really did have a great deal to do, Nathaniel Hicks compunctiously said, "I can believe that." He waited for the rest of it, which was plainly going to be one of those disorganized reaffirmations of Captain Andrews's singularly naïve and simple notions about life.

To help him bear it, Nathaniel Hicks had his liking for Captain Andrews, who, over many months, appeared always, in every circumstance, as what it was simplest to call a decent guy. This was a rare and agreeable phenomenon. Perhaps it had to be coupled with the paraphenomenon of a naïveté; a reluctance to admit any of the ample evidence that most motives of most men were low; a readiness to believe, as he had just said he did, that justice and equity framed the nature of things and must prevail. The natural attitude, even among those much Captain Andrews's inferior in charitableness, was an indulgent, perhaps patronizing, regard for this good, lovable innocent. It was not an easy attitude to take in Captain Andrews's case. This innocent, Nathaniel Hicks was satisfied, had a brain of the very first order, a brain whose specially developed capacities exceeded those of the ordinary, so-called intelligent human being's as much as the ordinary, so-called intelligent human being's brain exceeded in its capacities those of, say, a fish's cerebellar nerve mass.

Without knowing anything about statistical work you could safely judge a man good when he could always supply whatever was wanted, and when what he supplied was always right. More arresting were certain spectacular little mental feats that Captain Andrews would perform when his natural amiability had been coaxed into prevailing over his disinclination to show himself off, or to show somebody else up. At what seemed one glance, he could memorize a whole page of figures. By looking at the hand exposed as dummy in a bridge game, and watching the fall of cards on the first two tricks, he could, with rarely an error, tell each player what he still held.

Some simple memory-training device might account for the first, and some obvious trick of calculation for the second of these feats that pleased and astounded a casual group. Nathaniel Hicks had been present at a display of Captain Andrews's abilities which went a great deal beyond devices or tricks, and which astounded people entirely competent to judge the mental work involved, though it could not be said to have pleased them. This was the scandalous occasion when Andrews broke a Navy code.

In Washington, during the idle waiting for orders at Gravelly Point, all sorts of people wandered in and out, seeking or bringing information. Colonel Van Pelt and the Section Chiefs were much of the time tied up in unproductive conferences, so many of the visitors had to wait a long while, sitting around the lumbered and disordered rooms talking to the AFORAD officers who had nothing to do. One such visitor was a Signal Corps lieutenant colonel, a cryptographic expert from Arlington Hall, on an unspecified errand to the colonel. He got to talking with Lieutenant Andrews and Lieutenant Hicks, telling them some interesting things about modern codes, and explaining the principles which, while keeping codes simple enough to be practical, made them next to impossible to decipher. As an illustration, he showed copies of five messages in a code the

Navy was using, and said, "What do you think you could do with that?"

Lieutenant Andrews whistled appreciatively. He said: "Would it be all right for me to look at them some more, sir?"

The Signal Corps man told him if he wanted to he could look at them till the cows came home. Lieutenant Andrews went off into the corner, sat on an upside-down waste basket and laid the messages out on a packing case. He sat there for about an hour. The Signal Corps man was finally let in to see Colonel Van Pelt. When he came out, he went over to get his papers.

Lieutenant Andrews stood up. Scratching his head, he said: "Gee, that's a tough one, Colonel. I don't know whether I've caught on or not. How about this?" He took a pencil and marked off, isolating them, successive groups of numerals in the first message. "Is that the idea?" he said.

Those cows had come home! It was true that, before Lieutenant Andrews began, the principles underlying such a code had been explained to him; but he had never seen one. He knew nothing about cryptography. He did not realize that, for all practical purposes, he had just broken the code. To be able to read the greater part of the Navy's top secret messages, all he needed now was more messages, including a few whose content could be guessed, by anyone familiar with naval procedure, from the time and place of sending.

The Signal Corps lieutenant colonel was, unfortunately, so flabbergasted that he said by God, that was right. He hastily took the sheet which Lieutenant Andrews had marked, lit a match, set fire to it, and rubbed the ashes to dust on the floor. Arlington Hall, not without reason, maintained meticulous security routines. The lieutenant colonel was obliged to go at once to a telephone and inform Counter-Intelligence, who, in turn had to notify the Navy. An hour later, the Military District of Washington sent over two MP officers to take Lieutenant Andrews in custody and escort him, along with Colonel Van Pelt, to the Navy Building where they confronted a lot of agitated admirals. The trouble seemed to be that what Andrews had just done, they said, no one could do in only one hour from only five messages. The absurdity of the necessary alternative—that Lieutenant Andrews had, for presumably sinister reasons, been long at work trying to break the code, and when he succeeded, he took care to demonstrate it in the presence of a man who was certain to notify Counter-Intelligence—aggravated their annoyance.

They questioned Lieutenant Andrews, mildly and sympathetically, and loudly and roughly. In true Navy fashion, the admirals used their two stars to dress-down and browbeat Colonel Van Pelt for having such a man in his command. They sent Wave messengers for more officers. Commanders and captains, Intelligence men and Navy cryptographic experts obsequiously came in. These new arrivals put to Lieutenant Andrews sudden technical questions supposed to make him betray knowledge he denied having. Finally he was given five messages in a former code-grouping of the same type and told that he had one hour to work it out.

Lieutenant Andrews proved unable to do it in an hour, perhaps because he was understandably nervous and because the experts kept asking him to explain what he was doing; but the progress he made seemed to persuade them that, after all, it might be possible—at least, for him. With a long, surly, and disgruntled warning about confining the exercise of his talents to his proper duties, they let him and Colonel Van Pelt go.

Nathaniel Hicks could grasp in a general way what these talents indicated. Here was intelligence in the real sense of the word—not in the misused sense of mere quickness or smartness, or knowing a few things most people had never troubled to learn. This was a strength and clarity of mind so great that it could hold and view simultaneously an infinite number, or at any rate, hundreds, of bare sequences of digits. Each sequence, and each digit, had, too, a limited, but still large, range of allowable random variations. Systematically, one after another, never forgetting and never mixing them up, each of these sequences with every admissible variation on it must be brought forward and set against the five collections of numerals until one sequence was observed to recur several times as a recognizable pattern interpolated among groups of digits without meaning.

The assumption behind the code, which was to give it its unbreakable security, was not that this logical operation couldn't be performed, but that it could be performed only by a number of men working with calculating machines for a number of weeks. That threat was easy to meet. At arbitrary short intervals a simple change in the sequence of interpolation reshuffled all the patterns. Anyone hoping to crack the code would then have to go back and begin over again, unless he was satisfied to read messages weeks or even months old. It was necessary to conclude that the brain behind Captain Andrews's high narrow forehead was no common brain.

Captain Andrews said: "You ask me how I tell what truth is. Well, a mathematical truth is a known fact consistent with all other known facts. Truth is a statement of relationship. It means, consistent with something else. Without the something else, the term can have no meaning. Like near. Near what? Near nothing is nonsense."

"Granted," Nathaniel Hicks said, "but—"

"How far is up? Where is under?" Captain Andrews showed himself much taken by the happiness of this illustration—"Heck, I never get to say what I mean. I certainly envy people who have a natural gift for words. Somebody like you or Jim Edsell, who knows how to write—"

"Don't mix me up with writers," Nathaniel Hicks said. "They're a bad lot. And don't mix me up with Edsell. He's a jerk."

"Don't you think he's a good writer? I read that magazine story of his, that one called 'Wait for the Wagon' about a month ago. The one you could see was about Gravelly Point, waiting around there for orders. I thought it was darn good. I know it was the way I felt. Didn't you think it was good?"

"Yes," Nathaniel Hicks said, "it was all right. He just makes me tired. Writers just make me tired. You often get that way on a magazine. However, you might consult him. I think you'll find he regards me as not so hot, too."

"He told me he thought you were the best man in Whitney's section. He also said you were a nice guy."

"He must be mad," Nathaniel Hicks said, though in spite of

himself he was not displeased. "All we do is row. He's going to get himself into trouble; and I expect that will prove your philosophical point."

Captain Andrews, walking beside him toward the back entrance, said in a low voice: "I think he *has* got into trouble. The Provost Marshal, that Major Sears, was talking to him a long time yesterday. He didn't say anything and I didn't ask him. I couldn't help wondering, though. I wondered if it was about that story. Do you remember it at all well?"

"Well enough. I daresay the Army doesn't take kindly to being shown as a bunch of boobs. That's an occupational risk writers run—"

"Did you think the captain, the one who was trying to think up all the useless things for them to do, was meant to be Whitney?"

"Obviously," Nathaniel Hicks said. "Anyone who lets himself stay around a writer may expect to be wounded by what he will consider malicious misrepresentations of that kind."

"I'm glad I thought to speak of it," Captain Andrews said. "I don't really believe Bill Whitney would do a thing like complaining to someone. But he only happened to read it the other night, and I think he was rather hurt. He happened to ask me, and I told him I certainly hadn't noticed anything that suggested him—it wasn't true, of course. Jim's captain was always saying things just like things Whitney says. I think he may ask you."

"I can lie as well as you can," Nathaniel Hicks said. "Don't worry about everyone so much, Don. You've just been telling me people only get what's coming to them."

✦

Colonel Ross said: "I think you should do it personally, Bus. Put in a call for Mr. Bullen about nine—he might not be there before then—"

General Beal sat on the edge of his desk. He had his sleeves rolled up as far as they would go—beyond his biceps—on his thin but strong brown arms. The habit was very common among young pilots, and Colonel Ross often wondered if there was some psychological or physiological reason for it. Rolling the sleeves only to the elbow, like most other people, did not seem to satisfy them. General Beal tensely swung his feet, making muscles move restlessly under the thin worsted cloth covering his narrow thighs. On his feet were so-called Texas boots, shabby but once-fancy, with decorated tops extending up his calves, and high heels. Whether because they were convenient for a flyer, whether because they appealed to youthful vanity, many flyers training ten or twelve years ago at San Antonio bought them; and once clear of Kelly Field, wore them on their first squadron assignments at Selfridge or Langley or Maxwell to show that they did not give a damn. Right this minute, over on the line at the Air Base, you would find dashing second lieutenants, fresh from transition training, stepping bright-faced, cumbered by their parachutes, from the wing into the cockpit elegantly displaying the same half boots, new, to their ground crews.

The pose on the desk edge, these details of dress; the intent, thin-cheeked, worried but almost lineless face; the hair now drying into its natural curl from the straight combing given it when it was wet earlier from the swim in the pool—they all combined, Colonel Ross must admit, to make you start when, on the open shirt collar you saw instead, of, say, two bars, two stars.

General Beal said: "You know more about things like this than I do; and I know you do; and I want to do what you think is right. But I can ask you why, can't I? Eileen!"

Through the open door behind the desk popped Sergeant O'Mara, a fat little Wac, pulling her chin in, pushing her bust out and holding her small pudgy hands firmly at the seams of her skirt. "Yes, sir!"

"Get me a Coke, will you?" General Beal said. "Here, wait." He dug from his pocket a handful of coins and loose keys, sorted them over looking for nickels. "Want a Coke, Judge? No? O.K., bring me two, and get yourself one."

"Yes, sir."

"And see if anybody knows where Colonel Mowbray is. I don't want him yet. Just ask him to call me when he can."

"Yes, sir."

Colonel Ross said: "As I see it, this is why, Bus. What he means here—" he tapped the paper—"is that he thinks he's more important than you think he is. Go along with him. It doesn't cost us a cent—"

"Well, how far am I supposed to go, for God's sake? Is he going to tell me how to run this command? What about those other things he says? What about that Public Relations guy? Do I blitz him? What about Johnny Sears? You want me to reprimand him? You want me to tell Pop he's got to backtrack on that bus deal? I won't do that, Judge."

General Beal put a cigarette in his mouth, then took it out again and held its ends between his thumb and first finger squeezing it lightly as though to test the strength of the paper. "Pop did the first aerial photography the Army ever did, flying a machine I'd be scared to get into if it was only standing on the ramp. When I was at Maxwell, first lieutenant, he was a lieutenant colonel, well, maybe a major; used to advise the men coming in. He was damn decent and knew what he was talking about, too. You'll never see me pushing Pop around. What we agreed; when he drops it, we'll just have to pick it up for him and go on from there—" The cigarette, curving more and more, suddenly snapped in half. "Hell!" General Beal said. He threw the fragments at the waste basket and brushed a few crumbs of tobacco from his trouser leg. "I admit I wish he hadn't done any of this about tomorrow. Why couldn't you stop him when you first heard about it? I'm throwing parties for myself! I'm supposed to be working here. I bet I catch something from Washington on that!"

"Maybe I don't like pushing Pop around either," Colonel Ross said, a little drily; both because of the difficulty of the feat proposed—without checking the act, he was to compass the result—and because the ingratiating appellation "Pop" in his own mouth always jarred his ear. Pop was a year or so his junior. "At any rate, don't worry about Washington yet. If Pop finds out I told you this, he'll think he can't trust Botty; so use your own judgment about whether you want to pretend you don't know. Nichols is coming down to give you the DSM. I don't know who fixed that up. About Mr. Bullen's other points, I suggest you don't do anything. I've heard about the police trouble from Johnny. It doesn't matter. When I get a chance, I'll have a talk with Captain Collins. If Howden or somebody squawks about anything in the paper, Collins better go down himself, and not send an assistant. I want to try to find out this morning where Bullen gets his Headquarters gossip—"

"For God's sake," General Beal said. "They send Jo-Jo Nichols all the way down with a medal? I don't want any more medals. You get to be a joke, that way. There are too many medals in this Army—"

"That may be," Colonel Ross said. "But you take this one and like it. I don't think it would be coming if anyone important was sour on AFORAD, up there. I think they still feel good about you."

General Beal said restlessly: "Could be. But I've seen a man get a medal because they had a kick in the teeth coming right up for him." With his finger he began to twirl a propeller of the shining metal effigy, mounted on a rod, of the new B-29 Very Heavy Bomber. "Seen this?" he said to Colonel Ross. "Pop sent it in Wednesday." He tilted the tail, putting the plane into an alarming dive. "Bet you that would leave the wings way back there." He smoothed the elongated shining nose. "Hear about the new fire control it has?" he said. "Two fifties and a twenty mm cannon in the tail they can aim and fire from the rear deck turret. I wouldn't mind seeing that. You know where they are, don't you? I was thinking we might hop out there, just overnight, one day next week. They don't want to advertise them, so they can't fly them around anywhere. But that's what we figure to mess up Japan with. AFORAD ought to have a look at it soon. I'd take Colonel Hyde, and maybe someone else from Bombardment, with me. You'd like to go, wouldn't you?"

"Not next week," Colonel Ross said. "I've got inspections every day."

"Well, maybe I'll just send Hyde. Or maybe we could get them to fly one here, at night—no, I guess we couldn't, not until we finish the new runway next month. What other things have you got, Judge?"

"Several," Colonel Ross said. "But let's get this Benny business over. It bears a little on one of them. What do you want to do about Benny, now you've slept on it?"

General Beal got up and walked to a window. "I don't know, Judge," he said without turning around. "I didn't sleep on it a hell of a lot. I couldn't get to sleep."

Colonel Ross looked at the general's straight tense back. "You'd better go see the Flight Surgeon," he said calmly.

"Yeah; I'd better see someone, all right," General Beal said. "That wasn't good, that business coming in. That never happened to me before. You got to have a better reaction time than that. If you can't keep up with it, putting down in that little rocking chair, where would you be in a plane?" He brought his thumb up and began slowly and purposefully to bite at his nail. "I've seen them. They go half-assing along, scaring the be-Jesus out of everyone. Telling you they're as good as they ever were, with so much rank hardly anybody can ground them—"

There was a tap on the door behind, and the general wheeled around. It proved to be the general's secretary, who was Sergeant Pellerino's wife. She was a slight girl with pretty features and a somewhat waxen complexion. Her perpetually worried look had disturbed Colonel Ross until he came to realize it was due to the fact that she needed glasses but would not wear them. It had nothing to do with her mental state. Her mental state was better reflected by her habit, as she worked, of quietly singing or humming to herself. She was a good stenographer and familiar with Army business, for she was the daughter of a non-commissioned officer stationed at March Field before the war, and had been working in Headquarters there when Danny met and married her. The general said, "Hello, Vera."

She said: "I was sorry to be late, sir. I had to make Danny go over to the hospital. His back was sore. He's all right, though, the doctor said."

"Well, tell him to take it easy," General Beal said. "And

156

tell them outside I don't want to see anybody until after Colonel Ross leaves."

"Yes, I will, General." She closed the door carefully. On the desk, the general's box buzzed, and she immediately opened the door again. "Shall I cut that, sir?"

"Yes—after this. I'll take this—" he went to the desk and knocked the key down. "Yes?"

The diaphragm squawked: "Coulthard, General."

"Hello, Hal."

"You tied up now, Bus? My Captain Hicks tells me you spoke to him about that matter we discussed the other night—"

"I am tied up now, Hal. I want to see Hicks later this morning. Why don't you bring him over with you?"

"Right you are."

General Beal sat in the chair at his desk.

He clasped his arms together, moving his hands slow and hard, rubbing his bare elbows. "I got rattled," he said moodily, "and that bothered me. So I took it out on Benny. I didn't have to say that about his running the show. So he got mad. So really I got him mad. And when he gets mad, he gets mad. He always has. I know how he works. See what I mean?"

"Yes," Colonel Ross said, "but I don't hold with it. It isn't suitable for general officers to have to worry about Benny's temper. Let Benny worry about it. I don't think he feels it consciously, but subconsciously he must be pretty well persuaded now that because he's a hot pilot, he can get away with anything. For his sake, and yours too, you'd better correct that. Don't make too much of this, Bus." He paused, considering whether to say what he had in mind: in substance, that General Beal was not a squadron commander any more. Now his duties and responsibilities were very different.

Squadron commanders, and even group commanders, had to take care of their people. This solemn, really sacred obligation was part of a Service code preserved not so much in written regulations as in certain little homiletic chestnuts. Earnest senior officers related them at the drop of a hat to any junior officers they could find.

Lieutenant Beal must have heard early, and probably often,

about the gruff old colonel and the young squadron commander summoned to his office. The colonel threateningly informed him that his conduct at the club last night did not become an officer and a gentleman. If it ever happened again, he would be court-martialed. Nonplused, the young squadron commander blurted out that he wasn't at the club last night, he had been engaged in his office on paper work all evening. The colonel answered that he now found him, as well as disorderly, insubordinate. If he did not shut up and get out, the court martial would take place at once. This, to be sure, dumbfounded the young squadron commander who had always regarded the colonel as a fair and reasonable man; but, outside, the Adjutant, seeing his distress, murmured to him that perhaps he ought to know that Lieutenant Jones, of his squadron, had taken a drop too much of the cup that cheers at the club bar last night. The young squadron commander then realized that this was the wise old, as well as gruff old, colonel's way of telling him that his command responsibility included taking care of his men, seeing they didn't get into trouble. A word to the wise, especially after a certain number of repetitions, may be expected to stick.

Colonel Ross said: "Your responsibility includes a good deal besides looking out for Benny. It includes seeing that people under your command, even if only temporarily, don't get punched in the nose every time Benny has the notion."

"I know all that," General Beal said irritably. The irritation could, and no doubt did, come from the ill-ease a man is bound to feel when, though knowing all that, the knowledge is simply there in his mind, idle, not coactive enough to silence the stubborn: Yes, but—of an instinct or feeling which was there first.

He said: "Benny can't do that. I agree. That's why I had charges drawn up. I wanted him to worry some. But you're wrong, Judge. Benny doesn't do it just because he thinks he can get away with it. Oh, no! That isn't Benny at all. Getting away with it has nothing to do with what he does. Benny is just Benny."

This emphatic truism would be adequately answered, Colonel Ross thought, by asking: who isn't who? He said nothing, though he could see that General Beal had stopped to let him say something, and that General Beal hoped that what he said would show he had grasped the point already, and that he, General Beal, could give over the exhausting work of making his meaning clear.

Disappointed, General Beal went on laboriously: "You have to take the good with the bad. It's like that thing last week— that kid who buzzed the nigger picnic. Of course, you take disciplinary action; but Folsom told me afterward he had to admit that was pretty flying. That kid came right down the shore between the water and the overhang of the trees. Of course, scaring all those colored women was bad; but in this war we're going to see a lot of close-in work on beaches; and do you want fighter pilots with the nerve and judgment to do that, or don't you? A man who's just a big-mouthed show-off, you bend his ears right quick; but you have to give a man like Benny a little latitude. Don't think Benny's just another pilot, Judge. He's a wonderful group commander. Best you ever saw. Brereton will say that, too. That's why we decided to send him home. We didn't want to risk getting him killed; and we figured, when he got burned, his luck was about out. He had over a hundred combat missions."

If you had any inkling at all of what over a hundred combat missions meant, that circumstance was bound to give you pause. Colonel Ross said: "It sounds like too many."

"It was too many, too damn many; but Benny wanted to fly with each of his squadrons—not to mess in with the squadron commanders, but just to watch them. He still did that even when he was going out with me quite a good deal, flying as my wingman on test missions." General Beal's expression warmed. He gave Colonel Ross a hopeful glance. "You ever hear how he got burned?"

"Well, I heard his plane caught fire," Colonel Ross said. He recognized his reluctance to hear more. Do what you would, you began to weigh in evidence, where it had no business to be, the hundred combat missions, the shocking burns covering almost all that third of the body which the medical officers regard as the very limit if you were going to survive.

General Beal said: "He went out with one of his squadrons

and what he usually did was fly a kind of top cover on them, all by himself. So he could see what they were doing. They were going to hit a Wop motor park we'd just found, and it didn't look like much. The Eyeties' AA always stank; they couldn't make their men stay at the guns; you'd see them running like rabbits. This time, we didn't know it; it was just one of those things, some German mobile AA stuff—about ten pieces—was withdrawing down a road beyond the park. Not part of the regular defenses, or anything, so we never knew they were there. They were always good, wonderful. They could get set and start throwing at you not more than one minute after they saw you. Red flight of this squadron of Benny's came down to dust off the park and never saw these Krauts; the road was in a little gully. The AA took out two planes right away, including the squadron commander, and were coming onto white and blue flights. Benny, upstairs, could see it. So he came down, slam-bang in a power dive, from the far side. The Krauts, shooting the other way, didn't see him; and with their guns going, didn't hear him, until he was maybe five hundred feet off, at fifty feet, coming up the gully, and opened on them."

General Beal sat up, his cheeks tingeing with color. He laughed shortly. "God, it was murder! Benny just mowed them down; set some trucks on fire, smashed some of the guns, must have drilled thirty, forty Krauts. Then he pulled around as hard as he could, and came back down the gully, which was not as fool a thing to do as it sounds. Those AA pieces, the gunners strap themselves in seats. When Benny came up the road, they were all aligned; they'd begun firing without taking time to move out of close column. He figured he'd killed all or most of the gunners. They'd have to clear the gun controls, those that weren't smashed, get new gunners in place, try and put out fires in the trucks—and, anyway, all they'd expect Benny to do was pull the hell out of there now; he'd spoken his piece, and he must have seen it was good enough for anybody. That's one thing about the Krauts—some of these things you hear, you'd better not believe—but this is nearly always so; they're good, but do what you aren't supposed to, and there they are with their pants down. Benny had it right. Not one of the pieces was able to fire; so he drilled another batch. Those he didn't get were into the ditch. Well, one of them must have had some kind of submachine gun, automatic rifle, or something, and Benny's plane took a long burst from it. First thing it did was smash the canopy-fastening so it slammed back and jammed. Same time, it hit a tank connection. About two minutes later the leak caught fire, came right on the cockpit."

General Beal drew a breath. He said: "Benny was at full throttle. He switched tanks, kept it there, and blew the fire out; but burning gasoline had sprayed all over his shirt—he wasn't wearing anything else. He managed to get the plane back, half an hour. He put it down. Cut the engine and he fainted. The plane ran right down the runway and off the end, and cracked up. Not too bad."

Colonel Ross said: "That was quite a trip."

"Oh, Judge!" General Beal said. "That boy is a honey! You can believe me. Because we have a few more like him, we're going to win the war."

It seemed more probable to Colonel Ross that they were going to win the war, not because they had a few more Bennys, but because they had thousands and thousands of run-of-the-mill pilots; and thousands and thousands of planes; and hills of bombs; and dumps of supplies as large as small cities, which could not be neutralized, as Benny had so nearly been, by one burst from one automatic rifle in one ditch. He said: "I don't think this is easy for you, Bus. But, in the law, you have to plead to the indictment. There is no off-set."

"All right," General Beal said. "I want to tell you one other thing, that happened at Batchelor Field, at Port Darwin where I first ran into Benny. We got a late alert on some Zeros, a lot of them, coming in, and Benny was in a flight that was the only one we had up. Benny did all right. He didn't get any planes, but he broke up part of the attack. Meanwhile several Japs went to work on the flight leader and took him; man who was Benny's best friend. Been to school with him and everything. He bailed out, the flight leader; but he opened his parachute too soon and a Jap shot him up and he came down dead. Thing was, his wingman left him. They started to attack as an element and the wingman, instead of covering his flight leader, dived out. If he *had* covered him, the Japs probably couldn't have got him—the Zeros were about the limit of their range and couldn't hang around. Well, this fellow got down; and Benny, and Benny's wingman, got down; and this fellow was saying why he dived out, his guns wouldn't fire; he was going to see what was wrong with the circuit."

Bending forward, General Beal began to pick at a little scab on his wrist. "Benny is a loyal guy. He knew the flight leader was dead: he dropped right on the field full of holes. Benny said: 'Leave that alone. I'll see what's wrong with it.' He climbed into the plane, hit the switches, and gave it a squeeze. The guns all fired. Matter of fact, the burst came within a few feet of killing some Aussies who were over across the field. So Benny got out then and really beat this fellow. He was bigger than Benny; but I think Benny would have killed him, except the crew chief and a couple of men finally got hold of him." General Beal looked sidelong at Colonel Ross. "You see what Benny thought. He thought the wingman had simply gone yellow. It looked too hot; so he dived out of it. Then he was going to fritz up his firing circuit and claim that about the guns. Benny didn't give him time."

"Obviously not," Colonel Ross said. It had been an old habit of his, on the bench, to relieve the frequent tedium of listening to testimony, by setting himself to observe, while witnesses related in chief their partial version of the facts, imprudent little admissions and implications that were sure to slip out as the story was illustrated and emphasized. Their anxiety to make the point foremost in their minds blinded them to everything else. Like those German AA gunners who never saw Benny coming, they looked the other way, engrossed in their job.

The account of Benny's African service told you that Benny, assured and probably arrogant, always acted as he pleased. A group commander's duty did not attach him to the mission every time one of his squadrons went out. Since the practice was approved, approval of the practice must be part of the necessary "latitude" not so much allowed Benny as exacted by him. From the incident of the fire in the plane, you learned, along with the fact that Benny's courage and endurance were great, that regulations about wearing flying clothes to fly were not for him.

What happened at Batchelor Field spoke for itself. It said more than General Beal (speaking at a disadvantage, since he was shy of saying in so many words the to-him-deeply-affecting things he meant) intended it to say. Benny beat up this wingman who in Benny's opinion killed his best friend because he was a loyal guy; still a loyal guy at Ocanara, the minute Benny was on the ground last night he went to beat up the man who, even if he hadn't killed his chief, might have killed him; and, anyway, who was wholly responsible for a stupid and dangerous act which upset the general enough to make him turn on Benny in anger. Colonel Ross was ready to accept this "loyalty" as an element in the complicated principle of action behind Benny's willful behavior; but the really relevant evidence now on the record was that Benny had done this before. It gave an impartial judge good grounds for believing that, when Benny could, Benny always took the administration of what looked to him like justice into his own hands.

Colonel Ross said: "This wingman; did he admit that that was what he did?"

General Beal said: "You can't admit things like that, Judge. He stuck to it that all he knew was, up there, he squeezed the stick; and no go. Could be. But Benny thought what he thought; and I know Benny thought right."

"You know that?" Colonel Ross said. "How do you know it?"

The tone, because of Colonel Ross's reflections of a moment before, was a little closer to the one a judge would use to a witness who was not being quite clear than the tone colonels use in asking a major general questions. Perhaps because Colonel Ross had been a judge much longer than General Beal had been a general, General Beal said with a defensive anxiety:

"Well, Judge, that was a rugged war then. They were dishing it out, but good; and lots of them. You were taking it, only a few of you. It gets on a man's nerves, and that makes him liable to do certain things you get to recognize. Sometimes, for a second or two, your hands can take off on their own. They do what they want to do, not what you thought you were going to make them do. That's how I know."

He shifted in his chair and clasped his knee, moving the shabby ornamented high shoe in jerky little kicks. "I don't say this wingman planned it, or even ever thought of doing such a thing. But then all of a sudden he'd done it. In a way, he had tough luck. That's happened to plenty of other people; but then they go back. Usually you see right away you'd better be dead than that. So very often you can cover it and nobody will realize what you did. But this boy couldn't get back. Not with those Zeros, with a P-Forty—you lost altitude, and you were out. So all he could do was think up that gun business coming down. See?"

"I see what you think Benny thought. I see why you think he thought it. But he could be wrong; and that idea never crosses his mind, does it?"

General Beal clasped his knee tighter. He said, more anxious, less patient: "What I'm trying to tell you, Judge. I know Benny wasn't wrong. Benny had been there. He knew. The wingman knew he knew. He wasn't sore at Benny. He saw he had it coming to him. It isn't that anyone thinks he's such a damn hero himself; he never said he was. You might be yellow yourself, looking at it from where the other fellow sat; but you can't let him do that, and kill your best friend. You can't let anybody get away with being yellow, just because you know you might be yourself. That makes it all the more reason. Sure, it could happen to anyone; but you can't let that be a good excuse." He paused. "I didn't mention this wingman's name, and I wouldn't; because it could happen to anyone. He's a good pilot. I think they may even be considering giving him a group when the Twelfth Air Force is operational in Italy. And if they asked me, I'd say yes. Anyway, I know you'd never repeat this—I wanted to tell you because it shows what I mean about Benny. We all kept it quiet—"

The small box on the stand behind the general's desk emitted a little buzz. Tilting back, he touched the key. Mrs. Pellerino said: "Did you want those Cokes, sir? Eileen has them here."

"All right—yes. Send her in."

The door to Mrs. Pellerino's office opened at once, and the WAC sergeant entered on tiptoe. She carried in one hand two bottles of Coca-Cola with straws in them; and in the other, some paper napkins.

Colonel Ross was glad of the interruption. He needed a moment to reconsider the case. He might as well abandon any notions he had of helping the general settle on the best or wisest course. What the general wanted to do about Benny was what they had done about Benny at Batchelor Field— they all kept it quiet! Granted that this might be neither right nor wise, it was now time to determine whether it was possible or practicable. The only argument that would ever stand against the plea that Benny was a wonderful group commander, best you ever saw; that Benny was a loyal guy, and here his loyalties had been involved again, so there was naturally no holding him, would be the flat impossibility of keeping it quiet. By an effort of mind and will, Colonel Ross forced himself to look dispassionately at the situation.

It was a good bet that Captain Hicks, the WAC lieutenant, Turck, and the colored T/5, had all told friends about their exciting evening at the first opportunity. Their friends had friends; and since the excitement involved the Commanding General and the interesting figure of Lieutenant Colonel Carricker, anyone in AFORAD might be expected to pay attention and to pass the anecdote on. That process was already out of control, so it would be sensible to assume that, by night, it would be known to all that Benny had punched a Negro pilot in the nose and been put in arrest by the general.

Dispassionate, Colonel Ross did not think this universal knowledge would make much difference. They might talk for ten minutes and remember for two days. Well, then, what about the punched pilot and the colored officers on the project?

Would they also co-operate by forgetting about it? On the whole, Colonel Ross had to admit to himself that he thought they would, or could, if handled judiciously, be persuaded to. Mr. Botwinick's report about the indignation meeting last night was probably accurate enough—there had been a lot of excited big-talk.

It must be remembered, first, that those talkers were little more than boys. Experience with juvenile court work persuaded Colonel Ross that boys did not get anywhere in sustained group enterprise without the support and encouragement of older, more experienced people. As a group, exciting each other, they might break the windows in an empty house when they thought no one was around; the sight of a lone policeman, or even the groundless rumor that a policeman was coming scattered them. They had no organization. Here, strangers and alone, the Army's overwhelming organization pressed them on every side.

It must be remembered, second, that they were colored boys. On the bench, Judge Ross would have silenced peremptorily and with indignation even the most indirect or guarded attempt to insinuate the distinction as affecting any cause in any way. It was necessary to insinuate it here. He did not pretend to that special knowledge of Negroes that Southerners always, and not, after all, implausibly, insisted was to them reserved. He did not (perhaps because years of patiently exercising his mind to compare equitably, to balance impartially, made it now impossible) give over the shamefaced feeling, common to Northerners who never really faced the problem as a practical problem, that it was unfair and unreasonable to blame any man for the lack of qualities which the power of an interested majority worked in a dozen ways to keep him from developing. Yet, instructed by experience, Judge Ross, Colonel Ross, had a gloomy working knowledge of what to expect when your fellow man's face was black.

Behind the black face might be a courageous spirit and a sharp intelligence; but you must expect both to be damped and spoiled by the inbred resignation, the experience of generations bitterly resenting, yet always resenting impotently, the white man's yoke. Every day the white man's greed and folly proved that his claimed superiority was a lie. He was not clever; he was not strong; he was not good; he was nobody's born master. All he was, was, to a black man's sorrow and his shame, a little too much for most black men.

While Colonel Ross pondered his lugubrious working knowledge of the Afro-American, Sergeant O'Mara came to General Beal's desk and laid down a paper napkin. The Coca-Cola bottles were dewed with moisture; and as she reached hastily to set them on the napkin and be gone, one slipped in her fingers. It fell free. It hit the carpeted floor, still upright. Out its mouth leaped a copious frothing geyser which splashed over General Beal's lap.

"Jumping Jesus!" General Beal said.

He started up, sending the chair back, for the iced liquid had obviously reached a sensitive spot. Colonel Ross, quite ready for the relief of low comedy, had to laugh.

From Sergeant O'Mara came an anguished sound. She dropped on her knees, snatched up the bottle, which had rolled over and was emptying itself. Scarlet to the tips of her ears and the back of her neck, she sprang to her feet. "Oh," she said, strangled. "It's on you, sir! I'll get a cloth—"

"Wait, wait!" General Beal said, brushing his trousers. He began to laugh, too. "I've got a handkerchief—take it easy, now! Don't do that—" Down Sergeant O'Mara's flaming cheeks, tears were beginning to course. "It's all right—" She turned in despair, however, with the apparent idea of running from disaster. The door, which she had left ajar, opened wider, and, moving blindly, she bumped hard into Colonel Mowbray, about to enter.

Colonel Ross took out a handkerchief of his own and wiped his eyes. "Good thing that was you, Pop," he said. "Eileen, wait a minute! Now, stop crying! First thing you know, it will be getting to Washington that Wacs are constantly running out of the general's office in tears. Vera! We spilled some Coca-Cola. Send somebody to wipe it up."

Colonel Mowbray, whether to steady himself, or to steady Sergeant O'Mara, put his arms around her. "There, there!" he said, getting his breath. "No use crying over spilt milk. Accidents will happen. You run along and fix your face, honey." He released her, and General Beal said: "Yes. Will all the women please leave? I want to get my pants off. Find somebody to take them over to the tailor shop."

When the door was closed again, Colonel Mowbray from the big armchair by the window, said: "Bus, I guess you saw the paper. Hope you aren't sore at me. We thought we'd just have a little surprise—" He scratched his whitening head, his wrinkled face and bright eyes turning in a penitent look. "Don't know how this fellow got hold of it. Oh—" he said, hitching forward. "Now, one thing, Bus. That's positively not true, what he says about the expense to the taxpayers. Anything coming from Orlando, or Hendryx, or Dale Mabry—the Three Thirty-eighth is putting down, they think, a couple of squadrons of P-Forty-sevens; just heard a minute ago—would be flying somewhere anyway on routine training. Same with our Airborne. We were going to do a drop near Tangerine City next week. All we're doing is doing it tomorrow instead, and at Ocanara. There isn't one thing that costs anybody any additional money. You see that, Norm."

The general, minus his trousers, walked up and down, pulling at the cloth of his shorts to help them dry. He said, "I'm not sore. But you better tell me another time you're cooking something."

"Couldn't tell you if it was going to be a surprise, could I?" Colonel Mowbray said, relieved. "Here, did I barge in on something? Were you busy with Norm?"

General Beal frowned. "We were talking about Benny Carricker. You know about last night? I was asking the judge what I'd better do."

Colonel Ross said: "This I think you'll have to do, Bus. Where's Benny now?"

"In his quarters, I guess. He's still under arrest."

"What he'd better do is go and apologize to the fellow he hit. In fact, maybe you'd better have them both here and see that he does. After that—"

"Just a minute, Norm," Colonel Mowbray said. "I don't mean I don't think that's right; but we got to look at this thing from all angles. Botty says he told you what he heard. You tell Bus?"

"Not yet," Colonel Ross said, annoyed. "I haven't had time, for one thing." He looked at General Beal. "We might as well fill you in. Botty says there was a little excitement among project personnel—the men with this boy told the rest of them about it when they got over to their quarters—"

"Yes," said Colonel Mowbray, "it seems they thought of organizing some kind of protest. Now, Botty tells me, he hears they *have* organized it. Now, Norm, you see about Benny? Sure, he ought to apologize; but if Bus makes him do it now —might look like a sign of weakness, don't you think?"

General Beal stopped his pacing. "What kind of protest?" he said.

"Twenty or thirty of them are planning to turn up at the Officers Club tonight."

"Well, what about it?"

"I mean our Officers Club, the Area club. Not theirs."

"I didn't know they had one," General Beal said.

"We had to give them one, Bus. You've got fifty or sixty of these colored officers. They all turn up, say, Saturday night at the dance. Not in Florida, Bus! That's asking for trouble. We've given them their own club. We've fixed it fine. We have the furniture from the old Base club; pool table; bar where they can get beer. We have it all arranged downtown with two of the churches; some colored girls coming out, so they can have a dance Saturday night—we put in a juke box. We even put in slot machines. They haven't any kick." He looked at Colonel Ross.

"You have this much wrong, Pop," Colonel Ross said. "This Area isn't the state of Florida; this is a United States Military Reservation. You'd better take a look at Army Regulation two-ten-dash-ten. Your new Officers Club is a public building; like all the other buildings here; and unless it wants to move out, it better extend to all officers on duty at the post the right to full membership. There is also an AAF Headquarters Letter on the subject."

Colonel Mowbray gave him a wounded look. He fumbled in his breast pocket and produced a folded paper. "Now, wait a minute," he said. Colonel Ross, not waiting, said: "I don't know why the Letter Order with the assignment of buildings didn't reach me until yesterday. As I remember, it was dated the first of this week."

Colonel Mowbray unfolded the paper. "Now," he said, "here it is. From War Department Pamphlet twenty-dash-six, Command of Negro Troops—War Department, mind you. It says in these exact words: 'The burden of deciding whether or not there shall be some separation in the use of camp facilities is placed on the local command'—now mark this—'with the assumption that local conditions will be taken into account.' I'm taking them into account. There's my authority." He looked at General Beal. "I know about this, Bus. You'd have trouble, sure as fate. A lot of these Southern boys just won't have it. We can't let Negroes use the Area club—for their own sakes—"

General Beal said: "This much I'm sure of: there will be no organized protests of any kind. I want to talk to the project personnel. Get them together. On the other hand; no Northern, Southern, Eastern, or Western boys are going to 'not have' what regulations provide—"

Colonel Ross said: "Don't do that, Bus! There's no reason to get them together. Ignore it. We don't know about it officially. That's why I want you to make Benny apologize. Get that much straight, and then we'll see what happens—"

✦

"This morning I am in the best of health, thank you, sir," Lieutenant Turck said. "And all goes merry as a marriage bell, thank you again."

Remembering it from yesterday, Nathaniel Hicks admired

and at the same time found himself touched by this controlled and composed, yet ceaseless struggle which, gracefully and even gallantly, she seemed to have to renew every day against that obsessive self-consciousness. She said calmly, though her color was up a little: "If you have a moment, Captain, I'd like to check over a list with you, a short one. We are missing some classified items. That is, somebody forgot to get signatures on the withdrawal slips, so we know only that Special Projects took them. I thought several of them might be with you, because of your fighter manual job. At any rate, I hope they are."

"I know several of them are," Nathaniel Hicks said.

He looked at her with liking; but self-consciousness, even when so admirably controlled, called to self-consciousness. He found himself frowning, overacting an effort of memory. "I know I have several Eleventh Air Force reports on arctic operations, and a Fifth Air Force Combat Evaluation of the P-Thirty-nine—some others, too. I can't get them for you until somebody opens the safe. I never learned the combination. Can you wait a few minutes? Sit down." He held out a package of cigarettes to her. She took one and sat in the chair beside his desk. He lit the cigarette for her and she turned her eyes down on the list in her hand.

"Yes," she said, "those are some of them. That is very good news." She, in her turn, spoke stiffly; for his awkwardness wasn't lost on her. She, too, frowned, studying her list again. "You don't have to give them back, if you aren't through with them. I'm just trying to straighten up the records." She determinedly raised her eyes. Nathaniel Hicks could see her take command of herself. She said: "While the cat was away, the mice seem to have been playing, poor dears." She had in hand now that wry raillery, aimed at herself; her defense against everything. She said: "My, what a dressing-down I did give them! I summoned them into my cubby-hole and I asked them whether or not they knew there was a war on; and whether or not they realized that in their custody were some of the nation's most important Military Secrets; and whether or not they were ambitious to be the first members of our Corps to face a firing squad. I could see them, out their eye corners, exchanging with each other intelligence to the general effect: *I hear her talking, the old buzzard!*"

Nathaniel Hicks said: "I really forgot I had the stuff still. I'm through with it. Miss Candee ought to be back in a minute. She and Edsell do most of the safe-opening around here."

"Oh," said Lieutenant Turck, "I have a communication for Lieutenant Edsell." She unbuttoned her shirt pocket and took out a folded paper. "It must be early, yet," she said, feeling the paper: "This still seems quite dry. Would you be gracious enough to give it to him. I suppose there's no reason why I shouldn't just leave it on his desk, but—"

"It it's anything important," Nathaniel Hicks said, "I know where to reach him. I'm not sure just when he'll be back. I'm afraid I'll have to go out myself before he does get back—" He found in his own phrasing a vaguely ungracious note, the exact opposite of what he intended. "I mean, if it's anything that shouldn't be lying around, we'll put it in the safe and Miss Candee can tell him as soon as he comes in—"

"No, please," Lieutenant Turck said. "It's absurd of me. There is no reason for you to bother. It is simply a note from Lippa. She couldn't get him on the phone."

Nathaniel Hicks said: "He left word that we could reach him over at the Public Relations Office. He went to see some newspaper man who turned up, some friend of his. And that reminds me, I think Captain Andrews was expecting to take him over to Personnel Analysis. I'd better tell them in Stat Control where they can get him." He took up the telephone and said: "Five-one."

"Look," Lieutenant Turck said, "you're busy. Suppose I come back later and check what you have?"

"No. Sit down," Nathaniel Hicks said. "I'm not busy at all. I am waiting for the colonel to tell me what the general says —Don, if you're going to want Edsell, he left word he could be reached on three-nine-seven. O.K.?" He hung up.

From the door leading into the next room where Major Whitney had his desk, Miss Candee appeared. She was a plump, blondish young woman. Pink and animated, she carried in one hand a large box of chocolates and, in the other, a box of cigars. "From *Major* Pound, Captain Hicks," she announced with a pleasing, since after all disinterested, delight. "Where's Captain Duchemin? I know Lieutenant Edsell is out."

"Captain Duchemin is off with the pigeons," Nathaniel Hicks said. "Here, offer Lieutenant Turck a cigar; the major mustn't be mean, now that he is of field grade. And, Palm, open the safe like a good girl, will you?"

Miss Candee giggled. "I'll put their cigars on their desks." She offered Lieutenant Turck the box of chocolates. "You don't really want a cigar, do you?" When Lieutenant Turck shook her head, she said, "I knew you didn't. Captain Hicks thinks I believe everything." She put the boxes on her own desk and went to the safe. "There!" she said. "You don't need me right away, do you?" She gathered up her boxes and tripped out into the hall.

To Lieutenant Turck, Nathaniel Hicks said: "That was about time! Pound came in with the National Guard or something, and he's been in grade and in grade—it must be two years. We were afraid they'd started some damn nonsense about merit. As Assistant Chief, Pound was doing a perfectly satisfactory job; you know, mixing up the papers and losing any that looked important. If they were going to start holding things like that against you—"

Lieutenant Turck said: "When I was at Des Moines this time, I met several women who were with me there in OCS. I would not have expected to care; but now they are all first lieutenants, drat them—"

In the hall door a tall man with a handsome, though fattening, young face under a shock of curly snow-white hair had appeared. Nathaniel Hicks got abruptly to his feet. "Yes, sir," he said.

"Ah. Busy, Hicks?"

"No, sir."

Lieutenant Turck had arisen, too. Now she came trimly to attention. Nathaniel Hicks said: "Colonel Coulthard, this is Lieutenant Turck, of Classified Files. She came for some papers of hers we had."

Colonel Coulthard ambled into the room and held his hand out to Lieutenant Turck. "Glad to know you, Lieutenant," he said. He turned on her an eye that plainly still took pleasure from the sight, or from the fetching effect of the sight on an old Army man, of these bright respectful women, all soldiers if often full-breasted ones, to the girdle; piquantly, all girls in skirts down from the waist. "These fellows of mine making you a lot of trouble?" he said genially. "Just you come to me and I'll take care of them! Sit down, both you. Hicks, I talked to the general about that. He's tied up at the moment, but he wants me to bring you over later. So, stand by, will you?"

"Yes, sir. Colonel, about that one-dash-fifteen material. I took it over and gave it to Mr. Botwinick, Colonel Mowbray's Warrant Officer. He said he would see that the general knew it was there. The general said he wanted it this morning, so I thought I'd better do that."

"Good. Yes, if the general wants it, I guess we'll let him have it!" He gave Lieutenant Turck a comradely wink. "All right; when I hear, I'll send for you, Hicks. Good-bye, Lieutenant." He turned and walked out.

Nathaniel Hicks went to the open safe and pulled some folders from the top file drawer. Returning with them, he said: "What do you think of that?"

"Why, I think that's lovely," Lieutenant Turck said. "Do you know some of the others? Do you know Colonel Jobson, of Personnel Analysis, for instance?"

"I also have a cringing acquaintance with Colonel Folsom of Fighter Analysis," Nathaniel Hicks said. "Oh, never think we aren't grateful. We keep his secret."

"What's his secret?"

Nathaniel Hicks tapped his head. "Are you old enough to remember Percy the Machine Man in the funny papers? I don't believe you are."

She shook her head.

"Brains he has nix," Nathaniel Hicks said. "I think these are all yours, if you'd like to check them. I don't think you want to carry them. It's quite a load, and I can see that another delightful day is coming up. This is when the sun gets over the pines, there, and hits the tiles." He went and switched on a big fan in the corner. He looked toward the open ceiling rafters. "Last week, Captain, now Major, Pound threw a string over the top cross member, hitched a thermometer to it and pulled it up. After it had hung five minutes, he let it down, and it said one hundred and seventeen."

Lieutenant Turck said brightly: "You should complain! You know, the reason I'm trying to get our records straight today is that I don't expect to have much time for them next week. Now that I am an authority on military law, the Staff Director tells me it's my turn to be Mess Officer for a month—in addition to my other duties, of course. I was hoping that would come in December or January."

She gave an exaggerated sigh. "That WAC mess kitchen is really formidable; and there you're supposed to be a good deal of the time seeing the nasty brats don't throw dish cloths in the mashed potatoes. The officer I'm relieving tells me that lots of them, who won't take their salt tablets, faint for lunch every noon. God, how sick I am of sweating! I think I have a complex—when I was younger, I used to douse myself with preparations that ensure personal daintiness. They raised the most horrible welts under my arms; but I couldn't stop until a doctor finally made me. What I hate, that I do! If this had happened to me then, I'm sure I'd have swallowed iodine—good morning, Major."

Major Whitney slipped through the door from his room beyond. "Hello, Lieutenant," he said. "No, don't let me interrupt you. The Photographic Section just got in some pictures I thought Nat might like to see. He's our fighter expert. Photos of the P-Fifty-seven, the jet job. They're secret, of course."

"I hope we have more than photographs," Nathaniel Hicks said, aware that he was rising, a little heartily, to his rôle of fighter expert. "Captain Wiley, at Orlando, told me we damn well better get going. He saw a German one on some mission. They didn't know what it was, at first. He was with a flight of British Spitfires, and it went by them as though they were standing still."

"Yes, I guess it's something," Major Whitney said. "Don't

forget and leave those photographs on your desk. We got another memo on security measures. It says secret and confidential documents when not actually in use shall be replaced in the files, and no files shall be left open if everybody is out of the room. There'll be periodical spot checks on it and appropriate disciplinary measures will be taken where necessary."

He set one thin buttock on the edge of Captain Duchemin's empty desk and nervously picked a package of cigarettes from his breast pocket. His intent, hollow-cheeked face twitched. "Nat," he said, "what are we going to do, the general taking you off this way? I know you can't help it; but we got five new projects in this morning. Fernald's busy; Goss is busy; Captain Adler's going to be at Wright Field another week. How's Clarence getting on with his pigeons, do you know?"

"He went out with his Signal Corps fellow. I think they were flying somewhere—"

"Look, if you go over with Colonel Coulthard to see the general, I wish on the way, if you can, you'd say something to him. You know, just indirectly, if you get a chance. We can't work like other sections. I mean, if we're going to write a report on a thing, a man has to know all about it. He has to spend a lot of time—like you going to see those people at Orlando and Sellers Field, and so on. We have to do that—" he pulled up, reminded of still another worry. "Say, just what did the general say about that Navy business at Jacksonville? I didn't like to ask you with the colonel there. Was he really mad? Nobody told us we couldn't go to the Navy. I guess you know we did, several times, on Hughes' life-raft report. That's why I told you to go ahead."

"He said Navy co-ordination was at HqAAF level, and we weren't to do any of it. If he doesn't like what we did do, he'll have to beat on Colonel Coulthard. The colonel fixed it up."

"And the colonel will have to beat on me, because I asked him to fix it up."

"Well, then you'll have to beat on me, because I asked you to ask him to fix it up."

Major Whitney grinned in a worried way at Lieutenant

Turck. "Think I could join the WAC, Lieutenant?" he said. "You don't have anything like this over there, do you?"

"No, sir, of course not. And I must get back over there. I have been wasting hours of Captain Hicks's time." She took the file folders. "If you're really through with them," she said, "I can manage; and you may trust me to tear up your slips. I'll leave Lieutenant Edsell's note on his desk." She hesitated a moment, then she said: "Incidentally, if you're not getting a better one somewhere else, we'd be enchanted to offer you a drink in our parlor after the parade Saturday—did you know we were having a parade? It seems so. Poor Lippa is going to have to march with her troops. We ought to be in by six. Mary has a brother in the Navy who sent her half a dozen bottles of Scotch—it sounds almost incestuous, doesn't it? You're welcome to it; and you, too, Major, if you're down that way." She smiled and walked out, erect, not quite easy.

Major Whitney, looking after her, said: "I always kind of like her. I think she's got brains. What's she doing with Jim Edsell?"

"Nothing I know of," Nathaniel Hicks said. "It's this Lieutenant Mary Lippa she mentioned. I, personally, don't know what they do. You might ask Duchemin. His crack was that Edsell hung around to eat, drink, and make Mary. A little labored, I thought."

Major Whitney frowned. "How about Jim?" he said.

He glanced behind him, as though to make sure that Captain Duchemin's desk was still empty. "He got into something or other night before last. The Provost Marshal didn't say what, said there were no charges, or anything; but he wanted to know a little about him. Asked me if he drank heavily. He came around to see me. I wish Jim would rein in. He's good; his work is good. I certainly don't want to push him around. But this morning, for instance, he just says he's going over to the Public Relations Office because a friend, some man he used to know, turned up there and was trying to get a pass or whatever they have to have to look around. I don't see that that's any of his business, except he seems to run with that Lieutenant Phillips—there is a little squirt, if I ever saw one."

"Why didn't you tell Edsell he couldn't go, you needed him here?"

"Nat, I will next time. But I don't like to act like that. I didn't appoint myself chief of this section; but I *am* chief, and so I'm responsible; and if I have to give orders, I'll give them." He paused. "Thing is, there's always something funny about what Jim's doing. You know, this fellow Lieutenant Phillips called him about, the one he went over to see, he's a colored man. He's from a Negro newspaper or something. Personnel Analysis has some project, some kind of all-Negro group, I don't know what. I suppose this fellow was sent down to write it up for their papers. But what I mean is, wouldn't you know right away that it would be Jim who happened to be a friend of a colored newspaper man? You never know what he's up to." He gave Nathaniel Hicks a careful, worried glance. "Didn't he use to be a Communist, or something, or write for some of their magazines? You know, I never told anyone this—" he looked around him again quickly "—but there was a special loyalty check ordered on him before we came down here."

"Maybe you didn't tell anyone," Nathaniel Hicks said, "but Edsell did. He told everyone. I guess he thought he was being persecuted; I don't know but that I thought so, too. Sure, he wrote for some radical magazines seven or eight years ago. He wrote for them because nobody else would publish him, and like any writer he wanted to get published. Edsell stopped writing for those magazines just as soon as the others thought his stuff was good enough to buy. Give it no thought."

Major Whitney straightened the desk sign on Captain Duchemin's desk. He cleared his throat. "They must think it's good enough to buy now, all right," he said. "Nat, I hope you won't imagine I'm sore because of that story. You know the one. I guess everyone could see it was supposed to be about me. Well, I admit right off, those two weeks at Gravelly, I didn't know whether I was coming or going. First Colonel Van Pelt would tell me one thing, and then Colonel Schermerhorn, who I guess knew Van Pelt was going to get the boot, would tell me just the opposite. I had to try to organize the section. I wonder just how much better Jim would have done?"

"He would have done much worse, Bill," Nathaniel Hicks said, embarrassed. He was on good terms with Major Whitney. Major Whitney had appealingly honest habits of mind. They kept him from pretending to more knowledge, or more authority, or more importance than was really his. In admitting deficiencies, he did not use the admission, as most people who make it use it, to excuse himself from further effort. Undaunted, he would still do the best he could.

Nathaniel Hicks said: "Look, Bill. I've worked with writers for years. I know a lot about them. When he writes, Edsell doesn't mean anything personal; any more than he means in that story he could do it better. He just sees a situation he thinks he can write a story about. Then he dresses it up and twists it around to make it a story. That's what they pay him for."

"I suppose that's right," Major Whitney said uneasily. There might remain in Major Whitney's mind a point he did not, or could not, phrase—what were you to think of a fellow free and friendly to your face, who, all the while, was working away at something that, at elaborate length, in the permanence of print, would hold you up to the ridicule of a large audience? Nathaniel Hicks could only answer by saying: "That's the way they are, Bill—"

Major Whitney opened his mouth and then closed it, smiling suddenly. He got off the desk. "Well, well," he said, "there he is! Come in, Major. Let's all look at it—"

Major Pound, his full, bland face warm and smiling too, came through the door. Major Whitney said, tilting his head: "Put something over that leaf, Bob. It hurts my eye. How about you, Nat?"

"On him it looks good," Nathaniel Hicks said, obliging himself to join in the banter. He shook Major Pound's hand. "Yeah," Major Pound said, "I thought I was the forgotten man, all right. Bill, now we got to get Nat one."

Discomfited a little by all these "Bills" and "Bobs" and "Nats," which persisted in ringing faintly false to him, being less the natural result of an established intimacy than an attempt made in all good will, but against the heavy odds of different backgrounds, attitudes, and habits of mind, to force an intimacy into being, Nathaniel Hicks said jocularly, "That's right; but first we have to get Bill made lieutenant colonel. We all lose face around here every day when the Chief of Section's only a major. They think it can't be much of a section. I may be seeing the general this morning. I'll speak to him about it—"

"Yeah, you do that, Nat," Major Pound said. "It says lieutenant colonel on the T/O, tell him—"

"Listen, Nat," Major Whitney said, "what you tell him is Colonel Coulthard's got to get me some more project officers, or some less projects. I don't give a damn which. You tell him I said that; hear?"

The telephone on Nathaniel Hicks's desk rang, and Major Pound, who was nearest, took it up. "Captain Hicks's office," he said. "Yeah, yeah. Just a minute—" He handed it over. "They have a call from Sellers Field, a Major Post. That the fellow you went to see?"

"Yes," Nathaniel Hicks said. "I don't think he liked seeing me very much. Yes, this is Captain Hicks speaking. O.K. I'm holding on—" he sat down and rocked back in his chair. "He lost an arm in China," he said to them, "and I don't think it helped his temper any. It wouldn't help mine—yes. Yes, sir. Good morning, Major."

Major Post's voice held a distant irritated squawking tone, but that was perhaps due to the telephone connection, for he said cordially enough: "Thought I'd better call you, Hicks. I guess you know about what's with us. I'm not going to be able to do that, what I said. Not to get it to you next week. I got to get a whole goddamn complete report ready to submit, by probably Tuesday or Wednesday—"

"Perfectly all right, sir," Nathaniel Hicks said. That Major Post should bother to let him know surprised him very much. He said, "It was kind of you to be willing to take the trouble. We'll be glad to have it whenever it's convenient for you to do it; but if you find you can't, I have all my notes on what you said. If you'd rather not bother, if it would be simpler for you, I could send you a copy of our draft, when we have it.

I wouldn't want that to go in without having you O.K. it—" he gave Major Whitney a wink.

"Well, things are in a mess, I can tell you," Major Post said. "I might not even be here after Wednesday. I don't know who's coming, yet. He could very likely want his own staff. I might even get assigned to Ocanara. You know Colonel Folsom, there?"

"Yes, sir. He's Chief of the Fighter Analysis Directorate. We've been doing some work with him on this job."

"Well, look, Hicks. I used to be in his squadron in Panama; he'll remember me. I figured you'd probably be in touch with him. I didn't want to call him directly, because he was kind of sore when I went into the AVG, and I don't know how he's fixed, anyway. But he might want to put in for me. How's about you just mentioning to him that you saw me here and I was saying I wished I could get assigned to Ocanara, AFORAD, whatever you call it? He couldn't do anything until this happened, until there'd probably be a change in staff here, anyway—".

"Yes, sir," said Nathaniel Hicks, astounded. "Well, Major, I'd be happy to do anything I could. You understand, of course, I'm not in Colonel Folsom's Directorate, I might not be able to get in to see him right away—"

"Well, could you see him by tomorrow?"

"Yes," Nathaniel Hicks said, suddenly remembering that the general's project might, after all, be used to get him anywhere he wanted to go. "In fact, I'll try this afternoon. I'm afraid I'll have to come right out with it; I mean, I don't know him very well, Major. Would it be all right if I simply tell him you want to come to Ocanara, if he can use you?"

"I guess so. I don't want to ask for any damn favors. I just thought if I could get it to him that I might be going to be available—I think he'd want me all right, if he had any place for me. See?"

"Yes," Nathaniel Hicks said, though he did not see quite how he was going to manage this artful presentation. "Incidentally, Major, I gather something has happened at Sellers.

I'm afraid I don't know what. Maybe I'd better know, in case Colonel Folsom—"

"Oh!" Major Post said. "Well, I thought General Beal would hear right away. Why, I thought you knew."

"Very likely he does know, sir." Nathaniel Hicks found himself adding, a little ashamed to be putting it on, "I haven't seen the general this morning yet. I'm waiting for him to send for me now."

"Well, it's out all over the place, so I guess I can tell you. The Old Man put a forty-five in his mouth and bumped himself off last night. We don't know who's coming down to replace him; why I say probably there'll be staff changes; why we all got to get full reports ready for a new CO—"

"Colonel Woodman?" Nathaniel Hicks said. He remembered standing on the cinder waste behind the Sellers Field Operations Building yesterday morning, talking to T/5 McIntyre by the truck; and the MP saying: "Colonel Woodman, sir!" He could see the stout, red-faced figure with the mustache and the riding crop acknowledge their salute with a negligent touch of his cap visor. "I'm very sorry to hear that, sir."

"He was boozed up," Major Post said briefly and bitterly. "I guess he couldn't take it, here. I know I can't. I got to get out. Maybe I shouldn't be spilling all this. I just thought, General Beal being up here yesterday—anyway, if you can get to Folsom, will you? Hell, they're hollering for me! I got to hang up."

"I'll see Colonel Folsom this afternoon, Major. I'll let you know."

"Roger," said Major Post.

Nathaniel Hicks put down the telephone. Whitney and Pound were looking at him with interest. Nathaniel Hicks said: "That's rather grim. His CO up there shot himself last night. I can't say I blame him. One of those tarpaper posts— never think we aren't doing all right! What he wants is for me, *me* to go to Colonel Folsom and ask Folsom to give him a job. Do you remember the last time we saw Folsom?"

Major Whitney shifted uncomfortably and grinned. As

Nathaniel Hicks's Section Chief, Major Whitney had gone over with him to explain the nature of Special Projects' directive to report on the revision of FM 1-15—in fact, to point out to Colonel Folsom that Fighter Analysis was required to co-operate in assembling the material; but that was all. The purpose of the report was to present a digest of the opinions of the best-qualified fighter pilots on changes which would make a revised manual square with the tactics and technique developed by actual combat experience in all theaters in this war. It was not up to Special Projects to say who was right and who was wrong. The AAF Board would decide on that. It was impossible for Major Whitney to agree that Captain Hicks must be guided by Colonel Folsom's opinions only.

Colonel Folsom answered, somewhat indirectly, that the whole project was a mess and there was no sense in it, and if they wanted to make fools of themselves and Hal Coulthard, go ahead, for all he cared. His only point was that Captain Hicks, there—his dark, even saturnine, profile jerked contemptuously indicating him—had asked for advice; but when he got it, he gave out that he knew more about aerial combat than Colonel Folsom did. Which Colonel Folsom sincerely doubted. He, Colonel Folsom, here and now, washed his hands of the matter; and, as he had a good deal to do this morning, that would be all.

Major Whitney said, "I don't envy you. You're liable to get thrown out on your ear. He's liable to think you've decided to take over his Directorate—"

"Maybe I will decide to," Nathaniel Hicks said. "Whether he can believe it or not, I do know more about fighter tactics than he does. I showed some of his diagrams to Wiley at Orlando. Wiley's comment was: 'That son of a bitch and his string formation would last over Germany about two minutes.' Speaking of that, Wiley ought to be here tomorrow. I spoke to Beaudry and the Charts and Plans Section will have a man to lay out Wiley's diagrams—"

There was a sound of steps and voices in the hall. In the doorway stood a tall, chocolate-colored Negro. He was in his shirt sleeves, carrying a blue serge coat over his arm. He was also carrying a straw hat and a worn leather brief case. He looked very warm. Seeing the three officers turned staring at him, he hesitated. Lieutenant Edsell appeared then at his elbow, took his arm and walked him firmly into the room.

Lieutenant Edsell looked very warm, too. His dark hair was disordered. He wiped his hand over his stubborn large nose which, like the rest of his face, shone with sweat. There was a tinge of color on his prominent cheekbones, and his dark eyes had a gleam which Nathaniel Hicks recognized as meaning that he was deeply and excitingly engaged in some contest or argument.

Giving his head a jerk, Lieutenant Edsell glanced at the three of them, and said loudly and coolly: "Bill, this is Al James of the *National Freeman.* Major Whitney, Al—Captain Pound—well, hell, Bob, when did that happen?—Major Pound, it seems; and Captain, or are you a major, too, Nat?—Hicks. Mr. James—"

Getting off his desk edge, Major Whitney nodded awkwardly, and Major Pound, arising, too, glanced at him, and then nodded himself. They drew away slightly toward the door to Whitney's office. Lieutenant Edsell showed a trace of a fleeting, almost triumphant smile. It was plain that the uneasy involuntary movement pleased him.

Nathaniel Hicks, who had been leaning back in his chair with his hands behind his head, was annoyed to see Edsell getting away with it. He arose, came around the corner of his desk, and held his hand out. "How are you, Mr. James?" he said expansively. "Anything we can do for you?"

He was correct, he saw, in thinking this would take a little wind out of Lieutenant Edsell's sails. He almost laughed, for Edsell's momentary expression was chagrin. Lieutenant Edsell said: "Sit down, Al. I'm going to call up Colonel Jobson's Executive." To Nathaniel Hicks, he said, "It's a stupid damn snafu. Al, here, came down to do a piece on the colored medium-bombardment group project. The War Department accredited him. In fact, the Air Forces Group of the BPR in Washington asked him to come down. Public Relations, here, gets him a gate pass and puts in to Colonel Mowbray's office for clearance.

That little rat Botwinick says it will have to have General Beal's personal approval, and it won't be possible for the general to consider it until late this afternoon because he will want Colonel Jobson's agreement before he authorizes anyone to interview the men in one of Jobson's projects. I thought I'd just call Major Blake, and tell him here is practically a War Department directive, and can't he speak for Jobson. The colonel's off getting in his flying time or something—"

Major Whitney, tightening his lips, said, "If I were you, I wouldn't mess into it too much, Jim. If Mowbray's office says you have to have the general's personal clearance, you both better sit still until you get it—"

"We'll get it," Lieutenant Edsell said. "Don't worry! Phillips went over to see Botwinick. He'll see Mowbray, if Botwinick won't give. I think I can talk Blake into—"

"Well, before you do," Major Whitney said, "come in here a minute. We have a lot of stuff this morning. I was waiting for you to get back—"

Nathaniel Hicks's telephone rang. It proved to be the colonel's secretary. She said: "Colonel Coulthard wants you right away, Captain. He's going over to the general's." Hanging up, Nathaniel Hicks said to Major Whitney: "I'm off."

Major Whitney cleared his throat. He looked at Mr. James. He said: "I'm afraid Lieutenant Edsell is going to be tied up for a while, and Captain Hicks is going to have to go out. Because of security regulations, we can't leave you alone in this office. Major Pound will bring you down to Reception, and you will have to stay there—"

Lieutenant Edsell said, "Wait, Bill. Let me call Blake. I can probably get the whole thing straightened up in five minutes, and you can show me the stuff then. Sit down, Al."

Major Whitney, quite white, said: "Lieutenant, what I just gave were orders. Major Pound, take this man down to Reception."

COLONEL Ross walked wearily into his office.

Lieutenant Colonel Howden, the Counter-Intelligence Officer, and Major Sears were both waiting; and since they were always punctual, they had surely been waiting twenty minutes. "Sorry, Luke; Johnny," he said. "We got tied up with the Old Man—"

Staff Sergeant Brooks, who was smoking a cigar at his desk by the window, got to his feet and said: "Judge, before you begin—just two things, sir. One, Mrs. Ross called and said she would not repeat not be at the Officers Club for lunch. She is there now, at Red Cross; but she has to go downtown with Mrs. Beal when they break, and won't be back until after two. The other: I have it written here—" He handed Colonel Ross a strip of paper on which were typed the words: *Colored Flight Officer TD Project o-336-3 Personnel Analysis did not wish give name feels should advise certain project personnel intend creating disturbance Area Officers Club approximately 2000 today.*

"Yes, I know about that," Colonel Ross said. "What did you make of this fellow?"

Sergeant Brooks shrugged. "Scared, sir. Trying to fix himself in case something happened. He wouldn't have told me, otherwise. He would have waited to see you. He didn't dare stay around here; but he wanted to get on the record."

"That's funny. All the people who come to Colonel Mowbray's office and tell Botty things do it because they have a high sense of duty."

"I bet," Sergeant Brooks said. He gathered up some papers and his half-smoked cigar, and went into the other room, where Miss Miller and Mrs. Eliot were typing, and closed the door carefully.

Colonel Ross held the strip of paper out to Lieutenant Colonel Howden. "This is something we may have a little trouble about," he said. "Botty got hold of it earlier from one of his Charges of Quarters. We've discussed the matter with the general. I don't like the position we're in; but we're in it.

The order is out, and separate Club facilities have been designated for the project. Show it to Johnny."

When Major Sears had read it, Colonel Ross said: "Now, here's what you do. I want you to have one of your best officers—Lieutenant Day, if he's as good as you think, at the Club right after supper. I want him armed; with an MP brassard. I want two patrol jeeps parked in the drive by the main entrance. Your officer will be in the bar. The bar has been instructed by Major Seely, the Club Officer, to refuse service to project personnel. When those who have asked for service are refused, I want your man to explain to them that the facilities of this Club are for permanent party personnel only. I want him to offer them a lift to the Project Club. He is not to put it as an order. I want it done with judgment."

"Yes," Major Sears said. "Day's the man. Would you give me the overall pitch, Judge?"

"It's fairly simple," Colonel Ross said. "Coming up to the Club, these boys will get a good look at the patrol jeeps outside. Inside, they'll find one of the Provost Marshal's officers right there when service is refused them. If he then speaks to them politely and offers to show them their own Club, I think, I hope, they'll just fold up."

Major Sears said, frowning: "You don't think it would be better to put Day at the door, stop them there? My experience, Judge, is that it's easier to keep people out than put them out."

"Not in this case," Colonel Ross said. "The plan, as it was reported to us, and it sounds likely, is for a certain number to come down, one or two at a time, and walk in quietly, and see what happens. The first few will be the leading spirits. If they aren't allowed in at all, they may go back and get the others together; if we let them in—the patrol details will, of course, pay no attention to them when they come up to the door—and confront them with a confusing situation, I think there's a good chance they will leave themselves. They'll have to decide very fast whether they're going to make a fuss, knowing the Provost Marshal has his men ready and waiting, or whether they're going to fall in with a civil suggestion that they didn't know that this was a Club for the permanent party only, and go along to their own Club. If they do go, that should be the end of the whole business. Some of them—this fellow who came over here wouldn't be the only one—can't be too keen about it, anyway. It's worth trying. What do you think, Luke?"

Lieutenant Colonel Howden scratched his head. He tapped the strip of paper: "Of course," he said, "if this fellow will talk, testify to the existence of a concerted plan to act contrary to regulations—I don't approve of fooling with things like that. If we know in advance, have the dope on them, I say smack them hard, before they ever get started. I'd get the fellow who wrote this. I'd make him give me a signed statement. I'd get whatever evidence Botty has, get it signed and sworn to. Then I'd put the whole lot of them under arrest, confront them with my evidence. I think, that way, they'd fold up even quicker than if you have one of Johnny's men babying them along. And it is babying them along! Didn't know this Club was for permanent party only! That's up to them. They'd better read orders, understand regulations. I mean, we're acting as if it were all right for them not to. No, Judge, it's wrong! They obey orders, comply with regulations; or we crack down."

Colonel Ross said: "That order of ours is, itself, contrary to AAF Regulations. I'll go along with Pop that, sometimes, in some places, it may have been the only way to keep the peace. We don't all obey all the regulations all of the time. But if there's trouble, and the trouble comes because you didn't follow the regulation provided, you're going to take a beating. Arrest those people; and you've got to charge them; and they can demand a court martial—no, that you don't want."

Lieutenant Colonel Howden, his long face set and stubborn, said: "All right. Even so. It needn't ever actually come to charges and specifications—court martial. You can arrest them, show them what you have on them, explain Article Sixty-six to them. Let's see whether they want to be up for mutiny or sedition, and suffer death or such other punishment as a court martial may direct."

"You couldn't make Sixty-six stick," Colonel Ross said impatiently.

"I never said you could, Judge." Lieutenant Colonel Howden's face lost some of its harshness in an expression nearly pleasant. "But you could scare the pants off them if you did it right! You could tell them, on the other hand, if they agreed to comply with regulations, they would be released from arrest and no charges would be brought. I just don't like that Club business, that waiting to see what they do. They have to realize they're subject to military law. We don't need to outsmart them, fool them, into doing what we say. The CG tells them what to do, and they damn well better do it."

Colonel Ross looked at him; but it was clear that Lieutenant Colonel Howden, no joker, was not being ironic. To him, there was no inconsistence. Forcing patience on himself, Colonel Ross said, though not without dryness: "Well, now we're getting somewhere, Luke. The CG told me what to do; and I've told Johnny; and he damn well better do it."

"Yes, sir," said Major Sears, grinning.

Lieutenant Colonel Howden said: "You don't kid me, Judge. I think somebody told the CG what to do, and told *him* he'd damn well better do it. And I'll bet it wasn't Pop."

"Colonel Mowbray concurred in the recommended action," Colonel Ross said. "Now, I'll tell you something else. Still another reason why we don't want any trouble. We got word this morning that Washington accredited a man and sent him down here to write up the project for the Negro press. That man is here. He is right over in the Public Relations office now. Colonel Mowbray is going to hold him off until tomorrow. Colonel Jobson has been briefed, and he flew out to Washington an hour ago to protest, on the general's behalf, to the Chief of Air Staff against allowing a write-up of an experimental project before it's even underway. I think we can get the War Department clearance cancelled. I think somebody got too smart in the Bureau of Public Relations."

Major Sears, standing up, said, "Damn if there aren't a lot of newspapers in this world! I told Luke about the other thing, Judge—the check on Headquarters personnel."

Lieutenant Colonel Howden said: "Judge, we'll do it; but I warn you, I don't think we'll get anywhere if you don't want them questioned directly. When Johnny called me, I had the records checked. There are forty-five civilians we'll have to find out about. You can't find out about that many without someone getting wind of it; and then you've probably tipped off the ones you're looking for. I think we'd do better to plant a different phoney item of the kind that's leaked in the classified material of each Headquarters section, and see which item or items turn up in the paper. Then we simply crack down on that office and give their personnel a going-over."

"Luke," Colonel Ross said, "I love you dearly, and I will go into that some other time. Now, I have to get back to the general's office. Steve!"

Sergeant Brooks opened the door.

"I'm going. Call Vera if you have to find me. She'll know where I am."

"Judge," Sergeant Brooks said, "you got an inspection schedule this afternoon. Going to keep it?"

"What is it?"

"WAC Area mess, barracks, and facilities."

"Oh, Lord!" Colonel Ross said. "All right. Tell the Staff Director I will be there at fourteen hundred."

✦

The new Officers Club was a substantial building of white-washed concrete-block set on an almost imperceptible rise above a small pond at the south end of the AFORAD Area. The pond, as was generally the case with the many ponds found in and around the small central Florida cities, was called a lake—Lake Titania. Two other ponds within the Area were named respectively Lake Oberon and Lake Thisbe. The existence of three "lakes" in the Area had adversely affected the architect's plan for the Club. The structure was well suited to the setting and climate. It enclosed on three sides an ample patio with arched, tile-paved, screen loggias. In the patio there should have been a pool surrounded by coconut palms. The coconut palms were there; but no pool. Pools were conventionally designated as auxiliary reservoirs for use in case of fire. In view of the fact that Lakes Titania, Oberon, and Thisbe were already storing in the Area millions of gallons of water for use in case of fire, the pool had to be disapproved.

Behind the screened arches of the long shadowed loggia on the west side a range of trestles had been set up with boards laid on them. This immense table was surrounded by chairs. Fifty or sixty of the chairs were occupied by women, all with cheese-cloth veils bound over their hair. They were engaged patiently and busily in folding more cheese-cloth into surgical dressings, a pastime more or less obligatory Fridays on the wives, and any other adult females of the families, of officers attached to AFORAD. The good example was set for them by General Beal's wife. She sat at one end of the great table, from time to time squirming to ease the discomfort caused a thin person by the hard wood slats of the chairs. She worked quickly and inefficiently, folding the smallest size of dressing, many of which she was obliged to refold when the Red Cross supervisor passed along the table and looked at the accumulated piles of work.

On Mrs. Beal's right, working more slowly, careful and deft, Mrs. Ross was doing the largest size of dressing, only allowed to experts. Next to her sat Mrs. Jobson, Colonel Jobson's wife, also doing the largest size of dressing. Mrs. Jobson, a stout woman, had pinned on her enormous bosom an appalling ornament in the form of a replica of her husband's Command Pilot wings set with jewels.

Mrs. Jobson said to Mrs. Ross: "Graham's just had to fly to Washington. I'm sure I don't know why. It's so inconvenient. Graham makes me give these buffet suppers and ask five or six of his officers with their wives, if their wives are here; and we have some tonight, and I don't know any of them from Adam. I don't even know which ones, so I can't postpone it. It is really too hard, with no help but these utterly worthless and undependable colored girls. I'd certainly fire mine, except the next one would be worse, and would want more money. Do you know Major Blake, my husband's Executive, and his wife? Very nice people, of the highest standing in Cleveland. Banking. Rosemary Blake told me yesterday that one girl she interviewed said flatly she would not work for less than—"

Mrs. Beal, who had been restlessly waiting on this almost endless monologue, now put out her hand and clasped Mrs. Ross's left arm. "Cora!" she said sharply.

Mrs. Jobson gave her a covertly hostile or affronted look, but necessarily yielded. "Cora," Mrs. Beal repeated, "I just thought of something. Something I saw at that other store. We might go there first—"

Mrs. Jobson waited a moment. Then laboriously, with an air of restrained offense, she arose, and passed down the loggia in the direction of the so-called Powder Room. Mrs. Beal said: "Praise God! Gab, gab, gab! The only thing is, I don't know how much money I ought to spend. What do you spend when you get presents for Norm?" She giggled. "We never used to have any trouble because we never had any money when Ira was a captain. Then he was away so much. I want to get him something nice, only if I spend too much he'll be sore. He keeps wanting to save some money. He says it's one thing to be a major general, with flying pay, and everything; but what about when the war's over? You know, he isn't even a permanent major yet. If the war was over tomorrow, he might have to just take those stars off and get out his captain's bars again." She smiled. "Colonel Jobson *is* a Major, USA," she whispered. "How would I like that? Oh, mama!"

She raised her chin and swept the long table with an imperial glance. "We've got a lot of people here this morning," she said, "do you think we could sneak out a little early? I suppose not." She moistened her lips with the tip of her tongue. "Oh, my poor fanny," she said, squirming. "These damn chairs!" She was silent an instant, her face intent and brooding. "Cora," she said suddenly, "I want to ask you something, sometime. It is a kind of intimate question. I don't want to ask you now, with that big cow maybe coming back any minute. I'll ask you when we get in the car. I have to ask somebody older. I have to know what you think."

Mrs. Ross said kindly: "Of course, Sal. I'll tell you anything I can."

Mrs. Beal said: "It's because I'm worried sick about Ira. He didn't get any sleep at all last night. He was stewing about Benny. He wouldn't even tell me what Benny did—he got into some trouble, I guess." Venomously, she said: "I'm good and tired of this Benny, Benny, Benny! I hope he did something bad. Ira just says: 'Don't bother me, will you, I'm worried about Benny, Benny, Benny!' Well, I know Benny has been running with this girl, and I hope he's in trouble about it, that's all I hope. She's a married woman, only her husband is in the Navy, and she lives with her father who has a lot of money—when she isn't living with Benny and that drunk Engineering Officer who used to be a prize fighter or something, that Captain Dyer who has the apartment with him. It's just disgusting!"

✦

The morning sun was bright and hot on the slats of the blinds; but they were tilted enough to keep the room in a stifling gloom.

Lieutenant Colonel Carricker went to the table by the window. Over his shoulder he said: "Now, shut up, Jane! I'm not asking you what I want to do. And you just stay there."

From a half-filled bottle of Porto Rican rum he poured a good deal in a glass. His solid body, harnessed with the marks of skin grafts was covered with sweat. Swaying a little, he drank the rum down.

She said: "I have to get home! Sweetheart, I've been here all night. Look what time in the morning it is! Daddy's bound to know I wasn't with—"

"You're not going anywhere," Lieutenant Colonel Carricker said. He came back to the bed.

Gasping, she said: "No, no, sweetheart! Ah, don't—"

The door opened abruptly, and she made a weak effort to pull together the damp and wrinkled dressing gown in which she lay. She said tormentedly: "Gus, please! Will you please stay out of here?"

Captain Dyer said: "Now, look, Benny. The general says you're to report right away. They've called twice. You better get up there."

Without raising his head, Lieutenant Colonel Carricker said: "Who's calling?"

"Botwinick, again."

"Tell him what he can do. I'm in arrest in quarters. If they want me, they can come and get me."

"See if I give a good goddamn, chum," Captain Dyer said. "I have to be on the line. I'm leaving now." He closed the door.

✦

In the dining room of the Headquarters Mess the Children's Hour was reaching its end. The coffee cups were pushed aside and the table was animatedly proceeding with Colonel Mowbray's coin-matching game which determined who would pay.

Colonel Mowbray slapped down his quarter, keeping it covered with his hand. "All right, you three," he said, "this is for odd man now." He lowered his grizzled head and peered cautiously under his palm.

Entering the room with an efficient unobtrusiveness Mr. Botwinick materialized silently two paces from Colonel Mowbray's elbow. Here, he uttered a gentle cough.

Colonel Mowbray, not taking his eyes off the game, said: "Now, what, Botty?"

Mr. Botwinick advanced another pace, bent his mouth to the colonel's ear, and whispered: "We cannot reach him, sir. I am afraid, from what the captain said, he may be intoxicated. Under the circumstances, would you wish to send down for him?"

Colonel Mowbray pursed his lips. He assumed an expression of reflective sagacity. Out of the corner of his mouth, he murmured: "May turn out just as well. Stop calling him. Tell Colonel Ross that we find the officer is in no condition to carry out his plan, and say I suggest postponing it. Anything else?"

"Lieutenant Phillips, Public Relations, is in the office, sir. He insists on waiting to see you. He says in view of the

WDBPR authorization he feels that it is vitally important to clear that man without delay."

"He feels, does he? You tell him he is meddling in matters that don't concern him. Tell him I want no more argument. The man is not going to be cleared today. He will not be allowed to interview project personnel. That's definite and final. Furthermore, I want him, James, whatever his name is, off the post immediately. Tell the lieutenant to get him, escort him personally to the gate, and then to report to me that he has left. I'll expect that report in not more than fifteen minutes. Go after it."

"Yes, sir," Mr. Botwinick said. He left with alacrity.

"Sorry, gentlemen," Colonel Mowbray said. He lifted his hand. "I have heads," he said.

All the coins exposed were heads; so he said: "Well, we'll have to do it again. This is still for odd man—"

✦

In the railed enclosure, beyond the passage to the door, Mr. James had been left seated on a wooden bench by Major Pound. He sat stolidly and patiently, ignoring the idle, surprised glances of the many people coming and going. Beyond the reception desk and the rail a number of enlisted men, Wacs, and civilian girls worked at typewriters, walked around collecting or distributing papers. Buzzers sounded; telephone bells rang; messengers and mail orderlies trotted in and out.

Opposite the bench, on the long wall was a big bulletin board whose top was crowned by artistically cut-out wooden letters reading: ARMY AIR FORCES AFORAD—5 DIRECTORATE OF SPECIAL PROJECTS. The board was divided into panels, each with its own fancy heading: *Research & Development Section; Photographic Section; Charts & Plans Section; Statistical Section; Reports Section.* Each panel was thickly pinned with sheets of paper. On the other walls were posters urging the purchase of bonds, warning about the dangers of espionage and sabotage, showing symbolically the Four Freedoms; stating that the target was Tokyo, that the target was Berlin. Suspended on wires, a great armada of black metal model airplanes hung in midair. They were keyed on a posted chart headed WEFT, under which somebody had scrawled in crayon (*Wrong Every Time*).

When half an hour had passed, Mr. James got up from the hard bench. He stood a moment, with nobody paying any attention to him. He moved toward the door. Down the long corridor to the right, a short man with glasses, a captain, approached, walking perkily and whistling. He looked benevolently, though with surprise, at Mr. James.

Mr. James said, "Captain, I wonder if you would be kind enough to direct me to the—" he looked at a scrap of paper in his hand—"Directorate of Personnel Analysis?"

The captain said heartily: "That's not here, my friend. This is Special Projects. How did you get here?"

"I was brought here by an officer who was going to take me to Personnel Analysis. I think he had to do something else, and I think I better not wait much longer. I am supposed to be interviewing some people there." He turned over his folded coat and displayed an Area Pass Badge.

The captain said genially: "I'm Captain Solomon, Special Projects Adjutant. Come along. Got a jeep out here. I'm going over that way, as it happens. I'll drop you off. How's that?"

"That would be mighty fine, Captain; if it's no trouble—"

"No trouble at all. What's your job? Are you working in the office there?"

"No, Captain, I'm from Washington. I'm down as a representative of the press. I have been authorized to write a piece on the proposed colored bombardment group. I wanted to interview some of the men."

"That so? Well, we'll fix you up in short order. Unless I'm very much mistaken, your men are in the Personnel Analysis Auditorium building for a lecture or something. I was going by about half an hour ago and I happened to notice, now you mention it, a lot of colored officers going in there. I'll drop you, and you can be there when they come out."

They went through the screened doors together, down the steps, and Captain Solomon waved up a jeep which waited with several others in the poor shade of a clump of poor pines. "Hop in!" he said to Mr. James. To the driver, he said, "Go by Personnel Analysis Auditorium, Mike, will you?"

◆

General Beal said: "All right, Hicks; off you go! Get your letter authenticated by Colonel Mowbray's office; and you'd better work out a schedule, so they can notify the local Commanding Officers that you're coming. You want to fly?"

"Well, sir," Nathaniel Hicks said, "if it's not too much—I mean, I suppose if I could have a car, I could manage as well—"

"You better fly," the general said. "You can have Lieutenant Noble, then I'll be sure you get there." He touched a key on the box and said: "Have Noble stand by with an AT-Six to fly out an officer after lunch." He leaned back in his chair, yawned, and said to Colonel Coulthard, "Weren't you at Rockwell when Woody was there, Hal? I was trying to think yesterday. Woody doesn't look too good. Neither does Sellers—tarpaper post, practically in a damn swamp. He thinks somebody's got a knife into him."

"How's that bottle coming along?" Colonel Coulthard said.

"He ought to lay off that; but I doubt if he will. He didn't like giving me the plane. I was sorry to take it when I saw what a stew he was in. I mean, it was just one more thing. Well, I guess he'll make out—"

Nathaniel Hicks debated with himself a moment. He then said: "General, I think I should tell you that I had a call this morning from the Operations Officer at Sellers Field in connection with the project I went up to see him about." He paused, finding himself at loss for words.

General Beal looked at him, surprised.

"He told me, sir," Nathaniel Hicks continued, "that he supposed word would have reached you. I gather it hasn't."

"What word?" General Beal said. "I don't think I follow this, Captain."

Nathaniel Hicks said: "I thought perhaps you'd better know,

sir, that the Operations Officer told me that Colonel Woodman last night shot himself to death."

IV

THE WHOLE morning had been upsetting, with too many things going on at once. Counting his own pulse, Colonel Ross could tell that his blood pressure, which troubled him occasionally, must be up, close to the point where the headache would begin. He took a pill and put the matter from his mind. The symptoms—where they were tending, where they were bound to end—disturbed him, of course; yet he was a good deal less disturbed now than when he first noticed them a few years ago. After all, the season was turning for his whole generation. You could tell the time of year, if you were a man of wide acquaintanceship, by the regular appearance in the obituary columns of the names of people you knew, or used to know. The size of it was: everybody over fifty lived under a definitive sentence of some kind, suspended during good behavior, perhaps. Nothing could be done about it; and while this acknowledgment might be regarded as a calm of despair, it was at least a calm. The last, best recourse was what it always had been: you thought of something else.

Colonel Ross did not lack other things to think about. Coming from his own office to the general's, after he had talked to Lieutenant Colonel Howden and Major Sears, he was intercepted in the hall by Mr. Botwinick. Mr. Botwinick, with the efficient, guarded brevity of a trained conspirator, murmured that Colonel Carricker was too drunk to report. To the best of Colonel Ross's knowledge, this was an unusual thing for Carricker to be at any time, let alone, at eleven in the morning.

Benny, then, recognized that he had troubles. Benny's limited world of hot pilots and hard men had its conventions, like other worlds. When its inmates found what they called All This Crap—the Army's arbitrary regulations and discipline—too much for them, they lodged their protest and demanded redress by getting stinking—really a ceremonial rite, undertaken with solemnity and deliberation. It showed that they were unhappy, and even, in a confused way, sorry. They wished they hadn't done it; but, like themselves, their regrets were rough and tough, their sorrow was of no whining, supine sort. Everybody could still go to hell.

Colonel Ross did not care much. It was clear that the matter was now beyond the stage where Benny's apology would be useful. Colonel Mowbray, through no fault of his own, had come to be right. The whole matter of Benny would better be postponed, at least until tomorrow. The evils thereof were sufficient unto today.

Colonel Ross intended so to advise General Beal. Bus would recognize the significance of Benny's being drunk. Under the stern face he was required as commander to put on, he might even respect Benny for acting exactly as any boy ought to act who was a honey; whose flying exploits were genius, God, were murder!

Colonel Ross went through the back rooms to Mrs. Pellerino's office. Mrs. Pellerino was distributing papers to the two girls who did the typing. When she saw Colonel Ross, she came over to him quickly. "I think you can go right in, sir," she said. "He's alone. Colonel Coulthard and a captain of his left by the other door some time ago." She moistened her lips uneasily, and speaking in a whisper said: "He was just calling Sellers Field, Colonel. He has just confirmed, I don't know whether you know, that Colonel Woodman, up there, shot himself. I thought if you didn't know—"

Colonel Ross was jolted.

Not normally a profane man, he ejaculated to himself: *God damn him to hell!* The shock of surprise had colored at once with an anger and disgust directed at poor Woody who, like the sot and the imbecile he was, took care to make his death the occasion for still another mess. Getting a grip on this senseless anger, he said calmly: "I didn't know. Thanks, Vera. Is it, ah, classified?"

"He knows that I know, sir. He asked me to transcribe the call."

"Good," said Colonel Ross, though he was far from thinking it was.

Mrs. Pellerino, back at her desk, glanced at him, and he nodded. She touched the key on the box and said: "Colonel Ross, General."

General Beal sat at his desk.

He said with composure, "Judge, I'm going over to the Base. If you have anything, ride over with me. I'm going flying."

"All right," Colonel Ross said.

General Beal said: "I'm going to take a Forty-seven up. I just want to fly around awhile. I'm not going anywhere." With no change of tone, he said: "Your man Hicks, Hal's man, had word Woody killed himself last night. I checked on it. It's true. Look, I don't think I do want you to come over with me, Judge. Anything you've got will keep, won't it?"

"Yes," Colonel Ross said. "It will keep." In this new distress of mind, the general would not want to be troubled about Benny. The unchanged tone disturbed him a little, and he said: "I'm sorry, Bus."

"Oh, the hell!" General Beal said. "Don't think I think the poor bastard shot himself because I took his plane away, anything like that. I'm not crazy. I just don't feel like sitting here; so I told Danny to get the Forty-seven he was working on out for me. I may see how high I can take it—something like that."

"That's a good idea," Colonel Ross said. "You could do that right over the field. Don't fly a fighter plane cross-country without a wingman along, Bus. It may be silly; but they weren't fooling about that. General Arnold would be very sore."

"I know," General Beal said. "I won't go away. I'll keep in touch with the Tower. There's the car, I guess. Hold the fort, will you, Judge?"

The fort, Colonel Ross decided, could be held as well from his own office, where he had work to do; but he did not get forward with the work. An unreasonable despondency filled him, an absurd superstitious conviction that, today, all their luck was out. Everything that could go wrong, would. He did not accept it; he opposed it with a firm mind; but not so firm that, after a half an hour, he could keep from calling Base Operations.

General Beal, flying a P-47, had taken off. Subsequently he had checked in twice, the last time about five minutes ago. He stated he was approximately over the field at thirty thousand feet, climbing. Did Colonel Ross want them to contact him? Colonel Ross said no; he merely wanted to hear whether he got off.

Against the remonstrances of reason, there stayed in his mind that silly ill-ease, the apprehensive pricking of the imagination which saw—and saw with clarity, with an alarming hint of veridical hallucination—Bus thundering slower and slower, driving up and up his P-47, a plane he had flown only once or twice before. Now, he was miles high, mushing, nearly slumping, in the rare air, the world lost under him in a vaporous haze. Mask clamped on his face, mouth raw from sucking pure oxygen, eyes goggling blankly at his dials, he was remote, beyond all aid, on his own, as much alone as a man dying; and this was not his lucky day.

The Operations Officer cut in then, saying: "Colonel Ross? Excuse me, sir. We had a message for you here from Colonel Mowbray about twenty minutes ago. I believe he thought you came over to the Base with General Beal. We were trying to find you. They said it was urgent; will you call his office?"

✦

The Headquarters Quadrangle buildings were air conditioned, so, though the temperature stood at 93 degrees outside at one o'clock, the windowless Staff Conference Room was cool enough. The surface of the long oak table, wider at one end than at the other, was flooded evenly with artificial daylight from fluorescent lamps. The walls were draped from floor to ceiling with folds of heavy red cloth drawn together to hide military situation maps and statistical tables posted with secret data.

When Colonel Mowbray's message finally reached him

Colonel Ross, who had not had lunch, sent Sergeant Brooks for a pint of milk and a couple of sandwiches which he brought into the conference room. When you breakfast at six-thirty, you get hungry by noon; and Colonel Ross, when he got hungry, knew that he got irritable. Methodically, he lowered the level of milk in the cardboard container through two straws and ate the sandwiches, allowing Colonel Mowbray to do the talking.

Colonel Mowbray was repeating himself. He wanted, he said, to get to the bottom of this. He did not like it; he did not understand it; and responsibility would have to be assigned and appropriate action taken. His audience, besides Colonel Ross, included Colonel Coulthard, of Special Projects, who had a bewildered air—no doubt, Colonel Coulthard didn't like it and didn't understand it, either. With him was his Adjutant, Captain Solomon, who kept smiling nervously. Also with him, though farther down the table, were Major Whitney and Lieutenant Edsell, of the Reports Section. On the other side were Captain Collins, the Public Relations Officer, and his Lieutenant Phillips. Next to them were Major Sears and an MP lieutenant of his named Kashkin. Mr. Botwinick sat beside Colonel Mowbray with a stenographic notebook. Among so many other things, Mr. Botwinick was an expert stenographer. Across from Colonel Mowbray was Major Blake, Executive of the Directorate of Personnel Analysis. There were, in short, far too many people here. On one of his ill-considered impulses, Colonel Mowbray must have summoned everyone he could think of who might possibly know anything about it. The undesirable result would be that all of them, in exchange for their trifles of information, learned much that it was not necessary for them to know.

Colonel Mowbray, having made his general remarks twice (or three times; or four times; for all Colonel Ross knew; assuredly Colonel Mowbray had not been sitting in silence while they waited for Colonel Ross) said: "Now, I hope it's clear to you that this is a very unfortunate and very serious matter. I don't know who's to blame, yet. I want to hear everybody's side of it. I want somebody, whoever can, to just start at the beginning. I want to plot out the movements of this fellow, this James man, from the time he turned up at the gate and was given an Area pass to the time he left."

Major Blake, who looked well-fed but was probably as hungry as Colonel Ross, touched the end of a mustache which while not waxed, was so neatly trimmed that it looked waxed. He said, with an air of great consequence: "I think that lets out PA, Pop. We know nothing about it whatsoever. Of course, Colonel Jobson mentioned the purpose of his trip to me, so I knew something was up, and I knew in general what it was. That is, I knew this nigger had turned up; but I also knew he wasn't to be cleared; and I certainly don't know how he got over to the Personnel Analysis Auditorium."

"Well, that's what we're here to find out," Colonel Mowbray said. "And I think you'd better stand by, Evan, if you will."

Captain Collins said: "I can start at what I guess is the beginning, sir."

Colonel Ross knew that Captain Collins had been sports editor for a large city newspaper, though he could not remember what city. Though he was now in his middle thirties, wearing glasses, and somewhat filled-out and softened, it was evident still that there had been a time when Captain Collins was an athlete himself—probably a football player at one of the big state universities where football was a business. It required, as well as more strength and speed, more brains, at least in the backfield, than were normal in the players of Eastern colleges, where football remained partly a sport. Captain Collins had a good-natured, well-featured face—outward evidence of a basic unexcitable assurance which often develops in a growing boy who looks able to knock down almost anyone, if he wants to. When you look that way, you don't have to be in a hurry about taking offense; and most other youths are in no hurry to offer it.

Captain Collins said calmly and mildly: "We got this call from the gate a little after eight o'clock. Mr. James had his War Department clearances, and a letter, attention PRO, signed by the Chief, Air Forces Group, Bureau of Public Relations in Washington. I told them to give him an Area pass; and I sent Lieutenant Phillips down to get him and bring him to the office." He closed his mouth composedly and sat silent.

Colonel Ross, who did not know Captain Collins very well, gave him in his mind a favorable mark, recognizing that astuteness, much too rare in human beings and almost unteachable, which never said unneeded words; and having said those that were needed, simply stopped and waited with attention but not impatience, for the response.

It was now up to Colonel Mowbray, who, not a very astute man, was taken aback by this competence of mind and manner. He cleared his throat in the silence. "Well," he said, "I suppose that's in order. Assuming, of course, his papers were genuine—"

Major Sears said: "That's our responsibility, of course, Colonel. They are required at the gate to satisfy themselves about the authenticity of any credentials presented before passing the bearer in. If we find out his papers were forged—"

"That isn't in question," Colonel Mowbray said. "Nobody says he had forged papers. I just want to get this straight, step by step. Have you anything further to say, Captain?"

Captain Collins looked at the palm of his hand reflectively. "I think not, sir," he said. "That, as far as I had anything to do with it, was how he came to be admitted, how he got his Area pass."

"Well," said Colonel Mowbray, "didn't you call my office and request a clearance?"

"Yes, sir," Captain Collins said. "That was after Mr. James was admitted, when he was in our office. Mr. James showed me his stuff, and explained what he had come for. We then put through to clear it with you."

"I know that. No, go on about that."

"I don't quite understand you, Colonel. That is all I know about that."

"What did my office tell you?"

Groaning silently, Colonel Ross contained himself by taking the last of his second sandwich in a large bite and chewing it.

"Why, sir, I believe your office, Mr. Botwinick—" Captain

Collins nodded toward him—"told us he would call back when he had consulted you. I think he said you were in with the general."

"And did he call you back?"

"I believe that he did."

"Don't you know, Captain?"

"Well, I was told so, sir. I didn't talk to him myself. Lieutenant Phillips took the call. I was out."

"Where were you?"

Captain Collins looked at him placidly. "Well, sir, as a matter of fact, I was in the can."

Colonel Coulthard emitted a grunt of laughter; and, thus encouraged, there were several smiles. To pay back despitefully, preferably with interest, the man who got them laughed at would be the natural next move of most people sitting in Colonel Mowbray's autocratic and powerful position. Colonel Mowbray blinked, and displayed instead that disarming, simpleminded magnanimity which so greatly inconvenienced Colonel Ross whenever he was about to pass a just judgment on Colonel Mowbray's character. The laugh, though more or less on him, was his own fault. Colonel Mowbray conceded it. He said, peering almost apologetically at Captain Collins: "Well, that's right, of course. It's immaterial where you were. I see that. I just wanted to get everything straight. You were out of the office. Now, what was it you were told by the lieutenant about Mr. Botwinick's message—"

"Pop!" Colonel Ross said. Though he admired magnanimity as much as anyone, though he even marveled at this saintlike little display of it, he never had been able to suffer a blundering examination silently. "Mightn't it be simpler to ask the lieutenant? Unless, of course, you want to ask Botty to tell us what he said."

"Yes," Colonel Mowbray said, relieved. "I will put that question to the lieutenant, instead. Reason I ask them, Norm, is I know what Botty told them. But they're the only ones that can tell me what they understood my orders to be, after Botty transmitted them. I want to get at the reasons for what happened next. Can you answer, Lieutenant?"

Lieutenant Phillips was tall, with fair, thin, wavy hair. He had the long, sloping forehead and thin, straight nose that often distinguished, in Judge Ross's experience, a high-strung, voluble witness, quick and fearless, but speaking before he thought. Unless the Bench intervened from time to time to save his story, a hostile attorney, trained to think before he spoke, would soon make a fool of him. When Lieutenant Phillips spoke, his voice, as you would expect, was high and clear. He had the accent, supercilious-sounding to most of the country, of educated New England; or, specifically, Colonel Ross was sure, of Harvard.

Lieutenant Phillips said: "As nearly as I understood it, we were given no orders. We were simply informed that we could not have a clearance for Mr. James because General Beal would have to approve it. As a matter of courtesy to his Directorate Chiefs, the general would not approve it until he knew that it was all right with Colonel Jobson. Colonel Jobson couldn't be reached because he was out getting his flying time." He paused and added: "That last, I gather from what the major, there, said a few minutes ago, was untrue. I gather that the colonel was warned, and then ducked out on it so the general couldn't ask him—"

Colonel Mowbray had disliked the accent at once. Given this good opening, he jumped in hard, with the grating disciplinary bark of the old Army: "I didn't ask what you gathered or didn't gather about Colonel Jobson, Lieutenant. Colonel Jobson has nothing to do with this. All I wanted was your statement of what you understood my message to mean. Do you concur in his statement, Captain?"

Adroitly grasping from the context that "concur" here meant "find correct," and nothing else, Captain Collins nodded. He said: "Yes, Colonel. I mean, I understood that that was the substance of what Mr. Botwinick said on the telephone. I did not understand that we had been given any particular orders."

"Surely you understood that nothing was to be done until General Beal approved the clearance. If not that, what did you make of the message? What did *you* make of it, Lieutenant?"

Lieutenant Phillips shrugged slightly. "Little or nothing,"

he said. "Frankly, I supposed that Mr. Botwinick, for reasons of his own, was disinclined to go to any trouble. I supposed it likely that he hadn't even bothered to mention the request to you."

Barking again, Colonel Mowbray said: "That is an entirely unwarranted supposition, sir! How dare you suppose such a thing? Go on, go on!"

Colonel Ross, his chin on his chest, his feet extended under the table, filled his pipe from a pouch. He looked up through his thick eyebrows in time to see Lieutenant Phillips repeat his slight shrugging movement of the shoulders. It was plain, then, that Lieutenant Phillips had been, literally, the reverse of intimidated by the old Army bark. That could be seen in the shrug, for it was unconscious, not a conscious shrug. The shrug, when it was conscious, was the cowed man's furtive little insolence, the sum of his impotent, frightened resentment. Judge Ross had seen it dozens of times—the shrugger, sore and surly about what the judge just told him, knew that if he didn't comply, the judge had only to speak a word and he would land in jail. He hoped his insulting little gesture would be noticed; but not noticed too much.

Lieutenant Phillips's unconscious shrug meant that his patience was giving out. He had tried to be civil, but enough was enough. Here, then, was a rich boy; or, at least, what had once been a rich boy; used to doing what he pleased. Half the time he would not be seriously opposed, because those with whom he came in contact would give way, believing that if they pleased him they might get a little of his money. When he was opposed and trouble resulted, he need not worry too much; some of the same money would pay the fines.

Lieutenant Phillips said: "Yes, I'll go on, if you want. The supposition seemed very well warranted to me. We had said that Mr. James was a Negro, down to visit a Negro project. I thought it quite possible that your office—and Colonel Jobson's office—" he gave Major Blake a contemptuous glance "—felt that it didn't really matter how they treated what the Major elegantly described as a 'nigger,' or how much of a runaround he was given. What Mr. Botwinick said, I considered mostly nonsense; for the simple reason that I was sure there would have been no difficulty in getting a prompt clearance if Mr. James had been the writer of some nationally syndicated column, instead of a representative of the colored press."

The moment's dead silence that followed, like the fact that Colonel Mowbray did not break in before Lieutenant Phillips finished, that Major Blake who had opened his mouth angrily to tell a second lieutenant where he got off, merely left it open, testified to Lieutenant Phillips's powers of presumption.

That dead silence could last only a moment, so Colonel Ross said instantly: "Aren't you making a good many gratuitous assumptions, Phillips? Did Colonel Mowbray's office ever, as far as you know, behave unfairly to Negroes? Had you, at the time, personal knowledge of definite facts that made Mr. Botwinick's statement to you nonsense? Unless the answer to those questions is yes, I suggest you moderate your language."

The glance Lieutenant Phillips gave him told Colonel Ross (not to his surprise) that he would get no thanks for his timely intervention. Lieutenant Phillips said indifferently: "Colonel Mowbray wanted to know what impression the message made on me. He then seemed to want to know why it made that impression. I have just told him, to the best of my ability."

"Yes," Colonel Mowbray said, finding his voice. "You considered the message I sent mostly nonsense."

"I don't think Lieutenant Phillips meant quite that, Colonel." Captain Collins spoke without haste or excitement, but firmly and loudly, taking and holding the floor. Captain Collins could see his man getting himself into a jam. Whether Captain Collins liked or disliked Lieutenant Phillips would not matter much. The proprietary, paternal instinct of command brought him forward to fight for what the Table of Organization said was his. "He was only trying to tell you what he told me at the time. He was not sure that the message actually did come from you. Anyway, he did not understand that he was being given any order, and neither did I. His job, as he saw it, and as I see it, was to act promptly on the War Department directive to the Commanding General, AFORAD, to clear Mr.

James. When a directive like that reaches us, we naturally take it for granted that the general will want to, and will, comply with it. Lieutenant Phillips was wrong in his opinion that the matter had not been mentioned to you. I don't think he was wrong, when that was his opinion, in trying to check with you personally. That is all he did, sir."

"That was *not* all he did!" Colonel Mowbray said. "His performance was extraordinary! Instead of waiting for General Beal's clearance, he decided to clear the man himself and send him over to the Directorate of Special Projects. Do you deny that, Lieutenant?"

Lieutenant Phillips said icicly: "Certainly I deny that I cleared him myself, or sent him anywhere. That is a deliberate misrepresentation, and you have no right to make it."

Adopting his booming courtroom voice, Colonel Ross said: "No one has the right to misrepresent you, Lieutenant. You, on the other hand, have no right to speak impudently to your superior officer. Don't do it again."

Captain Collins said: "Colonel, I think I am responsible for what my office does. If I may, I will explain as well as I can what was done in this case. I accept all responsibility for the results."

"You don't have to tell me that!" Colonel Mowbray said. "Explain, by all means, if you can. Explain to me why that man, who has not been given a clearance, was permitted to leave your office and to wander around the Area unaccompanied."

"Yes, sir," Captain Collins said. "Mr. James did not leave our office unaccompanied. I can't say how he came to be wandering around later; but I accept the full responsibility—"

From down the table, beyond Colonel Coulthard and Captain Solomon, Major Whitney said: "I don't think the full responsibility is yours, Captain. Not for his being unaccompanied, or for wandering around. I think I'll have to take that. Lieutenant Edsell brought him to our office, and I had some things to discuss with Lieutenant Edsell, so I had the man James escorted out to Special Projects Reception and left there by himself."

Colonel Coulthard, with the same half-jealous alacrity Captain Collins had shown, came forward now to cover his command. He said: "Well, Bill, did you know he hadn't been cleared? Understand he had an Area Pass—" he looked at Captain Solomon, who said: "Yes, Colonel. He had. He showed it to me. I can swear to that—"

Colonel Mowbray said: "A pass does not constitute a clearance. The pass was given him so he could come to the Public Relations Office. It is up to the office that gets the pass issued to comply with regulations. The regulation, and there is no excuse for anyone being ignorant of it, is that a civilian, admitted to the Area on a pass, shall be accompanied at all times by a commissioned officer."

Major Whitney said: "I guess I knew it, all right. I just didn't think. He was accompanied by Lieutenant Edsell until I ordered Lieutenant Edsell to do something else. I should have provided somebody to stay with him—"

"I don't see why you should," Colonel Coulthard said. "My God, we're so short-handed now we don't know where to turn! Why should we have to provide wet-nurses for people on projects that have nothing whatever to do with our Directorate? What I want to know is, who assigned Bill's officer to taking this fellow around? Bill didn't. Now, who did? It was Manny, here, who give the man a lift over to the Personnel Analysis Auditorium, Pop, if that will clear that up. No reason why Manny shouldn't. The fellow showed a pass and said he was trying to find Personnel Analysis. That has my approval. I'll be responsible for that. He hadn't any business with us; so the sooner we got him out, the better. How he got to us; that's another matter—"

Major Whitney said: "Colonel, I gave Lieutenant Edsell permission to go to Captain Collins's office to see this James. I didn't know he was going to bring him back with him; but—"

"Well, now we're getting somewhere," Colonel Coulthard said. "Why did you go to see him, Edsell? What was the idea in bringing him back?"

Lieutenant Edsell said: "I wanted to go over because I knew him, and I thought perhaps I could—"

"Who did you know?"

"Mr. James, Colonel." Lieutenant Edsell looked at Colonel Coulthard with a faint, elvish or perverse smile. "He's an old friend of mine."

Colonel Coulthard looked back with the expression you might expect to see on the face of a man, asked to meet someone's old friend, who found an ostrich nodding civilly to him, or a horse holding out his hoof.

Lieutenant Edsell let his smile grow a little. "I brought him over to our office, sir, because I wanted to talk to him. We had a project yesterday, I was working on it with Captain Andrews, for Personnel Analysis, which I could see was related to this colored bomb project. I thought I might be able to help with the clearance. I had been talking to Colonel Jobson's Executive about the other, our project. I thought if I told him Al James was O.K., he might be willing to tell Colonel Mowbray that Personnel Analysis approved the clearance. I was, of course, unacquainted with Major Blake's racial prejudice—"

Major Blake said: "You're unacquainted with a lot of things, Lieutenant. If you thought I'd approve a clearance without Colonel Jobson's knowledge, you're even stupider than you look. Now, suppose you leave me out of this."

Lieutenant Edsell said almost gleefully: "Where I'll leave you is just where I found you, Fatso! In case you want to make anything out of it, take those brass leaves off and see me behind some barn somewhere. I'll wax your whiskers for you—"

"Here, here, Edsell—" Colonel Coulthard said.

Major Blake who, though fat, looked in good shape, more than a match for Edsell, pushed his chair back, getting to his feet.

"Silence!" Colonel Mowbray roared. "Both of you! Sit down, Evan! Are you crazy? As for you, Lieutenant—"

Colonel Ross said: "Major, you seem to have offended these young men by calling their friend a nigger. It is an opprobrious term. Neither the War Department nor the Army Air Forces countenances its use to or about colored persons. If you must use it, use it in the privacy of your office or your quarters. Lieutenant, the epithet you applied to the Major is also opprobrious. If I understood you to be challenging him to a fist fight, you are insubordinate and disorderly. You will both state in my presence that you withdraw your expressions. Lieutenant?"

Lieutenant Edsell looked at him a moment. "O.K.," he said, "I withdraw them—if he does."

"And do you, Major?"

"Yes, sir; if this is an order."

"It is an order."

"In compliance with your direct order, sir, I withdraw my expression."

Lieutenant Edsell's lips went through a sneer; but he turned it, for present practical purposes decorously enough, Colonel Ross decided, toward the floor beside him. Colonel Ross said: "Pop, I think I'm the only one who's had anything to eat. How about all of you getting some lunch? I think we now have a clear enough idea of what happened. I have an inspection at two o'clock. I'd like a statement, for my own information, and for the record, on the final action taken about Mr. James. Who handled it? Johnny? And did Mr. James actually interview project personnel?"

Major Sears looked at Lieutenant Kashkin, who said: "He had been talking to some of them, sir. I don't know how long, nor what about. My orders were to find him, lift his pass, and escort him to the gate." He glanced at a little notebook in his hand. "I found James at one one four five hours outside the Personnel Analysis Auditorium, in conversation with project military personnel. I advised him, as I was instructed, that his presence in the Area had not been authorized, and he would have to leave. He did not make any trouble. There were some remarks made by project military personnel in the vicinity of the auditorium entrance, which I ignored. No one attempted to interfere. I entered a squad car with James and rode with him to the gate. I personally saw James off the Area. I observed that he took an Ocanara bus."

"Thank you," Colonel Ross said. "Could we now adjourn, Pop?"

"Yes," Colonel Mowbray said. "That will be all for now. Will you wait just a minute, Norm? Something I want to ask you."

When the others were out the door, he said, lowering his voice, anxiously inquisitive: "This business of Colonel Woodman at Sellers. He was Bus's first squadron CO, you know."

"Yes, I know," Colonel Ross said.

"I think it hit Bus pretty hard. Do you know anything more about it? I just heard the bare details, what Botty got from Vera. Is there anything we ought to do about it? Anything we could do about it?"

"I'm afraid not," Colonel Ross said.

V

THE CAR slowed and halted. Seeing the card with the colonel's eagle and the words *Base Administrative Inspector* on the windshield, the two guards started up from the bench under a little canvas tilt and saluted. One of them ran across the road and unhooked the chain from which depended a sign: WAC AREA OFF LIMITS.

When the car moved again, Colonel Ross lifted his sun helmet and fanned his face with it. Sergeant Brooks held up the clip board with the check sheets, and looked at the list on top of them. "Then, the last thing," he said. "General Beal called—"

"Why didn't you tell me that first?" Colonel Ross said irritably.

Undisturbed, Sergeant Brooks said: "The general said it wasn't important, Judge. He only wanted you to know he was back. He asked where you were going to be, and I told him he could reach you through the Staff Director's office, here. He said not to bother you; but when you got through, he wanted you to come around. He was going to get some lunch. That is all, sir."

Colonel Ross said, "Oh, Lord!"

They were approaching now the yellow-painted frame

building which housed the Staff Director's Office and Detachment Administration. In front of it, in the stunning blaze of early afternoon, about twenty WAC officers were drawn up in a double row at attention. In front of the double row, also at attention, stood Captain Burton, the Staff Director. "Who in God's name told them to do that?" Colonel Ross said. "It must be a hundred and ten in the sun, there. She must be crazy—"

The car came to a stop. Colonel Ross got out of it heavily, and pulled himself up a little, answering the salute. He could see sweat running on the nearer faces, stiffly and ostentatiously eyes-front. "Good afternoon, Captain," he said. "At ease, everybody! Fall out, before you melt—"

There was a simultaneous relaxing murmur of sighs, little groans of relief, and a few giggles. The formation broke up. Captain Burton, a large stout woman, produced a handkerchief and wiped her face, which was almost scarlet. To her officers, she said: "Company commanders in the staff room, please. Others are dismissed."

Colonel Ross said: "Captain, I think in the future we can arrange inspections without putting everyone to so much trouble. We could work out some kind of a schedule so that there will be a company officer at each barracks building when we reach it. I don't think it will be necessary to assemble them first."

Captain Burton said: "I see, sir. I thought possibly you would want to inspect the company officers as a group—personal appearance. They understand they are to set a proper standard for the enlisted women to emulate and respect. They are a very fine body of girls, Colonel, and I think they do set a high standard."

"So do I," Colonel Ross said. "They do you credit, Captain. Are there any general matters, before we begin?"

Captain Burton, her broad and beefy but not unhandsome face regaining some of the scarlet it had begun to lose when they got into the shadows of the hall, said: "I'm afraid there is one matter, rather unpleasant, Colonel. That is why I asked the company commanders to come in."

She ushered him into a long narrow room with unfinished board walls. Two big fans were stirring the warm air and

Colonel Ross took off his helmet gratefully. "I thought we might sit here," Captain Burton said. She drew out a chair for him at the head of the table, a gesture of deference, whether to his rank or to his gray hairs, which Colonel Ross found irritating. "Yes, close the door," she said, "and sit down, all of you." Sitting down herself beside Colonel Ross, she said: "This is a matter I don't quite know what to do about, Colonel; but I felt it should be brought to your attention. A number of women made the same complaint to their officers, and I will ask those officers, or some of them, to give you any details you may want."

She paused awkwardly. "In general," she said, "we are not very well satisfied with the arrangements the Base Hospital makes for the regulation physical inspections of enlisted women. It isn't convenient, having to send them all over there; but I quite understand that until the infirmary here in the Area is finished, those are the nearest adequate facilities. Though, of course, they aren't adequate, either, Colonel. The girls reporting have no proper place to undress. It is right next to an orderly room, or something of the sort, used by male enlisted personnel. Though I think disciplinary action was taken in one case, some of the men continue to make little holes or openings through the walls so they can see in, and the girls know that, and I think if they can't stop the men from doing it, then they must give them a different room. I brought the matter up with Major McCreery, but he said there was no other room, and anyway, a thorough inspection did not disclose any such holes now. There had been some, but they had been stopped up. From what I am told, this may be true; but they are stopped up in such a way that they can be, and are, reopened whenever the girls are undressing, and then covered up, so anyone inspecting doesn't find them."

"I see," Colonel Ross said, sternly putting down the ribald, highly unsuitable impulse to laugh. "I will discuss the matter with Major McCreery. I think I can promise you that it will be corrected at once. Make a note of that, Steve."

Captain Burton cleared her throat. "That is one thing, Colonel. The other is in connection with the same thing. There have been specific complaints, quite a number of them, that the Medical Officers, or some of them, at any rate, regularly make vulgar and obscene comments to the personnel they are examining. There has been some difficulty in identifying the officers in question—the girls have no way of knowing their names—but we pretty well identified one of them as a Captain Raimondi—" She looked down the table. "Lieutenant Lippa," she said, "will you tell Colonel Ross what your girls told you?"

"Yes, ma'am."

Colonel Ross looked down the table. Lieutenant Lippa had a sober, pug-nosed little face. She arose and stood straight, showing a neat little figure. She said: "In the course of the last two weeks, sir, four enlisted women came to me separately and said they did not want to go over to the Base Hospital for PI. I thought this might be due to extreme shyness, bashfulness; and I tried to overcome it, reassure them. I asked them what, specifically, they objected to. They were reluctant to say anything specific, at first. But I finally learned that, in addition to those peep holes in the wall, the Medical Officers, in the course of the required pelvic examination, often made coarse remarks to them and sometimes treated them with undue familiarity." She paused, grave and alert. The little pug face, Colonel Ross observed, was one that grew on you. "I think I should say, sir, that none of them, none of my women, accuse any Medical Officer of attempting to assault her, anything like that. There were just these wisecracks and unnecessary liberties—"

"It is still despicable!" Captain Burton said. "Taking advantage of a girl that way! I asked Lieutenant Lippa and the other officers who had the same complaint made to them, to note down the exact remarks. I have a list of them, which I can turn over to you, Colonel. Some of them are so obscene and offensive that I hesitated to have them typed out. Furthermore there is reason to believe that those who complained were not by any means the only ones who were obliged to submit to it—that some Medical Officers, at least, made a regular practice of insulting all the girls they examined. Go on, Mary."

Lieutenant Lippa, her face grave and intent—you could see that here would be a first-rate company officer; the small, quaint, grave face, the air of energetic resource, must strike most troubled people as a present comfort and a reassuring promise of help—said: "Well, sir, after the second one had come to me, I thought I'd better make a check. So I talked to a number of others, women I knew to be particularly truthful and intelligent, to find out whether they had any similar experience. Two or three told me they had not; but most of them admitted that there were wisecracks, more or less regularly. One said that a Medical Officer did try to get fresh with her; but—" the trace of a triumphant feminine smile appeared around Lieutenant Lippa's mouth "—she managed to give him a good hard kick. So he stopped; and she didn't have any more trouble."

Colonel Ross, wholly won over, repressed a smile of his own. He said: "Was this officer, who had to be kicked, identified?"

"Well, sir," Lieutenant Lippa said, "I think I know which one it probably was—the one Captain Burton mentioned; but she, this woman, didn't want to make a fuss. She said she guessed he was just fooling; only she didn't feel like being fooled with; and after she made that clear, he stopped."

Captain Burton said: "Naturally enough, none of these girls wants to be called as a witness, to have to testify, or anything. I think the Medical Officers concerned know that; and that is why they behave that way."

"Yes," Colonel Ross said. "We must remember it's one of those charges that can easily be made against an innocent man; so even when we're sure it's true, there would have to be very conclusive evidence. I would rather see what I can do by having a talk with the Medical Officers who make the examinations."

Captain Burton said: "I think, Colonel, Lieutenant Lippa has a suggestion to make in this connection." She looked at Lieutenant Lippa with the generous encouragement of a proud teacher who wants her best pupil to show off a little and thus do them both credit. "May she make it, sir?"

"By all means," Colonel Ross said. "Let's hear it, Lieutenant."

Lieutenant Lippa said: "I don't know whether it's practicable or not, sir; but I wondered whether, instead of sending our women over to the Base Hospital, we couldn't have them send us a Medical Officer. We could fix up a room here in the Administration Building; and then there wouldn't be any men peeping; and, well, being over here, the Medical Officer might not feel so free to, well, do any fooling. If you see what I mean."

"A very good suggestion, Lieutenant," Colonel Ross said. "I know of no reason why it couldn't be put into effect at once. You provide the room, Captain, and we'll arrange to have any needed equipment installed. Major McCreery can detail a man for certain hours of duty here every day. Make a note of that, Steve, will you?"

"That would be a great help, Colonel," Captain Burton said. "Other considerations aside, there was the serious loss of time—"

A telephone attached to the wall in the corner rang abruptly. A middle-aged lieutenant at Captain Burton's left started up and went to it. Turning, with an expression of what appeared to be awe, she said: "Excuse me, ma'am! Colonel, General Beal is on the wire. For you, sir."

Colonel Ross pushed back his chair. Flustered, Captain Burton said: "Well, we'll just leave you, Colonel. We'll be waiting outside. I'm afraid that telephone isn't very convenient to use—"

"It will serve," Colonel Ross said. He went over to it.

General Beal said: "I called you when I got down, Judge. I guess your man told you. I stayed over the field, all right. Made it forty-one thousand and a couple of hundred, uncorrected. I might have made a little more, but the head was getting hotter than hell and I was getting colder than hell. So I quit then; I didn't want to get Danny sore by messing the engine up. He really had it going."

"Yes; good," Colonel Ross said. He did not know quite what to make of the call, of the general's wish or need to give him this information about cylinder head temperatures, altitudes, and Danny's care of engines. General Beal might be still working to exorcise Woody's sottish specter, back with him now that he was down. Colonel Ross said: "Everything O.K., Bus?"

"No," General Beal said. "It isn't. Far from it. We got a very bad break. Judge, it looks like we've bought it. Here it is. Jobson got to Washington at one o'clock and went right over to the Pentagon. I've just been talking to him, and to the Chief of Air Staff. First off, what you thought; they don't like our Letter Order—the thing about the separate club."

Colonel Ross's glance showed him the room empty and the door closed. He said angrily: "How did they ever see it? Do you mean Jobson showed it to them? We'd better have his head examined! Didn't he understand his only job was to get that clearance canceled? He had perfectly good grounds for asking it. He didn't have to bring up anything else!"

"Well, Judge, I don't think he would have brought it up himself. I told you we got a very bad break. It wasn't Jobson. They called me; and I had to read it to them myself, on the phone. When Pop ran this man James off, know what James did? He must have gone straight to a telegraph office. The Air Forces Group got a wire from him. I guess somebody should have thought of that. It might have been a smart thing to hold him out here."

Colonel Ross said bitterly: "To do smart things, you need smart people. Have we got any? What did James say?"

"I don't have the text, Judge; but I gather he said we'd put him off by force, that he hadn't been able to reach me; and would they confirm to me personally the WDBPR authorization."

"What did Jobson do then? Go to pieces?"

"What happened was: an Air Forces Group officer brought the wire up while Jobson was with the Chief. What tied it was James went on to say he thought the reason we threw him out was we were trying to cover a deliberate segregation policy he understood was not in accord with AAF directives. Naturally, they said: 'Anything in this? Have you a segregation policy? Tell us exactly what goes on.' Jobson was on a spot."

In justice, this would have to be admitted. Colonel Jobson's intelligence and judgment, as far as Colonel Ross had observed them, never were of a high order; but he wasn't a fool, and he was an old Army man. A direct question had been asked him;

he could not tell a lie. There was the Letter Order. Colonel Mowbray had laid a tortuous train which, fired at any point, must lead to this resounding mess. By bad luck, Benny might punch the wrong person in the nose; by bad luck, Mr. James might arrive at Ocanara on the worst possible day and get himself turned loose in the worst possible place; by bad luck Mr. James's telegram of protest would be carried upstairs and laid on the desk between Colonel Jobson and the Chief of Air Staff; but if it weren't any or all of those, it would be something else.

Colonel Ross could have wished that Wilbur Wright had never taught Pop to fly. At this point, he could even wish that Wilbur Wright and bright young Lieutenant Mowbray had broken their damn necks in the historic cow pasture. He said: "So now what?"

General Beal said uneasily: "I don't think we can do what we were planning to do, not the way you planned it. They want action taken at once."

"What action?"

"They want us to amend the Letter Order by adding two paragraphs to read roughly—wait; yes, give me that, Vera. All right, Judge, I'm reading Paragraph Four: 'In order to promote the close integration essential in a self-sustaining combat unit, all project personnel will use the same facilities, as assigned in Paragraph Two above. They will regard as off limits AFORAD Area facilities provided for permanent party personnel, with the exception of the Post Office, the Finance Office, the Main Post Exchange Building, and such buildings or parts of buildings in the Directorate of Personnel Analysis Center as may from time to time be assigned for lectures or demonstrations.' End paragraph. Paragraph Five. 'This order will be distributed to each officer presently assigned to Directorate of Personnel Analysis Project zero-dash-three-three-six-dash-three, and will be read by each officer and returned by him to this Headquarters when he has accomplished the first indorsement form below certifying that he has read the order and that he fully understands it.' End paragraph. End order."

Colonel Ross said glumly, getting time to think: "In Paragraph Five, make them take out 'presently,' Bus; and farther down, put 'when he has signed' instead of 'when he has accomplished.' In Paragraph Four, add to the exceptions: dispensary, chapel. Do we want to deny them medical care and religious consolation? Who's going to handle this, and when?"

General Beal said: "Hear that, Vera? Please change those things for the Judge. Well, I'll get it mimeographed. It ought to be ready a little after four. I ordered Personnel Analysis to assemble the men at four-thirty. Here's how it was put to me; I got myself into this, I would have to get myself out of it. So maybe I'd better handle it myself, not delegate it. I wouldn't want Pop to do it, certainly."

"No," said Colonel Ross. "Let's not have him do anything more." He did not intend the tone to be so pettish; but it broke from his control. "Don't take that, Vera," he said. "And, like a good girl, get off the line. I might say something else we won't need a copy of."

"Me, too," General Beal said. He laughed shortly. "You can hang up now, Vera."

Colonel Ross said: "Bus, can you tell me anything more about the attitude in Washington? Were those paragraphs dictated to you as a suggestion or an order? Were you authorized to, or ordered to?"

"Judge, can you tell one from the other, coming out of there? It was an authorized course of action; but the heat was right on me. I got myself into it; I get myself out of it—but quick, but quiet. I have an idea there may be trouble of the same kind somewhere else. I know there has been a little trouble in the Training Command, in Texas. Club stuff. That's what Pop was thinking of. It's a damn hard thing, you know. You have in training, say, a big group of white bombardiers and a very small group of colored bombardiers. The Training Command, the AAF, doesn't give a hoot in hell what color skin a bombardier has, just so he's been trained to dump it on the target— or, if our big friends ever want to stop kidding themselves, within a few thousand feet of the target. It's a tough course, and there really isn't enough time anyway, and the CO has got to produce on the deadline. He gives with the bombardiers; or else! If the big group is going to sulk around because the little group drinks beer with them, there's a morale problem. If one group or the other is going to be demoralized, which group would it better be?"

Colonel Ross said: "There's no use going into that. Let's stick to what we do now." He looked at the blank board-wall on which was centered a poster showing three wooden crosses, one capped with a banged-up steel helmet, against a clouded sky. It said: *Women! They can't do any more—but you can! Join the WAC now!*

Colonel Ross said: "You're holding the bag, Bus. If you follow their suggestion, and that doesn't get you out of it, it's going to develop that you should have had more judgment than to follow their suggestion. You were there; you knew the conditions obtaining."

In one way, General Beal was right; a suggestion out of HqAAF could not be distinguished from an order for the good reason that every suggestion restated an order, detailing or delimiting it. Here, the order was: *you are directed to get yourself out of this in a hurry.* The suggestion defined 'out of this' for you. To be considered successful or satisfactory, your escape must work all the ends implicit in the suggestion. Rightly read, read this way, Paragraph Four said: *In getting out of this, you will repair injury to morale by somehow persuading project personnel that the order is acceptable to them.* Paragraph Five said: *In getting out of this, you will not undermine discipline by causing anyone to imagine that you gave ground under pressure, and so might do it again.* Taken together, they said: *In getting out of this, you will under no circumstances, by any action of yours, make such a stink that HqAAF, to the detriment of the war effort and to its own great embarrassment and inconvenience, will have to stand on the front porch juggling a red hot poker while it squares enunciated theory with expedient practice.* Not added (but only because Major General Beal surely knew it by this time) was: *Failure to comply with these orders, for any reason at all, will constitute disobedience and insubordination; so, watch yourself, Mac!*

Colonel Ross said: "Bus; add Paragraph Four to the order. Omit Paragraph Five. I will read the amended order to them, and then dismiss them. Nothing could possibly be gained by giving them the indorsement to sign. Nothing could possibly be gained by having you read it yourself. In the first case, somebody will, sure as fate, hold his hand up and say: 'I can't sign this. I don't fully understand this'; and you might have fifty men in arrest by five o'clock. In the second case, if I read it, and somebody sounds off in the back, I don't have to hear. You do; you'd have to blitz the guy right then and there. As soon as they find out what they're assembled for, as soon as they hear the order, they'll know that we know what they were planning. They'll have a couple of hours to decide whether to go on with it. We'll have to handle the Club differently. Johnny can get his men there at four-thirty and keep them there. The officer who is acting Provost Marshal will have to be stationed at the door and refuse them admission, if they show up. The other was the best bet; but after reading the order, we can't pretend it was just a misunderstanding on their part."

General Beal said: "Can we be sure it will work, Judge? If I follow their suggestion exactly and don't get out of it, that's bad, all right. But if I don't follow it exactly, and don't get out of it, that's worse."

Colonel Ross said, "You have it the wrong way. Do you want to be perfectly sure you have trouble? Follow their suggestion exactly. You'll have it. The other way you might not."

"You think we aren't just dodging the issue?" General Beal paused. "I have word Jo-Jo Nichols will be in, six, seven o'clock. He would still have been at the Pentagon when this broke. He's going to know about it, know what they suggested. I don't exactly like having to tell him I did something else." He paused again. "Jo-Jo's a very good guy, Judge. I don't know whether you know him or not. He wouldn't trot back with any stories he didn't have to tell. But I know they trust him, up there; and he knows they trust him—you wouldn't find him not-seeing anything a Deputy Chief of Staff ought to see. I sort of wish I could get it cleaned up before he came in."

"There isn't any way," Colonel Ross said. "He'll have to see what he sees."

"I guess so," General Beal said. "We certainly screwed up that business with this James man. That's why we're up the creek, here. Without that—well, it's too late now. Pop told me about your meeting."

"It was his meeting," Colonel Ross said.

"Well, I guess you'll agree I'd better blitz those two lieutenants. Pop thinks the Eleventh Air Force might be a good place for them. That could be arranged. They're short on most MOS's up there. They'd better find out they're in the Army."

Colonel Ross drew a breath. "For the love of God, Bus," he exploded. "Never mind what Pop thinks! Just think yourself! It is alleged we are discriminating against Negroes. We put a reporter off the post. There were two men who tried to work a clearance for him. Next thing they know, they're out on a rock in the Aleutians. And in case you hadn't heard, one of them writes for magazines."

General Beal said, "O.K., o.k. Don't *you* blow your top, too, Judge! Everybody else around here has. And come over as soon as you get clear, will you? Pop just thought—"

"He never did! He never did in his life!" Colonel Ross hung up without ceremony, somewhat shaken to hear himself pronounce so poor a jibe with so much ill-temper. Normally profane or not, for the second time today, and fervently, he said: *God damn him to hell!*

He meant Pop, poor old Pop; but the feeling was the enraged feeling he had about Woody, poor, no doubt, if not so old Woody, whose little weaknesses (like Pop's, too much indulged by those around him) could be counted on to make mess after mess faster than anyone panting along behind could hope to clean them up. And who panted along behind? Poor old Judge; poor old Norm; poor old Colonel Ross, IGD, SWAAF. He got no help; it was all up to him; something he could take care of in his spare time.

Wiping his forehead, Colonel Ross got hold of himself sternly and marched out of the room. To Captain Burton, waiting for him in the hall, he said: "Sorry to keep you waiting. Shall we get on with it?"

At half-past three Colonel Ross, followed by Captain Burton and Sergeant Brooks, came up the plank walk laid on the loose sand, burning in the sun, to the screened doors of the WAC Detachment Mess. He pushed the screened doors open and walked blinking into the shadows. The usual taut, agitated, female voice called out: "Attention!"

"At ease," said Colonel Ross. He looked at the line of cooks and bakers, kitchen police and dining room orderlies ranged stiffly down the side of the room. Captain Burton said: "This is Lieutenant Miller, the Mess Officer, Colonel. And Lieutenant Turck who will succeed her as Mess Officer next week."

"Yes," said Colonel Ross. Blinking, he said to Lieutenant Turck: "How are you, young lady. Thought you worked in Files?"

Captain Burton said: "In accordance with Headquarters policy instructions, Colonel, we have arranged a schedule to ensure rotation of duty assignments of junior officers in order that they may receive experience in all detachment duties. The assignment of Mess Officer is made in addition to other duties."

"Quite so; quite right," Colonel Ross said. "I would like these two officers, the Mess Sergeant, the First Cook, to go along with me. Other personnel may return to whatever they were doing, or if they weren't now on duty, they may be dismissed."

"Yes, sir," Lieutenant Miller said. "This is Sergeant De Luca, the Mess Sergeant, and Sergeant Loveman, First Cook."

"Come along, please. We'll look at the kitchen. First of all; Bulletin Board. Posted: Daily Inspection Report; Garbage Disposal Orders; Menu for the Day; Food Handlers' Cards—all these up to date, Sergeant?"

"Yes, sir."

"Names of cooks posted, yes; name of Mess Sergeant, name of Mess Officer. All right, check off, Steve. Now, let's see.

Floor; scrubbed, rinsed, mopped dry; baseboard clean, corners clean. Very good, Sergeant. Stoves. Tops clean; open all ovens, please. O.K. Work table, O.K.; serving counter, O.K.; meat block—that has a crack, Sergeant."

"Yes, sir. We have a new one requisitioned. We can't seem to get it."

Lieutenant Miller said: "I believe they had to send to some Army Service Forces depot, sir. They say it hasn't come."

"If they still say that Monday, you must stir them up a little, Lieutenant—that will be you, Lieutenant Turck. Note it inspected and condemned," he said to Sergeant Brooks.

Sergeant De Luca said: "Can we use it tonight, sir?"

"Not if I am here to see it. I will not be here. Now, the ice boxes, please—"

VI

As NATHANIEL HICKS stepped out the door of the Directorate of Fighter Analysis Administration Building he saw Lieutenant Turck pass, striding fast and erect along the cinder walk.

Though Fighter Analysis Administration was not, like the Headquarters Quadrangle, completely air-conditioned, Colonel Folsom, as a Directorate Chief, rated one portable window unit in his office. From the cool room, you walked into heat that seemed solid, dense as water. The surface of the paved road beyond the path wavered away, shakily reduplicated, trembling in a mirage which, a hundred feet off, was a foot from the ground. Up the road, the group of library buildings and the pines left standing around them trembled too. The clear sky looked pale, filmed with hot dust. Breathed, the burning air half-suffocated you.

Lengthening his own stride, Nathaniel Hicks overtook Lieutenant Turck. She started when he came beside her, turning her composed face which shone with a dew of sweat. When she saw who it was, she drew a breath. She said: "The Lybian air adust—do you care for Milton? I try and try; but, no! I thought, Captain, you were to be off into the wild blue yonder.

Did you get to see the general?" She held a step, fell back, and came up on his left. "Excuse me, sir," she said. "We have just been inspected at the mess within an inch of our lives and I am now very much in accordance with regulations, rules of military courtesy, and customs of the service."

"I thought you didn't have to take over until Monday."

"I don't, thank God. But Captain Burton thought I'd better see what I was going to be up against. It was Colonel Ross. He is a nice old lamb; but if you think his chivalrous regard for the weaker sex will help you when he sees a roach in the store room, you are wrong, as our Lieutenant Miller found. There was also a little difficulty about outside purchases from the General Mess Fund. I shall have to get, and worse, read, TM ten-dash-two-oh-five; TM ten-dash-two-fifty; TM ten-dash-three-ten; TM ten-dash-four-oh-five. Either that, or leave it all to the Mess Sergeant, which would probably be easier and better. But she is a very fat girl and her Christian or given name—not a nickname; she signs the pay roll with it—is Billie. The combination makes me uneasy. I do not think she is firm with the little slatterns and sneak-thieves under her. What about the general?"

"It was somewhat complicated," Nathaniel Hicks said. "I was to go off right away on a grand tour of our outlying installations; but other matters came up; there was a certain loss of interest in me; I could not get hold of Colonel Mowbray who had to authorize personally the authentication of my letter telling everybody to do everything I wanted. So finally I called Operations and told the general's pilot—how do you like that? —who was standing by with a plane, that we were not going anywhere. I don't think it went down very well. He had been waiting some time. I expect I won't go until Monday. Though, of course, as soon as I dismissed my pilot, the Adjutant General's office called and said to pick up my paper, it was done. Just then, they brought me a TWX from Orlando saying my Captain Wiley was flying over and ought to be here by four-thirty. He wasn't supposed to come today. Is all this interesting?"

"Very," Lieutenant Turck said. "It has the bustle and stir of life. Do go on, Nat."

"Well, I have plenty more," Nathaniel Hicks said, not unaware that it was the first time she had called him by name. "While I was studying this dispatch, Lieutenant Edsell came in and I gave him Lieutenant Lippa's note, which he seemed glad to get; but he remarked that he would probably be in the guard house over the weekend; so then he got to telling me how he had pinned back Colonel Mowbray's ears and terrorized several other officers of field grade in the course of a conference they had just been having on a little administrative snafu that involved us. So, when I had stood all I could, I remembered I had to see Colonel Folsom. So I went and got my letter, which proved to be a good idea. When the colonel, with whom I was not on speaking terms last week, took a look at that, our relations improved wonderfully. What I really went in for was to ask him if he would give a job to a man who asked me if I would ask him if he would. He said he'd see; he thought he could arrange it. Well, it looks as though, from now on, I'm going to be a pretty good person to know around here."

"I will have no trouble remembering," Lieutenant Turck said. They were in front of the library buildings. "Would it get me anywhere if I invited you to my office and fetched you a bottle of Coca-Cola? We have a machine that really works; so they come out cold."

"That would usually be a deal, thanks, Amanda," Nathaniel Hicks said. "But I have to send a message to the man about Folsom; and then, Wiley. I have to pop over—his phrase; he's an Alabama boy; but the RAF corrupted him a little—to the Base; welcome him; get him a place to stay; and take him to the Officers Club and give him a few slugs from that bottle with my name on it—you see how it is. There are so many demands on me."

"I want but little," Lieutenant Turck said. "Just get me promoted to first lieutenant, and tell the Staff Director to let me and Lippa live off the Area in a lovely apartment or snuggery I happen to know we can rent. You might mention those things when you talk to the general again. Be seeing you, I hope, sir."

228

She pulled herself up, saluted him precisely, and went into the library entry.

The plane was a beat-up P-40 with stained and flaking camouflage paint. It came noisily around after the jeep with the sign: FOLLOW ME, and aligned itself in the row of parked planes. The engine revved up, shaking the wings until they seemed about to fall off, and, with a pop or two, fell silent. Emerging from its blur, the propeller took shape in expiring slow twirls.

Captain Wiley, wearing a white coverall and a white cloth helmet whose strap was unbuttoned, erected himself in the cockpit. He lifted a hand to Nathaniel Hicks, put a long leg out on the wing, and jumped down.

"How's that?" he said. "Jesus, I didn't know whether I was going to get here! That's a real old-time son of a bitch!" He gave the shabby fuselage a punch. "First, I couldn't get the landing gear up. Couldn't find the damn handle." He began to laugh. "Never checked out on the son of a bitch," he said. "Told the Operations Officer; sure, sure, just like the Kittyhawk. Only, never flew one of those either. Why tell him that? Here," he said to the ground crew corporal who had rammed the chocks under the wheels and now stood waiting, "Here's your paper, son. Never mind anybody servicing this. God Almighty couldn't service it."

He turned and began to untwist a wire which apparently was all that held the storage compartment door closed. He jerked out an old musette bag and a frayed manila envelope full of papers. He said: "Say, Nat; I didn't know whether you expected me today; only, for God's sake, I found they had me down for duty officer Sunday. So I got to get back tomorrow. So I figured maybe I'd better come this afternoon. O.K.?"

"Fine, Gene," Nathaniel Hicks said. "I have a car right over there."

Captain Wiley stood about six feet four. Being unusually tall, without being unusually heavy, he looked thin, but he was very strong and solidly made. Fitting himself into the cockpit of a fighter plane took skill and ingenuity; and Nathaniel Hicks had

heard, when he was in Orlando, Wiley's Division Chief kidding
him about flying a Spitfire with his legs over the sides. Captain
Wiley's face, with a big wide mouth, big strong nose, big dark
eyes which he had a habit of narrowing at the corners, was remarkable for an almost satin tone of skin, and a coloring, warm
and even, that, in a woman, would certainly be considered
beautiful.

In his movements, Captain Wiley showed traces of the awkwardness common to people who are taller and have longer,
larger members than usual. He was not ashamed or embarrassed, and consequently belligerent, as undersized men often
are; but being oversized meant being conspicuous, even if in a
manly and agreeable way; and he felt it. So many people must
have kidded him about where he put his legs in a plane, or
asked him wittily whether it was cold up there, that he was
ready, whenever anyone looked at him, with a mobile, good-
natured smile; and, if the subject was pressed, the ejaculation
of a few filthy words, genially spoken and in his mouth so
worn with use that they sounded quite clean and innocuous.

Captain Wiley stood on the ramp, smiling down at Nathaniel Hicks for a moment, rocking gently from his heels to
his toes. "Hell," he said, "I better get out of this. They probably peg you for wearing it off the line." He began to remove
his white flying clothes.

On the cloth helmet Nathaniel Hicks observed a bit of tape
printed in ink: *P/O Grummet*. On the strap of the goggles was
another, littler, bit: *F/O Dell*. It occurred to Nathaniel Hicks
that these articles belonged once to members of the squadron
who had been killed. Their flying kits were divided, for a com-
plexity of reasons; beginning with the economical consideration
that somebody might as well get the use of them; but unquestionably going on to a casual, tough gesture in real or affected
contempt of death; and, beyond that, to obscurities of meaning
where deep feeling might mix with the usual mawkishness to
say: though they were dead, yet shall they live; they were not
forgotten, and they would not be unrevenged.

Underneath, Captain Wiley proved to be wearing eight-
point-two pants, somewhat short for him, and a bleached chino

shirt with the sleeves rolled up. The captain's bars on his open collar were tarnished until they looked like gun-metal. Above his left breast pocket he had a pair of illegal miniature wings, and the diagonally blue-and-white-striped ribbon of the British Distinguished Flying Cross. Above his right breast pocket he had faded Royal Air Force wings, shy one of the snap-on fasteners. Taking a soiled overseas cap from his back pocket, he unfolded it and propped it, Royal Air Force fashion, over one ear.

"Wait," he said. "I better take that damn parachute! I don't want that swiped. You can't get them like this here. This one hasn't been unpacked for three years, so I know it's all right." When he had dragged it out of the cockpit and slung it cumbersomely over his shoulder Nathaniel Hicks was not surprised to read on the cover: *F/O Johnson*. Since Flying Officer Johnson would not be likely to have a spare parachute in his locker or quarters, there was a good chance that this one had been recovered from the plane in which he died.

Captain Wiley, seeing the car, said: "Say, this is all right! I got to get me a car in Orlando, if I stay. It's like here; the School of Applied Tactics is way the hell out in the woods. Not good, not having a car. They give you enough gas? Another thing: it lets you take her away from it all. Fine for Operation Nooky." Lolling in the seat, his shoulder and long bare arm half out the window, he said: "How are you coming with this Folsom jerk, that his name? Don't let him give you any, Nat. On Malta's where I'd like to see those nice types—three, five interceptions a day. Shakes the dust off you!" They had reached the gate. "Patience, Bud," Captain Wiley said to the guard. He contorted himself, got a wallet from his back pocket, and waved open an isinglass face with his folded AGO card under it.

The guard said: "Excuse me, Captain. In case you're a transient, I have to inform you you will be out of uniform anywhere in Ocanara after seventeen hundred hours without a necktie. It is now seventeen ten."

"Thanks, pal," said Captain Wiley. "That's with us, too." From his trousers pocket he extracted a handkerchief, and, tangled with it, a crushed and wrinkled necktie.

The guard said: "Sleeves are also required to be rolled down and buttoned, sir."

"Be right there," Captain Wiley said. "How's about my fly? Closed or open after seventeen hundred?"

✦

Under the white square of a screen on which motion pictures could be projected Colonel Ross sat waiting. Major Blake and a lieutenant from Major Blake's office were on the raised platform with him. The lieutenant, standing to the front with a list in his hand was engaged in calling the roll. Major Blake sat at a bare table next to Colonel Ross. He had the roster sheets spread out and was checking names as the responses came.

The Personnel Analysis Auditorium, which could seat several hundred, echoed emptily behind eighty or ninety men in the front rows. It was very warm. It seemed warmer because floodlights, hanging from the beams of a half-dozen, great bowstring trusses that supported the hemicylindrical, flattened round of the roof, were turned on. Between the few windows, the dingy, concrete-block walls were decorated with pictorial charts, bold in line and color, having to do with AAF personnel.

On one chart little blue men marched briskly into tubes displayed like veins or arteries, the various times of entrance being indicated by a list of months along the margin. The tubes swept down, approaching each other, joining. Toward the bottom, all merged; and, two years after the first little blue men (pilots) entered, out came: ONE COMBAT GROUP.

Another showed, foreshortened, the picture of a B-17, bomb-bay doors open, bombs tumbling against a ghastly sky filled in letters of flame by the words: *Bombs Away!* Below, was stated starkly: *What it takes*—. Files of rigid scarlet mannikins showed how many men it took in Air Crew, in Operations, in Maintenance, in Transportation, in Administration, in Housekeeping, for just that one bomber.

Much of the wall opposite was covered by a huge graph headed: GROWTH OF THE ARMY AIR FORCES. Square-jawed silhouettes standing at parade rest succeeded each other. They grew from an homunculus four inches high, labeled 1938, to a prodigy thirteen feet high, labeled 1944.

Colonel Ross eyed these charts, which, while not uninteresting, did not interest him at the moment. He sat motionless, his mind troubled, breathing with a sense of weariness and oppression—the heat of this cavernous hall; the hard long day; the dubious, disagreeable job. He had taken another pill before coming in. He attended the far-off ringing in his ears with glum bemusement, for no gain in cheer or assurance could be expected if he diverted thought from himself to the business on hand. He had tried that. As soon as he sat down he had begun dispassionately to look over the assembled personnel of Project zero-dash-three-three-six-dash-three, to judge their temper as a group; and, if he could, to identify what was probably no more than the handful of hardy spirits on whom any organized action must depend.

Colonel Ross soon observed, as his gaze moved, that each man—they were boys, really—feeling Colonel Ross's eyes on him, glanced aside. This was natural enough. Boys planning mischief, or knowing of mischief that was planned, acted this way whenever they found authority looking at them. It was not these boys' fault that the movement of white eyeballs in dark faces was more noticeable than the movement of white eyeballs in white faces. It was not fair to form the conclusion that they were an unusually furtive, sullen, and shifty lot.

On the other hand, it was not easy for a man, tired, irritated by difficulties not of his making, and maybe, beyond his power to resolve, to practice a full, calm fairness; to remember that this furtiveness, sullenness, shiftiness *were* conclusions, reached in his own mind, existing only there—not qualities inherent in those he looked at. Looked at sympathetically, with friendliness or good will, the ill-ease showed by these boys might be appealing—they were young; they were nervous. They had faced the standing injustices of their world; they had overcome great handicaps, with little or no assistance, in order to sit here as commissioned officers. Those who wore the wings of pilots, navigators, bombardiers could be regarded as achieving more

233

than white men who wore the same wings. It had been harder for them to get the early schooling, simple as that was, which would fit them to enter the training courses. It was fair to form the conclusion that they were an unusually sensitive, intelligent, and courageous lot.

That this was the right view, that reason must in justice endow them with qualities like these, was Colonel Ross's settled conviction. His difficulty in interrupting the vicious progression, born in resentment at the heavy burden of trouble that they put on him, and at each stage assisted by this resentment, exercised him. From the unfavorable judgment passed by the irritable mind on that shift of eyeballs, resentment would go on to stir a deeper antipathy.

To see where you were going you did not always have to go there. Colonel Ross could and did stop himself at the first step; yet a reflective man must be disturbed to know that he has such stuff in him, ready to be jarred off, like a chemical or physical chain reaction. It would be almost a relief to let his brooding mind rest on himself, desponding over these slight telltale symptoms of the stroke he was going to have if he did not take care; and the thought of death which, after that, a man ought to see as a friend, yet seldom did.

This would not do, either. Granted, the miserable condition of humanity, the corrupted, unsound mind in the unsound body, both unnerved by aging. It remained necessary to make a shift at bearing yourself like a man; not mumping, not moping. Staring at the big pictorial charts, Colonel Ross set himself to his task. In a minute or two now, it would be up to him. It was time to consider what, if anything, he wanted to do, besides read the order. Since anyone could read the order—Major Blake: Major Blake's lieutenant, for that matter—he must have come hoping to accomplish something else. Why, then, was he here? What decided him to come?

There was a plain answer to that.

He came because he did not think General Beal ought to be here. He was here because there was no one on the general's staff that he would trust—not, trust to fix the matter up; he was uncertain that he could fix it up himself; but trust to avoid making the matter much worse. Mowbray; Jobson, if he were in Ocanara; Johnny Sears, as Provost Marshal—each of them, if he hadn't shown often a basic lack of judgment, had sometimes shown himself liable to sudden losses of judgment.

Colonel Ross did not mean to say that they were complete fools—not even Pop. In some ways Pop was astute. It was the habit of all of them to look straight, and not very far, ahead. They saw their immediate duties and did those, not vaguely or stupidly, but in an experienced firm way. Then they waited until whatever was going to happen, happened. They sized this up, noted whatever new duties there were, and did those. Their position was that of a chess player who had in his head no moves beyond the one it was now his turn to make. He would be dumbfounded when, after he had made four or five such moves (each sensible enough in itself) sudden catastrophe, from an unexpected direction by an unexpected means, fell on him, and he was mated. Colonel Ross could not risk it. Somebody would have to look out for Bus, and it mustn't be one of those people. They would do no better than Bus himself.

That he, Colonel Ross, should be ready, should even, under the weariness and oppression of the hour, be eager to save Bus from these other officers, and from Bus himself, touched his favorite speculation about motives in men where, naturally, it most interested him; and where, just as naturally, it was most obscure. What motives had he? He weighed the general; in this matter he found him wanting. He then dismissed the finding, usually of the first consequence, as, here, of no consequence. Clearly, he acted for cause; and it occurred to him, though it did not soften his opinions on the subject, that in some ways, and perhaps some important ways, his relationship to the general might resemble the general's relationship to Benny Carricker.

General Beal might jealously brood, irrationally dote, on his honey of a flying, fighting Benny. That far-from-paragon, that difficult, erratic brat, put only one real claim on General Beal; Benny needed somebody to look out for him; and who

235

else was there? Who else would? Who else could? Benny, no doubt, did all anyone had a right to expect of him if he just allowed General Beal to serve him well.

Major Blake's lieutenant called: "Willis, Second Lieutenant Stanley J.?"

There was no answer.

Suddenly roused by the name, Colonel Ross turned his head and said: "Check him off. I know about him."

Somebody from the rows of seats said then: "In hospital—"

There was a stir and a subdued murmuring noise.

The lieutenant faced about and said to Major Blake: "All present or accounted for, then, sir."

Major Blake lifted himself from his chair. He touched one end of his mustache. Leaning forward, his knuckles on the table, he said in a formal, loud voice: "You men have been assembled so that Colonel Ross, the Air Inspector, representing General Beal, can read you an order amended to clarify your status as project personnel on temporary duty at AFORAD. Pay close attention. This is important. Colonel Ross."

Colonel Ross got to his feet.

"First of all," he said, "I want to speak to you about the purpose of this project, and the reason for your presence here."

He closed his mouth and let his gaze go slowly and carefully over the ranks of dark faces. "You are picked men," he said. "Each one of you was selected in preference to many others because you demonstrated, in the course of your previous training, abilities and qualities of character that fit you to be leaders in a project of great importance to the Air Force, and to our country."

Colonel Ross paused again, searching the front row of faces. He saw the movement of eyes. He heard, or thought he heard, the murmur again, now hardly perceptible. He said: "The accomplishments of pilots of the Ninety-ninth Fighter Squadron are known, I am sure, to all of you. Their courage and skill in combat convinced the Commanding General of the Army Air Forces that, as soon as enough trained men were available, colored flyers, bombardiers, navigators, gunners, could be

236

formed into an equally valuable and effective medium bombardment group. That time has come. You are the men."

Whether to stop once more, to test the ascendancy he meant to get by voice and manner, engaged him over the last words; but they were going to hear him out. Even those who might be listening rebelliously could guess that he had something on them; and they might hope to learn how much, and what he planned to do about it. Colonel Ross said: "You know the plan. On the basis of tests and exercises here, a group organization will be set up. You will proceed then to the School of Applied Tactics at Orlando where courses for squadron leaders and group administrative officers will be given you. You will then form a nucleus around which a full-strength group can be assembled and trained. I believe that in the future a man who served with one of your squadrons will feel the pride that every flyer of the Ninety-ninth Fighter Squadron feels today."

Without pausing, he went on: "I will now read to you this order. It is the order you saw on your arrival, with the addition of a paragraph defining restrictions imposed on you as members of a group in the process of function analysis and organization. We ask you to observe these restrictions conscientiously. Your efficiency as a group depends on observance of regulations, on military bearing and attitude, on prompt and cheerful obedience to orders, as much as on your proficiency as air crew members. This is the order. 'Headquarters of the Army Air Forces Operations and Requirements Analysis Division, Ocanara, Florida—' "

Colonel Ross read clearly and slowly.

"—by command of Major General Beal," he concluded. Looking at them over the top of the paper, he tried to take in the quality of the moment's silence; and he could not help being aware of sullen emanations—some points of resistance. With only a moment to make his mind up, he made it up, and said: "Any questions on this order, gentlemen?"

He could hear Major Blake's chair move, doubtless indicating that Major Blake, though impotently, did not approve of offering what might be considered malcontents this fine opening. Colonel Ross waited.

A voice from one of the back rows said then: "It says in Army Regulations, two hundred ten, ten, paragraph nineteen, about Officers Clubs; it says they have to be open, extend the right of membership to all officers on duty at the post."

Colonel Ross could hear Major Blake's chair move again.

Colonel Ross said: "Will you stand up, please? I can't see to whom I'm talking. Thank you. Yes, that is correct. That is what the regulation on administration of posts, camps, and stations provides. No public building can be used for the accommodation of any self-constituted special or exclusive group. The order just read has nothing to do with that. General Beal states in the order his reason for putting AFORAD facilities, other than those named, off limits. The use of them, along with permanent party personnel having no connection with your group, would work against the development of that group spirit which it is one of the most important objects of this project to inculcate. You understand that, don't you?"

On the opposite side, another man stood up. He said: "Colonel, those Jim Crow cars they have on the railroad down here; they inculcate group spirit, too?"

"That is something those who make the local laws will have to explain," Colonel Ross said. "This is the Army. There are no Army Regulations that make any distinction on the basis of race, creed, or color. You know that. A soldier is a soldier; and that's the end of it as far as the Army is concerned."

The first man arose again. He said: "We saw them put a man off the post this morning, Colonel, for talking to some of us. I saw that."

"The man you saw put off, Lieutenant, was put off because he had failed to comply with the regulations which govern visits of all newspaper men to this Area. He came to talk to you without waiting to get General Beal's permission. This can't be allowed. In this Area are activities and equipment, which, if they were mentioned in a newspaper, would unquestionably be picked up by enemy intelligence. No unauthorized person can be allowed to see them or know anything about them. Many lives, and even the outcome of important campaigns, may depend on the effectiveness of our security measures. I am glad you brought that up. There should be no misunderstanding about it."

Colonel Ross looked at his watch. He said: "I will not have time to answer any more questions now. However, you all know, I'm sure, that as Air Inspector, that is as General Beal's Inspector General, it is my duty to investigate complaints and irregularities. Any man is free, at any hour when he is off duty, to come to my office and tell me what's bothering him. I hope, if any of you have other questions, you will see me in my office, and we can talk them over."

Someone, not clearly, but loud enough to be heard, said: "Talk; all they will do—"

Giving it no heed, Colonel Ross said: "You may dismiss the group, Major."

He walked across the platform, went down the steps, and out by the side door.

VII

ON TOP of the high southwest corner of Hangar Number One, enclosed by a great hexagonal glass cage filled now by the afternoon sun, which was toned down, because the glass was tinted blue-green; and which was not too warm, because the air was cooled and re-cooled by air-conditioning units, four Wacs, staffing the control tower, looked out over the vast triangular intersections of the Ocanara Army Air Base's six-thousand-foot runways.

The whole face of the field, along with the hangar roofs, had originally been the subject of an elaborate experiment in camouflage meant to transform it into just a few more of the farms and orange groves surrounding Ocanara. On the roofs, and on the concrete runways, colored a neutral shade, the tree plantings were represented by painted black spots, with a dirt road or two, also painted, running through them. On the ground between the runways, actual trees continued the pattern, and the painted roads became real roads passing carefully constructed roofs of houses and barns, raised a little off the ground to cast shadows. Pilots just out of training were occasionally enough confused by it to have to go around again; and perhaps, at the time the work was done, there had been psychological value in implying that this was war; that there was danger, that the Base was alert and ready.

None of it would have fooled for a minute enemy flyers properly briefed to bomb the installations. The hypotenuse of the northwest-southeast runway was juxtaposed with one of the large local ponds, called Lake Lalage, of distinctive shape and size. Unless this pond, which was very deep, fed by springs, and which measured a mile by more than half a mile, were to be drained and filled-in, or boarded over, the position of the Base was clear. This had come to be admitted, so the camouflage scheme was no longer kept up; the paint was faded; the various simulated objects were sagging and falling to pieces; and the runways were given their conventional numbers and markings indicating approximate magnetic bearings and length, for anyone who wanted to know.

A similar relaxation had overtaken last year's rigidly enforced rules for dispersal of aircraft. The grim pretense that German bombers might be here any night, entailing as it did so much inconvenience and loss of time, was at last abandoned. Now, on the big field, you could see impressive massings of planes—a whole squadron of underslung, whale-like B-24's lined up wing tip to wing tip; flights of high-finned A-20's painted black as night fighters; a half-dozen beautiful, silver P-38's; row after row of miscellaneous types; transports, medium bombers, training planes.

From the high post of the control tower, much activity was visible. Two miles away, along the dull-blue waters of Lake Lalage, an array of earth-moving machinery—drag-lines, scrapers, bulldozers, steam shovels—was busy at the head of the long runway, extending it. Lines of trucks, each flying a square yellow flag, moved in and out a temporary gate in the fence at the far hem of the field. Off to the left, where earthbanks had been piled to form butts, some old P-40's were in the sheds to have their guns bore-sighted or aligned. Periodically, bursting puffs of dust left the surface of the banks as the guns were test-fired. Down by the highway fence, gasoline tank-trucks came and went in the underground storage area.

On the big triangular wind-rose beyond the taxi way several painters worked from a wheeled stand giving the diagonal stripes a new coat of staring yellow and black. On the parking aprons, mechanics were busy with a number of planes. Here and there engines fired up, now swelling, now throttled down; and sounds like thunder reached the control tower.

Within the convex glass-walls, twangings and a variety of disembodied voices constantly filled the cooled air. Paying no attention to them, T/3 Anderson, the Chief Control Tower Operator, stood beside T/5 Murphy, staring with interest down on the extension of the ramp between the hangar and the low, long roofs of the Operations Building.

A marching column, approximately a squadron, had come through the gate from the barracks area to the field a few minutes ago. It had been disposed, not without trouble and confusion, in platoons to form three sides of an open square facing the ramp. At the right of this formation, near the palms before the Operations Building, field music from a Negro Base Services unit was drawn up. The men, decked out with white helmets and white leggings, stood in three rigid rows—eight trumpets; eight fifes; eight snare drums. In front of them a black drum major held a baton. Near the center of the open square several marks had been chalked on the concrete and a handful of officers had found the marks and were jostling around, arranging themselves in a line.

T/3 Anderson, focusing a pair of field glasses, said: "I know him, in front, there. That's Colonel Mowbray—"

At the operators' positions, facing the sunlit field across the cased transmitters and banks of dials and controls sat T/5 Bell and T/5 Keller. From time to time they spoke into their microphones in answer to the medley of voices that came and went on the sounding air.

T/5 Keller said: "Wind is L—love; over—"

Out of nowhere a dogged Texan drawl went on: "—I have on board Brigadier General J. J. Nichols, Deputy Chief Air Staff, and party. Brigadier General Oliver H. P. Baxter, Junior;

Captain John T. Stenhouse; First Lieutenant Maitland Darrow. This is Major Bert Rogers, pilot. Have you got that now—"

T/5 Bell said: "Five-zero, Ocanara Tower. Roger. Operations has your list. They are ready. You are now cleared to land. Runway one four. Notice and overshoot construction in progress. Wind is L—love, gentle—." She said to T/3 Anderson: "They are on their base leg."

T/3 Anderson caught up a telephone and said into it: "On their base leg, now, sir!" She put back the telephone.

T/5 Murphy said: "Oh, that's it! I see it. What kind of plane is it, anyway?"

T/3 Anderson said: "C-Sixty, Lockheed, hon."

"Oh, my; she knows them all—"

The speaker on the frequency of the range station at Orlando fifty miles away said softly: "—cleared to Jacksonville to cruise at thousand—"

A squawk protested: "I don't read you. Say again—"

"I say again. To Jacksonville; at *four* thousand. Over—"

Higher and louder, someone else said: "—four-five to tower for a check line! Go ahead—"

"—when I read you, I receive your Roger-five-Sugar-five. Okey-doke—"

T/5 Keller, staring at the sky beyond the field, said: "Botheration! There's that one again, west—" She brought up her microphone. "C-Seventy-eight about two miles west of field! This is Ocanara Tower. Do you hear me? Rock your wings, please. Over—"

Someone said promptly: "And if you hear me, toots, rock your tower. I am four-five miles northwest. C-Forty-seven, not Seventy-eight. You catch? Army nine-nine-three. I want to come in."

T/5 Bell said to her microphone: "Army nine-nine-three, Ocanara Tower. I have advised you field is closed for a period of approximately three zero minutes. Hold and circle left. Watch traffic. You will be number two to land when we advise you field is open."

T/5 Keller said to T/3 Anderson: "He just doesn't receive; or he just doesn't listen! I don't know what he's trying to do. We better gun him, hadn't we—"

"Yes," said T/3 Anderson. "Gun him, Murphy! See? Right over there—" T/5 Murphy raised and tilted the bulky light-gun tube. "Now, aim, hon," T/3 Anderson said. "He can't see it if it's slanted off, any. Give him red steady and watch his ailerons and rudder. He's supposed to acknowledge that way—"

"—Ocanara Tower, this is Navy Able-one-three—"

T/5 Bell said, "Oh, that fellow! He's one of those flying boats from Sanford or somewhere. He might be lost; but I think he's kidding. He wants to know where he is—"

"—there! He did kick his rudder."

"All right, he'll go around. Now, hon, watch the C-Sixty. They're down, see? They'll turn in a minute to taxi. Give him a green light—short flashes—that's right!" T/3 Murphy raised her field glasses, following the C-60 up along the hangars.

"Oh, I want to see this," T/5 Bell said. "Can I see them get out?"

"All right. And you can, too, Keller. Only, bring your microphone. It'll reach. So if anyone calls—"

Shoulder to shoulder they pressed against the convex glass panel.

Under them, the C-60 wheeled and swung broadside. There was a pause while the engines were run up. Then the cabin door opened. A faint harsh voice arose, bawling: "Present—arms!" The big black drum major let his lifted baton fall; the eight snare drums, beaten, jumped to a fine muted racket of ruffles; the eight lifted trumpets blew out a high blaring flourish.

"My, he's cute!" said T/3 Anderson. "General Nichols! Unless this is the other one. He looks like, you know in the movies, that tall, quiet man—"

T/5 Murphy said, clasping her hands, "Oh, let me see, Mona! Just for a minute—"

T/3 Anderson handed the glasses over.

"That other one, I don't think he's so hot! General Baxter! Who is he, anyway?"

"Search me! They have hundreds of generals—"

"Oh, can I see now! Please, Rose—"

"Oh, I guess they're going to inspect the guard—"

The two generals, who had been shaking hands with the short

243

row of officers in the center, moved across the pavement to the head of the platoon line on the right. The drum major lifted his baton, and the fifes came up as one fife. He dropped it; and they broke, piercing, into a sweet, shrill whistle, high and jaunty against the drums. At the bar's end, the bugles came up, too; and threw in their emphatic three notes' worth—a musically hot arrangement, almost an orchestral effect, of which the drum major was reasonably proud.

With jubilation, T/5 Bell began to sing: ". . . flying high, into the sun . . ."

From the void, a voice of reproach said: "Ocanara Tower! Nine-nine-three, for God's sake! When do we get to land?"

T/5 Bell sang: "We'll live in fame, or go down in—"

T/5 Keller lifted her microphone and said: "Army nine-nine-three! This is Ocanara Tower. A plane with high officers on board is being received on the ramp, and the field is closed until the ceremony is over. I will advise you."

The voice, sepulchral, said: "Nuts to them, sister. Don't they know there's a war on?"

T/5 Keller said: "Army nine-nine-three! We are required to report superfluous transmissions, or abusive and profane language received. Acknowledge!"

"Wilco, lamb pie. You doing anything tonight?"

T/5 Keller suppressed a giggle, but she said curtly: "Army nine-nine-three! Kindly vacate this channel, or I will be obliged to report you. Out!"

✦

Preceded by an MP jeep, and followed by two more staff cars, they passed the gates of the Ocanara Army Air Base and headed down the highway toward the AFORAD Area. The jeep, opening its siren at a column of Quartermaster's trucks that lumbered along half a mile ahead, summoned them with stentorian wails to move over.

In the back seat General Nichols sat on the right, with General Baxter in the middle, and Colonel Mowbray on the other side.

General Nichols's face was nearly triangular. He had a wide forehead with harmonizing height, and well-marked thin eyebrows above clear, dark-brown eyes tilting slightly down at the outside corners. A narrow but strong chin supported a straight, ample mouth with lips firmly delineated, almost chiseled. As though to emphasize this feature, which gave his whole face distinction, and at the same time, force, General Nichols wore above it a dark mustache clipped thin and flat. His face, turned to Colonel Mowbray, had a mournful, vacant expression. The distinguished, even beautiful, lips parted. He said slowly: "Only one thing I'm a little sore about, Pop."

To facilitate conversation across him, General Baxter tilted up his smooth chin, pulling his head back and blinking benevolently through his glasses. He kept his face straight, though he naturally recognized the sober-sided start of one of those deadpan sallies for which Jo-Jo Nichols was widely remembered and appreciated. "Personally," General Nichols said, "I'm a simple soldier. I wish I could get away from all this fuss and falderal! Of course, I realize that when I stand in the place of the Chief of Air Staff, I'm not free to consult my personal likes and dislikes. I have to accept honors appropriate to my station. Formal reception by officer of suitable rank; O.K.! Field music, ruffles and flourishes; O.K.! Escort of Honor; O.K.! But let me ask you one question." He bent forward and barked suddenly: "What happened to those fifteen guns I consider the representative of the Chief of Air Staff entitled to? I didn't hear them!" He reached across and slapped Colonel Mowbray's knee. "Pop, you old so-and-so," he said. "How are you, anyway? How's Bus?"

Colonel Mowbray, emitting a cackle, said: "Bus? Bus? Bus is just fine, Jo-Jo. He would have come over, only we never expected you as early as this. He was still tied up. You certainly got here!"

General Nichols said: "We had a tail wind the whole way down. From Charleston to Savannah we worked it out on the computer we were making about two hundred and seventy; and I don't think it could have been much less the rest of the time. We never left Bolling until two o'clock. I had to wait for Ollie."

"Well, why did you do that?" Colonel Mowbray said, peering at General Baxter. "We never knew Ollie was coming. We never invited him. There isn't any place to put him up. He's going to have to sleep on a bench in Sunshine Park. What did he come for anyway?" Though Colonel Mowbray spoke so playfully, the sharp inquisitive note in the last question was strong enough to make General Baxter laugh.

"I came for the ride," he said. "I came mostly for the ride." He continued to laugh. "Why?" he said. "Aren't you glad to see me? A few little things you don't want the Air Inspector's office to know about? Well, I may find time to look into them."

"You can look all you like," Colonel Mowbray said. "We're always ready for inspection. Bus is doing a wonderful job here, I can tell you." He leaned forward. "Had I better butter him up some, Jo-Jo? Congratulate him on those stars? How did he get those anyway? Buy them at the PX?"

"Why, no," said General Nichols. "Didn't you hear about that? It was something I was able to do for him. You see, this list, promotions the Old Man wanted, went over to the Hill; and of course Ollie wasn't on that. But when the list came back through Legislative Liaison a lot of names had been added. You know—colonels who'd been pulling strings and pestering their home-state politicians to get made. Naturally, Ollie was there. Now, one morning this returned list had just been sent in to the Old Man when I found I was out of cigars, so I dropped around to get a couple from the box on the Old Man's desk. Fortunate thing for Ollie!"

"Wasn't it, though?" General Baxter said blandly.

"Yes. That very minute the Old Man, reading the list, had reached Baxter. He gave a kind of disgusted grunt—you know the way he does—and grabbed a pencil to strike it out. I was bending over the desk, filling my pocket with cigars, when I saw what he was going to do. I yelled: 'Good God! What's that behind you?' He drops the pencil and looks around. 'Why, nothing!' he says. 'Check!' I said. 'Just thought we'd better make sure.' So then, by the time he picked up the pencil which had fallen on the rug, and was ready to read again, he'd lost his place in the list and went on from farther down. So that's how Ollie got to be a BG."

Colonel Mowbray laughed until the tears came into his eyes. "Tell Bus," he said. "Tell Bus that one!" He got his breath and wiped his eyes. He said, suddenly serious: "Bus is a little bit upset, Jo-Jo—oh, one thing I did want to speak about before we get there. I suppose you heard, before you left, about this little difficulty this morning, that Negro newspaper fellow raising the fuss. Now, that man was entirely in the wrong; and I was surprised to hear any attention was paid his telegram. As Graham Jobson must have told you, he should never have been sent here. Those public relations people seem to be so busy sucking up to the newspapers they don't care what they authorize, or how much harm it does."

General Baxter said: "That isn't quite the way the newspapers see it, Pop. They yell bloody murder. They tell you WDBPR is a special agency to see that no reference, direct or indirect, to the Army or the war appears in print."

"And that might be a good thing! What they did here, without consulting us, sending a man down to write up a project that didn't even start until this morning, and might not work out—somebody is nuts! Now, I admit our people, one of our Public Relations officers, and another, pulled some bad boners; and we'll have to take disciplinary action there. But the point is, Washington had no business to say he could come down; and he had no business to sneak off by himself, when he knew he wasn't cleared, and start trying to get a story. He ought to be struck off the accredited list for that. He ought never to be allowed on any AAF post again! That's what I think, Ollie."

Colonel Mowbray did not wait for General Baxter's agreement, since he did not expect to get it, and he probably felt he had not too much time for what he wanted to say before they reached AFORAD Headquarters, none to waste in hearing a defense of the War Department Bureau of Public Relations, or its Air Forces Group.

Public Relations in the peacetime Army, the old Army, were usually handled by those officers whose poor or mediocre performance of other duties made them the easiest to spare. In this new, wartime Army, Public Relations, at least at the higher level, was of course in the hands of commissioned civilians— publicists, advertising men, newspaper editors. While able enough in those fields, and never wrong about what the papers and magazines wanted, the smarter ones might practice a kind of collusion. They now had the power to accommodate those who would have the power later, when the soldier-suits were taken off, to accommodate them with valuable jobs. Colonel Mowbray did not trust them. He did not even trust General Baxter on this point. Not all general officers were insensible to the advantages of a press friendly to them personally.

Bending forward to engage General Nichols, Colonel Mowbray said: "What I wanted to tell you, Jo-Jo, before you see Bus, was that I think Bus very rightly feels that Washington didn't back him up. He sent Graham Jobson to explain the situation, why James ought not to be cleared. There really couldn't be any argument about that. Bus was right. But what do they do? They take this entirely false and misleading telegram that James sends the Air Forces Group and take action on that. They use that as a basis to intervene in a purely local thing, a little personnel difficulty which we were already acting on and had under control. Bus didn't say this, you understand; but I'm saying it because I'm pretty sure I know how Bus felt, how he naturally would feel. He has a right, on his record, to have Washington stand behind him. That's what I think, Jo-Jo."

While he listened, General Nichols's face relaxed from the blank, mournful expression fixed on it when he told his story about General Baxter's promotion. He smiled lightly but firmly. His eyes grew intent. Like a man who has enjoyed a short rest, but who sees now that his time is up, General Nichols, with an almost visible gathering of muscles, arose and shouldered his load—heavy, but not too heavy for him, because he was strong and he was used to it. He said: "Pop; two points about that. One: your purely local thing isn't purely local. For some time now the Secretary of War has been doing everything possible to make the Negro press change its tone and attitude.

The Administration is disturbed by the incessant attacks on Army policy, very often AAF policy, and the playing-up of unfavorable stories. Next year there is an election. Two: I wasn't there when they talked to Bus; but I heard the transcript of the conversation. I think Bus was fully backed up. He was told to repeat his order and to make it stick. We suggested a way to handle it. In view of the other point, we didn't like the order because it left us open to the charge the James man, in fact, made; that segregation, on the basis of color, was being practiced. We asked Bus to state that this was not the case. He wasn't directed to revoke the order. Now, what more could he ask?' "

Colonel Mowbray said: "Jo-Jo, I want you to know, because I don't think Bus would tell you, that Bus never saw that order until after it was published. There was some slip-up in distribution in Headquarters. I wrote it. I put in what you didn't like—the separate Officers Club. Bus had nothing to do with it. In my judgment, it was absolutely necessary. If Bus is in trouble about that, I want you to be able to tell them how it happened—whose error in judgment it really was. I know Bus will have to take the formal responsibility; but I think the Air Staff, the Old Man, should be told it wasn't Bus's idea. Bus would not have approved that order."

General Nichols, still smiling patiently, said: "Did you know Bus wouldn't approve it when you wrote it? Come on, Pop!"

"I didn't say that," Colonel Mowbray answered stubbornly, his face somber. "When I wrote it, I did think Bus would approve it. Now, I don't think he would have. If there hadn't been that hitch in distribution, Norm Ross would have got a copy before it was published, instead of after. He would certainly have talked it over with Bus. I know Norm didn't approve of it. He said so right away; before we heard anything from Washington."

"Ross is your Air Inspector, isn't he?" General Baxter said. "I think I knew him when he was in Washington. We wanted to get him."

"Yes; he's an awful good man," Colonel Mowbray said. "I don't know what we'd do here without him. Bus depends on him a great deal. We all do." He looked moodily out the car window. They had turned east off the highway and were running, the car's shadow stretched far ahead of them, through the pine woods. On the right, those miles of steel mesh fence, topped with barbed wire, which enclosed the Area, had begun.

Colonel Mowbray said: "Mind you, Jo-Jo; about this policy business. I don't agree with Norm. He thinks your policy is right. It isn't. It's wrong. It's bound to make trouble. It's bound to lead to the very thing you're trying to avoid. A colored boy may have the same legal rights as anyone else, and we can see nobody takes those away from him; at least, where we have control. We can't impose him on the community, on Ocanara, for instance. In Ocanara, there isn't a hotel used by white people which would dream of letting a Negro register; there isn't a restaurant used by white people that would serve him a meal. I don't think you'd suggest we try to change that. In short, you know better than to insist that the municipality of Ocanara stop segregating Negroes socially. Your theory says they ought to; but before you start a fight about that you better finish the fight you have in Europe and the Pacific." He wagged his head knowledgeably. "That's your real policy, off the post; and it's right. First things first! On the post, your policy should be the same and for the same reason. The Negroes aren't the only ones who have rights. If the Southern boys don't want to spend an evening socially with Negroes they have a right not to."

General Baxter, benevolent, beaming through his glasses, said: "Pop, who abridges that right not to? Nobody I know of."

"Don't give me that, Ollie!" Colonel Mowbray said, bristling. The air filled suddenly with a faint but sickening stench. To the right could be seen the neat concrete vats, thickly creamed and mantled under the sprays revolving, of the Area sewage disposal plant. "That's what that smells like!" Colonel Mowbray said indignantly. "All right. So there's no regulation that says every man will report to the Club every night and have one or more beers standing next to a Negro. If they don't like it at the Club, they don't have to go to the Club. Sure! Sure!"

Colonel Mowbray squirmed in his corner; but he had the air of hopping up and down; of being ready to fly, fearless and furious, like a bantam or a terrier, at the monstrous nonsense confronting him. This was engaging, and General Baxter, with a grin, said provokingly: "Sure! Glad you admit it."

"Yes, and you tell me why a club, established for the pleasure and convenience of its members, should offer a lot of boys from say, Georgia, nothing but a chance to pay their dues and then take a free choice between not liking it, or not going to it! I tell you, they won't stand that!"

"Too bad!" General Baxter said cheerfully. "Just what will they do?"

"They'll make trouble, and it *will* be too bad! You're deliberately taking a social matter, a matter that a great many of the best men we have feel deeply and strongly about, and making it an issue of discipline. They won't submit; and you know in advance that they won't. Go on! Do your damnedest! You can arrest them; you can court-martial them; you can dishonorably discharge them. In short, if you're that much of a fool, you can arrange to get rid of a lot of your first team and see how you make out with strictly second-string colored boys!"

Colonel Mowbray's face had turned scarlet. The consternation that his idea caused him brought him close to stuttering. He said furiously: "Someone's crazy—stark, raving mad! This bomb group, here—if and when activated! Does anyone in his right senses think it will stack up with a good white medium-bomb group? I don't say they won't try. But can they? Jesus God; by and large, man by man, they just haven't got it! The Bible says hewers of wood and drawers of water, and that was no fooling! Look around you, use your eyes, ask anyone! Talk to Colonel Mandible, commands the Engineer Corps troops here. He was telling me last week. What those jigaboos can do to machinery and equipment would break your heart! Give them a new truck, and in a week it's ruined. Give them a machine gun and in ten minutes it won't fire. Take away the white officers, and by night your squadron paper-work will be screwed up so nobody can ever straighten it out; your barracks will be a pigsty; your mess will be serving cold burnt beans three times a day and piling two weeks garbage on the back porch. Jesus God, I'm glad you can laugh! I feel more like crying!" Indeed, a suggestion of angry tears appeared glistening in Colonel Mowbray's eyes. He tightened his lips and clamped his jaws together.

"Now, Pop!" General Baxter said. "Nobody's going to swipe your air force."

On General Nichols's face the firm quiet smile remained unchanged. His expression was both abstracted and attentive. He did not waste his mind's time on trifles like this poorly conducted and futile debate; but he did not overlook or miss trifles either.

General Nichols said lightly: "We're going to have to use them, Pop; and I don't think they're all as bad as that. I think, given a chance, a lot of them will do all right. We have some reasons for thinking they will. I hope you won't feel bad about this, but I brought down with me a Distinguished Flying Cross for one of your bomb group project boys. A Lieutenant Stanley Willis, I think the name is. I have the citation in my brief case. I'll have to ask you to have him looked up for me."

"Willis?" Colonel Mowbray said. "Willis?"

"I'll give you the full name and serial number. He's one of the pilots. They put in for an Air Medal for him from his last station. Awards and Decorations had it pending, we happened to discover, and the Old Man himself changed it to the DFC. Willis was in a B-Twenty-six, flying with three other B-Twenty-sixes out of Del Rio on a cross-country exercise and they hit weather. By the time they worked through, they didn't have gas to get home. They were talking back and forth between the planes and the other pilots, who, incidentally, were white, thought the best thing would be to bail out. This fellow, the colored pilot, had noticed a little field—the sort of place they fly Cubs off Sunday afternoons. He took a turn over it and decided he could put down. He had a co-pilot and a navigator along—both white—and they were willing to try it with him. He'd go first, and if he cracked up, the other planes could bail out. So he did. He ran off the strip, or what passed for that, of course; but he'd lost enough speed to use his brakes by then and he managed to swerve it a little and keep on hard, fairly level, ground until he stopped. So he pulled off to the side, and the other three came down, while he talked them in, telling them where to touch and where to go, and they all landed O.K., too. I don't think you could call that second string flying, Pop. Those B-Twenty-sixes aren't for children. The Old Man figured half a million dollars' worth of planes rated a couple of dollars' worth of medal, all right; and under the circumstances, awarding it here and now might be useful."

"Sure, sure," Colonel Mowbray said. He swallowed. "You have me all wrong, Jo-Jo. I don't hold a thing against a Negro because he's a Negro. I'll give him every bit of credit he can earn every time he earns it, and maybe a little extra—A for effort. But one swallow doesn't make a summer." He moistened his lips. "Well, I got off the point, I admit it. You're the policy people. We have to do what you say. And you know Bus. If he's overruled, he doesn't sit sulking about it. Just, as I say, he had troubles enough today, enough on his mind. I guess you know about Colonel Woodman at Sellers Field."

"Yes," General Nichols said. He looked at General Baxter. General Baxter said: "We know, all right. It was decided for various reasons that we'd take the matter over from the Training Command. The fact is, Pop, I'm the Investigating Officer. Since Jo-Jo was flying here today, they thought I'd better come down with him, get a statement from Bus, and go on to Sellers tomorrow."

Colonel Mowbray said: "Then you did know Bus went up there yesterday? I was going to tell you. That's a mighty upsetting thing to have happen, you know. Of course, he was Bus's first squadron CO, too. You knew that? I never knew Woodman, myself; but he had a lot of hard luck. He didn't get the breaks at all. Norm Ross told me that Woodman had this idea that somebody higher up was out to get him." He shook his head sadly.

General Baxter said: "The presumption of AR six-hundred-dash-five-fifty is always that a sane person doesn't commit suicide. We wouldn't mind finding he had delusions of some kind. Self-destruction while mentally unsound. Some people went up with Bus, didn't they?"

"Norm Ross and Benny Carricker."

"Of course, I know Woodman was hitting the bottle, and that doesn't help. If I have to find he was drunk at the time, and I guess at Sellers I will find that, it could be mental unsoundness due to his own misconduct, so his death becomes due to misconduct and is not in the line of duty. If Bus and his people can say he was acting queer when they saw him, it would be a help."

General Nichols said, almost derisively: "Don't get in a sweat, Ollie. You'll have plenty of help." He looked steadily at Colonel Mowbray, no doubt considering his own findings on Colonel Woodman. They were clearly at variance with the findings General Baxter hoped for, the findings General Baxter had probably been told to bring back.

Smiling, General Nichols said: "It isn't much of a secret that Woodman had his neck way out; and he knew they were looking over the axes at Fort Worth. It's tough to have a lot of hard luck; it's tough not to get the breaks at all; but these are tough times, Pop. We have a job; and a man who's given part of it to do has to do it right—or else!"

He spoke quietly and carefully, without special emphasis, as though spelling-out principles about which General Baxter, and perhaps still higher authority, were showing themselves a little remiss. General Nichols gently dissociated himself from General Baxter's mission. Smiling still, he seemed intent on stating the simple, irrecusable considerations, before which every other purpose, hope, or wish ought to give way—even including, it seemed, that piteous or compassionate wish to say, or at least to report officially, no evil of the dead. It was plain that General Nichols could continue to look at the facts of ruin and failure long after other men, though reputedly tough and hard, shifted their eyes and, shrinking to think that they also were mortal, wanted to cover them over.

He said: "A man like Colonel Woodman, who has been regularly falling down on his job, and knows he has, could do a lot worse than shoot himself—I think. What else is there for him to do? We aren't taking any excuses. Not even in cases where something can be said on both sides. I know of several cases like that. The Old Man would have given almost anything to be

254

able to let it ride, to save somebody's feelings, to excuse somebody who perhaps did a great deal for the Air Corps in the old days. He couldn't. He had to act. There is too much at stake."

General Nichols's serious smile deepened. He said: "An idea seems to be around in some quarters that we're pretty near out of the woods, that winning the war is just a matter of time, now." He shook his head. "We don't know what might happen. The whole picture could change tomorrow; and not for the better. We needn't take our hair down about it; but in this thing too many good men have died, and too many good men are going to die." He paused. "I don't mean I think you don't know that, Pop; or that you'd want it any other way. But remember, they are just as serious as hell up there."

Colonel Mowbray said: "Down here you won't find anyone who isn't just as serious as hell, too."

"Let me tell you something, which you will treat as top secret," General Nichols said, still smiling. "I was at the conference at Quebec last month. A certain intelligence service, which seems to be smarter than ours, laid before the meeting some information of great interest. It was a minute of the specific terms on which one of our important allies offered to join the Axis in nineteen-forty; and on which they offered, this year, to make a separate peace. They were turned down both times because the Germans thought the terms too high—"

They were at the gates of the Area. All other traffic had been halted and moved over to the side. The guard was drawn up at attention by the gate house. General Nichols absently touched his cap, and they went through the arch. He said: "We don't know whether the offer, or a modification of it, still stands; but it is obvious that we would be unwise to trust these friends or count on them very far. If the Germans changed their minds, we might have to throw away our operational planning for next year." He laughed quietly.

"Yes," Colonel Mowbray said. He sat a moment, his mouth open in brooding surmise. "Yes, I see that could be pretty bad," he said.

General Nichols said gravely, "It reminds me in some ways of a situation that developed at Keesler Field a few weeks ago when I was down there. Off the shore, there are a couple of small islands, a few miles out in the gulf. One of them is un-inhabited, and it had been used for some time as a gunnery range for fighter planes. The other island belongs to an old woman, somewhat eccentric, who lives there alone; has a vegetable garden, some chickens, a cow. There is a house on it, and a barn; but they don't amount to much."

General Nichols cleared his throat. "Well, it happens that, from the air, it looks a good deal like the other island, about the same size and shape; and they're right there together. As I say, the house and barn don't amount to much, and the other island had a couple of sheds on it, which I think fishermen used for something sometime. The planes would fire at these old sheds. I suppose it was remarkable that it hadn't happened before; but at any rate, one evening a pilot who wasn't very familiar with the range took out a P-Thirty-nine to try a newly installed cannon. He made a run on the island, put his sights on this shed, and opened up. It happened to be the wrong island, and the shed was the barn, and the old woman was in the barn, milking the cow."

General Nichols shook his head. "It was good shooting. The pilot lobbed in four or five thirty-seven-mm shells, broke the roof all to bits, scored two direct hits on the cow, which just disintegrated. My, it was a mess!"

Colonel Mowbray said: "What happened to the old woman?"

Mournfully, General Nichols said: "Pop, she was left hold-ing the bag."

VIII

AT QUARTER to six Nathaniel Hicks drove Captain Wiley into the parking space beyond the low white masses of the Officers Club. They had been by Visiting Officers Quarters to get Cap-tain Wiley a room and to leave Captain Wiley's stuff. Then they went over to the Special Projects Building to catch Major Beaudry, of the Charts and Plans Section, before he left, so that he could arrange to have a draughtsman in the morning to lay out the formation diagrams.

Evidently reflecting on these glimpses of the AFORAD Area, Captain Wiley, as he got out of the car, said: "Say, you got quite a thing here, Nat; quite a thing!"

Going along with the fighting man's usual view, Nathaniel Hicks said apologetically: "It's mostly a lot of crap."

"Sure it is," Captain Wiley said. "But I love to see a lot of anything. Here's all this; here's all that. You been around the Training Command much? Why, they have more damn fields, more damn planes, more damn men! It makes you think, Nat!" He narrowed his eyes pensively as though to undertake this exercise. "In England, in 'forty-one, when they had us really on the hooks; in Malta, when I was there, I've gone up to intercept with only part of one tank full. All we had. You could make one pass and you were through; and if they didn't hurry up, you couldn't even make that. You'd have to get down and drag your plane in a hole in the cliff and watch the bastards bomb." With a negligent imitation of a British voice he said: "Dashed enervating. Bloody awful." They were walking around to the Club door and he added: "Say, is the place pinched?"

In the drive curving up to the front entrance stood two jeeps full of military police. In the arch of the doorway a stocky red-faced lieutenant with a gun strapped around his waist and an MP brassard on his arm came to attention and saluted them.

"I don't know," Nathaniel Hicks said. "I saw at Operations when I was waiting for you that they had some brass coming in. Maybe it's an escort. I hope General Beal isn't here. He thinks I'm off on a job for him."

"How's with Beal, anyway?" Captain Wiley said. "Is he a good Joe?"

Not sure about his competence to decide this point, Nathaniel Hicks said: "They seem to like him."

Captain Wiley said: "I heard he was a fugitive from Bataan; but, hell, you can hear anything you want. A fellow who knew him in the Middle East said he was a nice type with an aircraft, only he flew his groups awful hard. When he finished with them, they'd had it! I heard he ordered them to hit Crete one day, along with some mediums, though he knew, like everyone else, they couldn't make it out and back. So, at least a squadron came down in the water. No lack of moral fiber tolerated."

From Captain Wiley's tone it was difficult to tell whether he regarded this as reprehensible callousness on the general's part, or as a good practical joke, humorous because it was so outrageous, on the squadron concerned. Nathaniel Hicks said: "What do you do when they tell you to fly somewhere you can't get back from?"

"Me?" said Captain Wiley. "I wouldn't know. I'm here. They never sent me anywhere I couldn't get back from. Why, Nat, it isn't a good idea. There might be only one chance in a hundred, but if the CO is smart, he'll make sure you have that one chance. If you haven't any chance, he shouldn't send you. I'd have to know more about that Crete story. Maybe never happened, anyway. But I'll bet if it did, there were these winds aloft or something they figured might just let them do it. This death or glory stuff is all bushwah, except with nuts; and those, you don't want. An outfit of smart guys, always trying to figure the opposition before the opposition figures them; they can take, any time, any day, an outfit of nuts wound up to crash their planes into something. That just isn't smart; and the smart guy wins." He smiled serenely, not pressing the implication that he must be smart himself since he had done a good deal of winning, but assured in it, and standing on his judgment of himself with no embarrassment.

The steps and arch of the entrance to the Officers Club led directly into a wide vaulted passage which ran the width of the building. It was open at the end, looking over a stone balustrade to Lake Titania. The right side was open too, facing the coconut palms and shrub-plantings of the patio. On the left side were doorways with ornamental signs above them to the lounge, the bar, and, at the end, to the dining room. Part of this wide tiled passage was furnished with little metal tables and wicker chairs. These were for the convenience of members who might want to offer female guests a drink. No women were allowed in the bar room. It was pleasant here on a warm evening, for a breeze off the lake was always stirring in the passage. "How will this do?" Nathaniel Hicks said. "Inside, it gets awful hot."

"Swell, swell," Captain Wiley said. He let himself down in one of the wicker chairs, heaved his long limbs around until he found a comfortable slouching position. He tossed his overseas cap on the table, and gazed with pleased attention at the only other table that was occupied. Two Engineer Corps lieutenants sat there drinking rum and Coca-Cola with three not-bad-looking girls, two dark, the third blonde. Nathaniel Hicks went into the bar room.

He came out with a colored boy in a white coat carrying glasses, ice, bottles of charged water, and a full bottle of Scotch on which was pasted a strip of paper printed in pencil: *Capt. N. Hicks 0-907360.*

"Swell, swell," Captain Wiley said. "Scotch, huh? I got so I liked that stuff." He dropped into his heroicomical British voice. "A bit all right, this!" To the colored boy he said: "No ice, my man. Not done, you know." He began to laugh. He poured himself a moderate amount of Scotch, filled the glass with water and inched himself lower in the chair. Enfolding the glass in his big, long-fingered hand, Captain Wiley said: "Cheers, chaps!" He tilted it up and swallowed half of it. He brought his hand down and, still holding the glass in his lap, said: "You say the general's got the thing now, Nat? Is that good?"

"I'm not sure," Nathaniel Hicks said. "But the general has actually flown in combat; plenty of times, I guess. I do know that. I figure he'll see your dope is right, and that might take care of Colonel Folsom, which would be good. I saw Folsom this afternoon on something else, and he was quite pleasant. I was up at Sellers Field yesterday talking to an AVG man. I have some notes he gave me I'd like you to look at."

Captain Wiley said enviously, "There's a piece of cake! I wouldn't have minded being out there, then. Cash money for every plane you got! Then you take it, and do a little trading with the Chinks, and pretty soon you have a packet. That part is still going, a fellow at Orlando, just back, told me. I'd like some of that; and I wouldn't mind seeing what those yellow-bellies fly like." He looked pensively at his glass. "Only, not till they give you something besides P-Forties. Once you fly a

Spit you don't want any of those." He laughed. "What I liked was a Spit-Nine on a Wop Macchi Two-hundred, or Two-oh-two. Definitely a swindle; but fun for all. They used to come over Malta with the bombers sometimes, doing a lot of phoney acrobatics. We generally got a pretty good alert, so you could be up, supposing you weren't grounded for parts or out of—ah—petrol. Wonderful feeling, Nat! You sit there waiting, and you see pretty soon a few V's of bombers lumbering along, and the Wop fighters doing barrel rolls and all the silly stuff around them. Screw radio silence! You'd hear the FL's suddenly yipping: 'Red Leader to you chaps; White Leader to you chaps; R for ravioli, R for ravioli—' One day," he said, laughing and slapping his knee, "I got to admit we had it back. A few Hermanns in One-nineties came over, way the hell up, at the same time. We never saw them. I was just bouncing a Wop, and I heard this goddamn firing in the air. When you hear firing in the air, it's only one place; right back of you. Goddamn bullets going through my wing! I leaned on it and went ass-over-tea-kettle. I swear, his prop nicked a piece out of my rudder. I figured afterward Hermann outsmarted himself. He didn't open early because he was trying to make sure; and then he was too close to correct his aim. He came over me, bat out of hell, probably so mad at missing, when he practically had me stenciled on his fuselage, that he stopped thinking. So he started to pull up. He never should have done that, naturally. You overshoot somebody, and you've put him on your tail; so you better begin evading quick."

Captain Wiley set his glass on the table to free his hands. He poised one above the other. "So me, I let it spin about one and a half, pulled out hard coming up, and caught him smack in the ring, almost stopped, trying to climb—" He tilted his left hand and shot his right hand toward it. "So, I socked him the business in a good long squirt; and he began to burn; and *alles kaput Hermann!*" He took back his glass. "That's something we want to keep saying in the manual, Nat. You look behind you, no matter what! You wouldn't get the break I got twice. They shot down two of our people on that same bounce—one of my best friends; fellow named Johnson. Drilled him through

260

the back of the head and he never pulled out of the dive he was making on this Wop—zingo! Right straight into the field."

Nathaniel Hicks said: "Isn't that his parachute you have?"

"Yeah, that's right," Captain Wiley said. "That was a funny thing. The way he flew into the ground, you wouldn't have expected to even find pieces; and they were spread around, all right. Somehow, you'd never figure out how, the parachute ripped off him, and there it was, a hundred feet away, good as new. Goddamn, I was sorry to see him killed! He was one of the best flyers ever lived—only, he forgot to look behind him once." Captain Wiley emptied his glass and put it on the table.

Nathaniel Hicks pushed the bottle of Scotch toward him.

Captain Wiley said: "I might have another short one, thanks." He poured a little more in the glass. "I'm supposed to have ulcers. We all had something from the food they gave you. Johnson used to get as sick as a dog every morning. Well, he's cured now!" He enfolded the glass in his long fingers again and tossed most of the contents into his mouth. He wiped his lips on the back of his hand and said: " 'Gashed with honorable scars, low in glory's lap they lie. Though they fell, they fell like stars, streaming splendor down the sky!' "

Astounded, Nathaniel Hicks said: "What's that, Gene? Bushwah?"

"It's a poem," Captain Wiley said, grinning. "Sure, it's bushwah. Here's some more I read." He frowned attentively. " 'Their shoulders held the sky suspended; they stood and earth's foundations stay; what God abandoned, they defended, and saved the sum of things for pay.' " He smiled with pleasure. "Makes you think, Nat!" he said.

It did, indeed; Nathaniel Hicks reflected. It was wise to bear in mind that the man who declaimed against bushwah usually concealed somewhere in him the ordinary deep human love of it. "Do you like poetry?" he said.

"I don't know," Captain Wiley said. "Those are just some things I read." He poured charged water into his glass, sloshed it around, and drank a little. "I used to read things now and then. Lot of the Britishers had a few books with them."

He rested at great ease, contentedly turning his gaze on the

261

blonde girl, who seemed to be a third or extra one at the other table.

Nathaniel Hicks saw that she was fully conscious of the gaze. While Captain Wiley told about his close shave that day over Malta and illustrated with "hand flying" the FW 190's unwise maneuver and its result, she must have been stealing looks at him. She observed, and might naturally like, the negligent disposal of the rangy muscular body in the wicker chair, the bold and open masculine face with the enchanting warm complexion, the inviting cast of the narrowed, roving eyes. She no doubt evaluated the wings on his shirt; and perhaps even the ribbon of the British, or Honest-to-God Distinguished Flying Cross. Sidelong, through her lashes, she now saw that she had his attention. She began at once to address herself to her companions, male and female, with animation, cocking her head, tossing her hair, moving her arms and hands with lively grace, while she displayed her teeth in frequent soft peals of laughter.

In a low, pleased, pensive tone, Captain Wiley said: "The time and place being given, to organize that would be possible. Nice little dish of a bitch, too. Wonder who she is?"

"I couldn't tell you," Nathaniel Hicks said.

"I don't want to know," Captain Wiley said. "Good I got to get me back tomorrow, or I might be trying to promote it, and my Orlando schedule is tough enough. Funny thing about the wars, that way. Types of chicks strictly no-no-no in peacetime just can't wait to lay it on the line. I guess I'm really a son! You'd think, when you have a good chick crazy about you, it ought to hold you; but every time I see a good new one, damn if I don't start wondering how that would be. Of course, it doesn't matter so much now; but if I got married. You're married, aren't you, Nat? What's your wife do if she thinks you're knocking a little off, every now and then?"

Though he was embarrassed Nathaniel Hicks could not very well take offense from the innocent, direct inquisitiveness of this, if not child, grown-young-man, of nature. "I don't know," he said. "I don't think she'd be very pleasant about it."

"What I mean!" Captain Wiley said, smiling. "Of course, you don't have to tell them, I suppose. But they get suspicious as hell. Even if you're only going with them, pretty soon they start asking questions. You take off for a couple of days, so they know you aren't getting it from them, right away they wonder who you are getting it from. Could be correct, too. What's your wife think you do?"

Nathaniel Hicks said self-consciously, since in Captain Wiley's eyes it surely reflected on his virility: "I don't know, Gene. Perhaps she does wonder if I'm shacked up with somebody. If she does, she needn't. I'm not. I haven't found it necessary, if you want the fact."

"Still, wouldn't it be smarter of her to come down and keep an eye on you?" Captain Wiley considered the question perplexedly. "I mean, what the hell, don't you miss her?"

"I miss her," Nathaniel Hicks said.

"Then, how about her? Does she miss you? What does she do to pass the time? That's something I'll bet I'd wonder about."

Nathaniel Hicks said: "I think there are quite a number of women in the world who don't give the ice man a lay every morning as soon as their husbands go to the office."

"I suppose not," Captain Wiley said. "I guess I just better not get married yet. I'd kind of like to. I'd like to have some kids. How many kids you got?"

"Two," Nathaniel Hicks said.

"Yeah, I'd like that. But I guess I'd better not. Not while they have so many of those around." He flicked an eye at the blonde girl. Adopting his British voice, he said: "That's but good. And there's jam on it, chaps!"

Moderately warmed by whisky, Nathaniel Hicks took a look at the blonde girl on what might be called his own account; yet where Captain Wiley saw such a temptingly available delicacy, all Nathaniel Hicks saw was a lot of trouble. Reason, indeed, overcomes the passions! If, by lifting his finger now, he could enjoy her, would he lift it? He would not! He would go further than that. If—an improbable hypothesis, since he was not exactly Captain Wiley—the propositioning was hers; if she provided, with no work of finger-lifting, the necessary time and place to "organize" her; if she then and there offered herself to him, free of bother and uncertainty of going after her, would he accept? He felt safe in saying he would, instead, get the hell out the shortest way.

Part of this chaste reluctance might come from what Captain Wiley had half in mind; a magic—indeed, Captain Wiley could not help feeling, incredible—purification by marriage of the appetite. Nathaniel Hicks had the general intention of being, or at least, the definite wish to be, faithful to his wife, whom he loved, and, in addition, really liked at least as well as, and usually much more than, other females who from time to time might catch the male eye. Yet this intention, or this wish, this love and liking, perhaps served, in the concourse of factors that operated together against the loose proposals of instinct, as no more than secondary, hardly needed reinforcements to a central disinclination sprung from lower considerations.

A man like Captain Duchemin (though so many years past Captain Wiley's flaming youth) sought with relish unimpaired and readily found the adventurous quest and the fun of the chase; the glee of capture and the titillations of variety. They all struck Nathaniel Hicks as highly undesirable; if not always in themselves, always in what experience knew they brought about. Though 'twas an angel, 'twas a she! Let irregularly into your life—oh, my God, the trials and tediums, the disgusts and annoyances, the quarrelings and repinings, with which she would quite justifiably plague you when, having enough, you thought of withdrawing! A short course in the dear school kept for fools would learn you that Peace, O Virtue, Peace is all thine own!

Captain Wiley had been waiting, apparently in the hope that Nathaniel Hicks would say more, give him some useful or interesting tip. Getting none, he looked away at last. Nathaniel Hicks, relieved, looked away, too, his eyes moving down the wide shadowed passage to the bright late sun beyond the arch of the entrance door. He saw several figures on the steps out-side.

Nathaniel Hicks opened his mouth idly, about to say Pope's line aloud—if Captain Wiley was made to think by poetry, that might stay him! An oddness in the gesture or movement of the figures beyond the door then brought his eye back to them. He studied them with perplexity.

There were a number of them. Because of the screen doors and the blinding gold light, they could not be distinguished ex-actly, though their silhouettes were sharp. The short, erect one, which Nathaniel Hicks recognized as that of the MP lieuten-ant, had moved from his post at the side of the arch. Being on the top step, inside, his head came higher than the others. They, standing together on lower steps might have gathered to listen to orders or instructions; but certainly they were not the MP's from the jeeps in the drive. The MP's all wore helmets.

A confused stirring, a movement of heads and shifting of shoulders took place in the listening group. The MP lieutenant, rigid, seemed to be looking them over, turning his face from those at the left to those at the right. Then he moved, too, mak-ing a smart stride to the rear, which brought his back against the wide screens of the big double door. With a motion inex-plicably like that of a man preparing to conduct setting-up exer-cises or taking a formal stance before doing a fancy dive from a springboard, he lifted his arms out from his sides and held them extended, straight and level.

His audience seemed disconcerted. They remained immobile a moment. Then one figure mounted a step, and another mounted two steps. The first figure joined him. The rest then moved, closing up, jostling each other. There was an indistinct murmur. The MP lieutenant, his arms still straight out against the door, did not budge. The two foremost figures, coming in under the arch, were now on the MP lieutenant's level, and they were taller than he was.

Nathaniel Hicks followed this amazing dumbshow with his lips parted. Captain Wiley said: "Say, what gives, Nat?" He pulled himself around and looked over his shoulder.

At the door, the silhouettes beyond the screen seemed frozen

265

again in their new positions. Then everything moved again, jerking forward. The larger of the two figures immediately facing the MP lieutenant lifted his hands and seemed to lean slightly. His arms spread in a slow sweep and came around the lieutenant. They drew instantly together, as though embracing or getting ready to dance.

Now the arch was filled by a general disorderly surge. The high screen doors trembled; they parted at the center, swinging in, admitting the whole group in a straining huddled mass that pushed before it the MP lieutenant, off his feet, clasped and carried in the big figure's arms. The others deployed past this embraced couple, their heads turning as though in search or inquiry. Their moving black faces shone; and Nathaniel Hicks saw that they were Negro officers.

The irruption, bringing all the actors from perplexing silhouettes to solid, three-dimensional people, ended, perhaps because of altered acoustics in the vaults of the passage, the dumbshow with its uncertain murmurs.

What was plainly the MP lieutenant's voice, high and angered, yet not uncontrolled, said: "—your hands off that! You see my brassard! You are not allowed—"

In answer, a deeper, African voice, speaking gruntingly, with labor, said: "I don't want to hurt you, lieutenant. He's taking that gun so you won't hurt—"

Another voice, urgent and excited, said authoritatively: "Set him down, I say. Set him down, now—"

"He want to arrest us, I guess—"

"That's all right, now. Carter's got his gun. Let him go ahead. Let him do that."

The MP lieutenant, released so suddenly that he staggered, said, breathless: "I order you to return my side arm! I order you to leave this building immediately—"

"Don't go, anybody!"

"No, don't go—"

Behind Nathaniel Hicks, at the other table, one of the women said: "Oh!"—a faint little scream. The abrupt scrape of chairs would be the Engineer officers getting up. Captain Wiley, with extraordinary quickness, already had his feet under him while

266

his chair fell over on its side. His tall form straightened with formidable alacrity; he wheeled easily, perhaps by an illusion of late afternoon light, towering in stature, as he moved on the group.

"Give that here, boy!" Captain Wiley said. His long arm went out and snatched the MP's holstered automatic and the dangling belt from the man who held them. In a tone full of danger, his soft strong voice broadening in an Alabama accent which usually appeared as no more than a trace of drawl, Captain Wiley said: "Get! All you!"

He swung the belt and holster lightly, advancing with so much purpose that there was a general stunned recoil. "Now, you heard the lieutenant," he said, earnest and even. "Now, you get! Right quick! You, too, there! Stay out of here—"

The MP lieutenant, disheveled, his cap gone, but dauntlessly stiff and erect, made a motion which proved to be that of bringing a whistle to his lips. The blast shrilled along the passage vaults. Nathaniel Hicks, still gaping, realized that this explained it—his men must have had orders not to interfere until he signaled.

Now they were coming, all right. Their metal heels stamped at the double up the steps outside. The round shapes of their bobbing steel helmets rose against the bright arch of the doorway. The screens swung in.

A female voice behind Nathaniel Hicks said: "Oh, my goodness—"

Nathaniel Hicks saw a stout sergeant, the rim of his helmet shadowing his eyes, a submachine gun laid over his arm, come through the doors. More helmets, more MP brassards crowded closely after him. Out the entrance to the lounge walked a thin, graying major. The major said to Captain Wiley: "All right, please. I'll just handle this—"

Captain Wiley, a little higher-colored, his eyes narrower and brighter, turned calmly and looked down at the major. He then looked at the helmeted sergeant with the submachine gun, and the crowd of MP's. He looked back at the major and laughed.

"You want to handle this, too?" he said. He held out the holstered automatic and belt.

The MP lieutenant said: "I'll take that, sir."

The major said: "I am the Club Officer, Captain. I have special instructions for dealing with this matter. Kindly return to your seat. I must ask all witnesses to remain." He faced the colored officers. "Now, you men, you will step outside, please. I'll want to see your AGO cards. You are in arrest, all of you."

IX

THE NIGHT was heavy and hot. Beyond the summits of the cork trees and the live oaks the sky, by some trick of refraction in the tropic air, or for some other reason unknown to Colonel Ross, was packed to bursting with stars—large ones like brilliant luminous blobs; small ones unnumbered in drafts of incandescent dust. They gave so much light that, except where the tree shadows held it, the darkness was no more than a deep dusk. From the bungalow verandah the spreading waters of Lake Armstrong could be clearly seen, and even the dark line of the far shore, more than a mile away.

Across the hollow in which the swimming pool and the tennis courts lay, the Oleander Towers Hotel bulked up in a long mound on which was imposed the pattern of a hundred lighted windows. All the windows were open on the breathless night. From them came out a medley of distant sounds; laughter, the humstrum of radio music, radio voices. Loudest of all, now rising, now falling, an unskilled male chorus raucously chanted: "I've got sixpence."

The singing had persisted to the point where the unflagging singers had only twopence, jolly, jolly twopence; a point people completely sober would be unlikely to reach, and Colonel Ross listened with disapproval. He did not think that this sound of revelry, particularly on Friday, not Saturday, night, would do anyone any good if it came to be noticed in General Beal's bungalow a hundred yards away. It would carry there to General Nichols and General Baxter, having a talk with General Beal in the dining room, just as well as it carried here.

Colonel Ross knew where Bus and his visitors were. Half an

hour ago Mrs. Beal, in an elaborate white dinner dress, had come disconsolately across the lawn. Pouting, she said they had thrown her out as soon as dinner was finished, and she was sick of sitting by herself. She settled in the hammock, tangling her voluminous skirt around her thin legs, carelessly crossed. With one of her infantile gestures, she thrust her right hand into Mrs. Ross's to be held. With her left hand she covered a little angry yawn. "What goes on around here, anyway?" she said. "Is there some trouble out at the Area?"

"Why?" Colonel Ross said. "What makes you think that? Is that what they're talking about?"

"I don't know what they're talking about," Mrs. Beal said. "But I'll bet *you* do, Norm! All right, see if I care! I know something happened. Bus came in with Jo-Jo and Ollie Baxter, and they were feeling pretty good—been having a few quick ones out at the office, I guess. Then that Mr. Bullen came with his photographer—" she giggled. "He called up and asked if he could, and I said, sure. Bus said all right, because you said he was to suck up to Mr. Bullen." She giggled again. "He said I wasn't to say that; it was unrefined. That's why I'm dressed up like Mrs. Astor's horse. Cora, there's something cockeyed with this dress. Will you look at it before I go? It needs something done to it. Well, anyway, they took a lot of pictures of Bus and me sitting on the couch; and Junior, who acted like hell. They'll be in the paper tomorrow, Mr. Bullen said. Then they called Bus to the telephone. That was you, Norm. I know it. I could see right away that something bad had happened. Did they have another crash? Was it that Benny?"

"No," Colonel Ross said, "there was no crash, and it was not that Benny. It was merely a little disciplinary difficulty I wanted to report. And that's all I'm going to tell you."

At this point Colonel Coulthard, who had been to General Beal's bungalow and found the general engaged, came across the lawn and tapped on the screen door to ask if he could sit with them. At Mrs. Ross's suggestion, Colonel Coulthard soon went out to the kitchen and made a pitcher of rum swizzle, a beverage he was supposed to be skillful at concocting.

Colonel Ross, very tired, could have done without these visitors; but, since they were putting up General Baxter in their spare room, and since Mr. Botwinick and Major Tietam, the Judge Advocate, were coming down with charges and specifications on the colored officers arrested at the Club, he could not have gone to bed anyway. Besides, it would be too hot to sleep, especially when he had much on his mind. Colonel Coulthard, probably tired, too, seemed content enough to sit silently sipping his drink and smoking his cigar. Mrs. Beal had subsided into a long murmuring conversation with Mrs. Ross at the other end of the verandah.

The far-off singers now had no-pence, jolly, jolly no-pence; and Colonel Ross arose wearily. He went into the bungalow. At the end of the hall a light burned by the telephone. He dialed the hotel and said to the switchboard: "This is Colonel Ross. Find out where that racket is coming from and give them a ring."

He heard the ring almost at once, showing that the party had made itself widely felt. Answering, a facetious voice snapped: "General Beal, here!"

"Colonel Ross, the Air Inspector, here!" he said as grimly as he could. "Break that up! If there's any more singing, I'll have to have your names and serial numbers, and you can all reply by indorsement tomorrow."

Taken aback, the voice said hastily: "Yes, sir."

Colonel Ross set down the telephone and made his way out to the verandah again.

Colonel Coulthard, who had guessed his errand, said, "We've got a lot of people around here who think this war is a picnic—chance to raise some hell."

"Well," said Colonel Ross lugubriously, "so it is, so it is. They aren't far wrong there. That's what makes war so popular with people."

"This one isn't popular with me," Colonel Coulthard said. He shook his handsome white head. "Not the way I fight it. If I could get out to a combat air force—"

"Oh, go on, Hal!" Mrs. Beal called across the verandah. Her waspish tone seemed to say that she too was discontented with this war as it affected her, and with much better reason. She said brutally: "You're too old and fat. You're too lazy. We gave you the easiest job we could find, and still you're kicking! Ira's changing your efficiency rating to 'poor,' you know. You'll never get anywhere."

"How'd you like to have a kid sister like that?" Colonel Coulthard placidly asked Colonel Ross. "Fresh brat, isn't she?"

"Oh, you!" Mrs. Beal said. "Why don't you ever do anything, Hal? Why don't you shake the lead out of your pants?" Dimly in the darkness, her white face, chin belligerently lifted, and her white dress, tensely stretched forward, could be made out. Her voice, throwing the fast jeering questions, trembled with impatience. Colonel Ross supposed that this tone had a long history. It might fetch back to days when she was indeed his "kid sister"; and Hal, complacent and handsome, from her standpoint failed her in some childish crisis, and so acquainted her for the first time with the more ungrateful truths of life—one of them, maybe: all that glisters is not gold! Her attachment to him was henceforth tinged with exasperation. She said goadingly: "What did you do about that stuff you were saying the other night, that wonderful officer of yours who was going to put everything in a magazine? Nothing, I bet!"

"That's where you're wrong," Colonel Coulthard said. "I did just what I said I'd do. I took Captain Hicks over to Bus this morning, and we planned it all out. He's starting on the project now. So, pipe down!"

"Oh, I'll bet you'll make a mess of it!" Mrs. Beal said. She drew a quivering breath. She said to Mrs. Ross: "I'm going to bed. I'm dead. There's no sense waiting up for those lugs over there. Bus and Jo-Jo will beat their gums for hours. I know them! By now, they're reminding each other of all the people they can think of, and saying: oh, he's no good; because of something he did at the Academy, or Kelly, or somewhere. Cora, would you please look at my dress before I go?"

Left alone with Colonel Ross, Colonel Coulthard said almost defensively: "Sal's bark is a lot worse than her bite." He took a swallow from his glass and drew brightly on his cigar. Colonel Ross could see that this was very likely the case. Colonel Coulthard defended, not himself, but his sister against Colonel

Ross's possible misunderstanding. Colonel Coulthard knew that no one could seriously consider him lazy. He worked loyally, long and hard, at a job that was not easy for him; and his Directorate had an impressive list of projects completed. Neither was he fat, by any means! From being obliged to sit at a desk so much, he was a little plumper in the face and fuller in the body than he used to be. Neither was he, as a field officer, old. He had his fine white head of hair when he was thirty and he was only forty-five now. Therefore, Sal, in her familiar fiery way, was joking. The point about the efficiency rating was of course an outrageous lie, a joke. Colonel Ross, who knew everyone's efficiency rating, because General Beal asked his advice in assigning them, knew naturally that Colonel Coulthard's was consistently *superior*. When you understood Sal, you knew she was just being funny.

Colonel Ross received and accepted this complicated message conveyed by the defensive remark, and by the kindly serious full face, a yard away in the dark.

The actual consideration in Colonel Ross's mind was the laborious one of whether it would have been wiser to have those men brought to him tonight; or whether he was right the first time in deciding that it would be good for them to wonder until tomorrow what they were in for. It would probably be necessary to court-martial the Flight Officer, whose name seemed to be Amos NMI Grandgent—the one who laid hands on a Deputy Provost Marshal in the person of Johnny's Lieutenant Day; and also Second Lieutenant Charles Carter, who, it was alleged, while F/O Grandgent held Lieutenant Day, wrongfully possessed himself of Lieutenant Day's side arm. The question, not quite settled in his own mind, was what exact effect might be expected if the other four were, or were not, charged, too? The ordinary presumption in law that the others, assisting by their presence, were equally guilty, was probably not here justified in fact—or at least might not be justified in fact. It did not follow that any two of the others would have assaulted the Provost Marshal if Grandgent and Carter hadn't made it unnecessary for them to assault him. Colonel Ross doubted that all six were equally resolute or firmly united in a business they could all be sure must have alarming consequences. It might be better to narrow it down—actual manhandling of a provost marshal in the performance of his duties made a military offense so flagrant that it ought to be possible, as it would certainly be very desirable, to appoint a majority of project personnel, colored officers, to the court.

This, of course, was taking a bright view. There was the possibility, in the dim view, that Bus would have what was substantially a mutiny to deal with. Mr. Botwinick's spies reported that, in one of the latrines, had been written by several hands: *This is Mr. Charlie's War;* and *Japs fight for Afro-Americans' Freedom;* there was also a sketch, showing a grave, with *For Whites Only* printed on the cross at its head. Counter-Intelligence would now have a spasm. Luke Howden would want to get to the bottom of this subversive plot before breakfast tomorrow. Without meaning to, Colonel Ross sighed aloud.

Colonel Coulthard, whose presence he had actually forgotten while his mind worked with weariness to bring order into this lumber of facts, conjectures, alternate possibilities, inconclusive conclusions, said: "It's a hard life, Norm. Too damn many things—you do all you can; and then somebody crosses it up. I hear Washington was onto that mess this morning. Did Jo-Jo Nichols say anything?"

"Not when I was there," Colonel Ross said. "Pop brought him and Baxter over. We had a social gathering. Bus gave them a drink and they talked about the flight down. Everybody seemed cheerful."

"Jo-Jo gives me the creeps, sometimes," Colonel Coulthard said moodily. "You don't know him very well, do you?"

"I never met him before. He seems to be something of a comedian."

"Funny kind of comedy, you'll find; if you see much of him. Before you finish laughing, if he decided that was the best thing, you might hear him say: 'Take that man out and shoot him.' He'd mean you. I knew him at Selfridge a good many years ago. He was Adjutant. He really ran the place. He runs

273

every place he is. You know; other people are horsing around, interested in different things; they get tired, they get sick of it all, they don't pay attention. Not Jo-Jo. He just drives right on. And, Norm, he isn't here for fun; don't think he is."

People in a service as close and clannish as the old Air Corps had a tendency to entertain extravagant ideas, whether hostile, or admiring, or, significantly, both, about each other. By and large, the airmen of the Army between the wars were a high-strung lot. Colonel Ross could see that it was natural, inevitable. They needed special psychological equipment—what amounted to a split in personality. To face the endless risks of aerial flight a man must have a sanguine, happy-go-lucky habit of thought; but replaceable instantly, at need or at will, by its very antithe-sis—a freezing into precision as the controls were taken. This was the condition of survival; the only way to put off sudden reali-zation of all those risks in sudden death.

Colonel Ross did not doubt that Nichols, like the rest of them who were still alive, would occasionally strike his fellow-psychopaths as psychopathic. He said, "He didn't come down because of the trouble this morning. It was all arranged several days ago. He was coming down for the party tomorrow."

"He must have had some other reason," Colonel Coulthard said. "And I don't believe Ollie Baxter's hopping the plane was any accident. Jingle Willie must have been told to send some-one from his office, too. Well, we'll find out, I guess. By the way, what did you make of my man Hicks, Norm? I meant to ask you."

Colonel Ross contemplated the subject of Captain Hicks with-out any eagerness. Though he had supported and advanced the scheme—indeed, largely arranged it—he realized that it was an incidental project, a possible opportunity to embellish or add a little something to his grand project, which he so clearly recognized when he sat moping in the Personnel Analysis Au-ditorium—General Beal. His judgment would not agree that it was a necessary job; and his experience assured him it was a useless one.

The public relations experts did have a basis of sorts for claiming their techniques were effective or even irresistible.

That they could mold opinion was proved by the way they had molded the Army's opinion, made almost everyone on the top level repeat meekly after them that public relations and its work of propaganda or, if you wished, "indoctrination," was of the most vital importance. Colonel Ross doubted if anything done since, and as a result of, this triumph at the top had produced advantageous changes in the public attitude; or that the war, due to these efforts, was in any way more popular— more vigorously pressed, more fully supported. Though they might like some of its effects, the people did not like war and nobody could make them like it. The effects they liked; high wages; the chance it gave a good many people to push in the name of the emergency other people around, needed like good wine no bush. Men did not have to be artfully persuaded to like what they liked. Where the persuasion was exerted to make them like what they didn't like, it was as always a complete and ludicrous failure.

The measure of this failure was clearest where its success was supposed to be most important. You had simply to contrast the time and effort put into "indoctrinating" the military rank and file, instructing the individual fighting man in "war aims," with the results as they appeared in his ordinary thought and real attitude. The average man already had firmly in mind the one war aim that carried or ever could carry any weight with him. His war aim was to get out as soon as possible and go home. This didn't mean that he wouldn't fight—on the contrary. Brought within fighting distance of the enemy, he saw well enough that until those people over there were all killed or frightened into quitting, he would never get home. He did not need to know about their bad acts and wicked principles. Compared to the offense they now committed by being here, and by shooting at him and so keeping him here, any alleged atrocities of theirs, any evil schemes of their commanders, were trifles. Though the level of intelligence in the average man might be justly considered low, in very few of them would it be so low that they accepted notions that they fought, an embattled band of brothers, for noble "principles." They would howl at the idea; just as, in general, they despised and detested all their officers; hated the rules and regulations and disobeyed as many as they could; and from morning to night never stopped cursing the Army, scheming to get out of it, and hotly bitching about the slightest inconvenience, let alone hardship.

On the face of it, Colonel Ross must admit, it would be hopeless to embark such an Army on a serious military campaign. Such men certainly did seem to need "indoctrination" the worst way—that is, if you knew nothing about the history of American arms. Colonel Ross could remember from his youthful enlisted days the attitude of the heroes of that war, the disgruntled volunteers. They had soon learned a song which—it was worth remembering, too—had drifted down to them from the Civil War. The song's enjoyable concluding couplet went:

"We'll hoist Old Glory to the top of the pole;
And we'll all re-enlist—in a pig's asshole!"

This irritable, almost infuriated scorn; this coupling of images, with the wish to outrage fancy sentiments entertained (they suspected) at home, summed up the American attitude. Colonel Ross, and anyone who used his eyes and ears, could see it had not changed. Colonel Ross doubted if it could be changed; and, as a matter of fact, whether from any practical military standpoint it needed to be changed. When the fighting began the bitchers would fight all right. Indeed, the event, the battle, proved that—still bitching, only more so; despising their officers still more; hating the Army still more, and regarding orders still less—they would usually fight to somewhat better purpose, man for man, than whoever was opposite them.

Considering this aspect of Captain Hicks's project a moment, Colonel Ross roused himself to an effort, not very successful, to recall the talk yesterday. He said: "I got the impression that Hicks could do it, if it can be done. If that's what you mean. I imagine he has contacts he can use if he wants to. I don't think he was too enthusiastic about the idea, as an idea."

"Why not?" Colonel Coulthard said. "I thought he was, this morning."

"I could be wrong," Colonel Ross said. "Only, I don't think I am. I think Hicks knows his field very well. I guess he was fairly important. He probably had a good deal of authority; I mean, he didn't have to ask anyone what he'd better think. Did he tell you he thought it was a good idea?"

"Not in so many words," Colonel Coulthard said. "I didn't ask him. He seemed ready enough to go ahead with it. I didn't get the impression that he was doing something he didn't want to. Is that what you think?"

"Did you get any impression about what he thinks of you?"

"I don't know," Colonel Coulthard said, surprised. "I really haven't seen a great deal of him. He's polite and pleasant. He doesn't seem to mind taking orders, even if he was some kind of big shot—"

Colonel Ross said: "You generally get to be some kind of big shot by using your head, one way or another. In the Army, you use your head by saying: yes, sir."

"I see what you mean," Colonel Coulthard said. The meaning apparently troubled him. He gave a short laugh. "Maybe Hicks thinks I'm just dumb. He could, all right. I wouldn't blame him. I guess he knows a lot of things I don't. There are some damn able men in my Directorate, Norm. If I knew all they know, I don't mind admitting I'd be a lot smarter than I am. At least five, I think six, are right there in *Who's Who in America*, so that shows you. Still, I don't think they dislike me—"

Colonel Ross said: "All I said was that if the project was left to him, Hicks might not, in his editorial capacity, be interested in the idea. That's all right. It needn't be left to him in his editorial capacity."

Colonel Coulthard said, uneasily, "I see that, Norm. Maybe I did give him a direct order to do it, and he said: yes, sir. But I definitely thought he was willing—"

"I think you thought right," Colonel Ross said. "I could see yesterday that he wouldn't mind the idea of doing a special job for the general. This morning, when he thought it over, he probably still liked it. Now, maybe when he's seen all we have to show him, he'll go back to his editorial capacity and decide there isn't anything he wants to do. We can help him with that. Maybe he'd better go to New York for a few weeks temporary duty to talk over the stuff with different magazines or people, see what he can arrange. I know his wife and family are up there somewhere."

"Sure," Colonel Coulthard said. "I suppose he ought to get something for it. I never know quite how to handle some of these—"

On the screen door at the end of the porch an apologetic tap sounded. Looking over his shoulder, Colonel Ross said, "Come in, come in!" Though he had not heard any car, he assumed, able to see the figure beyond the screen, that it was Mr. Botwinick. He saw now that it was General Baxter.

Getting to his feet, he said, "Come in, General! Your things were sent up. Care for a drink? Hal Coulthard has something in a pitcher there, if he hasn't drunk it all."

"Thanks very much, Colonel," General Baxter said. "I don't think I will. Hello, Hal. Colonel, Bus asked me to tell you he telephoned the Judge Advocate and had him hold those papers. He thought it would save time if the three of you considered them together in the morning. I will sit down a minute, if I may." General Baxter groped for, and found, the couch. He let himself down on it heavily.

"Not tonight," he said, "but sometime tomorrow morning, if you can, I wish you'd write or dictate a short statement for me on Colonel Woodman. I'm flying up there at noon for the investigation."

Colonel Coulthard said: "That was a damn awkward thing, wasn't it? You know who Bus first heard it from? My man, Hicks! I was there. That was damn awkward, too. Bus said something that showed Hicks he didn't know. Hicks knew, because he had a call from a fellow up there about a job he was doing. He thought he'd better tell Bus. Bus got white as a sheet. I think he really cared a good deal for Woody."

General Baxter said solemnly: "I'm sure everyone who knew him was shocked. That's why it was decided to appoint an Investigating Officer from HqAAF. The Old Man wanted to get to the bottom of it."

"What I hear," Colonel Coulthard said, "he might better not get there."

General Baxter frowned; but he said smoothly enough: "We'll find what we find. Since you saw him yesterday, Colonel, it would be a great help if you'd set down anything you observed about Colonel Woodman's state of mind. Bus said you had quite a long talk with him alone. I daresay you formed an opinion about the rationality of some of the ideas he expressed."

"I see," Colonel Ross said. "I'll have a statement ready before you leave."

"Bus said, among other things, that he thought Woody's behavior when he came down to meet you on the ramp was quite clearly distraught."

"That's true," Colonel Ross said. "I had forgotten that."

"I think we may find," General Baxter said, "that Colonel Woodman hasn't been right in the head. Not for some time. There were some very strange unauthorized communications from him to Headquarters. Well, I mustn't keep you up to talk about it now. I hope I haven't kept you up. It's very kind of you and Mrs. Ross to be willing to take me in, Colonel."

"I'll show you your room, General. We're very glad to have you."

✦

Lying on his back, frowning at the ceiling in an effort to keep awake, Colonel Ross said: "You know Captain Hicks. He was the one who took us out to the Club in his car. His wife was down visiting him."

Mrs. Ross, who was at the dressing table methodically administering to her hair the hundred brush strokes it got every night before she retired, said: "Oh, that one! Yes; she was quite a nice little thing; but not very sensible. I never knew what he did before he was in the Army. She told me she wasn't able to come down to stay because they had children in school up North. She thought it would be bad for them to be dragged around the country. I could have told her she was much mistaken. Disturbing their routine would do them more good than harm. A child will take almost anything for granted, if you let him. He's not nearly as sensitive as you are; and he adapts himself very easily. They seemed to have plenty of money; so there was no real reason why she couldn't come, if she wanted to."

Colonel Ross said: "I think, in many ways, a man is wise not to move his family down here. Where is he going to put them? It isn't entirely a matter of money. I've heard you find fault from time to time with what *we* have; but this is the very best there is; and the only reason you have it is that you happen to be married to a chicken colonel."

Mrs. Ross said: "That's a man's argument, Norman. Any woman knows perfectly well that she is either married, and so lives with her husband; or she isn't married at all. It may be very uncomfortable, and very inconvenient; but she ought to be with him, if it is in any way possible. Unless he has been sent overseas, she can always make it possible. She has no right to let him live alone. It isn't good for him; and what isn't good for him will not, in the end, be good for her."

Colonel Ross smiled drowsily. He said: "I suppose you mean you think he's bound to take the opportunity to misbehave himself. A good many undoubtedly do; but I think Hicks is quite a steady, sober fellow."

"That wasn't my whole meaning," Mrs. Ross said. Laying down the hair brush, she began to braid her hair. "But, yes. Certainly. I know about men. There's not one of them, get him away from his wife and family, who doesn't begin to kick up his heels and look around for chances to show what a gay dog he is. I daresay the chances available often don't quite suit him —they look risky; or they cost too much. Though, of course, he wouldn't pinch pennies the way he would at home. Or the girl sees right away that he's a married man on the loose, and that doesn't happen to be what she wants. So, if he does behave himself, you can be sure it is for one of those reasons; and he needn't give himself virtuous airs."

Colonel Ross laughed. "Which reason do you think was mine

when I spent those months in Washington last year? I can assure you that I never misbehaved."

"You would assure me that, even if you had, Norman. I admit it would be the least you could do. It's not an assurance any sensible woman wastes breath asking a man for. I meant 'risky' as covering quite a wide range, not just whether his wife would catch him. An older man may feel, and how rightly, that he'll look ridiculous tagging after some little creature half his age. He might not be able to face what other people would think of him. If he knows he's not as young as he was, he may be afraid of things the little creature herself might have occasion to think. Those are risks to his dignity."

"I admit I am not as young as I was," Colonel Ross said; "but for my age, I feel—"

"There was nothing in the least personal about that, Norman; though I don't know whether I could speak for little creatures half your age, if you were ever silly enough to take up with some. I'm simply saying that any intelligent woman knows you can't be married on a part-time, or spare-time, basis. Men have no sense about themselves, left to themselves. Unless a woman wants him to get into all kinds of trouble, she has no business to leave him for months and months. I didn't leave you for months and months, you may remember. And it was not convenient traveling on those trains, or comfortable living in that hotel weekends; and I had a hundred things to do at home, closing up, and so on."

"Why, my dear," Colonel Ross said, "I imagined that it was pure affection that prompted your visits."

"So it was! Do you think any woman who wasn't devoted to you would take all that trouble to see how you were, whether you were eating properly, whether your laundry was being done—and, of course, yes, to see that you didn't, like a certain number of men your age, and you know some of them, develop notions. Every cocktail lounge in Washington was full of them, picking up girls and drinking, if not actually too much, more than they were used to. If you remember what they looked like, you'll agree that no woman who was really fond of a man could let him make such a spectacle of himself.

And it *would* be a case of her letting him. He'd never be doing it, if he wasn't left at loose ends, with no one to look after him."

"He certainly wouldn't be doing it if he had no opportunity to do it. I see that," Colonel Ross said. "I am very glad indeed to have you looking after me; so you will not mistake me if I say that I think it quite possible that a fellow like Hicks, who seems to be happily married, with a home and children, might refrain for months and months from doing anything that would hurt his wife for no better reason than that he was fond of her."

"The weak point there, Norman, if by any chance you aren't perfectly aware of it, is the definition of 'anything that would hurt his wife.' He'll always end by deciding it isn't a matter of what he does, it's a matter of what she knows. He is wrong, of course. Either you see why, or you don't. It is a matter of falsifying a relationship, which has to be a kind of common trust, between two people. If he is, in the very exact phrase, untrue, and she doesn't know it, he may think he's getting away with something. He isn't. He has made it no longer a common trust. He's made an unstable arrangement of ignorance on one side and deceit on the other. However, that isn't what I wanted to talk to you about. Sal is very unhappy about Bus."

"Why?" Colonel Ross said.

Mrs. Ross had taken an orange stick, twisted a little cotton around the end with neat firm movements and applied vaseline to the bases of her nails. "She finally told me what I think is the principal thing. He doesn't sleep with her, Norman. He hasn't for over two weeks. She is very much upset. She was crying about it."

"The confidences of women seem to me extraordinary," Colonel Ross said. "What did you say?"

"I told her I thought it showed nothing but that he was very tired. I told her she should insist on his taking a week's leave at once and going away somewhere. He could surely do that. Couldn't you talk to this Nichols man, get him to tell them, when he gets back to Washington, to order Bus to take a week's leave? I told her I would see you did."

"I don't know that I can," Colonel Ross said. "I never met

General Nichols before, if I could be said to have met him now. I shook hands with him in Bus's office. With somebody I knew well, I might do it. I'd know how to put it to him. Incidentally, Baxter is here on his way to investigate the business at Sellers Field. I think he intends to find that Colonel Woodman was overwrought. I would not want it to get back to Washington right now that General Beal's staff was worried about him."

Mrs. Ross faced around. "I think you have something on your mind, too, Norman. Sal says she knows that Colonel Carricker is in some sort of trouble, and that's part of what worries Bus. Is that what worries you, too?"

"There's nothing much to that," Colonel Ross said. "Benny is impetuous in his habits. He lost his temper and punched another officer in the nose. I wanted Bus to come down on him. Bus didn't want to. We had a long talk. Bus is very strong for Benny."

"Yes, I know that. Sal is quite savage about Benny. I don't like Carricker at all. I don't see how anyone could."

"That's because you are looking for the wrong things," Colonel Ross said. "Benny represents something to Bus. It isn't entirely unreasonable. I don't suppose one man in a thousand has what Benny has when, as Bus would say, the chips are down. I can see it. I suppose you never have to wonder if you're covered, where your wingman is, if Benny is your wingman. I suppose Benny can just naturally outfly and outshoot anything that comes up against him; a beautiful sight. I suppose, when there's one second to do it, and you must be right or you'll be dead, Benny sees it and does it before he or anyone else has time to think. I have some reason to believe that last. I have seen Benny pull out a plane that, I expect, anyone else would have crashed; and I was on it."

Mrs. Ross said: "You never told me that. Yes. You're quite right. Never tell me. I don't want to know. I wish you wouldn't go flying all the time. I know it's useless to say that. I don't understand what you mean by saying Benny represents something to Bus."

"Maybe I don't understand myself," Colonel Ross said, "but something occurred to me this afternoon. I am not sure Bus understands it. He may; in an intuitive way. I think Benny is what Bus wishes he were; what Bus thinks he might have been, if they'd only had the war fifteen years ago, not now when he's forty and too old. Though I am sure Bus doesn't know this, I am also sure that nothing flatters him so much as to have Benny accept him as an equal, talk back to him, disobey him sometimes. That way, he knows Benny respects him. I think Benny does, too. I think Bus is one of the very few people Benny has any use for. They make sense to each other."

"I think it is dreadful!" Mrs. Ross said. She spoke with such unexpected intensity, and so vehemently that Colonel Ross opened his closed eyes. She had arisen from the dressing table and put out a hand that shook a little to snap off the light there. She said: "I think it's dreadful that they make sense to each other. They really make no sense at all! That's what is wrong with all this. That revolting young thug is supposed to make sense! If he does, then certainly nothing else does. Have you heard anything about Jimmy that you haven't told me?"

"Why, no, my dear," Colonel Ross said, "I am not sure I see the connection, if there is one."

"There is," Mrs. Ross said. She came over to the bed and sat on the edge. She bent and removed her slippers. "Believe me, there is." She snapped off the light on the bedside table and tensely lay down in the dark beside him.

"You must not worry," Colonel Ross said. "He will be all right."

"No," she said, "he won't be all right. He is never coming back. He is going to be killed."

Colonel Ross drew a deep breath. "That is absurd, Cora," he said. "I can tell you that our overall bomber losses are proving light. Only a fraction of what we anticipated, what we were prepared for. His chances are excellent. They will soon be even better, because we will be in a position to rotate the crews, bring home those who have flown a certain number of missions. Those are military secrets, of course."

"Who would I tell them to?"

"You read what he wrote himself. He—"

"I suppose they see to what he writes. I suppose he tries to write what he thinks I want to read. Even so, I know he was afraid when he wrote that letter, that last one."

Since that letter had been dated 18 August, Colonel Ross thought this likely. Every bomber base in England must have known by then what happened on the seventeenth. They must have known, too, that this wasn't the last, this was the first, massive strike at the German fighter-plane production complexes. That day, there was probably no member of any bomber crew at any base who was not afraid when he thought about it. Of course, most of the time, he didn't think about it.

Colonel Ross said: "I suppose you have me to blame, my dear. But I did not see what else I could do. And I don't see now."

"No; it's everything. I blame everything. I worked so long; I tried so hard—then something comes along, I don't know what, and just knocks everything over. What is the use of it?"

Colonel Ross said: "Don't press me on that point. I will not conceal it from you. I often wonder. I was wondering this afternoon. I am an old man; and the longer I live, the less I know, and the worse I do; and what, indeed, is the use of it? You can't do anything with people; I have been trying all day. I think Colonel Mowbray is a good man, and he is the biggest fool I know. We are having a little trouble with some Negro officers. They feel they are unjustly treated. I think in many ways they are; but there are insurmountable difficulties in doing them justice. The only people who stood up for them were two offensive young fellows, I think principally interested in showing off, in making themselves felt. I really saw nobody all day who was not in one way or another odious. I speak with confidence; for the certain number who looked all right, looked that way, I understand by now, only because I really knew nothing about them. And, of course, in every situation, I was odious, too."

"I know," Mrs. Ross said. She moved until her head rested against his shoulder. "Let's not go on about it."

THREE
SATURDAY

T HE COLORED boy thrust his head out the elevator door, looking up and down the corridor.

"Hold it!" Nathaniel Hicks said. He broke into a trot while he fumbled with the strap of his wrist watch which he had been putting on. It was five minutes of seven in the morning.

The waiting elevator contained a bald and solemn lieutenant colonel with Chemical Warfare insignia, probably a visitor down on temporary duty; and Major Beaudry, of Special Projects' Charts and Plans Section. Major Beaudry, a diffident-looking little blond man with glasses, said: "Hi, Nat." With a plaintive volubility well-known to Nathaniel Hicks, he continued at once: "Look; what time do you think you and your friend will be around about those diagrams? The Photographic Section put in for a rush job on some lettering. It wouldn't take very long, and if you weren't ready until nine o'clock or so, say, I'd let McCabe do that first. I tell you, I'm going crazy! Everyone thinks we can do everything on one minute's notice! I didn't mean you. You told me about this job a week ago. I hadn't forgotten it. Then, coming around yesterday, you give me a chance to see how much there is, and to keep McCabe clear for it today. If you have to start early, if your man has to get back to Orlando, or something; why, the hell with Photographic! They'll just have to wait. I told you you could have McCabe, and you can."

Nathaniel Hicks said: "Claude, you let him go ahead. I'll find out as soon as I can, and call you. I don't know what's going to go on this morning. After we talked to you, I took Wiley out to the Club; and there was a fuss there, and some people got arrested. The Club Officer took our names as witnesses, and said we'd probably be required to attend some hearing or whatever they have this morning. I don't know when or where. Are you going out now?"

"Well, that's all right, Nat. If you're delayed, McCabe can do the other. But just let me hear if you can't get over at all, will you? Yes; I thought I'd go right out. If I'm not in an hour before anyone else, we never get going. Couldn't give you a lift, could I?"

"Will you?" Nathaniel Hicks said. "Don Andrews has my car. He went to meet his wife at Orlando. She was coming on an Eastern Airlines plane, due at two or three. And there wasn't any way she could get over."

Major Beaudry said: "I wish I could get my wife down. My, I'm sick of living in a hotel. But, honestly! You ever try looking for a place to live around here? I swear to you, I was offered a two-room shanty with a pump and an outhouse at a special rate, because they were patriotic and I was in the Army, of one hundred dollars a month! If I didn't want it, there were plenty of people who did."

"I know," Nathaniel Hicks said.

"I suppose you're in the same fix," Major Beaudry said. "You don't want to ask your wife to come and live in a pigsty, or one room in a hotel. Then, when you have kids, they're probably in school; and then you probably have a place somewhere; and if it isn't in the city, maybe you could rent it, and maybe you couldn't, what with people not being able to get gas, or even maybe fuel oil to heat it. Oh, I tell you, it's a mess!"

The elevator doors opened on the lobby. Major Beaudry and Nathaniel Hicks drew back to allow the Chemical Warfare lieutenant colonel to precede them. He nodded in solemn acknowledgment. Major Beaudry said: "Say, isn't that Andrews?"

Looking, Nathaniel Hicks said: "Yes; and that's his wife, all right. You know, that's typical of Don! He probably got in here around five o'clock. He's going to put her up in his room in our apartment; but he didn't want to disturb us, I suppose. So they just sit down here and wait until we show."

"He's an awful nice fellow, I think," Major Beaudry said. "I hear he's a mathematical genius. Somebody told me he invented the secret code the Navy uses."

"Not quite," Nathaniel Hicks said, amused by this fine

example of the relationship borne by what you "hear" to what is actually the case. "What he did was break the Navy code, to pass an idle hour; and I suppose they had to overhaul the whole thing. It was at Gravelly. I was there when he did it. Well, I won't need the lift, thanks, Claude."

"But you'll let me know as soon as you can about whether you need McCabe, won't you?"

Captain Andrews had now seen Nathaniel Hicks. He arose from the couch and came rapidly to meet him. "Thanks a million, Nat," he said. "Here's your key. We used about eight gallons of your gas, I figured. I'm sorry about those coupons. I just hope you aren't going to need them. But here's the cash for the gas, anyway. You got time to come and meet Katherine?"

"Of course," Nathaniel Hicks said. "Look, you dope! She must be dead. Why didn't you bring her up when you came in and let her go to bed?"

"Oh, we thought we'd wake you if we came banging in there. She slept some in the car. We stopped and got some breakfast at a road stand, so we weren't here until quite a bit after five."

"Well, Clarence ought to be down in a minute. I ordered him to give the place a good scrubbing before he left."

Though a photograph of Captain Andrews's wife stood on his bureau (along with a photograph of his mother; and of a sister of his), Nathaniel Hicks was not sure that he would have recognized her. The photograph must have been taken a number of years ago, and he got from it the casual impression that Mrs. Andrews was a plumpish, probably short and heavy girl. She was, instead, he saw, thin and tall with a somewhat oblong face, which was thinned down from the curves of the photograph (probably a bad one) with a wan, not-young look— Nathaniel Hicks guessed she was in her early thirties. She had narrow graceful eyebrows of a light reddish brown, and matching hair—rather thin and brittle-looking; no vigor of red in the tone. Her eyes were a pale blue with, as she turned them, a tinge of green. Her thin body was sunk in lines of exhaustion against the faded cretonne cushions of the lobby couch. From the way she drew in her breath and moistened her lips before smiling at him, Nathaniel Hicks concluded that she did not feel very well.

She offered him a thin narrow hand that proved to be cool, even cold. Her clothes were simple and unnoticeable and had not cost much. The shoes of some reptile skin on her slender feet were scuffed. Nathaniel Hicks found himself touched in a mixed way—by the inexpensive, no, cheap, yet not tasteless frock, the old shoes; by the thin face, when, in a tender tired way, she passed her eyes over Captain Andrews; by the staunch effort of will which enabled her to smile.

"It was so nice of you to lend Don your car, Captain Hicks," she said. "I don't believe I ever would have managed to get here by myself. Oh, it was so wonderful when I saw him in front of the airport waiting at the fence there! It was all I could do to keep from bursting into tears."

"Well, we're very glad you're here," Nathaniel Hicks said. "Don's been fretting so, and fussing around, and biting his nails, that if it had been any longer we'd have had to shoot him, I guess." She lifted her eyes and looked at Captain Andrews wordlessly. Captain Andrews said: "That's a fact! I never thought of it, but I guess I drove them all crazy. You just couldn't get any space anywhere. As I told you, I finally had to ask Nat and Clarence if I could bring you in here."

She managed to get her eyes away from Captain Andrews and said to Nathaniel Hicks: "I do think it's awfully hard on you, Captain Hicks. And on Captain Duchemin."

"You're quite wrong," Nathaniel Hicks said. "We had to straighten the place up for the first time, though I doubt if you see where we did it. Under various things, Clarence found forty-one cents in cash; and I found a Club coupon book of mine with a dollar-ten in coupons in it. So, you see—there's Clarence now. It's all clear; and all yours."

Captain Duchemin, his big body rolling limberly from foot to foot, came across the old marble slabs. "Katherine," Captain Andrews said. "This is our other victim—"

His eyes bright and smiling, his wide, placid face grave, Captain Duchemin inclined his big cropped head, and when he saw she was holding her hand out, took it with a trace of awkwardness. Nathaniel Hicks had observed before that Clarence was not easy with women on whom he could not very well be forming any design. He said, gravely: "How do you do? I'm Captain Hicks's orderly, ma'am. I have to report to the captain: mission accomplished. Kitchen scrubbed; bathroom scrubbed; wet towels taken out of corners; old shirt removed from light fixture; empty bottles pushed under sofa; dirt swept under rug—it's in apple-pie order."

"I think it's so kind of both of you," Mrs. Andrews said. She got to her feet, and put a hand as though steadying herself, on her husband's arm.

"Not at all, ma'am," Captain Duchemin said, "I speak for Captain Hicks, too. Because he's my senior in grade, he makes me do most of his speaking for him, while he lolls around all day—"

"Nat," Captain Andrews said, "I'll be out as soon as I get her settled. Will you tell Woolsey, in case he tries to call my Section for anything?"

With Captain Duchemin, Nathaniel Hicks moved into the stream crossing the lobby to the front doors. Captain Duchemin said: "I think I'll be bivouacking in the field tonight, Captain. My young pigeoneer seems to have recovered from his indisposition of yesterday and we're concerting a joint operation on the unfinished business out there."

"All right," Nathaniel Hicks said.

"A serious understatement!" Captain Duchemin said. "I suppose it's the best you can do."

They crossed the high verandah and went down the steps into the already-hot sunlight. Blinking in the bright glare, Captain Duchemin cut a mock caper. Ebullient, light-hearted, he began to hum. Then, pitching his lowered voice to a reedy feminine falsetto, he began happily to sing.

"Oh, please do to me," he sang, "what you did to Marie—" he rolled his eyes up. "Last Saturday night, Saturday night—"

◆

Down the long hall, cool, empty, and shadowed, of that wing of Headquarters Quadrangle which contained General Beal's office Mr. Botwinick walked rapidly. Electric light fell out the door of the Message Center and the drumming click of the battery of teletype machines came with it. There was no other sound and no one in sight. Above the long range of closed doors, neat gold-lettered signs hung on metal brackets: *Assistant Adjutant; Adjutant General; Cryptographic Security Office; Judge Advocate General Section; A-1, A-2, A-3, A-4; Executive Officer;* and at the end: *Office of the Commanding General. Enter through 101A.*

Mr. Botwinick opened an unmarked door between *A-4* and *Executive Officer* and entered briskly. "Oops!" he said at once. "I beg your pardon, Colonel! I didn't know anyone was in yet."

The room held several desks, some pushed together toward the corner, some at a careless angle, which gave them an unused or little-used look. At one of them, with his feet on it, and a paper opened to the comic section in his lap, sat Lieutenant Colonel Carricker. He said, "Hello, Botty."

Mr. Botwinick gave him an attentive, furtive look. Lieutenant Colonel Carricker raised a cigarette burning between his fingers and took a puff. His hand was not steady. He spit a fragment of tobacco from his lip and ground the cigarette end out on the surface of the desk. His face looked damp, pale under the tan, and slightly tumid. His eyes were markedly bloodshot.

"I just wanted to get some forms from the filing case there, sir," Mr. Botwinick said. He went briskly over and pulled a drawer out.

Lieutenant Colonel Carricker said: "What's the pitch, Botty?"

Mr. Botwinick said: "Today, I really don't know, sir. We were trying to get you yesterday. I believed the general wanted you for something."

"What did he want me for?"

"I wasn't told, sir."

"Don't give me that, Botty! What was it? Is he sore?"

"Well, Colonel, we telephoned your quarters several times. Colonel Mowbray said finally not to call any more. I suppose the general knows."

"What's he doing this morning?"

"Why, I think the general is pretty well tied up, Colonel.

General Nichols, Deputy Chief of Air Staff, and General Baxter of the Air Inspector's Office, flew in late yesterday afternoon and I imagine he will be tied up with them, though I understand General Baxter is leaving at noon."

"What'd I better do?"

Mr. Botwinick, who had possessed himself of a handful of printed forms from the file drawer, shut the drawer carefully. His sharp eyes brightened. He pursed his lips thoughtfully. "Suppose I inform Colonel Mowbray, as soon as he comes in, that you are here, Colonel? It might be a good idea to have a talk with him. Though I don't know definitely, I think there was some plan yesterday to ask you to apologize to the officer with whom the—er—incident took place Thursday night. He was seriously injured."

"Where is he?"

"At the Base Hospital, I believe, sir."

"Do any good if I went over there now?"

"I wouldn't do that, sir, until I talked to Colonel Mowbray."

"I'm in a jam, huh?"

"I'm afraid so, Colonel. I happened to know that the general directed that papers be drawn, charges and specifications."

"I know that, too." Lieutenant Colonel Carricker lit another cigarette shakily and threw the match on the floor. "What happened to them?"

"They were held," Mr. Botwinick said. "I got the impression that Colonel Ross was opposed."

"Colonel Ross?" Lieutenant Colonel Carricker pondered a moment. "I don't believe that," he said. "He'd sure as hell slap it on me if he could. Come on, Botty. Give straight. What's happening?"

"Quite a good deal has been happening." Mr. Botwinick looked out the window into the quadrangle. "Some friends of the officer you struck, sir, were incensed, or pretended to be. A group of them attempted to force their way into the Area Officers Club, which is off limits for them, late yesterday afternoon. They overpowered the Provost Marshal's officer and six of them are in arrest. I understand that the general has been in communication with Washington." He paused. "I will tell you

295

in confidence, Colonel, that there is a TWX in this morning which the general has not yet seen, though he will see it within the next half hour. I delivered it with the other messages to Colonel Howden, who went down a few minutes ago. One of the press services picked up a dispatch with an Ocanara date line about a colored officer being assaulted by white officers and hospitalized. It seemed to be a garbled version of the occurrence Thursday. HqAAF requested immediate action."

"What do you think that means?"

"It could mean trouble, sir. I believe Washington took a strong line on the desirability of avoiding disturbance and publicity over the difficulty with the colored personnel. I suggest you talk to Colonel Mowbray, sir. I was just going to get myself some coffee, Colonel. Could I bring you some?"

"Yeah, will you?" Lieutenant Colonel Carricker said.

✦

Area Officers Mess Number Two was a long, low, yellow-frame building, with a kitchen wing built at right angles to it, between the row of BOQ's along Lake Oberon and the most easterly of the Directorate centers—Bombardment Analysis.

At quarter past seven the line always began at the door, or even on the steps outside, and extended the length of the room. It then doubled back along the cafeteria counter. The ranges of bare board tables, each seating twelve, were, in spite of the crowd, half empty; for most people ate in haste and the stream going out equaled the line coming in.

Behind the serving counter the mess orderlies were really sweating. The in-and-out doors to the kitchen wing swung constantly. Stacks of metal trays came banging to replace the piles at the head of the counter, diminishing as the line moved. Plates with slices of three kinds of melon were hastily dealt out onto the beds of crushed ice. The dozens and dozens of glasses of fruit juice embedded in the ice bed were renewed as fast as they were taken. Wheeled conveyors came from the kitchens to the steam tables with full pans of scrambled and fried eggs, of bacon and sausage and ham. Another was dropped in place over the hot water as soon as the servers, filling and passing out the plates, emptied one. Metal baskets of rolls and muffins and biscuits were pulled from the warming cabinets and dumped into the open compartments in the counter. One man did nothing but lay out on wide trays inch-square butter pats which came from molds that impressed on them: *Buy More Bonds; Remember Pearl Harbor; Keep 'Em Flying.* Another man ceaselessly replenished the ranks of pint bottles of milk in a trough of ice. Two others filled coffee cups from the big urns and handed them forward.

At the end, a checker, a WAC corporal, surveyed the approaching trays, punched her machine and dropped checks on them. The cashier, a civilian woman, took the checks and money and feverishly made change. Carrying their trays, the breakfasters distributed themselves, glancing around at the tables which a half dozen men kept clearing of used dishes and wiping with damp cloths. Big fans in the corners of the room had already been turned on. Over the tables and the line and the counters arose a steady din of talk, the scuff of moving feet, the bang and clatter of trays and dishes. The warm, damp air smelt of bacon and coffee and tobacco smoke.

Down near the door, at a table for the moment otherwise unoccupied, Captain Burton, the WAC Staff Director, sat eating a good breakfast with Lieutenant Lippa and Lieutenant Turck. Since it was more convenient for conversation, they sat two—Captain Burton and Lieutenant Turck—on one side; and one—Lieutenant Lippa—on the other.

Lieutenant Turck, whose breakfast was a glass of fruit juice, a cup of coffee, and a roll, was already through. Having carefully wiped the edge of the table with a paper napkin she put her elbows on it and lit a cigarette. Lieutenant Lippa, who had a half a melon and a bowl of corn flakes, was not so far along. Captain Burton, who had melon, and oatmeal, and ham and eggs, and two muffins, was a good deal slower. Although she ate steadily and with appetite, Captain Burton's full, sunreddened, well-scrubbed face was troubled. She said, "As of

One September, it was still the same. It was in the Headquarters News Letter. Regardless of assignment, no branch insignia other than Pallas Athenae may be worn by Wacs. I think they are going to change that; but they have not changed it yet. If Colonel Folsom told Wister differently, he was mistaken. She may not wear Air Force insignia, even if she is assigned to Fighter Analysis. She must take it off at once. I will, of course, order her to, if it comes to that; but I would rather one of you told her in a friendly, informal way."

Lieutenant Lippa said, "Colonel Folsom gave her the insignia himself and told her to put it on. He said it was authorized by Air Force Headquarters. I expect she thought she had to. There's been some hand trouble with Folsom. Somebody told her the best cure was to get three walnuts, you know those big round nuts, and put them under the edge of her stocking top." She chuckled. "It gives them pause, it seems."

Lieutenant Turck pulled down the corners of her mouth, directing at Lieutenant Lippa, with a shake of the head, a meaningful, warning look. Captain Burton grew redder. She flicked a muffin crumb off the full-busted front of her immaculate khaki shirt. She said: "It is perfectly true that certain men, given any opportunity at all, behave like beasts. When a girl knows that, I think she has a special obligation not to offer them, by her attitude or by any act that might be misinterpreted, any opportunity, any incentive. I don't think she does right to treat the matter lightly or jokingly. She has, as well as her own reputation, the reputation of the whole Corps to consider. A girl who is an officer has an added responsibility to set a tone or standard which the enrolled—the enlisted women can respect. I don't mean that I think Lieutenant Wister is to blame in this case. But I think she can, if she wants to, make it abundantly clear to Colonel—to any man, that familiarities would not be welcome." Captain Burton's distress was visibly increasing. "It's just not laying yourself open to misinterpretation." She came to a painful pause. She took her knife and fork and began to cut up the piece of ham on her plate. Lieutenant Turck transferred the cigarette from her right hand to her left, lifted her right hand and, frowning ferociously at Lieutenant Lippa, tapped a finger across her lips.

Without looking up, intent on cutting her ham, Captain Burton said: "I know neither of you will misunderstand me if I say I hope you'll both be particularly careful about that—possible misinterpretation. You're in town, down at the Oleander Towers, most weekends. It's quite natural for you to entertain male friends, offer them a drink, when you have a sitting room you can invite them up to. Nobody but a very narrow-minded kill-joy could see any harm in it. I certainly don't. But I do hope you'll be careful—I mean about having them up there too late; or letting them drink too much—you know; a party that attracts attention, that people hear down the hall."

Lieutenant Lippa said to Lieutenant Turck, "Do they hear us down the hall?"

"They might have once," Lieutenant Turck said. "The time that Britisher, the Squadron Leader, was doing the singing. We never asked him up. I don't know where he came from. He was wandering around, and the door was open, so he came in."

"Well, I do hope you'll be careful—"

Firmly interrupting her, Lieutenant Turck said: "Captain Burton, this is Lieutenant Edsell, of Special Projects."

He had walked up, balancing his tray, and stood with a confident familiarity that Lieutenant Turck did not much like behind the chair next to Lieutenant Lippa. "Greetings," he said. He acknowledged his introduction to Captain Burton by bowing negligently. "Good morning, ma'am. Mind if I sit down?"

Captain Burton said in confusion: "No. Not at all—"

From the confusion it was clear to Lieutenant Turck that Captain Burton had been hearing the rumors. In one connection or another, little tattletales, often well-meaning, would have apprised Captain Burton of the interesting circumstance that Mary was seeing a lot of a certain officer. Since Mary was not any too discreet about it, they might feel they had good grounds to hint further that Mary's virtue had been surrendered to him. Captain Burton, trying for weeks not to understand hints, determined never to believe any such thing about the girl well known to be her favorite subordinate and freely admitted to be her best company officer, now showed distress. Her flabbergasted look at Lieutenant Edsell proved that her real meaning a moment ago was just what Lieutenant Turck thought it might be. The hope reiterated was her fervent pathetic plea to Mary to make it not true.

Lieutenant Lippa, casually pushing out the chair for him, said: "Hello, Jim."

That was all Mary had to do. She made the non-committal words into a dead giveaway. Her clear-eyed, pleasant, pug-nosed little face suffused suddenly and strongly with an eloquent, distinctive shyness, delicate and high-strung. She was transfigured. Any woman, even Burton intent on blinding herself, must know intuitively what had come over Mary. The light tremble of the heart, the low quiver of the womb were too intelligible. It would be hard to misunderstand the lover's query that now posed her, and by its desperate importance, now reduced and humbled her. Afraid to allow herself to look directly, she waited with averted eyes, stretching her nerves to feel the answer in the ringing air.

Since this trembling and quivering, this supine reduction, very well illustrated an indignity that life tried to put on all women, Lieutenant Turck felt, besides concern about what Captain Burton might be seeing, indignation on her own part. She said in a consciously crisp voice: "I thought you were to be in the guard house today, Lieutenant."

She gazed at his face, of which the features were not bad; but she could count on its habitual expression to irritate her and fill her with distaste. There was a rude, overweening gleam of the eyes, and a cocky, loutish outthrust of the jaw that made Lieutenant Edsell look always as though he thought he had just scored off someone and was now pushing exultantly for a chance to do it again.

"Huh!" Lieutenant Edsell said. He stared at her cordially, for any remark that could be considered hostile, critical, or sarcastic, he probably took as a favor to him. The rough and tumble could begin without delay. He could run atilt immediately and start exchanging hits. "Where did you hear that?" he asked brusquely. "Nat Hicks?"

This hit was a good one; and it would be too much to hope that it was just lucky, that he didn't know it was good, or hadn't planned it that way. Practice in giving and taking injuries and insults had plainly taught Lieutenant Edsell to study anyone with whom he found himself often in altercation; and the insight he then demonstrated was disconcerting. He knew where to aim; and the same practice taught him the rapid expert jab that pinked you right there through any offered opening. His hit made, Lieutenant Edsell, too delighted by his success to be very malevolent about it, savored your reaction. Whether you howled, or whether you ludicrously pretended that he never touched you, it was all one to him—equally satisfactory.

Lieutenant Turck, with her own imprudence to thank—where else would she have heard it?—supported as well as she could the uncomfortable notion that rumor now had her "seeing a lot" of Captain Hicks; and that everyone in Special Projects leered and coupled their names. She said coolly: "Oh, word gets around."

Lieutenant Edsell said: "Doesn't it, though! Well, don't give up hope. I may land there, yet. The day is young and the trouble is plenty. The Brass bit a lot of it off yesterday, and I want to see them chew it."

"Oh, dear," Lieutenant Lippa said. "What have you been doing now?"

Lieutenant Turck could have slapped Mary gladly for the tender assentative tone and the silly admiring look; but, that would involve reaching across the table, so she said only: "He has been making trouble for poor old Colonel Mowbray; and now Colonel Mowbray wants to make trouble for him; but that wouldn't be fair, would it?"

Lieutenant Edsell said: "That old dodo! I hope to see him try! Not that I think he means much harm. He's just so goddamn stupid."

Lieutenant Turck could observe that Captain Burton, distress piling on distress, liked neither the profanity nor the contemptuous reference to a full colonel, General Beal's Executive Officer. Heedless, Lieutenant Edsell said bluffly: "I don't know how much you know about what happened yesterday; but I think we have them on the run. You may have heard that a special group of colored officers was brought in this week on a new project. The unreconstructed Confederates and other poor white trash, some of it from West Point, got all hot and bothered. Next thing, people might start treating a Negro like a human being! Can't have that! So, a lot of them decided to strike a blow for White Supremacy. I suppose they got liquored up, they usually do. The night before last, they gathered in suitable force—about twenty or thirty to one makes them feel fairly safe; and when a colored medium bomber crew came in and landed, they jumped them, over by Base Operations. It got hushed up, of course; but I guess the Confederates hadn't had such fun since they nailed the cat to the kitchen floor. I happen to know that at least one of the Negroes is still in the Base Hospital. That was the beginning of the trouble."

"I don't believe that ever happened," Lieutenant Turck said flatly. "I—"

"No, you don't. That's right," Lieutenant Edsell said. "That's the reason a lot of sadistic sub-morons down in dear old Dixie can do whatever they want to any Negro, any time. When you're told about it, you don't believe it. Those charmin', romantic Southern boys couldn't be that unkind, could they, sugar? Well, just take my word for this. It did happen. A lot of things you don't know about happen every day in the South. And a lot of things you don't know about happen every day in the Army. But never worry your pretty heads! Just keep not-knowing about them, and you'll be fine. Now, I'll tell you what happened yesterday, which, of course, you want to be careful not to believe."

Lieutenant Edsell had forgotten his breakfast after he had taken it off the tray and arranged it in front of him. Leaning across it, he said: "What really started the trouble yesterday was that Prescott Phillips, one of the Assistant PRO's, had the guts to try and get a square deal for a colored newspaper man; to get him the treatment any white newspaper man would damn well get. This man was accredited in Washington and sent all the way down here specifically to do a story on this bomb group project. Understand that. There was no question about his right to do the story. General Beal had orders to let him do it. Furthermore, I happen to be able to say that the man sent was topnotch. Of course, because he has a black skin, the reactionary press, the big papers, can't employ him, won't give him space; but he has about three times the intelligence and ability of the average nationally syndicated lug. I'm not guessing about this. I know him personally. I was at college with him. He worked his way through waiting on tables; and that's what I did, too, if you want to know." He looked past Lieutenant Turck and gave Captain Burton a hard, disdainful smile.

Lieutenant Turck could see Lieutenant Lippa listening with a doting absorption that must be second only to Desdemona's while hearing Othello tell what a remarkable man he was. Lieutenant Lippa goggled, finding all this passing strange, wondrous pitiful.

"Well," Lieutenant Edsell said, giving the air a short cut with the edge of his hand, "our local authorites took it on them to decide he couldn't do what Washington said he could do. They certainly didn't want that. Not after what they let happen the night before. And considering the fact that they secretly set up a lot of Jim Crow regulations to segregate the project personnel and were trying to keep it quiet. Of course, we didn't, then, know their reasons for being in such a panic. I saw right away that something smelled; but I didn't know what. Pres is a little naïve, in some ways. One thing: he's always had a lot of money. His old man is richer than hell—you know: Phillips. Though he's certainly been in the Army long enough to understand that when you see somebody getting a raw deal, you look the other way, but quick, the poor damn fool thought that if he brought it to Mowbray, Mowbray would fix it. Quite apart from the fact that Mowbray was, for these special reasons, scared to death, that was a laugh! Pres seriously thought a man, an old Trade School man from way back, who'd spent his whole life in the Army—I guess he would have starved to death anywhere else—gave a hoot about justice, for God's sake! What is that?"

Lieutenant Edsell noticed his coffee and took a gulp of it. Captain Burton arose. Her face was set and red. She said: "I've got to get over to the office." Her lips trembled; but she either could think of no more to say, or could not trust herself to say it. Bumping a chair indignantly, she marched to the center aisle and down toward the door.

"She get her ear burned?" Lieutenant Edsell said. "She won't beat on you, will she?"

With a hoyden air disagreeable to Lieutenant Turck, Lieutenant Lippa said: "The heck with her."

"I see what you mean," Lieutenant Edsell said. "It's a type I'm really awfully fond of."

"Rest easy!" Lieutenant Turck said. "You're a type *she* doesn't like at all. I have an office of my own I've got to go to, but I don't want to miss any of this. Could you hurry it up some?"

"Yes, I could, sourpuss," Lieutenant Edsell said. "But why should I? I'm really talking to Mary. You just happen to be here."

"I know all that," Lieutenant Turck said. "I'm only waiting for how you told Colonel Mowbray, the old Trade School man, where to get off. Does it come soon?"

"It comes this morning, maybe," Lieutenant Edsell said. "If he wants to go on with the party, that is. He may get a little surprise before noon: and I think he may be a good way up the creek, which is all right with me. In addition, he had to arrest quite a number of colored officers last night. They were all told that the Officers Club here was for whites only—part of this secret segregation scheme. And I'm very glad to say that some of them decided not to take it lying down and went there anyway. So, of course, they had to rush in the MP's."

"Tell me," said Lieutenant Turck, "just why are you very glad to say that? I can see you are; but tell me what there is about it to make you feel good."

"I don't like to see people walked on," Lieutenant Edsell said. "Four freedoms, you know. What we're fighting for."

"What who's what?" Lieutenant Turck said.

"Ah!" Lieutenant Edsell said, laughing delightedly. "Don't go losing your temper, Amanda. What did you really mean by that crack? That I just talk, that I'm too yellow to fight? I don't think I am. I wouldn't like getting killed any better than the people getting killed every day like it; but I don't think I'd run away. I can't help it if they put me here instead of there." He looked at her admiringly. "You know, something might be made out of you. You have a nasty disposition, which is the first thing you need if you're going to stand up to these sons of bitches. Now, I don't think you'd get so sore at what I say if you didn't pretty well know at heart that that's what they are, and that you ought to be doing something about it. You should have seen that roomful of smug bastards yesterday! They nearly died when Pres Phillips told them straight out what they were trying to do—old Mowbray chattering like a monkey; old Ross, the General's Air Inspector, pretending he was the impartial judge, boom, boom! A foul little squirt of a Personnel Analysis Major named Blake asking what difference it made what happened to a 'nigger.' Our dimwit of a Colonel Coulthard hanging his big mouth open—ah! Don't tell me you like swallowing their crap! I don't think you want to see people walked on, either!"

"Oh, no!" Lieutenant Turck said. "No, you don't! I don't have to join up with you—or else! This is a free country, my fine big-hearted liberal friend!"

II

GENTLY PUSHED, the door of the Public Relations Office swung wide open. Miss Crittenden, a thin, dark-haired girl in a bright red dress, nipped the tip of her tongue intently between her teeth and advanced with a cardboard box cover which served her for a tray. On the tray were several paper cups of steaming coffee and several sanitary glassine envelopes containing doughnuts. She made her gingerly way through the outer office, which was deserted, and into the small room behind where Captain Collins had his desk.

On the desk Captain Collins was resting his feet. He had tilted as far back as his chair would go. This put his well-featured, somewhat full face almost on a level with his feet.

Above his face, where he could stare disgustedly up at it through his heavy-rimmed glasses, he held a mimeographed release of several pages. He was reading rapidly, raising his other hand as he finished a page to throw it over.

"Them Pentagon jerks!" he suddenly said. He fired the sheets at the tray marked *File* on his desk, missing it. Then he took his feet down and said: "Thanks, Caroline."

He removed his glasses. Lifting a finger, he poised it. When she had set down the coffee and a doughnut, he shot the finger suddenly toward the chair by the window. "Leave those other coffees lay, honey child," he said. "Sit yourself down a minute, first closing the door about two thirds or three quarters, but not so much you can't see if anyone comes in out there. I have something on my mind, so-called."

"You want me to get my book, Captain Collins?"

"I do not! I just want your counsel and advice while I belly-up to this here piping hot Java." He pried the cardboard lid off the container, opened the doughnut package, bit a doughnut in half, and dipped it in the coffee.

"You, too," he said. "You can't counsel on an empty stomach, can you? Now, here's the business." He stopped and chewed the moistened doughnut thoughtfully. When his mouth was empty, he said: "Mr. Bullen, our pal Al, rings up here at eight o'clock sharp. He is not home in bed. He is down at the gate. He craves in. He has to see me right away. Why eight o'clock? Why me? Very unexpected and delicate subject. To wit: uh, now, racial relationships. Say no more on telephone."

Captain Collins drank some coffee. "This is hot!" he said, spilling a little on his blotter. "Watch it! Well, 'no more on telephone' is plenty for us old-newspaper-men-ourselves. I sent Pres Phillips, who for some reason was here on time, down to the gate right away. I had to. I was advised to stick to the phone, in case Colonel Mowbray felt ants in his pants early. So, now where are we? What is your impression of the character and temperament of Mr. A. Bullen, Ocanara *Morning Sun*, under stress? Will he, on sight, drag out his shooting iron and blow down Lieutenant Phillips, after what he wrote yesterday about what he thought of Lieutenant Phillips? Would I have been wise to give Mr. B. a different escort from there to here?"

Miss Crittenden looked at him with perplexity. She said: "Oh, I can't tell when you're kidding, Captain Collins! Why, Mr. Bullen would never do any such thing! He's the gentlest, kindest man. Why, I used to work for him, on the paper; I mean, back before the war. I don't know what Lieutenant Phillips could have done to make Mr. Bullen take offense that way. It must have been just a misunderstanding, is all."

"Good!" Captain Collins said. "I thought you'd know. Now, honey child, rack your brains. Any time yesterday, did you say anything to anyone outside this office touching on uh, now, racial relationships? You know; about our little unpleasantness yesterday? Honor bright, Caroline."

"Why, Captain Collins!" she said. She set the paper coffee cup agitatedly on the window sill. She turned almost as scarlet as her dress. "I'm sure I don't know—why, I wouldn't breathe anything that violates security! I declare; I don't know just what to say—"

"Well, if you can, please do think of something, honey child. You did maybe mention it?"

The color began to leave Miss Crittenden's scarlet face. She grew quite white under the rouge applied all over her cheeks in Southern small-town style. She said: "Captain Collins, I never, never breathed one word that violates any security. I never, never! Sometimes I might tell Daddy at supper little things that might have happened, that didn't have anything to do with classified material, anything like that. I might have just said we had some trouble about this colored man. I never thought that could matter—"

"What does Daddy do for Mr. Bullen? Something, doesn't he?"

"Why, he's chief press man on the paper," she said faintly. "Oh, Captain Collins, that's downright absurd! Why, he wouldn't think of telling silly little things—"

"Caroline; you ever mention to him this birthday shindig for the general? Back a few days?"

"I don't know, Captain Collins. I just don't know. I guess I could have, maybe—"

307

"Caroline, Caroline!" Captain Collins said. "Those pieces of poop, for reasons unknown, were stamped real pretty, top and bottom: *Confidential*. As a result, one Lieutenant Colonel Luke Howden, Counter-Intelligence, is steamed up over who poured the whisky in the well. We could be in a jam, you and me."

Miss Crittenden began to whimper. "Oh, Captain Collins! I never, never—"

Captain Collins looked at her compassionately. He drew a breath and let it hiss out between his teeth. "I don't think you did, either," he said. "Lordy, Lordy! Quick," he said. "Out of here, and go wash your face! They'll be along in a minute. I'll have to see what I can do. I'll see if I can fix it. Don't say anything to anyone."

"Captain Collins, I'd just lie down and die if—"

Arising, he went and took her arm, drew her to her feet and pushed her gently into the outer office. "Beat it to the ladies' room," he said. "Leave it to me." He closed the door after her and took the telephone from his desk.

The answering voice said: "Air Inspector's Office. Sergeant Brooks."

"Captain Collins, PRO. Colonel Ross there?"

"No, sir."

"Do me a great favor. When he shows, ask him if he will see me for five minutes. I have some important information bearing on an investigation I believe he ordered. I will have to give it to him verbally, and in his office. See if you can get me in before he leaves or somebody ties him up, will you?"

"I will tell him, Captain."

Captain Collins put the telephone down. As he expected, a knock came almost at once on the door to the hall. He opened it and confronted Lieutenant Phillips and Mr. Bullen. "Very kind of you to come out, Mr. Bullen," he said. "Come in. Would you care for some coffee? That was brought about five minutes ago. I think it's still hot."

Mr. Bullen inclined his head courteously. "No, thank you," he said. "I had myself some breakfast." He half turned and took hold of Lieutenant Phillips's arm. He said gravely: "That little misunderstanding between the lieutenant and me, I'm glad to say we got cleared up. Hasty words on both sides; and more of them on mine than his, I must admit. I think he knows I understand he was doing his duty; and he tells me he believes I hadn't any intention of disseminating anything that could hurt or embarrass in any way the war effort. Thank you very much for your trouble in fetching me here, Lieutenant."

Captain Collins said: "Well, Mr. Bullen, they make us lay down some laws, sometimes, that, personally, I don't think are necessary, at all. Frankly, there are times when I think we act crazy. We'll surely do our best to go along with you, just as far as they'll let us. Have a chair, sir. Pres, stick around out there, will you? We may have something. Bob Breck isn't in yet; but when he comes, tell him to stick around, too."

He closed the hall door. He said to Mr. Bullen, who stood politely near the chair by the window until Captain Collins had reached his own chair behind the desk, "The War Department Bureau of Public Relations is improving its policy line, Mr. Bullen. They do things better than when I first came in. I don't have to tell you I'm no soldier. I was in the ROTC at college, a good many years ago; and so I was suddenly jerked off the City Desk and put in khaki pants and told to buy myself an Officer's Guide. Here I am."

Mr. Bullen said: "I was well aware that you were a newspaper man, Captain Collins. That's really why I thought I'd take the liberty of coming out here this morning. I say that, because you might be surprised some at my coming to you about this matter." He lifted his spare, dry, tanned face and gazed earnestly at Captain Collins. "I have a number of reasons for it. I don't care to approach the Executive Officer, Colonel Mowbray, for any cause whatsoever. Though I had the pleasure of seeing General Beal personally yesterday evening, Mrs. Beal was present, and the general had guests, and asking him for a few minutes private conversation would not have been opportune. I thought of you, because I knew you were a newspaper man. I hoped I could talk frankly to you. I presumed it would be part of your duties to advise the general on any matters pertaining to public relations."

"That's what's in the book, Mr. Bullen," Captain Collins

said. "But I ought to tell you that the general wouldn't expect me to advise him unless he asked me to, first. He never has asked me yet."

"Yes," Mr. Bullen said. "I quite understand that. My thought, Captain Collins, was that I would give you, if I may, certain information that has come into my hands, so that someone on the general's staff here would know about it. Now, in one sense, this matter, at the present stage, is none of my business, none at all—a category of things I don't greatly enjoy mixing into. But it could get to be everyone's business in Ocanara. First of all, Captain, information has come to me about some quite serious trouble involving relations between blacks and whites out here. Would you feel able to tell me whether that is the case?"

"Not unless it's off the record," Captain Collins said.

"You have my word of honor, Captain Collins, that I will make no use whatsoever of your answer, in the paper, in any writing or conversation, at this time, or at any future time. I ask only for my own information, and I feel I can say my motives in so asking are not idle and impertinent ones."

"I'm sure of that," Captain Collins said. "I will tell you, then; yes. There has been trouble. I think 'quite serious' is an exaggeration; but I'm not free to tell you what happened. I completely accept your assurance that what I say will go no further than you; but, Mr. Bullen, that wouldn't change the fact that they told me what little I know with the tacit understanding that it would go no further than me."

"Of course!" Mr. Bullen said. "I ask nothing more. I asked what I did ask only because the information I have might be meaningless, a waste of your time, if there was, in fact, no trouble at all. You will understand, Captain, that any disturbance of relationships between whites and blacks must cause, anywhere in the South, the gravest concern. I feel that concern deeply; and I am sure everyone in Ocanara, black and white, feels it."

Captain Collins said: "Well, Mr. Bullen, I think we all understand that. There just doesn't seem to be any final answer. It's certainly a tough problem."

Mr. Bullen said quietly: "Like you, Captain, I came from the North. I was not born here; but I have lived here the best part of twenty-five years. I have formed certain conclusions in that time; but I won't trouble you with my conclusions. If there are differences of opinion, I think most of them are differences that always arise between those who have to deal with facts, and those who are free to deal with theories. In that encounter there is a good deal of heat and never very much light; but I believe reasonable men, whatever their opinion, can meet on one point. Violence and disturbance will not help anybody. The interests of those who promote violence or disturbance are certainly not the interests of those, black or white, who must live together, and who want to live together amicably."

He put his hand inside the breast of his loose coat of faded wash material and brought out several folded papers. "What I have here," he said, "are copies of some telegrams dispatched from Ocanara yesterday. The first, you will see, is to the War Department, signed 'James.' One of the others is to a well-known Negro organization. Also signed 'James.' The third of this group is to an individual in Washington, from James, too. To this same individual, there is a telegraphed money order, the record of which shows that it was paid for by a Lieutenant J. A. Edsell, though the accompanying telegram is, again, signed 'James,' I assume this lieutenant sent it, because his name is noted as a return address on the original. Put together, I think we get this. In connection with the events truly or falsely described in telegrams one and two, somebody named Stanley was injured and put in the hospital. This Willis, in Washington, to whom the third telegram went, is ostensibly a relative of Stanley's. He is urged to come at once. We haven't got his answer; but probably he didn't have the money. The money was then sent him by this officer, Edsell. In view of the sending times, Willis could be on the train due here at ten o'clock."

Captain Collins took the papers and spread them out on his desk. He put his glasses on. After a moment, he said: "I see. This telegram to the War Department, I think Headquarters here knows about. As far as I know, this Stanley, whoever he is, is not connected with the other. Nobody was injured then. I know that." He paused and looked at Mr. Bullen. "I must ask you a question, if I may, Mr. Bullen. To use this information, I would have to know how these copies came to you."

Mr. Bullen said thoughtfully, "Yes. I think you are right to want to know that; but if it means that you would be obliged to make a statement about it, I don't want to tell you. Let me make myself clear. I have no objection to your saying that *I* showed you the copies. In fact, I will leave them here with you; and if an inquiry is made, it can be referred to me."

"That is satisfactory," Captain Collins said. "I won't ask you, then."

"I would prefer to tell you, for your own information. I think you have a right to know," Mr. Bullen said mildly. "Police Chief Lovewell, in an official capacity, asked to inspect the files. He thought it proper to do this on information which reached him through an ordinary police channel on the contents of telegrams one and two."

"I see," Captain Collins said. He looked at the copied telegrams again. "You say you think Willis may be here on the ten o'clock train. Is the Chief of Police interested in that?"

"He will be at the station himself. Mr. Lovewell would want to know who meets Willis, and where he goes. If Willis is really down here to see a relative, who is in the hospital at the Base, that's all there is to that. I suppose the military authorities will decide whether he can see him or not. You tell me you don't know of anyone's being injured; so that may increase a possibility, that Mr. Lovewell wouldn't overlook, that it is a blind. This man Willis might represent the Negro organization to which the second telegram went. Or some other. If he is in Ocanara with the idea of arousing any kind of disturbance, Mr. Lovewell would not want to be taken by surprise. I thought it possible that someone out here might want to check on the man in the hospital and look up this officer, this Lieutenant Edsell. I imagine he would be a colored officer. Well, Captain, I thank you very much for your time and patience. That's the sum of the thing." Mr. Bullen arose and took his hat.

"Thank *you* very much, Mr. Bullen," Captain Collins said. "I'll make some inquiries. In fact, I can call right now and find out if there is anyone named Stanley at the Base Hospital, if you like."

"I would be very glad to give Mr. Lovewell that information," Mr. Bullen said.

Captain Collins took up the telephone. "—yes, Stanley," he said. "No, I don't know his first name, or his rank. He may be an officer, he may be an enlisted man, he could be a civilian. You haven't? O.K., thanks."

He looked at Mr. Bullen. "Could he be in a hospital downtown? No—it says Base Hospital. That's that, I guess. Of course, he might have been discharged last night, I suppose. Maybe I'd better check that."

Mr. Bullen said, "I'm afraid, Captain, you'll find Mr. Lovewell's idea was right. It fits together. Thank you again for your trouble."

"I'll make some inquiries," Captain Collins repeated. "I don't quite know—well, we'll see. Just a moment, sir, and I'll have Lieutenant Breck go with you." He opened the door to the outer office and said: "Bob, will you take the car and drive Mr. Bullen downtown?"

When they were gone, Captain Collins called out: "Pres, can you come here?" With Lieutenant Phillips in the office and the door closed, he said: "Hear anything from Mowbray's office?"

Lieutenant Phillips shrugged. "Not yet," he said.

"Well, we'll keep our fingers crossed. I've got to see Colonel Ross, if I can, about something else this morning. I may be able to find out what's cooking."

Lieutenant Phillips picked up the metal model of a P-47 which Captain Collins used for a paper weight and looked at it. "Frankly, Dick," he said, "I don't give a damn. Though I'm sorry you got dragged into it."

"I'm sorry, too," Captain Collins said. "And I *am* in it; so will you not give your damn in as inconspicuous a way as possible? I don't blame you, Pres; but for God's sake try not to stir it up. Incidentally, have you any idea what your friend Edsell is doing, or thinks he's doing?"

"Yes, I know. But I don't think I'll tell you. It wouldn't do any good. It might just involve you some more."

"Even so," Captain Collins said. "If you know, would you just as soon tell me who in hell this man in Washington, name of Willis, is that he wired money to? I might as well tell you the Ocanara police think he's some kind of professional agitator. Now, what is Edsell; nuts?"

Lieutenant Phillips laughed. "That's a good one," he said. "These bastards certainly shake in their big shoes! I guess the wicked are still fleeing when no man pursueth. The man Edsell sent the money to, and if you want to know, I put up half of it, is a waiter in a Washington restaurant. His son was one of the colored officers sent in on this project. The other night I understand he tried to use the can in the Operations building —he'd just flown in—and some white officers took him out and beat him up so badly they had to take him to the Base Hospital. I suppose Mowbray wanted to hush it up, and they were hushing it up. James heard about it from some of the project personnel yesterday morning before they ran him off. He told Jim. Jim figured that if they got that boy's father down here, even if he was just a colored waiter, Mowbray would have to let him see his son, and would have to explain what happened, and take some action against the people that beat him up. I go right along with that, Dick." He put down the P-47 model.

Captain Collins said, "If that's true, I go along with it, too. I'd better call the general's office—no, wait; first—the boy who was hurt was named Willis too, then?—" He rocked back with the telephone. "Outside," he said. "I want the Ocanara *Morning Sun,* Mr. Bullen's office—yes. Captain Collins, Area Public Relations Office. Will you see Mr. Bullen hears, as soon as he comes in, that a—please write it down—Stanley Willis was injured, was sent to the Base Hospital. This bears out certain messages he knows about. This is Captain Collins. I will give you my extension, if he wants to check it." He put the telephone back.

"Going to call the general?" Lieutenant Phillips said.

"Well, hold on," Captain Collins said. "First I'd better get my facts straight. And I think I'd better check with Colonel Ross. He must know something about it. I'll try him again."

"You won't get anywhere that way," Lieutenant Phillips said. "He isn't going to buck the system. What's in it for him?"

✦

Profoundly disturbed, Colonel Ross could see—or, better, feel; for there was nothing arresting or notable to see—that some grave change had taken place in General Beal. Something had gone out of him; some distinguishing inner mettle, a sustained tension of nerves, a spirit wound up to act; something so much a part of Bus that it was hardly noticeable, taken for granted. Its characteristic look was always on Bus's face, immediately beneath surface expressions of pleasure or good humor, of irritation or anger. Its characteristic sound was in his voice, whatever his mood of the moment, whatever he was saying. A series of random pictures passed in Colonel Ross's mind: Bus turning his tense face sharply, the assured snap of the brown eyes, the lips parting with decision. Casual fragments of speech, firm through all the various tones of the occasion, came to him:

"—I don't like rubbing it into Woody, throwing my weight around with him—hell! You hungry?—"

"—Oh, Judge, that boy's a honey! You can believe—"

"—I just don't feel like sitting here; so I told Danny—"

"—don't *you* blow your top, too, Judge. Everybody else—"

Colonel Ross did not know if others at the breakfast table saw it; but he saw it. In the morning shadows Bus was calm to the point of indifference. At the head of the table, his back to the closed door, Bus sat listening, with an appropriate enough expression of mute reserve, but also with small signs of a profound detachment, to Lieutenant Colonel Howden's not too well organized remarks on the importance, when a first sign of disaffection appeared, of getting to the bottom of it, nipping it in the bud.

Colonel Ross now thought it significant that Howden, like Major Tietam, the Judge Advocate, had been asked to come into the dining room and bring his business. What they said would necessarily be heard, too, by General Nichols and General Baxter. Bus might feel that Nichols and Baxter knew plenty anyway; they might as well hear more. That was reasonable; but it became easy, once his apprehension about Bus had formed, for Colonel Ross to read into it a sullen passivity. Bus resigned here and now his right and his responsibility (nothing could separate them) to handle this himself; make his decisions; give his orders—in short, run the show, command the situation.

Colonel Ross asked himself whether General Nichols was also feeling this. He could not tell. General Nichols's face was composed, serious but easy, and nothing could be learned from it. General Nichols was beautifully shaved and beautifully dressed—no doubt, because he had official parts to play today as the Chief of Air Staff's proxy. He wore a so-called battle-jacket, the first that Colonel Ross had ever seen made of light material, a fine thin tan gabardine. Under the Command Pilot's wings, General Nichols had four rows of ribbons. Colonel Ross observed that the collection was unusual. It included none of the combat theater throwaways of this war—the Silver Star, the Distinguished Flying Cross, the Air Medal. Since he could hardly have come back without them, this would indicate that no combat command had yet been given General Nichols. The ribbons he did have—the Distinguished Service Cross, the Distinguished Service Medal, the Legion of Merit—might explain that. The first two probably dated from before the war, when medals were hard to come by. The Legion of Merit would be for recent services. Taken together, they would show that he failed to get a combat command not because somebody thought he didn't rate it, but because somebody couldn't do without him yet at Headquarters. General Nichols was a bombardment man, Colonel Ross knew. It was safe to bet that there would be something good for him when the apocalypse of the Twenty-nines was opened to Japan.

Except for the theater ribbons, showing that General Nichols had been allowed at least to visit overseas, Colonel Ross could identify none of the others he wore. Then they must be foreign; and that, too, was significant. They were probably picked up in the course of service as an Air Attaché at several capitals between the wars. Since governments to which he was accredited gave him medals, he pleased them. Since he could not have so many unless the War Department found him useful, his work had pleased all his superiors. It took a man of parts to play at once the charming guest and the industrious spy.

Lieutenant Colonel Howden's voice broke into Colonel Ross's brooding by saying his name. Howden said: "I can't quite go along with Judge Ross's opinion, sir—" he looked apologetically at Colonel Ross and then back to the general. "I feel it does point definitely to disaffected individuals. The nature of the thing—being the Japanese propaganda line—makes it grave. In my opinion. I don't mean I think there's any actual plot— yet. Writing things up on the walls that way is a kind of sounding-out—to get to know who else feels the same. You have to watch it. You may remember all that 'OHIO' stuff back in 'forty-one."

Colonel Ross stirred and said: "How many of them *did* go over the hill in October?"

"Not too many," Lieutenant Colonel Howden said. "Because we paid attention. We were ready to act. I was at Chanute then, and I know what the problem was, Judge."

"The judge could be right, though," General Beal said laboriously. "It's a way to let off steam. If somebody is going to duck out, or do something treasonable, does he go advertising it? I don't know; but I don't think they write it up in latrines."

General Nichols said gravely: "The last thing I saw written up in a latrine was: 'Kindly do not throw cigarettes in the urinals as they are hard to smoke when wet.' What do you suppose that meant?"

General Baxter laughed; and so, as though against his will, did General Beal. Colonel Ross, involuntarily, taken by surprise, joined them; but not against his will; for this coarse conceit unreasonably relieved him, restored the practical sense

317

of proportion which he had been losing in his alarm about Bus and Bus's state of mind. Lieutenant Colonel Howden smiled in a worried acquiescent way, not willing to give up his point, but not insensible to the privilege of being in attendance while generals familiarly joked. Major Tietam's round, solemn, little attorney's face assumed hastily a similar unreal smirk.

And another thing, Colonel Ross thought, anxious to hold his recovered balance: it ought not to be forgotten, while they beat their brains over this teapot tempest in a Zone of Interior installation, while the Charge Sheets that Major Tietam had passed to him—incidentally, why, when it was sure they would have to be handled a lot, did they print WDAGO Form No. 115 on such poor paper?—lay there specifying under Article of War Sixty-four the offense of six men in their willful disobedience of the Assistant Provost Marshal's order not to enter the Area Officers Club; now, at this very moment, if the weather had been at all possible, Eighth Air Force bombers were turning, a certain number of them damaged with engines out and dead and wounded on board, to try to make their English bases. Perhaps also at this very moment Fifth Air Force fighters were dropping belly tanks as the Zeros came climbing at them over some formerly unimportant Indonesian harbor.

General Beal said: "What about it, Judge?"

General Nichols looked at him, too. General Nichols's civil interest probably included a wish to satisfy himself about this elderly colonel's (no Military Academy ring; no wings; he would have noticed) part in the administration of the Operations and Requirements Analysis Division.

Colonel Ross said: "I think you sized it up, General. I think Luke put Counter-Intelligence's angle on it very well. I think he could keep his eye on that. But in this particular case I would certainly go along with you in feeling we don't have to act on it now. It's relevant. It might come to be important; but for the present it tells us only what we know already—

318

some of the project personnel are in a resentful mood. Let's deal with that first."

General Baxter said: "Bus, if I could put in my two cents' worth, I'd say that was just exactly right. The feeling in our office is that the purpose of any investigation is to develop facts in doubt or dispute. If that isn't necessary, the investigation isn't necessary. If it isn't necessary, it is undesirable; and I don't mean just because it makes work for our Special Investigations Division! It wastes everyone's time, and often it aggravates the trouble. In this case, if these colored boys have got it into their heads that they're being persecuted and badly used—"

"Is that what they say?" General Beal took up the sheaf of TWX messages next to his empty coffee cup. Leafing them over, he pulled one out and extended it to General Nichols. "Read that," he said. "Now, who gave that out? It's not true. There was no riot here. Why does a press association pick up a thing like that without bothering to find out whether it's true or not? Why do the Air Forces Group people in Public Relations fire that upstairs when they don't know whether it's true or not?" To Colonel Ross's renewed disturbance, the general spoke without anger or even emphasis, as though the question were real, not rhetorical; and the answer must be something beyond him, something he wouldn't even try to figure out.

General Nichols gave the lines of typed tape a comprehensive glance. "Well," he said, "they were probably told to send up anything their Press Section found that mentioned Ocanara. About the newspapers; that's always interested me. Most of the things you read in a newspaper you naturally don't know anything about, except what they tell you. Did you ever happen to read a newspaper account of something you did know something about? It's always more or less wrong, usually more. I'm told it's because most stories are rewritten when they get to the office by somebody else, not the man who covered the story. They have to make them fit between the advertising. I don't think it's done on purpose. I don't think they'd mind if they had it right. There's nothing you can do about it."

"I'm not going to try to do anything about it," General Beal said. "All I say is, if it happened, I don't know about it.

So I can't give them any report on it. I suppose I'd better tell them the business last night before the newspapers do. I don't know what they want. I don't even know whether they think I have some plan to persecute Negroes, or whatever Ollie said. Is it all right for me to court-martial these people? Did they tell you?"

General Nichols said: "As far as I understood the telephone conversation, they told *you*, Bus. I certainly didn't hear anything to make me think they weren't leaving you free to do whatever you needed to do to maintain discipline."

General Beal said: "Even if I get in the papers? We have a leak here to the papers. The Judge can tell you about it. Whatever I do is going to be in the papers. I'm not going to act in this without an Air Staff directive. Can you give me one?"

General Nichols shook his head. "Not me," he said. "I don't have any with me. I don't think you need a further directive, Bus. Some men willfully disobeyed an order and aggravated it by assaulting a provost marshal. What's the normal procedure? Is it to ask Washington for a directive?"

General Beal said: "Damned if I know, nowadays. This is their party, not mine. I've thought about it; and there are things they can't do to me, Jo-Jo. They can't give me the responsibility and keep the authority; and if I have to turn my suit in and join the Marines, I'll do that. I hear it's good. I hear they gave anyone with a military pilot rating a second lieutenant's commission right away."

Colonel Ross said: "Before you do that, General, let's give the AAF one more chance. Why don't we work out a course of action right now. Call Washington then, if you like, and tell them what it is, and if they don't like it, why they can suggest something else." He glanced at General Nichols who was lighting a cigarette. "Why let them suppose we haven't any plan?"

"Well, have we?" said General Beal. "Have you?"

"I think we can offer some suggestions," Colonel Ross said. "You have three members of your staff here, and this is a matter that comes more or less in their fields. If they can't offer you practicable suggestions, you'd better get a new staff." He took up the Charge Sheets. "We have six of these," he said, "all the men involved. I'd like to suggest, if court martial is indicated, that we narrow it to the two who assaulted the provost marshal, and that we make it a joint charge."

He looked at Major Tietam who said, "I quite agree, Colonel. This was simply tentative—in case, for some reason of policy I might not know about, the general might desire to prefer the charges separately and hold separate trials—there are different specifications, you see."

Colonel Ross turned the sheets over. "Yes," he said. He turned them back to look at the witnesses. "Who is this Captain Eugene P. Wiley, AFSAT, Orlando? How does he happen to be here?"

"I don't know, Colonel. I believe he was in the Club as the guest of the Captain Hicks, there. I don't know who Hicks is, either."

"I do," Colonel Ross said.

"Hicks?" General Beal said. "That Hal's fellow, yesterday? I thought I sent him to Boca Negra. Well, anyway, that's one project we'd better stop. I guess we're getting all the publicity we can stand. Anyone talk to these witnesses?"

"There was no investigating officer appointed, sir," Major Tietam said. "I based my summary on what Lieutenant Day, the Provost Marshal's officer, said."

"We'd better appoint one," Colonel Ross said.

"All right," General Beal said. He yawned. "You're it, Judge. Now, do what you want."

"What I want is a telephone," Colonel Ross said. "I can start my people rounding up the witnesses. I think we could have a hearing by ten. Let me do that now."

"Do whatever you like," General Beal said. "One thing; I think we'll cancel this show this afternoon. Jo-Jo's seen a parade. He doesn't need to see another. Have someone telephone Pop and tell him it's off."

"I don't think you can do that, General," Colonel Ross said. "It's in the paper this morning. A lot of plans, both here, and at other installations, have been made."

General Nichols said mildly, "I like parades. When I fly all the way to Florida to see one, I want to see it."

"If you like them, you can have them," General Beal said.

Colonel Ross had started toward the door; and, though he hesitated, he saw that he might as well go on. He went on quietly, opened the door; and stepping through, bumped fairly into Mrs. Beal.

Sal's right hand was raised, the wrist pressed against her mouth. In her left hand, hanging at her side, she clenched absently, probably unaware of it, a folded newspaper, twisted and bent in her tight fingers. She dropped the wrist from her mouth, showing her lips puckered, as though in pain. For the dumbfounding instant, Colonel Ross wondered if, bumping into her, he had hurt her. Then, quickly, he drew the door closed behind him, shutting them out into the hall together.

She said: "What is it? I want to know, Norm! I have to know—"

"Why, yes," Colonel Ross said. The need to know must be an insupportable need, if it brought her to come close to the door, perhaps made her put her ear to it. He said, "Come along down here. I have to telephone. Let me telephone, Sal. I have to get word to my office about some things Bus wants done. You'll let me do that, won't you?"

She said: "You won't tell me."

"I will tell you," Colonel Ross said. He put out an arm and pressed it against her, making her move. "But you'll let me telephone first, won't you?"

"No," she said. "What are they doing to Bus? You tell me now! You know. You have to tell me." She got her breath. "If you don't, I'm going right in there."

Colonel Ross said: "What will they think if you do that, Sal? What will Bus think? I'll tell you all there is. Bus has to decide what to do with some people who disobeyed orders. That's all we were talking about. I am trying to help him get the matter cleared up. That's why I came out to telephone."

"No," she said. "That isn't all. I heard more than that.

You're not telling me. I told you you wouldn't!" She stepped unsteadily sideways, as though to get by him; and Colonel Ross moved heavily, blocking her. Blocked, she let the folded newspaper fall to the floor. She doubled both hands into fists, and, frenziedly, her face contorted in the shadows, she began to beat the fists against his big chest.

Appalled, he said: "Sal, Sal!" He managed clumsily to catch her thin wrists and hold them. "You can't do this!" he said. "You've got to help Bus. You can't act this way—"

The wrists relaxed in his hands and he let them go. The disheveled blonde hair was half over her face. It swung back listlessly as she turned away. She put a hand on the stair rail, and held it. Still holding it, sliding her palm along it, she began to climb. Without turning her head, she said woefully: "Go on and telephone, Norm. I'm going upstairs."

Colonel Ross, still unnerved, noticed the newspaper on the floor where she had dropped it. The air of disorder it gave the hall troubled him. He went back, stooped, and picked it up. It was this morning's Ocanara *Sun*, and on the rumpled front page was a large photograph showing General Beal sitting on the living room sofa, his expression stern but boyish. Mrs. Beal, in the elaborate white dress, sat beside him, one arm through his, the other around her son who leaned with a petulant stare against her knee. Mrs. Beal was grinning engagingly at the camera. The caption said: *Happy Birthday to You!*

III

FROM BASE GATE NUMBER THREE, First Sergeant Charles Augustus Lindbergh Rogers was marching the three platoons of a Negro Engineer Corps company in column of fours across the level coarse grass and less-firm stretches of bare sandy soil of the air field toward the construction work on the extension of the long runway by Lake Lalage.

Though the company had the informal bedraggled appearance that went with field hats and herringbone twill work uniforms, the marching was good, the pace steady, the lines and files commendably true in spite of the often changing character of the ground. Off to the column's right, Sergeant Rogers, imposing in carriage and stature, his gleaming black face cocked up, boomed resonantly: "Hut—two—three—four! Hut—two—three—four!"

He turned in his stride, prancing backward with a shortened step, so the first platoon passed him, and the second, stiffening into greater precision under his ranging eye, came abreast.

"Count cadence three times!" he sang out suddenly. "And make me hear you!"

"Count cadence three times," chorused the Platoon Sergeants.

"Now, count!"

An exuberant hundredfold bellow broke from the column, shaking the bright morning air, certainly audible a mile away: "Hut—two—three—"

Spinning on his heel, Sergeant Rogers faced front again, surveying the runway ahead, now near at hand. "Column half right," he shouted, "march!"

He watched them vigilantly as they came up to the turning point and bent past him, moving parallel to the runway pavement. When they were all by, he called: "Company, halt! One: two!"

He stalked up to the Second Platoon. "You, there!" he said. "And you! What did you push him for? Fall out, both you!"

He stood brooding over them while he looked up toward the construction work. "That bulldozer," he said. "Not the first, the far one. At the double, up there and back! And go on doing it until I tell you. Start running and keep running!" He saw them off, watching them a minute. "And don't run funny!" he roared. " 'Less you want to run all day! Hold yourself up! Don't run like a monkey, run like a man!"

He faced the waiting platoons. "Company, at ease!" he said. "I said: 'at ease,' not 'at rest'!" Leisurely and severely, he passed his eye over the platoons. "At rest!" he said. "Nobody get out of ranks. Nobody start hollering or yelling, or you'll be at attention. Sergeant White, you take over. I got to find Lieutenant Anderson."

"He right there, Sarge."

"He coming now, Lindy."

"Who asked you, Bo? All right! Company; attention!"

The company commander, First Lieutenant Anderson, was approaching with an Air Force captain. Lieutenant Anderson, his shirt collar open, his sleeves rolled up, was deeply sunburned. He shot an anxious look at the company, and returned Sergeant Rogers's magnificent salute. "Fall out, everybody," he said, "and get around here. You can all sit down. I want to explain this to you. Hurry up; get settled, please."

With the company sitting and squatting in a big semicircle before him, Lieutenant Anderson consulted a paper. He said: "This afternoon an exercise in the defense of an airdrome will be performed. There will be a simulated attack by a force of paratroopers. That is, paratroopers are going to be dropped in strength on the field here with full equipment and they will endeavor to seize this area. For purposes of the exercise, it will be assumed that the runway under construction is an advanced landing strip that the enemy is trying to prevent us from completing and making operational. The Aviation Engineers working on it are to beat off the attack and hold the runway. What we're going to do this morning is lay out proper defense positions, fox holes, automatic weapons' emplacements, obstacles, and so on, according to plans which I have here. We won't have time to complete all of them; some of them will just have to be simulated; but I want to complete some of them so they would really be defensible. Regular camouflage procedure will be followed, and Captain Dobie, here, of the Post Engineers office, will show us where to find camouflage material, and any other necessary material. Is that clear? Any questions?"

Among the seated crowd there was an inquiring turn of heads, some quiet pushing, some nodding, grinning, and muffled laughter. "None of that!" Sergeant Rogers said. "Anyone got a question? Don't keep the lieutenant waiting!"

Someone said: "He want to ask: planes really coming? They really drop them on us?"

An indignant voice broke out: "You asking that, not me!"

Someone else said: "Who they? They not Germans?"

Derisive snorts of laughter arose around the questioner.

"All right," Lieutenant Anderson said, laughing too. "Now, everybody, get this straight. The planes are really coming. They are our planes, AFORAD planes from Tangerine City. They are really going to drop paratroopers and equipment. They are our paratroopers, the units stationed at Tangerine City. They are doing it as a tactical exercise, for practice and training; just as we're going to prepare real defenses for practice and training. It is being carried out in connection with the special parade and retreat ceremonies this afternoon. General Beal himself, and I understand also some other generals from Washington, will be present. They might come over and inspect what we've done; and, anyway, Colonel Mandible or Major McIlmoyle will be around to inspect the work shortly before the drop is scheduled. You will then be briefed on the part you are to play in the simulated defense. Everybody understand?"

There was a general murmur and nodding of heads.

"Now, one thing we want to remember. Those paratroopers think they're pretty good, and we want to show them that we're good, too. That the Aviation Engineers are just as smart and tough as they are. We want to show them that, if it was a real attack, not just a pretended one, if they were really the enemy, why, we made such good defenses that they'd all be killed before they took this landing strip away from us. Any more questions?"

Sergeant Rogers said: "And the lieutenant don't mean any more fool questions! You got any good questions, ask them quick, so we get them over and get working." He surveyed the circle an instant. "There are no more questions, sir," he said.

"O.K.," Lieutenant Anderson said. "Here is a list of the works assigned us, Sergeant. The figure in parentheses is the estimated number of men to be detailed for each job. When you see how it's going, use your own judgment about increasing or decreasing the details. I want to be sure at least one job of each type is really finished, camouflaged, and so on. Captain

Dobie is going to let us have some automatic weapons to mount in the emplacements. He'll send for them as soon as we're ready to set them up."

"Yes, sir," Sergeant Rogers said. He wheeled around imperiously. "Fall in, all you! Over there! I want to count you off, first. Then we'll get the tools from the tool wagons." He moved away.

Captain Dobie said, "I'll be back pretty soon and give you a hand with staking out the rest of the positions. I guess we have enough marked to hold them for now." He stood looking a moment at the men milling around to form platoon lines while Sergeant Rogers belabored them with short threatening cries. He said curiously: "How do you like it with them? Lot of headaches, I guess."

"I guess you get those anywhere," Lieutenant Anderson said, somewhat coldly. "This is a good company. Rogers, there, is good. He can get anything out of them, more than you'd get out of most white companies. Some of them are pretty ignorant, of course—just barely read and write—"

"You're telling me!" Captain Dobie said. "Let me tell you what some of them from one of the companies helping on the runway did yesterday! We have a twenty-seven-foot sea sled we keep over by the little pier with the shed for a rescue boat. Some machinery was being shifted and somebody decided the boat was in the way, so he told some of these jigaboos to move it—he meant work it along, push it or pole it, a hundred feet or so. The boat was out of the shed, up against the bank and the maintenance people had been overhauling the engines and they'd drained all the oil out. Half the spark plugs were out, too—I mean anyone could see it was being worked on. The men weren't there—the truck had come around and taken them over to eat."

Captain Dobie gave his head a disgusted shake. "Well, one of these jigaboos figured it would be easier if they made it move itself. He was a truck driver, or something; so he knew all about it. He put the plugs back and fired up. They have quite a power plant in those boats—do pretty near fifty miles an hour. So this lame-brain opens it good and wide without a drop of oil in it and freezes both engines solid. So this morning Colonel Uline is busy trying to requisition two new engines. You can have them, brother, you can have them! Be over in the shed there if you want anything."

Lieutenant Anderson, alone, stood watching while the platoons broke up in groups and moved away. Sergeant Rogers came back and said: "They have their tools in a minute, sir. I see those stakes. Any special place to start first?"

"No," Lieutenant Anderson said. "They're numbered; and here are the drawings. They're numbered, too. What about chow?"

"Corporal McIntyre's got some men, sir. I left them at the mess over in the Area. They're making sandwiches, and some milk cans of lemonade. Come noon, these'll be too hot to want to eat a whole lot. When they get done fixing the stuff, Corporal McIntyre is to bring it in a truck. The truck is there."

"Good," Lieutenant Anderson said. "What do those two think they're doing?"

Sergeant Rogers turned around. "Oh," he said. "Why, they're doing a little doubling, sir. They're disorderly in ranks."

"Well, stop them, now," Lieutenant Anderson said, frowning.

"Stop, you!" Sergeant Rogers shouted. "Get over there with your platoon!"

Lieutenant Anderson looked around. No one was within earshot, so he said: "You have to quit doing that, Sergeant. I spoke to you about it before. If one of them squawks to the Air Inspector—"

Sergeant Rogers said: "Sir, some of them don't know much, but every one of them would know better than going squawking behind my back. I wouldn't do it, I could help it. Some few, they get too big for their pants."

✦

Miss Candee, frowning at one of the many corrections in the text, sucked coffee slowly across the rim of the cardboard cup. Leaving a smear of lipstick on it, she put the cup down

328

then, nodding suddenly. Her hands fell to the typewriter keys; her fingers, as though of their own motion, danced over them. "Oh, the things Lieutenant Edsell writes!" she said with pleasure. She slipped out the typed page, deftly put together a new sheet with two carbon copies and rolled it into the machine.

Captain Duchemin, hunched over a typewriter of his own on a table beside his desk, puffing intermittently at his pipe, muttered: "Oh, the things the anonymous author of Technical Manual eleven-dash-four-ten writes!" A copy of the manual was flattened out on the desk next to him. "He says the sex of pigeons is difficult to determine without experience, and it is often necessary to observe their actions when together. A coarse idea, isn't it? Hm! Some common distinctive actions of the cock are—hm! Pecking the head of the hen when she shows no desire to mate. Hm! Wonder if that works? Palm, would you desire to mate if he kept pecking your head?"

"Oh, Captain Duchemin!"

"Say, am I crazy?" Captain Duchemin sat up. "Why should I be copying stuff? Where are your scissors, Nat? I'm going to cut out the paragraphs I need and paste them up."

Nathaniel Hicks, who was looking at the Ocanara *Morning Sun*, said absently: "My scissors are in your drawer there, where you put them the last time you swiped them."

"Captain Hicks!"

He glanced from the paper to Miss Candee. "Yes, yes, yes," he said.

"Captain Hicks, listen to what Lieutenant Edsell says in this story."

"I will not. And furthermore, it is now after eight o'clock. To the abstraction or misapplication of the Army's typewriter paper, carbon paper, typewriter ribbon, and typewriter you are adding a defalcation of man- or at least woman-hours belonging to and paid for by the Army."

"Oh, I only have one more page! You haven't anything for me to do yet. Neither has Captain Duchemin. What does defalcation mean? Unless it's something awful."

"It means embezzlement of what is held in trust."

329

"Well, I'm certainly not doing that. Am I, Captain Duchemin?"

"Polysyllabic humor!" Captain Duchemin said. "Polysyllabic humor! Ye Editor is quipping. Quip no more, Editor. Be quiet, everybody. How am I going to finish this first section before I fly away? Did I tell you what happened yesterday? Due to the navigational errors of Lieutenant Eusner, whom Manny gave us for a pilot, we dropped our collapsible, cylinder-type, four-bird container square in a pond, and so they all drowned. You'd think we were made of pigeons."

Miss Candee said: "He says about this man: 'Circumspective meanness of spirit, the unswerving allegiance to stupidity taught by thirty Regular Army years had perfectly qualified him to become a general officer.' " She giggled. "How does he know General Beal or somebody won't see that? What's 'circumspective' mean?"

"It means cautious, being careful," Nathaniel Hicks said. "Looking all around before you do it."

"Oh. Well, this is a very good story, I think. Only I don't get the title. It's about this boy at Officer Candidate School who went crazy. Oh, it's awful! Some of the things he says they made them do! Did they really?"

"You can't tell by us," Captain Duchemin said. "Captain Hicks and I went to the Gentlemen's School. Captain Hicks never had to do anything but try and keep awake through the interesting talks on company administration and sex hygiene until it was time to don his whites and go boozing in the downstairs bar at the Cromwell, a luxury hotel. What they did to those hotels! That *was* awful. It gave me an acute anguish in the business instinct. Now, you know as much as I do. What is the name you don't get of this story which the lieutenant is so economically having typed for him by the AAF?"

Miss Candee turned over the pile of pages. " 'We Go Rolling, Rolling Home.' I don't get it."

"You don't know the song," Captain Duchemin said. Beaming, he chanted: " 'Happy is the day, when the airman gets his pay—' Ah, now, can we help you, Sergeant?"

"I'm looking for Captain Hicks, sir—"

"Hello, Milt," Nathaniel Hicks said. "Come on in. Say, you didn't have to bother to come over here. I told Beaudry we'd come there. Wiley ought to be along in a minute. I went around to his VOQ earlier, but he was out getting breakfast. Milton McCabe, Clarence Duchemin."

"And that beautiful girl in the corner is Miss Candee; but mustn't handle," Captain Duchemin said. "And that lug right behind you is Lieutenant Edsell, who now gets gigged, as I believe they said at OCS, for being eleven minutes late. Mister, may I touch you?"

Lieutenant Edsell said: "Nuts to you, Captain. Hello, Milt. What have you got there?"

Sergeant McCabe had under his arm a large light drawing board with a folding support which could be adjusted to hold it on a table at any desired angle. He set the drawing board against the front of Nathaniel Hicks's desk and laid down a pencil case. His narrow dark face showed a patient smile. "I thought I'd see if we could do it here," he said. "Our place is full of carpenters and builders. Nobody knows why. They seem to be constructing a course for obstacle races. I can rough your stuff out on this, and take it back and finish it when they get the step ladders out of my corner."

"What are you doing?" Lieutenant Edsell said.

"What is it, Nat? Plane formation diagrams?"

"For God's sake!" Lieutenant Edsell said. He looked sympathetically at Sergeant McCabe. "They take one of the best artists in the United States and put him to drawing diagrams! That's typical of the Army mind!"

Sergeant McCabe looked embarrassed at this forthright compliment, or at the categorical statement of it. He said: "Thanks for the kind words, Jim; but—"

"No, no," Captain Duchemin said. "Don't thank the loot! You'll spoil everything! If you'll just grasp the offered opportunity to realize that the typical Army mind is also taking one of the best writers in the United States and putting him to doing Special Projects reports, he will gladly call it square. Won't you, Loot?"

Sergeant McCabe, more embarrassed, said: "I'm not kicking. I have a pretty easy time. Major Beaudry's been very decent to me. He fixed it so I could get out of barracks and live off the Area, so I have a place now where I can work evenings."

"That's dandy, isn't it?" Lieutenant Edsell said. He walked around behind his desk and sat down. "How do you like having a former Vice-President-in-Charge-of-Art-Calendars from a second-rate advertising agency deciding what you do and what you don't? I think it's a hell of a note. He *lets* you live off the Area! That's mighty white of him."

"Well, he didn't have to," Sergeant McCabe said. "I'm not kicking. When you're drafted, you're drafted; and you could land in a lot worse places than this—"

Captain Duchemin said: "Listen, boss; some of my best friends are advertising agency vice presidents. Can't you see how your contemptuous reference must wound me? And anyway, how do you think we crass business men would like being pushed around by some typical esthetes of finer clay? Comes the revolution!"

"Huh!" Lieutenant Edsell said. "Go carry Sir John Falstaff to the Fleet!" He took his telephone and said: "Outside. Look, I haven't a book. Get me the railroad station, will you?"

"Not leaving us, I hope?" Captain Duchemin said. "Not going away for a long, long trip?"

Lieutenant Edsell said, "I want to find out how late the morning train is. I have to meet it, if you don't mind."

"I don't mind. The Chief of Section, W. W. Whitney, your Commanding Officer; how does he feel? Does he mind?"

"He isn't going to know about it. You'll be covering for me."

"Wrong," Captain Duchemin said. "Any minute now I become airborne. Just as soon as Lieutenant Pettie catches a new case full of pigeons. And I won't be back until it's time for me to review the parade this afternoon."

Miss Candee said: "Lieutenant Edsell! Both Major Whitney and Capt—Major Pound are at a conference Colonel Coulthard called. So I guess Captain Hicks is in charge."

"Oh, no, he's not," Nathaniel Hicks said. "Captain Hicks is not mixing up in this at all."

"Major Whitney said you were in charge."

"Not to me. I didn't see him. Listen, Milt; I just thought of something. Would you be interested in getting on TD for a couple of weeks and being sent around the AFORAD installations to do sketches, water colors, anything you like, that they could use to illustrate some magazine articles? You wouldn't get paid for them—I mean, anything paid would have to go to the Aid Society, probably. But if you'd like to do it, I think I might be able to get you assigned."

"Absolutely!" Sergeant McCabe said. "Any time!" He laughed. "I get a little tired doing lettering," he said. "I never did have much practice at it, and it's a job. Could you really work it?"

"I think there's a good chance. They're trying to get some stuff about AFORAD into the magazines. They can't do it with a hand-out; they know that. I'm trying to work up some angles and see if I can sell somebody the idea of sending a good man down. I think if I could tell the general it would help sell the articles to be able to promise them illustrations by you, he'd go along. That would be true, too. I'm fairly sure we'd have to have a very good writer, and very good pictures to interest anybody worth interesting."

Lieutenant Edsell said: "On time? Thanks."

He put back the telephone, and said to Nathaniel Hicks: "Who's going to write these articles?"

"Why?" said Nathaniel Hicks. "You wouldn't want to do them. I was just telling Milt. No money."

"Though good, money is not everything," Lieutenant Edsell said, thoughtfully picking his nose. "Where's the money in writing an evaluation report on Thirteenth Air Force findings on the use of synthetic-rubber radio-range towers for underwater installations of the Army Airways Communication System? I would do quite a little to get W.W.W. off my neck for a while. Can you really say who's going to write them?"

"I'm supposed to find the material, and then I'm supposed to find somebody to work it up. But—"

"You've found him," Lieutenant Edsell said. "I'll do it."

Nettled by this peremptory settlement of the question, Nathaniel Hicks said: "Have you ever done any article stuff? If you have, I never heard of it, and I know pretty well everyone in the business. If you haven't, you just think you could. One of you prose artists can screw up a simple, factual story until hell won't have it. You never know anything about organization of the material, and most of you won't learn; you think you know it all."

Captain Duchemin said: "Bravo, butch!"

"Five gets you ten," Lieutenant Edsell said coldly, "that I can, right this minute, turn out a better article on any subject you care to name than any of those old line-hacks you think are writers. O.K., you haven't heard of my doing it; and I'll tell you why. Under ordinary circumstances, I wouldn't be seen dead in your big-circulation magazines. For reasons of my own, at the moment I'm willing to help you out. Now, another five will get you ten more that the magazine that sees the articles will write me direct to find out if I'm interested in doing other things for them—which I won't be. These, I am willing to do, and you'd better take me up." Lieutenant Edsell smiled calmly at Nathaniel Hicks. To his added irritation, Nathaniel Hicks found himself, against his will, impressed a little by this colossal conceit. "Yes; think it over," Lieutenant Edsell said disinterestedly.

"Why, damn it all—" Nathaniel Hicks began; but the telephone had rung, and Miss Candee, taking it on her extension, lifted her head and called: "Captain Hicks!"

The voice on the telephone said: "This is Sergeant Brooks, sir; Office of the Air Inspector. Colonel Ross directs me to notify you that there will be a hearing on an occurrence yesterday. The Charge Sheet lists you as a witness. You will please report at ten o'clock to the Staff Conference Room, Directorate of Personnel Analysis Center. One more thing, sir. Could you help us locate Captain Eugene P. Wiley? We understand that he was with you—"

"Yes," Nathaniel Hicks said, "I can. I am expecting him

here any minute—in fact, I see him now. He's coming in. I'll tell him."

Moving with his distinctive, long-limbed swing, a casual, easy swagger, Captain Wiley came smiling down the office. He said: "Say, I'm a little late, Nat! I was getting coffee in the PX when I saw this RAF chap, he's a Liaison Officer here, or something, I used to know in England. So we had to see what's with everything; and I never noticed the time it was. Jesus, I was surprised to see him!"

He caught sight of Miss Candee, viewing him with the mute, fascinated expression to which he must have been well accustomed. He acknowledged the tribute with his genial, lady-killing, frank smile and said: "Excuse the language, ma'am."

"That is Miss Candee," Nathaniel Hicks said. "And Captain Duchemin. You know Sergeant McCabe. Lieutenant Edsell. Gene, that call I just had was about the hearing this morning. They want us at ten. It's a hell of a nuisance; but maybe we can give Milt enough of the stuff first to hold him while we're over there."

"Sure," Captain Wiley said. He dug into his breast pocket and produced a folded wad of paper. "I took that list of diagrams we worked out in Orlando and made some drawings I thought I might as well bring over. They're not so hot, but they might help. Suppose the sergeant sees if he can figure them out. Might save him a lot of time. I don't know what order they're in." He flattened out the penciled sheets on the corner of the desk. "Well, here's a beam-rear attack on a bomber, for instance. See; element leader and his wingman, overhauling, here. See; fire opened here in two or three second bursts, at not more than two hundred fifty yards. Then, there; the break-away, sharp down; and then out, with plenty rudder."

"Yes," said Sergeant McCabe, "that's perfectly clear. If they're all like that, I could work from them. I think what I'd better do is rough this one out now, so you can see whether I have the right idea about how they ought to look finished. You want these real planes, or just symbols? I'll do symbols now, because I might not be able to do particular types from memory; but we have all the models over at the office, if you'd like to have them."

Captain Wiley said, "How about it, Nat? Real planes would be pretty good, I think. Kind of make them more interesting. If it isn't too much trouble."

"It's not," Sergeant McCabe said. "I'm getting pretty good at sketching planes."

He had set his drawing board up on the table by the windows and began swiftly to block off his sheet.

Captain Wiley watched him with interest for a moment. "By God," he said admiringly, "I like seeing a man who knows what he's doing! Look at that, Nat! Always wished I could draw! It looks so easy till you try it." He let himself down in the chair by Nathaniel Hicks's desk, clasped his hands behind his head, and tilted until he balanced himself and the chair delicately on two legs. "About this thing, this hearing, Nat. Do you know if they're going to have a court martial? If they are, I got to try to get out of it, give them an affidavit or something. They usually take that. I have this schedule of lectures and crap they make me give at Orlando. Having to come back here a lot of times wouldn't go down so well. It was all I could do to make them let me come now."

Nathaniel Hicks said: "I don't believe they'll want anything from us except a statement that we saw them pushing the Provost Marshal around, and maybe an identification— though the truth is, I doubt if I could identify the one who held him, or the one who had his gun."

"I'd know that boy, all right," Captain Wiley said. "He's a type you got to watch. Lot of white blood in him."

"What is this?" Lieutenant Edsell said. He had been looking at the manuscript Miss Candee had typed for him; but now he put it aside. "Is this what happened at the Club last night? Were you there?"

"It seems we were," Nathaniel Hicks said. "How did you hear about it?"

"It's all over the place," Lieutenant Edsell said. "Don't worry, there won't be any court martial. They wouldn't want to give the arrested officers a chance to get on the record in their own defense. They'll try to hush it up. The colored officers shouldn't let them. Every night a new bunch ought to go over to the Club and get arrested. The trouble is, they may not see the chance they have."

Captain Wiley, balanced on his chair, looked over at him. "I don't believe I get you, Lieutenant," he said. "What chance have they?"

"They have a chance to force the issue, and maybe end this whole segregation business, once and for all. The Army can't afford to practice segregation, if it's known they do. They'd have to allow Negroes the same rights as white men; and once that was established, I don't think the rights could later be taken away, even in the South—"

"They don't rate the same rights as white men," Captain Wiley said gently. "That's why the same rights aren't and can't be allowed them. The worst thing that could happen to them would be to end segregation. That would mean that a white man in the South would have to act every day as an individual to protect himself. That would be very bad for the Negroes. With segregation, now, both parties know where they stand, so there's almost no friction, see? Except when somebody from outside comes in and stirs it up. Your idea is mighty dangerous, Lieutenant."

Nathaniel Hicks said to Lieutenant Edsell: "For God's sake, Jim, do you have to argue all the time? Can't you just think what you think, keep still, and let us work?"

"Don't worry," Lieutenant Edsell said. "I'm not going to argue! I can see the captain is from the South; so I'll only point out to him that, like too many Southerners, he is under a grave misapprehension. The dangerous idea is his. It is very dangerous to deny people their rights. It means that, in the long run, you drive them to take their rights by force. Is that what the captain wants?"

Captain Wiley shook his head. "That, friend, they never will do, because they can't," he said. "What you're trying to say is that a Negro is equal to a white man. Don't you see that if he was equal, you wouldn't have to be demanding 'rights' for him? Like you say, he'd have them by force, if no other

337

way. He hasn't got them, though they gave them to him, and more, after the War Between the States. But he couldn't keep them; he wasn't up to it. That's where the North was wrong then, and that's where you're wrong now. The two races just aren't equal. Anyone who says they are, either doesn't have good sense, or doesn't know Negroes."

Captain Duchemin said: "Please, gentlemen, please! The captain has mentioned the War Between the States. In that dire conflict, sir, my dear old great grandpappy, a distinguished bounty jumper from Ohio, ran like hell from many a bloody field just to settle the momentous question for his posterity. Must we go through it all again?"

Captain Wiley smiled. "Our friend, here," he said, "seems to think so. I don't. The matter is good and settled. It's been proved, plenty times. They don't make the grade."

"For God's sake!" Lieutenant Edsell said. "I suppose you're talking about the AGCT tests! Granted, one Negro in twenty comes in Grades One and Two. Granted, for every Negro in those grades you'll find eight white men. What do you learn from that? You learn what we all know. In education, as in everything else, the Negro is systematically done out of a fair chance. You've just been explaining that, Captain. You don't want them to have a chance."

Captain Wiley said: "No, I'm afraid I don't know about these tests, whatever they are, you mention, Lieutenant. I don't believe you really have to give a lot of tests or anything. And it isn't a question of what you call a fair chance, or what I want them, or don't want them, to have. No amount of chances, and nothing I could do, would change the fact that a Negro happens to be a member of a relatively inferior race; physically, mentally, every way. It may be too bad, from his standpoint, and yours; but it's true."

"Very far from being true," Lieutenant Edsell said, "that is simply an absurd lie. There is no scientific basis for it whatsoever. Outside some of Hitler's phoneys, you couldn't find an anthropologist who would accept such a statement about the Negro race. If you don't even know that, there's no sense discussing it."

Captain Wiley said: "Please don't call me a liar, Lieutenant. Not here. Not now."

"Who called you a liar?" Lieutenant Edsell said. "A liar is a person who says what he knows isn't true. What you say isn't true; but it never occurred to me that you would know it wasn't true and still be saying it. That leaves you out, as far as I'm concerned. However, if you mean I'm not free to say that a statement which I know to be untrue is a lie, get rid of the notion, Captain. I believe you can't help your prejudices. I think, if you could, you surely would; because nobody likes to make himself absurd. I wish I could help you straighten out your thinking; but it doesn't look as if I could, and I've got to get downtown; so we may as well drop it."

"I believe that would be a right smart thing for us to do," Captain Wiley said. "I appreciate your wanting to help me, Lieutenant; and I am glad that you did not call me a liar."

The telephone rang. Miss Candee, rousing herself from the absorption with which she had closely if silently followed the debate, took it. She said in a hushed voice: "Reports Section; Miss Candee." She listened a moment and nodded at Nathaniel Hicks.

"Captain Hicks."

"Captain, this is Sergeant Brooks again. The hearing at ten o'clock has been postponed. We will notify you when it is scheduled, sir."

Nathaniel Hicks said, "You won't have it this morning? Well, now, Captain Wiley has to report back to Orlando today. He is only here on temporary duty. If Colonel Ross, or whoever will be conducting the hearing, could take an affidavit from him, and excuse him, it would be a great help. Can you find out if that would be possible and—"

The other telephone rang. Miss Candee pressed the switch on her desk and took up the receiver. She looked at Nathaniel Hicks and nodded again. "O.K.," Nathaniel Hicks said. "All right, Sergeant; if you will."

"You see?" Lieutenant Edsell said. He picked up his overseas cap and paused in the door. "No hearing, no court martial. I just hope they don't get away with it—"

Nathaniel Hicks waved an impatient hand at him and turned the button on the base of the telephone to pick up the other line.

"Captain Hicks," he said.

Lieutenant Edsell said: "Well, make up your mind about those articles. I'll have to tell Pound or Whitney if I'm going to do them—"

The voice in Nathaniel Hicks's ear was indistinct and Nathaniel Hicks waved his hand again. "I'm sorry," he said, "I can't hear you. Will you speak louder? And will you shut up, Jim?"

"Is this Captain Hicks?"

"Yes, it is! I still can't hear you very well. Who is calling?"

"Captain Hicks, this is Katherine Andrews—Don Andrews's wife—"

"Oh, yes, Mrs. Andrews," Nathaniel Hicks said. "I'm sorry. We must have a terrible connection."

"Do you know where I could reach Don? He left about an hour ago; but he isn't at his office. The number he gave me doesn't answer." There was a long pause and she said, "So I asked information for your number. I hope you don't mind. I—"

"Of course not!" Nathaniel Hicks said. "I'll see if I can locate Don. He may be in a conference—" Something in the uncertain quality of her voice made him add quickly: "Or is there anything I could do? Is everything all right?"

"I don't know," she said. "I don't know. I—Captain Hicks, it's—I'm horribly ill. I can't seem to—look, I am afraid I am going to faint. I will have to hang up. Could you—" The connection broke.

"My God!" Nathaniel Hicks said. "That's Don's wife. There's something wrong with her. I think she just fainted. They can't reach Don—"

Captain Duchemin said, taking the phone on his desk, "Better call the Base Hospital. They can send someone down." He bent his head toward Miss Candee. "Whip along to Stat Control, honey, and see who knows where Captain Andrews is."

340

IV

Sergeant Brooks put down his cigar and got to his feet. "Judge," he said, "I managed to reach all the people and they'll be there. However, there's one little technical difficulty I had with Personnel Analysis. The arrested officers don't really belong to any organization yet. You see, there was a tentative group organization set up, but only on paper. Group and squadron officers hadn't been formally designated, and as it happens, I don't know that it makes any difference, the man who was going to be temporary group commander is this Lieutenant Willis, who is in the Hospital. I have some more information about him, incidentally, sir." He looked at a pad on his desk. "Well, at any rate, the thing at Personnel Analysis was who would order these officers in arrest in quarters to report for the hearing. Major Blake said—"

"He says too much," Colonel Ross said. "That's an absurd quibble. Their present duty status makes General Beal their commanding officer. Tell them I order them to report by command of General Beal."

"Oh, I did, sir. Colonel Jobson made a night flight down from Washington and had just got there, and I think he was trying to stick his oar in. I took the liberty of calling Major Sears and asked him to send someone around to tell the officers to report. So I presume he did."

"Good, good. What's this information about this Willis?"

Sergeant Brooks looked at his pad. "Well, first," he said, "Colonel Mowbray called. He thinks it's very important for him to see you for a few minutes right away. He said to tell you that Colonel Carricker was in his office. I thought you should know that before you saw this officer outside. It's Captain Collins, Public Relations. He seems to have a lot eating him. About an hour ago he called up and said he had something to communicate to you verbally about an investigation he understood you ordered. I think it must have been Colonel Howden's thing—civilian personnel check in connection with Mr. Bullen and the *Sun*. Then he called again—Captain Collins—and said he'd had something else that might be even hotter. I told him he'd better come over, so he did. I asked him if he could give me an idea of what it was. He said he had information from Mr. Bullen that this man Willis's father was coming in this morning to see him—Willis, and that the Ocanara police were interested in it and in view of the story he had heard about how Willis came to be injured, he thought you should know."

"Well, I'd better see him," Colonel Ross said.

"Well, now, also waiting outside, sir, is Major McCreery."

"What's he going to do? Squawk about assigning a medical officer for the WAC business? If he is, you'll have to get rid of him. I haven't time to see him this morning."

"I thought of that, sir. This is entirely different, and he says it's very serious. I told him, would he indicate its nature to me and so on and so on; so he said he had word from the Air Surgeon in Washington about a discharge racket operating through the AAF hospitals—or one; at Mitchel Field, I think it was; and all Post Surgeons are to check; and he thinks you ought to help him. At Mitchel, they thought Medical Administrative Corps officers were taking bribes. A lot of people had been assigned to the section of the Base Unit running the motor pool. All men discharged from the Hospital; and one or two of them were shooting their faces off—saying they came from hot outfits that had overseas orders. It was supposed to cost about five hundred dollars. For two thousand dollars, you could get yourself a CDD and go home."

Colonel Ross sat down at his desk. "I don't see how it could be done," he said.

"I can see one way, Judge," Sergeant Brooks said. "Any military personnel can report sick to any regional hospital. Now, if a fellow got a furlough from a hot outfit, to let him go home a few days before he was sent overseas, he could report in sick at any hospital. If he was admitted as a patient, they would TWX for his papers. Once the papers were sent, his former outfit wouldn't have any more record of him; he wouldn't belong to it any more. When he was discharged, they could cut orders for him to be assigned anywhere—a Base Unit here, for instance. The thing would be getting entered as a patient.

I suppose there's some officer who has charge of that, an Executive Officer or something, maybe. If he could happen to be amenable to five hundred dollars. Well! What do you think of that, Judge?"

Colonel Ross said: "I think you're going to be a very successful lawyer, Steve. I regret that military service is interrupting your career. I can only hope you are smarter than any of our Medical Officers. McCreery didn't say he had any reason to think it was going on here?"

"No, sir. He was just jumping up and down."

"Well, that does no harm." Colonel Ross put out his hand, flipped the key marked Executive Officer on the box, and depressed the buzzer switch. Through a light crackling sound, Colonel Mowbray's voice broke out in the room: "Oh, Norm! Good! You couldn't come over here a minute, could you?"

"I'm pretty well tied up, Pop. I just left the general; and I've got people here."

"There in the room?"

"No, they're outside."

"I didn't want this to be heard, is all, Norm. Look, Benny came in to see me. I haven't told Bus yet. I wanted to know what about that suggestion you made yesterday. There's one other factor, Norm. Jo-Jo, General Nichols, was directed to bring down with him and award this Willis the Distinguished Flying Cross—something he did when he was in transition training or somewhere. Do you know whether Bus said anything to him about Willis being in the Hospital, the circumstances and so on?"

"I don't think so," Colonel Ross said.

"Well, you see what I mean? He's going to have to give him the medal, I guess. I contacted the Hospital and they said Willis was perfectly all right—that is, he could leave there. I told them not to discharge him until they heard from me. Now, I thought of this. If you and Bus still want Benny to apologize to him—why, Benny will. He's a pretty downhearted young man this morning. I could have him here and Benny could apologize; but then there's Jo-Jo and the award. Norm, it just looks pretty thick to me. Do you see what I mean? As if

343

we were trying to hush him up, sort of bribe him. Somebody's got to tell Jo-Jo the story, too. I can see why Bus might not have—he might want to keep Benny out of it, not let Jo-Jo get the idea it all happened because of what Benny did. I mean, the other part, the Officers Club thing. What is happening about that, by the way?"

"We were going to have a hearing at ten o'clock," Colonel Ross said. "I have just canceled it." He looked at Sergeant Brooks and pointed at the telephone. "Now, Pop, I have information, which I haven't checked yet, that the father of Lieutenant Willis was told the boy was hurt and is arriving here this morning to see him. He's coming from Washington, and so he'll be on the morning train, presumably. Will you have a staff car down at the station, with an officer, make it a captain, to meet this man and bring him out to the Base Hospital?"

There was a pause and Colonel Mowbray said: "You want— look, Norm, this is a colored man, isn't it?"

"That would seem very likely," Colonel Ross said.

"Isn't that—well, overdoing it again a little, Norm? He won't expect anything like that."

Colonel Ross said: "Pop, are we sorry this happened, or aren't we?"

The box carried the mechanically stepped-up sound of Colonel Mowbray clearing his throat. Colonel Ross said carefully: "Bus is not going to do anything about this, you know. We're going to have to do it for him. You understand that? The shortest way out is the best way."

Colonel Mowbray said: "Norm, Benny shouldn't have hit Willis. We are sorry about that; and so is Benny. But how about Willis, now? He never should have brought that plane in without being sure he was clear to land. I know his radio was out; and probably when he saw the runway lights come on, he figured that they must have heard his engines, and the lights were for him. But it was still his responsibility to make sure about other traffic before he put down. He should have gone around again. It wasn't his fault, no thanks to him, he didn't kill Bus and you and all the rest of them. That's what made Benny sore, and you know as well as I do, that that's why

344

Benny hit him. Everybody seems to be going at this as though Willis was just an innocent bystander and Benny went over and broke his nose because he was a colored boy, and for no other reason. Now, if we were being really just and impartial about this thing, it seems to me along with Jo-Jo's medal and an apology and sending cars for his father, Willis ought to get a reprimand, be grounded for a while, and docked some pay for reckless flying. I'm not suggesting that; I'm just saying it. You're a judge, Norm. You ought to see that."

"I see it," Colonel Ross said, "but I am not being a judge this morning. I think I have other responsibilities here and now." He looked at Sergeant Brooks who was quietly busy at the telephone at his desk in the corner, with a surprising, unmoved patience calling all the people he had called before to cancel the hearing. Colonel Ross supposed that this manner of Sergeant Brooks showed more than anything else that though Sergeant Brooks might well regard him as a trying old man, he had come, over the months, to respect the old man's judgment.

Colonel Ross said, "We have to get Bus out of this. He cannot or will not get himself out. We will have to disregard everything else." Talking to the box with his hands lying on the blotter of the desk in front of him was much like talking to himself, Colonel Ross felt, much more like it than speaking on the telephone, which was like speaking into a tube that clearly must lead somewhere.

Nonetheless, the box's electric silence seemed able to relay Colonel Mowbray's astonishment or sharp surmise. Colonel Mowbray must be well aware that the general often took action that Colonel Ross suggested—really, told him to take—but the perfunctory form was still important; you tacked on a *le-roi-le-veut*, which cleared you to act; you got your authority by a formal avowal that you, personally, had none. The silence meant of course that Colonel Mowbray was jibbing.

Colonel Mowbray said then in a dazed, but definitely reproving tone: "That's going pretty far, Norm." The plain implication was that Colonel Ross didn't know what he was saying—how could he? Fair-minded, simple-minded, Colonel Mowbray at once excused and criticized him. He was not Regular Army,

345

he was not an Academy man. In a crisis, these defects in him, these things he was not, would come out—in the same sense that Colonel Mowbray made it felt, though he had carefully not said it, that Lieutenant Willis, when he landed his B-26 without making sure he was cleared to land might be evidencing his defect—Negro blood—in what was ostensibly a rated pilot.

Colonel Mowbray said: "I think we'd better take this up directly with Bus, Norm. I don't think we ought to act for him, beyond a certain point, without informing him fully. For all I know, he may not want this man's father out at the Hospital. I wouldn't feel justified in sending a car—having him escorted there, unless Bus knew—"

"See if you can get in to talk to him now," Colonel Ross said. "I would like you to do this, if you will. Ask him if he means to be present at Retreat this afternoon before you ask him anything else."

"Why—" Colonel Mowbray paused, plainly dumbfounded. "Why of course he's going to be—he has to be. I don't think I understood what you said, Norm."

"That's what I said," Colonel Ross said. "And let me know, will you?" He flipped up the box key and pressed a button under the edge of his desk. Mrs. Eliot appeared in the door behind and he took two handwritten pages from the corner of his desk and said: "Would you knock this out, please. It's a statement for General Baxter and will need a witness to my signature. Or, better, give it to Miss Miller. I may want to have something taken down in a minute. Steve, was Captain Collins there before Major McCreery?"

"Yes, he was, Judge."

"Have him in. And when he is in, tell Major McCreery that I will be going over to the Base Hospital shortly and will see him there; that I am sorry to have held him up; but there is a matter which must be finished for the general. Tell him I'll be very glad to help him in any investigation he thinks necessary. In short, fix it."

✦

To Captain Raimondi, who was sitting on the edge of the desk in an open white jacket, slowly swinging a stethoscope,

Lieutenant Werthauer said: "Don't ask me. I haven't had time to look at the Night Reports yet—Prissy has them. I'd just come on, when there was this call to the Oleander Towers. Clark was Duty Officer last night, and he was supposed to stay; but Prissy told me the major was in early, and then went rushing over to the Area in some kind of a tizzy; so Clark, the bastard, must have thought with McCreery out of the way nobody would know if he left and went to bed, so he did. So I had to ride the ambulance." He took a pen and on the upper corner of the Admission Form lying in front of him wrote: *Andrews, Katherine L. (Mrs.)—Capt. Donald B. Andrews, AC; Special Projects, AFORAD.*

"It was this woman," he said. He looked at the laboratory slip beside him and began to write on the form. "Hyperglycemia," he said. "Blood sugar about two fifty. You could smell the acetone across the room. I didn't have a damn thing in my bag, so we wrapped her up and got her out here—that corporal, I think his name is Buck, or Bucks, they have driving, is going to kill somebody sometime, and I thought it was going to be me. I'll report him to Captain Vaughan. He shouldn't be allowed to drive a car. Anyway, we got her out and shot her up, and she'll do, I think. I don't know what the history is. You couldn't get any from her, of course. She was out like a light, lying there on the floor. I could see she'd been vomiting in the bathroom. Her husband turned up with another officer just as we were putting her in the ambulance; but I didn't have time to get much out of him, except that she'd never been under treatment for diabetes. She's about thirty-four—very thin; but I don't think it's a pathological emaciation. She would have been bound to have symptoms—polydipsia, polyurea, and so on, enough to make her see a doctor. I think it's a new case. She'd just come down to see her husband, and I think it just hit her. You know—prolonged strain, anxiety, there's a war on; all that. I'll have a talk with her husband. He's waiting around outside somewhere. He was in a state, poor guy. Of course, he didn't know what was wrong with her; but he'd developed himself an idea."

Lieutenant Werthauer threw the admission form into the

file basket. "He said she was all right when he left. But I could see something was bothering him. So then it came out. He got me off a little way, and said maybe he ought to tell me—er—though she'd had a pretty tough trip down, flying to Orlando last night, driving over here, and maybe—er—he oughtn't to have; why, she—er—wanted to; so he—er—had—er—connection with her as soon as they got upstairs, about an hour before—"

Captain Raimondi broke into a cordial guffaw. "Let this be to you a warning," he said. "Never do it in the morning!"

"Yeah; I told him I didn't think it had any special significance. She ought to be all right—a good insulin customer the rest of her life. The shots were starting to pull her out when I left. She's over in the Women's Ward—Wing E. Give her a look when you go by, will you?"

✦

Captain Andrews said: "I wish somebody would come out. Do you think we have the right place?"

Nathaniel Hicks, who could not help agreeing in his own mind that the long delay must be a bad, not a good sign, bent and crushed out under the sole of his shoe the cigarette he had been smoking. Testing the flattened end between his thumb and forefinger to make sure that it was really out, he arose and crossed to the other corner of the narrow hall and dropped it in a metal rubbish container. "I'm sure this is it," he said. He nodded at the sign by the door off the small office opposite. It said: *Women's Ward I.* Under that were the words: *On Duty;* and under that, a narrow slot into which a removable card could be pushed. The card said: *Lt. Isabella Shakespeare, ANC.*

Nathaniel Hicks considered this improbable name again. It was, he supposed, a rough anglicizing of some Slavic name. He said: "I suppose she's out having a quick cup of coffee at the Mermaid Tavern. There's a telephone in there. In about a minute, I'm going to see what it connects with." He came back to the small folding chair next to the one on which Captain Andrews sat.

Captain Andrews acknowledged the poor pleasantry about the Mermaid Tavern with a feeble smile. "Look, Nat," he said. "There's no reason why you should be wasting your whole morning this way. I certainly appreciate all the trouble you've taken; but I don't think there's anything more anyone can do. You must have been right in the middle of something with your Captain Wiley—"

Nathaniel Hicks said firmly: "He's all right. Beaudry sent McCabe over and Wiley's working on some diagrams with him. They don't need me. I'd rather wait until the doctor says it's all right, and then I can give you a lift back to the Area."

He hoped that the insinuated idea of everything bound to come out right would be of service to Captain Andrews in his pitiable state; but Captain Andrews, speaking distractedly, in a low voice, said: "You can't tell about these doctors. I don't know whether they're any good or not. This one, this Lieutenant Werthauer—it's silly; but when I see he's a lot younger than I am, I just wonder how much a kid like that can know."

"He looked competent to me," Nathaniel Hicks said, not sure that this was the case. "He certainly seemed to be on the job—I mean, he acted as if he knew what he was doing—you know; quick about it; and, well, absorbed in his job. I think I'd be willing to trust him."

Captain Andrews sat silent a moment, distrait, perhaps passing in his mind the natural, unreasonable retort: *yes, but what's it to you? You don't need to trust him!* He moistened his lips and said instead: "I don't know whether I really understood him. He said it was a coma; which I could see wasn't good. I don't think they use that word unless it's pretty serious. I think he said he thought it was a diabetic coma. I don't know anything about it; but I guess I always thought diabetes was a chronic disease, not something that could just suddenly happen to you. I could see she was awfully tired when we went upstairs, but I don't believe she could have been feeling really sick. Of course, you can't tell; she might not have wanted to worry me. She'd taken her things off—when I left she was going to try to get some sleep. I don't think I ever should have let her come down, especially when it was still so hot. I think the trip

349

exhausted her more than she knew. I suppose I should have asked her not to come. But I mean, Katherine's always been perfectly well. Except, about six years ago, we lost a baby—"

Captain Andrews broke off. He gave Nathaniel Hicks a sidelong, bewildered look, as though he could not imagine how he had come to proffer this intimate and purely personal piece of information.

Nathaniel Hicks said automatically: "That's tough."

Since now it was too late to recall the statement, Captain Andrews must have decided that if he went on it would be less awkward for Nathaniel Hicks than if he stopped dead or shied away. He said: "Yes, it was. You see, we'd been married a number of years, and we hadn't had any children; really, because a doctor thought she ought not to. I guess I was thinking of that—I mean how you can't tell about doctors. Then Katherine went to another doctor some friend of hers knew; and he told her there was no reason why she shouldn't."

Captain Andrews once more paused painfully, perhaps considering whether he could leave it there. He then said: "So I suppose we believed him; or Katherine did, because she wanted to very much. I guess I believed him, too; though I was a little nervous about it. But if I hadn't believed it, I know I wouldn't have wanted to take a chance. Well, at any rate, it wasn't true that there was no reason why she shouldn't. The first doctor was right about that. And it wasn't that the other doctor, the doctor who told her to go ahead, was ignorant or anything. But he was a Catholic, I found out afterwards. I should have found that out first, of course. It just never occurred to me that any doctor would tell a person it was all right to do something, when he knew all the time it had a good chance of killing her."

He looked worriedly away from Nathaniel Hicks. "I ought to say he took wonderful care of her, and got her over it very quickly, without any permanent bad effects. I don't want to be unfair to him; and I see that, believing what he believed, he had to tell her to go ahead. They feel they have to leave it up to God, or something; that it was wrong to say, like the first doctor, that she couldn't have a child, because you were only guessing until you actually tried. I don't know; but I know she meant much more to me than any child ever could; and when I was the one who didn't want to run any risk, I was to blame for not finding out that he said what he said because he believed special things, things I didn't believe. I don't blame him; I blame me. Well, I didn't mean to bore you with all that—it was just that that was really the only time she'd ever been sick. I can see that was my fault; and this is, too—"

"That's absurd, Don," Nathaniel Hicks said. "If I understand what the doctor told you, she must have been going to have an attack anyway—"

Captain Andrews shook his head stubbornly. "I think she had it because she was so worn out. I don't mean only this trip down here. The whole thing is too much for her. Living the way she has to. She has a job. She had it before we were married and she didn't have any trouble getting it again when I went into the Army. You see, I wasn't making enough money as a first lieutenant. I don't mean I ever made what you might think was much; but we could get by. You see, she has a brother who suddenly went blind when he was about fifteen and when her father died she had to pay his expenses. So because I went in the Army, she had to get her job back. So she has to live up there while I'm down here, and work too hard—it wasn't right."

He pulled up, brought his hands together and interlaced them tightly in his lap. "I shouldn't have done it," he said. "I'm not doing anything that's any use. I would have been more use with the company. There were Navy contracts they were consultants on even then, and now they have more of them, and I know they don't have anybody who has as much experience in some special lines as I have. I didn't see things very clearly. I mean; I did see a lot of men no older than I was, with kids and everything, going or having to go, and it made me kind of uncomfortable. And I knew the company was trying to get me classified indispensable. I know I sounded a minute ago as though I thought I was; but I wasn't, I was just convenient. I was pretty sure they'd manage to get me deferred on that ground, and I thought I couldn't do that. When it wasn't true, with everybody else having to go. I couldn't see that all I was after was to get a uniform to make me feel more comfortable—"

"Hell, Don," Nathaniel Hicks said. "Why do you think I'm here? It's only natural. Everybody was figuring as fast as he could, if he had any choice at all, what would be easiest for him. I don't suppose there's a man in Ocanara, unless he was Regular Army, who ever considered, five years ago, anything so crazy as being an Army officer. I think what you did, and the way you felt, was to your credit. Much more so than what I felt. I—"

Captain Andrews interrupted him. The interesting feelings experienced by Nathaniel Hicks during the first months of 1942, which Captain Andrews had been about to hear, Captain Andrews had no time to hear. They were trivial compared to what was in his own mind. He had come to the limit of his limitless consideration for others; he could be pushed past it. Nathaniel Hicks found himself shaken; guessing how intolerable must be the distress that pushed him.

Captain Andrews said: "It was just the last straw, the trip down here. I see now that when I got her upstairs I should have called a doctor right away. I guess I was just so glad to see her that I never noticed, when she got off the plane, when I was driving her over, the shape she was in. She could hardly take her things off. She wasn't strong enough to take her girdle off. I had to do it for her—"

He paused, moistening his lips, looking at Nathaniel Hicks with an expression of anguished inquiry, of a man listening desperately to hear something which was not being said. Nathaniel Hicks was unable to say anything.

✦

Captain Raimondi looked at his watch. He had still a few minutes before he began his rounds and he lit a cigarette. He said: "You know what I got this morning, Doctor? Orders to Randolph Field all signed and sealed. Aviation Medical Examiners' course starting fifteen September."

"You must be nuts!" Lieutenant Werthauer said.

"Far from it!" Captain Raimondi said happily. "I gave it

352

careful thought and listened to sound advice. What do I do? I take nine weeks of something from those chiropractors or whatever they have down there, and the world is mine. This war could last another five or six years. You might as well go along with it. I have my certificate from them, and a year from now, with fifty hours flying time, I'm a goddamn flight surgeon, with beautiful gold wings. A bit of wangling, so I get my time every month—you only have to be a passenger—and I also draw flying pay, beautiful flying pay. Now, why don't you get some of that?"

"To hell with them," Lieutenant Werthauer said. "At Carlisle they gave me all the Army crap I can take. I came in to practice medicine, not do monkey drill, and have a lot of little twirps instruct me in my military duties. You make Flight Surgeon, and you really are up Mike's! That's what you'll be doing—giving physicals to flying personnel all day, every day. You'll certainly be a lousy operator by the time you get through!"

"What do I do here?" Captain Raimondi said, yawning. "I pulled two appendixes in the last three months. Rest of the time, I'm studying the back ends of little tarts from the WAC; standing out on a small-arms range waiting for them to shoot each other; and walking the wards to see that you and Clark and Hinault, and especially Yensen, aren't killing more than your quota. I don't have a thing to lose. What have you got?"

"I'm not going to stay here," Lieutenant Werthauer said. "They'll start rotating combat crews pretty soon; and whether they realize it or not, there's going to be plenty of psychoneurosis coming into the general hospitals. That's for me! I just keep my three-one-three-zero MOS shined up, and I'll be out of this hole six months before you finish collecting your phoney wings."

"That may be for you," Captain Raimondi said. "But will they know it? If they need a supplemental staff for—ah, now—anxiety reaction cases, you know who'll get to go? Every experienced otorhinolaryngologist they can screen out, and maybe an occasional orthopedic surgeon. Listen to me, and buck for your examiner's certificate."

"You don't have to tell me what those dim-wits do," Lieutenant Werthauer said gloomily. "But at least I have a chance. At least I won't get packed off to be Squadron Flight Surgeon and officer in charge of requisitioning the booze at Little Nooky, Hants, Eng."

"None so blind," said Captain Raimondi, "as those who will not see! Where is Prissy and those reports? Sometimes I think we could do with a new Nurse, Administrative, around here. Speaking of administration, know what that tizzy of McCreery's you so well observed was based on? Prissy told me—that's one thing she's good for. He got word about a station where an administrative officer was entering so-called patients in return for a cash consideration and coaching them in what to put on for the Board to get a discharge. He wondered about us."

"I could have told you weeks ago," Lieutenant Werthauer said. "Any fool could see it. A lot of Section Eight stuff going through. There was no more wrong with most of them than there was with me—less, in fact; they hadn't been here nine months. I reported the first few I saw to McCreery. He told me I was mistaken. O.K. To hell with them. I'm mistaken. If McCreery hasn't sense enough to see when a man's faking, and the Board hasn't, what's it to me? Only, I didn't know he was getting paid for it."

"Well, *he* wasn't. Maybe that's what burns him up. Somewhere they were, though. And there's always your friend Captain Vaughan. Maybe he handles the Section Eight stuff."

"That's no friend of mine," Lieutenant Werthauer said. "Snotty little bastard—"

Captain Raimondi stood up abruptly and stepped to the window looking out on the poor strip of sand and sparse grass, across which a plank path led from the Base street, bare and hot in the sun, to the Hospital doors. "I thought so!" he said. "We've got visitors. That's the general's car. And there's the general! You don't suppose they're pulling a surprise inspection, or something? McCreery isn't with him. I think he's alone. My God, do you think I'd better get out there?"

"No," said Lieutenant Werthauer. "If he wants anything, let him come and ask. Don't start a lot of military crap here.

It's the only place you ever get away from it. You know what happened to me yesterday? I was downtown, and walking along Sunshine Avenue, I met a goddamn chaplain, a captain. I don't know where he came from—not one of the ones we have poking round. Well, as I say, I did my saluting for the whole war at Carlisle; so I favored him with a blank look. I don't know whether his holiness thought he was turning the other cheek, or whether he was reproving me for unsoldierly conduct. Anyway, he looked right back, hauled off, and saluted *me*. I thought: 'Oh, no, you don't, Bud!' and kept looking through him. I hadn't gone a yard, when two MP's step out from the arcade of the Scheherazade Hotel, throw me a ball, too; and one of them pulls a notebook, and says: 'May I have your name and serial number, Lieutenant?' Well—"

Captain Raimondi was listening inattentively. He said: "Yeah; but I think I better—"

The door opened and General Beal walked in.

Lieutenant Werthauer instantly put a hand out and took back the admission form from the file basket. Frowning, he studied it. With his other hand, he busily took a pencil. He wrote on a scratch pad: *Andrews, Katherine L. (Mrs.).* He compared the note with the name on the form, tore the sheet from the pad, and crumpled it up, throwing it in the wastepaper basket.

Captain Raimondi dropped his cigarette in an ash tray and jerked himself to a sort of attention. General Beal said: "Oh! I thought Major McCreery might be in here."

Captain Raimondi said: "Why, no, General. I don't think he's in the Hospital at the moment. I'm Captain Raimondi, sir. Is there anything I can do?"

General Beal looked away from him toward the window. "No, I guess not," he said. "I wanted to see McCreery—"

Taking advantage of the general's looking-away, Captain Raimondi made a hasty surreptitious movement with the hand at his side, jerking the thumb to indicate to Lieutenant Werthauer that he should stand up. General Beal was not so absent as he seemed. His glance came back. "No, no!" he said impatiently. "I'm just trying to think! Don't bother the lieutenant!

He's busy. I don't want to upset things. I just came over to see the Post Surgeon—"

Since the general's eye nonetheless now rested on him, Lieutenant Werthauer arose rebelliously, with a direct stare and stood behind his desk. A surge of sound, for the last moment or two sweeping nearer across the Base, was suddenly on them, a stunning hammer of engines from a big plane taking off. The whole room seemed to shake. You could feel the vibrations in the floor. General Beal made an involuntary wincing grimace, bit his lip. "Hell of a noise!" he said through the retreating racket.

Lieutenant Werthauer's direct attentive gaze had not left him, and General Beal hesitated. His mouth moved a little, twisting out a smile. He said in a voice of formal, cordial inquiry: "What is your name, Lieutenant? What's your job?"

"Werthauer, sir. I'm a neuropsychiatrist and internist."

"Oh," said General Beal. "Yes, yes. That's good. I've meant to get over here and meet the Medical Staff. I get good reports of your work. Sit down, sit down. Don't let me interrupt—" His eyes went away from Lieutenant Werthauer's and back to Captain Raimondi. "Would anyone know where Major McCreery went?"

Captain Raimondi said: "Sir, I think his secretary might know. I'll find out right away—" He went with alacrity.

General Beal said: "Sit down, Lieutenant. I don't know that I have any special need to see Major McCreery this morning. You're a doctor, aren't you?"

Sitting down, but looking at General Beal with still closer attention, Lieutenant Werthauer said: "That's right."

"Well, give me a slip for some of that sodium amytal stuff. I won't bother McCreery."

Lieutenant Werthauer shook his head. He said: "No. I couldn't do that."

"Why not?" said General Beal, astonished.

With a faint, remote smile, Lieutenant Werthauer said: "Because I don't prescribe anything for anyone until I'm satisfied that I know what I'm prescribing for. I can see that you are in a somewhat nervous state; but I would have to know much

356

more than that. If you want me to treat you, I'll give you an appointment for a thorough examination. Until I've done that, I can't do anything for you. Have you been taking sodium amytal? Did a physician prescribe it?"

General Beal said: "A flight surgeon in Australia gave me some, when I got out of the Philippines—"

"What was it?" Lieutenant Werthauer said, frowning quickly. "This so-called narcosis therapy? Was it enough to knock you out for twenty-four hours or so?"

"They were little green pills," General Beal said, staring at Lieutenant Werthauer. "No, they didn't knock me out. I've taken them now and then. He said they were perfectly harmless."

"That's one opinion," Lieutenant Werthauer said. "Been taking it ever since?"

"I told you I'd taken some now and then." General Beal looked at him with growing amazement. "What do you mean I do, take drugs? What—"

"How do I know?" Lieutenant Werthauer said. "If it isn't something you've been taking, what makes you think you want it now?"

"Just a minute!" General Beal said. "I don't get this, Lieutenant. I didn't ask you to ask me questions. Stand up!"

Lieutenant Werthauer got without haste to his feet. He fixed his stubborn and baleful eye on the general. "Put down that pen," General Beal said. "Now, just let me see you come to attention."

"All right," Lieutenant Werthauer said, not without satisfaction, "but it's no good shouting at me, General. I'm a physician; and I told you that, until I know what I'm prescribing for, I don't write prescriptions. So, if you think you're now going to order me to write one—"

General Beal said: "That will do, Lieutenant. Get out of here! Go to your quarters and stay there until you hear from me."

Lieutenant Werthauer said: "I'm on duty this morning. You want nobody to be here?"

"You'll have to find someone to relieve you," General Beal

said. "Get after it! And if there's any argument, or any more delay in obeying me, you'll find yourself in a very serious situation." He turned and walked out of the room.

Lieutenant Werthauer put his papers away and took his cap from the table. At the door, he met Captain Raimondi, who said: "Where are you going?"

Lieutenant Werthauer said: "Kind of you to ask, Doctor. I've just been ordered to my quarters."

"Are you kidding?" Captain Raimondi said. "Look, I've got to start my rounds. You can't leave—"

"You'll have to find somebody else," Lieutenant Werthauer said. "Mr. Iron Pants doesn't like the way I wear my hair."

✦

Looking in vain at the screen before the ward door, Captain Andrews rubbed his finger along his lips and said: "I ought not to be here. It is all crazy. I don't mean for me, any more than for you. You ought not to be here. It's different for some people —like Clarence. It's fine for him; it's right for him. What has he got to lose? He gets everything he wants. It all suits him—" Probably aware that he was becoming incoherent, Captain Andrews stopped.

Nathaniel Hicks remembered unexpectedly Captain Andrews's expressed convictions, yesterday morning, on how things come to be as they are, and events to happen as they do; and their exchange, then far from urgent, while they walked across the parking lot behind the Special Projects Building: *You can be sure of getting pretty much what you work for. Since when? Since always.*

Had Captain Duchemin, then, worked for this state that so well suited him? Was Captain Andrews getting what he worked for? Were there, perhaps, temporary wartime restrictions on getting what you worked for? No. Not if you could face the too-little-faced fact that war really brought you nothing that peace, mere living, couldn't eventually bring. The large-scale operation was what impressed you—some millions of men receiving at the same time through the same historical events their varying allotments of discomfort and disappointment and discouragement; some hundreds of thousands met occasions to dissolve in unthinkable fear or scream in unthinkable pain; some tens of thousands got an early death; but from which of these would a just and lasting peace secure you? Disappointment? Fear? Pain? Death?

Captain Andrews said: "Even the jobs he has to do suit him. All this about pigeons! He likes it. He has fun all day long. Of course, you can see that's what he had all day long in his work, whatever it was, representing those hotels. So, it's the same to him. Nothing makes any more sense than anything else. Take all those women he has. What does he get from them?"

Most people, when they put a question like that, put it puritanically and righteously, with the real idea of directing attention to their own virtuous behavior—which, unless it got attention, seemingly did not compensate them for all they feared they were missing. Their offensive low motive asked for an offensive low reply, an obvious one. Captain Andrews had no such idea. The question indicated only, though it indicated accurately, the nature of his dismay at his own life and times, as today developed them. The pandemonium of these days, the wreckage of sense and order, the all-involving débâcle—this, sport to Clarence, was nearly death to Katherine. It could not be right. Captain Andrews did not think life ought to be like this; and Nathaniel Hicks must agree. Though previously persuaded that so life was, and as a result not now surprised or shocked, Nathaniel Hicks, too, could never think that so it should be. The times, with their premium on Clarence's fun all day long, were wrong.

By "wrong," Captain Andrews did not mean "wicked" or "sinful"; he meant ill-advised, ill-considered. What Clarence got, what his lovely little Emerald, what all the others to him just as lovely, sometimes sooner, nearly always later, gave him in long, nuzzling clinches, in an abandonment of rucked-up skirts, in a convulsive fold with lips glued on lips, was not to Captain Andrews's mind bad or disgusting. How could it be? How did it really differ from what *he* got, what Katherine gave him? But to get it like Clarence with false variety in an in-

359

finite sameness, on any hammock on any porch, on any sofa in any parlor, on any bed in any hotel room, had to mean that that was all you ever got. Such fun all night, like fun all day, precluded the use of reason. You were, to be sure, free of reason's bonds and responsibilities and obligations. Once free of those, whether you wished to be or not, you were free also of affection and understanding, of trust and devotion.

At least, Captain Andrews must see it that way; and Nathaniel Hicks would again have to agree with him. Presumably, men being men, he must sometimes have thought of being unfaithful to his Katherine; but Nathaniel Hicks doubted if he ever had been. And for better reasons, surely, than those Nathaniel Hicks thought of when he was talking to Captain Wiley at the Club. Captain Andrews would probably see it as unfaithfulness not merely to a person, but to the basic human relation, the vital understanding between human beings. This went beyond anything sexual. It was a trust grown up joining two people together, a solidarity of common interest and common effort—the valuable part of any human relation, the thing that makes it agreeable and good, must be the mutual act of faith and trust: your friend does not hurt or humiliate you. It occurred to Nathaniel Hicks that the fact of physical "unfaithfulness" would never be the thing of moment to the average woman—sexual fastidiousness was probably a male concept. It would be, not the fact, but the thought of it, with its implications of people knowing, and always somebody must know, if only the man himself and the other woman. That was enough. He had joined with someone else to make a fool of her. And she was right, surely; and that was no trifle, unless all trust was also a trifle, without security, without confidence, without comfort.

Nathaniel Hicks found himself immediately thinking of his own wife, and even pluming himself a little on a continence that, after all, did not come very hard; and was—you had only to look at Don and Katherine—worth in the long run so much. That touching relationship affected him, as he thought of Emily, with a sensation that he did not for a moment recognize. Astounded, he recognized it then as an approach to tears.

"For God's sake!" he said to himself. "Buck up!"

He turned his head, his involuntarily reddening face, sharp away, and saw a nurse come out, moving aside and then replacing, the screen across the door of the ward.

At Nathaniel Hicks's first thought, his heart failed him. It would be impossible to support that. If it were that, though he could not go, how could he stay to hear? He saw then that the nurse had not come to report anything. Her surprised stare made it clear that she did not know anyone was here. She stared, frowning, for a moment; and then she came right over to them.

"It's against the rules for you two to be here," she said briskly. "This is a women's ward, you know. I think you must have come to the wrong place. Were you looking for someone?"

Captain Andrews got up in a diffident distressed obedience. Nathaniel Hicks got up too, but belligerently. With Captain Andrews too far sunk to fend for himself, Nathaniel Hicks was ready to fend for him. He felt the rise of ire, vigorous and free because it was patently disinterested. To be obdurate, and even to be obstreperous about it, was easier on someone else's behalf than on one's own. He said just as briskly: "Are you Lieutenant Shakespeare?"

"Yes, I am, Captain. And you can't—"

Measuring her, Nathaniel Hicks said menacingly: "Don't you think, Lieutenant, that when you're on duty it would be a good idea to stick around? You haven't been near your desk for over half an hour."

The success of this maneuver, the quickness with which she wilted, her defensive, harassed expression, made Nathaniel Hicks ashamed of himself. She said: "I am the only one on duty this morning, sir. I have patients to take care of. Lieutenant Roche is sick this morning. That's why there's no one out here. I'm sorry if you had to wait—"

Nathaniel Hicks, absorbed in mounting his little counter-attack, had observed hardly more than a short figure in a white uniform with a second lieutenant's bar on the collar. Now he observed that Lieutenant Isabella Shakespeare would certainly be called by Captain Wiley a dish of a bitch. Under the cap, her dark thick hair was a mass of curls, the work of nature, not any machine. Her small face, with its brooding, pouting expression had a natural rich color, not from any compact. Though her hands were short and chubby, her figure was very good. She must have heard soulful whistles in her time; and her body's air of blood-warm bloom, of endocrine well-being, suggested that she often heeded them. It occurred to Nathaniel Hicks that Captain Duchemin would be a good man for her to know.

He said, still confidently, though he suspected he would now throw away his advantage: "We're waiting to hear about a patient, the captain's wife, Mrs. Andrews. The doctor told him to wait. He's in there with her now."

"Oh," Lieutenant Shakespeare said; and Nathaniel Hicks could see he was right, she was much relieved to learn that he wasn't someone in authority checking on her. Doubtless she had been in disciplinary trouble before—late into Nurses' Quarters, and so on. The average Chief Nurse would not miss opportunities to make her pay for looking like that. She said: "What doctor? You mean Doctor Werthauer's case? Doctor Werthauer left long ago. He wouldn't have told you to wait here. You must have misunderstood him."

Nathaniel Hicks said: "Doctor Werthauer said to wait; and he told us where this ward was, so I think he meant here. Why don't you call him and ask him? Captain Andrews doesn't want to go until he hears Mrs. Andrews is all right."

Lieutenant Shakespeare looked at Captain Andrews and maybe the sight touched her. She said: "I'm not supposed to; but I can tell you the patient is all right, now. That's why I wasn't able to get out before. Doctor Werthauer wanted her pulse and respiration watched until she became conscious. She's conscious now; but of course she mustn't be disturbed. It might set her back very badly. She's in no danger."

Though she said this to Captain Andrews, she must have realized that Nathaniel Hicks was the one who might be intractable. She took a step close to him and turning from Captain Andrews put, to Nathaniel Hicks's surprise, her chubby hand pleadingly on his arm. "Now, won't you please go?" she said to him. "There's a place you can wait over by the Admissions Desk in the Administration Building. Probably Doctor Werthauer is looking for you there. Doctor Raimondi will be making his rounds in a minute, and if he finds you here, Captain, I'll get into trouble. You don't want me to get into trouble, do you?"

The gesture could be taken to indicate that Lieutenant Shakespeare found all men alike and knew the way to handle them. Nathaniel Hicks would like to have laughed—those wide, melting eyes; those parted, and at such close range, moist-looking, lips; that wealth of curls from which arose a not-unpleasant odor, mixed with traces of perfume and the also not-unpleasant muskiness of her slightly sweating body! There was something so absurd in the all-out appeal to his senses—was he now supposed to stammer, intoxicated: "How's about a little kiss?"; or "Doing anything tonight?"

In this amusement Nathaniel Hicks recovered at once from the disconcerting sensation that had, in fact, passed through him when the hand touched his arm, the damp lips tilted up, and the mixed odors invitingly reached his nose. It was not a sensation sorting too well with those chaste reflections of a few minutes back. It might even suggest that there was a basic, objectionable truth in Lieutenant Shakespeare's experienced idea of all men, and of their usable, pandemic impulses.

V

CAPTAIN COLLINS's manner and person, which impressed Colonel Ross favorably at Pop's "conference" yesterday, were the same today. While Colonel Ross listened, he looked at Captain Collins's amiable, intent face. He liked the intelligent brown eyes gazing, mild and direct, through the horn-rimmed glasses; the strong frame of the slightly fattened former athlete in unstrained repose. Economical, well-ordered, and earnest, Captain Collins's speech recommended him as much as ever. Colonel Ross thought again: *Very good man; he would get results anywhere you wanted to use him; is he wasted as PRO here?*

He overstated it a little, emphasizing the favorable estimate to counteract that unreasonable, almost uncontrollable, impatience he felt. There was on him the load of Bus's business—the enormous difficulties to be met and solved if he was somehow to get General Beal through the day with no co-operation from Bus; nor even, perhaps, from Pop. Pop, if he wanted to, could help little; but Pop, if he demurred and scrupled, could hinder plenty. Most of what was done might have to be done in front of General Nichols. Colonel Ross did not really know General Nichols. At what point would Bus's old pal, Jo-Jo, decide that this went too far, and silently transform himself into the eyes and ears of the Chief of Air Staff, of the CG/AAF?

General Nichols would not do it hastily or out of hand—that was plain at breakfast. Bus could behave badly, childishly—he wasn't going to do anything about anything; no, he wouldn't go to the parade; to hell with them all; to hell with the Army; he would join the Marines; and General Nichols listened unmoved. In Bus's high position, a man had a right to take his hair down occasionally. A man could say, or even do, foolish, violent, and perhaps shameful things, as long as he did them in a certain way and in the right place (meaning, in a place where his loyal staff surrounded him so he would not be seen). General Nichols, the Chief of Air Staff's deputy, the eyes and ears of the Commanding General, would see nothing and hear nothing. General Nichols would not have his job if he could not distinguish what signified from what did not signify. Yet, Bus must stop somewhere; and who but Colonel Ross must decide where and, probably, find the means to stop him?

Certainly not Captain Collins. Captain Collins wouldn't have to do that; and so Captain Collins, in his earnest concise way, naturally thought that the day's important business was this of his. Even about that, Captain Collins did not know the half of

364

it; and much of what he did know was wrong. To assist him in self-control, Colonel Ross began to make useless notes on a memo pad. He wrote: *Mr. Willis,* and he reflected with irritability that Pop would probably think *"Mr."* was going pretty far. This was a colored man. He wrote: *lives in Washington:* and then, *waiter in restaurant.* He wrote: *Edsell, Special Projects, believed sent money;* and then: *story from Lt. Phillips.* He could not understand why Pop was so long in calling back— God alone knew what the old fool was up to!

He said, more coldly than he intended: "Yes. Well, Captain, you're mistaken in thinking General Beal doesn't know the circumstances of the incident at the Air Base the other night. Your Phillips has it all wrong. The only thing even partly right is that Lieutenant Willis, a colored pilot, was punched in the nose by a white officer. General Beal himself happened to witness it, as I did. It will be taken care of. Racial friction was not involved in any way. Though I think the incident, or misunderstandings about it, did help to precipitate the difficulty yesterday. In any event, there would be nothing General Beal could do. I don't know quite what you thought he could do. You might tell Lieutenant Phillips, who struck me yesterday as a young man who talks too much, to stop spreading that story around. He has invited disciplinary action already; and I think he would be well advised to watch himself."

Captain Collins colored a little. He said politely, unruffled: "I hope I haven't butted into something that is none of my business, Colonel. I thought you ought to know what Mr. Bullen told me. Lieutenant Phillips's story is, at least, the story that seems to be going around; and, if you saw that Press Association dispatch this morning, not merely around the Area, here. I thought there was, or might be, a Public Relations angle. I think there still is. Since it didn't happen, the general may want to consider whether it should be denied. If it had happened, and he hadn't been told about it, I thought, again from the Public Relations angle, we ought to give prompt publicity to any action taken against white officers who beat up a colored officer. The general would surely want to use his authority to show he and the Army Air Forces don't countenance things like that."

Perhaps, Colonel Ross thought, he'd better buzz Pop and find out what Pop was doing. It was almost certain to be foolish and harmful, if it went beyond calling the general. Calling the general couldn't have taken all this time—he would give Pop three more minutes.

He said: "We are a little upset this morning, Captain. Your information is valuable. You did right in bringing it to me at once. About Lieutenant Willis's father—I may want you to help with that, if you will. I am waiting for a call from Colonel Mowbray. Will you wait, too, please?"

"Yes, sir. Colonel, about the other matter—"

"What other matter?" Colonel Ross said, frowning.

Captain Collins said, "About that investigation you ordered on a possible leak in Headquarters to Mr. Bullen's paper—"

"Oh; yes, yes. Steve said you knew something about it. I'm sorry. I forgot. Have you anything definite?"

"I'm afraid I have," Captain Collins said. "I'm afraid I know all about it. It's from my office. I had a hunch when Mr. Bullen called me this morning. So I investigated at once—"

Colonel Ross drew two savage lines across the memo sheet. Getting hold of himself, he wrote carefully the name: *Caroline Crittenden* and then underlined it. He looked at Captain Collins. He supposed his look must have been ominous, for Captain Collins stumbled over a word. "Go on, go on," Colonel Ross said. "I don't quite know what you mean by 'more or less of an accident.'"

Soon he looked at the clock, and saw that Pop's three minutes were up. Distracted, he said: "Yes. I see."

The comment might sound weak and indecisive to Captain Collins, a token of uncertain authority and a slow, troublous old mind—like Pop's. Exasperated at the notion of Captain Collins remarking the loosened grip, the poverty of command, he said sharply, as if with superior acumen: "You seem greatly disturbed about this, Captain."

"I am, sir," Captain Collins said.

"Just so!" The swelling irritability filled Colonel Ross's chest and even his throat, where it duly produced that spiteful bark by which authority, making someone jump, confirms itself. Colonel Ross heard the sound with disrelish; but he felt the relief it gave, too. "Answer me one question, Captain. This young woman. You don't happen to be shacking-up with her, or anything, do you?"

He had nonplused Captain Collins, all right. He had that satisfaction, for what it was worth; and, of course, it was worth nothing, nothing like what it cost. He succeeded in blanking Captain Collins by obliging Captain Collins to trade whatever estimate of Colonel Ross he had been forming for a lower one. Captain Collins's lips parted; then, quietly, he brought them together and held them closed a moment. He opened them again and said: "No, sir. I don't happen to be." Then he said, "I don't know much about Miss Crittenden's private life, Colonel; but I would bet a good deal that she doesn't hell around. I don't think you'll find anything like that."

"I have no intention of looking," Colonel Ross said bitterly. An old man's cruelest loss of face had now to be acknowledged and the knowledge swallowed. He must—what was the phrase?—digest his spleen! Perhaps to some benefit; a late lesson! Captain Collins, half his age, passed him in deportment, in judgment, in show of true experience. Colonel Ross said: "I have no occasion to investigate her private or love life, if any. It occurred to me that you might have some special reason for going to bat for her. If so, I wanted to know it. That was all. Your private life is your own, too, Captain."

Captain Collins, who must have seen his advantage, made no attempt to use it. He said: "Well, sir, I know what you mean. It could happen, according to all I hear. And I guess you're right; I have a special reason, though not quite that special." He smiled pleasantly. "I felt sorry for Caroline, for one thing. It gave her a bad scare, and it seemed to me she hadn't meant any harm. She isn't too bright; but she's a good girl. And I

367

don't want to lose her, if I can help it. I'm the only other person in my office who can type worth a damn; and it's so hard to get anybody, I could see myself doing all our typing, in addition to my other duties."

"That is an admissible motive," Colonel Ross said, the smart in his mind easing. "However, Colonel Howden is conducting this investigation, you know. What do you want me to do?"

Captain Collins said, "It is kind of you to put it that way, Colonel. I want you to let her off, if you will. Though I know it is Counter-Intelligence's investigation, I understood that you ordered it; and I hoped if I could get to you before Colonel Howden got to her, and could explain the case satisfactorily, that you'd give her a break. Colonel Howden, the little I've seen of him, doesn't look too fond of giving people breaks. And anyway, if he wanted to, could he? I thought you could, sir, if you wanted to—I mean, of course, if you felt that you conscientiously could, you would have the necessary authority."

"Yes," said Colonel Ross.

He had been regarding himself this morning as half-helpless, overcharged, with few means given him; but that view depended on where you sat. Looking from below, Captain Collins saw him in his kingly state, caparisoned to act for General Beal; all the paraphernalia of authority at hand. Badly scared, not-too-bright, yet a good girl, Miss Crittenden, with hundreds of other people, waited for his word.

At a word from him, Miss Crittenden would weep no more, she could go free and clear. At a different word, if he chose to say it, Miss Crittenden's case proceeded to the War Department, and from there to the Department of Justice; and the Federal district attorney was advised to move to indict her. A Federal grand jury, importantly reflecting on catastrophes that resulted (a million posters told them) from even a little loose talk, could hardly argue about finding a true bill. Miss Crittenden would stand her trial.

What the trial jury found depended on many factors, some favorable to Miss Crittenden. Though she hadn't ought to have told, still she only told her Daddy. Mr. Bullen and his political friends would have retained the right lawyer, someone to show a Florida jury that the real issue was whether or not they wanted a new carpetbagging era. Was the Yankee government to have their help in hounding a pure young Southern girl to ruin and disgrace? After many months of cruel anxiety and humiliating public exposure, Miss Crittenden might hope to be declared not guilty.

Colonel Ross tore the sheet with Miss Crittenden's name on it from the memo pad. He said to Captain Collins, "Of course, this must stop. If it doesn't—"

"Yes, sir. If it doesn't, I will gladly take the rap."

"You can do that," Colonel Ross said, "but unfortunately, not until I have taken it first. Bear that in mind. I won't take it gladly, either." He tossed the crumpled sheet into the waste basket.

"I understand that, sir. And I very much appreciate your kindness—"

Colonel Ross said: "Collins, that is a highly improper remark. Withdraw it. The matter is in my discretion and for reasons I find good and sufficient, I have disposed of it. Unless you think you have influenced me improperly, by fear or favor, what are you thanking me for?"

"I was thanking you for letting me present my version of it, sir."

Colonel Ross said, laughing, "Do you like your job, Collins?"

Captain Collins hesitated. "I don't suppose anyone likes being a flexible gunner, either. Us; you fight it, as they say, and we'll write it! There isn't much to do, really. I have two assistants, and any one of us could handle it. You pass things out pursuant to the latest poop from Washington; and maybe arrange a tour of the installations for the Combined Committee on Something or Other. I don't really mean there isn't much to do; you never catch up with it; but when you've done it you haven't done anything. But I would be a liar if I said I wished I were out being shot at somewhere; and maybe I never had it so good."

Colonel Ross said: "This office is getting a new table of organization. I have Major Hill—he's at Boca Negra this week—on technical inspection; and he needs an assistant. I take care of administrative with Sergeant Brooks. We just barely manage that: and we really don't manage all the other things. I'm arranging to have an executive officer. He wouldn't have to do anything about the inspection end of it; but people come in— like you, for instance. I need somebody here; so if the general has me over at his office, or I'm out on inspections, everything doesn't stop."

Captain Collins looked at him alertly.

"The T/O would call for a lieutenant colonel; but we could get by with a major for a while. Anything about it interest you, Captain?"

"Yes," Captain Collins said. "I'm sorry I'm not a major, sir."

"It is a matter of judgment," Colonel Ross said. "If somebody came in and told you the story about the colored officer, or about your girl, you'd have to decide what to say to him, and what to tell me. There would be things you could handle yourself, and things that you would have to clear with me. Would you like to try?"

"Very much, sir. However, I don't know about the rank, sir. I have only been in grade six months. If I have to be a major—"

"Yes, you'd better be a major," Colonel Ross said. "You need the rank to do the job. It won't be necessary for you to have your time in grade. We'll take care of that right away." He made a note on his pad. He pressed a button on his desk. Sergeant Brooks opened the door and looked in. "Steve," he said, "call Colonel Ehret's office and ask them to add to the next Special Orders: Captain Collins, Public Relations, relieved from assignment and duty effective Monday, and assigned to us."

"Yes, sir."

"There you are, Collins," Colonel Ross said. "I think we can get your promotion next week."

The warm feeling which came from power to arrange so quickly a considerable favor for somebody else, which was also reasonably sure to be a good stroke of business for himself, lasted him, Colonel Ross supposed, half a minute. In this life, you succeeded when you were young because you never risked letting anyone do anything for you; and when you were old you succeeded, if you did, because you never risked doing yourself what you could pick someone to do for you.

Captain Collins showed signs that his equanimity was shaken, though not unpleasantly. Color came into his face; and he stuttered a little. "That was quick, sir!" he said, and laughed. "Well, I will certainly try to—I hope I can—"

Interrupting him, Colonel Ross said: "Unless, of course, an ax drops on us suddenly—"

The telephone rang.

On the line, Mrs. Eliot's voice said: "Colonel Mowbray calling you, Judge."

Colonel Ross was conscious of a sinking sensation. He said: "Where is he calling from, do you know?"

"His office, I think, sir. His girl is on the line."

"Well, what's wrong with the box?" Colonel Ross said. "All right; let's have it."

He could hear Mrs. Eliot saying: "I have Colonel Ross—" There was a pause and Pop's voice said cautiously: "That you, Norm? That you?"

"Yes, it is."

"Look, I didn't call before because I couldn't. Jo-Jo and Ollie Baxter are in my office. I'm using Botty's phone, see? I didn't know they were coming. They went out to the Base to see that P-Forty-seven with the you-know—"

"Yes, I know," Colonel Ross said. The you-know was a special small radar unit installed in the plane's tail which beamed its impulses through the whole rear quadrant. If anything approached within three hundred yards of the plane a warning signal lit up on the instrument panel, or at least it did sometimes. General Nichols tactfully expressed a wish to see it, so that Bus would be free to go to his office and get on with his work this morning. "I know, I know," he repeated.

"Well, look, Norm. Nobody knows where he is."

"Where who is?" Colonel Ross said automatically; but he knew who, before he finished saying it.

"Bus," whispered Colonel Mowbray. "He told Vera he was going over to the Base Hospital. He was there. He asked the

Officer of the Day for Major McCreery. He didn't stay there. Nobody knows where he went then."

"Did you call his car?"

"Yes. Picked it up on the way back here. The driver said the general had told him not to wait."

"Did you check at Operations?"

"No."

"Well, better do it. He may have gone flying. See where that AT-Seven and Sergeant Pellerino are."

"But he couldn't do that, Norm! He has Jo-Jo here; and—"

"I don't know who could stop him."

"Well, what are we going to do? Jo-Jo'll know there's something wrong in a minute. Look at the mess here! Bus can't walk out on that."

Colonel Ross said stoically, "I told you before. We will just have to go ahead as if he were here. Did you send that car?"

"Car? Car?"

"Never mind. I'll send it. I'd better come over."

"Yes. Look, Norm. I had to tell Jo-Jo about Benny's trouble. He came in wanting to find that Negro. You know, about the medal. I couldn't stall him off; I had to say where the man was. I don't know whether Bus wanted it that way, or not. But what else could I do?"

"Nothing else. Bus will have to want it the way we do it. Did you tell General Nichols that you didn't know where Bus was?"

"Of course not! That's what I don't want him to know. We have to find Bus. We have to get him back here. We have to do something."

"Let's begin by keeping our shirts on, Pop," Colonel Ross said heavily. "You better get back to Nichols and Baxter. I will see what I can find out from Operations; and we can try to reach the plane. If Nichols wants to give the medal, let him. It will take some time."

He hung up and said to Captain Collins: "Are you free for the next half hour or so?"

"Yes, sir."

"My car, and the driver, are by the side door. Take it. Go

372

down to the railroad station and meet Lieutenant Willis's father. Bring him to the Hospital, and wait with him until I get over. If there is any question at any point, you are acting on General Beal's orders. You can tell Mr. Willis that his son is all right. I know they were preparing to discharge him from the Hospital this morning, so he must be, more or less. It is being arranged for them to see each other. That is all the information you have. Can you handle that?"

"Yes, sir."

✦

Colonel Ross felt a faint disgusted pity for those two upset old men—himself, and Pop. Though Colonel Ross had a poor opinion of Pop's ordinary discernment or intelligence, and though anything or nothing could throw Pop into a spasm of agitation, the pathetic pitch of this spasm might actually have a reasonable and adequate basis. Pop had the advantage of him here in information and experience. Colonel Ross, in many senses an old Army man himself, was nevertheless once and for all excluded from the inner circle and its sacred and unfailing bond.

That mystic order, the West Point Benevolent and Protective Association, included Pop. Pop was a proficient in its never-written constitution and by-laws, in its precedents and procedures. Colonel Ross could only guess, from an outsider's incomplete view of some of the Association's past workings, at the admissible latitudes, and at the fixed limits—how far and in what directions its compassionate indulgence and long-suffering love would reach; how shortly and how arbitrarily both could end. Pop exactly apprehended both. He would not be confused by the occasional apparent paradoxes and inequitabilities. The principles were imbued in his mind.

Colonel Ross was sure these principles were few and simple. One of them might seem to be: you can do certain things if you just don't say anything about them; you can say certain things if you just don't do anything about them. Thus, Nichols and Baxter, Association members in good standing, thought nothing of Bus's outbreak at the breakfast table about turning in his suit—this language of sports or the locker-room was significant. It declared a whole ethos or set of attitudes. On, brave old Army team! Could a member of that team ever, by his own disgruntled choice, make the slightest actual move to leave the field and go to the showers? Obviously, no! That was unthinkable. That was not the good old Army way at all. That, or anything remotely like that, seen or even suspected, was beyond compassion and would not be suffered long.

Colonel Ross was ready to believe that Pop, the old fool, in this one matter, acute and right, knew that Bus was near the invisible edge, that the unthinkable opened only a step away, and yet Bus still moved, still did not look or did not care where he was going. Pop would know too what it meant, in terms of the whole long life, the whole career, the years of care and denial and disciplined patience at last rewarded, and all, in a moment, thrown away—why didn't you do it twenty years ago if you had to, when it would hardly matter to Pop or to you?

Colonel Mowbray said: "Now, I don't want you to think we were holding out on you, Jo-Jo. It wasn't that at all. This young man here"—he shot a look at Benny—"lost his temper. He admits it. He's sorry. He's ready to go right now and apologize to Lieutenant Willis. We feel, and he feels, that he may deserve some other punishment, too. Company punishment, I mean. Now, Bus did talk about court martial—"

Colonel Mowbray got up and began to ramble around the room at the mention of General Beal—surely, Colonel Ross thought, all the tip-off General Nichols could possibly need. "But I know why he did that," Colonel Mowbray said. "He wanted Benny, here, to realize fully the seriousness of what his temper had made him do. That's why Bus had charges drawn, ready to be preferred. But I don't think he ever meant to prefer them. I don't know whether you know Colonel Carricker's record. I don't think there's a fighter pilot in the service with a better one. In my opinion, a man who has been cited twice for the Distinguished Service Cross oughtn't to be court-martialed—

374

which, if they convicted him, would just about have to mean dismissal from the service. Not unless he was known to be guilty of some serious dereliction of duty, some disgraceful criminal offense. I know that's what Bus feels. You feel that too, don't you, Norm?"

Colonel Ross's first impulse had been to interrupt Pop, cut off the torrent of words before Pop said something he didn't mean to say. However, he did not think Pop would be physically or mentally able to keep still; and it might be better to let him talk himself out on Benny. Colonel Ross simply nodded in answer. He looked at Benny. Benny sat red-faced and stolid, gazing straight in front of him at a large aerial photograph of Maxwell Field framed on the far wall. He showed no reaction either to Pop's declaration of how bad he had been, or of how good he was. It occurred to Colonel Ross that Benny was not listening, not hearing any of this. This was more of the crap he had to go through; so he shut his mind and waited for it to be over.

General Baxter showed embarrassment—this was none of his business, really. He had time to put in before he flew to Sellers Field, so he tagged along with General Nichols, who also had time to put in while Bus was busy with his regular duties. Baxter did not like being set up, along with General Nichols, as a sort of court of appeal to hear what was strictly Bus's affair—disciplinary action involving a member of Bus's command. General Baxter cleared his throat. With the plain idea of keeping things on the basis of a discussion of theory, not of actual cases, not of this case of Bus's, he said unctuously: "I believe you're quite right there, Pop. Unless a commissioned officer's conduct should warrant or require dismissal from the service, he ought not to be court-martialed. That's our line. Of course, the Manual for Courts Martial defines offenses that require court martial. If I recall, assault *not* with a dangerous weapon isn't included in the mandatory paragraph." He turned courteously to Colonel Ross. "Would that be your recollection, Colonel?"

Colonel Ross said: "That is right, General."

"Yes," said General Nichols, who must have decided, not to Colonel Ross's surprise, that the real point ought to be made plainer. "It would be for Bus to say. And I hope I didn't give the impression I thought you were, as you said, holding out on me, Pop. We're just the visiting firemen." He laughed. "Bus would tell me as much or as little as he wanted to. I didn't speak to him about Willis's medal. The truth is, it slipped my mind. The feeling in Washington was, simply, that presenting the medal, which Willis had earned, all right, might be made something of a show. Good for the morale of his outfit. That was the Old Man's idea. Of course he didn't know anything had happened. It hadn't happened then. As soon as I heard about the arrested officers this morning, I thought Bus would probably feel, and so would the Old Man, that it would have to be done differently—not Bus pinning it on him in public. Until all members of the group showed they meant to obey orders and behave themselves, better keep it a strictly individual matter—"

"Just what I think, Jo-Jo," Colonel Mowbray said. "What I said to Norm about Benny apologizing, when he first said Benny should. Before I even knew about the medal. Do we want them to think we're trying to bribe them? No, sir! Let them toe the line first! I think, I admitted right along, that Benny's apologizing was the right thing for him to do. Looking at it as a thing in itself. Same way, if this colored boy earned a medal, he ought to get it. But not in any way that might look to the other men like a kind of weakness, a kind of weakening, on our part."

Colonel Ross thought disagreeably: yes, if you have to weaken, always do it where not many people see you; and be sure you get something for it. He did not feel quite disagreeable enough to say, with Benny sitting there: "Is Colonel Carricker going to toe the line first? Might it look like a kind of weakness, a kind of weakening, on our part, when he gets away with murder?" He said: "Would you sit down, Pop? You make me dizzy."

Colonel Mowbray pulled up. "Sorry," he said. He went obediently and put himself in his chair.

General Nichols, his chin in his hand, looked reflectively from Colonel Ross to Colonel Mowbray. He said: "You think I shouldn't give him the medal, Pop? I have to do that. The Old Man told me to."

"That's up to the Old Man," Colonel Mowbray said.

There was, Colonel Ross must agree, a saintlike humility in the statement, an honestly respectful, trustworthily familiar forthrightness as he said the words from which no one could ever tell there had been a time when he and his "Old Man" were second lieutenants together, young aviators together, and one, sitting stiffly in the stick and fabric frame of a preposterous flying machine, looked no more nor less a likely lad than the other.

Pop started to rise from his chair, and then pressed himself back into it. He planted his elbows on his desk and twisted his hands together. "No. No. I was just agreeing with you, Jo-Jo. We ought to do it privately, if you have to do it. Only, that changes the picture about Benny, it seems to me. First Benny apologizes, and then you give him a medal; or first you give him a medal, and then Benny apologizes. Isn't that laying it on pretty thick? I mean, wouldn't he, Willis, even, think so? Norm thinks I don't want Benny to apologize. I do, Norm; only at the right time. Is this right? Is it, Jo-Jo?"

"I really don't know," General Nichols said. "That's for Bus, not me, Pop. I can't mix into that. It is to the prejudice of the best interests of the service for officers to go around hitting each other in the nose. The one who started it would do well to apologize. When, where, and how would be properly determined by the commanding officer. I'm not it. But I have to give Willis the medal. Willis doesn't seem to have done anything—disobeyed orders, misbehaved himself—to excuse postponing it. If you think I'd better talk to Bus before I do it—"

"I didn't mean that," Colonel Mowbray said, half rising. Clutching the edge of his desk, he pushed himself back into his chair and swung it from side to side on its swivel. "Why don't you go over to the Hospital and give it to him now, then? Take Ollie along to read the citation. That boy couldn't ask better than two general officers coming in to decorate him. Norm or I could go along, representing Bus; but not Bus himself, see? Could you go, Norm?"

"I could go, if General Nichols would like to do it that way," Colonel Ross said.

Colonel Mowbray said, "Naturally, I agree with you, Jo-Jo. What you said. Under the circumstances, Bus oughtn't to do it personally. Willis is a member of this group that disobeyed orders. Matter of fact, I saw the project T/O's which Colonel Jobson's office prepared, and Willis was slated for temporary or provisional group commander. It would be really his job to take responsibility for the actions of his group. Certainly it would be if he had been present for duty with them."

"Yes, but he wasn't," Colonel Ross, tried beyond endurance, said. "And probably he didn't even know he was to be provisional group commander. I think we will have to hold him harmless. Perhaps if he *had* been there, none of it would have happened. Perhaps it's a pity he had to be in the Hospital."

"Well, I don't know about that," Colonel Mowbray said rebelliously. "That boy was picked tentatively because he was supposed to show qualities of leadership. If he'd been there, the trouble might have been much worse. See what I mean? If he does have qualities of leadership, and it was decided to make trouble about post regulations, it would have been worse with a man who showed leadership to lead it. That's aside from the point. All I was saying was Jo-Jo, if he wants to, should go ahead and give him the medal at the Hospital, where it would be private. Bus shouldn't be involved in it personally; but he couldn't have any objection to your doing what the Old Man said had to be done. So I don't think we even need to bother Bus about it. You want me to call the Hospital and brief them that you're coming over?"

General Nichols looked at Colonel Mowbray indulgently, a shadow of smile on the fine lips under the cropped mustache. Lugubrious, Colonel Ross thought to himself: "*Who do we think we're fooling?*"

General Nichols said: "Do that, Pop. I don't think we need to drag poor Ollie over. Would it be convenient for you to represent General Beal, Colonel Ross? If you approve, that is. You haven't said what you thought."

"I think he should be given the medal, sir. Of course, I don't

378

know what his frame of mind is. Would you like me to go over first and have a talk with him?"

"No," General Nichols said. "I don't think you need to bother to do that, Colonel. If you don't mind coming with me." He smiled. "Sometimes I've heard talk about it," he said, "but I never knew a man to turn down a good medal yet. Have I got it?" He reached for a pigskin brief case on the table and took from it an envelope, and a morocco-covered jeweler's case, which he opened with a flash of red, white, and blue ribbon. He gave the envelope to Colonel Ross. "That's the citation," he said, "if you'll be kind enough to do the reading. Shall we go?"

Colonel Mowbray struck down a key on the box and said: "Botty. Get my car right away to take General Nichols and Colonel Ross to the Base Hospital."

General Baxter said, "I don't mind going, Jo-Jo, if you think it would swell the parade."

General Nichols said: "I think this has been a hard morning for a fat man, Ollie. Never volunteer for anything is the way in the Army, they tell me. We'll be seeing you."

VI

AT THE Admissions Desk in the hospital headquarters building Captain Andrews and Nathaniel Hicks were asked to wait. They waited on one of the benches arranged along the walls, with a good view of a big diagram whose black graph line showed the venereal disease rate week by week, under the arresting announcement: SHE NEVER TELLS YOU SHE HAS IT!; and over the admonition: GET SMART, SOLDIER; and the street addresses of the downtown prophylactic stations.

They had been waiting about five minutes, all the other benches empty, and no one in sight but a Wac typewriting under a sign: *Information*, when General Beal strode from the Officer of the Day's room and passed the railed enclosure, headed for the door.

Nathaniel Hicks murmured to Captain Andrews: "Look who's here!"

General Beal's eyes swung levelly from right to left, taking in the open space and the benches around it. The general's face had a tight, taut look. The sweeping eye was cold and hard. It rested an instant on Nathaniel Hicks; and the general turned then and came that way.

During another instant Nathaniel Hicks was not certain, for General Beal's face was expressionless, that General Beal was actually coming to speak to him. If the general *was* coming to speak to him, he ought to get up; if the general was really headed for the side passage beyond the bench, his having got up would be awkward. Belatedly, Nathaniel Hicks did get up; and astonished, Captain Andrews got up with him.

General Beal said: "Hicks, that project of yours is off. Drop it. We aren't going to do it. Tell Colonel Coulthard I changed my mind—"

In confusion, Nathaniel Hicks said: "Yes, sir."

With no pause, the matter curtly opened and now flatly closed, General Beal turned on his heel, crossed over, and went out the door.

Whether because Captain Andrews believed the nurse and was reassured; whether because the dearest anxiety fades as time passes, Captain Andrews had become more like himself. With the general gone, he said sympathetically: "Gee, that's tough, Nat. That sounded like a good thing."

Nathaniel Hicks found that he was both jolted and disgruntled. "Maybe he thought I was making it too good," he said, disconsolate. "And maybe I was. I was throwing my weight around with Colonel Folsom a little yesterday, and he may have squawked."

Captain Andrews said: "It didn't seem to me he was exactly sore at you, Nat. Of course I don't know what he's usually like. That's the only time I ever saw him close up. I thought he was thinking of something else, more—I mean, I think he would have come right out, if it was anything he thought you did wrong. Gosh, I'll say for him he looks the part—I mean, like a general. They don't, all."

"I guess he was acting the part, too," Nathaniel Hicks said.

The now-canceled project had restored him, for twenty-four hours, to something like his lost and gone civilian status. Though without noticing, gratefully he must have resumed the attitudes that went with that status. He had tasted again a sample, at least, of his old prerogatives to decide, direct, do what he wanted; and to have what he said always (or nearly always) go. He tasted with relish, for they were better now; not, as they used to be, a mere matter-of-course. Absence from them had made the heart grow fonder of them.

It would take time to pack the attitudes back where they came from and to re-reconcile himself to his low military status —by this uniform identified as one whose only real work or reason-for-being was to await orders and then obey them; by his captain's bars certified as a mere line officer, a junior, casually to be nodded up or nodded down. He might be expected, when asked, to supply his superiors with information; but he would not be asked, and was not expected, to supply them with opinions. No explanations were owed him. It was enough for him to hear General Beal's wishes. The general wished one thing yesterday, and another thing today. Need more be said?

No! More need not be said; yet Nathaniel Hicks stirred with rebellion. He was not willing to let go so easily. What the general wished, went; and what the general wished today did not suit him. But how about tomorrow? Could nothing be done about that? Nathaniel Hicks would damn well see what could be done about that. He would have a talk with Colonel Coulthard. And, probably better, he would also have a talk with Colonel Ross. This project, promising so much good or advantage to the Army Air Forces and to General Beal personally, ought not to be lightly abandoned. He must exercise his wits and apply his ingenuity.

Unfortunately, it was an abject exercise and a low application. He would need to be ingenious in flattery, and quick witted in misrepresentation. To be clear about his illaudable purpose, he had only to remember that when the project was first put to him, his instinctive editorial judgment rejected it—in the limits that security set there could not be enough interesting material. It wouldn't make a story.

Still, it was true that, written by a first-rate article man, something might be got-off on someone. And where or how would he get a first-rate article man to do it? A first-rate man would see as easily as he did that there wasn't any story—still, of course, Edsell was a professional writer; he might be out of his field, but he probably couldn't be wholly incompetent; and Edsell wanted to do it enough to work at it. McCabe, of course, was really first rate; only it meant an expensive reproduction job and if the article wasn't too hot, instead of being carried by the art work it might be rejected because the art work cost so much. Of course, if they did an article on the general himself—the inside story of the victory of air power in Africa? the boy general who showed them how?—McCabe could do his portrait. A point to suggest to Colonel Coulthard; who would doubtless see that Mrs. Beal heard. If Mrs. Beal knew who McCabe was—it would be important to impresss McCabe's standing on Colonel Coulthard, who would certainly never have heard of him as an artist—she would be a very odd woman if she disliked the idea or failed to press the general to go along.

Nathaniel Hicks would not, could not, guarantee to get a portrait of General Beal in full colors into a magazine of national circulation; but he could sure as hell try. The best way of trying would be to fly north for a couple of weeks' temporary duty, and see what he could promote by a little personal string-pulling with various publishing friends and acquaintances. It might even be necessary to make several trips—in short, get home several times.

The discomfiture of stooping, as he must, to say what he did not fully believe; and of doing, as he must, what he did not fully approve, was strong; but not strong enough to stop his mind's eager and lively outpouring of possible means to such desirable ends. And it wasn't as if the whole thing were fake, as if he knew it was wholly useless or completely impossible. There was a chance; and certainly, if anyone could pull it off, he was the one. He had the connections and he knew how to go about it. Moreover, he didn't invent the project; Washington, Colonel Ross had said, and so had General Beal, considered such projects important and desirable. That made sense. The scope of Air Force activities ought to be impressed on the public; how else could the public be made to understand the Air Force's needs? And was there, after all, anything more useful to the war effort that he could be doing if he wasn't doing this?

Nathaniel Hicks's weakening discomfiture, hearing these arguments, asserted itself enough to sneer faintly at such a lot of intelligent self-interest, and at the commanding position held in all he thought by the simple consideration: *what's in it for me?* Well, what else did a man consider, anyway? Even a man like Captain Andrews, rushing to his country's aid, admitted that he had in mind the uses of the uniform to keep him in countenance. This was war! Nathaniel Hicks could almost hear the myriad-voiced, confirming and sustaining murmur from a hundred circling camps, counseling him to do as he planned to do. It was the righteous sentence of the day: *Screw you, Jack; I've got mine!*

Overhead, among the open rafters, a loudspeaker made a throat-clearing sound and said hollowly: "Captain Donald Andrews. Captain Donald Andrews, please. Kindly come to the Officer of the Day's room."

Captain Andrews started up, crossed the open space and went between the two railed enclosures to the door at the head of the central hall. Left alone, Nathaniel Hicks glanced around, thinking that, if he could get a telephone, it might be a good idea to call the office and see how Wiley and McCabe were getting on. The WAC Pfc. with the sign: *Information* on her desk said she guessed he could use the telephone at the next desk, and she opened the gate in the railed enclosure.

Several enlisted men came in the front entrance then—one with crutches and a heavily bandaged foot; one with a patch over his left eye—and sat on the benches which the Wac, nodding at them, indicated.

Captain Duchemin answered the phone.

"Swimmingly, swimmingly, they say they're getting on," he said. "There is art all over the place. They do not need nor want you. How's with Mrs. A.?"

"Don's seeing the doctor now, I think. They sent for him. The nurse said she was doing all right."

"Why don't you ask how I'm doing? I am at a standstill. Manny's plane, or more properly in the present use, my plane, cannot be made to fly this morning. I am grounded; and so are Pettie and pigeons. Miss Candee keeps going to the Ladies Room and leaving me to answer phones. The captain and the sergeant keep putting out their cigarettes on me. Oh, say: Three-W's is trying to locate your buddy or side-kick, Edsell. I had to say he stepped out a moment. You don't know where he is, do you? Major P. has been sniffing around suspiciously. I think a high sling will soon be rigged."

"I don't know where he is; and they can put him right in it, any time, tell them."

"Good. Wait! If you're going to be there at the Hospital give me a number, will you? Here I am, left as Acting CO of the Reports Section and I want to know the disposal of my forces. Let's synchronize our watches, isn't it?"

"You can get me here for a while," Nathaniel Hicks said, giving him the number on the phone. "I ought to be along pretty soon and I'll relieve the hell out of you."

Putting the telephone back, Nathaniel Hicks said thanks to the Wac, and stepped out of the enclosure. He had reached the bench where he had been before and seated himself when the screened doors of the front entrance opened again.

They admitted Lieutenant Edsell.

Lieutenant Edsell held one door a moment, his face turned away from Nathaniel Hicks, while he ushered in somebody with him. It proved to be a heavy squat man, bareheaded, carrying in one hand a soiled, pale-gray felt hat, and in the other a straw suitcase with a piece of rope around it. He wore dark wrinkled trousers and a dark wrinkled coat, hanging wide open

384

on taut damp expanse of green shirting patterned with darker green flowered sprigs. He had tucked a large bedraggled handkerchief inside his collar and tied it around his neck. On his big feet were new sport shoes in an arrangement of black and white leathers.

Nathaniel Hicks stared at him; and at once, in anguish, his throat aching, he had to swallow down the violently eructed laugh. It was too much; it was too funny; it went wildly beyond the mere laughable incident into the high fantastic. The man with the suitcase turned his broad anxious face. Lieutenant Edsell's companion was another Negro.

Lieutenant Edsell, letting the door go closed, passed the back of his hand across his sweaty forehead and gazed challengingly around. When he saw Nathaniel Hicks, he said: "What the hell are you doing here, Nat?" Not waiting for an answer, he piloted his companion over. "Mr. Willis, Captain Hicks," he said. "This is Lieutenant Willis's father." With a triumphant glint of eye he examined Nathaniel Hicks's face for signs of understanding and astonishment. Nathaniel Hicks dared say he found them, for, wiping more sweat off, Lieutenant Edsell said in a satisfied tone: "Just set your bag down and sit here with Captain Hicks, Mr. Willis. Captain Hicks is from my office. I'll find out where Stanley is." To Nathaniel Hicks he said, as an afterthought, "Got the pip, or something, Nat?"

"Don Andrews's wife is ill," Nathaniel Hicks said with dignity. "I'm waiting for him. And, look. I was just talking to the office. Whitney is steamed up about where you are. You'd better check in."

"Nuts!" said Lieutenant Edsell.

Mr. Willis sank heavily on the bench. He turned his head to Nathaniel Hicks and, apologetically wiping both his face and his sparse fuzz of tight, woolly, graying hair with the full ends of the handkerchief knotted around his neck, said: "Mighty hot out in that sun—"

Lieutenant Edsell remained a moment, surveying them with continued satisfaction. He said: "We took a taxi to the Base gate; but they wouldn't let it in. They gave us a pass, all right; so I don't think that was an accident, if you get me. It's quite a walk from the gate to the Hospital area. Good exercise." He nodded significantly.

Nathaniel Hicks said: "As far as I know, they never pass in taxis, or any car that hasn't a Base sticker."

"Yeah?" said Lieutenant Edsell, favoring him with a look of derision. "Well, they had instructions to pass in Mr. Willis and escorting officer. Some Ocanara police were at the station and I suppose one of them tipped off the people here. Somebody, old Mowbray probably, must have told them they'd better let us in; but not to be too nice about it. So they fixed Mr. Willis a good long walk. However, this time I have them by the short hairs, and they aren't going to get away with it. I'm going to raise some hell around here. I'll see the Post Surgeon." He went off with assurance, down the central hall.

Mr. Willis lifted the knotted handkerchief again and sopped up sweat on his chin. He said to Nathaniel Hicks: "Reason I come down; I got a boy here, Stanley, who got hurt. The lieutenant's going to get me to see him, he says. I surely worry about him—"

From the inside pocket of his coat Mr. Willis produced suddenly a long fat brown envelope, slightly damp at the end. "He's a flyer, officer, second lieutenant, a pilot. He fly those bombers. Look here." Mr. Willis took a rubber band from the envelope and extracted a mass of folded papers. A photograph fell to the floor and, grunting, he recovered it. "See there, that's him," he said. He offered the photograph to Nathaniel Hicks. "Then, this other. That's when he's in training. That's the plane he had. Then, look here, that's a paper, certificate. You read it. Says he's head of his class, basic training—no, advanced training, there. He got those for all the training. He got others, in academic. Say he's first. They give him a prize for that. War bond. That's it. He goes to bomber school. See, here's a picture. He flew that plane. There's a letter I got. United States senator. They come in this restaurant where I work. I know lots of them. See, that recommends Stanley to have flying training. To the Secretary War. That's way back—"

Clasping the papers, Mr. Willis peered at Nathaniel Hicks. With no warning, enormous fat tears began to issue from his eyes, running quietly with the sweat on his now bulging coffee-colored cheeks. He drew his breath with a low wail. "I don't know what trouble he get into," he said. "I don't know what they do. Lieutenant say they beat him up. Hurt him—"

"No, no, Mr. Willis. You mustn't—" Nathaniel Hicks said. "I—" about to say he did not know what—just anything that might stop the overflow of great tears—he pulled himself up. The natural impulse might be to take over, to say that Edsell knew nothing about it, while he, Nathaniel Hicks, had been right there, seen the whole thing—but would the account of what actually happened reassure Mr. Willis? Mr. Willis would clamor to know more than the bare facts. He would want to know how badly his boy was hurt. Nathaniel Hicks could not tell him. He would want to know how Lieutenant Colonel Carricker came to hit Stanley. Nathaniel Hicks did not see his way clear to explaining. He said inadequately: "I'm sure you'll find he's not seriously hurt. I don't think he did anything to get into trouble. You mustn't be upset—"

The inanity of these remarks, the best he could venture, made him angry. It was just like Edsell! With characteristic assurance, yet not knowing what he was talking about, Edsell improved the fine occasion in any way he could. The more upset Mr. Willis was, the better for Edsell's purpose. This purpose was not primarily to aid and comfort Mr. Willis; and Edsell would be the first to admit that; he would not pretend to be doing anything but what he was doing—conducting an action on principle. Trifles like Mr. Willis's peace of mind, or (it was fair to say) Edsell's own comfort and convenience, weren't worth consideration if sacrificing them could really give him a grip on those short hairs he spoke of. Edsell was exultantly dedicated to making all the trouble he could. It might be a good deal, if Mr. Willis went on like this.

Nathaniel Hicks said sternly: "You must get hold of yourself. That record of your son's is a fine one, and nothing's going to happen to him. If you act this way, all you'll do is make him feel bad—"

Nathaniel Hicks let his eyes move away, looking, the truth was, for means of escape. There was no sign either of Lieutenant

Edsell or of Captain Andrews. He looked at the enlisted men on the benches across the room and was relieved to see that they had either not noticed Mr. Willis crying or, if they had, they were not interested.

Opening his mouth to admonish Mr. Willis further, a task for which he felt little fitted and to which he was not inclined, Nathaniel Hicks heard the sound of steps beyond the door. He looked that way. The screen swung and in walked a trim, tall man with a little cropped black mustache. On his chest ribbons made a wide blaze and, jolting the eye as only they could, general's stars were on his shoulders.

This spruce apparition was greeted by a fractional pause while those who saw it took it in. One of the enlisted men, a thin redheaded boy by the door who must have been reading his *New Soldiers Handbook*, started erect. He blurted: "Attention!"

The others jumped. Even the man with the crutch tucked it clumsily into his armpit and made to rise. The general, observing this, said with affable alacrity: "No, no, there! At ease! Sit down!" He turned his head, perfectly composed, to speak to the person with him. Nathaniel Hicks saw that the person with him was Colonel Ross.

✦

General Nichols, in arranging to drive to the Base alone with Colonel Ross, undoubtedly planned either to ask him something, or to tell him something. General Nichols, while he listened to Pop's ill-sorted argument explaining Benny, was looking at Colonel Ross much of the time. General Nichols might easily have read in Colonel Ross's face the question: *Who do we think we're fooling?* At that point the situation became ridiculous. Must they keep up the pretense that I don't know that you know that I know?

Sure of General Nichols's intention when General Baxter was so firmly kept from joining them, Colonel Ross resolved that, while he would not volunteer any information, he would answer a direct question directly: they didn't know where General Beal was. He need not decide what else he would say until he saw how General Nichols took that; but he intended to present, in whatever way seemed best when the time came, an obiter dictum—the learned judge's incidental or collateral opinion, which, while not binding, could be so stated that dissent would be impertinence and ignorance.

He would say that Bus's going-off was natural and sensible. It showed basic good judgment. Bus recognized that he had a problem. He also recognized the effect on himself of the heavy strains and responsibilities of his position. Bus saw that he was in danger of acting precipitately, without due consideration. The way to avoid this, to give himself an uninterrupted chance to think the thing through, was to duck out without telling anyone. Bus had probably gone flying. That would be the easiest way to make sure that nobody could reach him unless he wanted to be reached. There was nothing for anyone, except a chronic worrier like Pop, to worry about.

As this was not Colonel Ross's real or full opinion, he supposed he still had a hope of fooling General Nichols; but his object was not really to deceive. The chance was as good as ever that General Nichols would be glad to accept any plausible line that comported with the facts, as far as the facts now went. To help General Nichols this way, a grave and formal attitude might be useful.

In the hall, Colonel Ross shifted himself, as junior officer, to the general's left and marched silently with him toward the side entrance. He was waiting with reserve for the general's first remark. General Nichols made it as they reached the corner. He put a hand on Colonel Ross's arm, directing them both to a door marked OFFICERS. "Let's go in here a minute," General Nichols said.

Colonel Ross preserved his grave and formal attitude in the lavatory. General Nichols, coming to wash his hands while Colonel Ross sedately washed his own hands beside him, studied his reflection in the long mirror above the basins. The sculpturesque, still face might give a vain man satisfaction; and a vain man's satisfaction is never quite concealed.

Inconspicuously Colonel Ross watched for it; but General Nichols's quick critical glance at the cropped mustache, the clipped hair, the perfectly tied tie, the perfectly fitted battle jacket, was that of the inspecting officer, who shows no interest in what is right. If everything is right, he passes on indifferently. Passing on, General Nichols reached for a paper towel.

The container, as usual, held none.

Colonel Ross turned around, pushed back one of the swinging doors with his elbow and reeled out a mass of toilet paper. He said: "I'm very sorry, General. We're having trouble getting towels."

"Thanks," General Nichols said, accepting a few yards of the flimsy stuff and rubbing it over his hands. "Oh, I know there's a war on." He looked amiably at Colonel Ross. He said: "And you could be still worse off, Judge. You might not even have this. I will tell you an important military secret. Halfway through the Conference sessions at Quebec last month they ran out of toilet paper. Completely. Even in the Governor General's house in the Citadel there wasn't any, and some very important people were tearing up newspaper. Of course we shot a plane off right away and flew in a load. Nobody knows whether it was enemy agents, or whether they just didn't realize how much it takes to keep up with a conference."

By deliberately calling him "Judge," by the joshing tone, and the man-to-man touch of scatalogical humor, General Nichols was deliberately inviting Colonel Ross to lay formality aside. In the whole history of war it was unlikely that a colonel had ever refused such an invitation from a general officer, so Colonel Ross saw that he would have to go along. He laughed appreciatively. "Yes," he said, "that seems to be a concomitant of any human assembly. The end-product does pile up."

As a matter of fact, he would be glad to hear more about Quebec. He did not mean the inside story—what momentous plans had been agreed on, what grand decisions reached. Not enough informed to appraise them properly, in no position to do anything about them, anyway, Colonel Ross would rather not know about those. What he might hear to his profit, what he wanted to hear, was quite different. Encouraged to go on with his experiences at Quebec, General Nichols might tell Colonel Ross a good deal about General Nichols.

Much might be learned, for instance, from his attitude, which would soon be plain, toward the great personages gathered there with him. All unknowingly, General Nichols letting it be seen that this or that interested or impressed him, would show Colonel Ross the way to handle General Nichols. He might, indirectly or incidentally, answer the most important question in Colonel Ross's mind—how General Nichols really rated, what his powers were, what kind of influence he had in high circles.

Colonel Ross got ready a deft, leading remark, which would keep General Nichols on that subject, surely as agreeable to the general as it was to most men, of himself and his exploits. He would incite General Nichols along the way he should go. Before Colonel Ross could speak, General Nichols tapped his arm casually, directing him out the door.

Colonel Ross was disconcerted.

Immersed in his idea, he had been choosing the course, directing things. He had forgotten that he was this young man's junior. Not he, but General Nichols was the one waited-on, the one who always gave the signal. Embarrassed by his own incredulous start, Colonel Ross made haste to obey. He walked into the hall. The original deft, leading remark was lost in this mental shuffle; and before Colonel Ross could find a new one to offer in its place, General Nichols said: "The Old Man had me along to run errands and hand him the papers, mostly."

He let his eyes, grave and candid, rest on Colonel Ross. "He thought I ought to be up on the diplomatic falderal because I'd had some assignments as an air attaché. Then, before we were in the war, they'd sent me to England as an observer in nineteen-forty-one, so I knew personally a good many RAF people and could be useful as a sort of liaison officer. It let me see a lot of what was going on."

He paused, with an air of reminiscent amusement. "They didn't get around to consulting me very much," he said. "One night I was given three minutes to tell the President and Mr. Churchill some grounds we had for our objection to a proposal that was made. The Old Man held a watch on me while I did it and it took me two minutes and fifty-two seconds. When I finished, the President yawned (it *was* pretty late) and said:

'Uh—thanks, General'; and Mr. Churchill said something like: 'Harrumph!' I was then excused." The air of amusement grew into a smile.

They had reached the door at the end of the side passage and Colonel Ross opened it and held it for the general. They stepped from the refrigerated hall into the full tropic morning on the steps. The car stood there with the driver in his seat, and at the foot of the steps, holding the car door open, Mr. Botwinick beamed obsequiously. He must have slipped out and run around to make sure everything was all right. General Nichols gave Colonel Ross another casual little tap and Colonel Ross, ducking his big shoulders, scrambled in and took his proper corner.

When General Nichols smiled, Colonel Ross had smiled in return, though weakly. While they came down the steps, while Mr. Botwinick facilitated their entrance into the car, he had the disturbing sense of now seeing, of having certainly felt, what they meant—what made Hal Coulthard say on the verandah last night that he sometimes got the creeps; what threw Pop into that rage of agitation over the idea of General Nichols coming to know too much; what Mrs. Beal—Sal—hysterically apprehended as she tried to learn at the dining room door what "they" were doing to Bus. They must all, from time to time, have been abruptly nonplused as General Nichols finished speaking and smiled.

In the supposed privacy of his mind, Colonel Ross had formed an intention. Before he could even set about acting on it, General Nichols had anticipated him and had offered him at once, still joshing a little, a good part of the specific information, summed up for his convenience, that Colonel Ross had planned to wile out of him.

Did General Nichols, then, for God's sake, read your mind, know everything you were thinking? For slow thinkers like Hal and Pop, for a whimsical and impulsive child like Mrs. Beal, it would be a short jump to that disquieting, even dazing, conclusion. Bewildered, persuaded that he was outclassed by unheard of abilities and up against inhuman attributes, Hal or

Pop began warily to study all his old friend Jo-Jo said or did, to find obscure meanings, sinister purposes, hidden dangers. Sal, working up a fright, doubled her fists and hammered them, like a child, on whatever she could reach.

All that was nonsense! When a man knew what you were thinking it was either because you had just told him by your acts or words or appearance, or because he judged you and your situation rightly, and to know what you had in mind, he needed only to ask himself what you would be likely to have in mind. Colonel Ross, restored, thought of other things he would like to know. He said judicially: "Still, the Conference must have been an interesting experience, General. A close-up of the people running things often helps to clarify the situation. I have had some experience in politics. It is very rightly called the art of the possible."

General Nichols gave him a quick, complimentary look. "Yes," he said, "the possible! That engaged them a lot. The problem is always, as I see it, to find out what that is; because that's all. You have to work inside that. The top echelon rides in the whirlwind, all right; but sometimes the storm seems to do the directing. That limits your choice, your freedom. Certain things that it might be wise to do can't be done. Of course, it doesn't mean you haven't, at the top, a good deal of choice, a good deal of freedom. You can't order a man to flap his arms and fly; but you can always order as many qualified pilots as you have to take as many planes as you have and fly the wrong way to the wrong place at the wrong time."

Colonel Ross stared at him with attention, pricking up his ears. In that sober, casual observation, if General Nichols would go on and interpret it, might lie some of what Colonel Ross had hoped to learn about General Nichols. It might express disillusionment; and if so, there was a simplicity here, since simplicity is a prerequisite of disillusionment.

General Nichols might be coming late to the realization of the important truism that men are men, whether public or private. A public man had a front, a face; and then, perforce, he had a back, a backside, and in the nature of things it was so ordered that the one was associated with high professions and

393

pronouncements and the other with that euphemistically denoted end-product. They were both always there. Which you saw best would depend on where you stood; but if you let yourself imagine that the one (no matter which) invalidated or made nugatory the other, that was the measure of your simplicity.

General Nichols said: "I've read, I think some Frenchman said, that though you sit on the highest throne in the world, you sit there on your own tail. It is a handicap to you; and it doesn't help much to inspire the people watching you with confidence."

That was helpful. General Nichols's inquisitive, reflective eye did not miss their human plights, their various mental and physical predicaments. He would, perhaps, observe that the Protagonist of the Bull Dog Breed was often grumpy, half a mind on his brandy-soured stomach and throatful of cigar-flavored phlegm. Grimacing, Mr. Churchill must taste, too, the gall of his situation. Fine phrases and selected words might show it almost a virtue that, far call'd our navies melt away; that, on dune and headland sinks the fire; but those circumstances also kept him from the leading position. Except as a piece of politeness, he did not even sit as an equal. His real job was to palter. His field and air marshals, on short commons of men and machines, his admirals of the outclassed fleet, all nerves bared by close to four years of war in the main unfortunate, supported him, courageous and proud, but also at the last word impotent.

Across the table, General Nichols's own side, the Union strong and great, was in a pleasanter position; justifiably cockier. They had the ships, they had the men, they had the money, too! However, the Champion of the Four Freedoms was, in cruel fact, not free to leave his chair; he could not do it unless somebody helped him. His top military chiefs, shown able enough as far as they had gone, were disadvantaged because they had never waged any war to speak of, fortunate or unfortunate. And then, too, though they had so much more of everything else, they faced what they called their opposite numbers with only four, instead of five, stars.

Thus, variously hampered and discontented, these great

personages showed General Nichols, the errand boy, the perhaps not-unartful nipper, how to make history. Their proceedings must often be less than sensible unless you understood the object of them. The object could not be simply to concert a wisest and best course. The object was to strike a bargain, a master bargain which was the congeries of a thousand small bargains wherein both high contracting parties had been trying, if possible, to get something for nothing; and if that were not possible, to give a little in order to gain a lot. Since, in each such arrangement, someone must come out on the short end, and since no subordinate could risk being the one, chiefs must meet and agree.

Agreement was ordinarily resisted by mutual misrepresentations, and obtained by a balance of disguised bribes and veiled threats. Plain honest people were often disgusted when they found out that high business was regularly done in these low ways. They were also indignant; because they knew a remedy for the shameful state of affairs. Let every man be just and generous, open and honorable, brave and wise. No higgling or overreaching would then be necessary.

"Yes," Colonel Ross said. "Yes, yes!"

General Nichols said: "I can tell you that the Conference, as well as naming a commander, set the date for the invasion of Europe. There was a certain amount of protest. An invasion plan for this year had already been given up. It was felt that the best use of air power was not being made if we were again prevented from completing projected operations on the scale and on the schedule we planned. The new directive was to do what many people considered the third or fourth best thing, depending on how you looked at it."

General Nichols drew from the inside pocket of his battle jacket a long, flat, silver cigarette case, on which Colonel Ross saw the crowned emblem of the Royal Air Force. Engraved below were several lines, of which he could read the beginning: *Presented to Colonel Joseph Josephson Nichols, USAAF, with the high regard and comradely esteem of—*

General Nichols said: "We are on a tough spot. If the operation is anything short of a complete success, it will be due to our failure to make the best use of air power. We know that. The Old Man knows that. We cannot fail to do what we know must be done merely because we are not to have all the time and all the priorities we thought we had to have. We must do it anyway. The Old Man thinks we can; so at any cost, we will."

By a momentary change of expression, by a movement of muscles that redistributed the lights and shadows on the surface of General Nichols's face, Colonel Ross gained the abrupt impression or illusion of another face suddenly showing through, making a different use of the same marmoreal features. Colonel Ross supposed that he had not quite dismissed those vague, ominous, stated or implied, opinions about General Nichols. Colonel Ross stirred in anxiety, thinking he might be about to discover the mean, plain truth—malice or ambition, coldness of pride, cruelty of self-interest. A human mind and will that saw itself interacting with great events often hid those qualities under the protestation of a higher necessity—*we cannot fail . . . we must do it anyway . . . at any cost we will . . .*

Anxiously poring on this other, underlying face, Colonel Ross concluded with relief that it was fundamentally innocent. It lacked the finish, the artificial guilelessness of the arch-villain or arch-conspirator. Its strength would be in candor, not machination. It was a hollower and an older face. It was severe and pensive, as though thinned and worn by strain or stress or trial. There was a clear mournfulness of eye, suggesting persistent if not deep ponderings, long unlighted vigils, an undeceived apprehension, a stern, wakeful grasp of the nature of things. While so mournful, the eye was at the same time singularly serene, without the slight clouding of subtlety, or the veiling blankness of devious design. General Nichols looked out calmly, in well-earned assurance of rightly estimating the possibilities and limitations of the Here and Now, and so of being ready for what might come.

Though not certain of all that these marks and signs portended, Colonel Ross could recognize their most important meaning. They showed a man past that chief climacteric, the loss of his last early involuntary illusions. A time of choice had come and gone. At least in a limited sense, it had been up to him whether he adopted, as soon as he could learn or invent them, new versions of his boy's-eye views; or whether he tried to go on without them. Colonel Ross was impressed; for if he was right about General Nichols, General Nichols had chosen the hard way, and now went on without them.

People like Bus, people like Pop, people like Colonel Ross himself, might, to this stripped-down, comfortless, plain and simple mind seem superannuated children. Bus and Pop more, he himself (Colonel Ross thought) less, carried over, gave a grown-up handling to, the boy's complicated world of imaginary characters; the boy's long, long, illogical thoughts; the boy's unwarranted entertainment and unfounded terror in a state of things systematically misunderstood.

General Nichols and the never very large number of men like him could watch them with calculating detachment—not underrating these persistent children, nor even despising them. They were boys in mind only. They had the means and resources of man's estate. They were more dextrous and much more dangerous than when they pretended they were robbers or Indians; and now their make-believe was really serious to them. You found it funny or called it silly at your peril. Credulity had been renamed faith. Each childish adult determinedly bet his life and staked his sacred pride on, say, the Marxist's ludicrous substance of things only hoped for, or the Christian casuist's wishful evidence of things not so much as seen. Faiths like these were facts. They must be taken into account; you must do the best you could with them, or in spite of them.

General Nichols said: "I don't mean that the air potential was denied. What we could certainly do—as you may know, Colonel, thanks to the new aids applied in March, the RAF really ruined Essen by July—and what we could probably do were both recognized. It was not denied that our course would be safer, might be cheaper, and could with luck be more quickly and completely successful. I had a little trouble getting the point; but I got it in the end. It wasn't desirable for us to be too completely successful."

Colonel Ross gave him a quick look.

"That's what I thought," General Nichols said. "Some people still think so. Of course, we've got to have a separate air force; and we'll have it. And there may be people who don't want us to look too good—but they aren't people in a position where they can do anything about it. That particular opposition's argument hinged on what we meant by complete success. The Old Man simply figured on beating the hell out of the back areas, blowing up the whole German war potential. That would take care of the German armed forces all right. The opposition felt that the way to take care of the German armed forces was to attack them directly and overpower them. As an operation in itself, they never said it was as safe, as cheap, or as good. They simply said: you want to make the biggest mess in history; and who's going to clean it up? Answer: we are; unless we assume, which we are not assuming, that we won't win the war. The Old Man said: that isn't what you asked us. You asked us how to make Germany quit fighting, and we told you. Say the word and we'll do it for you; we will obliterate them, and obliterate them, and obliterate them again."

General Nichols smiled faintly. "The Old Man's ideas are thorough-going," he said. "He didn't say it was the best thing to do; he just said if that was the thing to do, that was the best way to do it. Naturally, there were compelling reasons why the course we recommended was not adopted. One of them may have been this not-making-too-much-of-a-mess. Then, of course, we weren't starting from scratch, or with a free hand. What we had done already was bound to limit what we could do next; and, of course, we could not do what we *might* not. We have to wait for the word to be said; and if the people who say the word can't see what you see, they won't say it and we don't get to do it. Short of a military coup d'état, which I did not hear anywhere proposed, we would have to make do with what they were able to see. The possibility exists that they are right. It's a matter of different opinions about the same thing. The other thing, the limit put on what we could do next by what we had already done, I heard an RAF fellow state in terms of airborne troops."

General Nichols held out the cigarette case. Colonel Ross did not like cigarettes; but he took one.

General Nichols said: "Once the jump master boots a paratrooper through the hatch, the paratrooper is on his own. How he lands will depend, among other things, on his training, his physical condition, his experience and judgment. He must keep looking to see what's what. He must make the right decisions at the right time. Now, suppose he gets down and it looks bad; the terrain, or enemy dispositions, make it dangerous to land, and he sees he'll probably duff it. What's his right course? Why, unless the man's a bloody fool, he climbs back into the plane and tries somewhere else."

General Nichols struck a match and lit Colonel Ross's cigarette. He said: "What did Bus do, Judge? Duck out?"

Colonel Ross, his eyes on the sheltered match flame, drew a mouthful of insipid-tasting smoke.

"I don't really know, General," he said. "Bus left his office without saying anything. Pop tried to reach him but he wasn't able to; so Bus may have gone flying. He had some things to think over. I could see when we were talking in the dining room there, he hadn't made his mind up about that business. That was why he threw it at me. I could hold it while he thought it over."

General Nichols said: "Did you decide not to have the hearing?"

"I decided not to have it this morning," Colonel Ross said. "I thought it over, too. When you've spent as much time in court as I have, General, you're inclined to keep things out of court if you possibly can. Once you initiate a process, the process takes over—like your friend's paratrooper jumping. Once our MP officer prefers charges, we begin to have a record. Because a record has to show certain things, certain things must follow. While we can still have them, or not have them, I thought we'd just pause for reflection. Bus may think of something. I may think of something. Washington might even think of something, I suppose."

General Nichols said: "Judge, I think you're all making a little too much of this. Bus is, certainly. He has the Washington angle wrong. He really knows that. You must have found out by now that Bus is a little temperamental, Judge. Bus was just feeling sulky this morning. He wanted to have it wrong, so he'd have something to sulk about. Now, no one blames Bus for what happened. Given the situation that exists, it, or something like it, must happen from time to time. Where does Bus come in? He didn't cause the situation to exist. Is the Old Man, the War Department, or anyone else, going to hold Bus strictly accountable for the facts that Southern whites feel that Negroes cannot be allowed social or political equality; or that Negroes don't enjoy being treated like animals? The situation is a nuisance to us, and we wish it didn't exist; but Bus isn't expected to find a solution for it."

"Sulk" was a good word for what Bus was, in fact, doing, and General Nichols used it, not contemptuously, but kindly. Colonel Ross nevertheless bristled in an irritability, already pricked raw by the morning's many cares and exasperations—too many to keep them all in mind; but while he concentrated on one, he felt the general soreness of the others waiting on his leisure for further consideration. Further consideration of some of them could only mean blaming himself more fully, in greater detail. With others, it could only mean angering himself again over the needless stupidities of someone else. General Nichols's little dissertation on the "situation that exists," the easy philosophic detachment, the pooh-poohing of Colonel Ross's infinitude of troubles by the bland opinion that too much was being made of this, provoked Colonel Ross. He said: "I'm not sure, General, that it's clear to me, or to Bus, what Bus *is* expected to do. Is it, by any chance, also not clear to Washington?"

The rude, railing tone was, Colonel Ross must confess, unbecoming. At the sound of it, General Nichols gave him a reflective look in which, while there was no visible displeasure or annoyance, there was undoubtedly a critical query, an un-shown surprise, a naturally menacing speculation. Was this surly old man being captious? Was he going to be difficult?

In a distress resembling the distress he felt immediately after suggesting to Captain Collins that he was in some rakish relationship with his Miss Crittenden; the distress of seeing himself put himself wantonly in the wrong, Colonel Ross felt immediately the hateful consequences—the despite he did his gray hairs; the loss of that precious aplomb of self-respect; the quailing of mind, no longer intrepid because the knowledge that he was wrong knocked all its props out, and left his mind with nothing to give him but the shamed, furtive counsel: *Take care; you don't want to go too far!*

General Nichols lifted his hand and looked at his fingernails. He said equably: "A problem in public relations required a statement of policy. That policy was considered, approved, and announced. Bus, and everyone else, will keep in line. If circumstances beyond his control, an accident, an unforeseen contingency, force him out of line, he is expected to get back in line as quick as he can. That's all there is to it. Bus is not expected to do the impossible; he is not expected to reverse himself, humiliate himself. He is expected to act, as far as other duties and responsibilities allow him, to smooth it over, not stir it up. I don't think there's any difference of opinion between us on that, Judge. From what you say you're doing, I can see we don't differ."

"I don't know that I have a plan," Colonel Ross said. "It isn't complete. It may not work. It doesn't go much further than this. When Pop was talking, I thought I'd have a talk with Willis. Incidentally, Willis's father had word he was injured, and he's expected in this morning. I sent an officer to meet him. I thought I'd have a talk with him, too."

General Nichols said: "After I've given the boy his medal, I'll bow out; and you have your talk. As I see it, he gains a good deal, everything he's worked for, everything he now almost has, if there's no more trouble, if he helps you. I don't think I'd pay a great deal of attention to Pop's notion about what's laying it on thick, and what isn't."

"I won't pretend I like it," Colonel Ross said.

"The boy seems to have a just complaint," General Nichols said; "but I think the question for him is whether he likes his complaint so well he'll trade a medium bomb group—at least three promotions, his name in the papers, all that, for it. That's just a statement of the facts. I don't think it needs to be regarded as a bribe, or as a threat."

"I will try not to so regard it, if he will," Colonel Ross said. He sat somber a moment.

General Nichols said, "There's this about Bus—there always was, Judge. There's you, and there's Pop; and you know him and you work for him and you go to bat for him. And if you will, other people will. They did; they have. The Old Man knows that. A man can't do everything himself—not if what he's doing amounts to much. Up to a point, yes; but then how much other people will do for him is very important." He paused reflectively. He said, "Nothing definite is decided yet, as far as I know. The Old Man doesn't project operations around any given individual. Flying is a hazardous occupation; and so is war. You can't be perfectly sure who's going to be here when the time comes. Circumstances may change; so you need a different person. A person may change. Someone else may get to be better. But the Old Man always plans in terms of alternatives, considered possibilities, a long way ahead. I say I don't know anything definite; in fact, I'm sure there isn't anything definite, because it isn't time to decide yet; but I think there might be this in mind for Bus."

General Nichols carefully put out his cigarette in the ash tray under the window. He looked a moment at the passing pine woods soaked in sun. He said: "I think the Old Man has it in mind to give Bus the Tactical Air Force for the invasion of the Japanese home islands; if and when. It would not be inappropriate. The AAF wouldn't mind cutting itself a little piece of that 'I shall return' stuff." He looked back from the passing woods to Colonel Ross. "It wasn't intended originally to bring Bus home this year. Bus pretty well proved in North Africa that he was the best man we had to command large scale fighter operations. A big fighter job was coming up—is coming up. You can guess it. In a few more months, we'll have the planes modified, and we're going to escort the bombers all the way. Of course, Bus wasn't the only one, or even the first one, to see we'd have to do that; but it was really his baby. He went to work. He managed to set up small test missions. From them, he developed some basic tactics and a good operational organization scheme. The Air Staff liked it. That was when the Old Man put him through for major general. I don't know how much of this Bus told you."

"None," Colonel Ross said. "Bus doesn't talk much, about himself, General. Of course everyone knew what he did in Africa. He's said a few things about that, but not much else—to me."

General Nichols said: "Bus got his second star and was pulled out a little before the African business was over and sent to England. Then the Old Man changed his mind. I think I know why. Bus was insisting he be allowed to fly the escort missions himself. He was always flying missions in Africa, you know. Of course, some operations he needed to see first-hand; and leading missions, especially in the early days, was good for morale; only Bus did it all the time. He seems to like it. The Old Man didn't want him doing it all the time over Germany. We can't afford to lose what Bus knows, on the chance that he might get to know a little bit more. It puts too much at stake; it's not a reasonable risk. And, anyway, when the Old Man says something, that's it. Believe me. You don't go on insisting on things."

General Nichols drew a breath. He said: "So it seemed a good idea to have Bus home, stop fighting the whole war with him, give him a chance to cool off. Moreover, he was just what they wanted for AFORAD, Ocanara, here. He certainly knew about operational requirements; so everything fitted in nicely. I know the Old Man had a talk with Bus, and Bus was satisfied. I imagine the idea is for Bus to hold this down until we go ashore in Europe. Then, shoot him over to that Tactical Air Force—not in any command capacity; but to observe how the air-ground co-operation works out. As soon as we get into Germany, Bus would be pulled out and brought right home to start the fighter organization for the Japanese business. That's what I think is in the cards, Judge. Or could be."

"I see," said Colonel Ross.

403

His mind, tensely following, paused a moment. Might all this be taken, too, as just a statement of facts, no bribe, no threat? He let the puzzle, if one was there, go in favor of another distraction, minor, outside or behind his first line of thought, but urgently relative to another line, to one of those permanent, underlying concerns which, while not often admitted to full consciousness, always waited there, listening for anything it could use. What this constant concern picked up last was General Nichols's matter-of-fact: *As soon as we get into Germany;* and it gave a bound, identifying itself, and revealing by its relief that that was not all it had picked up in the course of this conversation.

The listening concern heard, and it trembled, when General Nichols spoke his doubt that the big brass, the VIP's at Quebec, intended to make the best use of air power. It heard again, and it shrank, when General Nichols proclaimed that, nonetheless, the air effort would proceed *at all costs.* When it learned that fighter planes would soon escort the bombers all the way, it blew hot and cold, considering first the new safeguard, and then the fearful danger which that decision attested. Now, it heard that at Quebec, at Washington, the places where people knew, doubt was not entertained; there was no "if." They ought to know; they felt no serious question; so, thank God, we must be getting somewhere! The identified thought presented itself for an instant in the picture of his son, Jimmy, crouched bundled-up in the bomber's naked, defenseless-looking, transparent nose, the bombsight cup against his eye; neither he, nor the plane whose run he now controlled, able to deviate one jot, evade one inch, while the guns below, with exquisite precision, preternaturally collecting and correcting their own data, laid themselves, and kept themselves, on this creeping, sitting target.

Colonel Ross said: "Then they brought Bus home to have a rest. Do they think he's getting all he needs?"

"They have to think so, Judge," General Nichols said. "I never heard it formulated as policy; but I know, in practice, the only people who get more rest in the Zone of Interior are those who can't be usefully employed. Bus is useful here;

and this should be useful to him—a fairly big administrative job. Bus knows he hasn't been sidetracked, or anything like that. It is all to the purpose. I don't believe anyone—not Bus himself—considers Bus an administrative type. They don't want to make him one, either; but he needs the experience that comes from having the problems dumped on him. Picking the right men to handle them for him. You have to have that to manage a unit as large as a whole Air Force. The Old Man doesn't miss much. Bus would be good for AFORAD; and AFORAD would be good for Bus."

Colonel Ross said: "His wife, and my wife, think it would be wonderful if they gave him a few weeks off; just let him go away somewhere and do nothing. They think Washington would do that if you suggested it."

General Nichols said: "Judge, it wouldn't be good to suggest that Bus ought to have some leave, go off for a few weeks. They would want a reason. Keep remembering that Washington has all the troubles it needs—I know nobody in the field ever thinks so—and things could also add up on them, if they let them. They could get in a state, too; except the Old Man won't have it. Nobody can be allowed to make himself a worry. Colonel Woodman was an example of that. He was about to get the ax, you know. I suppose you could say little things had been adding up on him, and he let himself get into a state. Sellers Field was relatively unimportant, and Training Command Headquarters stood between Woodman and Washington, at least until Woodman did some funny business out of channels. In short, they don't like to hear that somebody needs a rest. It's always bad news in their business."

Colonel Ross said: "Isn't it worse news when somebody like Woodman blows his brains out?"

"If he'd been told about Woodman, the Old Man would have had him relieved some time ago," General Nichols said. "He can't be told everything—the day isn't that long. So other people have to take the responsibility of deciding what he must be told, and what he needn't be told, or maybe, mustn't be told."

"I see that," Colonel Ross said.

"Yes; well a couple of people took the responsibility about Woodman. They knew that if the Old Man heard that Woodman was letting things add up on him, that finished Woodman. There is no time for rests. Everyone just has to take it, carry on anyway. It's a little like our pilot-training theory. We don't say too much about it; but you know and I know that it's better, more economical, to push a boy hard, throw it right at him; if it comes to that, let him crack up in a training plane here at home; instead of babying him along so he can crack up a fighter in an overseas theater."

The car was approaching the intersection where the road from the Area joined the highway to Ocanara, beyond the Air Field and the Base. On the highway, in ponderous motion, also approaching the intersection, crawled a tractor-mounted gasoline shovel with a crane boom. Colonel Ross saw it first; but the driver immediately saw it too. He leaned forward and set off the staff car's siren. The tractor halted, the high boom wagging back and forth, and they passed it, turning north ahead of it.

Frowning, Colonel Ross made an instinctive move to push back the glass panel between him and the driver. The great machine with its heavy-lugged tread was hacking up the road surface, and they would assuredly hear about that from the State Highway Department.

"Want to stop?" General Nichols said.

Colonel Ross brought a notebook and pencil from his breast pocket. "No. I won't hold you up, General," he said. He took down the Engineer Corps serial number under the white star on the cabin. "I don't know what makes them do it," he said. "They have definite orders not to move heavy stuff on its own tread over a public highway. They pay no attention. It wouldn't surprise me if that's come a mile or more, all the way down from Gate Number Three—"

"I guess we're going to stop anyway," General Nichols said.

The brakes let out a shriek as the driver stepped hard on them. Around a bend in the scrubby woods a low-bed trailer on multiple sets of wheels stood in the middle of the road. Fallen off the trailer, directly in front of the car, was a great mass of metal, the whole battered fuselage and the torn-off wings of an A-20 attack bomber, painted black as a night fighter. A sergeant and two men, standing idle, started at the sound of the brakes, and turned to look.

Colonel Ross opened the car door and got out. Around the bend behind, the crane boom poked its way, jerkily advancing. Colonel Ross faced it, bringing up both hands in the airplane taxi signal to stop; but though he could see the operator peering from the cab window, this signal was presumably unknown to the Engineers. The crane kept on coming.

Colonel Ross faced around and called: "Sergeant, come here! Who's in charge?"

The sergeant gave him an alarmed salute. "I guess I am, right now, sir. The lieutenant went to telephone. He didn't come back. Then this captain, I don't know his name, from the Post Engineer, came, and went off. We're waiting for that crane, sir. We couldn't do anything—"

"When you block a road," Colonel Ross said, "always get somebody up above there to stop traffic! You come around the bend right into this without any warning. There could be a bad accident. Go on, son," he said to one of the enlisted men. "Double up there to the intersection! And tell the fellow in the machine to stop, back up, get off the road. General Nichols, Deputy Chief of the Air Staff, is in this car, and you have him blocked here, now." He turned back to the sergeant. "What is this, anyway—oh, the one that went down by Pine View Monday night?"

"Yes, sir."

"Well, what happened? How did you drop it?"

"It fell off, sir."

"Hitting it up around the bend there?"

"Oh, no, sir! You couldn't, with this. I don't think it was loaded good."

"Well, why wasn't it?"

The sergeant said: "I don't know, sir. We didn't do it. A detail went up to where they found the wreck yesterday, and they did the loading. I guess it got to be pretty late at night when they finished, and it was pretty thick in there, bad, swampy. I guess they didn't want to take it out in the dark, or something. So they brought that crew back, and Lieutenant Walker took us up in a jeep to drive it in this morning."

"Unless you were coming around that curve fast, I don't see how it could roll off a thing as big as that trailer."

The sergeant said: "I didn't think they had it secured any too good when I saw it, Colonel. They had like these chocks and a mess of cables; but it didn't look secure to me. I told the lieutenant it looked like it might shift; but he said it was O.K., so—" There was an understandable note of righteousness in his voice.

The noise of the big tractor engine continued, growing louder, behind him; and Colonel Ross turned around. The crane was still approaching. The man he had sent running up was now running back. "He says the ditch is too deep there to move it off the road, sir. He thinks it isn't so deep here. He's going to see."

"All right," Colonel Ross said. "Get on up to the intersection, and halt all traffic." He went to the car. "I'm afraid we're stuck for a moment, General. When they move the crane, I think we can turn around and go in by the upper gate."

"Quite all right, Judge," General Nichols said. He opened the door and stepped out. "That hit good and hard," he said, looking at the smashed A-20. He moved toward it with interest.

"It's ours," Colonel Ross said. "We lost it early this week. One of those things. It was a routine night interception exercise —two flights up, and nobody reported anything unusual. This just didn't come back. We had quite a time locating it. With that paint job, it doesn't show up very well to an air search—"

Standing by the plane with General Nichols, Colonel Ross became aware of a pervasive stench spreading from the fuselage. Blood must have run down, collected in a pool somewhere inside the wreck; and the heat had turned it rotten.

"Well, as you say, General," he said. "They'd better do it here, not over there. This was one of our best crews, however.

Acting as instructors. We don't know just what could have happened to them."

"Hm!" said General Nichols, who must have caught the sickening whiff too. "*Was*, is right! I see it didn't burn. Probably means they crashed out of gas."

"Probably," Colonel Ross said.

He could feel the blaze of sun stinging across his neck and on the backs of his hands. Sweat dripped steadily from his armpits and ran tickling down his sides. More sweat had gathered in his eyebrows and now worked through them, so that the battered black painted wreckage, fallen inertly across the road, swam distorted by sweat entering his eyes. He wiped the sweat away. On the side of the plane's black nose, spiritedly sketched in dark red paint, was a cavorting skeleton who danced with a nude woman. Under it, in fancy letters, were the words: *Tarfu Tessie.*

Colonel Ross swallowed against the revolting smell of the decayed blood—it must have taken lots of blood to stay wet, to stink after nearly a week! Well, hundreds of planes ended like this—right here at Ocanara in the bone yard they had what could be collected of a couple of dozen—and there would be hundreds more. It could not be helped; and it was impractical to mix personal feeling with impersonal fact. Colonel Ross could manage not to mix them with a surface composure; but how could he control the subconscious cross-reference, that constant relation of anything that was relative to that constant concern of his? In a smashed plane somewhere, perhaps soon, blood stinking the same way would have leaked from his son, Jimmy.

Since it was useless to pretend that he would then so easily make the practical separation between feeling and fact, in his malaise of shame and remorse, his composure could be no more than surface. The telegrams went out yesterday. Last night, or this morning, the people for whom this *was* Jimmy opened and read them. He only hoped, as they read, they would tell themselves philosophically that it couldn't be helped.

Behind him, the tractor engine fell silent; and Colonel Ross, still swallowing against his nausea, left General Nichols and walked over. The bulk of the machine had been pulled to the side far enough to let a car pass.

Colonel Ross looked up to the cabin and the stout red-faced T/3 leaning out. He drew a breath and said: "Son, don't you know there's a regulation against running anything with lugs on a paved highway? Just look back there! You hacked it all to pieces!"

The T/3 said with an injured air: "Well, what do I do, Colonel? They tell me, bring it here on the road. I bring it here."

Colonel Ross said: "You could have brought it down the inside of the Base fence, had a section taken out, and come through. Who told you to bring it down the road? Who gave you your orders?"

From his shirt pocket Colonel Ross produced his pencil and notebook again.

VII

It was a setback for Nathaniel Hicks when Colonel Ross and the general with him came into the Hospital. Nathaniel Hicks had been planning, as soon as he got over to the Area, to go first to Colonel Ross's office. He planned to find Colonel Ross there. He planned to find him at the moment unengaged. Colonel Ross would ask Captain Hicks cordially what he could do for him. Captain Hicks would tell him, with respectful concern, about General Beal's change of mind; he would venture the opinion that it seemed a pity to drop the project at this point. Captain Hicks had given the matter careful consideration. If General Beal could be persuaded to let him go on with it, they might be able to place exactly the sort of stuff Washington said was wanted in some good magazines. Captain Hicks had also been thinking along the lines of Colonel Ross's suggestion about something on General Beal personally; and he had this angle on that. Colonel Ross would then say that he agreed; that he would go right now and put it to the general; and that he didn't doubt—

But Colonel Ross, out of his office, with visiting brass in tow,

410

might not be able to receive the urgent little sales talk for hours. There might be no chance to see Colonel Ross at all today. This was bad. When you wanted to protest, it was always better to protest promptly. When you took your time there was a loss of force; if your reasons were good and strong, why were you so long thinking of them?

Important as it was to the plan for Colonel Ross to be in the right place at the right time, it was still more important for Colonel Ross to be in the right mood, receptive and cordial. Nathaniel Hicks was not sure that he had read Colonel Ross's look correctly, but Colonel Ross had seen him and identified him. There was no doubt about that. Colonel Ross's methodical glance-around as he came in had stopped on Nathaniel Hicks and Mr. Willis. Colonel Ross's expression hardly changed; yet there might have been an increased sternness, an increased beetling of the gray brows.

For this change, if there had been a change, Nathaniel Hicks could think of several reasons, all disquieting. He was, for instance, only hoping that Colonel Ross did not know of General Beal's decision. Colonel Ross himself might have done the deciding as soon as he saw the file copy of that wonderful letter. He might feel that it far exceeded anything General Beal wished or intended, and that getting it authenticated in the Adjutant General's office had been a great piece of impudence.

Then, too, it was an uncomfortable chance that Nathaniel Hicks should be sitting here with Mr. Willis. Colonel Ross might not know who Mr. Willis was; but he undoubtedly knew that Captain Hicks was down as a witness to last night's affair with the colored officers. He might be irritably wondering what the devil Hicks was up to now with this colored civilian.

Colonel Ross and his general crossed over then and passed between the railed inclosures. They disappeared down the central corridor. Mr. Willis, who had opened his mouth when the enlisted man called the others to attention and left it open while he stared after Colonel Ross's companion, now asked who that was.

Nathaniel Hicks, preoccupied, told him that was a general.

Still staring, with a pleased air, at the head of the passage where the elegant figure had disappeared, Mr. Willis observed that, in addition to senators, he also often served a general at the restaurant. "Old man, now," he said. "He don't wear uniform. You know him?" He mentioned a name that Nathaniel Hicks associated indefinitely with the last war. "He's a delicate eater. He say to me: 'Robert'—that's my name—'you seen those lobsters. You take that one you saving to eat yourself later, and give it to me—'" Mr. Willis's face clouded. "I got his letter, too; War Department; saying about Stanley—"

Nathaniel Hicks said: "I'm afraid you'll have to excuse me for a moment, Mr. Willis—"

Colonel Ross was back at the head of the passage, alone. He looked directly at Nathaniel Hicks and beckoned to him.

Nathaniel Hicks got to his feet and came over.

Without speaking, Colonel Ross touched his arm, bringing him a little way up the passage. Colonel Ross said: "Hicks, who's that with you? Willis's father?"

Nathaniel Hicks said: "I believe so, sir."

"What do you mean, you believe so? Is it, or isn't it?"

Caught up so sharply, Nathaniel Hicks colored. He said: "I mean that I never saw him before. He started to talk to me, and he showed me some papers about what he said was his son, Lieutenant Willis—" he cut himself off, aware that he had the sound of answering back. He remembered that he did not want to make Colonel Ross, already irritable, angry.

Colonel Ross said: "There seems to be a mystery here, Hicks. I sent Captain Collins, the Public Relations Officer, to meet Mr. Willis at the station. Now, where did you come from, and what became of Collins?"

"I came over to the Hospital with a man whose wife was suddenly taken ill, sir. I think I know the Captain Collins you mean, by sight. I haven't seen him here."

"You didn't see him at the station?"

"I was not at the station, sir. I went down to the Oleander Towers with this officer, and then brought him out here in my car. That was almost two hours ago."

Colonel Ross's look was full of severity; and Nathaniel

412

Hicks, to his annoyance, found himself starting with alarm—like a guilty prisoner at the bar, he supposed. Colonel Ross said: "Well, who brought Mr. Willis to the Base, then? Do you know anything about that?"

Nathaniel Hicks hesitated. He had no desire to make trouble for Lieutenant Edsell—quite the contrary! It was not because he liked Edsell, or wished him well; but because he didn't like him, and would not mind at all if Edsell got some of the trouble he was always asking for. This ill, or at least, not good, feeling obliged him to lean backward to avoid doing or saying anything that might strike a knowing, skeptical third party as done in spite or said in malice.

Observing the hesitation, Colonel Ross said: "Hicks, are you mixed up in this business, too? Did you help get Willis down?" He spoke with an impatient reproach, an incensed disappointment, that Nathaniel Hicks found hard to support. He had tried, for those reasons of delicacy, not to drag Edsell in, not to be the one to testify against him; but was he going to submit for one minute to being regarded by Colonel Ross—whose good regard was so important to him—as "mixed up in it"; as another sedulous smart-aleck, like Edsell; as Edsell's partner in Edsell's bumptious and self-conceited effort to make himself felt?

Nathaniel Hicks said: "I don't know just what's going on, Colonel. Whatever it is, I had nothing to do with it. I can guess who got Willis down—"

Colonel Ross said: "I know who wired him and who sent him money for his fare. Now, what else do you know? Just what is this fellow, Edsell, up to? Do you think he had anything to do with the trouble at the Club last night?"

"No, I don't," Nathaniel Hicks said. "Because I am pretty sure he didn't know about that until this morning, or at least he didn't know what had happened. He was trying to find out from me and Captain Wiley. Then he left to go to the station. He did not, at the time, say what for."

"He must have beaten Captain Collins to it. So Mr. Willis came out with him. Where did Edsell go?"

"He said he was going to see the Post Surgeon, sir. He was going to arrange for Mr. Willis to see his son."

"We have already arranged that," Colonel Ross said. "Edsell will be quite a while getting to see the Post Surgeon. The Post Surgeon is very busy this morning. We'll just take Mr. Willis off Edsell's hands." He looked thoughtfully at Nathaniel Hicks. "That was General Nichols with me; and I don't want to keep him waiting. Ask Mr. Willis to step over here. He'd better see this. You'd better come along, too."

What "this" might be, Nathaniel Hicks did not know; but, disturbed, he could guess why he was to come, too. Colonel Ross must want to keep an eye on him. Colonel Ross did not choose to have him get together with Edsell just yet; so, presumably, Colonel Ross did not quite believe him, or quite trust him.

He walked up the passage and across to Mr. Willis. He said: "Colonel Ross is going to take you to see Stanley now."

Mr. Willis arose impetuously. "I don't wait for the lieutenant?" he said.

"No," said Nathaniel Hicks. "Just come with me."

Colonel Ross shook hands with Mr. Willis. He said, "I'm the Air Inspector. I sent a car down to pick you up at the station, when I heard you were coming, Mr. Willis; but I'm afraid it must have missed you."

Mr. Willis said: "The lieutenant bring us out all right, part in a taxi, part walking. I never mind, so I get here. Only, I leave my grip there, I hope no one going to go off with it—"

Colonel Ross said: "We'll take care of that. Hicks, bring his bag over and put it inside the rail, will you? The girl will see it's all right."

When he came back, Colonel Ross was saying: "General Nichols is here now, Mr. Willis. As soon as the presentation is over, you can spend the day with Stanley. You heard he was hurt?"

"I heard that," Mr. Willis said. He shifted heavily on his waiter's flat feet. "I know."

With an eloquence that Nathaniel Hicks found extraordinary, since the means by which it was expressed were so simple and so few, Mr. Willis made clear what he now thought he knew.

The shadow went over the wide sloping face, bent aside in bitterness; the dark eyes closed up, turned brooding inward; the lips set themselves forlornly under the broad, nearly simous nose. Never resigned to life in the land of Egypt, yet wasting no breath on useless protest, he mourned the recurrence of a phenomenon of insult and injury for which he found no understandable explanation, a woe of his people about which he could not do anything. "They beat him up," he said. "He hurt bad?"

Nathaniel Hicks, confronted earlier by this same lament, with tears, had been greatly discomposed. Abashed, he could not think of any relevant response; there was no answer to it. Colonel Ross said: "Oh, no, Mr. Willis. Stanley's not seriously hurt. I'm sorry you've been worried about it. He wasn't beaten up—it didn't really amount to a fight. There was a little squabble; and Stanley was hit by another officer. That is, the other man started it; and he's sorry; he's going to apologize. It had to do with flying—a misunderstanding. The other man lost his temper. You know how these young fellows are, Mr. Willis. Stanley has a pretty sore nose; but there isn't any permanent damage done."

This might be no answer to the deep question; but it came with composure to the immediate point, and at the same time, by a compelling mein and manner, assumed full direction, disposing and proposing. There was an easy disposition of Mr. Willis's lament. There was a flattering proposition. If he would go along, Mr. Willis could associate himself with Colonel Ross in dignity and authority, his welcome equal.

Mr. Willis saw this chance. The brooding eyes brightened, but holding his face still bent aside, he said: "He not in trouble, then; Stanley?"

"Quite the contrary," Colonel Ross said. "You can be sure they wouldn't be giving him this medal if they weren't pleased with him. The Commanding General of the Army Air Forces, when he saw the report, personally directed that Stanley be awarded the Distinguished Flying Cross for what he did in saving his own plane, and two others, besides. Did Stanley tell you what he did?"

Mr. Willis, reanimated, said: "He wrote me that. These others afraid to try; but not him. He wrote he showed them."

"Yes," Colonel Ross said. "You ought to be very proud of him."

Observing the simplicity of this management, the perfect firmness that kept Mr. Willis going along, and that, as he went, petted and pleasured him, Nathaniel Hicks began to guess with interest where they were going. He began to see, not sorry, that though Edsell might be right in his often displayed assumption that there was no fool like an old fool; yet, as well as old fools, there were smart old men.

While you applauded yourself for the way your young ingenuity and vigorous enterprise confounded the gaffer and gave you an advantage he never expected you to have, he, unruffled, looked over this advantage of yours and then looked back into that length of experience, which he had and you hadn't, to find the usually simple measure that would turn the tables, take your advantage and make it all his.

Colonel Ross said: "You know, too, of course, that Stanley has a good chance of being named commanding officer of this bomb group we're going to try out. It's a big job, and he'll have to prove he can handle it before it's confirmed; but, at this point, our Personnel people think he can. That means they consider him, as well as a fine flyer, outstanding in qualities of intelligence and leadership. You must have given Stanley a good upbringing, Mr. Willis."

"That's right," Mr. Willis said eagerly. "I bring him up good. I make him go to school; two years college. I make him study what they teach him. I tell him he has to be first, the best. The same in the Army, in training. I got papers right here—"

"I'll be glad to see those papers," Colonel Ross said. "But right now, I think we'd better go along. The general will be waiting. Stanley doesn't know you're here yet. It will be a surprise for him. I'll introduce you to the general, and then we'll have Stanley in. I'm going to read the citation, so you just stand with Captain Hicks until I finish and the general pins the medal on him."

✦

It was the usual Conference Room, with the usual bare table and a dozen folding chairs. Windows on one side had awnings let down to cut the sun glare that reverberated off the hot empty road and the faded camouflage paint of barracks buildings, rowed monotonously beyond it. The wall at the end was covered with a collection of staring colored cautionary posters from the Training Aids Division, or the Flying Safety Division, which showed comic blockheads, now grinning or gaping their way into asinine plane accidents; now maiming themselves as they fumbled with tools and weapons, or carelessly became entangled in machinery.

There were only three people in the room: the general; an irascible-looking, redheaded major with Air Surgeon's wings; and a melancholy-looking, lanky lieutenant with Medical Corps Administrative insignia. Since he had no proper business here, Nathaniel Hicks thought he ought not to push himself forward. He closed the door and lagged behind, staying near it, while Colonel Ross introduced Mr. Willis to the general. Colonel Ross then said: "And Captain Hicks, Directorate of Special Projects." He half turned, and not finding Nathaniel Hicks where he must have expected to find him, frowned. Nathaniel Hicks hastily inclined his head to the general, and made to join them.

Before he could move, there was a knock on the door; and Colonel Ross said to him with impatience: "Open it, Hicks, open it!"

However, the door opened without his help.

A sergeant, with a rigid knock-once-and-enter formality, stood aside, and Lieutenant Willis walked in.

Nathaniel Hicks stood aside, too; but Lieutenant Willis had turned his face toward him as the first person he saw. Nathaniel Hicks made a mute movement to indicate the general. He realized at once that Lieutenant Willis could not see very well—and with reason! Carricker, though not big, must be brutally strong; and when he hit somebody, he hit him! Lieutenant Willis's face was greatly swollen. His colored skin did not show bruise marks as clearly as white skin might have, but his whole nose and his upper lip, across which a narrow dressing lay in a slant, were grotesquely puffed. The same tumid enlargement extended out both cheeks, almost closing his eyes.

Nathaniel Hicks, drawing further back, as Lieutenant Willis belatedly turned where he indicated, now moved uncomfortably to join the others.

The general, the major, the lieutenant; Colonel Ross and Mr. Willis, were all looking at Lieutenant Willis. They all gave him, fleetingly, the same stare, shocked to a pause by the battered face and the half-blind motion of the head. Coming next to Mr. Willis, Nathaniel Hicks eyed him sidelong, with apprehension, while the pause hung, a sort of subdivided long second of time; for who knew but what Mr. Willis, seeing the reality of that "pretty sore nose" would suddenly roar with grief and indignation?

Beyond Mr. Willis's black face, Nathaniel Hicks could see the general's white one, already past the pause he had been given, coming out of it with a clear speaking calm, informed with meaning, ceremonially transformed from the taken-aback man to the high officer, the image of authority, tranquil in his great place. The dignity that sat upon him as he assumed his rôle was so persuasive that, without resistance, those who had supporting parts found themselves falling into their rôles, too.

Lieutenant Willis brought up his hand to his swollen face and saluted. The major and his officer had come to an unpracticed attention; and so, Nathaniel Hicks, realized, had he himself.

Colonel Ross said: "This is Lieutenant Stanley Willis, General, at present attached to Operations and Requirements Analysis Division Project zero-dash-three-three-six-dash-three. Lieutenant, this is General Nichols, Deputy Chief of Air Staff."

Below Nathaniel Hicks's ear, Mr. Willis murmured vigorously: "Now, he see me! Now, he see me! Look! He surprised—" Nathaniel Hicks could, indeed, see a blink of the nearly closed eyes, a start of the stiffly held frame.

General Nichols said: "Lieutenant Willis, I have been directed and commissioned by the Commanding General of the Army Air Forces to bring here and award to you the Distinguished Flying Cross. Will you now read the citation, Colonel?"

Colonel Ross raised a paper, and peering through his glasses, read: "For extraordinary achievement while participating in an aerial flight."

Mr. Willis's voice, very low, with a sound of shaky smothered mirth said, as though to himself, but Nathaniel Hicks could hear it: "What a wallop he got! What a wallop—"

Colonel Ross said: "On April seventeenth, nineteen forty-three, Second Lieutenant Stanley M. Willis, Army Air Forces, piloting a B-Twenty-six medium bomber in company with two others on a routine cross-country training flight, found his scheduled return to base delayed by adverse weather conditions. In overcoming these conditions all three planes were obliged to use most of their fuel. Because of the distance to the nearest suitable air field, and the rugged desert country over which they were flying, no landing appeared possible; and a proposal to bail out was made. However, Lieutenant Willis, with less than fifteen-minutes fuel in his tanks, located on the map and accurately led the flight to a small auxiliary field intended for the use of light planes only. Examining the unimproved strip from the air, Lieutenant Willis judged a landing might be possible, and resolved with the agreement of his crew to go first and make the very hazardous attempt."

Mr. Willis's hand came against Nathaniel Hicks's arm and clutched it fervently. "That's it," he said approvingly. "That's it."

Colonel Ross read: "Lieutenant Willis, by his great skill and coolness succeeded in landing his plane undamaged, and by radio directions from the ground, he guided the other planes to safe landings. By his courageous good judgment and his superior airmanship, Lieutenant Willis thus prevented the certain loss of three valuable medium bombers, and possible death or injury to members of their crews. Lieutenant Willis's conduct on this occasion reflected the highest credit on himself and on the Armed Forces of the United States."

"Lieutenant Willis," General Nichols said, "it gives me pleasure to present to you on behalf of the Commanding General, the Chief of Air Staff, and the United States Army Air Forces, this medal in recognition of your achievement."

Colonel Ross held out the case to him, and, lifting the medal from it, General Nichols stepped forward. He freed the catch, and pinned it neatly on Lieutenant Willis's shirt. He held out his hand and shook Lieutenant Willis's hand. Stepping back a pace, he stopped and saluted him.

Mr. Willis left Nathaniel Hicks. He darted forward. He said loudly: "Boy, you got a funny-looking nose, there! You get in the way of something?"

He began to chuckle, shaking; and then, almost simultaneously, he began to sob. He seized Lieutenant Willis. He wrapped his thick arms about him. Still chuckling, still sobbing, he rested his cheek, for he was a good deal shorter than his son, against Lieutenant Willis's shoulder. "Be a good boy!" he said. "You see? You always be a good boy."

VIII

IN THE observation post, elevated by a frame of galvanized-steel cross members on the sand hill between the Chechoter range house and the big range panel, white side turned to show the range was open, Lieutenant Wierum, the Range Officer, leaned on the guard rail of the narrow walk. Field glasses hung off his chest from a strap around his neck. He held a microphone whose long wire went back to the radio inside the glass housing.

Lieutenant Wierum, looking out west, had a view of twenty-five square miles of the so-called Chechoter Forest—slightly rolling scrub lands; a thick undergrowth of hollies and heaths and saw palmetto, with stands of sand pines and, usually around springs or small ponds, clumped cabbage palms and groves of big live oaks. Within the confines of the hot horizon the whole vista showed few signs of human occupancy. Far to the west, a drift of pale, voluming smoke arose from the sawdust pile of a mill that could not be seen. Here and there were glimpses of the scraped course of raw-sand roads, often topped with a different-colored clay to make easier going for military vehicles. Five miles to the east, the Chechoter Demonstration Area, carefully concealed in one of the larger oak groves, could be located approximately by the undisguisable break in the scrub of its steel-mat landing strip.

Lieutenant Wierum on the tower walk looked directly across the clearing of the range, a sand waste now growing over again with grasses and low bushes. In the center, a circular bombing target had been laid out. At the end, beyond a foul line, were the big gunnery targets in a long slanting row.

Lieutenant Cross, the Assistant Range Officer, who leaned on the rail not far from Lieutenant Wierum, said: "How long is this? I think they have gall sending this hot-shot up, when it's well known to be time for me to eat."

"He can't have too much more in his magazines," Lieutenant Wierum said. "Not the way he's socking it out."

He lifted his glasses and turned them south. A mile or so away a single plane, a P-47, flying a right-hand, ground-gunnery pattern at about twelve hundred feet, moved on its base leg. "I'll tell him we're closing in a minute. Micky here?"

"Half an hour," Lieutenant Cross said, nodding over the rail at a jeep standing before the range house.

Keeping his glasses on the P-47, Lieutenant Wierum watched it as it turned level and began to drop on the range in a long dive. Approaching at this angle, it seemed not to move so much as swell, larger each second. Abruptly, midway out the leading edges of each wing, bright pale blurs of flame trembled on the blast tubes. Shifting his glasses, Lieutenant Wierum could see a lively commotion across the surface of the target third from the end. Wood splinters flew. Blotches broke out on the painted circles of the canvas covering. Over the slope behind walked spurts of sand kicked by the fifty caliber slugs burying themselves.

The noise of gunfire, a hard, high-noted knocking hammer came clear for an instant. Then it was overlaid by the deep snarl of the engine pulling out. The plane banked hard, bearing east, climbing away at full throttle. Its roar trailed fading down the hot noon.

Lieutenant Wierum wiped sweat from his tanned forehead and brought the microphone to his mouth. He said: "O.K., Eight-four! Now, that was somewhat better. Your run was good. You leveled off correctly, and you were right on the target—very good. However; here are things you need to work on. You still don't follow instructions. Remember: your guns are bore-sighted for two seven zero miles per hour. You were considerably exceeding it, weren't you? You want to watch that. You are also still making your bursts a lot too long. You got eight fifties there, remember. Just make sure your ring's on whatever you're shooting at, and a very short burst will take care of it, don't worry! If you overheat your guns, you can get a stoppage and be out of luck in combat. And pouring it in isn't only bad for your guns, pal; it beats hell out of our targets."

He screwed his eyes up thoughtfully. "Now, about your flying. I can see you've done quite a bit; but not in a Forty-seven, huh? You make your pull-outs very dangerous. That time, it seemed from here practically a sixty degree bank. I'm telling you; quit trying to look so hot, or we'll be shoveling you up and sending you home in a box! Your Forty-seven has marked mushing tendencies. It's a whole hell of a lot heavier than the Forties you may be used to throwing around. And just keep in mind that when you bank that way, your stalling speed is up forty per cent, or more. And another thing, for the same reason; always pull out at not less than seventy-five feet. That time you may have been a little higher than the time before; but you still looked a good deal under seventy-five feet to us."

Lieutenant Wierum looked at his watch. "Now, because of these things I mention, I can't rate you satisfactory for P-Forty-seven gunnery on your passes so far. Now, if you think you have ammunition, and want to make one more, go ahead. Only, make it snappy. We want some lunch, and we have to close the range. We have a schedule this afternoon early and the targets have to be patched. Oh. Let's have your name and AFORAD organization, please. We didn't get that when they notified us you were coming and I need it for my records. I say again: this will be your last pass. The range will then close. Acknowledge."

Lieutenant Cross reached over and took Lieutenant Wierum by the arm. With his other hand, he pointed into the southern sky. Then he brought his glasses up and studied the small shining dot there for an instant. "P-Thirty-eight!" he said. "Now, for Christ's sake—"

"He may not be coming here."

"He sure as hell is. They got no right to do that. We didn't get any notification. They know we have an afternoon schedule—"

The outside loudspeaker under the eave of the metal roof said: "Eight-four, Range. Wilco, thanks. I will make one more pass. I can't seem to contact anyone on my B-channel. I want the Demonstration Area landing strip control. When I finish this pass, I want to set down there."

Lieutenant Wierum said: "Eight-four. Notice a P-Thirty-eight approaching southwest high. Keep looking until you see it. It may be coming onto the range. Do not attempt to set down on that strip. The reason you can't contact control is that they are on duty there only when they expect planes in. That is a prohibited area, and except in emergency, you must not land without specific authorization from Ocanara Operations. Are you in trouble?"

The loudspeaker said: "I am O.K. Can you get somebody on the telephone over there?"

"We could, yes," Lieutenant Wierum said with exasperation. "But unless you're in trouble, you must not land! Now, it's nothing to me, bud; but they'll burn you bad. You'll get grounded and fined some pay; so make your pass, and go home. You see the P-Thirty-eight? Where you are now, look about two o'clock level. And kindly vacate this frequency. I got to find out what he thinks he's doing."

He said to Lieutenant Cross: "Smart bastard, it seems! We got two of them. The air's full of them." He said into the microphone: "P-Thirty-eight about two miles southwest, this is the range tower. Observe P-Forty-seven flying gunnery pattern.

Do not come into pattern or on the range. You are not scheduled, and the range is closing. Acknowledge!"

The loudspeaker said: "Eight-four, Range. I see the plane.
Ring up Demonstration Area Headquarters, please; and say
I will be coming in. I want some lunch. This is General Beal
speaking."

✦

Master Sergeant Dominic Pellerino, General Beal's Crew
Chief, had gone early to eat, at half-past eleven. Quickly fed,
he put a toothpick in his mouth and sauntered, by an inconspicuous route, from the Ocanara Base Mess to the Electrical
Shop abutting on the vast cavern of Hangar Number 2.
Tracing his way through the machines and work benches to
the supply section and stock room, he signaled the clerk at
the issue window. The clerk pressed a button that unlocked
the side door. Sergeant Pellerino passed along the ranges,
dimly electric-lighted, of racks and bins. At the end was another door, with the words: *Knock and Wait* stenciled on it.

This had been the darkroom of a photographic laboratory
before the laboratory moved to a building of its own. Nomi-
nally, the present use of the old darkroom was miscellaneous
storage—a place to put those bits of equipment and odds and
ends which had been dropped from accountability, but which
a wise Shop Chief never threw away. They, or parts of them,
might come in handy on some job sometime; and, anyway, he
might want to fiddle with them for his own amusement. Thus
in one category were used motors and generators of various
sizes; resistors and condensers; relays and solenoids; thermal
overload resets and AN connectors. In the other category was
the most considerable item; a whole Martin power-operated
gun turret, without the guns, from a crashed B-24. Master
Sergeant Storm, Chief of the Electrical Shop, had ideas about
rewiring it.

While this storage use was real, and enough to justify the
assignment of space that would be little good to anyone else,
it was not the principal use of the darkroom. The darkroom
provided quarters for what was known, not unnaturally, as the

Knock and Wait Club. This was an informal group of the top sergeants in engineering and maintenance, crew and shop chiefs, marked out from the common run by their important positions, and by their resulting special attitudes of mind and manner. Their habits were unhurried; they spoke with laconic assurance. They had extra privileges and established perquisites to which they helped themselves with authoritative aplomb.

Almost everyone in the Air Service Group knew of the club's irregular existence, and knew who belonged to it; but as a matter of form, the members acted as though all was very secret. This was one of those practical, give-and-take arrangements, a co-operation with their various commanding officers, who tacitly agreed to be ignorant as long as they plausibly could be ignorant. It was a practicable arrangement, because membership in the club was self-limiting.

To be free to frequent the darkroom, a man had to be good. Unless he knew how to organize his work and discipline his personnel so that his absence for an hour or two made no difference in the progress of the jobs on hand, he could not go to the club without soon losing his stripes. He must have the judgment and experience to know exactly what his valuable abilities entitled and enabled him to get away with. A competent organizer and disciplinarian endowed with judgment and experience was a treasure. He was much more important than most of the officers supposed to be over him; a point made plain by the fact that he had more real power and far more effective authority than most of his officers.

The lieutenant could give all the orders he wanted, but none of them would be carried out until the sergeant decided whether it was necessary and reasonable. If it was held to be unnecessary or unreasonable, it would never be carried out. Busy motions might be made, but one thing after another would go wrong until carrying it out was patently impossible. The lieutenant learned, if he was capable of learning, not to give that kind of order. If he was not capable of learning, he found himself fixed up for royal chewings by the higher echelon, and for eventual reassignment as unsatisfactory. When a top sergeant gave orders, it was different. Reasonable or unreasonable, necessary or unnecessary, they were really orders. Any GI who didn't jump to obey, fully and completely, then and there, without argument or stalling or gold-bricking, was asking for, and would certainly get, the dirty end of every stick. They would ram him so full he wouldn't be a week in wishing he were dead.

Sergeant Pellerino, whose qualifications for Knock and Wait club membership were as high as possible, came to the supposedly secret door, rapped out a supposedly secret knock, and was admitted.

Though the club furnishings were meager—a table and seven or eight folding chairs, ringed closely around by the accumulation of electrical junk—Sergeant Storm had provided several ingenious conveniences. Fluorescent lighting was artistically let into the ceiling behind a glass panel. There was an exhaust fan and a salvaged air-conditioning unit. There was an intercommunication circuit connecting a squawk box in the wall with the desk by the shop telephone out front. When not out front himself, Sergeant Storm kept a man on duty at the desk to relay messages.

When Sergeant Pellerino came in, three members were there already; Master Sergeant Storm; Technical Sergeant Gonzales, the Paint Shop Chief; and Technical Sergeant La Barre, the Armament Chief. Storm and La Barre crouched on their heels by the half-dismantled power turret in the corner.

La Barre, who had the gun controls in his hands, said: "Look, dope! The deadman switch got to be there. That you can't change. That's where you want it, what it's for. What it says; the gunner gets drilled—" he went through a pantomime of taking a bullet in his head. "His hands drop off the handles. The switches, right away, snap free and cut the action. Now, you show me where else it could do that—"

At the table Sergeant Gonzales methodically turned dominoes from an emptied-out box face down. He was by birth a Porto Rican; and dominoes, as a game of skill and chance, was his introduction. The others had been dubious; but they were not long in seeing that the form of dominoes called Muggins, or All Fives, at a dollar a point, made money change hands as effectively as shooting craps; and did not drag out the process, like poker; while, as in poker, consistent winning took, as much as luck, a sharp eye and a crafty mind. Moreover, it was a game with a cachet—no mere GI's pastime in a corner. It suited the club and its members.

Sergeant Gonzales said: "Heads up, you two. Here it is." He said to Sergeant Pellerino: "What you eat so long for, Danny? You don't need to. Look at that pot on you!"

"Bite it!" Sergeant Pellerino said amiably. He pulled his shirt out of his pants, unbuttoned it, and shrugged it gingerly back on his shoulders, exposing to the grateful cool air a fleshy chest covered with sleek black hair, against which gleamed his dog tags and a gold medal of Saint Christopher. Moving his back stiffly, he eased himself into a chair and took the seven bones Gonzales pushed toward him. He stood them on edge in a little row like a wall with the pips facing him. He said: "You like to know something, Spic, you don't know, that's for you? You got a job. Vera saw it in the office. Be coming at you in a week, ten days."

"Like what?" Gonzales said. "And how do you get calling me Spic, you fat Wop?"

La Barre and Storm left the gun turret and took chairs. Gonzales pushed them their dominoes. Storm said: "How's the back, Danny? You act like you want us to think it hurts."

"The hell. I only bumped it."

"You got a good cut on your face, there," La Barre said. "Vera catch you out?"

"The hell. We had rough air. I wasn't strapped, so I took this bump."

Gonzales said: "Come on, Danny. What job?"

"How'd you like to change all plane markings?"

"They just changed, for God's sake! It wasn't two months. Not much more."

"Now, they just change again. No red at all. The bar edge is blue; and no red rim around the circle. All blue."

"What's better about that?"

"I don't know. I'm only saying what it's going to be. Anybody beat this?" He slid out a double-six for a set.

In the wall, the squawk box said: "Sergeant Pellerino."

"Now we go round again!" Sergeant Pellerino said. He turned, wincing, in his chair and addressed the wall: "What?"

"Telephone."

"Who's it?"

"Botwinick for Colonel Mowbray, Sarge."

"No!" Sergeant Pellerino said. "I went to eat. I told you before."

"I told them. They checked the mess. They say: aren't you back yet?"

"No. I'm not back yet. You don't think I'm coming back to Electrical. Maybe I'm on the line. Maybe I taxied a plane out to test the brakes. Don't bother calling me for that any more. Except it's Vera; or Colonel Ross, his office."

"Okey-doke, Sarge."

Storm, a small man with a shrewd little pointed face, put the six-three against the set. La Barre promptly put the six-two against the other side and said, pointing at Gonzales' pad: "My five. Let me see it there. What's chewing Old Wobbles, Danny?"

Sergeant Pellerino shrugged.

Gonzales added the double-three to the six-three and said: "My five."

"To really bitch this, I got to draw," Sergeant Pellerino said. He took one and turned it in his palm. It was the three-blank and he put it against the double-three. "I guess he thinks I might know where the general is. Maybe I do; but why tell him? He don't need to know."

Sergeant La Barre said: "What's all the ammunition for? We gave him a maximum load. Those Forty-sevens really carry it. Four-twenty-five rounds. You know that?"

"Ammunition could be to shoot," Sergeant Pellerino watched the play critically. "Here's where I make money," he said, when it was his turn. He slid out a domino dramatically, and, indicating with his forefinger, said: "Five into twenty-five. Thanks, all! Why, he never shot with one. He might want to try it at Chechoter range. He wouldn't get found there, too soon."

"What pitch is that? Why don't he want to get found?"

"He might like to be away from it, Joe. Maybe he don't like it all the time here. Do you?"

"Make me general, and I might like it all the time," La Barre said. "Go on; try me! I'll tell you then whether I do."

"I can tell you now. You'd like all the horse sugar he has to handle. You'd never get tired."

"What's Beal?" Gonzales said. "Tired? Can't he take it? Losing his grip? Bucking for Section Eight?"

"You ever know anything?" Sergeant Pellerino said with acerbity. "Name one single thing! He never lost a grip yet; and I've seen him places that would make you for Section Eight. So don't give me the argument, you goddamn AUS draft dodger."

La Barre said: "In there, it ever pinch your nose any, Danny?"

Sergeant Pellerino laid both hands on the table. "Let's make a check," he said. "I ask him in a nice way to lay off. Now, you; if you're kidding, I'm asking you not to kid any more. You're not kidding, we better go back to the hangar and analyze the project."

"You scare me to death!" Sergeant La Barre said.

Storm said: "Do you have to be so hard? Sure, Joe *was* kidding. Now you rack him back, so he can't be sure. A couple more, and he'll *know* he wasn't kidding."

Sergeant Pellerino said: "You were listening. I never sucked around anywhere in my life; and I can tell you, information and guidance all concerned, you wouldn't make any time there if you happened to try. Now, why wouldn't I get hard? I got a right—"

The squawk box said: "Sergeant La Barre."

"Saved by that bell!" La Barre said. "Oh, the Jesus, Danny! What did I say about you, or him, the general? It just gives me a laugh, the way you arch your back, anybody says anything at all the least little bit—yeah?" he said, tilting his chair.

"Captain Dobie, Post Engineer's office, over at your place.

You got any belts of thirty cal blanks anywhere? They need some for something this afternoon."

Sergeant La Barre said: "Yeah. Well, there's some in Magazine A, tell them. Only I got to get an authorization from the Operations Officer I can give them; and I got to get a receipt he took them. See? Not one or the other. Both. Tell me what they say." He looked back to Sergeant Pellerino and said: "We still fighting?"

"Last I heard, Joe, you're having your laugh," Sergeant Pellerino said. "Have that. I don't mind. What I mind is cracks to me about what you don't know. You and Gonzales want to really know, you ask anybody overseas with him. They won't say he's easy. You try and lay down—officer, enlisted man, anybody—and he'll ream the guts out of you. But he don't ask you to do anything he wouldn't."

"Aaah!" La Barre said. "Where did I hear that sometime?"

"You just heard it right now," Sergeant Pellerino said doggedly. "I said it. And he can do anything you can do better. Now, you want to go 'Aaah!' again?"

"Lay off, Lame Brain," Storm said to La Barre. "You see, or don't you see?"

"I see," La Barre said. He sat back, his face serious. "Now, catch, Danny! You can get hard. I give you that. But, don't, right now; I wouldn't. You got a bum back, there; and that cut, I could open in one minute. Nothing I said was against you. I don't need to fight you. But I can still think what I think."

Sergeant Pellerino said slowly: "I just care what you say; and then I only care when I hear it. I don't have to listen. Any more than you have to listen, somebody saying your mother's a bitch."

They locked eyes a moment; and Sergeant La Barre began to grin. With a relieved, loudly hilarious note, Sergeant Gonzales said: "Hey, who's whose mother here? You the general's mother, Danny? The general your mother? I got to know."

"He's the general's mother," Sergeant Storm said. "He's like this hen that only got this one goddamn little chicken."

"Bite it!" Sergeant Pellerino said amiably. "We going to play a game; or we going to beat our gums?"

The squawk box said: "Sergeant Pellerino."

"Yeah, for God's sake?"

"Colonel Carricker, Sarge."

"No."

The squawk box said cautiously: "He's not telephoning, Sarge. He's here—"

There was a pause; and Lieutenant Colonel Carricker himself said suddenly from the box: "Come on out, Danny. I want to see you."

✦

Mrs. Ross pushed open the pantry door and looked into the back hall of the bungalow. "Oh!" she said. "Norman! I thought you were Sal. She's coming over and we're going down to the Scheherazade to get our hair done. We have appointments at half-past one. Do you want some lunch? I can't give you much; but I was just fixing something for myself. I thought you'd probably be at the Club with the generals."

"Don't bother, my dear," Colonel Ross said. "I'll pick up something. I just came down to get my pills. I forgot them this morning."

Mrs. Ross let the door swing behind her and advanced on him. "Norman," she said, "I don't think you've been feeling very well for the last few days. Now, please go and see a doctor. You know what Doctor Potter said. You are driving yourself too hard."

"I feel as well as can be expected," Colonel Ross said. "Because I know what Doctor Potter said, there is no point in wasting another doctor's time. And not one of these young doctors. Your doctor should always be older than you are, I begin to realize. If he isn't, he doesn't know what you are talking about. Doctor Potter said to take the pills; so I came to get one."

"You look tired," Mrs. Ross said.

"I am tired. There was a lot of stuff this morning; and General Nichols was on my neck."

Mrs. Ross looked at him with reflective concern. Then she said: "Norman, get your pill and come out to the kitchen. I'll give you lunch. I want you to relax for a little while. If you have a car waiting, tell the man to go and get something to eat. You don't have to go back this minute."

"I do; but I guess I won't," Colonel Ross said. "I more or less deserted Nichols. I was at the Base with him; so I sent him back to the Area in Mowbray's car. Young Hicks gave me a lift down here. He was coming down with another officer. His wife was ill at the Hospital and he wanted to get some of her things for her. My car will pick me up. It ought to be here presently."

"Hicks's wife? When did she get down?"

"She didn't. I seem to be a little fuddled. It was the other officer's wife. It is my age coming out. Do you remember old Mr. Barry? The last years he was practicing he was always having pronoun trouble. I used to have to straighten him out from the bench. All the words tired him. Yes." He sighed. "Hicks, I'm afraid, has suffered a blow. He dropped the other officer off at the hotel drive and insisted on bringing me over here. He had a matter he wanted to speak to me about, of course. Bus decided against that magazine project. He told Hicks it was all off. Hicks feels this is short-sighted of the general. He does not want it to be all off. So he bent my ear with several urgent reasons—though not his chief one, I think —why the project ought to be all on again. He wants me to see what I can do."

"Why did Bus decide against it?"

"I don't know. Neither does Hicks. I think Hicks had been happily making a lot of plans. He put it delicately to me that in New York he was not without influence. If he managed it personally, he felt that he could overcome the natural editorial suspicion of War Department hand-outs. He had an angle on General Beal, which, if handled right—that is, by him, and by a writer he thought he could find, would appeal to a certain editor with whom he had worked, in fact, who used to work for him. His anxiety, though covered, was apparent. I thought it bore out very well what I said last night. Hicks

432

is a steady, domestic type. Far from liking to be a gay dog in Ocanara, he is intensely intent on being sent to see his wife and family. It would have edified you."

Mrs. Ross said: "He could want both, of course. You don't seem much edified."

"Ah, well—yes, yes I am," Colonel Ross said. "But I don't think Hicks credits me with all the acumen you know I have. I told Hal Coulthard I thought TD orders, sending Hicks to New York for a while, might be a useful incentive. Thou shalt not muzzle the ox when he treadeth out the corn! But, today, I don't particularly want to work on Bus. Also, today, I feel a little glum. That makes me sensitive to all this self-interest—other people's. Their anxiety is indecent. I don't like the way they please me. There is a tang of purpose. They butter me up, but not disinterestedly. They are afraid they won't, otherwise, get something they want. I am disappointed in them. They should put more art into their bamboozling."

"You exert yourself too much," Mrs. Ross said. "I wish you'd do something about getting an assistant."

"I have done something," Colonel Ross said. "I have one. I have Captain Collins. I took him from Public Relations. I think he's a good man; but I am afraid he's not perfect; I am afraid he's human. I had him, as well as Hicks, in mind. I sent Collins on an errand this morning. Through no fault of his, he fell down on it. I told him to do something that he couldn't do, because somebody else had already done it, without our knowledge."

"I don't see, then, how you have any grounds for being disappointed in him."

"I didn't say I had grounds, I just said I was. I didn't hear from him for quite a while; I suppose it took him some time to find out what had happened. When he finally reached me on the phone I could see he had been more anxious than I realized to get out of Public Relations. Since he had balled up, he thought, the first thing I asked him to do, I might not give him another chance; I might revoke the orders. He would be stuck forever in Public Relations. Now, I am a hard man to please; for though I blame myself, I was disappointed to see how frightened he was. He was not the man he was yesterday. He had been tampered with—by me. Lord Acton stopped on a half truth; and that, the less important half. Power corrupts all right. If you have enough of it, it may, in the end, absolutely corrupt *you*; but you only need the least little bit, a modicum of power, the power of a staff officer, to do a good job corrupting other people."

"I don't want you to be glum," Mrs. Ross said. "That may all be true; still, you wouldn't have given Hicks the project, or this Captain Collins the job, if you hadn't thought they were all right. Sometimes you are too scrupulous, Norman. You brood on things. I was really still asleep when you left this morning. I meant to say something about the fuss I made last night. I was depressed. There was no other reason for it. I hope you haven't been thinking about it."

"Is that so?" Colonel Ross said. "If I answered: 'Why, I never gave it another thought—' well! Much of what you said was true, my dear."

"All I said was true! But I wouldn't have said it if I hadn't been depressed. I wouldn't have got to thinking about it. I think you are depressed this morning. I know something is bothering you. I suppose you aren't able to tell me what. But you should remember that you are tired. I kept you awake too late last night; and—"

"I would not put it quite that way," Colonel Ross said. "I feel my time was well enough spent. I might even undertake to speak for young fellows half my age, if you should ever be silly enough to take up with some."

Mrs. Ross, coloring, smiled faintly. Lifting her hand, she gave his chin a couple of possessive taps. She said: "Go take that pill. I'll have lunch for you right away. Oh; Zinnia isn't here, as usual. She sent some excuse by Mrs. Jobson's maid. I'm awfully fed up with these colored girls."

When Colonel Ross came into the kitchen, cold ham and potato salad were laid out. Mrs. Ross was slicing an alligator pear She said: "I don't think I'll give you any coffee, Norman. Perhaps you could get a short nap after you finish. I'll just see your car waits. This parade or review or whatever it is will probably keep you standing around for hours. And then there'll be more of it at the Club. I hope you won't have to drink much."

"I never drink much," Colonel Ross said. "Only more than I'm used to."

"Now, you've teased me enough about those things I said. There was a great deal of sense in them."

"Quite right. But I can't take a nap. I must go as soon as the car comes. There is too much to do. So I must have some coffee."

Pouring him coffee, Mrs. Ross said: "I'm not going to bother you with questions about what's going on. But two things I would like to know, if you can tell me. I have a reason for asking. Is Bus out at the Area?"

"You mean, right now?" said Colonel Ross. "I really couldn't say. I haven't seen him since eight o'clock. I was tied up; and then I had to go with General Nichols—why do you ask?"

"Because I wanted to know. I said I wouldn't bother you; so never mind that. Sal thinks the trouble, or whatever it is, is connected with General Nichols and General Baxter coming down. Is it?"

Colonel Ross said: "Baxter, my dear, as I told you, simply got a lift. He is going right on to Sellers Field. He wanted a statement from me about Colonel Woodman, which he had to have this morning. He may have left already."

"There was a flight set up at one o'clock," Mrs. Ross said. "General Baxter was here, an hour or so ago, to get his things. He was elaborately civil to me. Sal happened to be here, too; and I thought he was a little constrained with her. So did she."

Colonel Ross said: "You should make allowances for the fact that Sal comes from an old Army family. When you live that peacetime life, special attitudes are instilled in you. You live in one long, very slow, intrigue—I don't mean it's venal; but you learn to watch out. If the colonel's wife thinks poorly of you, or of your wife, that will do you no good. When some brass turns up, you'd better mind your p's and q's. Years later, you may not be given the assignment you'd like to have because you said or did the wrong thing that day."

Mrs. Ross said: "I don't know how special those attitudes are. I remember putting myself out quite a good deal to be pleasant to Governor Clark's wife. It was not always easy; she was a stupid woman. That was when they were trying to get you to enter the primaries. I didn't want you to; because it was certain you'd be nominated, and virtually certain you'd be elected. You being you, you wouldn't have got on in the State House at all. I did what I could, even so, because I saw the idea of being governor appealed to you; and I knew if I argued, it would simply appeal to you more—"

"It appealed to me very little," Colonel Ross said. "If Clark wasn't going to run again, I simply felt for a while it might be my duty. Of those who signified their willingness to run, I didn't see a man who would be willing, or if he would be willing, who would be able, to keep the State Chairman reasonably honest."

"I know," Mrs. Ross said, "and you wouldn't have been able to handle Oswald, either. That's what I had in mind. You don't understand politicians."

"That's a mortifying idea," Colonel Ross said, somewhat huffily, "I would have thought that few people understood politicians as well as I do."

Mrs. Ross reached out and patted his hand. She said: "I meant: you don't understand, or at any rate you never want to do what must be done to work with them. In politics the first job is to get elected and stay elected. If you can't do that, nothing else matters; because you won't be able to do it. With politicians, the question is whether they're going to use you, or you're going to use them. I didn't mean they were too clever for you. I think you see through them; but that isn't enough. To use them, you must begin by making them think they're using you. You don't have to warn them in advance—"

"Well, I find that I do," Colonel Ross said. "If I feel it my duty to put an honest man, meaning in that case, myself, in the State House; my first care will certainly be to see that my man, meaning myself, *is* honest. A piece of calculated dishonesty, deceiving Oswald or allowing him to deceive himself, seems a poor way to start."

436

Mrs. Ross said: "You are getting me off the track. It is only that I think you should notice sometimes that you see your duty as what you would personally prefer to do, not what you know would be in the best interests of other people. Now, eat your lunch." She sat silent while he finished what was on his plate. She said then: "I gather you saw a good deal of General Nichols this morning. What did you make of him?"

Colonel Ross said, "I think people usually make of General Nichols what he wants them to. I think he has a strong purpose. Like the Apostle, he may serve it by being all things to all men. I think he often suits what he says to his hearer—I don't mean, saying one thing to one person, and the opposite to another; but saying the same thing different ways. I'm impressed by anyone who keeps himself in hand; and also, I suppose because I have been in the law so long, I have a partiality for a man who isolates an issue and pleads to it, not all around the bush."

"He made you like him, in short."

"At least, I see that possibility," Colonel Ross said. He drank some coffee. "What did Sal say about him?"

"Several things. One was that he would shoot his own mother if he thought she wasn't on the ball."

"Well, tell me another thing," Colonel Ross said. "I know about that. Hal Coulthard was muttering something last night about Nichols shooting people. Personally, I doubt if he ever shot anyone."

"She thinks he's here to do something to Bus—do him dirt, was her phrase. She says he's the Chief of Air Staff's private assassin. I don't know anything about that; but General Baxter, as I said, was acting in that absurd way men often act when they know something you won't want to hear, and are trying to get away before you find out. At any rate, I think General Nichols is a dangerous man."

Colonel Ross said: "I have a considerable liking for Sal; but I cannot think of anything I would trust her judgment about."

"This isn't a matter of her judgment," Mrs. Ross said. "General Nichols frightens her. You may laugh at this, Norman;

437

but the reason *I* think General Nichols is dangerous isn't anything I know about him. I don't know anything. It is not anything Sal says. Sal says all kinds of things. It's that while Sal's afraid of him, afraid he may do Bus dirt, she doesn't dislike him—not the way she dislikes Colonel Carricker, for instance. I was interested to hear you say that about all things to all men. I don't suppose General Nichols is, by any means. I don't suppose Saint Paul was; that was probably just Saint Paul's idea of himself. But at least it showed the lengths he was ready to go to influence people. That's a very dangerous type of person. They often have what I think must be an hypnotic effect."

Colonel Ross said: "I see nothing to laugh at. However, I will say I don't think Nichols has the faintest interest in doing, or intention to do, Bus, or anyone else, what Sal calls dirt. In any human situation, even the simplest, there are more variables than any human mind can properly take account of. The phenomenon, which you put very well, about being afraid of him but not disliking him, can be explained. He puts it to you that certain things are self-evident; and he puts it to you so strongly that you feel, in light of them, you and he have common aims, plans. After that has worked on you awhile, he might show you that among the chief obstacles to your common plan was you yourself. You might find that really he was right; and if you did, you might have to help him see what could be done about removing you. I think he would be quite grave and friendly. You would not dislike him."

Mrs. Ross said: "I wish I could talk to him. I'd find out what he was up to; and I'd also see how to handle him. I don't doubt he has himself well in hand as you say; but what shows he's such a brilliant thinker? Tell me something he said."

Colonel Ross said: "That was not quite it, Cora. I said I was partial to a man who can isolate an issue and plead to it. I think he isolates the issue, winning the war, with great clarity. I don't say he had any brilliant thoughts about it; just that he can disentangle facts from impressions. He doesn't let himself be confused by accidentals—because a thing is big, or because it is small. He commented on one big thing—problems at the Quebec Conference; and one small one—the disciplinary difficulty which I mentioned to you last night, about some colored officers. His thought in both cases was that you will not do what you cannot do. Do you find the thought impressive?"

"No," said Mrs. Ross.

"It is quite important, however, if you have to make the decisions. A great many people, maybe most people, confronted by a difficult situation, one in which they don't know what to do, get nowhere because they are so busy pointing out that the situation should be remade so they *will* know what to do. Whether you like it or not, there are things you can't buck—no matter how much you want to, how vital it is to you. A parachutist who jumps from an airplane cannot climb back, no matter what. Even if he sees he'll be killed when he lands, he can't. Gravity is a condition, not a theory. In our trouble with the colored officers, we also have a condition, not a theory."

"You didn't tell me what that trouble really was."

"It is always the same," Colonel Ross said. "It is the standing trouble. You read about it in books, where it is often tragic. In life, as well as tragic, it tends to be tedious. A number of Negro officers came in on a project, and Mowbray assigned a separate officers' club for them. They considered it racial discrimination; and a few of them tried yesterday afternoon to use the Area Officers Club. It is off limits for them. There was a very moderate fuss; no real violence; Johnny Sears's men arrested five or six of them. We didn't know quite what was going to happen, then; now, I think, nothing is. I have talked to the officer who is in line to be their group commander, and he is co-operative. He happened to be in the Hospital when this happened; but he is getting out now. I think he can manage them. There weren't many of them, and, of those there were, I doubt if more than one or two wanted to do it."

Mrs. Ross said: "I should think they would all want to! It seems to me that if a man is qualified to be an officer, he is qualified to go to the Club. I don't see how he can be one and not the other."

Colonel Ross said: "If you'll confront our condition instead of your theory, you'll see. This is how he can be one and not the other. For reasons of justice and decency; and also for reasons of political policy, the War Department decided that colored men must be given a chance to qualify as officers. We have about a thousand of them in the Air Force. In the Air Force, we have now somewhere around three hundred thousand white officers. A certain number of these, I don't know how many, but in relation to the whole, a proportion infinitely larger than that of colored to white officers, an unmanageably large number, hold that a nigger is a nigger. They will not have anything to do with him socially. That is their decision, inculcated in them from their first conscious moments, handed down to them with the sanctions of use and interest. I don't say this couldn't be changed, or that it won't ever be; but it won't change today, tomorrow, this week. A man cannot choose to see what he cannot see."

"It is outrageous!" Mrs. Ross said. "I don't doubt there are quite a number of ignorant and prejudiced young louts, like Colonel Carricker, who feel that way. There must be many more, a big majority, who feel that a Negro is a human being, and who want to see him treated fairly. Why does what the majority wants make no difference?"

Colonel Ross said: "Carricker, as far as I know, has no feeling about it at all. I have seen a good deal of him, and I don't think he gives a hoot in hell who he has social contacts with. Racial prejudice may be low and infantile; but it is a form of social consciousness. Any form of social consciousness is too advanced for Benny. Benny, as Bus once remarked to me, is just Benny. My dear, you still confront the theory. What the majority wants makes a great difference. That big majority may feel that a Negro is a human being all right; but when you add that they want to see him treated fairly, you're wrong. That is not the condition. The condition is that the big majority doesn't *mind* if he's treated fairly, a very different thing. The big majority does not want him to marry their sister. The big majority does not want to insult or oppress him; but the big majority has, in general, a poor opinion of him. It gets awfully fed up with these colored girls."

Mrs. Ross said: "If I had a white girl working for me and she was dirty and lazy and unreliable, I would be just as fed up with her. I am certainly not fed up with Zinnia because she happens to be colored."

"That's not this point, my dear. Your remark stated a conclusion. It was in the phrasing. You were stating that your experience and observation convinced you that these colored girls were nearly always dirty, lazy, and unreliable—"

"I think there are reasons for that—"

"There are reasons for everything that is," Colonel Ross said sententiously. "They're often interesting. Figuring them out increases our understanding. They may arouse our indignation or our compassion. They add up to say that if things had been different, things might be different. That seems quite likely; but things aren't different, they are as they are. That's where we have to go on from."

"What is that?" Mrs. Ross said.

"It sounds like someone in the hall," Colonel Ross said. "Perhaps it is Zinnia, risen from her bed of pain to come and serve you. It might be my car, but I think they would have rung."

"Zinnia wouldn't come to the front door," Mrs. Ross said. "Sal would call. Go and see, Norman. It's such a curious sound."

Colonel Ross arose and went through the pantry door. The door opposite, to the hall, was open; and he could see, down the shadowed length, the shadowed screen door framing a hot oblong of sun on tropical foliage, and above it, beyond the hollow, the faded pink stucco of the Oleander Towers Hotel. The hall was empty.

The sound, which resembled light but uncertain footfalls, somebody walking with difficulty, was suddenly repeated. "Who's there?" he said.

There was no answer. From the dining room at the right came a succession of small bumps, and the noise of a chair's legs scraped along the floor. Colonel Ross went and opened the dining room door.

The chair at the head of the table was pushed aside. Sitting on it, one hand holding the table edge, the other pressed to her forehead, was Mrs. Beal. She gave her head a jerk, whipping the free-swinging hair back from her face. "What do you know?" she said. "Hello, Norm! Where did you come from?"

She started to get up; but her hand slipped on the table edge and she bumped her elbow. "Oooh!" she said, clasping it. "That hurt! Wait a while, I guess."

Colonel Ross let the door close behind him.

Mrs. Beal said: "It's all right, Norm. I'm just plastered. Sit down. Let's sit down a while. I want to talk to you. Cora's going to get our hair done pretty soon. Not yet." She took her left hand in her right and turned it carefully, gazing down at the watch on her left wrist. "Go in a minute," she said. "You don't know where Bus is, I bet."

Colonel Ross drew back one of the other chairs and sat down on it. "Where have you been, Sal?" he said.

"Nowhere," Mrs. Beal said. "Over at our place. I had a little drink. Oh, you think somebody saw me! Nobody saw me. I came around by those bushes. Almost stepped on a snake. Coral snake."

"Did you really?" Colonel Ross said.

"No, silly!" said Mrs. Beal. "I just said that. You don't know where Bus is, I bet."

"Where is he?"

"You wouldn't tell me anything," Mrs. Beal said. "Why should I tell you? I know."

"How did you find out, Sal?"

"Easy," said Mrs. Beal. "Made them ask Danny." She brought her fist up to her lips and took one knuckle between her teeth. "He knew."

"Who asked Danny?" Colonel Ross said. "Colonel Mowbray?"

"No," Mrs. Beal said. "Who'd tell him anything?" She sat still, gnawing lightly at the knuckle.

Colonel Ross said: "Where did you get the drink, Sal?"

"Out of a bottle, silly," Mrs. Beal said. "A great big stinking bottle of Scotch. I drank it all; what was in it. Funny face, what's his name, Mr. Bullen, and the man with the camera, it was for them last night. I just saw it; and I thought: 'How's about a little drink? That'll put some lead in your pencil!'" She giggled. "Everybody out," she said. "Dinge's day off.

Junior's at nursery school. Bus at Chechoter. Nobody but me. I feel fine."

Colonel Ross said: "Chechoter? You mean the Demonstration Area? When did Bus say he was coming back?"

"How should I know?" Mrs. Beal swayed a little, sitting straighter in the chair. "Ask that Benny, why don't you? Benny knows everything! He knows where Danny goes. Benny found out. Benny said—" very pale, she broke off and swallowed laboriously.

Colonel Ross said: "Sal, do you feel all right?"

"No," she said with difficulty. "I'm going to be sick. Get away; go away! Going to be sick in a minute—"

Colonel Ross got to his feet. From the kitchen, he heard Mrs. Ross calling: "Norman! Where are you? Norman—"

"All right, Sal," he said kindly. "You go right ahead."

He went out the door. In the pantry he met Mrs. Ross. She said: "Norman, where on earth—"

"It's Sal," he said. "She is being sick."

"Sal? Being sick? What do you mean?"

"I mean, she is throwing up; as indeed you can hear."

Mrs. Ross made to push him aside. In consternation she said: "Norman! Did she take something? What did she say? Get a doctor at once—"

"No, no," Colonel Ross said. "It was just whisky she took. A lot of Scotch, she says."

"She's drunk? You mean she's sick because she drank a lot of Scotch? I don't believe it. She might have said that; but —call a doctor, quickly!"

"Oh, she was drunk, all right," Colonel Ross said. "She drank all that was left in a bottle she saw. Too much at once, I should say."

"Why should she do that? Norman, this may be serious. You call a doctor. I asked you where Bus was, remember? Either you don't know, or you wouldn't tell me. I said I had a reason. Sal doesn't know where he is either."

Colonel Ross said: "Sal knows where he is now. She found out by asking Colonel Carricker. It was the only way she could find out. So she drank a lot of Scotch. It seems quite simple."

"Benny?" Mrs. Ross said.

"Exactly!" Colonel Ross said. "I understand she doesn't like him much. I don't think she liked having to do that."

"Ah," Mrs. Ross said. "Poor child! Norman, I think your car has just come. There's one at the steps. You go along. Don't let anyone in here. I'll—"

"First of all," Colonel Ross said, "you'd better get a rag or something."

IX

FROM THE windows of the barracks they screamed in delighted, taunting chorus: "You'll be sorry! You'll be sorry!" It was varied by individuals who yelled dolefully: "Oh, you won't like it here! Oh, you wait! You won't like it here!"

Thirty or forty WAC enlisted women, replacements fresh from the Second Training Center at Daytona Beach, waited in a defensive huddle sitting on their suitcases and barracks bags in the slight shade of three pines beyond the boardwalk that crossed the waste of sand to the barracks door. They heard the chorus with fixed, consciously game, smiles. They exchanged brief whispers among themselves. They looked around with covert apprehension, trying to size this place up. Some of them chewed gum, and some smoked cigarettes, and some did both. The smokers, when they finished their cigarettes, showed their good basic training by tearing the butt open, scattering the remnants of tobacco, and rolling the bit of paper into a minute ball before throwing it away.

The chorus suddenly died. Looking over her shoulder, one woman started up and called out attention. They scrambled to their feet. A WAC officer and two sergeants had come down the steps of the building across the road and were approaching them.

The officer, surveying the group pleasantly, said: "All right, everybody! At ease. I'm Lieutenant Lippa. You are to be in my company. This is First Sergeant Levy, and Staff Sergeant

444

Hogan. I understand you had lunch downtown before the trucks brought you out."

Several voices said: "Yes, ma'am."

One said cheerfully: "Heck, no! Call those little measly sandwiches—"

She was instantly answered.

"Oh, you!"

"Oh, listen to her!"

"Oh, Lardsy has a tapeworm—"

Lieutenant Lippa smiled. "Well, if anyone's hungry, she can go to the PX coffee shop later. Sergeant Hogan will show you your quarters. I'll come over in an hour or so and see how you're getting on. This afternoon, the whole Detachment is parading at Retreat. Don't worry; we don't always do it. This is just a special occasion. Anyone who wants to be excused today is excused. Of course, if anyone wants to march, we could fit her in. It won't be more than a few miles, and I don't believe it will be more than a hundred in the shade. Just speak to Sergeant Hogan."

There was a general squeal.

"Lardsy! Lardsy wants to march—"

"Oh, my feet!"

"Oh, dummy up, Jones!"

"One more thing," Lieutenant Lippa said. "I'm sure you know the other women were teasing you. They always do that when new groups come in. You aren't going to be sorry. I think you'll like it here. This is a good post. So you won't think I'm just saying that; the percentage of women dropping out here last month before we were sworn in to the Army was smaller than at any AAF installation of comparable size. We are very proud of our record. All right. Dismissed. You needn't form up. Just take your things and go along with Sergeant Hogan."

Walking back across the road, Lieutenant Lippa said to Sergeant Levy: "They don't look so bad, Norma; do you think? We can certainly use them. I hope too many of them haven't got job ratings."

Sergeant Levy, a tall stout dark girl, said: "I saw only about

445

five. Motor Transport Course at Daytona. I suppose they'll grab them at the Base."

"Yes."

They went up the steps and through the screen door, and into Lieutenant Lippa's little office. Lieutenant Lippa jerked her cap off and sailed it neatly onto a hook on the wall. She snapped the switch of an electric fan in the corner and plumped down on the chair behind her desk. "Now, where were we?"

Sergeant Levy scratched her head. "Oh, there's the form for that letter Captain Burton wanted. They can all be the same, I guess." She drew a sheet of paper from the basket on the desk.

"Oh, bother!" Lieutenant Lippa said. "Oh, damn! I thought she'd forget."

Holding the sheet up, Sergeant Levy began to read aloud: "Dear Mrs. Blank. Your daughter parenthesis name close parenthesis is now an enlisted woman in the Army of the United States, Women's Army Corps. During the time she has been stationed at this post she has not only done an excellent job, but she has been a definite asset to our company—" Sergeant Levy made a face. "Each one is to be typed individually, so it looks like a personal letter from you, it says. Now, don't fret. I'll put Straus and Cheney both on them Monday. I know where I can get another typewriter."

"All right. What else?"

"You were going to find out about duckboards for the laundry."

"I did. Captain Burton says we can get them. The Post Engineer will bring them over. Look; we have to do something about the way they wreck those electric irons. They mustn't disconnect them by jerking the cords. They must take hold of the plug itself, only they must be sure their hands are dry. Me, I never took hold of the plug itself in my life. How am I going to make them do it?"

"We could put a sign right over each outlet. That might remind them."

"Good. Do that. Anything else?"

"About Vanderbeck's assignment to the Beauty Shop."

"Yes. Here's what we have to do. She has to be covered by insurance. We use unit funds. It's authorized. She has a license from her State Board to operate a permanent wave machine, so there's some standard policy she's eligible for. Only, it has to cover not only her, but me, and Captain Burton. The Judge Advocate's office says any one of us could be sued if somebody had her hair all burned off. Do me a fund requisition when you have time. Just leave the amount open. They're finding out about that. That's all, isn't it?"

"Nope," Sergeant Levy said.

"Ah, Norma, no! Not Buck!" Lieutenant Lippa said. "Please, please. Not today! Not this afternoon. Monday. I'll talk to her Monday. I can do it much better Monday. Saturdays, I'm so pooped I don't know whether I'm coming or going. Monday I'll climb all over her."

Sergeant Levy said: "Monday, you'll say it was too long ago. You'll say: wait until she does something else."

"Oh, God; oh, God," Lieutenant Lippa said. "I suppose I will." She lifted a hand to her open collar and, taking the lieutenant's bar between her thumb and forefinger, began to rub it distractedly with her thumb. "Maybe she did feel lousy. She did get up in the end, didn't she?"

"She got up at eleven o'clock," Sergeant Levy said grimly. "Fighter Control reported her absent from duty in the Filter Room. I had to say she was sick."

"Did you report her sick?" Lieutenant Lippa said hopefully. She reached into the basket and took out a carbon of the Morning Report.

"No, I didn't," Sergeant Levy said. "I wasn't going to report her sick when what she was doing was refusing to obey orders. Buck gets away with a great deal too much. Last Saturday night she was at that Roadside Rest with some AA men. A woman who saw her told Hogan she was pie-eyed. And furthermore, she went out to a car with them, and everybody knew what she was doing."

"But she got in all right?"

"If you call drunk all right. She was walked in by a couple of others. She never could have made it alone. She was a mess, someone who saw her in the washroom said. Lipstick all over her face; stockings down around her ankles. No girdle on."

"Well, why wasn't she reported?"

"Hogan didn't see her. The others didn't want to report her. They told Hogan because they thought Hogan could talk to her, make her stop acting that way. Just one like her, and the word goes around with the men; and a girl can't have a date without the lug who asks her thinking because she's a Wac, she'll roll right over. And getting sore if she doesn't."

"I know, I know," Lieutenant Lippa said. "Well, if you told them she was sick at Fighter Control, we'll have to report her sick. Do you think she wasn't?"

Sergeant Levy shrugged. "Not as sick as that. She may have had cramps; but anyone but her would have stood roll call; and if they were bad, Hogan would have reported her sick, and let her lie down. I know what she was doing. Hogan did speak to her about Saturday; and she was sore at Hogan, trying to make all the trouble she could. She just said: no, she wasn't going to report sick, she wouldn't go to sick call. Hogan says: then she has to get up. She says: no she won't, she doesn't feel like it. Hogan gives her a direct order; and she says: 'Let's see you make me.'" Sergeant Levy had grown red. "I know what I'd feel like doing," she said. "Hogan isn't husky enough; but I'd just want to take that cot and dump her on the floor. She'd be up, all right."

Still rubbing the insignia, Lieutenant Lippa said: "Whatever you feel like, don't ever lay a hand on anyone, Norma."

"I wouldn't have touched her. I'd just have taken that cot and turned it upside down." She made a muscular gesture showing how she would do it. "All right, ma'am! I know what I'm supposed to do. I'm supposed to report it to the Company Commander who will take appropriate disciplinary action."

Lieutenant Lippa said: "Send for Buck. Only you'll have to get her on today's sick report. To explain why she wasn't entered this morning, you'll have to call Unit Personnel. Say it was overlooked because medical attention wasn't required; it was just dysmenorrhea, and I let her stay in quarters. They'll accept that; and we'll have the record straight."

"Is that fair to Hogan, ma'am?"

"Will you please not call me ma'am all the time when there's nobody here? And stop getting mad. I want the record straightened out because otherwise we'll have a fuss with Fighter Control. I'm not going to tell Buck that I did it. Now, do you mind that?"

"Can I stay?"

"Yes, you may. Don't ride me, Norma! I know I have to do it. I just can't help not wanting to. It's just Saturday afternoon."

"I don't blame you," Sergeant Levy said. "I wouldn't ask you to, except if she gets away with it, it will be worse later. One thing; she's put in for overseas. I guess the little bitch figures that there, with less competition, they'll really go after her. You might try that angle; though God knows she certainly oughtn't to be sent."

"She does all right at Fighter Control, doesn't she?"

"They say she's a good plotter," Sergeant Levy said with reluctance. "Well, I'll get her in. I have her waiting in the Orderly Room, as a matter of fact. I thought a little waiting would do her good."

"What's her first name? I forget."

Sergeant Levy pursed her lips, turning at the door. "I got a good mind not to tell you," she said. "She *is* a little bitch; and don't forget that! Sybil, she calls herself."

With Sergeant Levy out of the room, Lieutenant Lippa stood up, tugged her girdle down, tucked her shirt in smoothly, adjusted her skirt band; and, lifting a little mirror from her desk drawer, held it in one hand while she patted her hair into place with the other. She then sat down, drew the chair straight, arranged the few things on her desk more neatly, and taking the morning report from the basket, began to look at it.

Sergeant Levy knocked almost at once. She brought in a pasty-faced girl with a thin sharp nose and blonde-colored hair showing darker at the roots. Contrary to regulations, the hair was well down on her collar, and her fingernails were covered with cracked and flaked polish in a shade certainly not inconspicuous. However, she pulled herself up and said, if sulkily:

"Ma'am; Private Buck reports to the Company Commander."

Considering Private Buck's described attitude that morning, it seemed safe to guess that reflection had intimidated her. Lieutenant Lippa said soberly: "Close the door please, Norma." She nodded at a folding metal chair and said: "Sit down, Sybil. How do you feel, now?"

Private Buck said: "All right." She paused and added, "Ma'am."

Lieutenant Lippa drew a breath. She said: "Sybil, why did you act that way this morning?"

Private Buck, looking toward the corner of the room, said: "I didn't feel well."

"When you don't feel well, you must report yourself sick. You understand that. If you don't feel bad enough to report sick, you don't feel too bad to get up. Now, you're here because Sergeant Levy tells me you refused to obey Sergeant Hogan's order. Why did you do that?"

Private Buck said: "Hogan's always picking on me."

Lieutenant Lippa said: "We are in the Army, Sybil. Sergeant Hogan has certain duties, just as you have, and just as I have. If Sergeant Hogan criticizes you, it is because she feels she has to. You've been in the Corps long enough to understand. If Hogan warns you about something, she is not picking on you. In fact, she is doing all she can to keep you out of disciplinary trouble. If you felt that you couldn't submit to discipline, you had a chance to leave without prejudice before the swearing-in last month. You decided to stay. Why was that?"

Private Buck shrugged her shoulder slightly. She looked at her hands and said: "They were saying I could go overseas. It didn't mean I wanted to stay here."

Lieutenant Lippa said: "Yes; but the conditions were explained to everyone who applied to go overseas. You are on the list, and it is quite possible you will have a chance to go. To be eligible, your record and conduct have to be excellent or better. If your disciplinary record shows a serious offense, like refusal to obey orders, you won't even be considered. Now, what am I to do?"

Private Buck said, "I don't know."

From progressive small changes in Private Buck's face it was apparent that she had not expected gentle handling. All morning her mind was doubtless oppressed by a wretchedness of apprehension, a fear that now she really had gone too far. She was in the Army, all right; and Sergeant Levy, grim and outraged, was going to tell the Army on her. Her ideas of what might happen then were probably indefinite and so all the more frightening. She would have heard stories, some true, of rugged corrections administered to men who displeased the Army. She had come cowering, prepared to have the Company Commander climb all over her. She was astonished and then emboldened by such mild tones. Warily, furtively, she took heart. Lieutenant Lippa, for all the bar on her collar, was younger than she was; and, Private Buck might believe, not so smart as she was—a college girl, probably; prissy, because she thought she was better than other people. Private Buck looked at Lieutenant Lippa with real, though still veiled, contempt. Sticks and stones would break her bones; but words, Private Buck surely knew, would never hurt her.

Seeing the sullen gaze, quickly turned away, Lieutenant Lippa drew another breath. She said: "Sybil, tell me something. For quite a while you haven't been getting on very well with the other women. And you haven't been behaving very well, have you? Are you in personal trouble of some kind? If you are, and feel you could tell me about it, I'll do anything I can to help you. Would you like me to ask Sergeant Levy to step outside?"

Private Buck said: "The only trouble I'm in is everybody reports me for everything, whether I did it or not. If you're going to believe them! A lot of little snitchers—"

Sergeant Levy said: "Look, Buck. There should have been a report on you Saturday night. There wasn't. Nobody did any snitching. Several girls spoke to Hogan and to me; but only when we promised we wouldn't report you. They asked if Hogan wouldn't speak to you. That's why she did—"

Lieutenant Lippa said: "Never mind, Norma."

"Let her go ahead," Private Buck said. "I don't care what

she says. I know she probably told you a lot of lies about Saturday night. I know who told Hogan, too. Then Hogan gets nosey—thinks she's such an angel!"

Lieutenant Lippa said: "You did have a little too much to drink that night, didn't you, Sybil?"

"I didn't; not any more than anybody else."

"That isn't what I heard," Lieutenant Lippa said.

"Yes; and I suppose you heard something else, too. Just because I was outside a few minutes—"

Sergeant Levy said: "You were outside an hour, in a car with some AA men. I won't say what you were doing; but when they got through with you, you didn't look like it was discussing our war aims. When you act in a way to bring discredit on the Corps—"

"All right, Norma," Lieutenant Lippa said. "That's nothing but hearsay. People exaggerate. But, Sybil, you know perfectly well that if you *do* drink too much and make yourself conspicuous at a place like the Roadside Rest, you *do* bring discredit on the Corps. The other women very rightly resent it. It affects them all in at least two unpleasant ways. They want to be able to go there on dates and have fun. If anybody acts up, and the Provost Marshal hears about it, that place, and even every place like it, is sure to be put off limits. Then, if a Wac misbehaves herself, the word, always exaggerated, goes around, and the men may get a wrong idea about them all. When you go outside and sit in a car and let men take liberties with you, if you did, it isn't just your business. You see, you do everyone an injury."

Private Buck tightened her lips and nodded twice. "So I do, do I?" she said.

"Yes, you do. And yourself, most of all. I don't have to tell you that. You know what men think of a girl. You know what they say. A girl simply cheapens herself—"

"Cheapens herself!"

"Yes, she does, Sybil. And you know it as well as I do. When they don't care anything about you, and you don't care anything about them—"

"Cheapens herself!" Private Buck repeated. She tossed her head. She said intensely: "You have a nerve!"

Lieutenant Lippa said: "I didn't say that to be offensive, or to hurt you. And I didn't say I believed that's what you were doing. If 'cheapens' hurts you, I'm sorry I said it."

Private Buck said: "She's sorry she said it!"

Lieutenant Lippa said: "Please don't speak that way. Why are you so rude? I'm trying to be as fair to you as I can."

Sergeant Levy said: "I wouldn't try any more, ma'am. That's the way she is all the time. I told you what she was."

Private Buck said: "And I'll tell you what you are, you dirty big Yid!"

"Buck!" Lieutenant Lippa said. "If I ever hear you—apologize to Norma! At once!"

Private Buck said: "No, I won't."

Sergeant Levy said: "I don't need any apologies from her. I consider the source. Only she might get the back of my hand all of a sudden."

Lieutenant Lippa said: "Buck, are you refusing to obey my order?"

"Oh, orders, orders, orders!" Private Buck said. "I have my duties, she says—just like Hogan; just like you have! Once in a million years about, I get off. You; every weekend you sneak down to that hotel—" Perhaps groping after some remembered rumor; perhaps only throwing out at angry random, she said vindictively: "I'm so awful, am I? What do you do, I'd like to know? Think nobody knows about you?"

All the color left Lieutenant Lippa's face. Involuntarily, she put a hand down on her desk, steadying herself. Seeing Lieutenant Lippa speechless, Private Buck, elated at her luck, burst out: "You certainly have a nerve!" In triumph, arrant and insolent, she said, "I cheapen myself, do I?" Inspiration visibly arrived. "You and that Lieutenant Turck!" she said. "I suppose you think everybody doesn't know what you two are!"

Sergeant Levy sprang up. She said: "Shut your nasty mouth, Buck!"

Lieutenant Lippa's color came back. She even laughed briefly. She said: "Norma; sit down, please." Looking soberly and directly at Private Buck, she said: "I don't suppose you really meant that, Sybil. If you did, I'll just have to assume that you're mentally unbalanced. I'll have to report to Captain Burton that you made that accusation. I'll give you a little time to think it over. You are restricted to limits. Monday, if your attitude is still the same, I will have to take action. That's all."

Sergeant Levy, who was still standing, opened the door. "Get!" she said, "before I boot you out!"

Closing the door after Private Buck, she turned and looked at Lieutenant Lippa.

"I told you!" Lieutenant Lippa said. She put her elbows on the desk and her head in her hands. "I made a mess of that! She's probably right. At least she knows I do go down there every week, while she stays out here in a barracks. I guess I have a nerve. How does she know what I do, or don't do, when I duck out? How do you know?"

Sergeant Levy said: "Now, take your face out of your hands. A bitch is a bitch is a bitch. I know all I need to know; and so does everybody else. There isn't a woman in the Detachment who doesn't wish she was in your company. That ought to be good enough for you."

"Oh, God!" Lieutenant Lippa closed her eyes and shook her head. She said, elaborately plaintive: "I don't think a woman ought to be in this business. She ought to have some kind good rich man to take care of her; and sit on a cushion and sew a fine seam, and feed upon strawberries, sugar, and cream."

"Heads up!" Sergeant Levy said, looking at her with tolerance. "When this shindig at the Base is over, don't you come back here at all. I'll handle everything. I'm going to bring your bag to Lieutenant Turck before we go, and she can take it in the taxi with her. Then when they dismiss, you go right to the Towers and get out of that monkey dress and fix yourself a good stiff drink and forget about us. I don't want you calling the Orderly Room tonight, either. If there's anything, and there won't be, I'll call you around noon tomorrow. See?"

✦

Miss Lang, Major Whitney's secretary, was pivoted about in her seat to look in a card index drawer behind her. She had crossed one leg over the other, and occupied in whatever her search was, she had not observed that her skirt needed to be pulled down.

Gently closing after him the door from the next room, Captain Duchemin smiled with benevolence at Miss Lang and expertly dropped his gaze, appreciative, to enjoy the great deal he could see of her knees and legs. He looked away with regret and said: "You want me, Bill?"

Major Whitney raised his worried eyes. He murmured, "Yes. Yes, I did. Just a minute. Sit down, will you?"

Captain Duchemin lowered his bulk placidly into a chair and took a more leisured notice of Miss Lang's legs. Major Whitney at last brought down his poised pen and signed the paper in front of him. "Look, Clarence," he said. "I hear they snafued the pigeons for you. Were you going to be able to do anything on that this afternoon?"

"I guess not," Captain Duchemin said. "Still no plane. Pettie's outside there. He's taking his mobile loft down the road to toss some birds. I was going with him; but I don't need to. I've seen a pigeon."

"Well, if you don't mind, would you do something else, then? We're in a jam. You got that Training Aids R and R, Helen?"

"I think Major Pound must have it, Major."

Major Pound, who had been scratching his head in cheerful bewilderment while he turned the sheets of a correspondence file back and forth, roused himself when he heard his name. "Huh?" he said. "Look, I don't believe this is the right one, Bill. I don't see anything at all about flexible gunnery here—"

"Got that R and R from Colonel Smith?"

455

"Yeah. I had it. Hold on. It's probably here somewhere." He began to shuffle up the papers overflowing his in-basket.

Major Whitney twisted anxiously in his chair. He said, "Anyhow, here's what it is, Clarence. The Training Literature Section, Training Aids Division, AC/AS Training, they're in New York City, are getting ready to prepare this new field manual, one-dash-twenty-six, I think it is: *Defense of Airdromes*. This Lieutenant Colonel Smith, their liaison here, was told to get all the stuff he could for them. Now, there's this thing this afternoon. I don't know why the hell he can't do it himself; but he got onto Mowbray's office, and they bucked it to Special Projects; so it ended up here. We've got to help him—"

"There!" Major Pound said. "Knew it was somewhere."

"Yes. Let's have it, Bob—"

The telephone rang. Miss Lang said: "Colonel Howden, Counter-Intelligence, Major."

"Who?" Major Whitney said. "What in God's name does he want?"

Lifting the phone again, Miss Lang said: "Major Whitney is tied up right this minute, Colonel. Could I give him a message, have him call you back?"

She listened a moment, covered the mouthpiece with her hand, and said: "He and Major Sears, the Provost Marshal, want to see you for a few minutes as soon as possible."

Major Whitney bit his lip lightly. "If he wants me to come over there, I can't for at least an hour."

"They want to come here."

"O.K. Tell him to come on. Sorry, Clarence. Well, anyway, they're having this simulated airborne attack on the field, part of the show this afternoon. The drop is by some new C-Forty-sixes they've been working with. They have them with some kind of double doors, each plane dropping two sticks of paratroopers simultaneously—"

"Mercy!" Captain Duchemin said. "In sticks, paratroopers come?"

"It says here. They want us to send an observer to make a brief report on the operation. There's a simulated defense set-

456

up, too. Would you go over and observe—I don't know what; whatever there is? I guess it's a kind of sham battle. They sent a couple of those." He pointed to some green brassards with white "O's" lying on the table. "I guess that's so nobody will shoot you. They must want you right in there."

"Ha!" Captain Duchemin said, animatedly facetious. "Hark, I hear the bugle calling! Hand me down my walking cane! No: give me my boots and saddle! No: where's my staff car?"

Major Whitney said seriously: "I would if I could; but I don't see how I can get you a car." He looked at the paper. "It's only going to be over around the new construction on the long runway at the Base. You reach it from Gate Number Three. There's a bus goes by there; and the Motor Pool says when there's a bus they aren't allowed to provide cars for anybody under the grade of field officer."

"What?" Captain Duchemin said. "A bus to the battle? That's carrying simulation and sham pretty far!" He had taken one of the green brassards, turned it around his arm, and fastened it with the safety pin. Lifting his elbow, he gazed at it admiringly. "Look," he said. "They sent four of these. They must want me to have some aides. Why doesn't Captain Hicks have to observe this, too?"

"Yeah, that car of his!" Major Pound said. "Only I'll bet he'll make you be his aide, you do that."

"Yes. Nat can observe, too; if he wants to," Major Whitney said. "Only he's got his Orlando fellow; he may be busy."

"They'll be through."

"Well, if they are; tell him I said: would he go with you. Maybe he'd like to see it. I wouldn't mind seeing it myself, but they got me stuck. Here are some people they want you to check with for your report. Better write these down. One. Captain Dobie, Post Engineer's office. He had something to do with laying out defense positions. Two. Lieutenant Anderson. He has an Aviation Engineer unit that's going to do the defending. Three. A Captain Larkin, commanding the paratroopers. He'll be jumping with them. I suppose you better get there a little early, so you can look it over. The drop will be at four-thirty."

"Four-thirty?" Captain Duchemin said archly. "Oh! You mean: one six three zero! Didn't understand you for a moment! Can do, Major!"

Major Pound, gazing at the green arm bands, said hopefully: "Maybe I could get to go on this?"

"No; I don't see how you can, Bob," Major Whitney said. "There's all that stuff we have to take to Colonel Coulthard; and I can't tell when this Howden will get here; what he wants; how long he'll take." He looked at Captain Duchemin. "Jim Edsell outside?" he said.

"He was when I came in."

"What's he doing?"

"Well, ah, he seemed to be conferring with, ah, Lieutenant Phillips, Public Relations Office."

Major Whitney frowned. "Tell Jim he's not to go anywhere, will you? I've got to have a talk with him, get a few things straight. You don't know where he went this morning, do you?"

"Not me," Captain Duchemin said. "I count only sunny hours."

"I don't blame you for that," Major Whitney said. "I wouldn't want to say anything myself. Only, I wish you and Nat would do more than just cover for him. I wish you'd make him see he's riding for a fall. I'm sorry he doesn't like me; I suppose I don't like him. But I think I can say I've tried to be as fair to him as I can. I'm not going to chew him just because he cuts out every now and then. I'm not running a stockade. But Jesus, what he gets into! Yesterday, he had everyone on his neck about that colored friend of his—Colonel Mowbray, the Air Inspector, Colonel Coulthard. They take it to General Beal; and he really may get chewed—"

Miss Lang said warningly: "Major—"

Major Whitney turned and got to his feet. "Oh. Come in, Colonel," he said. "Come in, Major. This is Major Pound, my assistant—"

Lieutenant Colonel Howden, his ungainly tall figure bent by a slight stoop, which was in fact arthritic but which gave him an aspect of grim purpose, advanced up the room. He nodded his head, without change of expression on his long cold face, dismissing Major Pound as of no importance. His light-colored, slow-moving, atrabilious eyes went briefly to Captain Duchemin, who was self-effacingly leaving by the other door. Duchemin checked on, Lieutenant Colonel Howden took a chair by Major Whitney's desk. Major Sears, following him, took the other chair.

Major Whitney said: "Close the hall door, will you, Helen? Yes, gentlemen. What can I do for you?"

Lieutenant Colonel Howden worked his jaw meditatively as if chewing, though with firmness rather than distaste, something hard and unpleasant. He looked searchingly at Major Whitney and said: "We'll see, Major. I'll let Johnny, here, tell you his story. It concerns an officer of yours, Lieutenant James Edsell." He stopped, held Major Whitney in a critical stare. "You don't seem altogether surprised, Major," he said. "Well, that's why I'm here. There are some things I want to know. Johnny tells me you gave him a good report on this Edsell earlier this week. It doesn't fit into our picture of him. We'll go into that later. Tell him about this, Johnny."

Major Sears's face and person, both of them trim and manly, Major Sears's calm manner of the alert and fit policeman, were all in contrast to Lieutenant Colonel Howden's large irregular features, his indifferently worn uniform, his air of waspish, perhaps old-womanish, menace. Major Sears said: "I'm sorry to have to trouble you about this officer again, Major. It's not the matter I mentioned the other day. I think I should say in this case, too, there aren't any charges against Lieutenant Edsell—"

"Not yet," Lieutenant Colonel Howden said. "There are grounds for charges. You'd better say why you haven't brought them, Johnny."

If Major Sears objected to this brusque supervision of his story, he gave no sign. He said: "Yes, charges could be laid, Major; technical charges, at least. We haven't brought them because I thought I'd better talk to you again. Frankly, I can't quite make this man out. Colonel Howden agrees with me in wondering if he might be a mental case. That's what we wanted to talk to you about."

Lieutenant Colonel Howden said: "In part; in part! This officer may be crazy, yes; but he also may be disaffected. That is, naturally, the angle that interests me. My office didn't come into the picture until this morning; but I put a number of people on it; and what takes shape isn't good. I've learned some things I think are significant. Now, I know he was involved with that Negro newspaper man yesterday. I've found out he's a radical writer. Of course, he never should have been commissioned! Most of those people are crazy; lots of them are, at least secretly, disaffected. Do you know that?"

Major Whitney shifted, bracing himself against the back of his chair. "I haven't seen any evidence, Colonel," he said. "If you're going to give me some, maybe I better hear the evidence; and then say what—"

Lieutenant Colonel Howden said: "You mustn't ever expect to see much evidence, Major. What's dangerous about the disaffection is that it's secret. It isn't easy to get concrete evidence of it; and we can't always wait until we have it. That would amount to leaving a man free to do all the damage he could as long as he did it with no witnesses. For my purpose, it's quite enough if a man acts in a suspicious way. Now, what I want to make clear to you is that, in my opinion, this Edsell already has acted in a suspicious way. I'm just warning you, Major. We don't fool around with disloyalty." He switched his head suddenly and nodded at Miss Lang. "I think you'd better step outside for a few minutes, young lady."

Major Whitney flushed. He said: "Miss Lang is entirely trustworthy, Colonel. I give you my assurance—"

Lieutenant Colonel Howden shook his head. "Unfortunately that won't answer," he said. "Civilian employees, and if they weren't regarded as entirely trustworthy they would not be allowed to hear or have access to certain information, have recently been repeating what they learned about confidential matters to outsiders."

He snapped his frigid, wall-eyed stare back to Miss Lang as though expecting to catch her in a start of guilt. "Now, it may

460

be necessary for me to give you information for whose security I have to hold myself responsible. You don't seem to appreciate the seriousness of what we're discussing, Major. I'll try to make it plain to you. Meanwhile, I must issue whatever orders I deem proper to safeguard the work of my office. When I issue such orders, they are to be accepted and obeyed, whether they proceed through ordinary channels or chains of command, or not. As a Section Chief, you must have been briefed on that."

Major Pound, with an air of intelligence, said: "We did have some directive, Bill, or something that had that. I might not have showed it to you."

Lieutenant Colonel Howden looked coldly and carefully at Major Pound for a moment. Then he looked back to Major Whitney. Major Whitney looked distractedly aside. With a plain bitter effort, Major Whitney said: "I suppose you know what your business is, Colonel. Hear that, Helen? The colonel says he wants you to leave."

Compressing his lips, Major Whitney forced himself to watch her while she arose, went to the door to the next room, opened it, went out, and closed it after her. By the time she was gone, Major Whitney had controlled the slight quiver of his cheeks. Lieutenant Colonel Howden said: "Go on, Johnny."

Major Sears cleared his throat. He said: "Well, this is the business this morning, Major. I've only had Lieutenant Kashkin's verbal report, so there may be some little inaccuracies, but not to affect the case." His tone changed as he became the experienced or trained witness; he went fluently into that special language that purports fact, as opposed to opinion. He said: "About the middle of the morning one of my officers, Lieutenant Kashkin, was directed by me to proceed to the vicinity of certain BOQ's assigned to the use of officers of this colored project. His orders were to observe the area and report immediately any developments that might, in his opinion, threaten possible disturbance or disorder. About an hour ago, Lieutenant Kashkin, who had parked his jeep where he could watch the BOQ area and the street leading to it, observed Lieutenant Edsell approaching. Kashkin knew Lieutenant Edsell—I mean, by sight; because he had seen him at Colonel

Mowbray's inquiry yesterday. Knowing that Edsell had been involved with the colored newspaper man, James, Lieutenant Kashkin considered it his duty to investigate. Therefore, he left the jeep, intercepted Lieutenant Edsell, and asked him please to identify himself and state his business. Kashkin was, of course, armed and wearing an MP brassard, so Lieutenant Edsell could have no doubt about Kashkin's position and authority."

Lieutenant Colonel Howden, perhaps feeling that this careful, detailed approach was a waste of time said: "Now, I'll just explain a few things to you, Major. A disciplinary difficulty with some of the Negro officers came up yesterday after Colonel Mowbray's conference, which I understand you attended. I won't go into the difficulty, if you don't know about it. It's unimportant. What is important is that information reached me this morning that indicates the existence of a dangerous subversive spirit among some of these officers, perhaps all— expressions of sympathy for our enemies; willingness to sabotage the war effort; intention to incite to mutiny. Now, we know, and you know, that yesterday your fellow, Edsell, had a leading part in introducing into a highly restricted Area what appears to have been a Negro agitator of some kind, passing as a newspaper reporter—"

Major Whitney said: "No, I don't—I can't say I do know that, Colonel. From all I heard yesterday, when Colonel Mowbray investigated it, that's what James was, a newspaper reporter. He was accredited by Washington, who certainly must have been satisfied who he was and what he represented. Edsell knew him before—"

"Yes," Lieutenant Colonel Howden said. "So I understand. That's one of the things that strike me as significant, Major. We will investigate Edsell's background thoroughly, I can promise you—" He held his hand up. "Just let me finish, if you will! I'll be ready to hear what you have to say later. Incidentally, Major, I will want to know how it happens that Lieutenant Edsell seems to have no regular duties. Never mind now! We also know, we were informed, that at approximately ten o'clock this morning Edsell went to the railroad station where he met another Negro civilian arriving from the north. I have men checking to find out who this Negro was, and where Edsell took him. He met him and took him somewhere before he turned up on his way to these Negro officers' BOQ's. Perhaps you begin to see how serious this is. Go on, Johnny."

Major Sears said: "Lieutenant Edsell showed Kashkin his AGO card, as requested; but he refused to state his business beyond saying he was looking for someone who might be in one of the BOQ's. He then questioned Lieutenant Kashkin's authority to stop him. Kashkin answered that he had the police authority to require any person in the military service to identify himself and show that he was on proper business in any part of the Area. During this exchange, Lieutenant Kashkin observed that Lieutenant Edsell behaved in a somewhat excited manner, and he did not feel he could let him proceed without a better explanation of what he planned to do."

Lieutenant Colonel Howden said: "What he planned to do isn't hard to guess. There's no reasonable doubt that he wanted to arrange somehow for some of the key men in the disaffected group to meet and talk with this new Negro civilian. We'll find he's another agitator, specially trained in the techniques of encouraging unrest, encouraging them not to quit, not to let the trouble get settled, peter out. In a way, I'm sorry your man stopped Edsell. If we'd known earlier all we know now, it might have been a good idea to leave Edsell alone until he had made his arrangements, lay this fellow by the heels, get enough for the Federal authorities to put him away for a while."

"That's an angle," Major Sears said; "but under the circumstances, Colonel, I think Kashkin did exactly right. His duty, what I put him there for, was to prevent further trouble in any way he could. That's what Colonel Ross, General Beal, wanted." Resuming his tone of testimony, he went on: "So Kashkin informed Edsell that he could not enter the BOQ area until he had checked with me, asked for instructions. Lieutenant Edsell repeated his assertion that Kashkin had no right to interfere with him; and said that if Lieutenant Kashkin wanted to prevent him from entering the BOQ area he would have to use force to do it. Lieutenant Kashkin advised him that he was prepared to use force if necessary; but he hoped Lieutenant Edsell would not make it necessary. Edsell then made a movement to brush by Lieutenant Kashkin, and Lieutenant Kashkin took his arm, restraining him. Edsell then made no further resistance or attempt to pass, telling Kashkin that he simply wanted it clear that he yielded to physical force." Major Sears smiled. "Lieutenant Kashkin said, as nearly as he could understand Lieutenant Edsell, who, though peaceable, appeared still more excited and spoke in a loud sarcastic way, that Edsell must have thought Kashkin violated regulations by touching him. Edsell did not seem to know that if it really went to extremes, if when ordered to halt he disregarded the order and went on, and if he could not have been stopped any other way—say, he was running and Lieutenant Kashkin could not catch him—Lieutenant Kashkin would have been fully warranted in drawing his side arm and shooting him down."

"Warranted, yes," Lieutenant Colonel Howden said, "but we don't like that stuff. You're liable to kill him and he's no good to us, dead—"

"Not with Kashkin," Major Sears said, "not with any officer of mine; and not with most of my men. One thing I see they can do is shoot. I don't mean just a Pistol Expert badge. With me, that's where they start. Kashkin is really good. Give him a gun; and at fifty yards he could put a slug through about any point in a man's leg he wanted. They wouldn't run much after that; and they wouldn't be killed by a mistake, either—"

Lieutenant Colonel Howden smiled faintly. "O.K., Johnny," he said. "I take it back."

Major Sears smiled too. "Excuse me, Major," he said to Major Whitney, "I couldn't let that go by." The smile faded and he said: "Well, that's about all. Oh; Lieutenant Edsell also attempted to insist that Lieutenant Kashkin arrest him. Lieutenant Kashkin said he would only arrest him if he persisted in entering the BOQ area in defiance of Kashkin's order as Deputy Provost Marshal. Edsell then made some vague remarks that Kashkin took to mean that Edsell felt the refusal to arrest him also put Kashkin in the wrong, that he had no right to restrain him by force and then not arrest him, something like that. Lieutenant Kashkin ignored these remarks; and Lieutenant Edsell then walked off, away from the BOQ area. Lieutenant Kashkin immediately returned to the jeep and reported on the radio to me."

Lieutenant Colonel Howden said to Major Whitney: "There you have it. You can judge for yourself how much sense your man makes." He worked his mouth thoughtfully. "As Johnny suggests, it may be a mental case, something for a medical board. If that's Edsell's trouble, that's all right with me. As a matter of fact, I'd much rather think it was that. I couldn't help wondering, Major, the way you reacted when I first mentioned his name, if you didn't know, hadn't known for a long time, he was pretty queer."

"No, I don't know that," Major Whitney said, frowning. "He's got a superior efficiency rating, just what I told Major Sears. I don't know whether you're suggesting I would have given Major Sears a good report on him, when I knew all the time he wasn't entitled to it. If you are, you're going to have to make that charge to Colonel Coulthard and prove it. I won't take that from you, or any man, Colonel. You seemed to be hinting awhile back that I'd done something irregular—you said you were going to ask me how it happens Lieutenant Edsell hasn't any regular duties—"

"Now, just calm down, young man," Lieutenant Colonel Howden said. "Was Edsell on duty this morning, or was he not? If he was, did his duties take him, did you give him any orders that made it necessary for him to be, where Johnny's man found him?"

Major Pound, who had been sitting staring with absorption, said: "Why, hell, no! What I told you, Bill. I was looking for Edsell all the time. He wasn't out on any project. I admit I didn't try very hard to find where he was—I didn't like to raise a fuss in there, account of that Orlando pilot and McCabe from Charts and Plans, they were in there working on Nat's job—"

Major Whitney said: "Shut up, will you, Bob? I've got enough on my hands—"

Lieutenant Colonel Howden said: "You have a lot on your hands, all right; but I think we can help you with it. That's what we're for. If you'll just stop acting as if this was a kind of contest, you on one side and us on the other, everything will be a lot simpler. I think you want to co-operate with us; but you're a little touchy. I told you we didn't fool with disloyalty, Major. When I'm dealing with it, or its possibility, I find it better to come right out and say what I have to say. Now I've said it. I'm not telling you what to do in your command. You can take any action you like; but I think you should know, and that's what I've been telling you, that, naturally, action we think is inadequate will have to be supplemented. Somebody higher up will have to act."

Major Whitney said: "What have I got to act on? I don't see any proof of disloyalty in what Major Sears says—"

"Well, we'll leave, Major," Lieutenant Colonel Howden said. He nodded several times, arising. "I think you can find something to act on. Unless you don't want to; unless you approve of your man's goings-on."

"I don't think you have any right to say that, Colonel," Major Whitney said.

Lieutenant Colonel Howden, halfway to the door with Major Sears after him, said over his shoulder: "Well, see to that, Major, see that I don't! That's all you need to do."

X

THE WAC messenger, a freckle-faced little girl, entered briskly and came to a halt. She held open the canvas carrying-satchel slung at her side, shook her head; and then placed on Miss Candee's desk the package tucked under her other arm. "That's all," she said.

"Well, what's that?" Miss Candee said belligerently.

Like most War Department civilian female employees, Miss Candee was hostile to Wacs on general principles. They

466

thought they were so patriotic, volunteering to live in barracks and wear that awful uniform; and take regular Army pay, as though the CAF rates weren't low enough! They probably imagined this made them superior to girls like Miss Candee, while as a matter of fact the only reason they went into the WAC was probably they never *had* been able to get any good job, or hold it; so they needn't think they were so much.

The Wac said: "I don't know. It's for Captain Hicks, it says."

"Well, what is it? Who sent it?"

The package, about the size and shape of a shoe box, was covered with worn, soiled wrapping paper and tied with an old piece of string. Apparently it had been through the mails, for there were stamps on it and an address had been inked out. Miss Candee switched it around disdainfully. Across the top, printed with pencil in capital letters, were the words: GIVEN TO CAPTAIN HICKS AC SOCIAL PROJECT SQUADRON AFORAD-5 AAF THANKS AGAIN FOR GET ME ON THE PLANE, CAPT. RESPECTFULLY YOURS TRULY T/5 MORTIMER MC INTYRE JUNIOR CE.

"For Heaven sakes!" Miss Candee said. "What is this? Who gave it to you, anyway?"

The Wac giggled. "I saw who brought it," she said. "It was this colored soldier. He drove up in a truck with some other colored soldiers; and he brought this in and said it was for Captain Hicks."

"Well, didn't he say what it was?"

"No. But everybody in the Message Center thinks it's *chicken*. You know, fried chicken. That's what it smells like." She giggled again.

"Well, I certainly don't want it!" Miss Candee said with distaste. "Don't give it to me. Leave it on Captain Hicks's desk, if you want."

Tilting her small chin, the Wac said: "No, I'm not allowed to. We aren't allowed to take things around *inside* any office. We just deliver it to the room, to the girl there. Sorry!" Shifting the satchel on her hip, she pranced out.

"Bitch!" said Miss Candee; but to herself only and under her breath. She got up, took the package and carried it down to Captain Hicks's desk where she deposited it beside the pad on which was scrawled boldly: *1320. Gone to eat. Back ½ hr. Gene.* Under it was neatly lettered: *Me too. MM.*

Miss Candee sighed, made a gesture to show that the heat here in the stifling early afternoon shadows was almost prostrating her, and went back to her desk. Taking up a much-handled copy of the Ocanara *Morning Sun* she looked at the photograph of General and Mrs. Beal on the front page. Then she laid it aside and picked a smoldering cigarette from the ashtray next to her typewriter. Holding the cigarette between her thumb and forefinger, she brought it to her mouth, puffed at it without enjoyment, and put it out. In an anguish of boredom, she gazed across the room at Lieutenant Pettie, who sat in the chair beside Captain Duchemin's empty desk minding his own business. From time to time, he re-examined a long scratch on his left wrist and for lack of anything better to do, picked off bits of the scab.

Miss Candee said desperately: "Lieutenant Pettie! I hope you don't mind my mentioning it; but I certainly like that Signal Corps insignia, those colored flags. I think it looks much better than the Air Corps insignia, don't you?"

The remark was not an easy one to answer; and Lieutenant Pettie's startled blank rosy face showed him at utter loss. He said indistinctly: "Oh, I suppose it's all right, if you like it." Sheepish, he smiled at her; but it was plain that he had no more to say.

Unsatisfied, Miss Candee sat brooding a moment. Then she had another idea. She looked down to the end of the room where Lieutenant Edsell, at his desk, and an officer she recognized as Lieutenant Phillips, from Public Relations, bent their heads together. Watching them, she saw that the inaudible conversation they had been carrying on was momentarily suspended. She sang out: "Oh, Lieutenant Edsell! Could I interrupt just one second? Lieutenant Edsell, are you planning to give me that report on one-point-release parachutes this afternoon? I just wanted to ask; because if I have to type all that, I'd better not start anything else, had I?"

Lieutenant Edsell looked up irritably. He said: "You know

I'm not! We have to hold it until the rest of the dope comes from Eglin Field."

Miss Candee said: "Well, then I haven't anything to do, unless Captain Hicks has something when he comes in. Gosh, I wish when it's as hot as this they'd let us off early! They did at Gravelly last summer, remember, when it wasn't half as hot. Well, anyway, we do get off an hour early, you know; because of the parade. We had a memo saying civilian employees would be allowed to attend. I think I'll go."

"I'm sure you will," Lieutenant Edsell said.

"I want to see General Beal. I think he's marvelous looking." She recovered the folded newspaper and surveyed the photograph. "Do you think Mrs. Beal is pretty? I do. I think she looks quite young."

"That's enough, Palm!" Lieutenant Edsell said. "Just quiet down, will you?" He turned back to his friend. "Gab, gab, gab!" he observed.

Lieutenant Phillips was still looking away from him. The observation, by its tone, was an indirect overture, but Lieutenant Phillips appeared to notice it no more than he noticed the considered use of Miss Candee's chatter, which was cut off only after it had continued long enough to close, put a natural period to, the previous discussion.

Lieutenant Phillips, the expression on his thin-featured face still aloof or remote, said: "Well, what it comes down to is you don't know what really happened; and you don't know what's happening now; and you don't know what's going to happen. I suppose the MP lieutenant reported you?"

Lieutenant Edsell gave him an angry look, perhaps stung as much by the accuracy as by the coolness of this summary; but the anger was not whole, as though his usual eagerness to trade blows was tempered by hidden injuries. He was coming up to scratch; but slowly, like a man not very anxious to be hit again where he had been hit, and been hurt, before. He shrugged. He said: "I don't know. He might not have. He didn't come out of that too well. He was scared. He knew he was in the wrong, and he might think twice—"

Lieutenant Phillips considered this suggestion with a derisive lift of his lip corners. He was, perhaps, considering, too, that whatever ascendancy in planning and direction he had allowed his friend to assume was all along unwarranted. He said: "How could he come out of it any better? He stopped you."

Lieutenant Edsell said: "I suppose he wouldn't have stopped *you!* They have radios in their jeeps, you know. That means, if I went on, everybody, the Provost Marshal, old Ross, that half-wit Mowbray would hear where I was before I even got there. I wouldn't have time to find Willis and talk to him. I had the MP in the wrong already; the only smart thing then was to stop. Let him stew. I just walked off and went and had lunch."

Lieutenant Phillips said: "And I suppose the only smart thing, earlier, was to leave Willis's father alone at the Hospital."

"For God's sake, Pres," Lieutenant Edsell said, "I admitted that once! I couldn't be everywhere at the same time. Of course I might have left him with you, if you'd been there."

"You know why I wasn't there. Collins had me stuck in the office."

"Yeah? Well, he"—he tipped his head toward Major Whitney's adjoining office—"thought he had me stuck; but that's where he was wrong. It was *that* son of a bitch who really fixed me." He nodded the other way toward Nathaniel Hicks's empty desk. "I suppose you'd say I might know he would. Well, I did. What I didn't know, what I couldn't know, was that old Ross would show up right then. Naturally, Hicks would make all the time with Ross he could."

Lieutenant Phillips said disdainfully: "But you don't actually know that Hicks had anything to do with it."

"The hell I don't!" Lieutenant Edsell said. "The Wac on duty there told me it was the officer I left with Willis who brought him over to Colonel Ross. And it also fits the picture. I knew he'd got himself this job from Ross to put some crap about the place here, building up General Beal, in some magazines, as he says, of national circulation. He was really throwing it around before I left the office this morning." Lieutenant Edsell warmed to something like animation. "Milt McCabe, the artist—we have him in a sergeant's suit over in Charts and Plans—came in to do some stuff for this jerk of a captain, fighter pilot from Orlando, who was helping Hicks on his project"— he nodded at the drawing board, and the plane-formation diagrams laid out on the big table by the window.

"So Hicks, fussing around, important as hell, tells McCabe he'll have General Beal assign McCabe to him to do some pictures for the articles. Then he gives out to me how he's the leading brain in the publishing world, a real literary guy, fine judge of writing—my God, did you ever read the tripe they publish? He was huffing and puffing about all he was going to do, and how he was like that"—Lieutenant Edsell held up two fingers and brought them together—"with the general and Ross and everybody. So I should have realized. The trouble at the Club came up, and he made it pretty plain he was on the side of this chivalry-of-the-South lug from Orlando; so I should have realized more."

Lieutenant Phillips said: "Well, I must say, when it was as clear as that that Hicks was against it, turning Willis over to him seems to me about as stupid as anything you could possibly do."

Lieutenant Edsell said: "Now, get this straight. Everything about this that was done, I did. You just sat around on your ass. Though I must say I'd rather have you doing that than screwing things up the way you screwed up Al James yesterday—"

"I screwed it up?"

"That's right; you. Why did you tell Mowbray's office he was colored? If you'd used your head you could have slid over it with that little rat Botwinick. The reason you're so useless for anything except talk, is that you're so goddamn naïve. Politically, you're infantile. You still believe all that crap they taught you up there at Saint Paul's, or wherever it was, and dear old Harvard."

Lieutenant Phillips's face showed the discomfited incensement of a man who sees, through grave faults in his friend, his own graver, greater fault. He has committed his self-regard by having such a friend. How can he explain or excuse his choice? Lieutenant Phillips arose with abrupt ostentatious stiffness, took his cap, and walked out the door.

Miss Candee, who had been studying the newspaper, lifted her head at once and said: "Lieutenant Edsell!"

Lieutenant Edsell took the telephone on his desk. Miss Candee poised with her lips parted while he gave a number. "Lieutenant Lippa there?" he said. "No, don't bother. Who's this; Sergeant Levy? Yes. Well, if she gets back, tell her to give me a ring right away, will you? I may not be here too much longer." He tossed the receiver carelessly into its cradle.

"Lieutenant Edsell!"

"Yes, for God's sake."

"You'll break that telephone!"

"I hope so."

"Lieutenant Edsell, did you see this story in the paper?"

"No."

"It's very interesting. It's about this man, this conscientious objector; what he said."

Lieutenant Edsell stood up, turning his back on her, and began to look at Sergeant McCabe's diagrams piled on the table, raising them one after another and tossing them down.

"Lieutenant Edsell!" said Miss Candee, "Will you please listen! I want to ask you something. Here's what he says." She peered at the paper. "He says, and I quote: 'I have insurmountable scruples against joining any fighting branch; but I expressed my willingness to go into the Medical Corps, where I might be of some useful assistance, as I am acquainted with First Aid. This has been denied me.'"

She looked hopefully, but Lieutenant Edsell, unheeding, continued to lift and lay down the big sheets of the drawings. More determinedly, raising her voice, she read: "'Though not a member of any church organization, I accept the Christian doctrine of non-resistance; and I regret so many of those who preach it do not practice it. I regard Hitler as evil; but I maintain that evil will not be overcome by more evil, that is, hate and violence; but on the contrary, by love and charity.' Close

472

quote. Lieutenant Edsell, do you think Hitler would be overcome by love? I don't."

"For God's sake," Lieutenant Edsell said, turning around. "What are you gabbing about, Palm?"

"It's this man in Tampa, what he says. He's a well-known baseball player, it says. I never heard of him. It's very interesting, I think. I'm surprised you're not a conscientious objector, Lieutenant Edsell."

"For God's sake, why?"

"Well, you're sort of against everything all the time, aren't you?"

"I'm sort of against a lot of damn foolishness all the time. Conscientious objection is a lot of damn foolishness."

"Well, I mean that's what most people think; so I'm surprised you do, too. You know—when you were talking this morning to Captain Wiley about colored people. I mean, you said everybody in the South was wrong. Don't you think a man has a right to be a conscientious objector?"

"He has a right to be anything he wants to be; if he can get away with it."

"Even if—well, here's what the man from the Selective Service Board said. And I quote: 'The protection of those rights of the individual which he enjoys and exercises when he practices non-resistance is provided by others. It is a mystery to me how he can accept those benefits, if he has so much conscience, when he is unwilling to join the men who are risking their lives to maintain them.' "

"Huh!" Lieutenant Edsell said, rousing himself. "What benefits is this sap accepting? The benefits of paying thirty-five dollars a month to be shut up in a concentration camp with a lot of other screwballs, run by some selected Christers?"

Her design at last succeeding, Miss Candee said with zest: "Well, I think the man, this spokesman for the Board, means he owes his country something, doesn't he? After all, over here, he does have benefits, like freedom, democracy, and everything. He wouldn't get them in Germany, would he?" She looked at Lieutenant Pettie, who was regarding them both with amazement. In the Signal Corps, plainly, the day's work was

473

never like this. The mute tribute, the sight of Lieutenant Pettie gawking, amazed by so recondite a colloquy, increased her happiness. She said graciously: "What do you think, Lieutenant Pettie?"

"Gosh, don't ask me," Lieutenant Pettie said.

Lieutenant Edsell said: "Don't ask anyone questions like that, Palm! There's no sense in them. What's what he would get in Germany have to do with anything? The point is: what does he get here? You've just been reading what he gets here. He gets held up publicly as a yellow bastard by some pompous jerk who crowded himself onto a draft board so he could push other people around. He gets to spend the war, and if it's like last time, several years after it, too, in a concentration camp. What's he owe his country for that? And what do you mean by his country? The state?"

"No, I mean the whole country; not just his one state."

Lieutenant Edsell allowed himself to smile. "All right," he said. "The Federal state, the thing that runs the country; the product of class antagonisms and the instrument of class domination. He owes it what? Whatever it calls itself, wherever it is—here, Russia, Germany, Japan—it's nothing but a set-up to keep in power a few people who lied and cheated their way there, and to make everybody else work for them. What he owes it is a kick in the teeth, every time he can give it one without getting himself liquidated. That's the point about your friend in the paper; by talking back to the draft board, he's simply liquidating himself. Of course, if he really believes in non-resistance, he'd be no good for constructive action anyway, so he might as well be liquidated—"

He broke off.

The door from Major Whitney's office had opened softly and quickly. Captain Duchemin, mimicking a man who ducks a blow, let himself nimbly around. He eased the door closed and set his big back against it. "Mighty near did get liquidated!" he said. "Brrrr! A real live cockatrice, this Howden colonel! Oh, no!" he said to Miss Candee. "Doesn't mean that at all! Hasn't anything to do with that! It means a fabulous monster that slays with looks. Often confused with a basilisk. Say, Loot," he said to Lieutenant Pettie, "sorry to hold you up so long. Can't go this afternoon. The major unloaded another job on me."

Miss Candee said: "Captain Duchemin! What's that on your arm?"

"I have been elevated to Combat Observer," Captain Duchemin said. "For valor. Where's Nat?"

Miss Candee said: "Captain Hicks called in, Captain Duchemin. He gave me a message for Captain Wiley; just, he'd be here by two o'clock or so. They went out to lunch, Captain Wiley and the sergeant. They ought to be back—"

"No doubt, no doubt," Captain Duchemin said. "Let them come. They come like sacrifices in their trim, and to the fire-eyed maid of smoky war—I've got to make Captain Hicks an observer, too. He's my transport officer." To Lieutenant Pettie, he said: "Want to come? I have another brassard and Captain Hicks has plenty of room."

Lieutenant Pettie had arisen. He said: "I guess I hadn't better; I told them to take the loft out. Some of them haven't had too much practice. I guess I'd better stay with them." He turned toward the door, and paused. "How about—I mean, later—will we—are we going to—"

"Ah!" Captain Duchemin said. "I was about to tell you when the major called me in. Yes, indeedy! All is arranged; and by the hand of a master. They're preparing some tasty home-cooking out there. June's coming to pick us up in her car. Pleasingly economical, isn't it? Meet you in the Oleander bar at six."

"O.K.," Lieutenant Pettie said, "I'll be there." He blushed markedly and went out in confusion.

"My Jocky is a bonny lad," Captain Duchemin said. "A dainty lad, a merry lad; a neat, sweet, pretty little lad, and just the lad for me! Old song." He let himself drop into his chair with a loud creaking, lifted his heavy legs lightly and set his feet on the desk. He gave Lieutenant Edsell a benign look, chuckling—at whatever he found winning in Lieutenant Pettie's shy little eager appetite; at himself, for the joking deftness he had probably shown in making the evening's fine

475

arrangement; and, blithely, at the sum of good things in life, at his inexhaustible oyster of a world.

Lieutenant Edsell, whose world, at least today, was not like that, returned the look moodily. He said: "What's this you're going to observe? Anything I want to see?"

"I don't know," Captain Duchemin said. "It is a parachute drop by some new troop-carrier planes. The Training Aids Division want a report on it. They are going to seize or attempt to seize the construction work at the end of the long runway."

"I guess I'll go with you," Lieutenant Edsell said. "What the hell, I can tie it in with that quick-release parachute report—" He got up and went down to the bank of file cases where he pulled out the drawer with his name on it and began to thumb over the index tabs.

Captain Duchemin said: "Well, ah—I think you'd better check with Three W's, Loot. He directed me to inform you that he wants you to stick around."

"Why?"

"I don't know. He said he wanted to see you."

Lieutenant Edsell brought back a file folder. "He can see me Monday. By that time he really might have something to see me about." He spoke scornfully, even threateningly, as though this would somehow show Major Whitney where to get off. "What's he want to see me for?"

"I don't know," Captain Duchemin repeated. He lowered his heavy-lidded, humorous eyes demurely. "Maybe he thinks you're in a rut. Maybe he wants to tell you to get out of the office more; get around; meet people; have outside interests." Lieutenant Edsell's astounded look, the incredulous gaze of utter outrage made Captain Duchemin laugh. With expansive bonhomie he said: "Yes, yes. All work and no play, you know! Now, look at me—"

"Don't think I don't!" Recovering from the stupor of outrage, Lieutenant Edsell found his tongue. With a vehement, studiously cutting disgust, he said: "I gave you a good look just a few minutes ago. It was quite a sight!" Considering, or perhaps just blindly feeling, the sum of affronts and injuries he had been offered today by the asses, apes, and dogs around him,

476

he said with elaborate hatred: "Is there anything at all you don't do to get it?"

Captain Duchemin lifted his eyelids wide, his bland eyes brightening. On his serene, full-cheeked face appeared the light of private entertainment, an alert grasp of the possibilities for fun. He assumed, however, a sober air. "Before we go into that," he said, "while we're still on your outside activities, I'd like to lodge a tiny protest of my own, Loot. I don't really enjoy being left hour after hour to fend off Three W's, and think up things you might be doing to tell Pound. I will co-operate, yes; but ask yourself: is this trip necessary?"

"I don't blame you for changing the subject," Lieutenant Edsell said contemptuously. "That was really something! You make them send the car to get you. You make them give you dinner—for God's sake!" he said, enraged. "Why don't you just put an ad in the paper, saying: 'At stud'!"

A mock expression of pain crossed Captain Duchemin's face. He uttered a delighted, deprecatory cough. "Really, such language!" he said. "Ladies are present! Miss Candee is horrified. We must elevate your mind and purify your sentiments. Yes; I will speak to you of love—"

Miss Candee stood up. She tossed her head and said: "I'm going out for a few minutes."

"No need, no need," said Captain Duchemin. "This discussion will be on a high plane. Nothing base; nothing coarse. That's what we must get him away from. Loot, abandon those crude propositionings, those callow grabbings and grapplings. Come here, Palm. Let's show him how it should be done."

"I will not!" said Miss Candee.

"Pity!" Captain Duchemin said. "One picture is worth a thousand words. Well, I'll instruct him verbally. It's simple, Loot. You, too, can be a success. Let the soul speak. Take her soft hand tenderly in yours; gaze reverently in those melting eyes (the light shouldn't be out yet); and tell her how beautiful she is! She'll do all the rest, bless her little heart!"

"Oh!" said Miss Candee with indignation. She took her bag and a towel from her desk drawer and went out into the hall.

Lieutenant Edsell said: "What do they do when you give

them that? Puke?" Captain Duchemin's massive sides were shaking quietly, though he struggled to keep his face straight. Lieutenant Edsell said: "What's so goddamn funny, you ineffable slob?"

"You, my friend, you!" Captain Duchemin said. He gave way and laughed until he cried. He wiped his eyes. "The fire begins to burn the stick; the stick begins to beat the dog!" he said. "What did they do this morning, Loot, confound your politics? You going to get square by shaking your head to hear of pleasure's name? Is it all my fault? You going to practice single strictness from now on, and make me sorry?" He gazed at him, merry and inquisitive. He said deliberately, "What's your little Wac going to say to that; or is it all her fault, too?"

"How would you like a nice poke in the teeth?" Lieutenant Edsell said. He jumped from his chair. "Go on; get up!" he said.

Captain Duchemin still reclining, laughed and laughed. "Yours in the ranks of death!" he said. "Sit down, Loot; I can't stand it!"

Lieutenant Edsell made a wild swing at him across the corner of the desk. Captain Duchemin still laughing, tipped his head away, and let it go by. Seeing Lieutenant Edsell move in to swing again, he lifted his foot adroitly, encountered Lieutenant Edsell's chest with it, and gave him a powerful light shove. Lieutenant Edsell, impelled backward, sat down hard in the middle of the floor.

"Excuse me, Loot," Captain Duchemin said, wiping his eyes again. "Slob, if you like. But big. But active. Don't forget that."

The telephone on his desk rang, and he took it up. "Captain Duchemin."

"Why, yes, ma'am," he said. "Right here."

To Lieutenant Edsell he said gravely: "For you, Loot. Lieutenant Lippa calling."

✦

The door that led into Mr. Botwinick's windowless small office from the larger room behind, where Mrs. Spann and

Miss Jelliffe had their desks, stood ajar; so Miss Jelliffe took the liberty of pushing it open wider.

"I'm back now, Botty," she said.

Miss Jelliffe's hushed, urgent tone showed that she knew something of, and shared as far as she was allowed, the great anxieties that weighed today on Colonel Mowbray, and so on those who loyally worked for him. Miss Jelliffe's tone showed, too, the zest that most people feel under their concern when they assist at exciting emergencies, not actually their own; or join in facing crises that are grave, but for somebody else. Miss Jelliffe advanced, her stout little body moving ebulliently on tiptoe, and laid on Mr. Botwinick's desk a few red-edged Immediate Action letters that she had typed before she went to lunch. "I thought you might want these," she said.

Mr. Botwinick was bending to his work in a pitch of busyness, of indefatigable industry, that he could, at need, sustain all day long. A telephone to which he was listening was propped against his ear, skillfully held there by his hunched shoulder. It could be seen that he had someone on his other telephone line, too; for he held the second instrument suspended, away a little. As he listened to the telephone against his ear he made rapid notes on a scratch pad. Every moment that he was not actually writing on the scratch pad, he scanned with dispatchful care a long report, uppermost on the heap of such papers in front of him.

Beyond Mr. Botwinick's desk a thin blond man with sergeant's stripes and glasses sat against the wall, waiting for Mr. Botwinick to get to him. In his manner there was nothing so bold as boredom or impatience; but he was ill at ease. He kept looking ostentatiously away, so that he could not be suspected of inquisitiveness about Mr. Botwinick's telephone conversation; but his eyes returned cautiously, cast down, at first only as far as the fancy wood desk sign that said: *Chief W/O F. X. Botwinick*; then, quickly to Mr. Botwinick himself. The sergeant, incredulous, wanted to see again what was perhaps the most remarkable of Mr. Botwinick's several small acquirements.

While Miss Jelliffe laid down her letters, Mr. Botwinick had been writing swiftly on the scratch pad, a pencil in his left

479

hand. He nodded Miss Jelliffe an acknowledgment. He put down, not hanging up, the second telephone, the one in his right hand, and took, instead, a pen. The pencil paused, and the pen unhesitatingly signed the paper he had been reading. Mr. Botwinick shot the pen back into its War Department inkwell holder and handed the signed paper with an explanatory twitch of his eyebrow to Miss Jelliffe. Then he took up the telephone he had put down and said to it, twisting his chin away from the other telephone, to which he was still listening: "Don't hang up. Just wait." He held it off again, suspended; and the pencil in his left hand started to write again.

Satisfied that it was really so, that Mr. Botwinick with apparent equal ease and legibility could write with either hand, the sergeant looked away again. His astonished eyes blinked behind his glasses. His ill-ease, if anything, increased. It was hard to see without heightened apprehension the marks of the common fanatic on Mr. Botwinick—the hollow cheeks; the sunk bright beady eyes; the pulled-in lips; the lank hair dampened with sweat in the cool room—borne out by this fanatic's fantastically difficult, but not actually useful or valuable, little feat.

In Mr. Botwinick's hunched brooding tension, in that astonishing habile use of his lean little hands, a disturbing, not wholly fanciful, resemblance was suggested. Mr. Botwinick was like a spider. Mr. Botwinick could be very well imagined squatting in the center of an intricate strong web strung across the whole AFORAD Area. Sensitive to every twitch on every thread; never sleeping, and though often biding his time, never tired or unready, Mr. Botwinick, many-eyed, eight-legged, could look to everything, reach everywhere like lightning.

Miss Jelliffe, receiving the signed paper, hesitated.

Mr. Botwinick said to the telephone to which he had listened so intently: "Good. Good. And he told him to drive over here? All right. Wait a minute. There may be something else." He looked at Miss Jelliffe.

"He in there?" Miss Jelliffe asked.

Mr. Botwinick said: "He went to lunch with General Nichols

at the Club. Mrs. Spann is in there watching the box. Tell her I'm going to call him now. Tell her the plane business is all right. That was Operations just talking to me. They're back."

"Who's back?"

Mr. Botwinick smiled faintly. "She'll know who," he said. "Tell her." He lowered his shoulder, releasing the phone against his ear. He said to it: "Worthington? Hang up; but don't go away, in case I have to call you back." He broke the connection with his thumb and gave a number. He said: "Have Colonel Mowbray called. This is his office. Mr. Botwinick." He started to bring up the other phone; paused; and said abruptly to the waiting sergeant: "Olmstead. Mind getting me some coffee?"

Sergeant Olmstead, starting out of his alarming reveries, jumped. Mr. Botwinick was not only to be feared. Afforded this favor, the chance to oblige Mr. Botwinick, Sergeant Olmstead could feel hope. A plain, or buck sergeant now, he would get eighteen dollars more a month if Mr. Botwinick, pleased with him, put him on an assignment that rated Staff Sergeant. "Sure thing, sir," he said eagerly.

Mr. Botwinick, a telephone in each hand, tilted back in his chair. He sent closed with his elbow the door behind him through which Miss Jelliffe had gone. He put the earpiece of the phone on which Colonel Mowbray would answer against his left ear and tilted the mouthpiece up over his head, out of his way. He raised the other phone and said: "Haight? All right. Now, Olmstead is over here. I'll be talking to him in a minute." He narrowed his eyes until they were nearly closed. His hollow face became sterner. "Now, first, what I started to say in that connection." He shook his head. "Don't ever do that again. What Olmstead might know has nothing to do with you; and what you know has nothing to do with him. What you find out, you find out for me, for the colonel. Don't tell anybody else. Don't go talking it over with your friends. You're no use to me when you do that. Now, get on with what I told you; watch for what I told you. If you see anything at all, get it to

481

me. You haven't been going good, Haight. You better get better quick."

Mr. Botwinick hung up. There was a tap on the door behind, and he said: "Yes?"

Miss Jelliffe opened the door a little. She said: "Botty, if you get the colonel, Mrs. Spann says will you tell him something?"

"If I know what, I might; but not if I don't know what." Pleased with his pleasantry, Mr. Botwinick smiled at her.

"You know what I mean!" Miss Jelliffe said, bridling. "Colonel Coulthard called on the box. He was pretty sore. He wants Colonel Mowbray to call him."

"Why is he sore?"

"Oh, he said something, as nearly as Mrs. Spann could understand it, about he was G.D. if he was going to have Counter-Intelligence, that Colonel Howden, and the Provost Marshal running his Directorate for him. I think they came over and saw some Section Chief of his without telling him; gave some orders, or something." Miss Jelliffe shrugged. "Mrs. Spann says he has brother-in-law-itis again." She smiled thoughtfully. "By command of Mrs. General Beal."

Mr. Botwinick indicated with the trace of a smile that he understood the jest; but he said primly: "We're always glad to co-operate; but Colonel Mowbray isn't going to have him running AFORAD for us, either."

"Okey-doke," Miss Jelliffe said. She closed the door. Immediately, the hall door opened and Sergeant Olmstead came in. He said: "No sugar in it, sir. I remembered you don't like any."

"Thanks," said Mr. Botwinick. "Now, sit down."

He took the lid off the container, and though it was very hot, steaming, indifferently swallowed the coffee. He wiped his mouth on the back of his hand and drew a breath. He said distantly: "Haight called me. He says he told you some things to tell me. Is Haight getting to be a special buddy of yours, or something?"

"We go around some, sir," Sergeant Olmstead said with alarm, sensitive to the tone.

"That's up to you. That's entirely up to you," Mr. Botwinick said, looking off to the corner of the room. "Haight hasn't been on the ball about this particular thing. I don't think he's been trying; and furthermore, I happen to know he talks too much. He was telling some people a lot of things they didn't need to know at the Non-Coms' Club the other night. You tell him things?"

"I never told him anything he didn't know, sir. I—"

"Never tell him anything at all," Mr. Botwinick said. "I get tired saying this over and over. Never talk to anyone. Never write anything down. Never give anything on the telephone, unless I particularly tell you to."

He brooded a moment on Sergeant Olmstead. He said: "There are people around who can tell me when somebody is shooting his face off. Don't forget it. Things I want reported are things Colonel Mowbray needs to know; but very often the whole point is for him to know without everybody knowing he knows; see? You got to use your head. Somebody shooting his face off could make us unnecessary trouble; and anybody who makes trouble won't have stripes long. Understand?"

"Yes, sir," Sergeant Olmstead said, appalled.

"All right. Remember it. What about this business?"

Sergeant Olmstead cleared his throat. "Well, sir," he said, "as soon as you called me, I kept an eye out, of course. So pretty soon, about eleven hundred, Lieutenant Willis comes in, with this colored civilian, old man. Somebody said, his father."

Mr. Botwinick said sharply: "How did you tell it was Willis? You'd never seen him before."

"Well, I saw they came in this Hospital staff car, sir; and the officer, his face was pretty well banged up. He had a small, kind of like a bandage on his lip. But I made sure. When he came in, I went up to him and told him I was Charge of Quarters, and was he Lieutenant Willis, because I would show him his room."

"All right," Mr. Botwinick said. "Be sure you never guess about who a person is. What then?"

"Well, sir, the word was kind of passed around. Haight said over in the other building somebody was yelling upstairs that Willis was there. Quite a few came over. I think Willis himself told somebody to tell the arrested officers he wanted to see them all right away. So they came down to the recreation room, my recreation room. It wasn't like a regular meeting exactly; but I could hear Willis giving them quite a long speech."

"What did he say?"

Sergeant Olmstead said reluctantly: "I couldn't hear that too well, sir. You said never let them see I was listening, so I have to be careful. They had the door closed at the end of the hall. So I took some towels and went up to the rooms at the end so I could be checking the linen; and I could hear this speech or something. Some of them answered; there might have been some argument; but I don't think much. I think he asked them to do something, agree to something; said, would they agree? They all talked pretty low. But I figured this, sir." He looked hopefully at Mr. Botwinick. "If they have any real serious argument, those jigaboos would be shouting and yelling; they wouldn't talk low."

"You mean you don't know what it was about, then?"

"No, sir! I'm pretty sure I do know, sir. I didn't, I couldn't, get it right then, listening to the meeting. But I did, a little later, sir. When they broke up in there, Lieutenant Willis came out and went down to this room where this colored civilian, supposed to be his father, was. I walked down the hall in a minute and heard him, his father, asking him what he was doing. And Lieutenant Willis said he was just talking to them about some trouble they were in while he was in the Hospital. He says, the old man: 'You better be the boss now.' And he says, the Lieutenant, he does not think they will do it again."

"That all?"

"No, sir," Sergeant Olmstead said anxiously. "Another thing I heard; I heard two others talking, one was one confined to quarters, Lieutenant Carter; one was another one. In the wash-room. You can hear pretty good anything in there because of the ventilators. Lieutenant Carter was saying it was all right; they would be released from arrest. Then the other one says, kind of making fun of him: 'They send you invitation pleasure of your company at that Club, too, I guess.' Carter says that was all right. They agreed to skip that for now, until they were in a better position. Here, they weren't in such a good position. They got to get activated as a bomb group first. 'Yeah,' says the other, 'and if the group don't get activated, Willis don't get major.' Then they said some other things—"

"What other things?" Mr. Botwinick said. "Don't leave something out you might think wasn't important, you didn't understand, unless it was about some entirely different thing. And tell me what they say in their words, not yours. I want to hear, when you can remember, just what they said; not, about what they said."

"Yes, sir," Sergeant Olmstead said. "Well, Lieutenant Carter was getting kind of mad, I thought. He says he's perfectly willing; Lieutenant Willis can get major, colonel, anything he wanted; because with him the group would get activated. Then, they all get overseas to a combat theater, they're all trained, they have all this expensive equipment; then somebody tries any Jim Crow stuff, they just don't fly, no matter whether Willis or anybody orders them to; because then they got a good position." He paused, straining in concentration. "The other one says just: 'I hear you talking!' So Carter says: 'Yeah, that's for you all right, talking. You're the big authority there. So where were you at the Club? I didn't chance to observe you. It wasn't just talking then; or writing something for Mr. Charley on the wall, be sure nobody see you.' He said then: 'Some of you no-goods had of come out, we might have gone some place. We did, six of us, all we ever said we'd do; you did nothing, seventy, eighty of you. So shut that big mouth,' he said. 'Why would we do any more, maybe take a court martial, maybe get in prison, for your kind? You don't have any head,' he said. 'You all just had your necks grow up and hair-over. You think—"

Mr. Botwinick had peremptorily raised his hand for silence. His voice alert, alacritous, he said to the telephone: "Botty, sir. That plane is back. So is Colonel Carricker's plane. I have most of the information, sir—" He reached out and turned over the leaves of the scratch pad. "I got through to the Chechoter Range Tower and was able to contact the Range Officer, Lieutenant Wierum. They were not aware of who it was at first; but they found out because he inquired about putting down at the Demonstration Area strip. He did not do that, however. They observed what was Colonel Carricker's P-Thirty-eight approaching right about then. It came up on his wing and flew formation with him for a while. Lieutenant Wierum reports they were talking on Channel A; but he just heard the Thirty-eight make contact. He did not listen. He was then contacted and told not to bother calling Demonstration Area Headquarters about landing. The two planes then headed south together. That is all he knows."

Colonel Mowbray said guardedly: "You don't know, was he mad? I mean, about Benny being supposed to be grounded?"

"Well, not positively, sir," Mr. Botwinick said with a scrupulous air. "However, I directed Worthington to be outside Operations when they landed. He observed them closely, and reports that as soon as Colonel Carricker was down, following the other, he came right over. Someone was ordered to get La Barre, the Armaments Chief. They all spent quite a few minutes looking at the guns, examining the blast tubes, having the magazines opened. He then said something to Colonel Carricker, who climbed into the Forty-seven, fired up, and informed the Tower he was going out a while—"

"Fine! Fine. Did he have his car?"

"Yes, sir. It was by Operations. He went over and waited several minutes there, watching Colonel Carricker's take-off. He then directed the driver to proceed here. I requested Mrs. Pellerino to let us know when he arrived. It ought to be any minute now, sir."

"Yes. The minute she does, call me here. General Nichols is talking to some people. I won't break it up until I know he's back in his office. Any idea where Colonel Ross is?"

"Yes, sir. I ascertained that he was downtown. I contacted his car. He is probably now on his way out. I could probably get through."

"Yes. Tell Norm. Tell him where I am. Tell him I suggest he might check right away on, you know, who will be at Retreat. Mrs. Beal told?"

"I called down there, sir; but could not get any answer. However, she was informed that Colonel Carricker was going up to the range. I know where Mrs. Beal probably is; but I did not want to call her there unless you thought it advisable. She was going to a hairdresser with Mrs. Ross."

"Yes. Let that wait. Better, if the general called her. Anyone try to get me?"

"Colonel Coulthard, sir. Colonel Howden has been over there, investigating that lieutenant you know of. Colonel Coulthard expressed some irritation to Mrs. Spann. I did not think it was necessary for him to reach you."

"No. No. Keep him off. About that other, Botty. I don't suppose you've been able to get anything yet—the reaction, there, I mean."

Mr. Botwinick smiled quietly at the corner of the room. "Yes, sir," he said. "I have all the information. It is satisfactory, I am glad to say. I don't see anything immediate to worry about there."

"They took it O.K.?"

"My information indicates that, sir."

"Be all right, you think?"

Mr. Botwinick's eyes brightened. "In my opinion, yes, sir. I judge it to be under control." With modest assurance he added: "In both matters, sir, I consider we are out of the woods."

XI

When Colonel Ross turned the corner of the hall approaching his office with Captain Collins, Sergeant Brooks, who had seen the car come up and park, was waiting at the hall door to intercept him. Sergeant Brooks had in one hand a half-smoked cigar, and in the other a copy of orders. He held the orders out to Captain Collins and said: "These are yours, sir. I marked the paragraph. Judge, we got a delegation in there. I tried to get the car again—but I guess you were talking to somebody."

"Botwinick was talking to me," Colonel Ross said. "What do you mean, delegation?"

"It's Colonel Coulthard and some officers of his. I told them you were on the way, ought to be here in a minute; so they waited. It's something about Colonel Howden messing around over there. Colonel C. is sore as a pup. He tried to reach Colonel Mowbray and couldn't. He has a major, one of his Section Chiefs, with him, and what I think is Captain Hicks, the magazine fellow you had on the general's job; and our old friend Lieutenant Edsell. I tried to get a line on exactly what was biting the colonel; but he just said he was goddamn tired of all this; and that you knew all about it, he was talking to you the other night; and he'd tell you, not me; and he'd stay here until he saw you."

Colonel Ross said: "I must see General Beal before I see anybody else." He looked with faint humor at Captain Collins. "You're the goat." He said, "Go in and tell the colonel that I'm over at the general's; and that you've been appointed my executive. See if you can get him to tell you what he wants. If he has all those people with him, it's very likely about Lieutenant Edsell and the thing this morning. Colonel Howden may have been checking up. You probably know; Howden doesn't have to go through channels unless he wants to. Smooth him down if you can. He might be willing to have them all make statements. If that would hold him, get Mrs. Elliot in. She is good." Colonel Ross turned in the door and went back into the hall.

Sergeant Brooks said: "They're in the judge's office, there, Captain. Know Colonel Coulthard?"

"Not too well," Captain Collins said. "I saw him at a meeting Colonel Mowbray had the other day."

"Regular Army. Old Air Corps," Sergeant Brooks said. Captain Collins, regarding him attentively through his glasses a moment, let his eyes drop toward the mimeographed orders in his hand. They were orders that Sergeant Brooks, the experienced factotum, might be in two minds about; and Captain Collins said: "What's the best line with him?"

Sergeant Brooks said: "I think he's gone off half-cocked, Captain. I think the lieutenant's in more trouble. I know he was in some yesterday—you know about that, I guess. Colonel Coulthard probably figures the judge was running that, so— I'd tell him the judge had to go to General Beal; but he sent you right in because he knew it must be important. Whatever it is, you'll find Colonel Coulthard hasn't got it straight. Better arrive out of breath. They've been waiting ten minutes."

"Thanks," Captain Collins said. "Here it is, then."

"If I hear a big bang," Sergeant Brooks said amiably, "I'll be in to get the body." He put the cigar back in his mouth and sat down, apparently contented enough, to go on looking at a copy of *Air Force* laid out on the table.

Captain Collins opened the door to Colonel Ross's office.

Colonel Coulthard was sitting in the best chair, the one to the right of Colonel Ross's empty desk. He cocked his curly white head in a petulant way. There was even petulance in the way one leg was crossed, thrown over the other. The lifted foot, in a neat strap and buckle shoe, twisted impatiently in quick circles. His eyes came over, and he gave Captain Collins a surprised stare. It was plain that he had long done that officer's duty of permanently attaching names to faces, so that in a whole Group he would call every one of his men right. Colonel Coulthard, hardly hesitating, said: "What do you want, Collins? Colonel Ross isn't here, if you're looking for him."

"I'm working for Colonel Ross now, sir," Captain Collins said. "The colonel is with General Beal; and he is afraid he may be quite awhile getting away."

"I thought the sergeant said he was going to be here in a minute, he was coming here. I have to see him."

"Yes, sir. He was. Colonel Ross was on his way here when Mr. Botwinick called his car. So he told me to see you right away."

"Well, what can you do?"

"I don't know, Colonel; but Colonel Ross told me to get in here and do anything I could."

Colonel Coulthard threw his hands up irritably. Pouting, he said: "I thought you were in Public Relations." It was plain that he liked things to be the way he thought they were.

Captain Collins raised the copy of the orders that he held. He said: "I really still am, sir, until Monday. Colonel Ross arranged it this morning; but I just this minute got my orders."

Colonel Coulthard said: "Let me see those orders, will you, Collins?"

Surprised, Captain Collins proffered them.

Surprised, too, since he probably spoke with no idea but to counter an uncertainty of mind by making a show of authority, Colonel Coulthard said curtly: "Thank you!"

Holding now the mimeographed Special Order, some thirty paragraphs covering three pages, Colonel Coulthard was obliged to go through the motions of reading it. He doggedly began, skipping with a frown from paragraph to paragraph:

3. Each of the following O is granted lv of absence for the number of days indicated, effective on or about . . . 6. So much of par 14 SO 101 this Hq 1 Sept 1943 as relates to Capt Charles C. Robinson 0491550 AC . . . 9. Pursuant to authority contained in par 1 a (3) AR 20-5 . . . 14. The following O have rptd at this Hq in compliance with . . . 22. The following EW WAC unasgd having rptd . . .

Colonel Coulthard was a few minutes in reaching and reading the marked paragraph on the third page: *27. Capt Richard P. Collins 0301376 AC is reld from dy Public Relations Office this Hq and asgd to dy Office of the Air Inspector . . .*

During the pause Captain Collins had time to look at the others present. Major Whitney perched uncomfortably on the edge of the small desk in the corner, where he aimlessly straightened and restraightened the desk sign which said: *S/Sgt Brooks*. He met Captain Collins's glance with a worried grimace of recognition, a turn of eye that seemed to deplore this situation, or doubt its utility.

On the first of two hard chairs against the wall across the room sat Captain Hicks. He stared absently out the windows, through the downpour of afternoon sun on the road, to the long, green-tinted, concrete-block mass of the Library and Files building, heat-struck, inadequately shaded in its meager pine grove. Captain Collins looked at him with interest, for he knew who Hicks was. Like many newspaper men, Captain Collins from time to time wondered if work on a magazine would not be easier, more interesting, and more lucrative than the daily grind in the city room. Captain Hicks reflectively rubbing the short hairs of his cropped blond mustache with his forefinger, now noticed Captain Collins's glance, and nodded civilly enough.

Captain Collins then looked at Pres Phillips's friend, Edsell, who occupied the second hard chair. Lieutenant Edsell stared absently, too; but at nothing, his eyes dark and baleful. The morose absorption left his face exposed in vacancy. For the moment, untended, Lieutenant Edsell's face relaxed, not to blankness, but to its cast of wont. Like an empty glove, it kept the shape of the hand that used it. Left to itself, it still expressed those mixed, sometimes antagonistic sentiments which it was most often called on to express—suspicion mingled with contempt; derision never wholly free of resentment; impulsiveness hampered by calculation; vanity unsettled by doubt.

Left to itself, not roused to fight, not exercised with scheming, Lieutenant Edsell's face expressed also despondency and defeat. While he brooded, faraway, he acknowledged some considerable reverse he must have suffered in his long standing quarrel with the state of things, some new disappointment added to that sum of disappointments whose galling recurrence was no doubt his real casus belli. It was the face of the unresigned man of sorrows, angrily acquainted with grief—the well-known sorehead.

Colonel Coulthard, official seal and the Adjutant General's signature closely examined, at last said; "Well!" He handed the orders back to Captain Collins. He said: "Thank you, Captain. That's that, I guess." Bluffly, but by indirection apologetic, seeking to establish again his momentarily slipping status of gentlemanlike senior officer—strict and firm; but fair and a good fellow, he said: "If they have all these people they can transfer around, they ought to give us some! We need them more than anybody else."

He cleared his throat and smoothed his curly white hair. "Well, now, Collins, I don't know what you can do. What I came here to find out, is what's going on—that's all. Do you know? If you can tell me, go ahead. I suppose you must know something about it. You were there yesterday. You know about that business."

Captain Collins said: "Yes, sir. I know about that. Colonel

Ross, who was present, told me about Lieutenant Willis getting hurt. I know Lieutenant Willis's father came down this morning. In fact, I was sent to meet him—" he could not quite keep from looking toward Lieutenant Edsell. Lieutenant Edsell had roused himself, though listlessly. It occurred to Captain Collins, and the idea surprised him, that Lieutenant Edsell was, as well as desponding, frightened; he did not want any more trouble.

"Well, yes, yes," Colonel Coulthard said. "Now, answer me this, if you can. Did Colonel Ross tell Colonel Howden to go talk to Bill, here?"

"I'm quite sure he didn't, sir."

"Howden's acting on his own, then! I'm not saying he hasn't a right to act as he sees fit. He has. Now, I don't know what he"—he twitched his head indignantly toward Lieutenant Edsell as though he disliked even to name him—"has been up to this time. He says: nothing. That's as it may be." Colonel Coulthard's face showed that he doubted, and doubted with annoyance, whether the queer duck there could even understand the terrible query put on him as an officer by the flat public declaration of his colonel that what he said might or might not be so. "Colonel Howden may have information I haven't. He may have reason to act as he is acting. But he has no business to threaten, make imputations about, one of my senior officers who couldn't possibly be involved, no matter what it is. If he's dissatisfied with that officer's official conduct, as a matter of common courtesy if nothing else, he ought to come to me and tell me so, and why. I've been offered no explanation at all. And I don't like it."

"I see, sir," Captain Collins said. "You would like Colonel Ross to find out what Colonel Howden—"

"Just tell Norm I think Colonel Howden owes me an explanation. I'm not going to Howden for it; but I want it; and I'll get it, if I have to carry the whole thing to General Beal. Look at the time we're wasting! I have work. Whitney has work. Hicks, here, is supposed to be doing something right now. We want to know whether he"—again, he indicated Lieutenant Edsell shortly with a jerk of the head—"is facing charges.

He has work to do, too. What are you supposed to be doing now, Hicks?"

Amazed, as he well might be, by the sudden demand, Captain Hicks started. "You mean, sir—" he said. "Well, I have this officer from Orlando, who has to fly back there this afternoon. I was going to help him get off; I mean, take him over to the Base; he's about ready to leave. Major Whitney wanted me to go out with Captain Duchemin to observe an operation for the Training Aids Division—"

"Training Aids Division?" Colonel Coulthard said. "What have we got to do with that? Anyway, I thought you were working for General Beal. I thought he sent you somewhere. That's why I didn't understand how you got in on this. Bill says you told him you were at the Hospital with this colored man, and Colonel Ross had you bring him in to see this boy get a medal from General Nichols—" in a gesture eloquent of utter confusion, Colonel Coulthard lifted one hand and slapped the back of his white head. "By God!" he said, "I want this straightened out! I want to know who's doing what, and why."

Captain Collins said: "Colonel, could we do this? Could we get it down in the form of statements? Then, if Colonel Ross is held up, you won't be—"

Colonel Coulthard said: "The only statement I can make is, Howden better have some good reason for—get a statement from Howden if you want statements, not from me."

"I meant, from these other officers, sir. Perhaps Major Whitney could summarize what was said to him by Colonel Howden. Perhaps Lieutenant Edsell—"

Lieutenant Edsell said: "I told Colonel Coulthard all I know. I'm sorry he doesn't find it satisfactory. I have nothing further to say."

Captain Collins said: "Well, sir, may *I* see if I have it straight? May I ask you some questions, sir?"

"I don't see what good it will do, Captain. I just told you I don't know. If I could tell you, I *would* know. What do you want to ask?"

"I'd like to ask first, sir, if I'm right in understanding that Colonel Howden, of Counter-Intelligence, sometime today came to Major Whitney and made certain representations about Lieutenant Edsell to him?"

"Well, tell him, Bill," Colonel Coulthard said to Major Whitney.

Major Whitney said: "Yes, he did, Captain. It was about an hour ago, longer now, I guess. After lunch. Lieutenant Edsell was stopped by an officer of Major Sears's, the Provost Marshal. Colonel Howden seemed to think that Lieutenant Edsell was, or might be, engaged in subversive activities. He didn't say exactly what—"

"See what I mean?" Colonel Coulthard said. "If he knows anything, let him say it. Not beat around the bush! Not imply Bill was to blame for where his officer was, where he was going."

"Yes, sir," Captain Collins said.

Up the road outside the windows a sound of gasoline engines had been growing slowly louder. Sedately, at about ten miles an hour, a command-reconnaissance truck passed. It was succeeded by the neatly spaced carriers of a motorized heavy weapons company—an 81-mm mortar platoon, three machine gun platoons; the trucks spic and span, the personnel, though in battle dress and surely sweating under the steel helmets, sitting at attention—somebody must have decided it would be just as well to look good while they went by this side of Headquarters quadrangle. They would be on their way over to the Base for the parade.

Reminded that it was getting late, Captain Collins said: "One other thing I didn't get, Major, was where Lieutenant Edsell was going—why the Provost Marshal's man stopped him."

Major Whitney said uncomfortably to Lieutenant Edsell: "Well, you were going to that project area, weren't you?"

Colonel Coulthard said: "Speak up, Edsell! You must know what you thought you were doing. Nobody else does."

The tone, so unmistakably that of testy impotence, baffled Captain Collins. One look at Colonel Coulthard showed that this angry, vain floundering was far removed from his nature and habit. Restraining influences, to which he submitted with

494

the worst possible grace, were laid on him. Captain Collins, blinking through his glasses, looked away.

Much more mildly than Captain Collins expected, Lieutenant Edsell said: "I was merely trying to find Mr. Willis, the father of Lieutenant Willis. I left him talking to Captain Hicks at the Hospital while I went to get the Post Surgeon's permission for him to see his son." Lieutenant Edsell's manner had a studied reasonableness which seemed in its way as unnatural as Colonel Coulthard's sulky complaining to and about a man, in the order of things, his to command. Lieutenant Edsell, intent only on what he was saying, into which he now put a suggestion of injured innocence, said: "They held me up some time, and I couldn't get to see the major—Major McCreery. When I came back to Mr. Willis, he wasn't there. I learned that Captain Hicks had turned him over to Colonel Ross. I don't know why—"

Captain Hicks said: "That isn't quite right." He looked at Lieutenant Edsell with annoyance. "Colonel Ross came in. He saw Mr. Willis, who was sitting near me. He motioned to me, and asked me who Mr. Willis was. He then said to get him, and come along. He took us both down to a conference room where General, I believe, Nichols, of the Air Staff, gave Lieutenant Willis the Distinguished Flying Cross. I was there, but I had nothing to do with any of it."

Outside a new noise of heavy vehicles had been slowly approaching. It proved to be a motorized anti-tank company, the carriers trailing the towed guns. While Captain Hicks spoke, Lieutenant Edsell, paying him no attention, watched the guns pass.

When Captain Hicks stopped speaking, Lieutenant Edsell went on: "I didn't, myself, see where Mr. Willis went, or whether anyone went with him. All I knew was what the Wac on duty told me." He looked at Captain Collins with an apparent appeal for understanding. "You may remember that the colonel"—in his turn, but with restraint, he indicated Colonel Coulthard by a movement of his head—"and Colonel

Mowbray were making quite a thing of it yesterday about a civilian wandering around without an escort. I'd brought Mr. Willis in. Unless I wanted another eating-out, I supposed I'd better make sure he did have an escort. I knew they discharged Lieutenant Willis at the Hospital. I thought the most likely place for Mr. Willis to go would be over to his son's quarters. So I went there. Or tried to. That's what I was doing when the MP lieutenant took it on himself to stop me."

"Well, why didn't you say that in the first place?" Colonel Coulthard said. "You had no business to be escorting him; but if you were, it was certainly your responsibility—why didn't you just say so?"

Lieutenant Edsell said: "I didn't say so because you didn't give me a chance. You simply came in, if you recall, and told me and Captain Hicks to come with you and Major Whitney and see the Air Inspector. Major Whitney hadn't asked me anything except whether it was true that the MP lieutenant had stopped me. He didn't seem to feel any interest in anything else. I suppose he was excited. He acted that way."

Captain Collins coughed. "Lieutenant," he said, "could you say anything about what the colonel just mentioned—how you came to be escorting Mr. Willis? I think Colonel Ross will want to know about that."

"Certainly!" Lieutenant Edsell said. "I knew he was coming down. Mr. James, the man Colonel Mowbray had run-off yesterday, knew about it. I knew that unless Mr. Willis had an officer with him, he might be all day getting onto the Base and finding where his son was. I was simply acting—"

Colonel Coulthard, apparently no longer able to contain himself, said: "You were simply acting like a damn fool! And I'll tell you this. You'd better see a lot less of your colored friends from now on. Don't think I'm accepting these explanations you make. Your conduct is highly unsatisfactory; and don't think you're in the clear. You're not, by a long shot! You never should have been given a commission—"

With dignity, quite steadily, Lieutenant Edsell said: "I was not given a commission, sir. I earned it at OCS. I think Major Whitney will say I have performed my duties. I don't think

I've disobeyed any orders, or acted contrary to any regulations. I know you can say anything to me you want; and I'm sorry I interrupted you; but I felt that I was entitled to resent that. I will not interrupt again."

Colonel Coulthard, coloring deeply, opened his mouth as though for air, and then closed it, and then again opened it.

From the road outside came now, ringing clearer and clearer, a count of cadence, and the audible measured scuff of marching feet. Colonel Coulthard involuntarily turned his head, for the key and timber of the counting voice, unsuited to this use, startled the ear. It was brisk, and carefully brusque; but soprano, just the same.

Up the baking asphalt, stiff, straight and neat-footed, came a WAC lieutenant; and after her, precisely posted, the guidon bearer, the platoon sergeants, the guides, and, in column of double platoons so they marched eight abreast, a WAC company in quite creditable array—all stiffly eyes-front; all determinedly stretching themselves with a quick snap of skirts to a thirty-inch stride. They were, it could be presumed, on their way to some point where they would take busses to the Base.

Colonel Coulthard, his mouth still open, gaped out at the marching files while the shrill female yelp continued snappily: "Hut, two, three—" Dazed, almost shaken, Colonel Coulthard could be seen considering this further sample of that heteromorphic and fantastical Army of the United States in which, after so many years of military service, he now found himself helplessly incorporated.

Recovering, closing his mouth, Colonel Coulthard swallowed and stood up. He gave Lieutenant Edsell a haggard look. "I haven't anything more to say to you," he said. "We can't spend the whole afternoon here! Get back to your jobs!"

✦

Observing Colonel Ross at the door, General Beal said: "Come on in, Judge! Take a look at this."

General Beal sat at his desk, surrounded by what appeared to be a throng of women—Mrs. Pellerino; Sergeant O'Mara; Miss Jelliffe and Mrs. Spann from Colonel Mowbray's office. They hovered eagerly over a shining, impressive-looking machine that had been wheeled up beside the general's chair.

"You never saw such a gadget!" General Beal said to Colonel Ross. "It came while I was out. You dictate to it; or it dictates to you; I don't know which." Frowning with interest he began to manipulate controls. A light flashed on; small gleaming parts began to shift and revolve; and from somewhere inside, General Beal's own voice burst like thunder. It roared: "But how does it work?"

"My God!" General Beal said, covering his ears.

"It turns down, sir!" Mrs. Pellerino said. "There! Set it back; start it again, Eileen—"

A low humming followed; but nothing else; and all the women exchanged glances of consternation. Mrs. Spann said: "I don't believe—"

The machine interrupted her, using Mrs. Pellerino's voice: "It's going now, sir. You see; you don't have to bother to speak right into it. It picks up just about everything. I think that's too slow. Eileen, twist that there, by you—"

General Beal's voice cut in: "Hey! Wait a minute, Eileen! Let's see that hand! What's that?"

The machine emitted the women's clamor of recorded cries and laughter. Hearing it, they immediately joined in with a fresh clamor. "Why, it got it all!" Miss Jelliffe cried. "It got it all!"

Mrs. Pellerino said: "It just gets everything—"

General Beal's voice continued: "No, no! No, you don't! Give it here! Let me look—"

Sergeant O'Mara's voice, fumbling in confusion, wailed: "Oh, sir; I meant to take that off—"

With merry excitement, Mrs. Pellerino's voice said: "She just got it! Isn't it lovely?"

"She think she's getting married? I'll see about that! I'm her commanding officer; she can't marry without my permission. Get me that regulation—"

"She can get engaged! She only got engaged—"

"You mean, now she's taken him for a diamond, she isn't going to come through? Who is this guy, anyway? He in the Army? Well, he's going to be transferred to Greenland tomorrow. I never said she could get engaged. I need her. I'll get some good out of this gadget—"

"What goes on here?" Colonel Ross said. "Is it a gag?"

"Oh, no, sir," Mrs. Pellerino said. "You see, it's playing back." Her pale face radiant, she seized Sergeant O'Mara's left wrist and drew the hand toward Colonel Ross. On the third finger was a ring with a small diamond.

"Well, well!" Colonel Ross said.

The machine cleared its throat and pronounced with gruff severity: "Subject: Disciplinary Action. To: Technical Sergeant Eileen O'Mara, WAC. One. Investigation has indicated that on or about four September nineteen forty-three you acted without authorization in becoming engaged to be married. Two. You are hereby reprimanded for conduct to the prejudice of good order and discipline; and directed to get disengaged. Three. In the event of indication that proper remedial measures have not been taken, necessary action will be initiated to secure compliance—"

The recorded voice was overlaid by the recorded squeals of protest and shrieks of delight. General Beal reached out and stopped the revolving parts. "How's that, Judge?" he said.

"Admirable!" Colonel Ross said, looking from General Beal to the machine. In his amazement, he doubted if he concealed his irony. He had not, he meant to say, been prepared to find so much fun and frolic here. He said: "A very useful device."

General Beal's face showed a generous color of amusement. "All right, ladies," he said. "You are now excused. Get! I want to talk to the judge. Oh, Eileen; any of your folks going to be able to get down for this?"

Sergeant O'Mara said: "It's quite a way, sir. My sister might, I think."

"No one else? You want me to give you away?"

"Oh, sir—"

"O.K. Tell the chaplain to see me. What do you want for a wedding present? A one-night pass?"

"Oh, sir—"

"Not enough?"

Rapt with happy embarrassment, Sergeant O'Mara said: "No, sir. Not nearly."

General Beal laughed. "Must be a good-looking young fellow!" he said. "I'll talk to his CO. We'll see what we can do. If you locate quarters, we might even let you live off the Area. Only, I wouldn't want you coming in here with circles under your eyes every morning."

"Oh, sir—"

"Oh, sir—" General Beal mimicked, grinning. "Beat it! Tell the chaplain."

When the door closed, General Beal said to Colonel Ross: "Eileen's a good kid; but I never thought she'd catch anyone. We'll give her a real wedding." He took up a slip of paper. "This is the fellow's name. Sergeant in Bombardment Analysis. Would you put through on him, Judge? We might as well make sure he hasn't a few other wives somewhere."

Colonel Ross took the slip of paper. "General," he said, "when you—"

General Beal had turned quickly to the papers laid on his desk. With great neatness, Mrs. Pellerino so arranged them, one above another, that the heading of each was uncovered and he could see without delay what they were. "Want a lawn mower, Judge?" he said. "Specially developed for air fields by the Repairs and Utilities Branch of the Office of the Chief of Engineers. Hitch it to a weapons carrier. Hm! Comes in nine sections, cutting a swath twenty-one feet wide—mow forty acres an hour—"

Colonel Ross said: "Bus, when you go off, would you have the kindness to tell Pop or me where you go off to? And how about flying cross-country alone? Were we discussing a directive the other day?"

"I didn't fly back alone, anyway," General Beal said. He went on, as though absorbed, leafing over the papers.

"That, I heard, too," Colonel Ross said. "I had the impression that Colonel Carricker was grounded."

"So did I," General Beal said. He looked up and grinned. "The gall of that guy! The Range Tower called me to say watch out for this Lightning coming up. I was busy flying gunnery patterns—the Range Officer eating me out the whole way—" He swiveled abruptly in his chair and hit the key on the little box.

Mrs. Pellerino said. "Yes, sir?"

"Vera," General Beal said, "call Chechoter and ask them for the name and serial number of the officer on duty at the gunnery range this morning, around noon. I want to write him a letter of commendation made part of his two-oh-one file. Remind me."

"Yes, sir."

To Colonel Ross, General Beal said: "He was on the beam, that boy, Judge. You know; really putting-out. Taking some trouble. I ought to get around more and see who's doing a good job at our other installations—let them know we know."

"I suppose it might not do too much harm," Colonel Ross said. "But remember you can't get everywhere; and what you'd mostly see wouldn't be what they did when they thought nobody was looking. And for each man you decide rates a letter of commendation, there'll be fifty others who, everybody knows, rate it more; and they don't get anything. You think the Chechoter fellow didn't know who you were?"

"He hadn't any way of knowing, Judge. I had Danny notify the range a plane was coming; but I told him not to say who, and I know he wouldn't. Besides, you should have heard this kid tear into me." General Beal laughed. "He said I'd better stop trying to look so hot until I learned how to fly a Forty-seven. He said I stank about ten ways; and exactly why. He was right. He saw I didn't quite have the hang of the plane, diving in. A pilot who listens to him really gets help." He looked at Colonel Ross and went on quickly: "That's a good plane, Judge. I like it better every time. All that turbo-supercharger weight does slow it some, makes it a little heavy to handle at low altitude; but that engine; that four-bladed prop; the power it's got! It's a hefty bitch, too. Nice thing to come home in, I bet. Take a lot of hits and still keep going."

Colonel Ross said: "I'm delighted to hear that. I understand the Materiel Command is buying seven or eight thousand for us. I'm glad to see you taking such a bright view of everything. You were talking about Carricker."

"Wait!" General Beal said. "Just remembered something I didn't take such a bright view of. I sent one of McCreery's men to his quarters—what's his name? Something like Eisenhower—you know about that, by the way? It's too bad Frank Andrews got killed, Jo-Jo thinks. I'll tell you later. Wertenhauer—no, Werthauer, his name was." General Beal reached out to the big box.

It said to him promptly: "Mrs. Spann, General. Colonel Mowbray hasn't returned yet. I believe he is at the Club with General Nichols."

"Botty there? Tell him to call the Post Surgeon. Say I am releasing Lieutenant Werthauer—want me to spell it? I don't think I can. He will return to duty. Get after that right away."

"Yes, sir."

"He was a little snotty; and I lost my temper," General Beal said. "I ought to stop doing that, shouldn't I?"

Colonel Ross said: "I hear you also didn't take such a bright view of Hal's man, Hicks—his project. I hear you told him it was off. Is it?"

"Oh, that!" General Beal said. "I didn't mean anything about Hicks. Did he think I did? I never saw what good that project was going to do, really. You think we ought to go on with it? Let's let it hang a minute. I'd like to put it to Jo-Jo; see what he thinks. Let me do that, Judge."

"You're the boss," Colonel Ross said. "Except with Benny, apparently."

General Beal laughed. "In carrying out orders, Benny shows a pretty high degree of initiative, inventiveness, and resourcefulness. What the book says. I saw this Thirty-eight coming right for me; and I was wondering. Then I saw it bank over, snap around to go on my left. As soon as I saw that, I knew it was Benny—he can show you how to fly. There wouldn't be two like that around here." Since Colonel Ross said nothing, he went on: "I watched him come in position, forming up as wingman. Then I could see him looking up at me, raising one finger for A Channel; but I just looked ahead, not paying any attention to him. I was turning on my base leg for the range. I knew he was turning with me; but I still wouldn't look at him."

General Beal began to laugh again. "What I didn't know; when he realized I wasn't paying any attention, he started to change position, coming above, moving in, still a little back. Then he gunned it gradually. First thing I saw was his fuselage pushing out, his right prop spinning practically in my eye, his wing pretty nearly on top of mine. He was looking down across the engine nacelle to see me jump. 'O.K., Hotshot!' I thought. I touched the stick to wing up a little, quick; and he did all the jumping."

General Beal paused on the recollection with a grim cheerfulness. He said: "Benny's had it close before; but I bet he never had it closer! I punched my radio button; and he came through, squawking: 'Don't do that!' I went on transmit and said: 'You know where you ought to be; and it isn't up here clapping wings with me. I grounded you. Now, what do you want? I'm going down to shoot.' I moved in on him a little; and he hauled off fast, yelling: 'Stay away, damn it, keep away!' Then he said: 'Go on, shoot your target, Chief. I want to go home.'

"I said: 'Who's stopping you? You get back and stay grounded.' He said: 'I don't go until you go; and I got more gas left. I could stay a couple of hours.' I said: 'You may have more gas; but I have charged guns.' He said: 'You think I haven't?' I could see him reach to knock down the safety hood on the gun switch and turn his sight on. 'All set!' he said. 'I'll see you, Chief! Show me how good that coal truck you have there is!' I couldn't help laughing."

Colonel Ross said: "You aren't both nuts, by any chance, are you?"

"Well, I hear you don't have to be," General Beal said. "But how it helps! Boys will be boys, Judge."

The tone of banter, the garish exuberance, the festive eye, made Colonel Ross say: "Well, you're a pretty big boy now, Bus. Been a fine thing, wouldn't it—fine example! Two planes playing—they lock wings and crash—you and Carricker. I can't seem to see the joke, General."

General Beal gave him a compassionate look. "Don't take it so hard, Judge," he said lightly. "It wasn't too dangerous. I knew what I was doing; you can count on Benny knowing what he's doing. He had no right to be there; but I knew why he was. I was telling you yesterday, Judge. You just don't understand Benny." Smiling still, but graver, he said: "I don't know how he even knew I went off, or where. He must have worked it out of Danny. So he just grabbed a plane and came up."

Colonel Ross said: "This is how he knew. Sal was pretty nearly frantic. We couldn't tell her where you were. We didn't know. Finally Botwinick decided he'd better see what Benny could do. He knew where to get hold of Danny. I don't mind about us—much! But sometimes you might give Sal a break. You worry her to death."

"That's so," General Beal said. "I'll give her a ring." He reached for a telephone.

"She's over at our place now, lying down. She'll come out to Retreat."

"O.K.," General Beal said. "But if I'm taking the salute, I can't have her on the stand. They may do the sisters and his cousins and his aunts stuff some places; but here it's strictly military personnel. I don't want her to be mad about that, too; so perhaps I better talk to her."

"You'd better let her alone," Colonel Ross said. "She and Cora can drive out together. Afterwards, I hope she slaps your ears down."

"She will," General Beal said. "She's the best little ear-slapper you ever saw. Another reason I can't have her on the stand. She might do it right there. I couldn't blame her; only, would it look good?" He paused. "Listen, Judge," he said, "I knew she was steamed up, this morning. I didn't feel like coping with it, right then. I was sorry; but there wasn't anything

504

I could do. She knows how it is, by this time. You just have to wait it out."

Colonel Ross said: "If I had a daughter, I'd see she never married a flyer. Why should she wait it out? In the end they all kill themselves; and meanwhile they practice for it by killing their wives."

"Sal talk about divorcing me?" General Beal said. "She's always saying that. It's just a passing whim, Judge. Don't you think?"

"Maybe," Colonel Ross said. "But she must be wondering why she married you, a lot of the time."

General Beal said: "She certainly didn't want to; but she knows why she did. She had to." Looking at Colonel Ross, he laughed. "I don't mean that way," he said. "It would be one brave man who fooled around with a daughter of old Colonel Coulthard's. Sal couldn't get to marry anyone else. Every time they posted me a good way off, she'd have a try; but she'd write me one of those letters about wanting me to be the first to know; so I'd wangle some leave or orders or something and fly back long enough to bust it up for her. She knew I wasn't ever going to be a general, and that killed her; but I guess she finally got in a panic about being over twenty. Then, I know Hal was sore at her for kicking so many of his friends in the teeth—wouldn't bring any more around for her; and the old colonel was probably giving her holy hell, telling her twelve broken engagements was enough, and if she did it any more, he'd take his razor strop to her. So she had to marry me."

In this joking relation were elements of complacence, and other elements of sentimental or self-interested reminiscence, the mind's flat lie about the past; but also, ingenuously full-hearted, wistfully it gathered a true tenderness around the more or less distorted facts. Unmixed with anything but sadness, fond feelings could live there, secure from the minute by minute test of verifiable truth and observable fact, unspoiled by the moving instant's irritabilities of sense, the separate discomforts, the incompatible wishes that greatly moderated, in any present, men's appreciations of one another, let alone of their women. General Beal looked back and saw himself with innocent approval; and, by extension, he also approved his girl. Colonel Ross did not doubt that Lieutenant Beal in his fur-collared jacket and snappy breeches and fine Peal boots, standing by a new P-12 which he had just finished stunting all over the sky, was something to see. A girl would be crazy to marry anyone else as long as he could be brought to keep showing an interest.

"I guess she did have to," Colonel Ross said. "Do you wonder what went on here while you left me and Pop running the Army?"

"Nope," said General Beal, smiling at him. "I know what went on, Judge. You fixed everything."

"Maybe I did; and maybe I didn't," Colonel Ross said. "I certainly split my old gut trying. You gave a few orders you don't know about; and I want them to stick. We're not going to court-martial those colored boys. Lieutenant Willis is back on duty as acting commander of the tentative group."

"O.K."

"I want Benny to apologize to him."

"O.K. Benny won't mind that."

"That's lucky for me!" Colonel Ross said. "The parade is, needless to say, coming off. In fact, it is coming off in an hour. Are you going to go to it looking like Joe Pilot?"

"You want me to doll up?" General Beal said. "All right. I got a uniform in the bathroom, there. After that Coca-Cola the other day, I figured I'd always better keep a spare. You never know what they're going to spill on you."

The box buzzed behind him. General Beal tilted back and hit the switch neatly with his elbow. "What?"

Mrs. Pellerino said: "General Nichols and Colonel Mowbray, sir."

XII

THOUGH THE windows had been left open, Nathaniel Hicks's car, standing in the full sun in the parking lot behind the Special Projects Building, was scorching hot. Nathaniel Hicks entered it gingerly. Captain Wiley opened the front door on the other side and got in, too. Captain Duchemin opened a rear door and toppled down on the seat. "Help!" he said. "Help! Get it going, Captain! Raise some wind!"

Nathaniel Hicks backed the car around and went out the lot entrance. He said to Captain Wiley: "I guess we've got everything covered, haven't we? Of course, there's no telling what General Beal may do with the text he has. He may not like anything I do now. I'll see those diagrams get to him as soon as Milt has them ready. They may help. You might show your copy to that fellow from the Pacific you spoke of."

"I'll do that," Captain Wiley said. "I haven't talked to him; but I hear he's had it. He hasn't been back more than two weeks; so whatever it is, it won't be past history. Like that Folsom jerk's crap. I'm sorry if what I told you to put in made him mad—I mean, if that's why he crossed up the other thing for you."

"Of course, I don't know he did," Nathaniel Hicks said. "But it was quite a coincidence. I might have guessed there was a hitch somewhere when he turned so pleasant all of a sudden. Probably as soon as I left he was on the box to the general. I guess he saw I pitched it pretty high. I feel a little sorry for this Post man at Sellers; he's probably cooked, too."

Captain Wiley said with indifference: "That guy is screwy —or out of date, anyway, Nat. If he got over here in Folsom's directorate or whatever you call it, he might even try to back Folsom up, make us more trouble. Don't listen to either of them. Folsom may be a flyer from way back; but when it comes to air fighting today, he doesn't know half what you know. With what you know now, Nat, you could take a plane and make a monkey out of him."

Not displeased by the idea that he impressed an experienced fighter pilot as potentially Colonel Folsom's superior in modern air warfare, Nathaniel Hicks said: "If I could take a plane! Folsom does have something there, Gene. Because I don't fly myself, he knows I don't know what I'm writing about—somebody else has to tell me."

Captain Wiley said: "Why don't you take up flying, Nat?

507

You'd like it. Wish you were at AFSAT. There's a BT-Seventeen I know I could get for an hour or so a day. I could teach you to fly in two weeks."

"I'm too old—" Nathaniel Hicks said.

"Horse feathers!" Captain Wiley said. "Are you too old, for God's sake, to drive a car? Well—"

Nathaniel Hicks said: "I mean, I'm too old to like it. I didn't start early enough. When I'm in a plane, all I ever want to do is get out as soon as I can. You're fifteen years younger than I am, and you're an experienced flyer; so you must have started about as soon as you could walk—"

"I'm not so damn experienced," Captain Wiley said. "I wouldn't say that. A fellow like this Folsom could show me a lot of things, probably. The only thing I say he can't show me, I can show him, is tactical stuff. He never had to learn it or be dead! I admit I started fairly early. There was this airport, they called it; a grass strip this fellow from the last war had near where I lived. I suppose I was horsing around there from the time I was fifteen. I suppose I got maybe three hundred hours in the kind of crates you find at a place like that. My dad wouldn't buy me a plane, though I had him about talked into it when I heard there was this chance to go to England."

Captain Wiley laughed. "He didn't like that, either; but he was on a spot. His father, this grandfather of mine, see, was a general nobody ever heard of with Kirby-Smith for a while. So we listened to a lot of that as kids. He was younger than I was when he went to the war. You couldn't talk that off! Anyway, in England they gave us all six weeks training—the first real plane I ever flew. Then they started us right away making operational flights, using Hurricanes—sweeps across the Channel. I thought I had quite some boat until the ME-One-oh-nine-E's joined up with us. They'd get up and hold at thirty-five thousand, waiting for us. We couldn't get there; we couldn't do anything, except make a banking turn, steep; come about; and try to squirt them when they went by, maybe six hundred miles an hour. You figure how many we got!" He shook his head reminiscently. "That was April, 'forty-one. We were outclassed as hell; but in a way, if they don't knock you down, it gives you

508

a good start. You're always up Mike's; and you have to get yourself out, not sit back and let your plane's superior performance do it for you. Makes you fast on your feet! Then, you ever get a plane that does have superior performance, like the Spit-Nine, you go to town! It's a great war, Nat; except there's a lot of waiting around."

Nathaniel Hicks said: "This waiting around's my fault, I'm afraid. I should have checked Operations earlier. I forgot they'd probably close the field."

"What the hell?" Captain Wiley said cordially. "If that jalopy I have will go at all, I can make Orlando in fifteen minutes, easy. Matter of fact, I'll be glad to see this. I never have. On Malta, we were looking for it any day. Had the operational areas all loused up with obstacles; resistance points manned all the time; everything set for them. There's something I wouldn't like to do! Jump into that; or come down in some goddamn cardboard glider! You can have it!" He shifted the worn musette bag in his lap, refolded his long legs more comfortably, and hung his bare arm out the window.

From the back seat, Captain Duchemin said: "How was everything in England, Captain? Natives co-operative? I mean, the female natives, of course."

"Not even rationed," Captain Wiley said. "Especially, if you settle for it standing up. Custom of the country. Damnedest thing I ever heard of! Lying down, you're a trot; that's evil; that's what bad girls do for money. Standing up, that won't count; our heroes, that's in aid of; that's for free."

Captain Duchemin opened his eyes wide, measuring Captain Wiley's slouched, rangy form. He began to chuckle. "How about the step ladder?" he said. "They bring their own?"

Captain Wiley gave him a startled look. Then he slapped his leg with delight. "You're in, chum!" he said. "Say, I got to remember that one!" He gazed at Captain Duchemin with generous admiration; and, indeed, Nathaniel Hicks could not recall hearing Captain Wiley attempt any wit of his own—he was perhaps too modest to imagine he could say anything funny; and probably his only humor would be the orthodox humor of the man of action, the practical joke, to kill time, ease that waiting-around which seemed to be the one evil he knew; a callously planned entertainment based on some unwarned person's anger when he found himself in a painful or frightening fix. Captain Wiley acknowledged now a higher art; and at the same time, a right view of life, or at least of women. His glance met Captain Duchemin's in mutual appreciation, in perfect understanding. It had not taken them a minute to cement a comradeship which Nathaniel Hicks, the least degree miffed, must see he had never managed and never could.

Nathaniel Hicks said: "Here's where we start saluting."

Still laughing, Captain Wiley and Captain Duchemin straightened themselves somewhat to answer the saluting guards at the gate.

Beyond the gate, a crowd waited at the bus stop. Pulling, one after another, slowly out into the road, a series of packed busses were beginning to move; so Nathaniel Hicks came to a second halt. Glancing at the crowd, he saw, standing a little apart, Lieutenant Turck. She stood disconsolately, her lips parted, her eyes, though in the shadow of her cap brim, narrowed against the painful glare. There were two suitcases resting on the sand at her feet.

Nathaniel Hicks let in his clutch and edged over to the roadside. "Give you a lift, Lieutenant?" he called.

"Oh!" Lieutenant Turck said, starting. "Why, thank you; no, sir—"

Her blink of surprise against the sun glare must have gone at first no further than Captain Wiley; and Nathaniel Hicks was interested, even touched, by this new evidence of her chronic slight constraint. To any invitation from any strange male, instinct answered for her in haste; no.

Then she recognized Nathaniel Hicks. Her face, already reddened with heat, reddened much more. Made to feel foolish, she said in agitation: "I'm sorry; yes, thanks! Thanks awfully. Thank God, in fact! There don't seem to be any taxis coming out here; and you can't even get on a bus—"

Captain Wiley depressed the door handle, thrust his leg out, and erected himself, towering, smiling civilly, over her. Captain Duchemin opened the rear door, shouldered his bulk through, stepped and took up her bags. Lieutenant Turck said to him: "Oh; hello, Captain! Please don't; I'll—"

Captain Wiley said: "Get in front, ma'am. We'll take those in back with us."

Realizing that this was no time to parley, that fifty people were watching, and that traffic was, or was about to be, held up, Lieutenant Turck ducked in and seated herself. She said to Nathaniel Hicks: "I never asked where you were going."

He said: "Where are *you* going? That might have something to do with it." The rear door slammed; and he let the car into gear, moving off after the busses.

"Well, I know you're not going downtown—"

"We have to go to the Base. We'll take you to the taxi stand outside there."

She said: "That's frightfully kind!" Nathaniel Hicks could see that this girlish overstatement embarrassed her when she heard herself make it. To mend matters, she became voluble. "Only, look; please don't go there first if you were going anywhere else. It doesn't matter at all when I get downtown. All my kids from Files were reporting for the parade, so I thought we'd shut up early. I'm just bringing down Lippa's bag and mine to get them out of the way. She has to march her company, poor wretch. So please just go wherever you were going—"

"We don't know where we're going," Nathaniel Hicks said. "We were directed to proceed to Gate Number Three and observe, whatever that means, this parachute drop they're having. We have plenty of time. That is Captain Wiley, behind you, by the way. He's trying to get back to Orlando; but they won't let him take-off until the show is over. So we're stuck with him."

Lieutenant Turck turned her head, inclining it, and said: "How do you do, sir."

Captain Wiley said: "Yours to command, ma'am."

Captain Duchemin, no doubt seeing a tactful way to save them the time it would take to go down to the Main Gate, several miles from Gate Number Three, said to Nathaniel Hicks: "If Lieutenant Turck doesn't have to get anywhere right away, what's wrong with her observing, too? We've got one more brassard." He laid it over the back of the front seat beside her. "She can cover the Woman's Angle for my comprehensive report."

With Captain Duchemin glinting his large benign eyes at her in his perhaps not really meaningful but automatically receptive, always ready, you-and-I-should-get-together expression—in fact, when necessary Captain Duchemin had made-do with much worse than her good figure and well-bred face—Lieutenant Turck, though not quite flinching, looked at random toward Captain Wiley.

Captain Wiley's expression was merely amiable and polite, but that could have been little relief for her. With new inner commotion, she probably found that she was not so immune as she wished to the attractions of masculinity when they were properly presented. From this choice of embarrassments, she turned to Nathaniel Hicks. Making herself rise to the occasion, she said resolutely: "Yes; why not? I'd love to! You don't mind? Would they let me in?"

Nathaniel Hicks said: "Pin that brassard on; and I want to see them stop you!"

✦

A camouflage fly-top whose overhead cover was net drape garnished with thick, convoluted strips of cotton dipped in paints, some green, some the colors of sand or dirt, threw a fretwork of thin shade over Nathaniel Hicks and Lieutenant Turck, who sat together on upturned ammunition boxes. Stretched over the ends of poles, supported by guys, the fly-top was joined to a large pile of used lumber that had been assembled near the point where the new paving of the runway extension began. This pile was twelve or fifteen feet high. Looking through the net drape above him, Nathaniel Hicks could see on top of the pile Captain Duchemin and Captain Wiley standing with a major of the Aviation Engineers named McIlmoyle, surveying the field.

Nathaniel Hicks could also hear their conversation—largely a loud monologue in Major McIlmoyle's rasping voice. The major was explaining the defenses; but almost everything he said made an occasion to acquaint them in more detail with his service on Guadalcanal last year; where, though himself apparently only an observer, he had shared in desperate fighting and played an important part in preparing the positions and developing the tactics that enabled the First Marine Division to hang on to Henderson Field.

Nathaniel Hicks did not doubt that these reminiscences were actually directed at Captain Wiley, whose two sets of wings and single valuable ribbon would always be taken as a challenge by those who served in other arms. The so-called Foot Army had a few things to tell the so-called Fly Boys.

That a reasonably peaceable relation had nevertheless come to subsist on top of the lumber pile was due, of course, to Captain Duchemin. Captain Duchemin, using, though without apparent effort or design, natural emanations from his big, bland, imperturbable face and his contented hulk of a body, could effect a preliminary easing of any relation. With inoffensive smiling tact, he then said at the right times the simple right things that insensibly worked on a man with his back up until he let his back down.

To start, the major had his back up, all right. When Nathaniel Hicks, bringing the car carefully over the temporary road, a thin cold-laid bituminous surfacing spread right on the sandy soil, and now much waved, cracked, and sagged by heavy truck traffic, drove in and halted near the lumber pile, Major McIlmoyle had come out from under the fly-top, his steel helmet shoved to the back of his head, his hands belligerently on his hips, and received them with an angry stare.

Nathaniel Hicks then got off on the wrong foot by inquiring for Lieutenant Anderson, the officer they had been told was in charge. The major said: "Well, he's not in charge. Anderson's at his command post. He's busy. I'm Battalion CO. Now, what do you want?"

Captain Duchemin produced a copy of Colonel Mowbray's directive. That, and the official-looking green brassards, had some effect; but Major McIlmoyle continued to stare at Lieutenant Turck and her brassard with an air of outrage; and at Captain Wiley and his wings with an air of contemptuous irritability and resentment.

Prevented by Colonel Mowbray's piece of paper from ordering them to get the hell out, Major McIlmoyle compensated himself by insisting that the car could not be left where it was. It must be run up close to the lumber pile, as far as possible into its shadow. When Nathaniel Hicks brought it up, the major, his red face running with sweat, shouted impatiently that it was not close enough, and directed him to back off and bring it closer. There remained then no more than an inch between the fenders and the piled boards, so Major McIlmoyle let it go at that, saying: "Goddamn it, camouflage discipline is being observed here, and you can observe it, too!"

Captain Wiley, no doubt tired of the irritable stares at him, and of the fussing, hectoring manner, commented disgustedly, not bothering to lower his voice in the least: "Ah, shove it, Jack!"

He then stepped out of the car and sauntered toward the lumber pile, which had been ingeniously taken apart and rearranged to leave under it, in the middle, a space wide enough and high enough to back in a combat half-track and so conceal it from the air.

The major had not failed to hear Captain Wiley's rude advice to him; but perhaps because of his experience at Henderson Field and his encounters with Marine and Air Force pilots there, he almost instantly thought better of his obvious first hot impulse to pull his rank.

Captain Duchemin, looking around, said: "All right if I go on top of the pile, Major? I'd like to see the overall layout. This is new to me. When you have time, would you mind if I asked you some questions? Say, is that a half-track in there? That looks like a pretty good idea!"

Major McIlmoyle said grudgingly: "You spend a while on strips exposed to enemy action, you learn to use cover. But don't get the idea this is a real defense layout. We had one company throwing up a few token installations this morning—"

They moved off toward Captain Wiley, who was looking at the half-track. Nathaniel Hicks watched with interest; but it was apparent that the major had definitely decided to forget that remark. He was soon saying loudly, addressing Wiley and Duchemin, both: "Yeah. Now, on Guadal, when I was there, first thing we did—"

Presently, all three of them mounted the pile by the boards stacked to form irregular steps against the side. Lieutenant Turck said to Nathaniel Hicks: "Do I dare get out?"

"You couldn't be safer," Nathaniel Hicks said. "Before we leave, he and Clarence will be agreeing to meet in the Scheherazade Bar tomorrow night, where Clarence will gladly introduce him to a couple of swell chicks. Let's get in the shade, there."

In the partial shade of the fly-top sat what proved to be that Lieutenant Anderson for whom Nathaniel Hicks had so inopportunely asked. Lieutenant Anderson, a thin worried young man, was at a field desk with a sign saying: *Company A Command Post.* He regarded Lieutenant Turck with due astonishment; but he said, sure, they could wait there. He even got up civilly and found the ammunition boxes for them to sit on.

Also sharing the shade, grouped together by the entrance to the space under the lumber pile, was the concealed half-track's complement of men, Aviation Engineer Negroes in work clothes, but wearing steel helmets and carrying M-1 rifles slung across their backs. Though Lieutenant Turck had astonished them, too, a point that could be read in nods, nudges, and jogs with the elbow, they instantly and ostentatiously averted their eyes. Sitting, kneeling, crouching on their heels, they were engaged in what was plainly a betting or gambling game, with much incidental mirth. A number of them lifted their hands simultaneously, and, at a signal, simultaneously brought them down showing one finger or more extended. The pay-off appeared to depend on how many hands, if any, showed the same number of fingers extended. Though no money was in sight, this was probably because of Lieutenant Anderson at the desk, and Nathaniel Hicks could see that a score was being kept on a scrap of paper. The excitement was intense.

In under the fly blew a fitful strong breeze coming across the wide airfield toward the lake water. The papers stirred on Lieutenant Anderson's desk while Lieutenant Anderson dealt with a succession of messengers, asking them questions, giving them orders. Occasionally he lifted a pair of field glasses and studied some point in the hot sweep of sand and coarse grass tussocks toward the declining sun. Occasionally he had another try at using the field telephone, whose wires, strung on low stakes, were supposed to connect him with two observation posts. The telephone did not work.

Within the sector limits marked by fluttering red flags Nathaniel Hicks could see a variety of defense positions—the dugout observation posts on the extreme perimeter, camouflaged with clumps of grass; groupings of shallow, prone trenches scooped from the sand; carefully sited machine-gun emplacements under small cantilever fly-tops of wire woven with grass hugging the ground. There were even a few simulated rocks of papier-mâché which covered sniper's foxholes. From the top of the lumber pile Major McIlmoyle's voice carried clearly, describing their purpose and construction.

Beyond this foreground, the airfield, shaken by heat, extended empty to the great line of hangars a mile or so away. Over there, in the shimmering distance, a good deal of activity was obscurely suggested. The great array of parked planes, seen in a mirage now settling clear, now swimming off the ground, interrupted a full view of the ramp, which settled and steadied, and rose and swam with them; but there was a persistent stir—perhaps, units forming; perhaps, the shifting of tiered faces and light-clad figures of people on portable grandstand sections beyond the Operations Building. Along the highway fence sharp little glittering flashes winked off the glass and metal of automobiles. Over the hangars and the extended jumble of hundreds of lower roofs of the Base, a late tropical afternoon growth of cumulous cloud towers stood immaculately white, theatrically motionless, against the enormous height of the deep-blue, northern sky.

Hushed grunts and guffaws sounded from the players of the finger game. Lieutenant Anderson said to his telephone:

"Command Post to OP Baker. Do you hear me?" On top of the lumber pile, Major McIlmoyle, answering Captain Wiley, said: "No; what they had then, they had mostly those screwed-up P-Thirty-nines they called P-Four-hundreds. Not the Marines, you understand. They had their F-Four-F-Fours—"

Nathaniel Hicks looked at his watch. He said: "As Captain Wiley feelingly remarks: it's a great war, except there's a lot of waiting around."

Lieutenant Turck looked at her watch, too. "I think they must be getting on, over there," she said. "Lippa was told to have her people ready at sixteen-twenty. It was very humanely decided that the detachment would only have to march past, not stand formation with the men. I suppose they didn't want to litter the place with swooning females—"

Major McIlmoyle said: "Of course, this here is a greatly reduced scale, Captain. Strong points, resistance centers, would be sited out a thousand, fifteen hundred yards from the strip. We'd emplace our automatic-weapons fire units in supporting distance; say, six hundred feet or so, from the perimeter of the strip; see?"

The Negroes smothered new laughter.

Lieutenant Turck said: "They were told to wait between the hangars where they'd be in the shade. They'd be given a signal to march out and insert themselves at some elaborately calculated point, I think, between the last of the men and the first of some mechanized units. Thank God things like that aren't required of me. Lippa will manage it perfectly."

Major McIlmoyle said: "They didn't do too much damage, not as a regular thing; but you didn't get any sleep. There was this Jap sub, or maybe several of them, used to surface off Lunga about twenty-hundred and throw us some shells. After midnight, there was this two-engined bomber, the same one; you could tell the sound; used to call it Louie the Louse—"

Nathaniel Hicks said: "Does she really like it?"

"I don't know," Lieutenant Turck said. "At least it takes her mind off her troubles. That is an important aspect of the WAC, remember. There are those, fortunately a good many, who, as advertised, would rather be with the men than waiting for them.

517

The rest, a lot of the officers you may be sure, are taking their minds off their troubles. I don't know that Lippa's troubles ever amounted to much—then. But I expect now she finds the exercise of command a great solace."

"She has troubles now?" Nathaniel Hicks said.

Lieutenant Turck said: "What do you think? You know him better than I do. Is he crazy?"

"Then came the main event," Major McIlmoyle said. "They let down some colored flares; and the Tokyo Express was heard from. That night they had it beefed up with what we found out damn quick was two battleships. We lost fifty-seven aircraft. In the morning, you never saw such a mess. We had troubles! They wanted to get the bombers left, the Forts that could fly, the hell out to Espiritu before the return engagement. Those Forts finally took off on eighteen hundred feet of runway, drawing seventy inches of pressure—if they blew their cylinders, too bad—"

"Jesus!" Captain Wiley said. "You're not kidding!"

Nathaniel Hicks said: "Opinions differ, though I guess not much. Our good colonel thinks so; he addressed him very harshly in my hearing this afternoon; but Edsell, though I think alarmed, stood his ground, and nothing much happened. I will say for him, he certainly makes himself felt."

"He isn't in arrest, is he?"

"Not as far as I know. Not when I left."

"He told Mary he was going to be. I expect he made quite a thing out of it. That was just before she had to leave for the Base. That's what I meant about taking her mind off her troubles. You know; the show must go on, the mails must go through. And there is this war we have, of course. They also serve who only stand and wait."

A poorly repressed shout arose from the half-track crew. Somebody cried: "Don't you change that hand—"

Lieutenant Anderson, holding his telephone, said: "Pipe down, you men!" To the telephone he said: "Command Post to OP Baker. Can you—"

Major McIlmoyle said: "Crack they did, brother, crack they

did! They'd stay in a slit trench, put their heads down in the corner and cry. Tell you confidentially; we shipped out I don't know how many. Submarine Amberjack took a whole load of nuts, one time. Well; what saved Henderson Field, and just barely. We had seventy-fives mounted on half-tracks. I got the CO to move them up and cover where they had to cross the Matanikau; and we knocked off ten Jap tanks, one right after another. They ever get those tanks across—"

"I am prejudiced," Lieutenant Turck said. "He makes me mad; and then she makes me mad; and then we make me mad, she and I. I mean; she seems to *have* to like him, an involuntary reflex. She knows I don't like her to like him; and she doesn't like that; and I don't like her not liking my not liking her to like him, if that's all clear. Our sentiments would seem to be somewhat involved, I must admit. I suppose I needn't have been surprised when I heard that one of her enlisted women very unpleasantly accused her today of a homosexual relationship with me."

Nathaniel Hicks said: "Did you ever try to work out your reasons for not liking her to like him?"

"Dozens of times," Lieutenant Turck said. "They are morbid; but not I think actually perverted. I suffer from squeamishness. She acts, if she will forgive me, like a bitch in heat. When she starts that, I feel like throwing up. I see that it could be, even if I didn't know it, because I wanted to stand in his relationship to her. It could be; but I don't believe it. It's more maternal. When she's nice, which is most of the time, I feel like patting her. I daresay to the male eye she's not beautiful; but she's beautiful to me. She is exquisitely neat in person and habits—and very clean; dainty is the word, I guess; but with no non-sense about it—very nice. Then she takes a fancy to that lout, and gets herself all messed up—listen!"

Muted, yet distinct enough, the warm wind brought suddenly a far-off soft blare of brass, a pulse of mixed drums—band music. "Off we go, sure enough," Lieutenant Turck said. "Listen—"

"And look!" Nathaniel Hicks said.

He stood up and stepped to the edge of the fly.

Beyond Lake Lalage, over the thin low pine woods of its far shore, close to the horizon, patterns of what appeared to be short dark dashes were developing on the stainless southern sky.

Lieutenant Turck came beside him. She screwed her eyes up. "What?" she said.

"Look lower; look there," Nathaniel Hicks said. "There, and there. They must be bombers. God, there must be a hundred of them—"

"Oh!" Lieutenant Turck said. Her taken-in breath acknowledged the sinister deployment, the pattern small and soundless, but visibly overspreading the sky, and growing.

Lieutenant Anderson, at the field desk, turned sharp. "See planes, Captain?" he said.

"B-Seventeens, I think," Nathaniel Hicks said. "I don't believe they could be your people."

"No," Lieutenant Anderson said. "But they're all due over about the same time, if they haven't screwed it up." Carrying his field glasses, he joined them at the edge of the fly. He said: "Those are flying at six thousand, or ought to be. Then, they have these two waves of fighters, at three thousand and two thousand. The troop carriers they said would come over at about a thousand, one batch, and another, five hundred— probably see them last—"

Nathaniel Hicks, taking a learned interest, said: "Isn't a thousand pretty high?"

"I guess so," Lieutenant Anderson said. "Probably part of them are new units and they want to give them more jumping room"—he glanced anxiously up through the net drape. It could be guessed that the major, whenever possible, must be allowed to see things for himself. However, Major McIlmoyle was faced the other way, his arm out, saying: "They generally figure they have to have a minimum clear area, five hundred yards downwind; so they'd have to start letting go about the middle of the field. Of course, you understand, Duchemin, this is not really a defensible position—"

Lieutenant Anderson saw that he'd better not wait for the

end of that. He called, somewhat diffidently: "Major! Bombers south!"

Major McIlmoyle whirled around. He roared: "O.K.; General Alert! I'm coming down." To Captain Duchemin he said: "Well, this is it! Better stay up here. You'll see all there is—"

By means of a chain attached to his shoulder loop, Lieutenant Anderson hooked a whistle out of his shirt pocket and thrust it in his mouth. His three quick blasts were suddenly taken up by a siren. In howling mechanical wails it repeated them over and over from the small shed by the landing on the lake. The players of the finger game broke their circle, starting to their feet, jostling each other as they ran under the pile to the half-track. Nathaniel Hicks said to Lieutenant Turck: "Want to go on top? I guess we'd better get out of their way."

There was now no missing or mistaking the approach of the bombers. Their vast column of staggered columns spread wide to occupy the whole southern quarter of the sky. Their measured advance was no longer silent. As the siren died away by the lake, a heavy mutter, the compounded vibration of many engines, beat, ominous, on the ear. It submerged entirely the drift of far-off band music. The air quivered; the earth trembled; the serried ranks prepared to darken the heavens. Here and there, the procession of majestic wing spans was touched with the bright wink of a sun-lit propeller arc. Nathaniel Hicks caught Lieutenant Turck's hand and trotted around the side of the lumber pile.

Major McIlmoyle, clumping down the descending levels of stacked boards, gestured at them: "If you two want to see this," he shouted, "will you please hurry up and go on top?" His look was again amazed; and, realizing why, Nathaniel Hicks dropped Lieutenant Turck's hand, which he had not, in fact, been conscious of taking. "Yes, sir," he said. "We're getting!" Lifting his eyes, he was able to add alertly, "Major! I think you have fighter planes, there. It looks like about a group, in squadron boxes."

Major McIlmoyle swung his head. To the east, a wide shoal of dark dots, ranged in fours, two high, two low, had appeared on the sky. "Sure, sure," Major McIlmoyle said, and rushed away.

Mounting the piled planks, Nathaniel Hicks said: "I believe he thought we were holding hands. Look; maybe we'd better do it again."

"If you please," Lieutenant Turck said, breathless. "I don't seem to be a very good climber." The step to the top was the highest of all; and she said: "Golly; can I make that?"

"Yes," said Nathaniel Hicks. He scrambled up. "Here."

She held her hand to him, and he caught her wrist. She managed to put her plain brown shoe on the edge of the top plank. Her pulled skirt uncovered her slip, and her slip slid above her bent knee, exposing all her straight right leg, straining on tiptoe—the tight hem of the nylon stocking; the garter strap that secured it to her girdle; the stretched edge of the girdle itself. She clapped her free hand vainly at the mounting skirt. Nathaniel Hicks gave a quick tug and brought her up beside him. She said, a little stiffly: "Thanks. Not too frightfully modest, I'm afraid." Captain Duchemin had turned to watch them. From his expression of benign enjoyment, she no doubt judged rightly that he, too, had been given an eyeful. She colored; her discomfort still greater.

Captain Wiley, his face lifted, his eyes narrowed, was gazing away east. "Yeah, they're from Orlando," he said. "Those are ours. Get a load of that, Nat! Now, those squadron formations are holding pretty good. But you can see right away they don't get to fly as a group much—too loose. They keep coming on and falling back—oh, oh! Watch the low flight, left! Ass-end Charlie's gone to sleep"—the sky was shaking with thunder and he had been obliged to raise his voice.

Clearly resolved, at any cost, not to stand there in prudish confusion like a stick, Lieutenant Turck said: "What kind are they, Captain?"

"Fifty-ones; Mustangs, ma'am," Captain Wiley said. "We just got them in." His eye, keenly ranging the volumes of hot golden air, was arrested on the cloud towers to the north. "Look!" he said. "See, on the clouds? Another group. Forty-sevens. Bet they're from Tallahassee! That's Ozzie's group, I bet! They moved up there from Orlando—"

"Mercy!" Captain Duchemin said. "Do you see what I see? Unless I'm much mistaken, this is—ah—it; here comes the—ah—main event. They look like Forty-sixes to me; supposing Forty-sixes look like what I think they look like."

He, too, had to raise his voice. "Enough of this is really too much!" he shouted. He put his hands over his ears. "I also consider those gadgets too low. Better duck, hadn't we?"

Captain Wiley, who had faced around, said seriously: "Hell, no! Good five, six hundred feet! Whoops! They're unloading."

Headed straight for the lumber pile, moving fast in a V of four, the troop carriers, appearing so suddenly over the buildings of the Base across the field, looked, Nathaniel Hicks must admit, very low. Behind each could be seen a rapid, evenly spaced train of falling objects, over which, in the same neat quick succession, parachutes began to open in explosive puffs. The four planes, the roar of their twin engines drowning out the high thunder of the bombers now overhead, came straight and level, right across and out over Lake Lalage. Behind them, they left a sky full of parachutes, all dropping, a monstrous snowfall, variegated by the colored silks identifying equipment.

"Say, is that a nice sight!" Captain Wiley said. "Pretty as a picture, you ask me! Say, I'm glad I saw this! Makes you think, Nat!" He narrowed his eyes with pleasure.

"There's another bunch!" Captain Duchemin said. "Coming in west—right out of the sun—"

Nathaniel Hicks could see a second V of four, considerably higher, the ones at a thousand feet, no doubt, headed slantwise toward them, with new trails of dropping dots and parachute bursts.

Out on the wide field, the first contingent, drifting and swaying slowly, was well down; and the men could be seen twisting their bodies and pulling their shroud lines. Then they began to hit, bowling over, scrambling on the ground, the great parachute bags collapsing, or, half-spilled, pulling away in the breeze. Dim in the noise came the sound of a whistle and a fast hammering burst of machine-gun fire. With a roar that made the lumber pile shake, the half-track, full of crouching men, rushed out the end and swerved off across the open sand.

"Right lively!" Captain Duchemin said. "Right lively!"

The second V of four carriers, flying fast and level, had disappeared behind the woods to the east under a swarm of fighter planes coming in. Against the hellish snarling racket they made, Captain Duchemin roared, shaking Nathaniel Hicks's arm: "Up! Look up! They're going to drop all over us, that last batch—"

Nathaniel Hicks turned his face up.

Two or three dozen open parachutes did, indeed, seem to be right over them, unexpectedly high and apparently motionless; the men under them, hung about with tools and weapons, distinctly to be seen, though in grotesque perspective, the pink, helmeted faces tilted to peer past the dangling heavy boots. "Gene!" Nathaniel Hicks shouted. "They *are* dropping on us! We'd better get off the top. If one of them banged into you, I don't think it would be too good. Here!" he said to Lieutenant Turck. "Down; quick!" He jumped over the edge to the descending levels of lower boards and held his hand to her.

Captain Wiley, whose attention had been on the fighter planes diving in, now stared up. He stood a moment without moving. "No, they're not," he said suddenly. "They won't hit here." He glanced out across the runway. "Where some of those sons of bitches are going to drop," he said, "is in the drink."

XIII

COLONEL Ross pronounced to himself: *All is best though we oft doubt what the unsearchable dispose of Highest Wisdom brings about, and ever best found in the close. Oft He seems to hide His face, but unexpectedly returns, and to His faithful champion . . .*

He was surprised. He did not know why he thought of those lines now; but he doubted if things like that were ever wholly random. His mind, finding him—though his conscious knowledge did not know it—in want of something, determined in its own way what he did not know he wanted, and went off to the past to turn over the litter of memory and see if anything was there. Finding something, if not the very thing, then something that might do, it was back with it, waiting for the first lull of activity on the conscious level to display its finding for what it might be worth.

The finding might, of course, be worth a good deal, if you only knew it. Here you had the answer; but unfortunately you might not yet have received the problem. The answer, moreover, came in the only terms possible for this kind of communication. They were terms of symbol or image, perfectly related to the meaning that was intended to reach you in the flawless logic that things equal to the same thing are equal to each other. It was again unfortunate that the conscious mind was not too bright, and so never could work out the perhaps-worthwhile meaning of most of these messages.

Now old Judge Schlichter, his raised finger oratorically pointing up at Highest Wisdom's home, heaven, boomed majestically on, while the sunlight of mornings years ago fell on the shelves packed with bound reports that lined the musty room where young Ross sat clerking for the Judge and reading for his bar examination. Bemused, old Ross contemplated the enigmatic spectacle.

Regardless of any service the recollection might be meant to do him, Colonel Ross was glad to have it. In recollection, the not-bright conscious mind, all meaning missed, could take it easy. Standing in the first line of the double row of General Beal's staff officers on the bunting-decked platform erected for the reviewing party, and already tired of standing, and of the late afternoon sunlight pouring across his face, Colonel Ross nonetheless rested in most senses.

The ample space, formally left empty, which surrounded the temporary scaffolding of the platform suggested a charmed area which it would be impossible for anybody to cross, bringing him business. He was a full hundred yards from the nearest telephones in the Operations Building. He was a full fifty yards from the convertible coupe with the top down parked with a few other favored cars farther along the ramp. That was the general's; and Cora had driven Sal out in it. Cora and Sal sat there together; and he knew that Cora was watchfully checking up on him from time to time; but she was too far away to advise him about not overdoing things at his age.

While he stood in this security, there were several bands to play for Colonel Ross and since it seemed to be agreed among them that the Air Corps song was most suitable for a march-past the music had an undemanding monotony. No sooner had it gone by, jaunty, passing farther and farther up the ramp to the right, and finally ceasing, than it began again from the left. Far down the hangar line, growing stronger, it came on, making the spine crawl with an ever-louder brave smash of drums, and the fine martial polyphony of mixed brass. Stepping out to it were five thousand marchers, with a good deal of mechanized equipment to come after that.

Colonel Ross noted, quite indifferent, that the marching was better than he would have expected. Fully half these units were made up of men who worked in shops or hangars or offices. The other half were tactical units of various sorts or arms; but tactical units at AFORAD were kept busy acting out field problems that the Directorate of Air-Ground Coöperation was studying and did no more close order drill than the average quartermaster company.

Colonel Ross noted, too, though not so indifferently, since they made a tremendous tiring noise, that Pop's grand aerial display, the contingents of visiting planes, actually were on their complicated schedule—a matter to which Pop at the head of the line called attention by winks and nods toward the south and east horizons. When the fighter groups came in sight exactly as the head of the big bomber flight passed throbbing above, Pop's satisfaction was so great that he lost all control and shattered the decorum of a reviewing party by lifting his hand to show Colonel Ross his thumb and forefinger joined in a triumphant circle.

In front of Colonel Ross, General Beal and General Nichols, with orderlies to right and left, really stood none the worse for all the Air Corps years between them and West Point. Chins up and alert, they put on the reviewing officer's show of ever renewed anticipation and unwearied interest as, through the band music and the noise of planes, new hearty barks and bawls came up, the advancing guidons dropped, the ranked faces in a simultaneous flash of changed color, snapped right.

Colonel Ross supposed that everyone was what passed for happy—the generals, as recipients of all this tradition, form and ceremonious duty, were getting a little of the least palling of human pleasures; the marchers, once they had done their eyes-right and gone by the stand, had the relief, at this point major pleasure, of knowing the unenjoyable exercise was for them nearly over; the spectators had the recreation of participating vicariously in martial, manly goings-on—war in stout-hearted terms of the "Soldiers' Chorus" from *Faust*; and a welcome change from their everyday war of ration books, Selective Service classifications, and the low diet of news that many of them would see was doctored by an omission of all happenings not desirable for them to know about, and by the insertion of much semi-fiction it was judged useful for them to believe.

Colonel Ross, too, might pass for happy. He enjoyed his hour or more of being left alone. There was nothing here he need pay any attention to. Shifting at intervals his main weight from one aching leg to the other, Colonel Ross contemplated in peace, with a melancholy no more than slight, the living, speaking image of Judge Schlichter, now twenty-five years in his grave.

At the time that young Ross's good fortune (joined, he might allow, with qualities of determined industry and reasonable intelligence) got him his chance to work in the judge's office, Judge Schlichter had come, now he was along in years, to conduct himself with a stateliness that extended to his smallest actions. Judge Schlichter's discourse—no homelier word described it—must dazzle any young man who had run away from school; and particularly one who regretted running away, and was resolved, at twenty, to recoup the losses he rashly incurred at sixteen. Judge Schlichter's range of vocabulary was so great that he seldom felt at loss for the long word to replace an ordinary man's short one. His learning was not confined in narrow legal bounds. He had familiarized himself with the best that has been thought and said, and quoted it freely. Young Ross wrote down a private list of authors to find out about, and of books to borrow from the public library. He regarded the judge with reverent awe.

This, no doubt, went on some months; but perhaps not very many, for the boy was observant and apt to learn. As he became more at home in legal circles, he would have to notice that the leading members of the local bar, though they listened all right, did not listen with awe to old Schlichter's circumlocutions. They did not hear with pleasure his spoutings of Milton, or twenty lines of Shakespeare declaimed like a ham actor, or verses from Whittier and Longfellow that had been boring everyone for half a century. A day came, of course, when signs that the judge was going to sound off pricked young Ross with anguish. He foresaw the pompous, struck attitude and the farcically affected boom; he anticipated with shame the eyes of visitors covertly rolled in resignation; the hand-covered asides, impatient, ironic, of counsel in court. How could the judge not know that everyone was laughing at him for a pretentious old windbag?

Here was a baffling question. Judge Schlichter had a mind, in the idiom of the day, like a steel trap. Bending from the bench, or sharply attending in his chambers, he missed nothing and he forgot nothing, and nobody fooled him. He could spot a lie a mile off. In a few minutes' masterly exchange, he was often pleased to demonstrate a slick scoundrel out of that scoundrel's own unwary mouth. When smart young attorneys, busy for several days, had finished crossing up an issue, old Schlichter, coming to charge, glancing at his notes, would strip off in ten minutes every expertly added non-essential. He rescued the lost point; he lucidly restated the evidence; and, in doing that, he made any chicanery on either side as clear

528

as day—most juries had no real need to leave the box at all.

It was too bad that Judge Schlichter could just as readily halt a pleading to bumble: Life is real! Life is earnest! And the grave is not its goal; or to flabbergast everyone by demanding of the prisoner at the bar when shall he think to find a stranger just, when he, himself, himself confounds, betrays, to slanderous tongues and wretched hateful days? What ever became of the steel-trap mind? What had become of the man nobody fooled?

What, indeed? What, indeed?

Colonel Ross, back in the present, caught a slight shifting and stiffening of bodies in the reviewing party. His eyes went left and he saw just in time the approaching break in the marching ranks, a color guard coming on. Colonel Ross, too, stiffened moderately with the line of staff officers. General Beal and General Nichols in perfect unison, with a snap of perfect precision, brought their hands up. Somewhat less perfectly, Colonel Ross brought his up.

It was, he saw, the colors of the WAC detachment; and he was not surprised, a moment later to hear, following a great shift of standing up and uncovering on the stands of spectators, a quick pattering outbreak of applause. In front of him he could see General Nichols, barely moving his lips, faintly smiling, say something to General Beal, who, faintly smiling, barely moving his lips, answered. Coming past now, all by herself at the head of a company, her hand rigidly to her cap brim, was the little snub-nosed lieutenant who stood to make her suggestion in the conference room the other day.

Colonel Ross said: "This is quite a war."

Startled, Major Tietam, next to him, whispered: "Sir?"

Colonel Ross shook his head. He let his mind move off again to find, where he had left him, old Schlichter being an ass in the cold-eyed younger world which, as the judge himself might have put it, knew not Joseph.

There were, of course, other ways in which Judge Schlichter proved less than perfect. Knowledge of them came more slowly;

and to be sure of them needed several years' loyal and discreet service. His discoveries affected neither young Ross's loyalty nor his discretion; but they disturbed his mind. Like Judge Schlichter's mental abilities, which were allowed to outweigh, if barely, his pompous foibles, Judge Schlichter's moral character was held in high regard. In many ways the regard was deserved. Judge Schlichter's professional integrity was absolute. He was incorruptible. In any matter having to do with money he was the soul of honor. The privacy of the judge's private life hid none of those sordid, not uncommon, secrets involving, at best, another woman; but, quite as often, through the modified impulses of senescence, little girls or young boys.

The judge's clerk, because he knew no better than to suppose that every man in high position would naturally have to have them, passed over these virtues and decencies. He expected the judge's character to deserve, not in many ways, but in all ways, the high regard people expressed for it. Young Ross had not liked his growing awareness that he could tell (though he never would) if he wanted to (but he did not want to) what seemed to him "plenty" about Judge Schlichter.

To the strait-laced, carefully respectable community it would also have seemed "plenty." Old Schlichter was a regular church-goer, a principal pillar of the church; and his severe public stand in issues of piety and right-thinking could be known when he flatly refused on one occasion to admit testimony from a man who declared with scorn that the Bible, brought for him to swear on, was all nonsense, and that he believed in no hereafter, and no God.

But when you heard Judge Schlichter's private opinions, you knew that in general he agreed with this view. Favorite quotations of the judge's came from the Bible, and many others seemed to postulate a Supreme Being and eternal life; but in private Judge Schlichter kept, at most, an open mind about all this. He appeared to consider the basic principles of Christianity consistent with right and reason; but in the doctrines of the Lutheranism he professed on Sundays, or in those of any other church, he certainly did not believe. He just pretended to.

The horrified community, informed of this unbelief, would

probably not have been surprised to hear that the judge went even farther. He also just pretended that he did not drink alcoholic beverages. At the back of his safe were hidden bottles of what the judge, perhaps by way of distinguishing it from liquor or booze, referred to as sound spirits. He regularly enjoyed a nip, either alone, or with one or two safe old cronies. The indulgence was always moderate. The judge never took too many nips, and never took them too often; but tippling in private was a hard thing to square with an uncompromising public stand for teetotalism.

The resulting disturbance in the callow mind of the judge's clerk might seem now something to smile over; but, at that time, young Ross did not suffer from any farm boy's naïve shock that such things as unbelief and whisky-drinking could be. In the Army he observed that most men put no stock in religion, and that most men took a drink whenever they could get it. What he troubled over was, then or now, no smiling matter. It was the indisputable plain truth that Judge Schlichter without the practice of these hypocrisies would be a better man than Judge Schlichter with them.

Judge Schlichter was well aware of this, for he said much too frequently: A wit's a feather, and a chief a rod; an honest man's the noblest work of God. Why then did he choose to live these lies? Young Ross already knew the answer. Old Schlichter weighed what he got from hypocrisy against what he might hope from honesty. He let honesty go. He did not have the nerve to be honest.

Old Ross, Colonel Ross, started from his thoughts. All of them had started, even jumped; General Beal and General Nichols as much as anyone else. They all then realized that it was, of course, the troop carrier planes; the sound of their coming not before noticed in the mutter of the big bombers. The carriers were on schedule. And, by God, they were really down, roaring over the Base! Heads had turned; General Beal did not prevent himself from looking right around. For one second they gave the illusion of barely missing the barrack roofs; it actually looked as though you would be able to reach up and touch them. In another second, you saw that you couldn't; for, on the third second, here they were, right above, breaking your ears with their engines; but a few hundred feet high, at least. Colonel Ross glimpsed the dark hatches open on their flanks. They and their big shadows fled out across the field, dribbling behind them, like an evacuation of their cylindrical steel guts, a string of tumbling paratroopers.

Colonel Ross shifted the tiring load of himself from his left foot, in whose toes he felt a cramp, to his right foot. He worked the cramping toes up and down, hoping to ease them. He heard the pumping of his mistaken heart, now back where it belonged; but still swollen from the bound of terror it took when that horrid irruptive roar of new engines coming too close, coming too fast, stormed his unprepared ears with a savage percussion that told his quailing brain he was surely a dead man. Whether other hearts there bounded as hard, or other brains quailed as much, he could not tell; but he guessed not. He was the oldest man here; and old men have a shameful lack of nerve.

Colonel Ross breathed in his breath and blew it out softly. For himself, for old Schlichter, for mankind, he could feel the same subduing mortification. There never could be a man so brave that he would not sometime, or in the end, turn part or all coward; or so wise that he was not, from beginning to end, part ass if you knew where to look; or so good that nothing at all about him was despicable. This would have to be accepted. This was one of the limits of human endeavor, one of those boundaries of the possible whose precise determining was, as General Nichols with his ascetic air of being rid of those youthful illusions, viewing with no nonsense the Here and the Now, always saw it, the problem. If you did not know where the limits were, how did you know that you weren't working outside them? If you were working outside them you must be working in vain. It was no good acting on a supposition that men would, for your purpose, be what they did not have it in them to be; just as it was unwise to beguile yourself, up there on top of the whirlwind, with the notion that the storm was going to have to do what you said.

General Nichols was indeed wise, young, if he had these points clear in his mind. The not wholly satisfactory idea—that wisdom, though better than rubies, came to so little; that a few of the most-heard platitudes contained all there was of it; that its office was to acquaint you not with the abstruse or esoteric, but with the obvious, what any fool can see—might as well be accepted, too.

This was not to say that General Nichols knew all the answers —yet! Now there would normally be a short delay while he passed through the season of tranquillity, the holy calm of the recent revelation which showed him this track was the right one, that the corner of the grand design had been uncovered, that the secret of it all lay this way, not far ahead. With that discard that impressed Colonel Ross, that choice of the hard way, without illusions, he had sagaciously bounded the possible on two sides. He would need time to see the side left open, and where that side must be bounded. To the valuable knowledge of how much could be done with other men, and how much could be done with circumstance, he might have to add the knowledge of how much could be done with himself. He was likely to find it less than he thought.

He—General Nichols, Colonel Ross, Judge Schlichter, every man—was so sure to find it less than he thought, because by the time he found it, he was less than he was. The drops of water wore the stone. The increment of fatigue, the featherweight's extra in every day's living, which could not be rested away, collected heaviness in the mind just as it collected acid in the tissues. The experience of seeing, of experiencing, briskly undertaken with the illusion of gain, was, of course, a work of destruction. You saw through lie after lie, you learned better than to believe in fable after fable, and good riddance, surely! Or was it? When you came, as you might if you worked hard, to finish your clean-up job; all trash and rubbish cleared from the underlying nature of things; not one lie and not one fable between you and its face; what would you do? You had what you worked for, all clear, open for inspection; and were you downhearted?

Downheartedness was no man's part. A man must stand up and do the best he can with what there is. If the thing he labored to uncover now seemed in danger of stultifying him, could a rational being find nothing to do? If mind failed you, seeing no pattern; and heart failed you, seeing no point, the stout, stubborn will must be up and doing. A pattern should be found; a point should be imposed. Was that too much?

It was not. This discovery wasn't new. What to do about it exercised the best minds of sixty centuries; and the results of the exercise, their helpful hints, their best advices, their highly recommended procedures, afforded you a good selection; you had only to suit your taste and temperament. Once you knew you needed something to keep you operative, playing the man, you could be of good heart. Your need would find it for you, and adapt it to you; and even support you in it, when those who had different needs, or thought they had none, asked if you were crazy.

Life, Judge Schlichter would agree, seemed mostly a hard-luck story, very complicated, beginning nowhere and never ending, unclear in theme, and confusing in action. Some of it you saw yourself, and while that was at most very little, you could piece out the picture, since it always fitted in with what other people said they saw.

Unhappy victims complained of their unhappy circumstances. The trusting followers of the misjudged easiest way found that way immediately getting hard. Simple-minded aspirants, not having what it took, did not quite make it. Conceited men proudly called their shots and proceeded to miss them, without even the comfort of realizing that few attended long enough to notice, and fewer cared. Any general argument or intention was comically contravened in reported or portrayed dispensations by which the young died and the old married; courageous patience overdid it and missed the boat; good Samaritans, stopping, found it was a trap and lost *their* shirts, too—everyday incidents in the manifold pouring-past of the Gaderene swine, possessed at someone's whim, but demonstrably innocent

—for what was a guilty pig, or a wicked one?—to the appointed steep place. Though so sad, the hard luck often moving, it was a repetitious story, and long; and what did it prove? Let somebody else figure that out!

Using the words of a Great, if perhaps not too Good, man, old Schlichter answered with sonorous piety and a noble gesture:

> *All Nature is but art unknown to thee*
> *All chance, direction, which thou canst not see;*
> *All discord, harmony not understood;*
> *All partial evil, universal good—*

Colonel Ross stood, every limb aching, bemused—some trucks or guns or something were passing with men on them sitting absurd and stiff, their folded arms held up—and he began to consider a few recent random contributions to discord, to harmony not understood.

The hulk of *Tarfu Tessie,* stupidly rolled off on the road, spread its stench of rotten blood. Lieutenant What's-her-name —Turck was sick in a paper bag in the plane they just didn't die in; and Sal threw up the rest of the bottle of Scotch and a few things she had eaten on the dining room floor. Nicodemus said: "I hopes I sees you—"; and the Ocanara *Sun* unfolded to *This & That by Art Bullen.* Through the hot night, he heard the drunken voices singing in the lighted hotel and got to his feet. Making impudent speeches, the snotty young lieutenants posed as, and were, the two, obnoxious, only champions of the dignity of man.

Saying: "I don't want you to be glum," Cora kindly pressed him with familiar warmth. The sullen, half-heartedly scheming, black faces, so suited to their old rôle of the abused, the betrayed, mooned up at him in righteous protest; but necessarily in vain. Colonel Woodman breathed whisky fumes across the desk, a palaver of nonsense, with ten hours to go before he put his pistol in his mouth. While Colonel Mowbray gently praised and gently blamed him, Benny, that young Mars of men, averted his hard, thoughtless stare indifferently, and slouched his strong scarred body, eyeing the aerial view of Maxwell Field. Bus, air-borne and all well in that fine hefty, though a little heavy at low altitudes, bitch of a so-called Thunderbolt, smiled like the restored Titan who touched his mother earth. Bus marked in the corner of his goggles the encroaching wing tip of the snappily flown P-38, moved his hand; and, Chief again, outsmarted his very best honey of a group commander; scared his nervy little murderer pissless.

Now Captain Collins said equably, of his idiot girl: "Not that special, sir"; and Captain Hicks with a great show of anxious candor said: "It's only that I feel, sir, something pretty good could be done." Arthritic, Luke Howden stooped along, never stopping to fool with disloyalty; and Johnny Sears quickly said: "It's easier to keep people out than to put them out." Poor old Pop, the brainless wonder, halted in distress, getting nowhere fast, up and down his office. General Nichols, so wise so young, let fall from his chiseled lips the calm word: "We must do it anyway."

Wagging his head, Colonel Ross pronounced: "From this, we learn—"; but a sudden sound interrupted him. It was a new noise breaking through the music of the last band, and the drone of plane engines still above the field. It came from a distance; and he was a moment in identifying it as a siren, across there by the lake, piling wail on wail.

When he looked that way last, inattentive in thought, the air had been full of the hosts of falling parachutes, the sus-pended jumpers from the carrier planes. They seemed to be all down now. Colonel Ross could see nothing at such a distance; but by the lake the siren persisted, far beyond any regular or prearranged air warning signal; and, with sudden attention, he turned his head to look down the line of the staff. He found Major Sears's head turned, too; and their eyes met.

Major Sears's lips moved, saying something. He stepped backward a pace, out of line; stooped, put a hand on the boards of the platform, and dropped lightly to the ground. On the ground, he began to run, heading for the open frame shelter beyond the Operations Building where, in constant readiness, waited the emergency vehicles—a crash truck, a field ambulance, and two fire engines.

XIV

NATHANIEL HICKS had no time to count the dropping parachutes, but his eye made a sort of calculation for him, an instinctive estimate of the scale of the disaster he might be going to have to see. He guessed that last plane load was thirty or more—three dozen, perhaps.

Meanwhile he was for several seconds engaged in minor but more immediate requirements put on his attention by getting down the lumber pile to the ground. Lieutenant Turck had clutched the hand he held to her; and she needed it, so he paused at each of the higher steps stiffening his muscles to give her a point to steady herself as she jumped. Captain Wiley and Captain Duchemin were down ahead of them.

Lieutenant Anderson, who must have been at his "command post" desk came out from under the fly-top, poised in indecision or dismay; and Captain Wiley put a hand on his arm, jerking his other thumb up. "Look, pal," he said, quickly, but not excited; "some of those are going in the water. I can't see any life vests on them; so maybe you better start making with a boat, if you have one. I don't think they'll swim so far with all that junk—"

Lieutenant Anderson said to a black sergeant who had come out with him: "Double over and let that siren off!" To Captain Wiley, he said: "We have a telephone hookup here. I better ring Operations, if I can—"

"To hell with that!" Captain Wiley said. "What can they do? You got a boat?"

Stepping clear of the corner of the lumber pile, Nathaniel Hicks could see a pattern in the floating parachutes. Though all one drop from one plane, they were in two groups, separated by an interval of altitude, each group strung out, scattered as though by a gesture of broadcast sowing. They no longer appeared all hanging together, all headed for the lumber pile.

A readjustment of perspective showed that the lower group, or most of it, could not get that far. The first parachutes, sown wide, were almost down, falling toward good ground—the sand and grass reaches within the defense sector, behind those installations on the perimeter which were engaged, not very convincingly, with short bursts of fired blanks, in repelling a "rush" toward them by paratroopers from the other flight who were coming in as skirmishers—not very convincingly, either—from the center of the field.

The defenders reacted to the new development of being taken in the rear with enthusiasm. A paratrooper hit almost on top of an automatic weapons emplacement; and was immediately surrounded by figures scrambling from under the camouflage cover. Two more hit; and then two more. All over the sector, yells were lifted, armed figures arose excitedly from prone shelters and slit trenches, swarming toward the rolling men and collapsing parachutes, plainly intent on "capturing" them.

From somewhere distant, Major McIlmoyle, perfectly recognizable, bellowed like a bull, chiding this mass maneuver, mixing curses and warnings that they were exposed, under fire; they were being attacked; they were exposed; to get down; one or two was enough, goddamn it!

Parachutes still in the air, a last few of the first group, all the second group, were getting lower now; and there could be no more question of hanging motionless, or even of moving slowly. The second group in a dispersed, side-slipping deployment, passed at a good clip, high over the lumber pile on an angle of glide that seemed to stretch as it quickened—not even Nathaniel Hicks could doubt where they would have to land. At the same time, under them, at angles of glide by contrast steadily steepening, the remainder of the first group came fast, landing nearer and nearer the pile; and now one last man was coming right at it. Astounded, Nathaniel Hicks saw that a descent by parachute was nothing like what he thought. It was a barely retarded plummeting; and a parachutist would hit no slower than a man would hit jumping free from, say the high top of the lumber pile.

In shocked alarm, Nathaniel Hicks stood stupid, seeing full

538

in front of him, beyond the pile, and already as low as its top, the swinging solid body in its baggy battle dress, the slightly drawn-up thick knees and big boots held together, the bent helmeted head and upstretched arms holding the risers. The figure fell like a stone; and it fell on stone—the broad, brand-new, never-used imitation stone of the concrete runway.

Since this man was facing downwind, his back was to Nathaniel Hicks as his boots struck. The flexed knees gave. He went over instantly, tilted sideways, rolling, legs slung limply out behind. His clutching fists grabbed in some of the sudden slack in the risers; but the parachute, which had tottered, starting to wilt as its great circumference swayed over and touched the paving ahead of him, felt the breeze and bellied full again. Now the slanting, rolling body landed, an audible smacking thud, on its side and shoulder. Expelled from the man broke a wordless cry, half scream, half groan. His chin strap must have come loose; for the helmet popped off his head and bounded on the concrete with a bright clang of metal. The filled parachute swung like a sail, straining the shroud lines taut, and began determinedly to drag its burden up the runway.

Held by this swiftly developing little horror in the foreground, Nathaniel Hicks's eyes nonetheless distractedly encompassed a background against which the dragged man on the runway moved. This was the sweep of placid blue water beyond the wide white paving, beyond the dun strip of sandy soil at the lake's bank. Into this background—an intolerable elaboration of simultaneous events—arrived the last group of parachutes, well down, well out—a hundred yards or more. The trailed figures rushed near the water; yet for a moment contact was delayed, as though they could not quite reach it.

At that instant three, maybe four, parachutes reversed their motion, rising slightly, puffing away, jostling into others. The phenomenon explained itself; they were freed of the men under them, who must have undone their harness fastenings, and who fell forward, the first down, hitting ahead with high splashes of spray. They were gone before the lifted water fell back. Beyond these plungers, those others still in harness struck with no more delay, plowed trails of foam, foundered under. The bevy of parachutes toppled low; and, quickly sopped, sank awash. There followed, for a gruesome drawn-out minute, a struggling commotion on or near the surface.

From the shed by the lake, the sound of the siren went wailing up. Nathaniel Hicks felt his throat contract to gasp air in, and then contract more, as though to use the air to shout; but nothing came. In his eye sockets, across his eyeballs he felt stabbing twinges like the pain of too much light—perhaps a spraining conflict of muscles caught at cross-purposes attempting to maintain one focus while irresistibly drawn to assume another. This ache of the overpressed eyes merged distractingly with the insufferable demands the eyes made on the mind, the impossible work of anatomizing into instants, enough instants to hold, one instant to one perception, the tumultuous few seconds with their multiple movements above and on the lake's surface, suddenly begun, suddenly all gone.

Meanwhile, the dragged man on the runway made hoarse sounds of anguish, which emerged indistinctly in the ebb of the siren howls spiraling over and over from low to terrible high. He worked with a fast frenzy to stop his rough progress. His clawing hands got the canopy edge, snatched at the wall of silk ahead, and dragged what he could reach down under him. The parachute shuddered, falling suddenly spilled; the lines dropped limp; the great cloth folds, collapsing, sank, and half covered the man, who now lay still.

Captain Wiley said: "Could this be dangerous?"

Captain Wiley was rising from a squat. He must have dropped on his heels, Nathaniel Hicks could not tell when. The realization filled Nathaniel Hicks with amazement; for he could see in it, dazedly, the work of a wonderful instinct. Economical of action, collectedly denying every vain impulse of confusion and excitement, Captain Wiley calmly crouched, appraising the situation; imperturbably doing nothing, watching for all this to resolve itself and show him something there would be some sense in doing.

While he made his survey, Captain Wiley had scooped up a handful of sand, which he weighed lightly, spilling it through his fingers. Straightening now, he let the remainder fall, brushed the last grains off his palm and walked toward the paratrooper up the runway. Nathaniel Hicks turned and saw Lieutenant Turck sitting on the lowest pile of stacked boards. Her lips were set tightly together and he could see her hands and even her shoulders shaking. Nathaniel Hicks said: "Where's Duchemin?"

Lieutenant Turck got to her feet. She said: "He ran over there—to that landing; whatever it is." She looked after Captain Wiley, and began to move. Frowning, she said: "He must let him lie; not move him. He has at least one leg broken—maybe both—"

Nathaniel Hicks said: "How do you know?"

She drew a breath. "I have all kinds of useless information," she said. "I have a lot of dismal acquirements. Did you know I was going to be a doctor? I happened to get married instead; but he was a doctor, too. I know about anatomy. Legs always bend back; not sideways, or forward." She gave him a distressed smile. "Yes; I was a librarian," she said. "Before and after. I can also operate a switchboard, and milk a cow; if you ever need anyone." She looked past him toward the lake shore. "I am, as usual, a little out of place, I suppose. Should we move on?" She began to walk again, catching her shoes in the loose sand.

Looking that way, too, Nathaniel Hicks could see the thickening crowd, the straggle of figures crossing the runway farther up. The siren had stopped; and there were, he realized, no more sounds of firing behind—all the sham fighting must have been abandoned. Not far away, in rapid movement on the lake bank, a dozen of the Negro engineers were stripping, peeling shirts over their heads, stooping hastily to get their shoes off. Several of them, black bodies now naked, jumped splashing into the water. Out a little way, their heads arose, and they set themselves with varying vigor, to swim—toward what, Nathaniel Hicks did not think they knew. Rather to the left of where they appeared to be heading, he could see, or thought he could, what might or might not be the light-colored cloth of a water-logged parachute or two. There was no sign of any heads there, any movement.

While Nathaniel Hicks looked, Captain Duchemin detached himself from the staring groups. His big figure came plodding over the sand, gained the runway, and moved toward them, preceded up the concrete by his long shadow. "Not working today, the crash boat," Captain Duchemin said. "Pity, isn't it? I don't think the bathers are going to get anywhere, either. Perhaps somebody ought to tell them to get out before they drown themselves."

"Not me," Nathaniel Hicks said.

"I was thinking of the loot, Anderson. Or our good major, McIlmoyle. I am only an observer, I informed them. A top sergeant, a fine black figure of a buck named Rogers, was the leading spirit. When I gave no orders, he gave some. Have we another casualty here?"

Captain Wiley knelt by the man on the runway, busy with the fasteners of his parachute harness. Lieutenant Turck said: "I wouldn't try to clear those leg straps, Captain—"

Captain Wiley said: "Let me get out that knife he has, there. I'll just hack off the suspension lines. Get him clear of his chute—"

"Yes. Good. Let's cover him with it. They must be sending medical people, don't you think? Would he have a first-aid kit? Could we find it without moving him?"

Around the corner of the lumber pile came trotting now two more paratroopers. One of them cried: "What you got, Shorty?" They came up the concrete with a clatter of steel heels. The other one, a corporal, said: "He hurt?"

"He's out," Captain Wiley said. He had drawn a jungle knife from the fallen man's sheath. Looking at the formidable blade with pleasure, he said: "The things they have!" Catching up the lines, he cut them with quick little slashes.

From Captain Wiley, and Lieutenant Turck bent beside him, the two paratroopers turned their sunburned faces to inspect Captain Duchemin and Nathaniel Hicks, an incurious flash of eyes under the helmet brims. With a direct and simple air of finding themselves alone and getting on with their private business, the corporal said: "Water! Here; my canteen—"

"No, don't!" Lieutenant Turck said. "That's the worst thing you could do. Let him alone!"

They had both crouched; and the corporal looked over at her, amazed. "We got to bring him to!" he said. "You want us just have him lay here?"

"Please do," Lieutenant Turck said. "We want to cover him up. We're getting the parachute clear. He's gone into shock. I think both legs are fractured. They must be splinted; and he mustn't be moved without a stretcher."

"You a nurse?" the corporal said.

"No; but—"

"Better leave us handle it, then, Lieutenant—"

"Uh-uh!" Captain Wiley shook his head. "What the lady says, friend! We cover him up and wait for the ambulance. Much better." Pressing with his thumb, he made a package of cigarettes rise out of his breast pocket and casually proffered it to them. "You got seven in the lake," he said. "This one's doing all right."

"Jesus!" the corporal said carefully. With a mechanical motion, as though involuntarily, they both took cigarettes. The other one said: "Thanks, Captain. We don't have a match." Captain Wiley flipped a paper book of matches at them. The corporal struck one and lit the cigarette in his own mouth. Cupped in his big hand, he then held it for his companion. He said to him: "What crossed? Who was flying you?"

"Lieutenant Tyler."

"Jeez, he's all right! Don't he look where the hell he is?"

With the same simple directness they had again withdrawn themselves, Nathaniel Hicks could see, into their real world, exclusively theirs, talking only to each other. "Didn't your light go?" the corporal said.

"Yeah; but I told you. What happened; number six in our file; his hook-on jammed on the anchor line cable, or something. We couldn't clear any more; maybe a minute. The lieutenant found it out. I guess he was watching to trim his tail up, whatever he does. Anyway, he sees something—I don't know. He bats the door back and yells what the hell. They got the hook-on moving then. I was right behind—next out. I hear our half-ass Powell yell back: 'Line stuck, sir. We're going.' Lieutenant says: 'Jeez, you ham-head, you better go! Think we stand still—' "

"Jeez, you should have held it!" the corporal said.

"Am I jump-master? He gives me the knee, and I went out. He stops counting between, I guess. Anyway, they fed so fast, one hits me—Shorty, here, I think. Say! I thought I had a tail surface across my neck! Then I knew something was buggering my chute up. Shorty's chute, probably." He cut the air with the edge of his hand. "Oh, mama, I said; here's mine! I bet I fell partly open, two hundred, two hundred fifty feet. When we bumped up there, I lost my auxiliary rip ring. Then, the rag snapped, O.K.; but how close it was; right away I landed—what a smack! Only, soft sand—not this."

The corporal looked over to the lake. "Who was after Shorty?"

"I'm not so sure. I'd have to figure. No one in the old platoon, I think. Yeah—that guinea fellow; the one we got right before they moved you, remember? Conti."

"Jeez, they ought to have Powell's stripes!"

"Yeah."

They paused, both open-mouthed, staring at each other in surprise. "Yeah!" the corporal said in turn. "Unless he never jumped, at the end."

"That half-ass would jump, all right. I give him that—"

"Something coming," the corporal said. "They take their time!" He turned his head. "Fire engine!" he said. "They bring a fire engine!"

Nathaniel Hicks, turning too, saw the fire engine succeeded by a heavy truck, and then an ambulance. On the runway paving, a jeep rushed up and halted. In large white letters the words PROVOST MARSHAL were painted on the drab metal below the windshield.

Captain Wiley said: "Better grab that, Nat; tell them this is for the ambulance."

Nathaniel Hicks walked over to the jeep. To the major getting out of it, he said: "We have a man with a broken leg right over there, sir."

"You have a man with a broken leg?" the major said. "Well, you made one hell of a lot of noise about it!" To the lieutenant with him, he said: "Tell them their man's over there!" Giving Nathaniel Hicks an irritable, critical look, he said: "Who are you, Captain? Are you in command here?"

"No, sir," Nathaniel Hicks said. "Major McIlmoyle, I don't know where he is, is in command, I believe. We're observers from the Directorate of Special—"

"Well, for God's sake, if you need an ambulance, someone's hurt, telephone for one! There's a connection right down at the crash-boat berth, there. Use your head, Captain! Don't set off a siren!"

Nathaniel Hicks said: "We had nothing to do with setting it off, Major. It was set off when seven paratroopers came down in the lake. We haven't seen them since—"

"Day!" the Major shouted after his lieutenant. "Get on the phone to Operations! Part of that drop went in the lake!" To Nathaniel Hicks, he said: "You see it?"

"Yes, sir."

"Stick around; I may want you later."

"Yes, sir," said Nathaniel Hicks. "That is Major McIlmoyle coming up to the fly-top, now."

"All right. Any other officers who saw it, tell them to stick around." He turned briskly and marched away.

Left standing, Nathaniel Hicks continued to stand. He supposed, indeed he knew, that the matter-of-factness he found himself feeling, was no more than nature, was no more than sense. The seven men—he would have said six; but he did not doubt that Captain Wiley when he saw anything, made no mistake about it—simply fell in, went down, and well-weighted, never came up.

He remembered disconnectedly someone telling him, as a matter of curious information, that Lake Lalage, though of no great area, was almost everywhere, even within a few feet of the shore, over a hundred feet deep; and that in some parts sounding lines, presumably because those using them had not come prepared for deep soundings, never found any bottom at all—an interesting geological formation. Nathaniel Hicks began to recall, but not accurately, accounts he had read of swimmers recovered after they had been under water—an hour?—a half an hour?—revived by the medal-winning patience of knowledgeable boy scouts, or of police pulmotor squads.

Then he thought of the six, seven, individuals dragged gently down the hundred-foot, or bottomless, gulf of water, choking and bubbling; those without parachutes, perhaps a little faster; but those with parachutes unsupported by them in this element. By now, at any rate—it must be ten or more minutes—though perhaps not all quite dead, there could not be one of them still conscious.

Someone behind him said: "Excuse me, sir—Captain."

Turning, Nathaniel Hicks saw, a yard away, poised hesitant, a thin, dark Negro. He wore much disordered twill work clothes, a helmet liner, but no helmet. Under his arm he pressed the butt of a rifle, hung at an awkward angle from its sling on his shoulder. Faded T/5 chevrons were stamped on his sleeves. He looked out from below the helmet liner with a diffident half-smile.

Nathaniel Hicks said blankly: "Yes. What is it?"

The Negro lowered his eyes. Moving one boot, he gave the sand, on which he stood beyond the runway, a gentle kick. "McIntyre, sir," he said.

"Oh!" Nathaniel Hicks said. "Hello! How are you? I didn't know this was your outfit!"

"Yes, sir," T/5 McIntyre said. "Captain, I only wanted—" he paused in confusion, "well, thank you; getting me that ride back, sir. Well, I bring this—something. I leave it for you, your building there. I don't know did they—"

"Yes," Nathaniel Hicks said, appalled. He found himself reddening.

"Only reason," T/5 McIntyre said. He coughed. "I wanted it for you—if they give it you. We bringing chow over here in the truck—so I have to go; I only leave it—"

"Yes," Nathaniel Hicks said. "I got it. I appreciate very much your wanting to give it to me——"

T/5 McIntyre's diffident smile reappeared. "I get it this morning," he said. "I—"

The sound of a new siren reached Nathaniel Hicks. Looking past T/5 McIntyre, he saw that it came this time from a car, a staff car, whose olive drab was waxed until it gleamed. The car came fast up the truck road, passed behind the lumber pile and wheeled onto the runway beyond. Seeing the small scarlet flag flapping on its bumper staff, Nathaniel Hicks said: "General Beal."

"Yes, sir," T/5 McIntyre said.

Nathaniel Hicks said: "McIntyre; it was very nice of you to want to give me that box; but I had to send it back to you. You see; if you gave me a present for anything I did for you —they could court-martial me for that—"

T/5 McIntyre said: "You don't keep it?"

"I couldn't," Nathaniel Hicks said. "Not in the Army, McIntyre—"

T/5 McIntyre said nothing for an instant. His eyes moved then, going past Nathaniel Hicks; and he shifted his feet quickly. He said: "I was only hoping you have it, Captain." He began suddenly to step backwards. "Well, thank you again, Captain. I got to get back—" he turned quickly away.

Looking where T/5 McIntyre had been looking, Nathaniel Hicks saw the Medical Corps men on the runway by the paratrooper. Coming toward him, almost at hand, was Lieutenant Turck. Still red, Nathaniel Hicks said to her, "That was our friend T/5 McIntyre—the colored kid on the plane. He had me on a spot. He tried to give me a present—"

Lieutenant Turck said: "General Beal's here. Look." She touched his arm; and he faced about.

General Beal had left the car. The general from Washington, Nichols, had come with him; and, moving together toward the lake, they had halted, and stood now not fifty feet away. The tableau, arresting in its grouping and lighting, was what Lieutenant Turck touched Nathaniel Hicks, perhaps involuntarily, to make him look at.

The hot sun, nearer the horizon, poured a dazzling gold light across the great reach of the air field. Under a pure and tender wide sky, empty now of all its planes, the flat light bathed everything; all the men, who appeared for an instant motionless; the lumber pile; the low lake shore; the wide, calm ripple of waters. The swimmers, who must have been ordered from the lake, were in the act of coming out. They emerged with shining limbs, their muscular black bodies brightly dripping. Mounting the low bank, they stole guarded glances at the two generals, then glanced respectfully away, going to the little piles of clothes they had left. They stood swinging their arms, slapping their chests and thighs in the easy exercise of drying themselves in the warm air.

Around the two generals a circle of officers had gathered, posed in concern. In this sad, gold light their grouping made a composition like that found in old-fashioned narrative paintings of classical incidents or historical occasions—the Provost Marshal indicated the lake with a demonstrative gesture; a young Air Force captain faced him, standing tense and stiff. Bulky in his fighting trim, a captain of paratroopers, and Major McIlmoyle, helmeted and dirty, waited in somber attitudes like legates who had brought news of a battle. To one side, a lieutenant colonel, probably the Post Engineer, in stylized haste gave grave tidings to a thin chicken colonel, that instant arrived—Colonel Hildebrand, the Base Commander.

A deferential distance behind these chief figures, touched with the same sunset light, the mustered myrmidons, token groups of the supporting armies, whispered together—the black engineers, the arms-loaded paratroopers; and in the middle background, borne on a stretcher as though symbolically, the wrapped form of the man who had fallen on the runway was passing.

Lieutenant Turck now stirred, in a quiet movement, facing away a little. With a recollection of decorum, a composed delicacy, she had moved so as not to be looking right at the husky naked black men preparing to dress. Nathaniel Hicks looked again at the silent circle of officers, and at General Beal's set face turned toward the water. He could see it clearly; and he was astounded to observe that tears were running down it.

548

XV

THE TELEPHONE call reached Mr. Botwinick in the Message Center at AFORAD Headquarters. Mr. Botwinick had gone down to the Message Center to check the in-coming log. According to schedule, General Beal, as soon as Retreat was over, would proceed to the Area Officers Club. Mr. Botwinick planned to be efficiently on hand, when the general arrived at the Club, with any late messages that might need immediate attention.

Though Mr. Botwinick had appeared casually, asked for the log, and set himself to reading it, standing informally at the counter by the wickets in the cage-like barrier around the door which prevented unauthorized personnel from just wandering into the Message Center proper, his presence caused a marked increase in busyness in the staff on duty. Everyone bent to his work. Papers were brought here and taken there with alacrity. The operator putting some long routine message on a teletype sending machine displayed uncommon speed. Of the receiving machines, only one was going. It carried the hourly weather report of the Gulf Coast sequence circuit. As fast as the carriage could get back to the left margin and take new reports fed into the line it clattered out the code symbols by which station after station reported, as of this minute, the temperature, dew point, relative humidity, wind speed and direction, cloud condition, type and amount of precipitation if any, and barometric tendency. Except in the Base Weather Office, where it was simultaneously arriving, this godlike survey, covering a quarter of the continent, had little use or significance; but an enlisted man, the newspaper he had been reading deftly concealed, followed it with anxious attention.

There was nothing much in the late messages. Mr. Botwinick handed the cryptographic clerk a short encoded piece that he thought might be more about that supposedly imminent surrender of Italy, and took a copy of a TO BEAL FOR NICHOLS FROM ARNOLD which read: RETURN EARLIEST URGENT HERE FIFTH INST PERMITTING WEATHER SUGGEST NIGHT FLIGHT. Then the telephone on the desk of the Chief Clerk rang. The Chief Clerk, a staff sergeant, said: "Operations, sir. They ask are you here." He arose obsequiously and turned over desk and telephone to Mr. Botwinick.

It was plain that the caller, with an intelligence quite usual in those who, in addition to their other duties were selected to keep Mr. Botwinick informed of important developments, knew what to do when he got no answer ringing Mr. Botwinick's office up the hall. From the time, he could guess where Mr. Botwinick was likely to be.

The time, shown by the first of a line of electric clocks set in the bare wall above the teletype machines, was shortly after five. Successive clocks went on to tell Mr. Botwinick what time it was now in San Francisco, in Honolulu, in Karachi, and in London; but Mr. Botwinick, though eyeing them, paid them no attention. Dropping into the chair, he had taken the telephone and said, "Botwinick!" briskly. Now he listened with an absorption, an absence from his immediate surroundings that made the continuing extreme busyness of the staff all the more unnecessary. An intensity, almost an anguish, of thought froze Mr. Botwinick's hollow face. For fully two minutes he said nothing. Then he said: "Wait."

With the quick ding of a warning bell, the press association ticker that printed news bulletins started up beside him, but Mr. Botwinick was oblivious. Clutching the telephone tight, he held it away from him a little. He worked his other hand into his pocket and found a soiled handkerchief which he wadded together and passed across his bony sweating forehead. He seemed to breathe with cautious difficulty. He sat for another moment, his thin shoulders in a tense hunch, his eyes narrowly regarding the line of disagreeing clocks, still as a stone.

Then he brought the telephone back against his mouth and said in sharp whisper: "Worthington."

"Yes, sir."

"Know where Colonel Mowbray is now?"

"He went to telephone, too. I heard him tell Colonel Ross he was going to call the Club—tell them it was off. Colonel Ross said yes, the general would be going directly to his office.

There were some other arrangements Colonel Mowbray was going to make, I don't know exactly what. I think it was the general himself who called Colonel Ross, told him to come over to the lake. Colonel Ross called his own office, I know; I think, about a press release. Before he went over."

"Who else went over?"

"Several people went earlier, sir, after the first call, the Provost Marshal's man calling the Operations Officer. He got Colonel Hildebrand and Colonel Uline—"

Mr. Botwinick said: "Now, listen. Did you hear anybody say anything about the crash boat being laid up? Or about the men being supposed to wear life vests?"

"No, sir. Not about the boat. I just heard the Operations Officer telling Lieutenant Nauroze he didn't see how seven of them drowned; weren't they always wearing Mae Wests? Lieutenant Nauroze said they probably figured they were wearing plenty without that; probably figured they wouldn't be jumping in lakes. The Operations Officer said: 'You jump in central Florida, there's nothing but lakes.' I heard that."

Mr. Botwinick compressed his lips. When he opened them he said casually: "Thanks, Worthington. That all? Anything else?"

"No, sir. Oh! Did you still want to know about Colonel Carricker? We had word finally. He developed engine trouble and decided to put down on Ocanara Number Three. He had to leave the plane. Captain Dyer went out with a jeep to get him. I know, before the parade, General Beal's office asked about him; he was supposed to be back."

"Yes. We heard that. The general knows. Now, in case he stops at the Base first, coming back, see he gets a message that the general wants to see him. Better see Sergeant Pellerino knows, too, if he's still in the hangar. They might just stop there, not come in Operations."

"Yes, sir."

"I'm going back to my office now. That is where I'll be."

"Yes, sir."

Mr. Botwinick put down the telephone and stood up. He said to the Chief Clerk: "Just hold that code message. The general is coming back here. He'll send for it if he wants it."

"Yes, sir." The Chief Clerk looked at him an instant with undisguised curiosity. He then disguised it quickly, looking away. Mr. Botwinick went to the gate in the cage of wire screening, slid his finger under the edge of the counter and pressed the release. He went out and closed the gate after him. Pausing at the hall door, he said, again casually: "Just an accident. Some people drowned at the lake." He went out into the hall.

The door of Mr. Botwinick's office was open and the light was on. Except for the faint sounds of the machines back at the Message Center, this whole wing of Headquarters was silent, the offices closed and empty. All Colonel Mowbray's people, and all General Beal's people had been allowed to go for the day.

Mr. Botwinick passed from his little office into the room behind. Mrs. Spann's and Miss Jelliffe's desks were bare and tidy. Though shadows were beginning to gather, enough of the strong evening sunlight in the open quadrangle was reflected through the windows for Mr. Botwinick to see easily the dial markings on the combination locks of the bank of file cabinets by the door to Colonel Mowbray's office.

Mr. Botwinick went to the first cabinet and turned the knob with practiced fingers. When he heard the click of the fallen tumblers he pressed the catch and drew the top drawer out. The drawer was almost empty; but lying in the bottom was a much-used file folder of heavy stock well filled with papers. Mr. Botwinick took it out. Holding it, he felt along the top of the cabinets until he found one of the sizeable red cardboard placards on which was printed: OPEN SAFE. This he set neatly in the drawer pull.

Carrying the folder, Mr. Botwinick went back into his own office, closed the hall door, and sat down at his desk. The folder had a label on its cover which said: *Miss Jelliffe—To file*. It held material that Colonel Mowbray sent back to Mrs. Spann today and probably also yesterday. Mrs. Spann separated this material, which Colonel Mowbray had marked to be filed, from material on which other action was noted and left it in the folder. It was Miss Jelliffe's job to do the actual filing. Miss Jelliffe was usually a day or two in finding time.

Mr. Botwinick pressed the folder open and began slowly, almost with reluctance, to turn the papers over. His finger tips fumbled the edges of the sheets, and from time to time, having turned over several at once, he had to stop and separate them. He was a minute or two coming to the sheet he had been looking for. He put his moist hands down flat on the surface of the desk and looked at it. The sheet was headed: HEADQUARTERS OCANARA ARMY AIR BASE. *Subject: Post Engineer's Report on Lake Lalage Crash Boat. To: Executive Officer, AFORAD.* It was dated yesterday.

At the upper corner of the sheet a form was rubber-stamped, with spaces for initials and for a check mark indicating disposal directed. Colonel Mowbray's imperial "M" was jotted there, all right; and after it—Mrs. Spann made very few mistakes— in Colonel Mowbray's scrawled script: *file.*

Mr. Botwinick extracted his handkerchief again and passed it softly across his forehead. Colonel Mowbray probably read no more than the heading—perhaps he was interrupted; perhaps he was thinking of something else.

Mr. Botwinick put his elbows on the desk. He clasped his lean little chin tight in one hand, looking at the paper. One of his telephones began to ring with a muted eager persistence; but Mr. Botwinick made no move. He let it ring, perhaps pondering what would happen to him if anything happened to Colonel Mowbray.

♦

Slumped down in the car's leather-covered seat Mrs. Beal said: "I'll bet they had a lot of fancy things fixed! I know they had a big stinking cake with the Air Force patch on it in colors. And candles. I don't know what they'll do with it now." The thought seemed to give her a faint, moody pleasure. "Down the drain!" she said. "Well, if Bus thinks he's going to suddenly decide later to bring Jo-Jo to our place and get something to eat there, he's wrong as hell. We haven't a thing.

I know him. He's wound up now and doesn't feel like eating. He'll make the fur fly for a couple of hours and then suddenly wake up and find he's hungry. He'll wish he had some of that cake. Well, I suppose they could sneak in the back and get it."

Mrs. Ross said: "I really don't think he could have gone right on and had a big party, Sal."

Mrs. Beal moved restlessly on the seat. "I'm not kicking," she said. "I don't feel too much like eating either."

Mrs. Ross said: "How *do* you feel, Sal?"

Mrs. Beal said: "I guess I'll live; only, what for? All I do is wait, wait, wait!" She had been listlessly holding a lighted cigarette between her slim childish fingers; and now she suddenly threw it out of the car. "Let them pick it up!" she said.

The car stood on the exactly raked and rolled gravel of the small parking space inside the Headquarters quadrangle just beyond the corner of the wing in which was General Beal's office. The entrance drive went past the general's private door. When they drove in, a blaze of last, late, gold sunlight lay in the drive, and Mrs. Ross had pulled around the corner so they could sit in the shadow. The bright light had now lost force; the sun was going. A tone, no longer of afternoon; but of early transparent evening filled the warm air. Above the tile roofs of the quadrangle buildings the blue sky was paled by a haze of tranquil yellow. "We could sit all night!" Mrs. Beal said. "Norm might have only thought they were coming over. Bus might decide they had to get those bodies; and he'd stay right there until they did. You don't know what he's like when something happens—some of his people get killed— I mean, and he doesn't think they ought to. I can tell you, it better not be anybody's fault!" She looked around her moodily. "Why do we wait any longer, Cora?"

Mrs. Ross said: "I think we might wait a few more minutes. Norman knows we're waiting here. If Bus can't come, I think he'll either come himself, or see somebody tells us. There are duty officers, people like that, he could reach."

"I suppose so," Mrs. Beal said. "I just hope he isn't acting too crazy, with Jo-Jo there. Only, Jo-Jo's seen him before, I guess." She brooded a moment. "You know, back when they

554

suddenly had the Air Corps fly the mail, that winter, and they kept losing pilots, one right after another—we were engaged then and Bus used to call me up every day. Then he didn't call me, and he didn't call me. So finally I called him; and he just said to me: 'What do you want?' That made me a little sore, so I said, I didn't mean it: 'Well, it might interest you to know that I'm sending you back your ring.' Did I lead with my chin! He said: 'You want a receipt or something?' and hung up on me. Hal told me afterwards—they had Bus on a desk job—Bus wouldn't stay in his office. He just stayed in the back of a hangar with Danny Pellerino—that's when he first had Danny for a crew chief—and took this plane apart, all apart. Then they put it together again. He didn't speak to anybody else for a week. Of course, he knew those people—is that a car?"

"I think there's one coming up the road," Mrs. Beal said.

"Well, it won't be Bus! I remember Father saying to me: 'You'd better be sure you want to live with a prima donna.' Man, was he right! It wasn't that he didn't like Bus, or thought Bus wasn't any good. Another thing he said was: 'When we have the next war, that boy will go places.' I always remember that; because Bus wasn't at all his type. He was just as Regular Army as you could possibly get—always running the Air Corps down; I mean, what they could do—" she broke off. "That *is* a car. It turned in."

Around the corner of the wing arose the sounds of a slowing engine, and of tires braked to a stop on the gravel by the door to the general's office. Craning out as far as she could, Mrs. Beal said: "I told you! It's a jeep. It's Benny and that Captain Dyer."

"I suppose they might know something," Mrs. Ross said.

"I'm not going to ask them," Mrs. Beal said.

From beside the halted jeep, over the idling engine, voices came clearly now.

Lieutenant Colonel Carricker said: "Thanks. Going to the Base?"

Captain Dyer said: "I'll go by, I guess."

"Well, brief Danny, then, will you? Make him come with

the crew tomorrow. Don't send that Brewer bastard. I could do it better myself."

"Yeah," said Captain Dyer. "And suppose we figure on putting in a whole new assembly. I know we got one. What are you going to do here? You going to be long?"

"How can I tell? This other thing; he may not get to see me tonight."

"Well, what do you stay around for?"

"Ah!" Lieutenant Colonel Carricker said. "He didn't say too much when he got back from Chechote⁻; so I guess there's some to come. I'll wait. He's had a beating, last couple of days. Old Ross is riding him about the niggers. The word from Washington, this Nichols, probably reads: assume the angle! The little woman's making him some kind of fuss. If he'll rack me back and get it over, I can kid him out of the rest, maybe. God damn; I don't think anybody over here thinks of anything but chicken. We got a war to win!"

"My!" Captain Dyer said. "Have you more bonds than I thought? What do I tell Jane?"

"What do you mean?"

"I mean; what do I tell Jane? She's down at the apartment by now. She called me. She was worrying that bad about you."

"What's she want?"

"It has all different names," Captain Dyer said. "They use like a bed for it. You ought to know, sonny boy."

"For Christ's sake! Tell her I didn't get back. Tell her I won't get back until next week. Tell her to go home and stay there. Tell her to lay off me. And tell her to give you that key."

Captain Dyer said: "You got that tired feeling, chum? You ought to learn to read them. I told you that one would take twins. What they say. Big girl, big time; little girl, all the time! I'll say you didn't get back. Tell her the rest yourself." He put the jeep in gear, rushed it away in reverse, cut it around, and went off with an accelerating roar.

Mrs. Beal began to laugh.

Mrs. Ross, who had not found the coarse casual exchange very edifying, looked at her with astonishment. Mrs. Beal said: "I guess he isn't so good as he thought he was!" She slammed her hand down on the horn and held it in a sharp prolonged blast.

Lieutenant Colonel Carricker, an old flying jacket thrown over his arm, his crushed garrison cap on the back of his head, stepped past the shrubbery at the corner of the building and stood staring at them. If Mrs. Beal had planned to embarrass him by letting him guess his conversation had been overheard she probably succeeded, for Lieutenant Colonel Carricker grew quite red.

Mrs. Beal, her chin up, surveyed him for a triumphant instant. She said then: "Benny!"

Lieutenant Colonel Carricker said: "Yes, ma'am."

"You just go to hell!" Mrs. Beal said.

✦

At half-past six the lobby of the Oleander Towers Hotel was full of people. All the shabby old chairs and sofas were occupied, mostly by women around whom centered various-sized groups of standing officers. The women could be recognized as officers' wives, with their husbands, and their husbands' friends. The Oleander Towers was not a good place for pick-ups. At the Scheherazade, or the Bimini, young women who wanted a little excitement could go alone—though usually they went in pairs, like a flight element; and with the flight element's purpose of mutual support and protection—to the cocktail lounge. A booth or table taken, a drink ordered, they could sit comfortably while alcohol did its genial work on all concerned, showing themselves to a good assortment of unattached men at the bar. Above the door of the Oleander Towers bar was a sign that said: OFFICERS CLUB—DOWNTOWN BRANCH. *Members and Guests Only.*

Tonight the bar was already full of members and guests. There was even a casually assembled line in the lobby waiting for tables. At the registration desk, a room clerk dealt as well as he could with a small crowd of people trying to check in and out. An island of their luggage had accumulated beyond the desk for the few overworked bellboys. Every minute, replenished, a stream of officers who lived in the hotel and who were now getting home from the Area and the Base, moved toward the elevators.

Coming into the thronged lobby with Nathaniel Hicks and Captain Duchemin, Lieutenant Turck said to them: "Thanks so much!"

"Well," Nathaniel Hicks said, "I see what you mean, Amanda; but—"

"Yes," she said. "Lippa's undoubtedly upstairs by now; and so is that Scotch I spoke of. She keeps it in a suitcase in the checkroom here—no liquor in barracks, you see. Why don't you both come right up and have a drink? I must say, I could use one."

Captain Duchemin said: "You're very kind, ma'am; but the fact is our pause to see the captain off to Orlando was just enough to make me the least little bit late for an appointment. I'd better pop in the bar there and see if my Loot has slid under some table waiting."

"Don't let us keep you," Nathaniel Hicks said. "Give me those bags. I'll see the lady to her quarters." He took the bags from Captain Duchemin.

Lieutenant Turck said: "We always have the same rooms; but I'd better check. You'll come up, won't you, Nat? I'll give Mary a ring, in case she isn't decent." She went over toward the desk.

Nathaniel Hicks said to Captain Duchemin: "If you're planning to get a bath, which you no doubt need, get up and get it; because I'm going to want one in a minute. Don won't be in, by the way. They were going to let him stay out at the Hospital tonight."

"And you," Captain Duchemin said, "have you got something on?"

"No," Nathaniel Hicks said.

"You wouldn't, ah—care to join our little *fête champêtre*? Comfortable furnishings, home-cooked food, charming com-

558

pany! Saturday night, I hear, is the loneliest night in the week."

"Not while I have a good book," Nathaniel Hicks said drily. "Go on. Find your Loot; and get that bath."

"Agreed," Captain Duchemin said. "But why don't you have a glass of the lady's Scotch? That way, you wouldn't be breathing down my neck while I dress for the ball. I feel I should pay my hostesses the delicate compliment of shaving. Makes me less abrasive, isn't it? If I knew you were boozing comfortably somewhere—"

"All right," Nathaniel Hicks said.

Captain Duchemin said: "I feel that your decision will make the lady very happy. *Bon amusement,* my captain! Don't—ah, do anything I wouldn't do." He marched over to the bar doors.

Nathaniel Hicks set down the bags next to one of the fancy pillars supporting the lobby vaults, and stood close to it, out of the way. There were, Nathaniel Hicks supposed, a hundred and fifty people in the lobby and very few of them were not talking. From the numerous small ambits formed around the seated women separate conversations all going at once joined to make almost a roar. Standing near the pillar, Nathaniel Hicks was well within earshot of two of these conversations.

To his right, a pretty girl who surely could not be over seventeen, sat stiff with inexperience and self-conscious cordiality. She was sunk down deep in a big chair, behind her pretty unstockinged legs. Her left hand wore an enormous diamond and a decorated platinum wedding ring, both obviously brand new. Encircling her stood three pilots, cropped-headed boys who looked no more than a few months her seniors—two second lieutenants, one of whom had the proud, dazed air of owning her; and so must be, brand-new like the rings, her husband; and a captain, in appearance not a day older than the lieutenants; but he had the DFC and the Air Medal and the Asiatic-Pacific ribbon with a few stars; so no doubt he commanded the lieutenants' squadron.

Amused by the extravagant diamond—the new wife's naïve-faced, fresh-colored young husband had probably never been away from home, nor had regular money of his own, before.

A little dizzy, he thought nothing of slapping down half a year's pay, plus perhaps some heavy winnings at cards or dice —Nathaniel Hicks let himself listen to the boy captain.

Closely attended by both lieutenants, who displayed a nice balance of respect and familiarity, and by the girl, who displayed a breathless interest that seemed to show she was not too young to have a sound instinct for ways to serve her husband, the captain, in a curt manly voice, proved to be talking about what happened at the lake.

Nathaniel Hicks's indulgent amusement at the oversized diamond, the raw young husband, the high school girlish bride, suffered a check. The ordinary preoccupations—the attention required in looking at and talking to his companions; in driving a car; in seeing Captain Wiley get his clearance, climb into, and while the crewmen held their extinguishers, fire up his old P-40, lift his long arm in farewell, taxi off to the head of the runway—all worked to keep Nathaniel Hicks thinking of something else for the last hour. He found now that what happened at the lake he had still much in mind, embedded there. With a tremor of nerves, he could clearly hear again the cry of the paratrooper breaking his legs on the runway; he could distinctly see the plummeting into the lake and the gruesome minute or two's vain commotion in the closing waters; the understandable but useless gesture of the excited black swimmers; and at the end, the generals, respectfully surrounded, standing a little too late on the sunset shore. Not very reasonably he now noted with irritation the callous casualness of people who talk about what they have not seen.

It was undoubtedly the biggest single topic in the whole hum of conversations. Everywhere everyone was describing it as an awful thing; but Nathaniel Hicks must note, and note with revulsion, the high conversational value of anything awful—it was not dull. Those who told so busily what they could not know spoke with the importance of men sure of an audience; those who listened heard avidly, with no feigned interest. Complementing the boy captain to Nathaniel Hicks's right, a speaker, quite as easily heard, held forth on his left. It was a gray-headed major with the gold Finance Department lozenge. For eager hearers he had a gray-headed lieutenant, also from Finance; two captains past their youth who wore the Adjutant General's colored shield; and two seated women, plain and middle-aged. The major was telling them that he knew, he had heard someone say, that General Beal had put what he cautiously referred to as "Colonel H." in arrest.

One of the women said: "But what did he do, Carl?"

The gray-headed major said: "It wasn't what he did, it was what he didn't do." Nathaniel Hicks, disliking the major's knowledgeable air, reflected sarcastically that now the story was going good. It was true that he had not been able to hear the orders General Beal soon began to give; but he was none-theless sure, since he had watched Colonel Hildebrand ener-getically assisting, that Colonel Hildebrand's arrest wasn't one of them.

To Nathaniel Hicks's right, the young squadron commander said: "Somebody'll probably get crucified. What I heard at Operations, it was the usual snafu. This was an exercise, trying out new planes, see? It was scheduled for Monday, see; and was going to be near Tangerine City. Different kind of country right around there. No lake, bodies of water, within ten miles. So they drew everything up for that jump, and didn't say life vests—they couldn't need any, see? Then, all of a sudden, they change it. The exercise is run off here, today. But somebody sure as hell forgot—"

The gray-headed major said: "—you've got to hit the man whose ultimate responsibility it is. Saying you forgot or you didn't know, won't do; not when there's a war on! If anybody makes a mistake, it's just too bad for him—"

The young squadron commander said: "What Nauroze was telling me, he'd been talking right to the lake, was the general really went into them about this boat. Said why the f— holy hell didn't they get a boat from Lake Armstrong; any num-ber of boats there, all kinds. Hire one, borrow one, steal one if they had to! Hoist it on a truck, low-bed trailer or some-

561

thing; cart it over to stand by if the regular crash boat wasn't working—"

The girl in the chair said: "Oh, how perfectly ghastly, Captain Burns! You mean they could have saved all those men—"

The captain made a deprecatory gesture, snapping his knuckles. He said: "Well, tell you the truth, I think the general was spinning there. I doubt if it could make a least bit of difference. A plane down in the lake might float a few minutes, see. Give you a chance to start up a boat, cast off, get out there. Now, I don't know where these characters jumped from, how high; but they're going to be down in ten, fifteen, twenty seconds. At the most. The idea is: get them down fast; see? Operationally, you don't want them hanging in the air like sitting ducks; see?"

To the gray-headed major, one of the Adjutant General's officers said: "What I heard, Carl, was the rescue boat had been laid up, engine trouble; and somebody didn't report it to the Post Engineer, Uline's office. Of course it wasn't manned; because it wouldn't go—"

The young captain said, shrugging easily: "Maybe they unloaded at the wrong point; maybe there was a stronger wind all of a sudden. But all I mean is, I don't see how any boat would do any good. Not when they didn't have vests to make them float. They're weighted the hell down—"

The lieutenant Nathaniel Hicks had picked as the girl's husband said: "Yeah; how about that, Hank? They must see where they're going, wouldn't they? Why don't they drop off all that junk, give themselves a chance? You wouldn't have to be so smart to figure that."

The young captain shook his head wisely. "You'd have to start early," he said. "Lots of them have special loads, too; demolition sets; communications stuff. That weighs plenty; and they put that on you to stay, you know—straps; buckles; zipped up. They make sure you don't lose any of it; when you get down, you could need it bad—"

The gray-headed major said: "No, you couldn't see anything at all from where we were, all the way across the field. I don't think anybody there knew anything had happened until they got the trucks out, over by the stands. Well, I wouldn't have wanted to see it, I can tell you! Those poor fellows coming down—"

The captain said: "And don't think it's so easy to be sure where you're going to land. I had to bail out once; and believe me, it's tricky as hell. When I got to what I thought would be around five hundred feet, I started to figure where I was going; and I saw it was right smack in this wood lot, big trees. Boy, I worked the head hard, trying to remember those pictures; put your arms over your face, all that. Where I actually hit was this open field. I swear it was more than two hundred yards from those trees—not that I minded! What I mean; by the time I saw the field was it, was sure of it, I didn't have only three or four seconds left—"

Nathaniel Hicks became abruptly aware that Lieutenant Turck was standing in front of him. He said: "I'm doing a little eavesdropping. Everybody here is—" Her expression made him break off.

She said: "Nat, I could die! Really, I can't bear it. It seems, as we all know, I was in Des Moines last weekend; and Lippa decided not to come down alone, so the reservation was canceled. Lippa did it. She must have thought they'd understand it was just last weekend we didn't want it. That is not what the dolts understood. They understood we would call and make a new reservation when we were going to want it again. Since no one called—you begin to get it?"

"Definitely," Nathaniel Hicks said. "Now, let's see—"

Lieutenant Turck said: "Ever since I got up this morning I've kept thinking: Saturday, thank God, Saturday!"

Nathaniel Hicks saw that she had interrupted him out of necessity. She could not wait to let's-see; she must attack and reduce immediately the ludicrous anguish which shamed her by forcing out, on so trivial an occasion, the wail that she could die, she couldn't bear it. She said briskly: "Whenever I wasn't being actively bothered, I'd sit there gloating, seeing myself, when day was done, panting up the corridor to dear old Three-

Ten-A, bursting open the door, setting out the Scotch with trembling fingers and slopping some stiff shots into glasses. When we were enough recovered, I would match Lippa— I would win, of course—for who got the bathtub first. I would soak for one half hour. Emerging fresh and dainty—but why go on?"

Why, indeed? Nathaniel Hicks, with real compunction, saw her failure. Her experienced sardonic portrayal of herself was not bringing its usual relief. The steady hand began to shake; the swift mocking strokes fell inaccurately. Instead of disappearing, the ignoble little disappointment grew—because, of course, ignoble or not, it was little only in the grim sense that the nail, want of which lost the shoe, was not a very big nail. Lieutenant Turck looked in despair at the wilderness around her. Essentially hateful in its upset values, its incentives to self-mistrust, its comfortless patchwork of unavailing efforts and disagreeable contacts; essentially frightening—the huge, going machine had no controls you could reach—this way of life made equilibrium precarious, dependent on a fantastic rigging job. The job was usually—it had to be—serviceable, and often most ingenious; but its safety factor, unless you didn't feel at all, was zero. It could not stand a prop knocked out here or a parted guy there.

Nathaniel Hicks said firmly: "Wait. Now, let's see—"

"There isn't anything," Lieutenant Turck said. "It's all at least two weeks in advance; so there won't even be anything next week. The room clerk, though an old friend of ours, was rather snappish. He had already had it from Lippa. She got in nearly an hour ago. She was, he said, very mad at him; but could he help it? She left word she was in the bar—he says she went in with an officer, almost certainly our ineffable Edsell, since you tell me he wasn't arrested after all. I can't face any of that. I won't face it. I will now take a taxi back to the Area. If I must weep, I will weep in the washroom out there."

"Come, come!" Nathaniel Hicks said. "Didn't you tell me something about the usefulness of men? I haven't even started yet. First of all, we get hold of Duchemin. I saw him go upstairs. He is better than any yak. He will get hold of the manager."

"Mr. Prouty? What good would it be, Nat? This room clerk we really know very well. If there was anything he could do, I'm sure he would. He says there's simply nothing at all."

"He isn't Mr. Prouty," Nathaniel Hicks said, "and you're not Captain Duchemin. That makes a big difference, you'll find. I don't say he can give you anything right now; but that doesn't matter. You don't need anything right now. By the time you do need it, somebody will have checked out and Mr. Prouty will be only too happy to see that any friend of Captain Duchemin is first to move in. I promise you."

"Do you?" Lieutenant Turck said. "Yes; please do! Only, I think I will go out. I mean; I'll come in later. I must have a bath."

Nathaniel Hicks said benevolently: "You can have one; and so can Lippa. We have baths upstairs. I don't think there's even a ring around the tub, because we also have a shower in a sodden little stall and I never knew anybody to use anything else. The tub is to keep extra ice in. Now, we'll go up. Duchemin can telephone Mr. Prouty. While he is getting out, we can sit on our balcony and look at Lake Armstrong. I'm afraid there is no Scotch; but there is plenty of bourbon which works the same way. When Duchemin leaves, you can call down and have Lippa paged. Don Andrews is at the Base Hospital. I will withdraw; and you can get yourselves all fresh and dainty. I will then buy you some dinner—"

"No!" Lieutenant Turck said. "Absolutely not! This has to stop somewhere. I don't know what you were planning to do, but it couldn't have been that. You will not buy any dinner. If we can just get clean—" she paused. "God knows about Lippa," she said. "Once that young man gets to work on her—she will have had a couple of drinks by now; and there's just no telling. If you have us on your neck, you may find him there, too. No. You see it gets too complicated. We'd better just skip it, Nat."

Nathaniel Hicks picked the bags up. "Come on," he said. "I'm running this. I don't give a damn about Edsell; and in many ways I don't give a damn about Lippa; but I am not going to have you weeping in the washroom out there—"

"There they are now," Lieutenant Turck said. "If I am any judge, and I am, I think you will find them inseparable."

Turning, Nathaniel Hicks saw Lieutenant Lippa, her arm through Lieutenant Edsell's, coming across the lobby toward them. He saw that it was undoubtedly true about the couple of drinks. Lieutenant Lippa looked flushed, which gave her a warm, somewhat starry-eyed appearance not unbecoming. Taken with her clinging hold on Lieutenant Edsell's arm the effect of sensual abandonment was so marked that she was getting a good deal of attention. As she and Edsell approached, she brought after her a train of turned eyes, glances that had fallen casually on her and then continued into stares. Nathaniel Hicks could see the young captain who had been talking to the two lieutenants and the schoolgirl bride rest his eye on her accidentally. He stopped talking, leaving his lips parted. His blue eyes flickered, irresistibly fastened. He forgot all about his companions, his mind overmastered by his fancy's absorbing suggestions.

Lieutenant Lippa, oblivious to all this, said to Lieutenant Turck: "Nice going, chum! We'll just leave everything to you."

Lieutenant Turck said: "Why didn't you say, when you canceled the reservation, that we wanted it again this week? Bert says you never told him—"

"I never told him not," Lieutenant Lippa said. "But it seems to me you might have checked. You said you'd take care of everything. What are you going to do now?"

Lieutenant Turck said: "Captain Hicks has kindly suggested that we could get cleaned up in his place as soon as Captain Duchemin, who is dressing, gets out. He thinks Mr. Prouty will be able to find somewhere for us to sleep later. We were just going up. Do you want to come and get a bath? I think it would be a good idea. I'm sure Lieutenant Edsell will excuse you."

"Oh, you're sure, are you?" Lieutenant Lippa said. A dark surge of anger showed itself in her face. "Well, I just happen to be fed up with all the things you're so sure of, Amanda."

Lieutenant Turck said: "Are you coming up?"

"No, I'm not. I just stopped to tell you that we're going out, and I won't be back tonight."

"Well, if you're spending the night somewhere," Lieutenant Turck said, "you'd better take your bag. You might need a nightgown."

Lieutenant Lippa said: "Oh, you make me sick, Amanda! Will you stop looking so damn refined?" Lieutenant Lippa moistened her trembling lips. She said loudly: "What in God's name would we want my nightgown for?"

"I don't know," Lieutenant Turck said. "Must you ask the whole lobby?"

With an air of pleasure disagreeable to Nathaniel Hicks, Lieutenant Edsell said: "Let's not have a cat fight, ladies!" He moved his eyes, examining Nathaniel Hicks's expression, which Nathaniel Hicks supposed was no friendlier than the feelings he had toward Lieutenant Edsell.

Derisively, with a mischievous attention, Lieutenant Edsell considered Nathaniel Hicks. He said then: "You wouldn't like to let me borrow your car for a while, would you?"

Nathaniel Hicks said: "I may need it myself."

Lieutenant Edsell laughed. "My pal!" he said. "Ask him any time! Well, don't feel too bad. We can take a taxi. Lou left me a key to his place when he went off last week. Here; give us the bag."

Lieutenant Turck said: "If you're going anywhere where there's a telephone, you'd better leave the number with me. If Sergeant Levy tries to get you for anything, I'd better know where to tell her to call."

Lieutenant Lippa said: "Oh, shut up!" She walked away toward the door.

Lieutenant Edsell took Lieutenant Lippa's bag. He said to Nathaniel Hicks: "I hear your friend Beal bought it again. Report on that to me Monday, will you? Good-bye, now."

Lieutenant Turck looked at Nathaniel Hicks.

"Well; we won't need to trouble Captain Duchemin to trouble Mr. Prouty," she said. "Now I *will* go along out to the Area. One thing. Do you know where this place he was given a key to is? I mean, if I can locate a telephone number for it, I'd like to. There isn't much chance it would be needed; but if it was—in short, she's not supposed to go where she can't be reached."

"Yes," Nathaniel Hicks said. "It's a Captain Adler of our Section. He's at Wright Field on some project. He has rooms in a house out Tropical Avenue. We'll get you the number. I have a list upstairs. And you're not going to the Area—not right now. I need a drink and so do you."

"Well, yes, thanks," Lieutenant Turck said. "I believe I still do."

She looked at the clock over the desk. It was seven. The throng in the lobby was thinning out. "But weren't you doing anything tonight, Nat?"

"Not me," Nathaniel Hicks said. "So I think we'll bring your bag up; and you get that bath and change your clothes; and then we'll have dinner. Now, don't say no. It's an invitation." Carrying the bag, he led her across to the elevators, and into one.

The elevator boy said: "Three, Captain?"

Lieutenant Turck said: "Thank you very much, sir. That would be most enjoyable."

"Three," Nathaniel Hicks said to the elevator boy. "And if you're sure you don't want to stay in, I'll run you out afterward. I'd have to do that. After all, I told Edsell I might need the car."

"Well, I would not want to make you a liar," Lieutenant Turck said. "You're very kind. No. I don't think I'll stay in alone. It's odd, since it's so utterly detestable out there; but the truth is, I would find it melancholy here. When I woke up and saw that Lippa wasn't around, I would start brooding about that all over again—"

Leaving the elevator, they walked down the long lighted corridor. Several doors stood open; several had the slatted second doors closed. The sound of radio music came from some, and the sound of talk and laughter from others. "Yes," Nathaniel Hicks said. "It is a damn funny way to fight a war, isn't it?"

Lieutenant Turck said: "I had, through no choice of mine, breakfast with our friend Edsell this morning, and I said something about that, rather offensive; and he answered very properly that he could not help it if they sent him here. I expect it's a point to be kept in mind. In fact, I don't know that one misses any part of the unpleasantness, except perhaps getting killed. Even that seemed quite well taken care of today. Oh, yes, I need that drink."

"You'll have it in one minute," Nathaniel Hicks said. "That's ours, right down there—"

As he spoke, the door at the end opened abruptly. Captain Duchemin, bright and clean, his bulk encased in a fresh, sharply ironed uniform, came out in a hurry, closing the door behind him. Seeing them, he pulled up. He tilted his cropped head; his broad, new-shaved face began to beam. "My error, my captain!" he said. "Set it right in a jiffy!" He dug a key out of his pocket, turned and unlocked the door, swinging it open and withdrawing the key.

"Did you leave the bathroom in a mess?" Nathaniel Hicks said. "Lieutenant Turck has been done out of her reservation, and I told her she could clean up here."

"The bathroom is spotless," Captain Duchemin said with interest. "I left it that way for you, of course. Want me to see if Prouty can do anything, or have you got it fixed?"

"Thanks awfully," Lieutenant Turck said. "Nat suggested you might be able to arrange something; but we changed our plans, and I won't be staying in tonight. So if I may just make free with your bathroom—"

"We're honored, ma'am," Captain Duchemin said. "Make free with all we have!" The humorous, heavy-lidded eyes slid off from her to Nathaniel Hicks. "I wish I could stay and help offer you refreshments; but I must get my Loot out of that bar while he's still mobile. He was sagging ever so slightly when I came up. So, bless you, my children! We, in thought, will join your throng, ye that pipe and ye that play—"

He went trotting off down the corridor.

XVI

OUTSIDE, IN the warm starlit night, several staff cars stood near the private door to General Beal's office. Inside, more lights than usual were on; but it had not been thought necessary to call back many people.

In the reception room between the hall and General Beal's outer office, Captain Collins waited with the draft of a press release that Colonel Ross had told him to prepare and bring over. In the outer office, Mr. Botwinick had established a little headquarters of his own. He sat at Mrs. Pellerino's desk to put through telephone calls. He had a couple of messengers waiting in case General Beal wanted anything. Down in Colonel Mowbray's office there were lights on, too. Colonel Mowbray was still over at Base Headquarters with Colonel Hildebrand, earnestly and no doubt inefficiently, busy with "arrangements"; but Mrs. Spann, whose sense of duty was strong and who liked to be in on things, returned to her post, though not sent for, as soon as she finished supper.

In General Beal's office the blinds were lowered at all the windows. Colonel Ross waited there with General Beal and General Nichols and Lieutenant Colonel Carricker. Colonel Ross had taken charge of the telephone, so he occupied General Beal's chair at General Beal's desk under the fringed and tasseled bright silk of General Beal's stand of colors.

General Beal and General Nichols sat in the comfortable leather armchairs across the room. General Beal was slouched low, his legs thrust straight before him. The only light came from the bronze lamp on the general's desk. The quiet reflected glow, easy on the eyes, glinted on the short, clipped wave of the general's hair. His face was tranquilly shadowed, his chin, because he was stretched out so fully in his chair, near his chest. He looked at his thin, strong hands, one of which was methodically engaged in turning, though without haste or impatience, idly and absently, his Military Academy class ring around and around on his finger. As far as Colonel Ross could see, he rested at ease.

In the other armchair General Nichols sat with his battle

jacket unbuttoned. He sat easy, too; but perfectly erect in the chair, his legs crossed neatly. Under the dark mustache his lips were closed with a firmness of habit. The ample intelligent forehead was smooth in a serene stillness. He let his eyes rest on the folded sheet of the TO BEAL FOR NICHOLS FROM ARNOLD message which had been given him when he came in. Colonel Ross guessed that General Nichols had his mind busy with a measured review of some important matters to which he was privy, comprehensively speculating on possible developments during the thirty hours or so he had been away from the Pentagon which might make the Commanding General want him urgently.

Lieutenant Colonel Carricker, who sat in a less comfortable chair, was getting, as nearly as Colonel Ross could judge, some form of what used to be called the absent treatment. It was a measure of discipline; but too capricious in its nature and method to satisfy Colonel Ross—perhaps because Benny accepted it so composedly, as a matter of course.

Benny had been sitting on the steps outside when they arrived. He tossed away a cigarette and got up, standing silent in the last dusk. General Beal, stepping out of the car, said nothing to him; so Benny said to Colonel Ross: "Mrs. Ross says to say they left, Judge. I think they were going home."

General Beal then said: "What did you do, crack up that job for me?"

Benny said no, it was all right. The generator quit charging. It must have been doing it off and on before; the battery must have been draining back through it. He hardly had any. So the prop kept running away; so he put it on manual and set down on Number Three. He'd take Danny out tomorrow morning.

General Beal said: "I don't know whether you will. Danny's doing a job tonight on General Nichols's plane. He has to sleep sometime."

"Well, when he can," Benny said. "It's not my plane. I don't want to fool with those prop assemblies."

General Beal grunted; but he made no objection when Benny came along. He simply paid no more attention to Benny. Benny took the neglect with composure, sitting down across the room and waiting with them.

They were waiting for Lieutenant Colonel Uline to call from the lake and report the progress of Colonel Mowbray's "arrangements." Colonel Ross was pleased to see Bus waiting so calmly, resting at ease. It was a lesson for him, Colonel Ross supposed; a demonstration of the avoidable expense of worry and alarm; and, he also supposed, a lesson wasted as usual, as far as he went. His experience fitted him to advise others, rather than himself. He could advise them very strongly to keep their shirts on. Just wait; it would all go. Give Time time; Time would take it away. Colonel Ross sat with a sense of spent storm, of ebbed action, of the charitable late coming of that wisdom which never could be expected until the day's prophecies had duly failed, the tongues ceased, the mistaken knowledge vanished away.

Colonel Ross, though subdued, was hopeful now. At first glance, a glance taken with the help of alarm and worry, what they had here was new bad trouble, more of the same, delivered to General Beal just when he needed no more. In a tizzy, Colonel Ross had his shirt off at once. Bus was barely worked free of yesterday's troubles—if he was free. Since the dubious job had been mostly his, Colonel Ross had a right to consider it a near thing, all precarious, all at hazard; no plan for it; and no theory better than anyone's good guess that the Nature of Things abhors a drawn line and loves a hodgepodge, resists consistency and despises drama; that the operation of man is habit, and the habit of habit is inertia. This weight is against every human endeavor; and always the best bet is, not that a man will, but that he won't.

Not seeing how more could be done, how he could do it again, Colonel Ross began to see—later, of course, than he would have seen it if he had just kept his shirt on—that this trouble, though new, though bad, was a good deal better suited to Bus's tastes and talents. Bus, not any less Bus than Benny, there, was Benny, reacted hard; but with assurance. The high strung gamut ran free from a first simple emotional response to the uncomplicated thought of the brave, the brave who are no more (in quaint, grim truth, all sunk beneath the wave!); through the explosion, simple and emotional, too, of anger rushing into natural patterns—no indecisive repinings about dear, dead days with that comical bastard Woody; no plaguing nonsense put on him by whoever gave their cry-baby prerogatives to a bunch of touchy colored boys, or by the finicking policies some Public Relations nut sold the Air Staff—of a known rôle to play, orders to give; then, with no real checks or crosses, on into the evening's wearing-out of anger, a subsiding, still simple, toward a common sense of mere regret, an acceptance (what else could you do with it?) of accomplished fact. The portentous truth appeared by intimation, full of comfort though so melancholy, touched with despair yet supportable, that nothing, not the best you might hope, not the worst you might fear, would ever be very much, would ever be very anything. Seen in this light, all other feelings must weaken, become more temperate—really, more indifferent. Since that was how it was, measures more moderate—really, more disinterested—suggested themselves.

Crumpling a cigarette package, General Beal said: "Benny. Get me a couple from that machine down there, will you."

General Nichols, stirring, produced the handsome silver case with the Royal Air Force emblem. General Beal reached and took a cigarette from it; but he said: "I need some anyway, thanks. Got change, Benny?"

Benny, getting up, said: "Yeah."

"Look," General Beal said. "If you mean that generator wasn't charging while I had it, and I never noticed, you're wrong. On those, if the generator quits even a minute, that prop circuit breaker goes, pops out. If your generator comes back, you still have to reset before the motor gets any current. If I didn't notice before, when I came in to land, I'd sure as hell find out. Use your head!"

Benny, scratching his nose, went on toward the door. He said: "I never said that, Chief."

"The hell you didn't," General Beal said.

573

Putting a hand on the door jamb, Benny turned. With an air of patient, technical reasonableness he said: "All I was figuring was how I might have drained the battery. I know one good way. The generator stops charging; but it isn't cut out. There goes your battery, drained back through it. It could have quit right after I went on cruise. The prop's fixed, stays set. I move my throttle; no juice for the motor, so the prop starts running away. I don't know. Danny might find something crossed, something grounded, something burned out. I could glide into Number Three, so I thought I'd get down. That's all I said." He opened the door and went out.

Lieutenant Colonel Carricker was hardly gone when the knock came on the other door.

Guessing it to be Mr. Botwinick, General Beal called, "Come in, come in!"

Mr. Botwinick came in.

Probably Mr. Botwinick did not see well in the shadows. No doubt he had most of his mind on the performance he proposed. He entered, his spare little frame moving formally front and center. At a proper number of paces from General Beal's desk, he halted and stood at attention. He then saluted Colonel Ross before he realized it was Colonel Ross.

Colonel Ross said simply: "For God's sake, Botty; what goes on?"

Mr. Botwinick, though discomposed, lost no time in right-facing. He saluted General Beal, stretched out in the chair. He said: "I feel compelled to report myself in arrest, sir."

What first went through Colonel Ross's mind was the surprised, but certainly not astonished, conviction that Mr. Botwinick, who was, after all, just the type, had at last cracked up. General Beal, astounded, hitched straighter in his chair. General Nichols's head turned with an alert inquiring look. Nobody said anything for an instant while Colonel Ross thought rapidly ahead—steps to take while they waited for the ambulance and the strait-jacket.

However, Mr. Botwinick, if not perfectly calm, immediately

proved himself perfectly lucid and collected. He said to General Beal: "I have now been able to check certain circumstances, sir; and in light of them, I see no alternative to reporting as I now do. I have no excuse, sir; but may I explain the situation?"

General Beal, sitting straighter still, said: "Well, sure! What situation?"

From the sharpness of General Nichols's continuing attention Colonel Ross could see that General Nichols, not familiar with Mr. Botwinick's habit of saying things the hard way, was half or more of Colonel Ross's first opinion. General Nichols managed by a slight turn of the eyes to query Colonel Ross. Colonel Ross was not sure he would be intelligible; but he answered as well as he could by shrugging slightly.

Speaking fast, Mr. Botwinick said that he was in a position to state positively that no copy of the memorandum from Colonel Uline through Colonel Hildebrand's office on the status of the Lake Lalage rescue boat was to be found in Colonel Mowbray's files. He had hesitated to reach this conclusion on the basis of his own search, which had been unproductive. Mrs. Spann had now come in; and since she could not find it, he would state categorically that it was not there.

Frowning, General Beal said: "Well, there was a memo, all right. Colonel Hildebrand showed us copies of it. It was sent over this morning."

"Yes, sir," Mr. Botwinick said. "Colonel Mowbray informed me that he had seen such a copy. He wished to know why it had not been shown to him." He paused as though in pain. "I presumed, and I told him when he called, that we could not have received it. That was incorrect. I have now examined with Mrs. Spann our correspondence sheet. It shows that we received something—it is noted by office of origin but, as is customary, with no subject, since a file number and a suspense reference number were affixed. I have no doubt that the notation refers to the missing paper."

"Then you think you did get it, you had it?" General Beal said.

"I must conclude so," Mr. Botwinick said laboriously. In spite of the artificial coolness of the room, sweat, Colonel Ross could see, was beading on Mr. Botwinick's forehead. Mr. Botwinick stiffened his slight frame and drew a breath. He said: "Having ascertained this, sir, I consulted further with Mrs. Spann. Though she is not prepared to swear to it, she is now decidedly of the opinion that she remembers in the mail today something, a heading, some subject, with reference to the rescue boat. She believes she must have seen it when she went over part of the mail after Miss Jelliffe entered it. She has called Miss Jelliffe, and Miss Jelliffe does remember entering such a memorandum."

General Beal looked at Colonel Ross; and Colonel Ross said: "You've covered that, Botty. The entry proved it was received, whether she actually remembered entering it or not."

Without taking his eyes from General Beal, Mr. Botwinick answered: "That is true, sir. What I wished to check was whether Miss Jelliffe remembered the subject. She is not perfectly sure. Entering the mail, she does not take time to read it; it is not part of her duties. Mrs. Spann, however, ordinarily does read it. As I related, Mrs. Spann went over part of the mail this morning; but not so thoroughly as usual."

General Beal said: "All right, all right. Now, what are you getting at?"

"I will be as brief as I can, sir," Mr. Botwinick said. "Colonel Mowbray was very much engaged this morning. He sent for the mail almost as soon as it came in with the intention of getting it out of the way, in case he did not have time for it later. Mrs. Spann had only started to look at it, therefore, when Colonel Mowbray buzzed me and said to bring it in—"

"I understand that!" General Beal said. "What I don't understand is why Pop didn't see it. Is that what you're going to explain?"

"Yes, sir," Mr. Botwinick said. "I can account for that."

"Well, account for it."

Mr. Botwinick said: "I destroyed it, sir."

"You what?" said General Beal.

"I destroyed it, sir," Mr. Botwinick said stoically. "I will explain, if I may. Colonel Mowbray had asked for the mail. I took it from Mrs. Spann, who had just received it from Miss

576

Jelliffe, who had entered it. At approximately that moment, General Nichols"—Mr. Botwinick glanced tensely toward General Nichols—"and General Baxter, who had, I believe, been over at the Base inspecting a plane, arrived, sir. Colonel Mowbray had been talking, I think, to Colonel Ross, on the box. Mrs. Spann told Colonel Mowbray that General Nichols and General Baxter were there, so he came out and brought them into his office. I felt that Colonel Mowbray would not want me to follow immediately with the mail; so I retained it until he should see fit to send for it. He did send for it presently." Mr. Botwinick looked at General Nichols. "Perhaps you recall that, sir?"

General Nichols said: "Yes, I do. We asked Colonel Mowbray to go on with his work. He sent for the mail. I remember your bringing it in."

"Yes, sir," Mr. Botwinick said. By his distracted solemnity he made it plain that he was about to immolate himself, and the moment was a great one—though the cost was high, ruinous, the drama was at any rate considerable. Now that Colonel Ross thought of it, Botty from time to time showed a guarded sense of drama in or under his monotonous industry. General Beal was frowning with bewilderment; and Colonel Ross began to frown thoughtfully himself.

Mr. Botwinick said: "Unfortunately, on my desk at the time, I had placed some classified material, certain documents and papers no longer required which I had taken from the files to burn. What happened is, I am afraid, obvious, sir. In picking up Colonel Mowbray's mail, it would have been possible for me to overlook a paper, Colonel Uline's memorandum. When I returned, I assembled all the material on my desk without further examination and myself took it to the disposal incinerator and saw it burned. I have no excuse, sir."

Since General Beal, staring, said nothing, Colonel Ross, assuming a professional forensic tone, said, "Let's go into this a little further, Botty. First, you don't actually know that's what happened; you just think it might have happened?"

Mr. Botwinick without turning his back on General Beal moved enough to look quickly at Colonel Ross. He said:

577

"Mrs. Spann and I are certain, sir, that the memorandum is now nowhere in our files, in our office. If it had not been destroyed—"

"Yes," Colonel Ross said, "I see your reasons for believing it must have been destroyed; but I would like to go over your reasons for feeling that you destroyed it. Let's do it step by step. Let's begin with your receiving Colonel Mowbray's mail from Mrs. Spann. It has already been entered by Miss Jelliffe, and we know from her record that a memorandum, almost certainly the memorandum on the rescue boat, was in the mail. Mrs. Spann herself, while not able to swear to it, thinks she saw it; and you and she conclude that she must have seen it then. While we have not proved that the memorandum was in the mass of mail you received from Mrs. Spann we can say that in the ordinary course of things it would have been, and so that it probably was. You agree?"

Mr. Botwinick hesitated a moment, his expression cautious and intent. He said: "Yes, sir."

"Very well. You have, you are carrying, a pile of papers, mail for Colonel Mowbray. You are prevented from bringing it right in, so you take it with you to your desk. On your desk is another pile of papers, old classified material to be destroyed. Where is this pile; where, on the desk?"

Mr. Botwinick said carefully: "It was approximately in the center, sir. On my blotting pad. I had been about to take the material out when I was interrupted by Colonel Mowbray's request. I make a practice of personally destroying such material."

"A very prudent practice," Colonel Ross said. "So you entered your office carrying the mail, and came up to your desk on which in the center lay this pile of papers to be burned. You put down the mail, a new pile of papers, for a moment. Where? On top of the old pile?"

"I am afraid, sir, that I did," Mr. Botwinick said.

"You surprise me," Colonel Ross said. "I would expect you to put them by themselves. When you saw the papers already on the desk, it would seem natural for you to recall what they were, why they were there. If you recalled that, it would seem natural for you to take at least ordinary care not to confuse the two piles."

Mr. Botwinick moistened his lips. He said: "I agree, Colonel. I must conclude that I did not recall. I acted with a carelessness for which I have—"

"Let's follow this further," Colonel Ross said. "You are informed, after a few minutes, that Colonel Mowbray now wants his mail. What had you been doing meanwhile, if you remember?"

Mr. Botwinick hesitated again. With a worried look he said: "It is my impression that I was talking on the telephone, sir. Yes. I had just completed a call when Colonel Mowbray spoke to me on the box."

"You had just completed a call," Colonel Ross said. "Let's visualize this. You put the telephone down. Colonel Mowbray spoke through on your box. You picked up the mail to take it in to him. The mail formed the top part of a pile of papers in the center of your desk. Would it have been possible for you, by accident, to pick up the whole pile, and not noticing what you had done, bring, as well as the mail, all the old papers in to Colonel Mowbray?"

Mr. Botwinick said slowly: "I think I would have noticed, sir. There was quite a considerable accumulation—"

Colonel Ross said: "Then you separated what you thought was the mail from what you knew were old papers. You wanted only the top part of the pile; yet it did not occur to you to stop and see whether you were taking any papers that were not part of the mail, or leaving any that were part of it?"

A tinge of deep red had risen in Mr. Botwinick's face; but he said firmly: "I took them up in some haste, Colonel. I ought not to have done it. I should have paid closer attention."

"I see," Colonel Ross said. "You wish General Beal to understand that through successive pieces of carelessness, the last of them caused by haste, you were personally responsible for the fact that Colonel Mowbray did not see, and so, that nothing was done about, Colonel Uline's memorandum?"

"I must accept that responsibility, sir."

Colonel Ross said to General Beal: "I don't think any action ought to be taken on this, General, until Colonel Mowbray has been informed. I suggest that, meanwhile, Mr. Botwinick return to his duties."

"Yes," General Beal said. "We'll have to talk to Pop. Let's do one thing at a time."

Mr. Botwinick said: "I regret this interruption, sir; but as soon as I knew what I had done, I felt I should inform you. I will be outside, sir, then." He turned and walked to the door, which he closed carefully after him.

General Beal stood up. He went over to a fancy little cellarette under the window. He found a key in his pocket and unlocked the cellarette, opening the top and front. A cluster of bottles stood surrounded by racks of glasses. He said: "Let's have a drink."

"A timely suggestion," General Nichols said. He looked curiously at Colonel Ross. "Interesting character, that man, Judge."

General Beal said, holding up a bottle: "This and branch water do you, Judge? Want some ice? I could send for some."

Colonel Ross said: "It will do very well without ice." Looking at General Nichols, he said: "Yes. Mr. Botwinick is an interesting character, General. In some important ways he might be said to run the Operations and Requirements Analysis Division. His carelessness surprised me. He's not given to making mistakes or overlooking things. I have trouble thinking of him doing anything by accident. However, accidents happen. The best of us make mistakes."

Smiling, General Nichols said, "I see that."

✦

Those qualities, the ones she ascribed to Lieutenant Lippa when she was talking under the fly-top at the lumber pile were, of course, her own, Nathaniel Hicks realized as he sat on the balcony with Lieutenant Turck. To her great advantage, he thought, a niceness of mind that seemed likely

580

to secure her, as Lieutenant Lippa was not secured, against unbecoming acts or even thoughts.

Admiring, Nathaniel Hicks could not help feeling a curiosity, not, he felt, impertinent, about that man to whom she was formerly married—this doctor, hadn't she said? What was it but a compliment if he did not very well imagine how she ever gave anyone good reason to want to divorce her? Could she mind if he felt she had a taste and a judgment that would be bound to keep her from marrying someone impossible, someone she would have to divorce? In the moment's easiness of liking, in a cordiality of discovered common attitudes and an esteem of opinions held in common, he had come near asking her directly. Given another moment, or, perhaps, another drink, there could have been no reason why he should not say, grave and sympathetic: "Tell me about this marriage of yours, Amanda."

As it happened, that was the moment she used to say: "Heavens! It's eight o'clock; and I think I'm the least little bit tight—how nice! But I'm not getting a bath myself; and I'm keeping you from getting one. And I'm keeping you from getting anything to eat. We won't get anything at all if we're not down by half-past eight, will we?"

Though he felt, in relaxed cheerfulness, no immediate need either of a bath or of dinner, Nathaniel Hicks got up obediently. "I'll fix that," he said. "I know the ropes here." Perhaps he was again making a favorable impression on himself—the dextrous manager; the man with a way with him. He said: "You won't have to hurry. Curiously enough, room service can be had after eight o'clock, and even until nine. They close the dining room at eight-thirty so that leaves some people free. They won't do anything fancy; but they usually have steak sandwiches. If you wouldn't mind taking what they feel like sending, I'll call down."

"No!" Lieutenant Turck said; but she was expressing only surprise. "How incredibly luxurious! I never dreamed of such a thing. Lippa and I sometimes bring things to fix in these nasty little kitchenettes, so we won't have to get back into uniform to go downstairs—"

"It's Duchemin again," Nathaniel Hicks said. "He has his uses. I now know plenty about hotels and how to make the best use of them. Sit still. I'll put your bag in Don Andrews's room. Then I'll trot down and see what Nick can send up. When I go out, snap the lock on the hall door. People wander in sometimes."

He went through the living room and briskly took up her bag, left by the door. In Captain Andrews's room he switched the light on. Laid over the back of a chair was the shabby dark blue coat and the thin print frock, wrinkled from hours of wearing, that Katherine Andrews had on when he was introduced to her in the lobby early this morning. Looking further, he found a faded pink slip; one stocking; and the old, much-washed girdle, limp and empty yet still stretched to the shape of her body, which, Nathaniel Hicks remembered, Don said she had not been strong enough to take off by herself. These used garments lay dropped on the floor beyond the bed. That they should have remained there, unnoticed, was affecting evidence of Don's state of mind when he came at noon to get Katherine's things.

Nathaniel Hicks collected the slip, and the limp girdle, and the stocking; and then the other stocking, which he found just under the edge of the bed. He opened a drawer in the bureau and at random laid these things with Don's shirts. He was lifting up the old coat and the cheap frock to put them on hangers in the closet when he saw Lieutenant Turck at the door.

He said: "You might well wonder. They're Don's wife's things. Don was in no mood to pick up, I guess. It was really a very tough break for them."

Lieutenant Turck said: "Is she all right?"

"They pulled her out of it." He spoke gravely, feeling again the compunction, the not-unpleasantly painful stir of mind he felt sitting with Don out by the nurse's office. "She was in a coma when they took her to the Hospital; so I guess now she's better. I gather it was a sudden attack of diabetes, which I don't think ever does you any good. Don was horribly upset. He is nice, and she is nice; and he is greatly attached to her."

582

Looking at the photograph on the bureau, Lieutenant Turck said: "Is that she?"

"It isn't a good photograph," Nathaniel Hicks said. "There. I guess that's as much in order as we can get it. The bathroom's right across—with the light on. I'll give you that full half hour."

She looked at him and colored faintly. She said: "What I came after you to say was—well, there's no earthly reason for you to vacate your premises just because you're kind enough to let me use your bathtub. I mean, I feel that every requirement of propriety would be satisfied if you'd just repose yourself on the balcony and enjoy another drink. You could call them downstairs. That's what you said you were going to do, first."

Respecting the delicacy of her balance between composure and embarrassment, Nathaniel Hicks said: "I guess I was being a little pompous about it."

"Oh, no, you weren't," she said. "Nothing could exceed the refinement, the graceful consideration shown and implied. It's just me. Thinking it over, I got to feeling like something in a book by Maurice Hewlett. Or one of those motion picture moments when the virgin heroine, keeping most of her clothes on, tucks herself into the one bed in the lonely cabin; and the camera takes tremendous care to show the hero with his collar turned up sitting on the steps outside all night. I don't need to be more of a damn nuisance than necessary. I'd feel much better this way, if you don't mind."

After he telephoned the dining room Nathaniel Hicks went back to the balcony. He had poured himself a drink, and he took it to the wicker chair in the corner. He settled down there sagely, looking out over the lake.

Now it was deep night; and, recognizably, the night was Saturday's. A majority of the Oleander Towers' military guests did not have to get up so early tomorrow. A period was put to the long week; and the new one could not start until Monday. Hotel noises, ordinary evening sounds, were subtly changed—a slight swell in volume, a minor definite difference in timbre.

By his stomach's calm steady glow, relaxing the nerves, yet increasing or seeming to increase, sensibility, Nathaniel Hicks saw how amusing it was. Saturday night might actually be present in the dim voices sounding off other balconies along the lake front, in the relaxed laughter coming out of other rooms, upstairs and down. But he himself, having his own Saturday night, must be contributing differences he could not doubt he heard in the several turned-on radios. A singing female complained, but softly, languid in what sounded like the same blessed reflection about sleeping late, lying late, in the morning, that you made her love you, she didn't want to do it. A man's incisive inflections were summarizing the news in a hurry, as though intent on getting it over and going out for the evening.

From the balcony underneath rang a joyful burst of laughter. Someone recovering from mirth, said: "Tell them that other one."

The answering voice, naturally nothing loth, began: "An unsatisfied damsel named Alice—"

More laughter pealed up at the end; and someone else said: "Come on, you guys! Let's go. Let's get started, if we're going to."

Gently the warm wind came off the dark lake. Nathaniel Hicks, hearing the men below leave, lifted his moist glass. Delightfully bemused, he drank. A quality in that last voice; scornful assertiveness, chiding impatience, reminded him of Lieutenant Edsell. At once, yet at leisure, he was in a speculation, necessarily loose, about the night of love in Edsell's borrowed apartment. He saw Lieutenant Lippa dropping her skirt, out of her shirt, finally in a state of nature—what would she want her nightgown for?—laying herself down to an unhalted running relation: sarcastic cracks about the military service; jeering comment on the follies, ineptitude, and false principles of General Beal, Colonel Mowbray, Colonel Ross, Major Whitney, and anyone else Edsell happened to be ranked by. Between kisses, poor Lippa could hear the arguments in favor of equal rights for Negroes. A denunciation of the whole system of private profit might prepare her at length for the dispatchful embrace. In short order, all incidental passion got over, spent, she could no doubt drowse off to a fuller account of her lover's triumphs today; of people rocked back, people demolished with a word, people deservedly made fools of.

Nathaniel Hicks contemplated with entertainment a little spiteful this grotesque picture. Not that he thought it was a true one; the Edsell he knew so well was not necessarily the only Edsell there was. In fact, that afternoon, the hard front seemed to be slipping when they were in Colonel Ross's office with Colonel Coulthard. Glimpsed there was a different, less annoying and amusing Edsell, standing not very resolute, hurt and downhearted, just behind his bluster. That miserable Edsell, Nathaniel Hicks could see, would be the one Lieutenant Lippa took in her arms and tenderly set about comforting.

Interrupting the thought, Nathaniel Hicks attended, listening. What was undoubtedly the hall door had opened; and now he heard it close. He jumped up in annoyance. He realized he had not set the latch on that door; and so anyone, probably someone with the idea of playing poker, could walk in.

Stepping through the French doors into the lighted living room, he saw astonished, that it was Captain Andrews. "Hey!" Nathaniel Hicks said.

Captain Andrews turned. "Oh; hello, Nat," he said. "I thought everybody must be out. I forgot some things. My things, I mean. I wanted to get a razor."

Nathaniel Hicks said: "How's Katherine?"

"Not too good, I'm afraid," Captain Andrews said. "They keep saying she's all right; but she looked awfully sick to me when I saw her. You know that nurse this morning—she's really been wonderful. I wish I could do something for her. She hasn't gone off duty yet, though she was supposed to. She's sitting with Katherine right now. Of course, I can't go in there" —he took his glasses off and squeezed his eyes closed wearily.

"Look, Don," Nathaniel Hicks said. "Come out here and have a drink. I think you need one."

Captain Andrews put on his glasses again. "I'd better not, Nat," he said. "I mean, this nurse, Lieutenant Shakespeare, is staying on until I come out again. She ought to have been off more than an hour ago. She was going to tell me how Katherine was—of course I can't go in the ward now. She was going to see the night duty nurse knew where I was. They're letting me use a cot in one of the empty wings. I'd better just pick up my shaving things." He looked at the bathroom door. "Clarence in there?"

"No," said Nathaniel Hicks. "As a matter of fact, we have at the moment a guest from the Women's Army Corps. It's Lieutenant Turck. You know her. She's taking a bath."

From Captain Andrews's incredulous, really jolted, glance, Nathaniel Hicks must see, with a sort of dumb start of his own, the interpretation Captain Andrews put on this news; an interpretation which Nathaniel Hicks had somehow—a little slow, being a little high, benignly elevated—actually forgotten about. Lieutenant Turck, in saying that every requirement of propriety would be met, overlooked this one, the unexpected visitor.

That Nathaniel Hicks had overlooked it, too; that when he told Captain Andrews who was in there and why, he spoke with never a thought of any implications, established, of course, his complete innocence; but unfortunately it established it only for him. He must realize that he now stood in a classic humorous fix—the innocent man surprised with every circumstance of guilt on a stage all set for a long comic misunderstanding. He alone could clear it up, because he alone knew how it came about; yet who on earth would, in the circumstances, believe *him?*

Captain Andrews plainly did not know what to say. He said: "Oh." He looked away from Nathaniel Hicks in great embarrassment. While all this was, of course, funny, preposterous, Nathaniel Hicks was annoyed to find himself coloring. He said: "She had a reservation for the weekend, and it got crossed up—"

The complications of the explanation, the need to detail so many involved factors all bearing on each other and all necessary to an explanation that would make sense, halted Nathaniel Hicks. The comedy had got going. Whatever he said would be just his story. Actions spoke louder than words; the thing itself spoke. The world, and anyone in it who wasn't born yesterday (even Captain Andrews, without guile if ever anyone was) had heard that one before. When a man and a woman withdrew themselves like this, put themselves alone together in privacy, they could have only one likely purpose; and the likelihood that they did have this purpose was not decreased any when it developed that the woman (never mind the man's offer to explain it all) was in the bathroom with no clothes on.

Asserting his composure, Nathaniel Hicks said: "I'm afraid her stuff's in your room. I thought you'd be out—I thought we could at least let her get a bath and change her clothes. I'm having something to eat sent up here; and I'll take her out to the Area afterwards."

But this, he saw at once, was not calculated to get him anywhere. Sure; he thought Captain Andrews would be out! Sure; she was taking a bath, and they were going to have dinner sent up; and then he was going to take her out to the Area! The hell you say! Nathaniel Hicks could not help laughing.

"Don," he said. "Don't worry; you haven't walked in on anything. I have no designs on Lieutenant Turck; and she hasn't the faintest intention of spending the night with me. She's taking a bath because they don't have bathtubs out there. She and a friend have a reservation here every weekend, with the principal idea of getting a bathtub. I happened to see her waiting for a bus and gave her a lift—"

That certainly left out a good deal; but it was a moment to be short and simple. He went on. "Through a misunderstanding, the reservation wasn't held for them this week. When she told me, I thought the least I could do was offer her our bathtub. She is now in it. And speaking of that, you'd better come and have that drink. She may be through in a minute. Since she thinks I'm out on the balcony and she has the apartment to herself, it might be awkward for her if she finds us both standing right here."

Nathaniel Hicks could see that Captain Andrews, by a stanch honest effort, was compelling himself to swallow the after all reasonably straightforward story. He wanted to; and he would! Captain Andrews said uncomfortably: "Gosh, Nat, I suppose I seemed pretty nosey! You mustn't think I thought—" but he couldn't quite complete the direct lie. He said instead, "What business would it have been of mine, anyway? I'd certainly have a nerve expecting you to explain to me; I mean, even supposing—well, yes; I guess we shouldn't stand here. But, Nat, I think I'd better not wait. I don't really need—I had to come down anyway; I wanted to send some telegrams—"

Nathaniel Hicks raised his hand. "I think she heard us," he said. He took a step up the passage. Lieutenant Turck's voice, distinct, speaking in query from behind the bathroom door, repeated: "Nat?"

"It's O.K.," he called. "Don Andrews came by to get some things. It'll be clear in a minute. We're going out on the balcony."

"Well, Nat, no," Captain Andrews said again. "As a matter of fact, I have another razor. There's another kit in my top drawer. Think it would be all right for me to go in my room and get it—I mean, now she knows we're here? I'll only be a minute—" he went and pushed back the door of his room.

Nathaniel Hicks could see Lieutenant Turck's open suitcase on the chair. Clean underclothes and a clean uniform shirt and skirt were laid out on the bed. Modestly averting his eyes from them, Captain Andrews went to the bureau. "Got it!" he said. "I don't really need anything else. I'm sorry, Nat, barging in this way." He paused. "Will you tell Lieutenant Turck why I couldn't wait? I hope I haven't embarrassed her."

"She's a very sensible young woman. If you'll try not to consider her abandoned because she wanted a bath, I think she'll settle for that."

"Gosh, Nat," Captain Andrews said, opening the door. "I don't see a thing—any reason. I mean, after all, I *do* know you're not Clarence. You know I know that—well, so long!"

"I hope Katherine has a good night," Nathaniel Hicks said.

In the roomy old-fashioned bathroom a big jar of bath salts whose odor of lavender pervaded the air stood on the clothes hamper. Lieutenant Turck must have overlooked it; but Nathaniel Hicks could see that she was a tidy young woman, for she left no other evidence of her bathing.

He hoped Katherine would have a good night. Standing listless under the shower, Nathaniel Hicks imagined for himself the unhappy joint vigil—Don stirring restless, lying with his shoes off on the mattress of a cot in the empty, not-at-the-moment used Hospital wing; and Don's thin, sick wife, half doped, half dreaming, her distracted head shifting about on the pillows while she wished herself away from the qualmish nightmare of whatever her complaint's discomforts were—there were sure to be plenty; no complaint ever lacked plenty.

Nathaniel Hicks was put in mind of recollected hospital experiences of his own—which, however, were Don's rather than Katherine's. From some years back he recovered the times of uneasy waiting when Emily was having the children. Absorbed in his own apprehensions, he was sure he portrayed very well, with no significant differences or variations, the conventional figure of fun. To some degree disheveled in appearance, more or less hang-dog in manner, the anxious father teased the busy staff with futile inquiries; and, though God knew they were hardened to it, in the end even exasperated them by his plainly shown notion that this was the world's first childbirth, and that he suspected them of being lax, slow, and probably stupid in meeting the unparalleled emergency.

Of course the doctors with their dayful of patients, the pestered nurses, were right about him, about that handful of funny men found hanging expectant around every hospital at all hours. Women had been having babies for a long time, and if they were moved to yell, that was just the way it was, nothing to get excited about. This was the job little girls were made for, so most of them would, however dolorously, get through it all right; and, moreover, would so far forget their groans that they were as likely as not to be soon back with a new big belly; not less self-important, though again plaintive and woebegone, and really no more frightened than last time. You would, in short, be wise, man or woman, to take what came with a minimum of fuss, because you were going to take it, fuss or no fuss. Unless you died and got over it that way, you would live and put it behind you the other way, by growing older.

Nathaniel Hicks turned the shower off and stepped out on

the mat. Viewing his bare wet figure in the mirror, he could see one working of that other way. Weighed by the pound, he had not acquired much fat in getting from eighteen to thirty-eight; but his body had a grosser look, a thickening in minor rearrangements of the older tissue on the older frame. Along the onetime youthful line of his jaw he could see those first hints of lumping and sagging where the folds of the old face would be. Emily, on the other hand—the relevance of the thought was plain—showed despite the violence done her body by two tight-stretched, distorting engorgements in pregnancy and two merciless rackings, tearing, joint-starting, in parturition, no sign he could see of being physically less young than she was.

But it would be inexpedient to dwell longer on this accidentally evoked image of Emily in her underthings at her dressing table, or lifting off her nightgown, or lying dim and bare on her bed.

Taking a towel to dry himself, Nathaniel Hicks turned his mind away. He got it only as far as a not-unrelated, though, in its effects on him, sufficiently different, thought—or, better, sentiment, since no real thought took form. It was just the still-incredulous amazement that this should be here and that this should be he. Pinching himself would do no good. It was not necessary; he felt already his cold, unconfused wide-awakeness, hopeless and helpless in its sense of time's great length; of all yesterdays gone; of life like this, and this war, lasting on and on; of the intolerable permanence of a situation which had been his, it seemed, not eighteen months but all of eighteen years, and from which he would be delivered, at this rate, never.

Putting on his bathrobe, Nathaniel Hicks remembered Captain Wiley speaking seriously in answer to a remark of Nathaniel Hicks's that had been only partly serious—that, with Fighter Analysis, with that jerk Folsom, holding out, the war must be over before the Training Aids Division even got the manual to write, let alone before the War Department published it, and any of the people it was meant for had a chance to read it.

Captain Wiley agreed about Colonel Folsom. He said what Colonel Folsom could do or have done to him; but he immediately added: "I wouldn't worry much about the war getting over too soon, Nat."

In all seriousness Captain Wiley seemed to assume that Nathaniel Hicks *was* worried, was able to share the quite real little worry that Captain Wiley might sometimes feel about the war ending too soon. Not that Captain Wiley lost any sleep over it, yet; but while he was doing his combat flying with a piece of chalk on an Orlando blackboard, he could be missing something. Captain Wiley had no flying cadet's illusions about combat. He came home with a bellyful—out there it was tough, it was dangerous; you could sure as hell get killed—the last damn thing he wanted! But though he knew all the cons, for him there were also important pros.

Out there, rid of this crap, they were fighting.

Swearing casually, rocking from heel to toe, Captain Wiley, somewhat limited in language, told the rowed young faces of a School of Applied Tactics cadre, picked squadron and group commanders, a little about fighting. When attacking bombers, for instance, they better sock it to the bastards if they wanted to live; get the hell in there, kill that gunner, before they broke away and gave him a flank shot at them for free.

While he talked, Captain Wiley, more and more restive, perhaps saw the fighter swarm, his preferred familiars, old squadronmates of his, coming off the runways at a hundred miles an hour; in thunder, airborne. The earth fell down under them; the winds aloft gave way. Not long after, the watchful far-off foe would note some specks on the sky. Stout he might be, skilled, sure of himself; but the man was not born yet who, seeing that sight, kept at that moment spit enough to swallow. He hadn't long to wait. On the heart's diastole, those coming fighters might look a mile off; and on the systole following, here they were.

The coming fighters had no waiting around to do, either. For God and country, for flying pay, for heart-in-mouth fun with death, for the hell of it, and in the excited hope to kill, they gave the incomparable two-thousand horsepower engines a good, swift, water-injection kick in the pants. To the expeditious brain, the expert eye said: *now!* A finger touch, light as the destroying angel's, broke simultaneous flame out all their guns. Behind this storm of lead, hand in experienced hand, they bored in—once more unto the breach, dear friends, once more!

Wisely smiling, Captain Wiley said: "Never think those Krauts won't need a whole lot of licking, Nat." Dispassionate, reflective, he said: "You ask me, we haven't really started. Up to now, we only kept them from licking us. Another thing; don't forget. They get the hang of their jets, and we could stop even doing that."

Nathaniel Hicks opened the bathroom door circumspectly and went down to his bedroom. Captain Wiley had reasons for his opinion; and, in light of them as Captain Wiley laid them down for his consideration, Nathaniel Hicks saw with inner dismay that Captain Wiley regarded his own discouraging summary of their progress as the brightest possible view of the bad situation. He said: "You see, we're a little bit bomber-happy, Nat. That's our biggest trouble. They got a lot of crap at Orlando about the strategic use of air power. It says there: we're destroying German war potential." He moved his head dubiously. "Know what I think? I think our big friends haven't done them any real harm to speak of. They don't mind getting destroyed at Orlando and in the newspapers. I think our pin-point bombing is a lot of bushwah; and that's the reason we get to do it. We waste bombs, we waste plane production, we waste manpower, and what more do they want? First time it gets to be a real nuisance, if it ever does, they'll probably pull a couple of fighter wings out of Russia and give the Eighth Bomber Command the works."

Nathaniel Hicks took insignia from his bureau top and attached them dejectedly to the collar tabs of a fresh shirt. Grim, though easy enough and undismayed, Captain Wiley said: "Wait and see! Some morning we'll throw them this nice thousand-bomber mission, and get back five hundred, four hundred, maybe less. That might wake even the bomber boys up; and we can start doing what we should have done first.

Get us enough fighters to come down on every German field within range of a mission and stop anything that tries to take off. No, I wouldn't plan on going home for a while yet, Nat. Even after that, don't forget, we'll have to go rescue the Navy from the Japs."

Nathaniel Hicks did not forget. Tightening his belt and centering the buckle, he snapped out the light in his room and went on up the little passage.

In the far corner of the living room Lieutenant Turck sat looking at a magazine. He noticed now that she had, when she dressed, done her hair a little differently, a tousled effect of curls, but more carefully arranged. She sat with grace, her neat slender legs lightly crossed under the edge of the neat, fresh tropical-worsted skirt. Putting aside the magazine, she smiled and said: "Isn't this nice? I feel so lovely and clean."

"And hungry, I expect," Nathaniel Hicks said. "The truth is, I don't dare call them again. They will get here; but not before they're ready." Though lovely and clean himself, he suffered a wave of intolerable loneliness and disconsolation— the pointless words, the pointless waiting.

Almost compassionately Lieutenant Turck said: "Poor man! I *am* quite a nuisance, aren't I?"

"Never think that," Nathaniel Hicks said. "I was reviewing the war. If you weren't here, I'd probably shoot myself. Anyway, let's have another drink."

"Yes. Let's," Lieutenant Turck said.

XVII

STILL SITTING at General Beal's desk, Colonel Ross reached out and drew toward him across the empty wide gleaming surface the jeweler's box, tossed there carelessly, in which lay General Beal's Distinguished Service Medal. Colonel Ross regarded the ribbon's wide white stripe, blue lines, and red edges. He looked at the bronze coat of arms set in its gold-lettered, dark-blue, enamel ring. Idly he lifted the medal out and turned it over, examining the reverse; the scroll, the trophy of weapons and flags.

General Beal said: "Anyway, let's have another drink."

General Nichols said: "That's real Scotch."

General Beal said: "It ought to be. Considering who gave it to me. But he wasn't supposed to get it, not by the case—austerity, they have. So it all comes under the Official Secrets Act. I took one of the cases up to Woody, poor guy. I don't believe even he could have got through a whole case after we left Thursday. I wonder who inherits that?"

"It's a point," General Nichols said gravely. "I guess it would be called personal effects. Maybe Ollie can make something out of it. You know; leaving several bottles with liquor still in them might be strong evidence that he wasn't himself at the time."

General Beal had arisen and gone to the cellarette with his glass and General Nichols's. "You're one cold-blooded bastard," he said, pouring the whisky. "You never knew Woody."

General Nichols said: "Bus, you can't sell me that guy, dead or alive. Let's just say he considerably outlived his usefulness, if he once had some. Let's just ship him to Arlington, give him a guard of honor, and put him in the ground."

"I don't know what good a guard of honor does him when he's dead," General Beal said. "Some more goddamn ceremony! How about you, Judge?"

Colonel Ross, not without grandiloquence, said: "It does us good. Ceremony is for us. The guard, or as I think we now prefer to call it, escort of honor is a suitable mark of our regret for mortality and our respect for service—we hope, good; but if bad or indifferent, at least, long. When you are as old as I am you will realize that it ought to get a man something. For our sake, not his. Not much; but something. Something people can see."

Laughing, General Beal said: "That's telling them, Judge! Only, what I meant was: how about another drink?"

"This one will do me," Colonel Ross said.

General Beal had turned around. Seeing Colonel Ross holding

594

the medal, he said: "Don't get that dirty. They may want it back."

General Nichols said: "Those are for keeps, I think. As the judge says, we encourage the spectators. Or do you mean you want the citation read, you want it pinned on you, so you'll know you've got it? I'm sorry about that. Pop was going to have quite a thing at the Club."

"Nuts!" General Beal said amiably.

On the desk beside Colonel Ross a light lit up. He put down the medal and taking the telephone said: "General Beal's office. Colonel Ross."

There was a knock on the hall door, which then opened and Lieutenant Colonel Carricker came in. He crossed over to General Beal and dropped two packages of cigarettes on the table. "You get lost?" General Beal said.

Benny said: "There weren't any in that first machine." He turned away, went over and sat down on the chair against the far wall. Looking across to him, General Beal said: "Want a drink?"

Benny said, "No. Not me."

Looking at him closely, General Beal said: "What's the matter, Benny? Do it all yesterday?"

Benny noticed a fly circling near his knee. Watching it, he poised his left hand and with a neat sudden motion closed it on the fly. Opening his hand, he flicked the crushed fly to the floor. "Could be, Chief," he said.

General Beal smiled faintly. He said: "Want to do something else?"

Benny said: "Sure."

General Beal looked over to Colonel Ross, who had tilted back listening to the telephone. General Beal said: "Could he use your car, Judge?" Colonel Ross waved his hand and General Beal said: "Take Colonel Ross's car and go over to Hangar Two and see how Danny's getting on, what General Nichols's pilot thinks about when they can get off. And tell the Weather Office we want to know if they hear any change north. When do you want to leave, Jo-Jo?"

"Sometime before midnight, if we can," General Nichols

said. "They seem to want us in early. I see by the papers Mr. Churchill is at the White House. They may want the Old Man over tomorrow."

General Beal said: "He working Sundays?"

"That's when we really work."

"Ought he to be doing that?"

"They make him take care of himself—some. If we can get off earlier I'd just as soon. I'd like to fly a little myself. I don't get any instrument time; but I could tonight if we get started before I go to sleep."

Colonel Ross said to the telephone: "All right. I'll call you back."

General Beal said: "Who was that, Judge?"

"Uline."

"They get those AA searchlights?"

"Yes."

"How are they coming?"

Colonel Ross shrugged. "They found bottom," he said. "About two hundred feet."

General Beal nodded. He said to Lieutenant Colonel Carricker: "Go on home after that, Benny. There's nothing to do here. You need some sleep." He bent on him a somber critical look, his face setting and stiffening. "Tomorrow, be out at eleven. I'll have the lieutenant in; and you can speak your piece."

Lieutenant Colonel Carricker nodded.

With sternness, General Beal said: "Now, get this. You better think it over before you hit anybody else. You busted the hell out of his nose." His indignation increased. "And, for God's sake, why couldn't you hit somebody who was white? You got us all in a jam. You made me trouble from here to Washington. You could have started a riot. You've had the judge splitting a gut for two days trying to fix up after you! Next time, you get the book. That clear?"

Lieutenant Colonel Carricker said: "All right."

"You bet it's all right!" General Beal said. "I haven't even heard you say you're sorry. I don't mean about his nose; you can say that to him tomorrow. What about yesterday? Colonel

Mowbray sent for you twice. You better make a quick check; figure out where you are. If that, or anything like it, ever happens again, you're all set for a reaming to remember. And here's something else. There seems to be a whole hell of a lot going on down at that apartment. You'd better start right now straightening out a few things."

Lieutenant Colonel Carricker said: "I'm sorry I made the judge trouble. I didn't mean to hit the dinge. I was sore." He turned his moody face down. "I got drunk yesterday. We have a little mix-up down there. I'm getting it straight, Chief." He swung his hand in a short gesture, as though snapping his fingers; but they made no sound. "Can I go now?"

"All right, Benny. Good night."

When the door was closed, General Beal said: "Think that will hold him, Judge?"

Colonel Ross shrugged. "It's better than nothing," he said.

"Well, it's all I'm going to do," General Beal said mildly. "I think it's enough. This time. If he does anything more, we'll see." He said to General Nichols, "He has woman trouble. She's probably chasing him; but he'll have to quiet it down. Even Sal knows about it." He turned back to Colonel Ross. "I know it's deep," he said. "I don't care how deep it is. I don't care how long it takes. They are to recover those bodies. What are you going to call him back about?"

"About that," Colonel Ross said.

General Beal said: "Call him now. Tell him to keep at it until they get them."

Colonel Ross said: "If they haven't got them by the end of the week, are they to keep at it? If they haven't got them by the end of the month—Uline doesn't think they'll have any luck at two hundred feet."

"Two hundred feet?" General Beal said. "They grapple submarine cables at thousands of feet. How do they do it?"

"I don't know," Colonel Ross said. "I suppose they use a steamer with special equipment. Shall we get one? I suppose the Navy might have something. I suppose we could bring it in by digging or dredging a canal to the Gulf coast. About forty-five miles, isn't it? Or we might set up a yard on the lake and build a ship here."

General Nichols made an amused sound.

General Beal smiled calmly. "Oh, no," he said, "we won't do either of those yet, Judge. They've got their lights; they've got their boats. They can drag all night. Tell Uline that. We'll go on trying this way."

"This way isn't going to work," Colonel Ross said. "But you're the general."

"You're damn right I am," General Beal said. "They have to prove to me they can't do it, not just say so. Wait. How about the press release on this?"

Colonel Ross said: "I had Captain Collins draft one. I think he's outside."

"Have him bring it in. We'd better write up something before our friend Art Bullen does it for us. Fine publicity! And speaking of that; tell Jo-Jo about the thing with Hal's man, Hicks. That project. Let's see what Jo-Jo thinks about it."

✦

"The real woman," Lieutenant Turck said somewhat owlishly, "the creature not too bright and good for human nature's daily food, has that advantage over men. Of course it would be Eve who ate the apple. She had no ethical sense. Anything women deeply and seriously want, or want to do, they *know* is right. It doesn't matter to them whether from the ethical standpoint it is good, bad, or indifferent. They know it isn't really wrong because it couldn't be when they want to do it so much. It is a sore point with me. Since I have the disadvantages of my sex, I want the advantages, such as they are. I don't get them. Not that I stop, not that it keeps me from doing it; but in the middle, when any real woman is nothing but eager and serene, it will as often as not be spoiled for me by the horrid, unwomanly suspicion that what I'm doing is contemptible. I have my memories—blast them!"

Smiling, Nathaniel Hicks scrutinized her amiably. That different arrangement of her hair, the tumble of short curls on top, somehow reduced at the sides of the head to flat well-dressed swirls, higher on the left than on the right, suited her features. Her lips, cleanly and lightly painted, parted enough to show her even upper teeth. Her candid eyes had her frequent rueful expression—as though, while she talked and with a glib ease, she worried over something else.

She said: "I can't be quite sober. How on earth did I get onto that? You were telling me about Mortimer McIntyre, Junior, and the, I must say, touching gesture of the fried chicken—"

"And now I wish I'd kept it," Nathaniel Hicks said looking at the array of used dishes before them. "It might have been quite good. Their steak sandwiches are hardly ever as bad as these. I'm afraid I didn't do well by you. You'll just have to piece it out with bourbon, which is also a food."

"I am doing all right with that," Lieutenant Turck said. "And now I'd better stop. Though I don't quite forget my many cares, I feel as disinterested about them as I ever will. Good; but the next step is, I get untidy. Or could I be already? Am I?"

"No," Nathaniel Hicks said. "I was thinking how wonderfully neat you looked." Though neat did describe her, he saw that some word he couldn't think of would probably be better. The thin wool cloth of the uniform shirt pressed in clean severe creases gave her a sort of austere beauty of order, an ascetic eschewal of female luxury, which was effectively continued and pointed up by what took the place of any jewelry—the bare, gold-colored second lieutenant's bar, the severe little classic profile and helmeted head of Pallas Athenae molded in non-precious metal.

"I am glad to hear it," she said. "I must stay that way. My mother once told me that it was far better to be very clean than very pretty. As a general proposition; I don't know. But I daresay every child should be encouraged to cut her coat to fit her cloth."

The wry phrasing, which would be in many mouths a standardized, not blamable yet tiresome, fishing for compliments, self-condemnation with a purpose, was in her mouth so clearly nothing of the sort that Nathaniel Hicks with a welling-up of good will toward her, would have been pleased to pay her compliments; but those most earned, and though not asked for, sure to be most wanted, resisted any simple statement.

She was now, she had with care remained, fresh from her bath; but like the austere order with which it consorted, this beautiful cleanliness was plainly inherent—not something that could be got just by washing the skin well. To Nathaniel Hicks it seemed more a work, incidentally involving lots of washing, of the constant wish and the sustained will; and so she kept it even in unlikely circumstances, whether she knew it or not. He remembered her in the terrible heat of yesterday's high afternoon pronouncing a little stiltedly: "The Lybian air adust—" it was defensive, he could see now. It intended the irony, for what that was worth, both ways. Though she reeked, she thought, of sweat, she quoted Milton; and though she quoted Milton, she reeked, she thought, of sweat. She also kept it after she had thrown up in Sergeant Pellerino's kindly offered paper bag, and stood ashamed, her knees weak, on the ramp.

Nathaniel Hicks said: "I think your mother would be pleased with you."

"Do you? That is kindly put," Lieutenant Turck said. "There are other things she told me that I might try remembering, too. One was that the best way to bore everybody was to tell them things about myself. It was a needed warning. I've always shown really extraordinary ingenuity in making occasions to bring the subject up. You might think I dearly loved the history of my life. I am getting back my fuddled wits. What you were talking about, of course, was General Beal and the magazine project."

"Oh, no; no, I wasn't," Nathaniel Hicks said. "Let me put it your way. That was just an example of my ingenuity. I was showing you that I was an admirable fellow with admirable principles. It was the sour grapes technique. I had been as eager as possible, all set, to fake, bluff, and lie my way through it. It was suddenly taken out of my reach; but I kept on jumping for quite a while. I wasn't at all ready to give up the chance to go north and waste the Army's time and money for as long as I could possibly drag it out. But after moping all afternoon I had to see it was off. That was when I called on you to admire my finer-than-ordinary feelings, my nice sense of right and wrong. It seems I was relieved, really relieved—"

"But I think you were," Lieutenant Turck said.

"Yes, I was. I am," Nathaniel Hicks said. "But it took a lot to get me there; and I don't need to give myself a medal for that. I realize now that Colonel Ross saw right through me. He is quite a smart old boy. While I gave him this disgraceful sales talk, he just sat looking at me. Of course, he never had the faintest intention of speaking to General Beal about it again. Of course, I'm really relieved it's off. I don't want to be like that; at least not when someone like Colonel Ross sees me."

Lieutenant Turck said: "I have a knack for forcing people into these awkward situations. Oh, I say, but I am an unworthy worm; and give a few examples. My reluctant vis-à-vis is obliged, it's like Oriental etiquette, to say that as worms go, I am not a patch on him; and he hastily invents some examples. This need never stop: versicle and response: You are *not* more unworthy. I am *so* more unworthy. But I will stop. I will stop drinking your valuable whisky, clean up these things, and with heartfelt thanks for your kindness and your cash outlay, make myself, as we said when I was young, scarce."

"No, don't do that," Nathaniel Hicks said. "These are the Oleander Towers's things, not ours, and we don't clean them up, we just put them in the kitchenette for the cockroaches. It isn't nearly time for you to go home. Go out on the balcony, make yourself comfortable, and I'll bring you another drink."

"Then you probably would hear the history of my life," she said. "You don't want to. I gave you some excerpts from it on the plane Thursday, remember? It gets more and more plaintive and less and less interesting as it goes on. You might think it couldn't; but it can. It would be a poor return for your kindness. So I'll just go home, if home it can be called—"

"No; don't do that," Nathaniel Hicks said again.

Looking at her, he saw that her face showed traces of strain or anxiety; her faint smile was pained, her eyes dissatisfied or unhappy, as though she stood in the distress of facing a choice; and, moreover, the choice was a choice of distresses. "You know," Nathaniel Hicks said, "I think this might be a fine time for you to get a few things off your chest. I think you have a lot of notions you don't need. Now, suppose we just sit down and have this history." He looked at her gravely. "How about this marriage of yours, Amanda? Do you keep all that to yourself a little too much?"

Though her direct gaze did not move, held firmly to meet his, he could see an instant's darkening flicker of the sad eyes, and she colored. "Now, none of that!" Nathaniel Hicks said. "I may not be old enough to be your father; but I am a lot older than you are—" in fact, he could not help reflecting, he felt quite old enough to be her father. He put out his hand and gave her shoulder a sharp fatherly tap. "Don't blush," he said. "That's the trouble. There's no sense in it. I already know much more about you than you think. Whatever it was, you wouldn't have done it if it were really anything to blush about."

Lieutenant Turck said: "Another thing. Speaking kind words to me is risky. I suppose I have such a yearning for them I take them at once to heart, where they inordinately move me. You see?" She had grown dusky red and her eyes, though still direct, showed an abrupt glisten, a collecting of tears.

"Yes, I see," Nathaniel Hicks said. Touched to a depth that surprised him by a grace in awkwardness, a pride in shame, he said, "And it's all right."

Lieutenant Turck said: "I am repulsive. You should believe Lippa. She knows me better than anyone else." She moistened her lips and said: "There used to be a *jeune-fille* gambit—and must be still, since it suits an adolescent female—that is, one not yet hardened to the way she is. It's a green-sickly quibble about the Girl You Think I Am, and the Girl I Know I Am. I will skip it. Yes; I'm going out on the balcony. But before I do, if I may, I will visit the bathroom." She paused. She said: "I manage to sound as though I wished I never needed to, don't I? I suppose that is the truth; and it's not a good sign."

In the kitchenette Nathaniel Hicks scraped the few plates, put the remnants of food in a paper bag which he dropped down the rubbish chute, and piled things in the sink. He took a little longer than necessary, waiting until he heard Lieutenant Turck leave the bathroom. If she wished she never had to go, she would doubtless just as soon not be met leaving. It occurred to Nathaniel Hicks, for he felt wonderfully better, far removed from the lonely disconsolation with which he came out of the shower, that there was nothing like getting your mind off yourself.

"I know now you can almost always tell by the eyes," Lieutenant Turck said. "They're usually somewhat large and a little—patulous is the word, I think. They have this curious, quite distinctive soft look, if you know what I mean. Humble, you might say, but hungry. I knew less then. Anyway, you must understand the whole thing was entirely my own fault."

A fitful waft of air came up, almost cool, from the lake. She shifted in her chair, lifted her glass in the reflected dim glow from the living room and drank. "You can see how long it is," she said. "Do you really want to hear any more? You can see it's basically one of those tiresome errors in judgment. A person, being stupid about it, makes his bed; and then he has to lie in it, and he complains and complains. The only pertinent comment or answer is always—you should have had better sense."

Nathaniel Hicks snubbed out a cigarette in the ash tray on the arm of his chair. He said: "I don't see any way in which it was your fault, Amanda."

"Let me help you," Lieutenant Turck said. "Malcolm really didn't want to marry me. I wanted to marry him. It was extremely complicated—everything. My feelings, his feelings; my situation, his situation. First of all, there was my situation. What I was trying to do—get a medical degree on the side—was impossible. Certainly for me; I think, for anyone. You see, being assistant librarian, I was on duty in the Medical School Library from two in the afternoon until ten at night. I could get through my lecture schedule in the mornings; and I wasn't so busy while I was on duty that I couldn't, most of the time, be doing my own work—but anyhow the whole thing was impractical. You have trouble enough in any Class A school when you have nothing else to do; and when you have a real aptitude."

"I can believe that," Nathaniel Hicks said.

"Yes. And I had something else to do, so I could eat; and I hadn't any real aptitude. It was just a notion I developed after I took the library job there. Once I got the notion, I was very determined, frenziedly determined—not because medicine fascinated me or anything like that. All that fascinated me was the idea of being a doctor, alleviating the ills of suffering humanity in exchange for a good deal of reverent awe and astonished respect."

She laughed. "I think it took about this form. A harried, frightened voice would call out: 'Is there a doctor in the house?' No answer. Then, unhurried, I would rise to my feet and say: 'I am a physician.' Obviously this is taking place in a theater; and I'm not sure an alert electrician wouldn't throw a spotlight on me. There would be an amazed murmur, a voice saying: 'Why, it's a girl!' That might perhaps be the real high point; but a few obvious good moments follow before I come to say, worn but calm: 'He will recover.'"

Nathaniel Hicks said: "Amanda, do you ever make fun of anyone but yourself?"

"A point," Lieutenant Turck said. "Am I afraid to? It's plain, about myself. I want to be sure I say it first. I seem to be dragging this out. Do I evade the subject? Well, I just couldn't do it—frenzies or none, daydreams or none. It was too exhausting. Of course, the dean was insane ever to let me try. I suppose I was about half through anatomy—most people's easiest subject—when I saw I wasn't going to make it. I don't think I was rational enough to really plan; but I had to have an out. That's where Malcolm came in, though he didn't know it; and perhaps, consciously, I didn't. I fooled him."

Nathaniel Hicks said: "I don't think you fooled anyone." The situation seen, not as she disparagingly described it, but straight, as those around her must have seen it, was probably appealing. The determination, the exhaustion, would move

604

more people than she then or now thought. The insane dean, for instance, while considering the plan impossible, might quite wisely reason that remarkable individuals are always turning up. Given any chance at all, they can and will do the impossible. This thin, fanatical young woman might be one of them. Why not allow her to matriculate and see?

"Well, I did fool Mal," Lieutenant Turck said bitterly. She sat brooding a moment in the dark. "You see, he thought he knew me very well. He was a third-year man and he worked in the library a good deal—in a way, I knew about that; I mean, about working because you don't seem to have anything else to do. I don't think he had any friends, because he wasn't liked. A good many of the other men had got to calling him—that forced institutional humor you'll recognize; very unwitty—the Terrible Turck. There was the colloquial sense—they meant he was just terrible, a mess; and also, though I never thought of it then, it was a meaningful oblique reference to a smoking room story about the irregular love life of the Ottoman Turks. This must be all very dull."

"Now, stop saying that," Nathaniel Hicks said kindly.

"Yes. I will. It's too late, anyway; isn't it?" Lieutenant Turck said. "I knew how unpopular Mal was. I was on pretty familiar terms with a good many of the men—they used to stop at the library desk and kid me; they were really very nice to me. Women medical students often have a tough time; but they more or less adopted me; and several of them did what amounted to taking turns tutoring me. That was the only way I got even as far as I did. But I thought I knew why they didn't like Malcolm. I thought it was because he was so gentlemanly, and liked books and music. Hardly anyone else in school had any manners."

She sat back in her chair. She said: "Did you ever notice that? You can think, right away, of one or two outstanding exceptions, I don't doubt; but, by and large, it's very rare to find a doctor who has any manners. Or who has any taste. It may be because they're worked so hard in medical they literally have to forget everything else, most of them. They haven't time or energy for anything else."

"I never thought about it," Nathaniel Hicks said. "But, yes. Could you be evading your subject again?"

"I suppose so," she said. "Well, I really liked Mal a great deal; and I think he really liked me a great deal. And we should have let it go at that; but I wouldn't. I didn't have an easy time, either." She drew a breath. "It's funny how you can know a thing instinctively, and also, theoretically by instruction, and still not admit it—refuse to really know it. When the other men found out their Miss Smith might be going to marry, for God's sake, the Terrible Turck, I think they elected one of them to tell me why I shouldn't. He made it as clear as he felt he could—it was none of his business, but; and so on. He was quite an honest man, and he had trouble because I suppose he didn't actually have much to go on, any real proof. Of course I understood what he meant. Being a great reader, I'd naturally read all about it. A problem in modern ethics. I could discuss the matter very learnedly, with clinical details from case histories. Anyway, this man took me to dinner and gave me a long brotherly talk—I inspire lots of those. But I just wasn't having any. He was a nice fellow; I liked him; but he was also pretty much of a roughneck; and that explained everything I wanted to have explained."

Thoughtful, Nathaniel Hicks finished his drink. He said sagaciously: "Now, wait, Amanda. Isn't there a little hindsight here? You say yourself these men didn't have much to go on, any real proof. You could see other perfectly adequate reasons why they'd have no use for him—"

"Ah!" Lieutenant Turck said. "But I know I knew. You see, I absolutely had to know, or I never could have got him. He didn't want women. It was a real revulsion. So, of course, I gave him quite skillfully to understand that he needn't worry about that with me, I wasn't really a woman. I don't mean I faked it entirely. By normal standards, I'm sure I was well and truly undersexed—that was what attracted him, why he could like me so much. And he saw the advantages, for him, of being formally, officially married; and he wouldn't mind having those."

In the dark she changed the crossing of her legs and adjusted her skirt with a jerk. She said: "I'm putting this too cold-bloodedly. Yes; I wanted to get married so I could bow out, quit killing myself trying to be a doctor. Yes; he wanted to get married as a kind of protective coloration. He thought he wouldn't stand out so if he was known to be regularly living with what passed for a woman. But—" she paused. "I'm afraid this verges on bathos, only there seem to be no other terms—I also wanted to be loved; and Mal also wanted to be loved, poor wretch. By the word, I think he knew what he meant better than I knew what I meant." She turned her head sharp, looking out toward the dim lake below. "Would I be going on like this if I weren't tight? Isn't it enough?"

Moved to a pleasant tingling solemnity, Nathaniel Hicks said: "I'd like to hear the rest; but I don't have to."

"My!" Lieutenant Turck said. She swallowed the rest of her drink. "I *am* laying it on! It's a habit I have. I will try to be less emotional about myself. Love is a composite female idea. What they mean is a feeling peculiar to women. This leads to misunderstandings. Really, I know a lot for my years, many as they are. Yet, correct me, if I'm wrong. I believe a man disjoins the several relevant feelings; they don't all blur together for him at the same time. Do they?"

"I don't quite know," Nathaniel Hicks said. "I wouldn't think a man's feeling was ever any simpler than a woman's."

"When you take all its aspects, I daresay not," Lieutenant Turck said. "But I get the impression that their regular practice is: one thing at a time. You know. He loves his love in the morning by feeling the friendliest affection for her; and perhaps he loves his love in the middle of the afternoon by feeling —she being absent at the moment; I'd think—a reverent regard for her beauties of character; and he loves his love at night by feeling an ungovernable urgency to have carnal connection with her. These are all O.K. with her; and she soon finds she'd better take them as they come. It's a matter of running up against the way people are. Since *that* you won't change, there's nothing to do, except the best you can. She may do it pretty well; but even in the happiest circumstances I doubt if she's quite contented. It shakes her sense of security.

It would be blissful if she could see all his feelings involved in her all the time, all at once."

Nathaniel Hicks said judicially: "If that's how it looks to her, for practical purposes it'll have to be called how it is. I'll say this. I think the average man in the mentioned urgency hasn't for a moment stopped feeling that affection or that regard. He will often be a little preoccupied with his immediate object; but, rightly understood, that should be an acceptable compliment, shouldn't it?"

"Oh, yes," Lieutenant Turck said. "Rightly understood! I knew better than to consider it gross or coarse. A human being's means, his facilities, for expressing his feelings are limited. I was only a little nervous; quite prepared." She raised her hand and ran her thumbnail across her upper teeth. Taking it away, she said: "As a tribute to physical attraction, it can't be regarded too seriously, can it? I mean, I understand that the response is more or less automatic, routine. As a compliment, I suppose one ought to be able to take it, or leave it alone. Shouldn't one?"

Perturbed, Nathaniel Hicks said: "You must not feel that way. Do you see what you're doing—"

She said: "And you see, nothing, nothing, can fix it. Everything makes it worse. The mortifications are indescribable. Believe me. You could crawl away and die of resolute intentions, manful endeavor, dogged persistence, even occasional measures of success—" she began, not quite silently, to weep.

"Amanda!" he said.

"Yes! I will please omit the clinical details, the case history. I was the last person in the world to have it happen to; but how about him, poor wretch, poor wretch. All my ethereal airs! All my unspoken engagements and delicate gabble, gabble, gabble." In a strangled voice she said: "For oaths are straws, men's faiths are wafer-cakes, and hold-fast is the only dog, my duck! A quotation wantonly misapplied if ever I heard one!" She stood up with a quick effort. "It is absolutely essential that I go home," she said.

In a spasm of agitation, Nathaniel Hicks said: "Absolutely

not! Sit down. I'll get you another drink. I was a damn fool. I had no right to—"

"You did nothing," Lieutenant Turck said. Standing, she continued to weep while she talked. "Can you think you made me talk to you? Can you think I didn't want to, more than anything? I couldn't help it. I can't help this. But I can go home."

Nathaniel Hicks had arisen, too. Facing her, he saw her shaking so hard that he at once put out an arm to steady her on her feet. Though he had moved with no clear conscious intention, the touch electrified him. The trembling of her shoulders under his hand seemed to transmit or communicate to him a trembling of his own, a surge of sensation, sharp-set, that instantly and unmistakably identified itself. He said: "Amanda. Look at me."

She said: "I am not responsible. Nat, let me go. You must —at once, I tell you!"

"I don't think so," Nathaniel Hicks said. He put his other arm around her, and she swayed a little, took a step, necessarily toward him, that brought her straight shaking legs hard against his. "I don't think so," he said again. There seemed to be an impediment in his speech connected with his now hammering heartbeat. Getting his voice clear, he said: "You couldn't imagine I'm just being sorry for you?"

"I don't know," she said through her teeth. "No, I *do* know. I am a damn liar. And also I know it has no conscience—has it? You see all I know?"

Drawing her tighter, Nathaniel Hicks said: "Could you stop thinking about all you know? Would you just—"

Lieutenant Turck's hands, until now resting nerveless, dropped limply at her sides, came up and pressed his back. She uttered a groaning sound, bumping her forehead with a movement of despair against his shoulder. "I can't help it," she said.

"Why help it?" Nathaniel Hicks said.

"I know one hundred reasons," she said. "One thousand." She brought her tear-wet lips hastily around and up. "Ah!" she said.

"Come in here," Nathaniel Hicks said. She was now, he realized, shaking no more than he was.

She made a slight resistance. She said: "Yes. I will. I'm going to. But could you put that light out first?"

✦

General Beal said: "Put that light on if you like, Collins. Right by the door."

Captain Collins said: "Thank you, sir."

In the ceiling fixtures the fluorescent tubes glowed white, flooding the room. Blinking through his glasses a moment, Captain Collins raised the typed sheet and read aloud: "Ocanara, Florida; September Fourth, Nineteen Forty-three. It was announced today by Headquarters of the Army Air Forces Operations and Requirements Analysis Division that a large scale experimental parachute drop staged here under simulated combat conditions this afternoon resulted in the death of seven members of an airborne unit."

Speaking slowly and distinctly, he continued: "The paratroopers were attached to one of the Division's satellite fields where development and demonstration of new tactics is carried on. Preliminary investigation indicated that the accident occurred when a mechanical failure caused one of the carrier planes to release part of its drop outside the designated drop zone. Names of casualties were withheld, pending notification of next of kin."

"That all?" said General Beal.

"Yes, sir," Captain Collins said.

"One thing," General Beal said. "Call Botty on the box, there, will you, Judge. Or wait. You'd better draft it. I want orders, I want them out tonight, within an hour. All AFORAD personnel at all AFORAD installations will wear life vests whenever engaged in any project that involves flying. Whether it's supposed to be over water or not makes no difference. You got copies of that thing?" he said to Captain Collins.

"There are five, sir."

"Give us each one. You read it, Judge. You read it, Jo-Jo. It sounds like hell to me."

Colonel Ross said, "I disagree. I think it fills the bill exactly. Captain Collins is an experienced newspaper man, General. I think we can leave it to him. There's enough information so we don't seem to be making a mystery out of it, but he hasn't said a word he didn't need to. That's for the press services. Mr. Bullen, the *Sun*, will have to have a somewhat fuller story. After all, several thousand of his readers were right there. Captain Collins talked to him."

"That isn't what I meant," General Beal said. "I meant it's certainly a hell of a story any way you read it. What business have we got to kill seven men like that?" He looked at Captain Collins. "What did Bullen say? Had he been hearing anything?"

Captain Collins said, "Well, General, he told me he'd heard the men had no life vests on; and that something was wrong with the rescue boat."

"What did you say?"

"I told him I believed that was the case, sir."

General Beal jerked his chin up. "You had no authority to tell him anything! Do you think we want that in the paper? What did you do that for?"

Colonel Ross said, "Captain Collins had this authority, General. I told him: Fix it with Bullen if you think you can. Personally, I've found it doesn't pay to tell a newspaper that facts are wrong when you know they're right. They don't consider it friendly. I think Captain Collins feels that, if you happen to want the newspaper to do something for you, you mustn't even tell them you don't know."

"What's Bullen going to do for us? Climb all over us?"

Captain Collins said, "I don't think so, General. He concluded by saying he hoped I'd convey to you the sincere sympathy, felt, he said, by him and by all Ocanara, city and county; and their regret that a tragic incident should have marred a most enjoyable occasion. He told me, sir, that he would be writing the *Sun's* story himself on the basis of whatever we decided ought to be released. I don't think there'll be anything in it we haven't released. I mean; since it's his paper, he says what goes into it. So I think we can rely on that, sir."

"Well, that's something," General Beal said. "Well, tell him we appreciate that."

"Yes; do," Colonel Ross said. "You must have worked hard enough for it."

General Beal said, "Somebody should have had sense enough to see they wore life vests. They have maps. They can see the drop area is right next to a lake a mile wide. How hard do you have to think to figure that one out? We need people with more sense around here. And that crash boat. What was wrong with those engines? Why should they have to replace them? I don't know how many hours they ought to be good for; but with the amount of use they got here, they ought to last forever—unless the people in charge of them never ran them up, let them corrode, or something. Uline better explain that to me."

General Nichols said: "It occurs to me, Bus, that a boat like that wouldn't be much use in a thing like this unless it was right out there at the time."

"And that's where it should have been," General Beal said. "Why the hell does nobody think of anything? Uline should have had it out. It should have been holding off there during the drop. Let's have another order, Judge. The Lake Lalage rescue boat will be manned at all times when the field is open. It will be taken out every day on a short test run. If it has to be laid up for any reason, even for half an hour, there's to be another boat of comparable performance standing by. Got that?"

"Yes," said Colonel Ross.

He opened the desk drawer and found a pad of memorandum sheets headed: *AFORAD. Office of the Commanding General.* Pulling a pencil from his shirt pocket, he began to write.

"By God," said General Beal, "I think I'll shake this place up! I want Lester in from Tangerine City tomorrow. Let him explain why his people came over with no life vests. Out he goes, it looks to me. If he didn't think of it, he should have."

"Colonel Lester is a pretty good man," Colonel Ross said.

General Beal said, "You think Uline's a pretty good man,

too, don't you? So do I; in a way. I don't think either of them is going to be good enough from here on in. We're going to get rid of some dead wood—"

The buzzer on the box sounded.

Striking the key down, Colonel Ross said, "Yes?"

A voice Colonel Ross did not recognize, probably one of Mr. Botwinick's "aides," said hollowly: "Colonel Mowbray to see the general, sir."

General Beal nodded at him; and Colonel Ross said, "He's to come right in." He looked at Captain Collins and said, "Think it might be a good idea to take that down to Bullen yourself?"

"I think it might, sir," Captain Collins said.

"I doubt if my car's back. Take one of the others. Have you had anything to eat tonight?"

"That's all right, sir," Captain Collins said.

"Yes. I suppose you might as well get used to it," Colonel Ross said. "I forgot to tell you, Collins. In our office, we hardly ever eat."

Perched jauntily on his grizzled head, Colonel Mowbray wore a faded, rumpled overseas cap to which his eagle was pinned not quite straight. His shirt sleeves were rolled up on his thin hairy old man's arms. On his chest, hung from the strap about his neck, was a new pair of field glasses. Around his waist, sagging at his thin hip, was a regulation broad belt of OD webbing supporting a forty-five automatic in its holster.

Though Colonel Mowbray's motions in opening, passing around, and closing the door were a little fussy and pottering, he turned from it with a certain brisk swagger. He peered at General Beal, his eyes bright in his grave gnome-like face. He said: "Just stopped by a minute, Bus. I'm on my way to the lake. I think we have everything there—or will have, by the time I get over."

"I'll say!" General Beal said, smiling. "What's the shooting iron for, Pop?"

Colonel Mowbray's thin gray cheeks took a tinge of rose;

but he said: "Well, you never know, Bus." Only a little at loss, he added energetically: "This is a serious thing. I just feel better with a side arm. It makes people understand it's serious." He advanced another step; and Colonel Ross could see that Colonel Mowbray had put on heavy GI shoes and a pair of leggings.

"Sit down," General Beal said. "Have a drink."

Colonel Mowbray said: "No, I don't have time, Bus. I want to get right over. Now; I guess Uline reported to you. Hildebrand and I got the boats, got the tackle. That AA searchlight battery ought to be there and set up now—give us plenty of light. Working parties are detailed. There's one platoon on now; and we'll relieve that at midnight and go on with a new one if we're not through. I had a restricted area laid off and posted guards. We got ambulances for the bodies. Oh! And Ehret says the telegrams to next of kin are ready; but I told him to wait, so they won't be received anywhere in the middle of the night. Oh; coffins are at the Hospital. I checked. The best thing, I thought, we'd send the bodies there—"

"If you get the bodies," General Beal said.

"Don't you worry, we'll get them," Colonel Mowbray said. "You needn't worry about a thing, Bus. Everything's taken care of. Why do you think we wouldn't get the bodies? We know within a hundred yards, less, where they have to be."

General Beal said: "Uline called and told the judge it was too deep."

In Colonel Mowbray's cheeks the tinge of rose returned, much stronger. He said: "What's he mean? He had no business —if he thought that, why didn't he call me or Hildebrand? We'll make any decisions. It isn't up to him." Colonel Mowbray frowned. "Tell you the truth, Bus," he said, "I'm a little disappointed in Gordon. Of course, I understand he feels a primary responsibility for the thing being crossed up, about the boat and so on. That's right; he ought to; and I see how that could upset him. It'd upset me. But a field officer, a man commanding troops—he's got to keep a cool head. Meet the emergency. Now, I don't think Gordon's measuring up too well. I wish I didn't have to say it. I'll see if I can snap him out of

614

it. I'd better get right over there. Oh. About funeral plans, Bus. What about that?"

"What about it?" General Beal said.

Brightening again, Colonel Mowbray said: "Well, don't you think we ought to do a little more than just nail them up and ship them off by express—I mean, supposing their people want a home burial. Would you like me to work out some kind of little ceremony, service, out by the lake? Tomorrow's Sunday; we could have something religious. Just a short thing. Parade a couple of squadrons—maybe use Johnny Sears's men, so they'd look good. Have a firing party; sound Taps. We could have the chaplains—I suggest Captain Appleton and Captain Doyle each read something appropriate. Better have Lieutenant Meyer, too; in case one of them was Jewish. I could check on that, of course. But anyway, it makes it more non-denominational. Might bring a plane over at the same time and drop a wreath on the water—"

General Beal said: "I don't think so, Pop. We have a press release here; and I don't think we need to do anything else to call attention to it. Our publicity hasn't been too good this week."

"Well, yes," Colonel Mowbray said. "I didn't think of that. Yes; I believe you're right, Bus. I was just thinking because there were so many of them, perhaps we ought to do a little something extra—Bus, I nearly forgot. I think this is important. That memorandum we never got. There's no doubt at all that Hildy's office received a report, all pertinent information; and that a memo was prepared and sent out. Now, that's a pretty serious thing. I think we'd better find out tomorrow, Monday at latest, how it could be possible. We'd better go over the whole system—Base Communications Center; our Communications Center; the courier service; everything. Take a fine-tooth comb to it. That's what I think. Don't you?"

General Beal said: "You didn't see Botty?"

"Not right now, Bus. He had a man on the desk outside. I think he said Botty went around to the mess kitchen."

"Yes," said General Beal. "He'd arranged to get us something to eat."

"Well, I don't need to see Botty. Not about that. I talked to him on the phone, right away when I saw the Base Headquarters copy of the memo. That paper, I know, wasn't in our mail this morning, which was when it should have been. We couldn't have overlooked it—Botty and Mrs. Spann between them; we don't lose things, Bus. The place to begin looking is the Communications Center and start tracing back."

General Beal said: "Tell him, Judge."

Glancing over his glasses at General Beal, Colonel Ross said: "All right. Well, we know what happened to that paper, Pop. Botty came in here half an hour ago and told the general he destroyed it. He had it. It was in the mail. It was noted in your memorandum record. He burned it, mixed up, he says, with some other papers."

Colonel Mowbray opened and closed his mouth. Colonel Ross could see the rise and fall of his prominent thyroid cartilage as he swallowed. Colonel Mowbray said: "We lost it? We had it and we lost it?"

Colonel Ross said: "Mr. Botwinick feels he must bear the responsibility. If the circumstances were as he described them, and he burned it, I suppose he must. I think there's no reason to doubt that he did burn it."

Colonel Mowbray said: "You absolutely sure, Norm? He's sure?"

Colonel Ross said: "He seemed sure enough to feel he had to report himself in arrest for dereliction of duty. That's what he came in here and did. The general told him to carry on; he'd talk to you."

Colonel Mowbray's mouth worked a moment. He said then: "Bus, that's a terrible thing! Hard to believe, I mean. Botty never lost a paper in his life, I know of." He paused and licked his lips. Feebly, not quite coherent, he said: "We want to remember that, don't we? Of course, I see why he'd feel he had to report—I mean; because the terrible mistake. I mean, because those seven men—that's a terrible thing to have to know you did! I'm not excusing him—"

General Nichols said: "Isn't that a little strong, Pop?" He spoke kindly. "I don't think anyone here has to know that.

From what I heard, the real reason those men were killed was that something happened to the hitch-ons. Before they got the lines running again, they were carried ahead for a minute or two. In this war, we're all just learning, Pop."

Colonel Mowbray made what sounded like a croak. He started to say: "That didn't have anything to do with—"

General Nichols proceeded firmly: "That jump master couldn't have had too much experience; and I daresay the men who jumped didn't, either. Maybe it wouldn't have mattered; but I think experts, men who've made a lot of jumps, can do a little more than these seem to have done about controlling their descent. I don't really know. But anyway, we see where the big mistake was. The jump master, instead of holding them, sends them out after the delay. That was a serious error. I agree; any unit commander ought to have a man's stripes for that. But when the man went on and jumped himself, you might say necessary corrective action was taken. You're protected from further errors in judgment on that man's part, at least. It was that error in judgment that caused the accident. Could you say your man Botwinick had anything to do with it?"

"No, sir!" Colonel Mowbray said. He swung his head in a series of distressed little wags. "That won't go down, Jo-Jo. That's what we're for, to provide for—when somebody makes mistakes. We can't stop that—that's the thing. We know somebody's always going to make mistakes. That's when we have to be ready, not go making one ourselves, too. What you say is no excuse—"

Colonel Mowbray stopped and swallowed; perhaps resting an instant from the hard mental labor that the involved statement cost him; perhaps casting about for thoughts that would carry it further or make it clearer; but he must then have recollected himself, remembered where he stood. He said: "Bus, I don't know what to say. I just don't know what to—"

Colonel Ross looked at him. Colonel Mowbray stood stricken in the middle of the room, aimless, all swagger gone. His thin frame stayed upright, propped by the stiff old backbone's years of habit in the position of the soldier; but Colonel Mowbray seemed to shrink or shrivel inside his clothes. He looked small

617

for his boots and leggings. On his withered little buttock the heavy automatic pistol was too big for him, outsized, a man's furnishings weighing down a child. The eagle inaccurately pinned to his limp overseas cap hung from its bent fastening pin, awry and loose. With a sad disturbance of mind Colonel Ross saw, starting in Colonel Mowbray's eye, what was indubitably a senile tear.

Brought so soon to his second pause, Colonel Mowbray twitched his head again, turning his face back from General Beal to General Nichols. He made a distracted explanatory gesture. He said: "Reason I say I don't know, Jo-Jo—of course what Botty did's inexcusable, unforgivable. But the other thing is: a man's usefulness. We want to try to see the overall picture. The good of the service. Not act against the best interests of all concerned. I don't mean, not take appropriate action; only not let ourselves go off half—"

General Beal stood up. He said: "Let it ride for tonight, Pop. We don't have to take any action right this minute." Approaching with purpose, he put a hand on Colonel Mowbray's thin shoulder. "You go along," he said. "I want you over at the lake."

Keeping his hand on Colonel Mowbray's shoulder, General Beal moved him toward the hall door, and moved with him. Opening the door, gently pressing Colonel Mowbray, General Beal went on out into the hall with him.

Alone with Colonel Ross, General Nichols put together the tips of his precise, shapely fingers. He studied them with gravity for an instant. He said: "Well, Judge?"

Sitting back in General Beal's chair, Colonel Ross found himself saying, in much the same tone: "Well, General?"

A rare, reflective smile touched General Nichols's mouth. His formal face, the not-quite-young but little marked mask he wore over that other face of his—the face of patience and watchfulness, of endurance and resolve—lit impassively with the mind's temporary pleasure, its enjoyment of the moment's agreeable interlude.

Colonel Ross waited, no less pleased than General Nichols to be party to this neat meeting of minds. He was pleased with so equal a display of the intellectual art that discerned, that asked, that answered, that perfectly agreed; but never once stooped to the low means of a spoken word. He was pleased with the top quality of those distinguished considerations of theirs, of the traded compliments on their seeing, both of them, a little more than some people saw, and on their saying, even now, nothing.

General Nichols said soberly: "Ought we to get on with the war, Judge? What about this project, this publicity thing, Bus wanted me to hear about?"

"Why, General," Colonel Ross said, "I think it's a matter of some interest. Bus is right about our publicity being bad this week, I guess you'll agree. Some of another kind might be opportune."

"Very," General Nichols said.

Colonel Ross said: "We're fortunate enough to have this young captain in the Directorate of Special Projects—as a matter of fact, he was the one at the Hospital this morning, the one I brought in with the colored boy's father."

"Oh, yes," General Nichols said.

"Now, in civilian life," Colonel Ross said, "he's a very important magazine editor or executive, or both. He really knows the business, and I think he has a lot of influential publishing connections. This man's name is Hicks—"

✦

The voices, there seemed to be only two—two advance members of some party somewhere downstairs which had not as a whole reached the singing stage—floated up the night to Nathaniel Hicks.

Because it was still early, because everyone else would need a few more drinks before he felt like joining in, the singers excused themselves by taking care, in mock expressiveness and kidding coloratura emphasis, to show that they were just being funny. They sang: "I wouldn't give a cent for the whole state of Florida—"

In the darkness Lieutenant Turck lay as though dead; but Nathaniel Hicks could hear her breathe. Her breathing had slowed; yet still it was quicker than normal, and a little rough —as though with a residue of her varied breath-taxing exertions in the last half hour. There had been those earlier labored tears begun on the balcony that dried in action; and the seizures of moaning that came on as the toils engaged her deeper. Some whimpered, not-to-be-contained cries were wrung out of her. Last came, exhausted and easier but copious, some final tears. These might acknowledge at first only the searchings of pleasure. Continuing, it was plain that they deplored more and more, helpless and too late, every circumstance that brought her here to be uncovered and looked at; to have the demented convulsions of her body noted and her mouth's hateful sounds heard.

Seeing tears to be idle, she had stopped them after a while, and made a slight eloquent movement, a sad pleading to be free.

Hearing her breathe, and hearing them sing downstairs, Nathaniel Hicks thought of things to say; but none of them seemed very good. Not sure what to do, he had put a hand out, found and touched her damp cheek. He moved the hand to her hair, which was damp, too. With a vague compassionate feeling he began to stroke it; but he had no more than begun when, on the shadowed obscurity of the bedside table, the telephone bell struck out its clear shocking zing.

Lieutenant Turck's start was violent.

She said: "Oh!"

Though he had started just as much himself, Nathaniel Hicks gave her bare shoulder a quiet tap. He turned, reached groping, and took the telephone. "Captain Hicks," he said.

The voice on the telephone was loud. It said: "Colonel Ross, Captain."

Nathaniel Hicks said: "Yes, Colonel."

"Wasn't sure I'd get you, Hicks—that you'd be in. Well, that saves us trouble. Not in bed, are you?"

"No, sir."

Colonel Ross cleared his throat.

"Good," he said. "You won't be going to bed. I believe you'll be pleased to hear that General Beal is sending you north on that project. Right now. General Nichols will give you a lift as far as Washington. You have half an hour. A staff car's coming down for you."

"Yes, sir," Nathaniel Hicks said. "Will I need orders—I mean—"

"Don't worry about that. We'll cover you. I'll see you at the plane. General Beal has a few instructions you're to follow; but we're going to leave you pretty much your own boss. You'd better fix us something good."

"Yes, sir," Nathaniel Hicks said.

"All right. Hop to it. Get your stuff together. We're giving you two weeks. You can have more if you need it. Better be downstairs when the car comes."

"Yes, sir," Nathaniel Hicks said.

He put back the telephone and said, shaken: "Well, I'll be damned! That was Colonel Ross. He says—"

"I could hear him," Lieutenant Turck said.

She sat up in the darkness. "I suppose I'll have to have a light," she said. "I'll have to find my clothes."

XVIII

AT NIGHT the glass box of the Control Tower was filled with a dim bluish light. This was intended to be light enough for eyes used to it to work efficiently in the tower; yet not so much light that an operator looking over the dark spread of the airfield would be totally blind.

At the moment, the bluish glow was modified weirdly by a strong radiance cast up against the glass from outside. The ramp floodlights were on. Under their focused, concerted beams the pavement before the Operations Building was lit like day. The universal warm darkness of the night seemed set back, arching above an open insubstantial cave of light. From the tower, T/3 Anderson and T/5 Murphy looked down into it like spectators from a balcony above a bright stage.

At the edge of the light flood, silent and shining, waited a midwing monoplane with a twin rudder empanage and a long pointed nose thrust ahead of its twin engine nacelles. Waiting around the plane were several line crew members in twill coveralls and cloth caps with brims tipped rakishly up off their faces. They had brought up the tanks and funneled hoses of carbon dioxide fire extinguishers. A portable generator had been wheeled under the plane. Crouched on their heels, examining some part of it with attention, were a couple of sergeants—the chief of the line crew; and Sergeant Pellerino, General Beal's crew chief.

Fifty feet from the plane, full in the flood of light, stood two cars. One of them was General Beal's staff car with the little flag on its bumper. The other was a convertible coupe with its top down. Beside it were General Beal, General Nichols, Colonel Ross, and Mrs. Beal. Still seated in the coupe was a woman T/3 Anderson thought was Mrs. Ross.

"But never mind them, hon," she said. Her tone was the preceptor's, kindly chiding, correcting yet encouraging a teachable pupil. "Just you look at the plane. You want to know all the planes, don't you? The C-Sixty, see? It's practically the same as the C-Fifty-six. A lot of the model designations only mean different equipment and things."

With an effort, T/5 Murphy transferred her attention. T/3 Anderson said: "Now, those wings, see? They're what they call swept-back, tapered, elliptical—the ends aren't round or square, that means—"

In the enclosed cool air around them the ceaseless hummings and twangings sounded. Remote disembodied voices rose and fell, came and went. A voice with extra sharpness said suddenly: "Hello Hiram twelve this is Lazarus. Vector two-six-zero. Orbit Honeybee Green. Angels ten and one half. Over."

T/5 Murphy turned in the gloom, gaping at this rigamarole; but T/3 Anderson said: "Now, that's got nothing to do with us. I just tuned that other speaker in on it. I wanted you to hear it, in case they were up tonight; so you'd know what

622

it was like. That's the Orlando fighter control frequency. It's Air Defense. They have planes out; and that's the Intercept Officer telling them where to go—"

T/5 Murphy said: "Oh, my; all you have to know. I don't think I'll ever—"

Not displeased, T/3 Anderson said: "Yes, you will, hon. I'll show you everything. This is your first time on at night; so you get some different things, that confuse you—"

Out of a crackling sound another voice said: "Zero-five to Tower, please. For a check line. Go ahead, please—" it went out in more crackling.

"Now, that's yours," T/3 Anderson said. "It's the pilot down there in the C-Sixty. He's seeing if his radio works all right. It does; only he's being intermittently blocked out by something—hear? When it's like that, ask him to say again. It could be something in his own equipment. Go on; go ahead."

T/5 Murphy brought her microphone to her mouth and said with little certainty: "Zero-five; this is Ocanara Tower. Will you say again to test—"

Another voice called out casually: "Tower! Exercise leader; Tactical Exercise Orion, White and Blue Flights. We have concluded. We are approaching the field south at three thousand. Will you clear us in?"

The first voice proceeded patiently: "—seven, eight, nine, ten, nine, eight, seven—"

T/3 Anderson said: "Tell Zero-five he's all right; and, out. Now, you know what Exercise Orion is. They're the P-Seventies, really the A-Twenties—*our* night fighter flights. You'll get to know them. They're up almost every night. Only, this is a new man, this leader—"

To her microphone T/3 Anderson said: "Orion Leader, this is Ocanara Tower. Wait. I will try to get you in first if I can. We have a plane that may be ready to go out." She lowered the microphone and said: "Hon, ask Zero-five if he thinks the general will want to take off very soon. Tactical flights have regular priority, remember; but when you can help it, never keep anyone like a general waiting for the runway. They don't like it."

T/5 Murphy spoke agitatedly to her microphone.

"You tell me!" the answering voice boomed. "They're all outside still. I don't know how long. They got another passenger to come."

T/3 Anderson put her microphone to her mouth. "Orion Leader; I am clearing you to come right in; two flights, six planes. Please make a three-sixty overhead approach on runway seven so I will know where you are. You will see the markers. Number one to land please call on his base leg. The glide beam is on; I say again, on. Wind is light, oboe at zebra. Acknowledge."

There was a silence.

"Damn!" T/3 Anderson said. "I'll bet he didn't listen. Orion Leader, this is Ocanara Tower—"

T/5 Murphy had taken field glasses again and turned them on the ramp.

Observing her, T/3 Anderson said: "Now, you just pay attention. You'll have to do this yourself sometime!"

T/5 Murphy gave a sudden sharp giggle. "Oh, you should have seen that!" she said, delighted.

"What?" T/3 Anderson said grudgingly.

"General Beal, you know what he did? He just suddenly reached out and pulled Mrs. Beal's hair; and she slapped him; and he twisted her arm around!"

Incredulous, T/3 Anderson said: "Were they sore?"

T/5 Murphy shook her head. "Uh-uh!" she said. She smiled in pleased reflection. "They were just horsing around."

"Well, now keep still, hon." To her microphone she said: "Orion Leader; will you kindly guard the frequency? I am trying to clear you in—"

From the void, the voice said: "Yeah, I heard you, sister. We're having a little—Leader to Blue One! Get on the hell down, will you—" the voice clicked out.

T/3 Anderson said: "I don't like *him!* I can tell by his voice. The other one was nice. I felt terrible about that."

"About what?" T/5 Murphy said.

"He and his radio operator were killed, hon. Monday night, I think it was. They crashed somewhere. They only just found them, someone said." She turned and stared into the darkness of the field. Low down by Lake Lalage the great searchlights turned on the water and the working parties made a glow. At this additional evidence of the perils and dangers of aerial action, T/3 Anderson said broodingly: "It's taking an awful long time over there. That must be an awful thing to have tó do! I wouldn't want to be doing that, I can tell you—"

"Ugh!" agreed T/5 Murphy abstractedly. "Here comes a car," she said. "Could that be what they're waiting for?"

Turning back, T/3 Anderson took up her glasses.

Through the gate in the fence between Operations and Hangar Number One passed a staff car driven fast. It ran straight across the ramp to halt near the other cars. The driver jumped out and lifted a flight bag from the front seat. The rear door opened.

"My goodness," T/3 Anderson said, "it's just a captain!"

✦

Except for him, in spite of him, they made a merry party on the ramp. Colonel Ross felt tired. He also looked tired—old and glum—he could be sure. Cora, sitting in the car, showed him how he looked by occasional glances at once critical and sympathetically concerned. She would recognize that he was tired and that he was, for that and other reasons, testy. She might even, he must admit, have a fairly good idea of what the other reasons were; and no doubt she considered it a pity that small things could so affect him. He was not being a credit to her.

General Nichols, debonaire in manner, was engaged in relating an anecdote. Not having attended to its start, Colonel Ross did not know what it was about, or apropos of; but it clearly concerned Air Force people well known to Bus. General Nichols said: "So Tooey gave them one of his looks; and that made them all shut up, except Pete. 'Sure, sure,' Pete said. 'It's like when you just put this regular small sum of money in the bank each week; and keep doing it fifteen, twenty years.

625

And you know, I swear to God, when you finally get to draw it out, you'll be surprised how little it comes to.' "

"He's got something there," General Beal said, grinning.

"Oh, you!" Mrs. Beal said. "How would you know? You never saved a nickel in your life. You just talk about it; and tell me I can't buy things. I'd like to know what cost Bus so much money overseas. If it wasn't poker, I'll bet he kept a harem. Did he, Jo-Jo?"

"Why, they don't cost so much," General Nichols said gravely. "I could name you someone in CBI who, we hear, has all these little yellow girls he even brings to the movies with him; but I think they get in half price—"

General Nichols could dismiss his concerns, it seemed. He could put it out of mind that he often sat in, or almost in, the councils of the mighty; that, if he did not yet say the word there, he assisted stern and vigilant at its saying. Somewhere along the line he also shed, it seemed, his pause-giving menace of resolve, his pitiless austerity of purpose, his stark speculations on the employment of air power and his wordless perfect perspicacity. Had Colonel Ross, this morning, let himself be taken in just a little? Had he, this evening, credited General Nichols with more subtlety of mind than General Nichols had?

As for Mrs. Beal, did Sal remember that this morning she had been filled with frenzy, and that as late as noon she had been filled with despair? Had she forgotten that General Nichols was the Chief of Air Staff's Deputy in charge of assassinations, that he would shoot his own mother, that he could only be here to do Bus dirt?

Mrs. Beal said: "Come on, Jo-Jo! Give. I want the low-down on that lug—"

General Beal continued to grin. With his grin, Bus wrote off, it seemed, all that formidable tale of worries so heavy on everyone over the last couple of days. General Beal had been, it seemed, in no special danger of sinking under them; so those who fell over themselves trying to lift the load could have their trouble for their pains. The not-unmoving picture of the simple soldier, fatefully set-on in his still unfamiliar high place by a host of mischances; dogged by disaster not his

626

fault; threatened with ruin by staggering irrelevancies—by Colonel Woodman, his bottle, his pistol in his mouth; by Benny persisting as Benny, the unreconstructable two-fisted fighting man; by the unrelated intrusion of a little history and sociology in the sullen contention of some colored boys that they were as good as anybody else; by a flustered jump master in a C-46 who hadn't sense enough to stop a drop and so got them in the papers again—well, it seemed, that picture was overdrawn. The only people who ever took the danger seriously were Colonel Mowbray, a simple dotard, and Colonel Ross—well, what was he?

Grinning still, General Beal with a sudden deft movement, ran his fingers into Mrs. Beal's hanging yellow hair and gave it a mischievous tug.

"Ow!" cried Mrs. Beal. Ducking her head to get free, agile on her small feet, she turned and neatly slapped his face.

"Ow," General Beal said, laughing. Quick as she was, he had been able to catch her wrist. "Now, just for that—" the strong fingers turned her wrist over, twisting it, doubling her up.

"No, no," Mrs. Beal squealed. She tried in vain to hit him with her other hand. "No! Fins! I quit. Jo-Jo, make him stop! *Ira!* Everybody's looking at us! I'll kick your shins—"

Indeed, she jabbed her heel at him; and so got her hand away. She snatched the car door open and got in with Mrs. Ross. "Now, you quit!" she said, giggling. "You started it. You tell him to stop, Norm. He only got what he asked for—"

"He is my commanding officer," Colonel Ross said. "I don't tell him. He tells me."

General Beal was not looking at him. Out of the night, down from the warm darkness came a heavy growing mutter of invisible planes. General Beal and General Nichols automatically lifted their eyes, listening arrested. Though no expert, Colonel Ross could tell, or thought he could, by the fairly deep pitch, the steady tone and rhythm of sound, that a number of light bombers, the night fighters, were coming over the field.

General Nichols said: "How are they doing?"

General Beal said: "That armament is lousy. These are the ones with a belly-mounting of four twenty-mm cannon. It ought to be machine guns. There's no sense throwing cannon shells at anything you don't actually see. Figure it this way. We get the contacts all right; but any least little deviation, and how are you going to determine that, in the angle of approach; and all your guns miss. It ought to be possible to put six fifties in the nose, bore-sighted to fire a good wide pattern. That's what they'll need."

"You want that, you can certainly have it," General Nichols said. "Gun mountings oughtn't to be hard; only, placing the magazines will take a little working out, I think."

Colonel Ross had observed the staff car coming through the gate. He said with relief: "There we are. Here's Hicks. Want to talk to him, Bus?"

"No," General Beal said. "You talk to him on the plane, Jo-Jo. I can't tell him anything."

General Nichols turned toward the waiting plane and raised his hand. From the control compartment window an acknowledging voice called down: "Let's go!"

The crew chief said: "O.K., Major. Fire up any time."

"Switch on! Left engine. Clear?"

"Clear, sir."

With a deep heaving grunt the left propeller moved, twitched over on the energized engine. It caught instantly, broke out with a bang. The propeller spun to a blur; the light beams thrown on it balanced, walking back.

The roar, throttled down, diminished a little; and bawling from the other window, the co-pilot's voice carried: "Switch on! Right engine. Clear—"

Colonel Ross walked over to the car.

"You're late," he said to Captain Hicks. "Though not very. You'd better get right on board. The general says he hasn't any instructions. General Nichols may want to talk to you about it." Colonel Ross regarded him attentively. He said: "You have what looks like a little lipstick on your face, Captain."

✦

Watching the plane taxi off, General Beal said: "Walk along here a minute, Judge."

At a strolling pace he moved from the lighted ramp out past the gaping opened doors of Hangar Number One. A B-24, its enormous four-engined wings spreading almost from wall to wall, had been moved in there. The monster was supported on massive steel trestles and men seemed to be working on a landing gear assembly. One rubber-tired wheel as big as the men had been taken off.

General Beal paused and watched a moment. He moved on then across the taxiway, out to the edge of the paving, facing the field.

General Nichols's plane, down past the long hangar line, had paused broadside at the head of the runway. Above it in the dark middle air, four or five hundred feet up, a shafting white wingbeam came on, slanting ahead for the ground—the last of the night fighters about to land. Colonel Ross could see the puff of flaming gases flicker out its exhausts. At this angle slowly, floating like a feather, the dim hulk came down, hit the runway with a soft bump, and swept on into darkness.

General Nichols's plane moved again, turning, the rudders twitching to align it. It trembled hard, gathering itself as the throttles went forward. The noise of its engines climbed to full roar. Irresistibly tugged, it began to roll. With a smooth rise of speed, its position lights fleeting in the dark, faster and faster it went humming away. Suddenly, in the everyday miracle, it was flying. The lights lofted gently, drew off the ground, parted from the earth.

"That's it!" General Beal said.

"Well!" said Colonel Ross. "Think he had a good time?"

"The end of a perfect day," General Beal said. "Jo-Jo is quite a man, Judge. It's a little hard to follow him sometimes; but he's a good flyer. I always remember that. I guess we got by. He likes you, Judge."

"I am complimented," Colonel Ross said. "I don't dislike him. I think that General Nichols may end by amounting to something. If that's true, he's more likable than many people on their way to amounting to something."

629

General Beal said lightly: "Jo-Jo thinks I need a nurse. That's you. I guess I do act that way." He laughed. "Don't worry, Judge," he said. He put his hand suddenly on Colonel Ross's shoulder. "Even Jo-Jo knows they could do without him before they could do without me. That's not boasting, Judge. There's a war on. Jo-Jo can talk to Mr. Churchill; but the war, that's for us. Without me—without us, he wouldn't have a whole hell of a lot to talk about, would he?"

Feeling the thin strong fingers, nervous but steadily controlled, pressing the cloth of his shirt, Colonel Ross almost started. The pressure was intelligible. It was the kindly hand laid on poor Pop to walk the distracted old boy out of the office, compassionately sending him on to the lake.

General Beal said: "It's late, Judge. I just wanted to say one or two things. How about that, tonight? Pop was really in a spin. After all these years, I don't think he has Botty figured out."

"After all these months I'm not sure I do," Colonel Ross said.

"Botty's a great little fixer," General Beal said. His tone was amused. "Not that it matters, but between you and me, what did that smart little son of a bitch do with that paper?"

Colonel Ross said: "Is there any reason to doubt that he burned it?"

General Beal said: "I watched you and Jo-Jo giving each other the eye." He laughed. "That incinerator is only going in the mornings, usually; so my guess is, when he got caught short, he tore it into little pieces and flushed them down the can. What do you think?"

Colonel Ross said: "Well, General—"

"Come on, Judge!" General Beal said. "You say why. Why did he think he had to get rid of it? Not so as he wouldn't be blamed, certainly. He keeps telling us and telling us he *is* to blame. Would you figure he must figure that's better than having somebody see it?"

"That's what I'd figure," Colonel Ross said.

"I mustn't see it; you mustn't see it; Pop mustn't see it. Make you think of anything?"

630

"It makes me think I sometimes take a good deal on myself, General," Colonel Ross said.

General Beal said: "Judge, I have some little weaknesses, like having to do things my way; and Jo-Jo thinks I'm just a fly-boy, and I am. No, I'm not any master mind; but spell it out for me and I'll pretty often get it. You tell me what you think I don't know, and I'll tell you what I think you don't know; and we'll get there. Only, I want you to pick up after Pop. It isn't really much, it isn't really often; but watch it, will you?"

"I'll try," Colonel Ross said. "An old man like me, a man I knew once—he was a judge, too—used to say: *sed quis custodiet ipsos custodes?* Know what that means?"

"Hell, no," General Beal said. "There are quite a few things I don't know."

"Well, in this case it might mean, who's going to pick up after me?"

General Beal slapped his shoulder lightly. "I could take care of that, when it happens," he said. "I'll do the best I can, Judge; and you do the best you can; and who's going to do it better?"

Back on the ramp an automobile horn was violently blown. General Beal turned; and Colonel Ross turned, too. Standing in the car, Mrs. Beal cupped her hands to her mouth and yelled: "Ira! We want to go home!"

"Why not?" General Beal said. "Shall we go, Judge?"

Yet he stood a moment, his eyes narrowed, raised to the night. The position lights of the northbound plane could still be made out by their steady movement if you knew where to look. The sound of engines faded on the higher air, merging peacefully in silence. Now in the calm night and the vast sky, the lights lost themselves, no more than stars among the innumerable stars.